THE MARTINELLI FAMILY

THE MAFIA COLLECTION

KRISTEN PROBY

AMPERSAND PUBLISHING, INC.

THE MARTINELLI FAMILY

The Mafia Collection

Kristen Proby

Cover Design: Emily Wittig Designs

YOU BELONG WITH ME

A WITH ME IN SEATTLE NOVEL

You Belong With Me
A With Me In Seattle Novel
By
Kristen Proby

YOU BELONG WITH ME

A With Me In Seattle Novel

Kristen Proby

Copyright © 2020 by Kristen Proby

Published by Ampersand Publishing, Inc.

DEDICATION

This book is for Rachel Van Dyken, without whom it may not have come
to fruition.
Thank you for your encouragement, and your friendship.
I love you.

PROLOGUE

~ELENA~

Twelve Years Ago

I've always hated this room. My father's office is grand, full of honey oak bookcases, a massive chandelier, and a desk in the center of the space that's bigger than the bed I sleep on. Floor-to-ceiling windows are at his back and look out over the estate that he insisted on but, in large part, ignores.

Whenever I'm due for a massive lecture, this is where he drags me.

"May I please speak with you?"

"What is it?" He doesn't look up from his computer, which doesn't surprise me. Paying attention to his daughter has never been a priority for this man. I'll just share my news and go straight to my room, pack my things, and be out of here for good.

I can almost *smell* the freedom. I can't wait to move in with my husband. *My husband.* That word makes me want to spin in circles of excitement. Archer and I will make a home and have babies. His family is wonderful, and there will be so much love in our household. Our kids will never question whether we love them. They'll never be afraid. And when the time comes, they'll be able to marry whomever they please.

"I got married." I square my shoulders and lift my chin. "Three days ago."

I'm not afraid of my father. Not now. But my stomach quivers with butterflies. I'm eighteen years old. An adult. And I'm able to make my own decisions without influence from my parents.

What can he do? What's done is done.

He looks up from his desk, and his cold eyes narrow.

"And who, exactly, did you marry, Elena?"

"Archer Montgomery."

He sets his pen aside and leans back in his big, black chair, silently watching me. His calculating stare makes me want to squirm, but I hold steady.

"Isn't that the boy I told you to stop seeing a year ago?"

"He's a good man, Dad. If you'd just give him a chance—"

He stands and paces behind the desk, looking out the windows and shoving his hands into his pockets.

Maybe he'll just tell me to leave. That would be the best-case scenario.

"What is your last name, Elena?"

"Montgomery."

"Don't." His voice isn't loud, but it's firm.

"Watkins."

He turns and stares at me impassively. "That's right. And that last name, along with the Martinellis', holds more weight than you can ever fully understand. It means that, as my daughter, you don't have the freedom to marry whomever you choose, whenever you decide to do it."

"I'm an adult."

"You're *my daughter*!"

I blink at the spurt of anger. He's not impassive now. His eyes shoot daggers at me, and sweat breaks out across my skin.

"Dad, I love him."

He shakes his head and waves off my comment as if it's an annoying fly buzzing around his head.

"We'll have it annulled immediately."

"No."

He lifts an eyebrow. I've *never* told my father no. I don't think anyone in his life ever has.

No one would dare.

"Excuse me?"

I lift my chin again. "No."

He stalks around his desk and grips my arm just above my elbow, almost painfully, and drags me through the house, up the stairs, and into my bedroom.

"You're putting me in time out?"

"I should have done this a long time ago. You're too spoiled. Too indulged. You think you can defy me, go against what's best for the family like this?" We keep moving quickly through the room to my closet, where he pulls a sash off my robe, yanks my arms above my head, and ties me to the light fixture in the middle of the room. He steps back, barely breathing hard. "This is where you'll stay until you come to your senses."

And then he walks out.

"Wake up."

I open my eyes and moan in pain. My shoulders are screaming. My hands are numb.

"Uncomfortable?" my father asks.

I don't reply.

"Was sixteen hours enough time for you to reevaluate your decisions?"

"Dad." I lick my lips. My voice isn't whiny. I'm not a little girl begging for a pony. I'm a grown woman, trying to reason with another adult. "What's done is done. We're married. We love each other. I didn't do anything to hurt anyone, and I didn't want to defy you. If you'd just give him a chance, I know you'd like him."

"It's not about *liking* him, daughter." He sits on my bench. He's in his usual uniform of slacks, a dress shirt, and a tie. He wears this every day of his life. "You're betrothed to Alexander Tarenkov. You've known that since you were twelve."

9

"I've never met that man in my life."

"It doesn't matter."

"This is ridiculous. I'm not marrying a stranger. This is the twenty-first century. Women can marry who they want."

"Not mafia women."

"I didn't choose this."

"It's a privilege," he insists. "You were blessed with this by birthright, whether you like it or not."

"I'm not divorcing Archer. I'm not giving him up, no matter what you say." I'm breathing hard now. The tears want to come, but I will them back. Just the thought of losing Archer sends searing pain through my heart. I can't live without him.

I won't.

"You'll do as you're told."

"No."

"There's that word again." There's an edge to his voice now. One I haven't heard before. "I'm not fond of it."

"Well, get used to it."

"I didn't raise you to be disrespectful to your father."

"You *didn't raise me*. Grandma did. Nannies did. Not you. And certainly not that pitiful excuse for a woman who gave birth to me."

He stands and walks to me. His face is inches from mine, and I can smell the coffee on his breath.

"You will watch your tongue."

"Or what?"

He rears his hand back as if he's going to slap me, but I stare him in the eye and tilt my head.

"You won't hurt me. The mafia doesn't hurt their women, remember?"

But he does. He follows through and slaps me across the face. The coppery taste of blood fills my mouth.

"I'm not just your father," he says calmly as he walks away and sets a briefcase I didn't see earlier on the bench. He snaps it open. "I'm a mob boss. I'm the one who protects the family, who oversees *everything*. Did you think I didn't know about you and Archer?"

My stomach jumps, but I don't reply.

I watch as my father unbuttons the sleeves of his shirt and rolls them up to his elbows. He unfastens the top button of his collar and then loosens his tie before taking it off.

He removes his Rolex and sets it aside, and then pulls his long, salt-and-pepper hair back at the nape of his neck.

"I know every move you make, daughter." He glances over his shoulder at me. "I gave you some slack to have your little romance. It kept you occupied, and you're right, Archer comes from a good family. You were safe.

"But to have the audacity to run off and get *married* when you knew it would be forbidden? That, I can't forgive. I've been too soft on you. The annulment is already in the works."

"I won't sign it."

He laughs now. "Do you think I need you to sign it? Elena, you disappoint me."

"I'll just marry him again. You can't keep us apart."

He sighs and reaches into the briefcase and pulls out a whip. It's long and well-worn.

"Dad."

He circles the room, walking around me. He rips my T-shirt in two, exposing my back, then returns to dragging the whip, flicking it with his wrist as if he's warming up.

He's just scaring me.

I'm so sick of this shit! Just let me leave so I can be with Archer!

He walks behind me, and to my utter shock and horror, he cracks that whip across my back, sending crazy, searing pain throughout my body.

"That's one," he says, his voice as calm and cool as glass.

I can't believe it. He *hurt* me.

"What's best for the family is always the priority," he says and lashes the whip over my back again, making me cry out in pain this time. "You know this. You *know*."

"I love him," I whisper, and am rewarded with another lash of the whip.

"Do you think I give a fuck?"

More lashes. He counts ten, then pauses and punches my face. I see stars when he hits me square on the nose, and then he picks the whip back up and counts another ten lashes. And when he's done, and I can no longer cry or speak, he simply rolls up the whip and tucks it into his briefcase.

I can't stand anymore. I'm hanging by my useless, dead hands. I can feel the warm blood trickling down my back, soaking my shorts. Blood also runs down my face, and my eyes are swollen.

"It looks like you need more time to think." His voice is calm again. His impassive eyes roam over my face before he turns and walks out, leaving me alone once more.

———

THE LIGHTS COME ON, blinding me.

"The annulment is complete."

My back sings in pain, as does my face. I have a headache the size of Texas. I can't see well.

But I'm going to live through this, and then I'm going to leave. I'm going to run away with Archer. We can live *anywhere*.

"I can get married again."

"Tsk tsk." He sets a laptop on the bench and opens it, then taps some keys. Suddenly, a video of Archer fills the screen. "Looks like he's having lunch with his sister."

Archer and Anastasia.

"This is live," Dad continues as if we're having a conversation about the weather. "Oh, see this man here?"

He points to the corner of the screen where a man I recognize as one of my father's goons sits at a table nearby.

"He's armed and has been given the command to kill them both when they leave this restaurant if you don't make the right decision. Right here, right now."

My eyes fly to his in shock.

"You wouldn't *kill* him." My voice is like sandpaper.

"You underestimate me, little girl. Even after the beating I handed out last night, you still underestimate me. Did you think I'd let you walk out of here and go off with him? Or let you sneak away?"

12

I can't reply. My eyes are on the man I love as he laughs with Anastasia. Oh, how I wish I was with them.

"I can't believe you're doing this."

"You have two choices. Either he dies, or you do what you were born to do and think of what's best for your family."

Archer is my family!

"Either way," he continues, "you won't be with him. You just need to decide if he lives or dies."

"This is so fucked-up."

"Quite," he agrees. And when I look into his eyes, I can see that he's enjoying himself.

He *wants* to hurt me.

He's getting off on it.

And I don't doubt that he'd kill Archer just to fuck with my head.

"Fine." I lick my bloody lip and feel everything inside myself break. I feel my heart die. How will I go on without Archer? How will I live for the rest of my life without him in it? But Archer losing his life isn't an option. I *have* to keep him safe. "You win."

"There." Father closes the laptop with a satisfied snap. "That wasn't so hard, was it?"

I expect him to untie me, but he turns away and picks up a lighter and lets the flame lick the big ring he wears with a prominent *W* on it. He doesn't wear a wedding band, but he's worn that stupid, gaudy ring every day of his life.

I want to shove it down his throat and let him choke on it.

"And this is so you always remember who it is that you belong to."

Before I can do anything, he presses the hot metal to my skin, high on my thigh, and I scream in pain as he brands me.

He fucking branded me!

I want to claw out his eyes. I want to spit in his face. But I go limp as a rag and wait as he unties my hands and helps me fall to a heap on the floor.

"I'll send a nurse up to tend to those wounds," he says. "And, Elena, if I find out that you have any words with Archer aside from breaking it off, or if you try to see him, I *will* kill him."

I watch his feet as he walks out of my closet, and then I curl in on myself, crying harder than I ever have in my life. Not from the open wounds on my back, or the burning flesh on my thigh.

No, the pain of losing Archer forever is far worse than any physical pain could ever be.

"HEY."

I'm holding the phone close to my ear, eager to soak in every word we say, even though they're going to be painful. He's going to hate me before this call is over.

"Where the hell are you, E? I haven't heard from you in *days*. A man shouldn't go that long without talking to his wife, you know?"

I close my eyes. *Wife.* Oh, how I long to be his spouse. To truly be his until the end of time.

"Yeah, we need to talk about that, Archer. We were really impulsive."

"Planned it for three months," he reminds me. "I don't think that's impulsive."

"Well, it was for me. You know, I think I just got really caught up in the idea of getting married and everything, but now that I've had time to think it over, I don't think this is what I want at all."

He's quiet for a moment. I want to scream, *I'M LYING! HE'S MAKING ME DO THIS TO US!*

But I can't.

"What are you saying, E? Do you want to go back to dating?"

"No." I swallow hard and hate myself for what I'm about to say. "No, I think it's best if we just go ahead and part ways now. Clean break. I'm sorry if I hurt you, Archer, but it's really what I want."

"I can't believe this."

I have to push my hand against my sore mouth so I don't sob out loud.

"You're *breaking up* with me?"

"Yeah. I'm just too young to be tied down, you know? I need to experience life and spend some time alone. You're just not what I want, Archer."

"But we're married." I can hear him pacing on the other end of the line.

"It can be annulled." Even the word tastes bitter in my mouth. It's the last thing I want, but my father was right. Neither of us needs to sign anything for the mob boss of the Watkins family to make it happen.

There's a beat of silence and then he hangs up without saying good-bye. I've just broken his heart, and I hate myself for it.

I hate my family. My father especially.

Rage flows through me, swift and hot. When it burns out, I feel... nothing. I'll never let anyone hurt me like this again.

CHAPTER
ONE
~ELENA~

Beep! Beep! Beep!

I roll over and kill the alarm. I've been awake for at least an hour already, lying in my warm, cozy bed, watching the sky turn from black to purple to blue. I've always been an early riser, which is why my job is so perfect for me.

Baby animals need their breakfast, and at the Oregon Coast Wild Animal Rescue, I'm the lucky woman who gets to feed them.

I stretch my arms over my head and then sit up, letting the blankets fall around my hips, exposing my naked body to the crisp morning air.

Summer is waning, and it won't be long before I have to turn on the heat. But I've been clinging to the season with all of my might. Once winter arrives, we'll have more rain and grey days than I care to think about. So, I plan to hold on to these nice summer moments for as long as I can.

I throw a robe around my shoulders, slide my feet into slippers, and pad downstairs to my small kitchen.

I live in what I lovingly refer to as a cottage. That's probably too grand a word for my little cabin in Oregon. My bedroom is a loft upstairs, and down below, I only have a kitchen, a small living space, and an efficient bathroom.

But it's only me here, so it fits me just fine. In the six years that I've lived in Bandon, Oregon, I've never needed more than this.

I come from mansions and a life of privilege, yet nothing has ever made me feel as safe as this.

I pop a pod in my Keurig, set my *Blow me, I'm hot* mug on the counter, and as my first cup of coffee brews, I step out onto the deck that gives me just a tiny peek at the ocean. The sky is clear today, and the wind is calmer than usual, so I make a mental note and promise myself I'll take a walk on the beach this afternoon after work and lunch with my friend, Lindsey.

With another deep breath, I turn back inside and pour some cream into my coffee, then carry it with me into the living room.

This is my typical morning routine, seven days a week, whether rain or shine. I sit on a small pillow in the corner of the room, crisscross applesauce, close my eyes, and begin my meditation.

I go to my happy place in my mind.

It's on a boat at a marina in Seattle with Archer. Even after all these years, following drama and hurt and more shit than I care to dwell on, it's always Archer I think about when I go to my happy place.

His smile. His gentle hands. Archer was my safe place, my constant source of stability in a life that was anything *but* stable.

When you're the daughter of a mob boss, life is damn scary.

Three minutes later, with a clear mind and relaxed shoulders, I retrieve my coffee and go about the rest of my routine. Shower. Makeup. Hair up in a ponytail.

When I'm dressed and have another cup of coffee in my trusty *Girls rule!* to-go mug, I set off for work in my old, rusted-out Buick. Saying it's second-hand is too kind. It was most likely fifth-hand.

But it does the job and gets me to and from just fine.

It also doesn't draw any unwanted attention.

It's a ten-minute drive to the rescue. I park in my usual spot and walk into the nursery, which is dimly lit as soft music plays through Bluetooth speakers.

It feels like a spa. Like someone's going to hand me a robe and a cup of tea and lead me back to a massage room.

But instead, we have mountain lion cubs, raccoon kits, and a baby sloth, all waiting for my attention.

"Hey, Ally."

I smile, used to being called Ally now. I changed my name when I moved to Bandon, complete with a credit history, passport, and driver's license. All after I spent two years in California under a different name. Unfortunately, I ran into a school friend unexpectedly at the vineyard that I worked at and had to run again.

The mob has connections for a girl who needs to disappear.

"Good morning, Chad." I smile at the man, who's feeding one of the mountain lion cubs with a bottle. "How did it go last night?"

"Pretty normal," he says. "Cleaned up a bunch of poop and fed roughly four hundred bottles."

I laugh at the exaggeration, although there have been times when it felt like that many.

"Is everyone healthy?"

"Raccoon kit red didn't want to eat," he says with a frown, nodding at the pen behind me. "Keep an eye on her."

"Will do. Thanks."

We tie strings of different colors around the animals' necks so we can tell them apart from each other and keep accurate records on each one.

I love this job. It's exactly what I always wanted to do, even when I was a little girl. I'm fiercely protective of it, and I don't even care that I work six hours a day, seven days a week since we lost an employee last year and haven't replaced her.

This is where I'm needed, and I love it.

Really. I do.

"THANKS FOR MEETING ME FOR LUNCH," my friend, Lindsey, says with a happy sigh as we sit in our booth at the diner downtown. "I feel like I haven't seen you in *forever*."

"I know. We had two bear cubs come in a couple of weeks ago after their mother was poached, and they require around-the-clock care. Work's just been really busy."

"Ally, you need to have more than wild animals in your life."

"No." I sip my Coke. "I don't."

"Sure, you do. You're a young, vibrant, beautiful woman. You need a man."

I shake my head.

"A woman?"

I laugh and sip my drink again. "I don't have time or the need for a relationship."

"We make time for the things that are important to us," she says with absolute sincerity in her voice. "I know some single guys—"

"Seriously. I'm fine."

"Okay." She sighs and smiles at the waitress who's just appeared to take our order. "Hey, Kate. I'll have the chicken salad sandwich with fries."

"Taco salad for me," I say, and we pass her our menus. "What have *you* been up to?"

"Work, mostly."

I raise a brow. "Hi there, pot, I'm kettle."

She snorts. "I know, I sound like a hypocrite. The spa has been super busy this summer with the crazy tourist season."

Lindsey manages the spa for a big resort that sits right on the water. I met her three summers ago when I went in for a massage that had been a gift from my boss.

"So, you must have broken things off with Peter?"

She wrinkles her nose. "Peter was a jerk. He brought me coffee to work one day—"

"Totally a jerk."

"—and he also had two donuts with him. He ate them *both* in front of me. I mean, what kind of monster does that?"

"I might have decked him."

"I thought about it." Lindsey shakes her head. "So, yeah, I broke that off. You know what we need?"

"I think you're about to tell me."

"A girls' night out." She smiles, clearly proud of herself, and I shake my head. "Come on, Al, we're not nuns. We should go out and let loose a little bit. Maybe meet a hot dude and have a little fun."

"I work super early in the morning. You remember that, right?"

"Everyone needs a day off. Even you."

"Until we find someone to replace Stephanie, it's not going to happen anytime soon."

Lindsey scowls and glances up at a TV that's silently playing the news above my head.

"Oh, man."

"What?"

She gestures to the TV with her chin. "I used to be obsessed with that family when I was younger."

"What family?"

I turn to look at the TV and freeze.

Matriarch of most powerful mafia family on the west coast dead.

That would be my grandmother.

My grandma is gone.

I watch the words scroll on the screen as blood rushes through my ears, blocking everything out. My grandmother, the most important person in my life, is gone, and I can't talk to anyone about it. I can't call my cousins or my uncle, Carlo, to ask how it happened or to find out when her service is so I can go home for it.

I can't do anything.

"Ally."

I turn and blink at Lindsey, who's now scowling at me.

"Yeah?"

"I called your name like ten times. Where did you go?"

I shake my head. "Sorry, I was just reading about the story."

"The Watkins and Martinelli families always fascinated me," she continues, sprinkling salt on her fries. "I mean, the sons on the Martinelli side? Have you *seen* them? Talk about hot. I might be willing to be a mobster wife if I could snag me one of those."

I blink at the plate of food in front of me. When did it arrive?

"I mean, how weird would it be to be part of that family?" she continues. "I always thought the mafia was something from the 1920s, not modern-day."

I nod, my mind racing.

"You know what? I forgot about an appointment I have this afternoon." I set my napkin on the table and reach for my purse. "I'm so sorry, but I have to go."

"You haven't eaten."

"I'm not really hungry."

"You can have it boxed up."

I shake my head. "That's okay. I'm sorry. Here's a twenty."

I toss the bill on the table and hurry away, trying to control the tears until I'm in my car alone. Jesus, Mary, and Joseph. I'm such an idiot. Acting this way will only draw attention to myself, and it'll have Lindsey asking questions later.

Like...why would the death of an old woman I don't even know make me so crazy?

I hurry to my car. Once inside, I drive away, leaving Bandon behind. Twenty miles later, I enter a Walmart and hurry back to the electronics section.

I can't call my family. They don't know where I am. My grandmother made sure of that eight years ago. I endured four more years of being under my father's thumb before he was sent to prison and was killed there. My mother was also murdered, and my grandmother sent me away, afraid that I would be the next target.

No one knows where I am.

But there's one person I *can* contact. I need to speak to *someone* from my life in Seattle.

I purchase the burner phone, and when I'm safely in my car again, I turn it on and punch in the number I memorized years ago.

I always send Anastasia the same text. Always. But not this time. Because I'm not just checking in to see how Archer's doing.

Me: *Have you seen the news?*

I sit and breathe, close my eyes, and do my best not to dissolve into hysterics. It won't do me any good to sob uncontrollably in the parking lot of a Walmart.

Get it together, Elena.

Less than a minute later, I get a reply.

Unknown: *I did. I'm so sorry, E. How can I help?*

The tears come anyway.

There's nothing Anastasia can do. There's nothing *anyone* can do. I'm on my own. I've been on my own for almost a decade, but I always knew that if push came to shove, I could contact my grandmother, and she'd help me.

But now, she's gone.

I haven't seen or spoken to her in eight years. She warned me then, sternly, that I had to stay hidden, couldn't blow my cover. She said when the time was right, she'd bring me home.

Even when everything went to shit six years ago at the vineyard, she never contacted me directly. My *situation* was handled quickly and quietly without a word from her.

Because one doesn't simply *leave* the mob. Especially the daughter of the boss. There's no way out. But I've had a reprieve. And I pray that I can stay hidden, that she took our secret with her to the grave. I hope that I'm as safe here in my little haven as I was the day I arrived.

I wipe the tears away and reply to Anastasia.

Me: *Nothing to do. I just needed something from home. Been to any new restaurants lately?*

That last line is my usual one, the one that secretly asks if Archer's okay. The man never stops eating. The response is always the same unless something is wrong.

So far, nothing's ever been wrong.

I need to check on him. To make sure he's safe and that my family hasn't done anything to him, especially after the way my father threatened to kill him.

Unknown: *Nothing new lately!*

That's the right answer.

I wipe the history on the phone, then place it under the tire of my car and drive over it, making sure it's good and smashed before I drive back to Bandon.

I don't even own a cell phone as Ally. I have a house phone at my cottage with old-fashioned voicemail where the few people who call me can reach me.

That's usually just my work and Lindsey. I stick to myself. I don't trust anyone, and truth be told, I'm not good with people. Because letting people get too close means establishing a relationship, and relationships only lead to heartache.

Been there, done that, have the scars to show for it.

I wipe my cheeks all the way home, letting myself cry and feel the absolutely stabbing pain the loss of my grandmother has brought.

I park in front of the cottage, hurry inside, and lock the door behind me. I run up to my bedroom and open the bottom drawer of my dresser.

Under my socks and underwear is a framed photo. The only one I allowed myself to bring with me when I fled Seattle all those years ago.

In it, I'm about ten, dressed in a white dress. It was my first communion. The mafia may be full of murdering philanderers, but they're staunchly Catholic.

Sitting next to me, smiling down at me, is my grandmother.

I hug the photo to my chest and give in to not only the tears from earlier, but also the sobs that have wanted to come since I saw the news report in the diner.

I wish, with all my heart, that I could go to the funeral. To be there to say goodbye to the best person I've ever known. I owe her that, especially after everything she did for me. But how? I can't be seen. It would blow my cover, and the last thing I need is for the family to find me.

All I know is, as I sit here sobbing, I *need* to go to Seattle. I quickly search my grandmother's name on my iPad and see that her funeral is in two days. I have *two days* to figure this out.

And that just makes me cry harder.

I'm not sure how long I sit there, rocking back and forth, hugging the image of us together, but finally the tears ebb, and I reach for a tissue to blow my nose and wipe the mess from my cheeks.

I carry the photo downstairs with me and pour myself a glass of wine, then curl up on the couch. I didn't take that walk on the beach. I could still go. There are at least two more hours of sunlight left. The beach helps to ground me, clears my head. And God knows I could use a clear head to figure this out. To remind myself that Grandma would *not* want me to go to Seattle for her funeral. Yes, a walk on the beach is exactly what I need.

But I'm drained. I'm so damn sad. I feel helpless.

Just as I resolve to spend the evening right here on the sofa with a bottle of wine and sappy movies on the TV, there's a knock on the door.

I frown. No one ever comes to my door unless they're lost.

Fuck. Did the family discover where I am? Did they come to find me?

My first instinct is to run.

But that's ridiculous. Grandma wouldn't have told anyone where I am, and she literally *just* died.

It's not the family.

Someone is probably lost.

However, when the knock comes again, I stand and tuck my trusty handgun into my shorts, then with the photo still in my hands, walk over to the door and look through the peephole. I feel my knees almost give out at the sight before me.

My eyes must be playing tricks on me. Maybe there was something in the wine. How long had it been in my fridge?

"Elena," he says, loud enough for me to hear through the door. "I know you're in there."

I swallow hard. This can't be happening.

"Open this door, Elena."

Elena.

No one has called me that in eight years.

I open the door and stare up at what must be a figment of my imagination.

"Archer?"

CHAPTER
TWO
~ARCHER~

I've been watching her for days. It sounds creepy as fuck, but once I found her, I just didn't know what to say. I thought I'd rush to her, yank her into my arms, and kiss her until we were both breathless.

But I couldn't approach her. Memories rolled through me as I watched her. The way we laughed, the long, deep conversations. How I couldn't bear to be away from her for more than a couple of hours, and each time I saw her again, it was a balm to my soul.

God, I loved her.

Instead, all I could do was watch her. At some point, she dyed her hair a shade darker than her natural color, but aside from that, she looks the same. Slim body, gorgeous eyes, and just like the last time I laid eyes on her, her bottom lip wobbles, and those interesting orbs fill with tears.

Except this time, it's not because we're standing in front of the justice of the peace, exchanging wedding vows.

"Archer?"

"Hello, Elena. Can I come in?"

She swallows hard and steps back so I can walk inside her tiny house. She's tucked in this little cabin at the end of a dirt road, all alone in a tiny town on the coast.

I have questions, and damn it, I'm going to get some answers.

"Did you see the news?" she asks.

"No, but Anastasia called me." I want to reach for her, wrap my arms around her and soothe her. But she's standing a good six feet away, cradling a picture frame to her chest. Her body language screams: *stay back.* "I'm sorry."

She nods once and turns away to sit on the couch.

There's an open bottle of wine on the coffee table, and a half-empty glass. So, before I sit next to her, I fill the glass and pass it to her.

"Thanks." She takes a sip and watches me silently for a moment. I can admit, after all of these years of being without her, this isn't exactly how I pictured our reunion going. But I'm letting her take the lead here because she has grief written all over her face. "What kind of car are you driving?"

I frown. "Why?"

"Just tell me."

"It's an Audi."

"Newer?"

"Yeah." I frown harder and then repeat, "Why?"

"My car is kind of a piece of crap, but that's on purpose. I mean, it's not so bad that it stands out, but it's also not nice enough to stand out."

She's doing her best to blend. "I understand."

"I just don't trust it enough to get me all the way to Seattle and back."

"You're not going to Seattle."

"Yes." She sets her glass down with a decisive *thud* and hurries past me and up the narrow set of stairs to a loft. "I am."

I follow her, not willing to let her out of my sight. "Elena, you can't go to Seattle. I don't know exactly what's going on here, but—"

"I'll tell you," she interrupts as she pulls a duffle bag out of her tiny closet and starts throwing things into it. "When my parents were killed, my grandmother wanted to get me the hell out of Seattle. We didn't know which family was responsible for Mom's and Dad's deaths, and Gran was sure whomever it was would come for me next. Rather than let that happen, she gave me a new life, out from under my family's thumb.

"She's the only one who knew where I was. She said she'd bring me back when the time was right, but it's never been right. And, frankly, I like it here. By the way, don't call me Elena. Call me Ally."

"No."

She scowls at me. "Yes. I'm Ally here and have been for six years. I've made a life for myself, and I *like* it. A lot."

"So you're not planning to go back to Seattle for good?"

"Hell, no. You know who my family is. I'm not going back to that. But Grandma was the most important person in my life, even if I haven't seen her in eight years." Her chin wobbles again, but she sniffs and pulls herself together. "So, I'm going to her funeral."

"If the family sees you, they won't let you leave again."

"They won't see me."

"Elena—"

"Ally."

"This is crazy. I'm not taking you back there, knowing that your life could be in danger."

To my utter shock, Elena pulls a small handgun on me and levels me with a cold look.

"Yes, you are."

I smirk at the gun. She won't kill me.

"You're right," she says as if she can read my mind. "I'm not going to kill you. But I could take out your knee, your shoulder. Your balls."

I drop the smile and narrow my eyes at her. She's not kidding.

I'm being held at gunpoint by the love of my life.

And she *is* the love of my life. Standing here, looking at her, has me aching. God, I missed her. And I'm smart enough to know that there's so much about her I don't know anymore. She's not the same woman she was when she was eighteen.

But I'm going to relearn her. Because letting her out of my sight again is simply not an option.

"Let's talk about this."

She doesn't blink as she cocks the gun.

I move fast and grip the wrist of her shooting hand as I pull her against me, the gun now pointed away from us.

"I'll take you," I say at last, my nose inches from hers. "But we do it *my* way, and you won't ever pull this shit on me again. After everything you put me through, I deserve better than a gun barrel pointed at my face."

I let her go and walk away, then turn back, soaking her in. "And we're going to talk on the way up there."

She lowers the gun and shoves it back into her waistband. "It's a long drive. I figured we'd talk. I have to call my job."

She pushes her fingers through her long, dark hair and hurries to the side of the bed to pick up a cordless phone straight from the nineties.

She dials a number and waits for someone to answer.

"Hey, Chad, it's Ally. Is Margie in? I was hoping to catch her. She's not? Okay. Well, I've had a family emergency. I need to leave for a couple of days." Her eyes well up again, and it tears at my heart. "Yeah, a death. I know we're already shorthanded, and I hate to do this to you. I know. Family first."

She lowers the phone from her mouth and wipes at a tear.

"Thank you, Chad. Really. I'll call you if I'll be out more than two or three days. Okay. Bye."

She hangs up, and I can't stand it anymore. I cross to her and gently pull her to me.

Elena's arms immediately encircle my middle, and she buries her gorgeous face in my chest, allowing herself a good cry.

I rock us back and forth, rubbing circles over her back and crooning to her.

"It's going to be okay, sweetheart."

She's got a death-grip on my shirt, and her tears rip at my heart. She's clearly hurting, and the only way to help her feel better is to drive her to Seattle.

So it looks like that's what we'll do.

"I wish we'd left last night," she says from the passenger seat, staring out at the pretty Oregon scenery.

"We both needed the sleep," I remind her. She slept hard. I offered to take the couch, but she said that was silly and offered half of the bed.

I took it.

I only touched her once when she whimpered in her sleep, and I reached over to rub her back.

Now that I've found her, there's plenty of time for the rest of it. I don't even know how she feels about seeing me again. But she didn't turn me away, and I'll take that as a win.

"The funeral is tomorrow at two in the afternoon," she says. "At least, that's what the news said."

"I can do a search to confirm it," I reply. "But you can't go in there like this."

"Of course, not. I'll buy a wig and wear sunglasses."

I glance at her and scowl. "You might as well wear a neon sign that says, *This is Elena, hiding from all of you.*"

"Well, what do you suggest I do?"

"I've got this." I reach for my phone and dial my baby sister's number.

"I haven't talked to you in weeks," Amelia says rather than hello. "Where are you?"

"In my car. Hey, I have a special project for you."

Elena grips my arm, and her eyes look panicked. She hisses, "No! Don't drag your family into this!"

"Trust me," I whisper.

"Who are you whispering to? What's going on, Archer?" Lia demands.

"I have someone with me who needs a disguise."

"Between you and Levi, I should go into the camouflage business. What do you need?"

"She can't look *anything* like herself. She's going to a place where if she's recognized, it could mean her life."

Lia's quiet for a moment. "Archer, did you find *Elena*?"

I smile. "Yeah."

"Oh, my God. This is so exciting. Is she with you? Can she hear me?"

"I can hear you," Elena says softly.

"Elena! We've missed you so much. Don't you worry, I'll make you look so different, even Archer won't recognize you."

"I'll always recognize her," I say and link my hand with Elena's, holding on even when she tries to pull away.

She won't be pulling away from me again.

"You can't tell anyone," Elena says, her voice laced with urgency. "This has to be absolutely secret, Lia. Please."

"I understand. Mum's the word. When do you need me? I have to get some supplies. Are you still the same size?"

Elena and Lia discuss the specifics, and once I've hung up with my sister, Elena bites her lip, looking unsure.

"Talk to me."

"This is a bad idea," she says at last. "What am I doing? I've been safe in Bandon for years. And now you and your family know where I am, and I'm walking right into the lion's den tomorrow. My grandmother would be so pissed."

"You love her," I remind her. "And you're allowed to go to your own grandmother's funeral. You're allowed to grieve and be a human being, Elena. Besides, *I* know where you are, but my family doesn't. And Amelia isn't a snitch."

"I know better than this."

"What are you afraid of?"

She laughs, but it's humorless. "Well, worst-case scenario? You and I are both killed."

"That feels extreme."

"You don't get it. I'm the daughter of a mob boss, Archer."

"A dead mob boss." I glance at her and see her bite her lip again. "And I never got it because you always refused to explain it to me, E."

"Doesn't matter that he's dead." She shakes her head. "I have responsibilities that I walked away from. There will be punishment for that. Grandmother warned me."

"Your father is *dead*. Who the hell would punish you?"

"Murdered," she agrees. "But it doesn't change the fact that I walked away from the family. That's not okay. I knew I'd have to go back one day, I'm just not ready. And any one of them could punish me for leaving."

I take a deep breath and decide that now's as good a time as any to ask some hard questions.

"Anastasia told me the real reason why you broke things off."

And learning that it was because her father had threatened my life was enough to almost destroy me.

"I wish she hadn't done that."

"So you'd rather I never knew the truth? That I remain clueless? I felt like a fucking fool, E."

"I'd rather you be *safe*," she stresses. "Your safety was always the goal. My father didn't hand out idle threats, Archer. There was no way in hell I was going to allow him to harm you. So, I did what he asked."

"And you never came to find me when he died."

"You don't get it." She growls in frustration. "My father made it clear to *everyone* that if you came around again, looking for me, that you were to be *taken care of*. That directive didn't die with him."

"You didn't give me a chance to make a decision for myself."

"What would you have done?"

"Gone to him," I reply. "Talked to him, man-to-man. Explained that I loved you and that I'd do anything to be your husband."

"It wouldn't have mattered. You're not from the right bloodline. You're not who he picked out for me. And *if* he'd been willing to give you a chance, he would have made you become part of the family. The mob family. And that's not okay, Archer. It would have only made things worse."

"I lost you," I say, frustration flowing through my veins. "It didn't get much worse than that."

"Losing you and the pain that came with it was *nothing* compared to the agony I knew I'd feel if he killed you, Archer. So, yes, I made a decision for both of us, and I'd do it again in a heartbeat."

"No. You won't. You won't ever make a decision like that for me, for both of us, ever again."

"This is ridiculous. I don't know why you're here. Why didn't you just move on? Find someone else and get married. Have a dozen kids. Live your life? Because you being with me puts us both at risk."

YOU BELONG WITH ME

"I tried," I admit. "I dated, and there was even someone who loved
me enough that I considered marrying her. But it wouldn't have been
fair to her because I never would have loved her the way I loved you."

We cross over the Oregon/Washington border, and I feel Elena
stiffen beside me.

"No one's going to hurt you, E."

She simply shakes her head once. "They hurt me. Every day. You
have no idea."

It's six in the morning when I pull up to my sister's home with Elena.
We spent the night in a hotel south of Seattle. Elena didn't trust me to
take her to my place, in case it was being watched, and I was inclined to
agree.

"You're here," Lia says when she opens the door. She immediately
pulls us inside, shuts and locks the door, and then tugs Elena into her
arms for a long hug. "Oh, I missed you so much. We have to do all of our
crying now so we don't mess up your makeup later."

"I missed you, too," Elena whispers into Lia's shoulder.

After a long embrace, Lia steps back and smiles at Elena. "I always
loved your eyes. The one brown and one green is *so* cool, but they'll give
you away in a heartbeat."

Now, she's all-business.

"I can't change my eye color," Elena says as we follow Lia through
her home to her studio. "What is all of this?"

"Oh, Archer didn't brag about his baby sister? Tsk tsk." Lia shakes
her head at me and smiles at Elena. "I do YouTube videos."

"This looks like more than the occasional video."

"She's being humble," I say. "She has five million followers on
YouTube and just launched her own makeup line."

Elena's eyes are huge as she stares at my sister in surprise. The last
time she saw Lia, my baby sister was still in high school.

"Wow. Good for you."

"Thanks. Makeup is my jam, and we're going to make you look not
only incredible but also completely unrecognizable."

33

"But how?"

"You're going to look like a man."

Elena and I both blink at my sister.

"There's no way you can make her look like a dude," I say.

"Of course, I can. I have wigs, facial hair, contact lenses to cover those amazing eyes, and I even bought her clothes. She'll be short, but she'll look like a guy in the next six hours."

"Wow," Elena says again. "Let's do it."

For the first time since Elena opened her door to me yesterday, she has hope in her eyes. If anyone can pull it off, it's my sister.

"I'll be back later to take you."

"Where are you going?" Elena asks.

"I need to get a suit from my house, and I have a couple of errands to run."

"You're not going with me to the funeral."

I shove my hands into my pockets, ready to go to battle. "Yes, I am. I told you we were doing this my way, and there's no way I'm letting you go in there without me."

"Then what's the point of this disguise? If you're with me, it'll be a red flag. You *can't* be there."

"You're not going in there alone." I pace away, frustrated all over again because she's right. If someone from her family sees me there, they'll know she's close by. I look at my sister and then Elena. "I don't want you going in there alone. So, Lia goes with you."

"Great idea," Lia says. "I'll put on a disguise of my own, and we'll look like a couple. We're about the same height. If I wear flats, we'll totally pull it off."

I nod, but Elena shakes her head no.

"I can't let you do that, Lia. It's too dangerous."

"She goes with you, or you don't go at all." I cross my arms over my chest, not willing to budge on this.

Lia nods in agreement. "No one will recognize us."

"I don't like it," Elena says, but then sighs in defeat when she sees the hard look on my face. "Okay."

"You don't have to like it. Keeping you safe is the most important thing." I cup her cheek, wanting nothing more than to kiss her, but we're not there yet. "I'll be down the street from the church in my car. I won't be far."

"Is he always this bossy?" Elena asks Lia.

"Yeah. He's the alpha type."

"I'm right here." I stare at them both, but they just smile back. "I can hear you."

"We'd better get to work if we're going to be ready to go on time," Lia says, gesturing for Elena to take a seat. "Would you rather have dark or light hair?"

"Let's go blond," Elena says. "And maybe spiky. Can you give me tattoos?"

"Like, on your neck?"

Elena nods.

"Heck, yes. Should it be a girl's name? That's super classy."

They giggle as they get down to business, acting as if they've been friends forever and saw each other just last week.

Elena always fit in well with my family. They accepted her unconditionally, and Elena spent a lot of time at our house while we were dating.

I, however, did not get the same reception from Elena's family. In fact, I never met them. Even when we ran away to get married, I never met her parents. Elena told me about them and explained that it wouldn't be safe if they found out about us.

I guess I just blew it off because I was in love, and I was young enough to think that love would conquer anything.

Until one day, she ghosted me. She was my wife, and she just disappeared, then called and said I wasn't what she wanted. I was fucking devastated. Angry. Hurt. It took years for me to move on.

"What do you think?" Lia asks, pulling me out of my thoughts.

After only ten minutes, Elena's face has already changed. I barely recognize her.

"You're a damn genius."

My sister grins and turns back to Elena. "I know. But thanks for acknowledging it."

THREE

~ELENA~

"Oh, God, why did I think I could do this?" I whisper as I drive Amelia and me into downtown Seattle where the funeral is being held. The thing about my family is, despite being kind of scary, they're also quite famous in the Pacific Northwest, so they needed a big church to accommodate all of the people that would come to pay their respects. Which works well for me, as it'll be easier for Lia and me to go unnoticed.

"No one is going to recognize you," Lia assures me and shifts in the seat next to me. Frankly, I don't recognize either of us.

I'm in a man's suit, black with a silver tie. My hair is blond and *not* spiky like I originally thought. We decided to go more conservative than rebellious. But I have a full beard, both of my eyes are brown, and I have sunglasses tucked into my pocket, just in case.

Lia covered her long, blond hair with a brunette wig. We both have prosthetic noses on, giving our faces an entirely different shape.

I park a block down from St. James Cathedral in downtown Seattle. I'm not willing to admit it, but I feel better knowing that Archer's parked not far from here.

I've been to this particular cathedral many times in my life, usually for baptisms and weddings. My parents' funerals were held here, but I didn't go.

I was already far away by then.

We're not early. I wanted to be right on time, when the church would already be full. My family never starts anything on schedule because they like being the center of attention, and they want to make sure the venue is packed.

Judging by the size of the crowd still outside of the church as we drove past, I'd say that hasn't changed in the past eight years.

"We're just going to slip into the back pew," I say for the fifth time since we left Lia's house. "If there's an open casket, which I would suspect there will be, we'll join the line to view her, but only if we can get in the middle of a line."

"You don't have to go," Lia reminds me before we exit the car.

"Yeah, I do. She was the most important person in my life, Lia. I need to say goodbye to her."

Lia nods and reaches over to pat my hand with hers. "Let's do this, then."

We get out of the car and link hands as we walk down the sidewalk to the cathedral. I'm relieved to see that I was right.

The crowd out front is big. People slowly filter into the church, mingling and chatting as they do.

"I guess one thing that never changes over the years is that funerals are social occasions," I mutter.

And now it's time to put on the show of my life.

I act the part of a man, escorting the woman he loves. My hand is on the small of Lia's back as I lead her up the steps and inside the church. So far, I haven't seen any of my family, which is a feat in itself since there are so many of us.

The church is massive inside. Hushed. Stained glass and old architecture surround us. The building is an architectural masterpiece, and I've always loved to look at the stories in the glass.

My goal is not to speak to anyone. I may look like a guy, but there's no way to change my voice, so Lia's agreed to do all of the talking.

It seems the family isn't here yet, which doesn't surprise me. Even though they do all kinds of shady crap, they like to be on display. So, it makes sense that they'd wait for the rest of the onlookers to be seated before they enter the sanctuary.

Grandma's casket is at the front of the church, and it's open.

"Let's go look before the family arrives," I whisper to Lia. She nods, and with our hands linked, we join the line of mourners waiting their turn to see my grandmother.

The closer we get, the bigger the ball in my stomach becomes. It's real. She's really gone.

When we reach the casket and stand near her head, I sigh deeply as I stare down at the woman who loved me so fiercely.

She looks peaceful. They have her in a red dress with her favorite signature strand of pearls. Her hair is salt and pepper and perfectly styled in the way she always wore it.

It looks as if she's sleeping, like she might wake up at any moment, smile at me, and suggest we have crepes for breakfast.

I want to reach in and touch her. I want to kiss her.

But as far as anyone knows, I'm a stranger, and it would only bring attention to myself.

"Let's go," Lia whispers.

She's right. We shouldn't hold up the line for too long.

I turn to walk away, heading down the center aisle to our seats in the back. I freeze.

Walking straight toward me is my uncle Carlo, flanked by Shane and Rocco. Carmine just came in the door behind them and is shaking hands with a man I don't know.

As far as I know, Uncle Carlo took over the role of boss. I loved this man. Aside from Grandma, he was the one I had the most in common with. He doted on me, as I was the only girl in the family for a long time.

But I also know what he's capable of, and he scares me more than a little.

No eye contact.

I glance at the floor and do my best to casually walk past him and my cousins. Lia's holding onto my hand.

Get to the back of the freaking church.

It's like I'm walking in slow motion. They're going to see me. One of them is going to *recognize* me.

But no one even gives me a second glance as they walk past and sit in the front pew.

Lia and I return to our seats, and both of us let out a long breath of relief.

"You did great," she says and loops her arm through mine, then leans her head on my shoulder. "The hardest part is over."

I nod, and we sit and listen for the next hour as the priest prays and gives a sermon. Family members get up to talk, sharing memories and stories.

That's the part that makes me cry the hardest. I wish I could do that, too.

Catholic funerals are long. So long. But it's eventually over, and we're all asked to sit and wait for the family to leave the sanctuary first, carrying my grandmother's casket out to the hearse and then on to the cemetery.

I blink and realize that I'm about to lose a contact. They're not comfortable, but until now, they hadn't given me any problems.

I continue to blink rapidly, and sure enough, the lens falls into my hand. I look up just as my cousin Carmine walks past, carrying the front of the casket on his broad shoulder.

His eyes lock with mine.

They narrow.

But he doesn't stop. He keeps walking past, and before anyone else can see me, I slip my sunglasses on my face.

Once the family is gone, Lia and I stand and slip out a side door, avoiding the front of the church where the family climbs into cars to go directly to the cemetery.

I won't go to the graveside service. It's just for the family, and we would absolutely stick out like sore thumbs there. But I did what I came here to do. I said goodbye.

Lia and I walk quickly, but not too fast, to her car. I drove to give the illusion of us being a couple. Once inside, I breathe a huge sigh of relief.

And the tears come.

"It's the adrenaline," Lia says, rubbing circles on my back. "And the grief. That was intense. Let's get back to my place where you're safe, and I'll make you some tea."

I nod and work on pulling myself together. "Can you please let Archer know we're okay?"

She reaches for her phone and dials his number. He's been waiting a block down the road.

"It's done. We're headed back to my place. Okay, see you soon."

THE MAKEUP IS GONE. I've had a long, hot shower, and I'm back in my regular clothes. I walk out to the pool area of Lia's home, where she and Archer are chatting with a man I haven't met yet.

"You look like you again," Lia says with a smile as she jumps up to give me a hug. "How do you feel?"

"A little raw. Sad. Relieved."

My eyes are on Archer's. He's clearly been worried sick. I can see it in the lines around his eyes. I want to cuddle up in his lap, and I know he would welcome that, but I'm not there yet.

I'm too vulnerable, and Archer and I still have some work to do. Who am I kidding, there's no work to do. I'm going back to Bandon. Alone. There's no reason to snuggle him because nothing has changed.

We can't be together.

"I'd like you to meet my husband, Wyatt," Lia says, gesturing to the handsome man who just stood to offer me his hand.

"It's a pleasure. I've heard a lot about you," he says. He has kind eyes.

"I can't say the same," I say with a smile. "But it's nice to meet you, too."

"I was just telling Wyatt that he would *love* the cathedral we were in today. He's an architect."

"You've never been?" I ask, surprised.

"Not inside," he replies. "But it sounds like Lia will be dragging me there soon. I mean, *taking* me there soon."

I sit on the loveseat next to Archer and watch the blue water shimmer in the pool. It's warm today, despite summer almost being over.

"How are you?" Archer asks.

40

"Exhausted," I reply honestly. "I don't think anyone recognized me, even after my contact fell out. I was afraid that my cousin may have placed me because, of course, he looked at me after the lens fell out, but he just kept walking."

"There's no *way* anyone knew who you were," Lia says with confidence. "You didn't speak, and your disguise was iron-clad. You're safe."

I nod. "Thank you. So much. I don't think I can ever repay you for today."

"You don't need to repay me," Lia says. "You're my friend, Elena. Even after all this time. And friends help each other."

The tears want to come again. God, how I missed this family. The Montgomerys were always so loving, so welcoming to me. I felt at home with them, and it seems that even after all this time, nothing has changed.

I wish things were different. I'd love to make a life with Archer and his wonderful family.

But that's not meant to be, and I have a life in Oregon to get back to.

"We should go," I say, turning to Archer.

He raises a brow. "Where are we going?"

"Back to where you found me, of course. I have work tomorrow, and I need to get out of Seattle."

Lia's face falls. "Can't you stay for a day or two? You can stay here, with us."

"Thank you so much for the offer, but no. I need to go. And as much as it hurts me to say this, I won't be back, Lia. Not anytime soon, anyway."

"But Anastasia hasn't seen you, and she'll be *so* upset."

My head whips around to Archer. "Does she know I'm here?"

"She knows I found you, but I haven't said anything else." He turns to Lia. "Did you?"

"Well, of course not, because Elena told me not to. But—"

"Good." I sigh in relief. "The fewer people who know I'm here, the better. I really do have to go. It's not safe for me to be here. For any of you either."

"I hate this," Lia says as we stand, and she hugs me once more. She's done that a lot today. I know she was young when everything between

Archer and me went down, but we always liked each other very much. "Please stay safe. And come home when you can. I've really missed you."

The guilt is swift and deep. I didn't expect to feel so much of that. "Same here. Take care, okay?"

Archer hasn't said much, and once we're in his car and headed out of town, he's still quiet.

"You don't agree with what I'm doing."

He rubs his fingers over his lips. "No. I don't."

"I've been gone for a long time. Grandma didn't ask the family for permission to help me disappear. For all I know, she never told them that she helped me. I just left one day. So, I don't know if they were looking for me. *I don't know anything* about how it went down for them. But it was made clear to me that there would be repercussions for my leaving. Because this isn't permanent. You don't just *leave* the mob, even if you're born into it and involved through no fault of your own."

"If you don't even know if they're looking for you, why do you have to hide?"

"Because they might be. Or worse, the people responsible for my parents' murders could be looking for me. I don't know what they were involved in that caused their deaths. It could have been as simple as being in the family, and someone was trying to teach us all a lesson."

"Why wouldn't your uncle and the others simply retaliate? Kill them all?"

"Oh, they will. Eventually. It's rarely swift. The mafia has a long memory, Archer. Which is why I can't risk my life in Oregon. I love it there, and if they find me, they'll demand I come back to work for the family."

"Work how?"

I shrug. "In any way they need me."

"Christ."

The farther behind us Seattle gets, the more I relax. I truly am exhausted. I lean my head on the passenger window and close my eyes, enjoying the sunshine on my skin.

"Hey, sweetheart. Time to wake up."

I blink my eyes open and frown when I see that it's dark and we're parked in front of my cottage.

"Holy shit, how did I sleep so long?"

"Exhaustion will do that to you," Archer says as I stretch my sore neck. "I tried to wake you when I stopped for gas, but you were out cold."

"I'm sorry that I didn't help with the driving," I murmur but realize he's already left the car and is rounding the hood to open my door.

I'm totally out of it.

"Come on." He holds out his hand for mine and then tugs me out of the car. He has my duffle bag in his other hand and guides me to the door.

Archer has always taken care of me. He's the kind of guy who fills your car with gas and makes sure you're fed. He always used to ask me if I was cold and offer me his sweatshirt.

I still have one of them. And I'm not sorry for never giving it back.

I unlock the door, and we walk inside, turning on the lights as we go.

"Are you headed back to Seattle tonight?" I ask.

"No."

I frown as he sets my duffle bag down and then turns and walks back outside. Before I can look out the window to see what he's doing, he walks back in with a bag of his own, shuts and locks the door, and turns back to me.

"Do you want me on the couch?"

"You're staying?"

"For as long as you'll let me," he confirms.

I sigh. "We clearly have a lot to talk about."

"Agreed. And it's not going to happen tonight. We're both exhausted, E. Let's get some sleep. We can talk tomorrow."

"I really should go to work in the morning."

Archer checks his watch. "It's already the morning. Just past midnight. You only took one day off, and you told them you'd be gone for a few days. Take one more day to rest up, Elena."

"I hate it when you're right."

He grins.

"So, am I on the couch?"

"It's too small for you," I reply, eyeing his broad shoulders and long, lean body. He grew a couple of additional inches after we broke up. "I don't mind sharing the bed."

He nods, and I lead the way upstairs. Despite a six-hour nap, I feel like I could sleep for another twelve.

"Why am I so tired?"

"You had a pretty wild twenty-four hours," he reminds me. "The adrenaline of not wanting to be recognized, the grief of the funeral. All of it. It's intense, and your body is ready to rest."

"You're not kidding."

"Can I use your shower?"

"You can use whatever you like," I reply as I shuck out of my shoes and stand in the middle of the room. "I usually sleep naked, but that probably won't work tonight."

"Not if you want me to keep my hands to myself."

I glance at him. "*Not* keeping your hands to yourself will only complicate things. So, I'll find something to sleep in."

"We're as complicated as it gets, honey." He kisses my forehead. "Go to sleep. I'm gonna wash up. I'll be back in a few."

I nod and watch him walk back down the stairs before I turn to my small dresser and forage for an old tank top and a fresh pair of panties.

I *love* having Archer here. And that's a problem. I can't get used to it. I can't just fall into his arms because that's where I feel safe. Because it feels good. I have to be smarter than that. He'll be gone soon, and I'll be left alone all over again.

I can't get used to him.

I hear the water running in the shower as I decide to quickly change the sheets on the bed. Sleeping in fresh bedding is the best. Not that I won't sleep like the dead anyway.

I've just slipped the cases on the pillows and slid between the sheets when Archer walks up the stairs.

"You must be tired," I say, watching in rapt fascination as a mostly naked Archer walks around my little loft-slash-bedroom. He's a big

YOU BELONG WITH ME

man, making the room feel even smaller than it is. And holy hell in a handbasket, his body has only improved with age.

He was something to write home about when he was twenty. At thirty-two? He's ridiculous.

It's definitely good that I'm wearing clothes. And that I'm so tired.

Okay, maybe I'm not *that* weary.

I shake my head and push my hand through my hair. *Pull it together, Elena.*

I mean, Ally.

I'm Ally.

Archer slips into bed next to me and reaches over to extinguish the light. In the darkness, we lie down, and my eyes instantly close. I've always felt safe here in my little cottage.

And now, with Archer here, as well, I feel protected. It's amazing.

And fleeting.

CHAPTER
FOUR
~CARMINE~

"I'm telling you, she was there," I repeat and lean over my father's desk, staring him in the eyes. "Elena attended Grandmother's funeral."

The thought still cuts me to the core.

"And why didn't you say something *then*?" Pop asks.

"Because I had Grams' casket on my shoulder. It wasn't exactly the time or place."

Rocco paces behind me. My brother shares my frustration. We were close to Elena, raised together like siblings rather than first cousins. In fact, there's nothing that my brothers and I wouldn't do for her.

She *knew* that.

So why did she run? And where the fuck has she been?

"She was disguised as a man," I mumble, turning to pace the office, as well. "But when she looked up, her eyes gave her away."

"I can't believe she could pull that off," Rocco mutters.

"Where has she been?" I demand, turning back to my father. "Do you know?"

He puffs on his cigar, sits back in his big, black chair, and seems to think it over.

"I thought she was dead," Rocco adds. "She just vanished."

"When Vinnie and Claudia died, the family was in chaos," Pop reminds us.

"Not so much that Elena would miss her own parents' funeral," I reply and walk to the window of my father's office that looks out over the city of Seattle. "We all assumed that she was killed too, and that we'd never find her."

"Jesus," Rocco mutters. "Who would have helped her leave?"

"Her grandmother," Pop says. "She must have helped her hide so she didn't meet the same fate as Elena's parents. My mother-in-law was a shrewd woman with a wide array of contacts."

"We can keep Elena safe *here*," I growl and turn back to the room.

"Of course, we can," Pop says with a nod. "So, we'd better find her."

"We need Shane," Rocco says. "He's the tracker in the family."

"I'll call him," I reply. "In the meantime, we need to step up the search through Grandmother's things."

"She lived in that house for sixty years," Rocco reminds me. "It's ten thousand square feet containing sixty-years-worth of shit. It'll be like finding a needle in a haystack—if there's anything there at all. Grandma knew how to cover her tracks and keep secrets. She wasn't the wife and mother of bosses for nothing."

"If there's anything there, we'll find it," I reply.

"What if Elena doesn't want to be found?" Rocco asks.

"That's not how this works," Pop says, his voice like steel. "And she knows it. There's no leaving the family, and she's had a long enough reprieve. It's time we bring her home."

I nod once. "I'll go through Grandma's house myself."

"One more thing," Pop says before we can walk out of the office. "Aside from Shane, this doesn't leave this room."

"Understood."

Rocco and I leave Pop's office, and I immediately reach for my phone. It's time for Shane to come home, too.

My brother answers on the second ring.

"We need you here, brother. As soon as possible."

"What's going on?" he asks.

"Elena's alive, and we need to track her down."

There's a long silence as Rocco and I ride the elevator to the parking garage. "I'll be there in seventy-two hours."

"Good." I hang up and slip my phone back into my pocket.

"She's going to be punished," Rocco murmurs, and my gut clenches.

"I know."

"How could she put us in this position?"

"We're going to find out."

CHAPTER

FIVE

~ELENA~

I smell coffee. And bacon.

I don't have any bacon.

I sit up and blink, surprised that the sun rose before me. The bed next to me where Archer was all night is empty and cool.

And it seems he's making me breakfast.

I glance at the alarm clock and sigh before rubbing my hands over my face and through my hair.

It's eight-thirty. I don't remember the last time I slept this late, especially after the long nap in the car yesterday. But Archer's Audi was so comfortable, especially with the heated leather seat, and I just couldn't keep my eyes open.

"You're awake."

Archer carries two plates and two cups of coffee into the room. How he's managing to hold it all is thanks to long arms and muscles for days.

At least he's dressed this morning. Because a mostly naked Archer is *way* too tempting to my long-ignored libido.

"I didn't have bacon in the fridge."

"A travesty I fixed first thing." He grins and sets the dishes on the bed, passing me one of the coffees. "I assume you don't take sugar in it since you didn't have any down there."

"Just cream," I confirm and take a sip, eyeing the eggs, hash browns, and bacon on the plate in front of me. "Where did you get all of this?"

"The grocery store in town." He digs in and takes a big bite of his eggs. "You didn't have anything down there. Are you trying to starve yourself?"

"You still have the same appetite, I see."

He grins and chews some bacon. "Don't worry, I bought us some stuff."

"Archer."

I set my coffee down and turn to him, but he reaches over and picks up a slice of my bacon and holds it up to my lips.

"Eat, E."

"Ally." I take a bite and chew, holding his gaze. "My name is *Ally.*"

"Ally what?"

I clear my throat. Lick my lips. *Shit.*

"Ally what?" he asks again.

"Look, thanks for the groceries, but I'm sure you want to get back on the road so you get home at a decent hour—"

He takes my chin in his fingers and makes me look him in the eyes. "Tell me."

"Montgomery," I whisper and close my eyes in embarrassment. "Ally Montgomery."

"Look at me."

"Archer, it doesn't matter what my last name is."

To my utter shock, he simply leans over and covers my lips with his own. Gently, but boldly. My inhale is sharp, but I don't pull away.

I've dreamed of having his lips on mine for *years.*

And here he is. Kissing me as if he does it all the time, like it's no big thing. Like my heart isn't pounding out of control. Like he isn't going to leave me alone any minute.

When he pulls away, his eyes are dilated, and his breaths come a bit faster than before.

"I'm not leaving."

"Archer."

"Just listen," he pleads. "It took me a long damn time to find you."

"No one was supposed to *ever* find me." I stop short and frown at him. "Wait. How did you find me?"

He pulls a piece of paper out of his back pocket and holds it out for me to take. I recognize the lined notebook paper. It's well-worn, the creases deep as if he's opened and closed it a thousand times.

I unfold it and sigh.

"My list."

"I remember that day like it was yesterday," he says, still eating his breakfast. "You told me all the places you'd run away to if you had the chance, and I wrote them down so I could take you to every one of them someday."

"And you kept it. These were just daydreams," I say, but lovingly read over the words.

Maui

Horse ranch in Montana

California vineyards

Tuscany

Bandon, Oregon

Beach in Mexico

I see each item has notes and check marks next to them, clearly written recently.

"You never talk about something flippantly," he says, making my heart skip another beat. "They may have been daydreams, but I know you, and I knew I'd find you in one of these places."

"I notice you didn't try Maui, Mexico, or Tuscany."

"I decided to start more domestically, but if I hadn't found you here, Maui was next on my list."

I've cried so much over the past two days, I wouldn't have thought I had any more tears left in me. But my eyes well as I stare at the list.

"We were on the boat that day," I say. "Drifting around Lake Washington, and you just let me talk on and on about these places that I'd like to visit. You were always a good listener, Arch. A good friend."

"I'm still a good listener," he says. "And your eggs are getting cold."

I take a bite of eggs with potatoes and fold the paper, then pass it back to him. "You can't stay."

"Why not? If you don't want me, if you've moved on with your life and you truly want *nothing* to do with me, then I'll go. Is that what you want? To never see me again?"

I can't lie to him. Even if it would be best for both of us. I should tell him that I don't want him, and send him far away.

To keep him safe.

He links his fingers with mine, the way he always did when we were so young and so in love we were stupid with it. And I know that I don't have the strength to tell him to go.

"I want you to be safe," I admit. "That's all I've ever wanted."

"I'm a grown man, perfectly capable of taking care of myself."

"Archer." I surprise us both and straddle his lap, framing his face with my hands. "I need you to *hear* me. I know you're able to take care of yourself, but my family is powerful. Ruthless. And if they find us here, they'll kill you. Don't you understand that everything I've done over the past twelve years has been to keep you safe from them?"

"I don't take this lightly. That's not what I'm saying, E. But the risk of being with you is better than the agony of being without you."

I lean my forehead against his. "We don't even know each other anymore."

"We'll learn." His hands, those big, wonderful hands, glide to my ass, over my loose T-shirt, and then he buries his fingers in my hair. "Maybe we won't like each other anymore, and I'll be gone in twenty-four hours."

That makes me smile. "You have started snoring in your old age. That could be a deal-breaker."

His eyes narrow. "I don't snore."

"Uh, yeah. You do."

He moves fast, pinning me to the bed.

"I think my ass is in my eggs," I say, giggling like crazy.

"Take it back."

"It's the truth. I can feel them through my underwear."

"No, the snoring. Take it back."

"Sorry. No can do. I could have sworn there was a freight train in here last night. But look on the bright side. I didn't have to use one of those white noise machines."

He barks out a laugh and buries his face in my neck, biting the sensitive flesh just under my ear.

"Are you still ticklish?"

Shit. I'm so ticklish.

"Archer, no."

But before he can do his worst, there's a knock on my front door, and we both freeze and stare at each other in surprise.

"No one ever comes here," I say as Archer climbs off of me, and I pull on a pair of sweats over my egg-soaked undies. "Stay here."

I hurry down the stairs and look out the window.

Lindsey's car is parked behind Archer's.

Double shit.

I clear my throat and paste a smile on my face as I open the door to my friend.

"Hey," she says. "I brought you some pastries from Marie's. I heard you've been out of work because of a family emergency. Why didn't you call me? I'm so sorry, Ally."

"Oh, thank you." I accept the box of goodies but don't invite her in. "I've been pretty out of it, and it was a complete surprise."

"I guess so. I mean, I was with you just a couple of days ago, and everything seemed okay. Whose car is that?"

She gestures to Archer's car, and I blink rapidly.

"Oh, it's, um, my—"

"It's mine."

I feel Archer walk up behind me, bracing his arm on the doorjamb above me, and I know he's smiling at my friend. Lindsey's eyes dilate at the tall drink of water standing behind me.

And honestly, I can't blame her.

"Archer," he says, holding out his hand for hers.

"Lindsey," she replies, shaking the proffered palm. Her eyes dart to mine with a silent *what the hell?*

"Archer is a friend of the family. He came to help when he heard the news. He'll be leaving soon." I clear my throat again. "Thanks for the treats, Linds. I appreciate it."

I back away, giving the universal signal for *thanks, now go away.*

And to my surprise, it works.

"Okay. Well, call me if you need anything. Nice to meet you, Archer."

"You, too."

We wave, and I shut the door then close my eyes on a sigh.

"Three days ago, I was safely hidden here. Nothing fishy going on to make me stand out or have people asking questions. Now, it feels like it's all slipping out of control." But it'll return to normal as soon as Archer goes back to Seattle. I know he said he's staying, but that's just not possible. I'll enjoy his company today, but then he has to *go*.

"There's nothing fishy about a family friend coming when there's been an emergency."

"Right. A charming, handsome guy like you is definitely the norm at times like these."

His smile would light up Times Square. "You think I'm handsome?"

"Have you *seen* you?"

"I mean, I clean up okay. I've never had any complaints."

"You're a smartass."

"That hasn't changed, sweetheart. Let's eat these donuts."

"WHAT IS it about Bandon that you've always liked so much?" he asks me later as we walk the beach. Large rocks stick up out of the sand around us. They remind me of Stonehenge. Sometimes, when I walk here in the very early morning, I expect to see witches and faeries in the mist. It's a magical place.

"The beach here is beautiful," I reply and step over a dead jellyfish. "There aren't quite as many tourists as northern Oregon, so I'm less likely to run into someone I know. That happened before, in California."

"So, you haven't been here the whole time?"

"No, I was Paige Williams and worked at a vineyard down in California for a couple of years. But one day, a girl I used to go to middle school with came through on a tour and recognized me."

I sigh at the memory and then point out into the ocean as a whale sprays water into the air.

Archer nods but doesn't let me quit the story.

"It's ironic that your last name was Williams. My cousin Natalie married Luke Williams."

"I know." I smile up at him when he glances down in surprise. "I've kept track of everyone. And your family is in the spotlight pretty much all the time."

"True. But you didn't know about Lia?"

"I knew." I shrug a shoulder. "I feigned surprise. I just didn't want to seem like a stalker or something."

"You're a stalker."

I wrinkle my nose. "Curious. I like the term *curious* better. Anyway, after Sheila saw me, I went directly to the place I rented and texted the number my grandma gave me. Within an hour, a man showed up at my door with a packet. No words were exchanged, he just gave it to me and left.

"Inside was my new life. Name, bank accounts, birth certificate, passport, driver's license. The works."

"Wow."

"Yeah, Grandma was impressive. I texted her after I arrived in Bandon and told her I was here but was vague. She didn't want to know specifics in case anyone came looking for me. We always knew how to reach each other, though.

"I *love* it here, even more than California. It was fine there, but I realized that I need to be by the water. It energizes and soothes me. But none of this is what we really should be talking about."

"There's something we should talk about?"

"So many things," I mutter. "Let's start with this. I know you said you're staying, but Archer, that isn't possible."

"I don't have to be in Seattle for a bit," he says as if he's being deliberately obtuse. "I guess I should catch you up on what I've been up to. I sold the fishing boat about five years ago. Now, I buy and sell real estate. Mostly commercial properties, but sometimes, I buy residential places here and there."

"You're a landlord?"

"Sort of. Anastasia works in one of my buildings. She used to live there, too. She makes wedding cakes. She was living above her shop, but since she recently got married, she's now living with her new husband out on one of the islands."

"Anastasia got married?" I feel immediate regret that I didn't know that. That whenever I contact her, I just ask about Archer, never about how she's doing. "Good for her."

"She's happy. She married Kane O'Callaghan."

"The artist?"

"That's the one. Anyway, my point is that I am self-employed. And as such, I think I'll take a look at some property around here. Mostly out of curiosity."

"I don't know what there is for you to look at," I admit with a gusty breath. "You can't *be* here. It's not safe for you. For either of us."

He stops short and waits for me to face him.

"I'm not trying to make things unsafe, E. I worked so hard to find you. I just want to enjoy you for a while. I'm flying by the seat of my pants here. All I know is that I don't want to leave here without getting to know you again."

I shake my head. "It can't happen, Archer. I wish it could. More than you know."

God, I missed him so much. It still hurts.

"You can't stay."

But he doesn't respond. He just looks down the beach and then gestures with a shake of his head.

"How far are we going?"

"Not much farther." I gesture ahead. "See those two rocks there?"

"The ones a half a mile away?"

I laugh and look up at him. "You're an athletic guy. An extra half-mile won't hurt you."

"You were never the sporty type," he says.

"I decided to start exercising more when all of this started," I admit. "I've always been an introvert. That hasn't changed, but I didn't realize that being isolated could be *so* lonely. And one of the things I found that helps is working out. I do yoga and meditation most mornings, and I like to come out here to walk or run in the afternoon if the weather isn't too bad."

"Run, you say?"

"Sure."

"I'll race you, then."

And he takes off jogging. I pause, just to watch his sexy body from behind. Tight ass, broad shoulders, muscular back. I need to soak it all in because in a couple of hours, he'll be gone, and these few stolen moments on the beach are all I'll have to hold close.

Holy hell in a handbasket, he's hot.

I take off, enjoying the push and pull of my muscles as I sprint closer to him and then run past him, reaching the rocks a good twenty yards ahead of him.

We stop and bend at the waist, trying to catch our breath.

"Holy shit," he says as he works to take in air. "You're fucking fast."

"Been doing it a while." *And I wanted to impress you.*

Which is kind of dumb, but there you have it. The appreciation in his bright blue eyes was worth every step.

"These are nice," he says, gesturing to the houses on the bluffs. "Why didn't you go for one? Looks like several are for sale."

"I don't make that kind of money at my job. I couldn't afford one of these," I say, shaking my head. "And, yes, my grandmother made sure my bank account has a couple million dollars in it, but it would look crazy if I bought one of these places and then collected my salary. I'd stand out, and the whole point is to blend. Besides, I like my little place."

"It's cute," he agrees. "Small."

"It didn't feel small until you were in it." I laugh and take a deep breath, soaking in the salty air. "It's always just been me."

"Always?"

I know what he's asking. Has there been anyone since him?

"I haven't been a nun," I admit, making him scowl. "But I haven't been in a serious relationship since you, Archer. How could I when the entire relationship would be based on lies? I couldn't even tell him, whomever he may be, my real name. You can't build anything on lies. And I have to be ready to leave at a moment's notice. So, yes, it's always just been me in my cottage."

"I shouldn't be jealous," he says. He's caught his breath, and with his hands in his pockets, he stares out at the water. "It's been a long time, and of course, you're not a nun. But I'm jealous all the same. And relieved."

"Relieved that I'm an old maid?"

He turns to me now. "You're not an old maid. But I am relieved that you don't belong to anyone."

"I belong to *me*. And that's how it will always stay, Archer."

He nods once and wraps his arm around my shoulders, pulling me against his side. "What are you going to feed me for dinner?"

"We literally ate lunch right before we came here."

"That was at least an hour ago."

"How do you eat so much and still look like this? It shouldn't be possible."

"Genetics." He kisses my hair, and I melt against him. Archer was always physically affectionate. It was something I had to get used to because my parents were distant, and the only one I was close to who hugged me was Grandma.

I didn't realize I was so starved for touch.

But not just any touch. Archer's.

I fit against him perfectly, my shoulder under his armpit. My arm around his waist. His lips planted on the top of my head.

I don't want it to end.

"We could do spaghetti," he suggests, making me laugh. "You always made a really good sauce."

"It's gotten better since I last saw you."

"Don't tease me," he says. "My fragile stomach can't handle it."

"I'll prove it. And just so you know, I know this trick. I'm not giving in to your reverse psychology."

"You totally are. It's okay. I'm charming, remember?"

"I never should have told you that. It just inflates your ego." I stop and turn into him, burying my face in his hard chest, clinging to him with everything I have. "You can't stay, Archer. This is me digging in my heels and telling you *no*. You can't stay in Bandon."

He doesn't say anything for a long moment, just brushes his fingers up and down my arms, and then circles his arms around me and pulls me close.

"You've been the love of my life since I was a junior in high school and I saw you sitting with Stasia in the cafeteria. You're *everything*, E, even after all this time. And that won't ever change."

"Archer—"

"Listen." He catches my chin with his finger and makes me look him in the eyes. His are that insane bright blue and churning like the ocean behind him. "You're *everything*. It feels like I've loved you my whole life."

He always was good with words.

He doesn't say anything else about staying with me. That was the best goodbye speech I've ever heard. He deserved to hear something that amazing when I left him all those years ago.

But I was young and didn't know what the hell to do, except get as far away from him as possible. To keep him safe. To keep him *whole*.

We're quiet on the walk back to the cottage. To my surprise, Archer strides right up the stairs to the loft and starts gathering his things, filling his bag.

"You don't have to leave tonight." I'm such an idiot, sending him mixed messages. But the thought of watching him walk away tears at my heart. "You could stay and get a fresh start in the morning. I'll make the spaghetti."

"It's okay." Once his bag is tucked in his car, he walks back up the steps to the front door and leans on the jam, smiling down at me in that way he always used to when he was particularly amused by me.

I have no idea what's so damn funny about this. We're saying goodbye for good.

"Thank you for coming. For taking me to Seattle. For everything."

He pulls me in for another hug, holding me firmly.

God, this is killing me. Why did he have to come here in the first place?

"I love you, Elena," he whispers. He kisses my forehead and then my lips. I feel it all the way to my toes, even though it's the barest brush of skin against mine.

Without another word, he turns and jogs to his car, fires up the engine, and drives away.

"It's the right thing to do," I mumble as I close the door and lean against it, willing the tears to stay back. It may be the right thing, but it still hurts, all the way to the bone. My cottage feels emptier than it ever has. "Get used to it, *Ally*."

I square my shoulders and get down to business, cleaning and scrubbing my little house and getting ready to return to the safe life I've made for myself in Bandon, Oregon.

To MY SURPRISE and delight upon returning to work this morning, I discovered that Margie hired a new employee. Which means I'll start to have days off here and there, and Chad and I won't be so slammed.

I almost kissed Margie on the mouth when she told me, but there was no time.

I immediately shifted into training mode and spent all day showing Beverly the ropes. It was a satisfying but tiring day.

Now that I'm home, I'm ready to go for my usual afternoon walk and then settle in for some alone time.

With my cropped yoga pants and tank top on, I set off for the beach, taking the same route I took with Archer just yesterday.

I hope I was able to cover the anguish I've felt since he left last night. If I looked sad at work today, maybe the others chalked it up to the family emergency that took me away from work, and not to me feeling heartbroken over someone I lost more than a decade ago all over again.

The beach is pretty much abandoned as I walk south. Fewer tourists is another sign that summer is almost over, and we're headed into the winter months. I'll miss the warmer weather and the sunshine.

I'm usually energized after my walks, but when I return home, I just feel tired. So, I take a quick shower, change into my comfies, and place an order for pizza delivery.

I'm going to give myself this one night to wallow in self-pity, and then it's back to business as usual.

When I'm armed with a large pepperoni, a full glass of wine, and the remote, I settle on the couch with my favorite blanket and snap on the TV. The regional news fills the screen.

"From what we've been told, law enforcement believes the Martinelli family may be behind this brutal murder, but the investigation is ongoing."

I quickly turn the channel to the home improvement network and set my pizza aside.

This. This is why I turned Archer away.

And it would be best if I didn't forget that.

CHAPTER
SIX
~ARCHER~

I could have stayed with her last night, but I have a shit ton to do in a short time. If she thinks I'm leaving, she obviously doesn't know me very well.

But I'll be happy to remind her.

Because I'm not going anywhere. If she needs space and time to get used to the idea of having me around, that's fine with me.

I'm in no hurry.

I've temporarily settled myself in a suite at a seaside resort, and I have a meeting with a real estate agent in fifteen minutes. I've had breakfast, and a five-mile run already, and am on my way to look at the house that caught my eye yesterday when I was on the beach with Elena.

Ally.

I need to get used to her name. She has my last name. I wonder if that's a coincidence or if she told her grandmother what name she wanted to use. She *should* have my name. And she would if she hadn't been afraid of her father.

"Mr. Montgomery?"

I nod at the woman standing by the front door of the large house on

YOU BELONG WITH ME

the cliffs. I can hear the waves crashing in the distance. "Yes, ma'am. Ms. Stebbins?"

"Cheryl, please." She shakes my hand and then opens the already unlocked door. Cheryl knows how to do her job well. She's an attractive woman, dressed in a simple, classy suit. Her blond hair is styled in waves down her back, and I can see she recently applied red lipstick to her pouty lips. But her smile isn't flirtatious, and she's all-business when she gestures for me to walk in ahead of her. All of the lights inside are already on. "This particular house has been on the market for about five weeks."

I nod again. I did a little research on this property last night while I ate takeout in my hotel room. The main living space is bright and open, with floor-to-ceiling windows that give me an unobstructed view of the ocean beyond. The furniture looks new, is simple, and fits the space perfectly. "Is it possible to buy the furniture with the house?"

"I'm sure we can make an offer and see what they say. They've already moved out of state."

The views from the kitchen and living room and then the master bedroom are simply stunning.

"The house was built in 1982, but as you can see, the current owners completely remodeled the home, updating all of the rooms."

"It's nice," I reply, taking in the white kitchen with black lower cabinets, the up-to-date light fixtures, and brand-new floors. It's better than nice. It's gorgeous. Living here while I win my girl back won't be a hardship in the least. "I'll take it."

Her eyebrows climb, and those red lips part in surprise. "Just like that?"

"Just like that."

"Do you have preapproval for a loan?"

"I'll pay cash. I'd like to close as soon as possible. And I'd like to ask the owners if I can move in right away, paying them rent, of course, until the closing date."

"Like I said, they've left the state, so I don't think that will be a problem."

"Great. You'll be able to reach me all day should you need to."

"This could be the easiest sale of my career," Cheryl says as we walk

63

outside, and she locks the door behind us. "I'll start making calls and drawing up the paperwork right away. I'll call the current owner and get back to you today regarding your questions."

"Thank you, Cheryl."

I shake her hand again and then lower myself into my car, headed back to the resort. The first matter of business for the day is finished. If E —*Ally* won't let me stay with her, I'll buy my own place. It's a good investment anyway.

I hurry back up to my suite and call my assistant, Leslie.

"Are you coming into the office today?" she asks when she answers the phone.

"No. I'm going to be working remotely for a while, Les."

"Killing me, boss."

I smirk and open my laptop. "There's nothing you can't handle in that office."

"You bet your ass about that," she says. "But I can't sign your name or write million-dollar checks. That's above my pay grade."

"No one writes million-dollar checks," I say as I press my finger to the pad on the keyboard and log into the computer. "We do everything electronically these days. Speaking of, I just bought a property in Oregon."

She's quiet for a moment, and I can just imagine the frown on her pretty face.

"Oregon?"

"Bandon, Oregon, to be exact."

"Commercial property?"

"A house. One that I'm going to be living in for a bit, and then I'll lease it out."

"I'm sorry, am I speaking to Archer Montgomery?"

"I don't pay you extra to be a smartass."

"You should. My smartassery is deeply undervalued. What are you doing in Oregon, Arch?"

"Let's call it a working vacation. I'll have my home office set up soon. You can reach me anytime."

"I have a list of messages for you," she says. "And you haven't answered your email in three days."

"I'll work on that today."

"Are you okay, boss?"

"I'm great. Better than I've been in a long time. But, Les, where I am is confidential. If anyone asks, I'm just out of town."

"That's the answer I give anyway. Please, and I mean this most sincerely, check your email."

"I promise, I'll do it today. I'll keep you posted."

"Be careful."

She hangs up, and I grin. Leslie's been with me since I started the business five years ago. She knows more about the day-to-day than I do, and that's no lie. We joke about her lack of compensation, but I pay her well for the job she does for me.

She's worth every penny.

Feeling confident that Leslie has the home front taken care of, I briefly think about what I should have for lunch, but my phone interrupts my decision making.

If Cheryl's calling already, it's either very good or very bad news.

"Hi, Cheryl."

"I have some excellent news for you, Mr. Montgomery. The sellers have agreed to your terms and are willing to include the furniture with the full price offer."

"Excellent."

"As I mentioned, they've moved out, so all of their personal effects are gone."

"When can I move in?"

"Immediately." She laughs as if she can't believe it. Truth be told, neither can I. "We have some paperwork to take care of, and then it's all yours."

"Excellent."

FOUR HOURS LATER, I've checked out of the resort and am unpacked in my new ocean-front house in Oregon. Setting up my office didn't take long, given that the desk and chair, along with shelves were already in the room. All I had to add was my laptop. I will need to find a store soon for a printer-slash-scanner, and I'm sure Leslie will give me a list of things I'll need, but this will work just fine for now.

I made a grocery run to stock up on the essentials, which for me is roughly five-hundred dollars-worth of food and snacks, some cleaning supplies, and a few bottles of the wine I saw at Ally's house.

Now, despite all of the food in the place, I decide I'm too tired to cook, so I drive to town and walk into the diner. I sit in a deep red booth, looking forward to the burger and fries I just ordered.

"Archer?"

I glance up, and there's Ally's friend from the other day.

"That's your name, right?"

"Yes, and you're Ally's friend..."

"Lindsey."

"Right. Nice to see you."

"You, too. I guess I'm confused. I saw her today, and Ally said that you left yesterday."

"Did she?"

"Yeah. She didn't look great, actually."

My heart stops, and my eyes narrow. "What do you mean?"

"Pale, quiet. I figured she was just still getting over the family emergency she went through. But here you are."

"Here I am."

I don't ask her to join me. That's not appropriate. But I also don't want her to rush off and call Ally. I want the news that I'm still here to come from *me*.

"I had some business to see to, and I didn't want to leave until I knew she was okay. I'll look in on her before I head out of town."

Lindsey's shoulders sag, and a smile spreads over her lips. "I understand. I'm glad she has you as her friend. I wish she'd told me about you before. I always thought Ally was a lonely person, but maybe she's just private."

"She's definitely private," I agree. "Have a good night, Lindsey."

"You, too."

She waves and walks up to the counter where a bag of food is ready for her to take away.

In a town as small as this one, I won't be able to be here for long without Ally knowing it. And that's okay, it's not a secret. But until this minute, I didn't realize how much I wanted her to find out from me, not someone else.

So, I'll have to make sure I *run into her* tomorrow and get going on my plan to win her over.

SHE NEVER DID GO for flowers. She wouldn't turn them away, but posies aren't the way to El—Ally's heart.

Donuts and coffee. Every day during her junior year of high school, when I was a senior, I picked her up for school with a bag of maple glazed and a white-chocolate mocha. It was a sugar shock to the system, that's for sure, but it never failed to make her smile.

I know that she works for the wild animal refuge just outside of town, so I park out front and, armed with all the sugar in the land, walk inside.

"We're not open to the public yet."

"I'm not here for the animals," I reply with a smile. "I'm hoping I can see Ally."

The man's eyes widen in surprise. "She's here, back with the babies."

"Can you please ask her if she has a moment?"

He nods. "Sure. Hang on."

He disappears through a door, and I'm suddenly as nervous as I was the other day when I rang her doorbell.

Here's hoping she doesn't pull a gun on me this time.

"Can I help—?" The words die on her lips when she walks out and sees that it's me. "What are you doing here?"

"I brought you breakfast." I pass her the bag and the cup of coffee with a smile. "I know you work super early and have already been here for a while, but I got a late start. Sorry about that. I hope you still like maple."

She frowns and glances into the bag.

"I haven't had one since the last time you..." She swallows, shakes off the rest of the thought, and looks back up at me. "You left."

"No, you kicked me out. There's a difference. You don't have to go home, but you can't stay here." I wink and lean on the counter that she's standing behind. "I bought a house. I think you're going to like it. I hope so, anyway."

"You bought—?" Her mouth opens and then closes again. "What in the hell, Arch?"

"We can talk about it all later." I tap the counter with my palm and step back. "I shouldn't hold you up. Enjoy your breakfast. I'll pick you up at six."

"For what?"

"Dinner, of course."

I turn and whistle as I step out of the building.

I WASN'T LYING the other day. She used to make a hell of a spaghetti. But she always loved it when I made tacos. So, for tonight, that's precisely what I'm going to make her. It works out well because I can prepare the majority of it early, then go pick her up and finish it up when we get back to the house—after I've given her a proper tour of the place.

With all the veggies chopped and ready, the cheese shredded, and the pico and guac made and in the fridge, I grab my keys and hurry out to my car, ready to drive across town to Ally's house to bring her home with me. I'm craving her company. Bandon is a small town, but I can't get to her fast enough. After I park and take a deep breath, I walk up and knock on the door.

There's no answer.

I frown and knock again, then walk over to look in a window.

No movement inside.

I head around the house, and there she is, sitting on her deck with her feet up on the rail and a glass of wine in her hand.

"There you are."

"Go away, Archer."

"No way."

She rolls her eyes. "Is the fact that I don't want you here really that big of a hit to your fragile male ego?"

I know what she's attempting to do. She's trying to piss me off and push me away.

It's not going to work.

"I've told you for days, I'm not going anywhere. You don't want me to stay here, and that's totally fine with me. I would prefer to be able to hold you at night, but I can respect your wishes."

"Obviously, you can't, because I told you to go *home*."

"Well, technically, I live here now."

"Tell me you didn't actually buy a house."

"I did. You're going to love it."

"Archer."

"Ally."

She stumbles over the next words and frowns. "You called me Ally."

"That's your name, remember?"

She blinks quickly, the way she does when she's surprised.

"Listen, I don't care what your name is, as long as I get to be with you. So, yes, I bought a house, and I'm here to get to know you better. To get to know you *again*."

"This is a *very* expensive courtship," she says, swirling the wine in her glass.

"You're worth it," I counter. "Now, are you going to come let me feed you, or what? I have everything ready for you."

"I shouldn't," she says. "I should demand that you respect my wishes and go."

"No, you should come and see this killer house and eat my tacos."

"Tacos?" Her eyes fly to mine, and she swallows hard, tries to seem unimpressed. "I don't even like tacos."

I step to her, and without touching her, lean in to brush my nose over hers. "Liar."

"Tastes change."

"Not when it comes to tacos, sweetheart."

"Did you buy a house on the beach?"

"Yup."

"Tacos *and* an ocean view?"

I simply smile at her.

"Fine."

CHAPTER
SEVEN
~ELENA~

Until I rode in Archer's car the other day, I didn't realize how much I missed heated seats. Yes, it's a first-world thing, and I'm not proud of it, but it's true. My backside just sinks into the warmth of the leather, and I could live right here, for a long time.

He drives us along the beach and pulls into a driveway that ends at a three-car garage.

"Are you telling me that you just bought a seven-figure house because you want to *date* me?"

Seeing him walk into my job today was a shock to my system, almost as bad as the day he came to my door. I'd been so sad, so *lost* since he left the other night. I was sure I'd never lay eyes on him again, and I was in the process of grieving not only my grandmother but also the loss of Archer all over again.

And then I walked into that room and saw him standing there, and it was as if everything in my world snapped back into place.

Which is crazy.

"Among other things."

I blink, confused. "Excuse me?"

"I bought the house because I want to date you, along with some other things." He unclips our seatbelts as the garage door lowers behind us. "Come on, I want to show you the place. And I'm hungry."

"You're always hungry."

He grins and pushes out of the car, hurrying around the hood to open my door before I can do it myself. He was always the type to open doors for me, and it seems that hasn't changed.

"It's better to walk through the front door," he says, opening the side garage door. "We'll just walk out this way."

"I'm sure it's fine through the mudroom."

"Next time. I want you to get the full effect this first time."

He takes my hand, linking his fingers with mine as if it's just second nature and not a conscious decision. The heat travels from my palm, up my arm, and settles in my shoulder, making me shiver in delight.

"Are you cold?"

I shake my head no and smile as he unlocks the door and leads me inside.

The view is incredible. I can see the rocky shoreline, the calm water beyond, and it takes me a second to catch my breath.

"Wow."

"I know," he murmurs, standing back with his hands tucked into his pockets as he waits for me to soak it all in. The view out the windows is beautiful, but the man before me is a complete shock to the system. He always was, even as a young man. But Archer in his early thirties? Holy shit. He's tall with broad shoulders and muscles in all the right places.

Sinew for days.

His hips are lean. And his abs? Well, let's just say if it were a hundred years ago, a girl could wash her clothes on his stomach.

"Keep looking at me like that, and my manners will fly right out that window, and I'll take you here on the kitchen counter, Elena."

Elena.

I quirk a brow.

"It's just the two of us, and I'm smart enough to never put you at risk out there." He gestures with a nod of his head in the direction of town. "But when it's you and me, you're Elena. I'll be damned if I'll say another woman's name when I'm being intimate with you."

"I never agreed to anything intimate." I lick my lips and will the damn butterflies in my stomach to get lost. "I agreed to tacos and a view."

"You'll get both." He reaches up and drags his thumb down my cheek. "And that's all. For now. Let me show you the rest of the house."

He leads me through bedrooms, bathrooms, and an office with a desk that's empty aside from his laptop. The house is big, much too big for one person, but it's comfortable.

"It's a lot of house."

"It's ridiculous," he agrees. "And the smallest one available with these views. So, I snatched it up."

"In one day?"

"I got lucky."

I give him a look that says *right.*

"I really did. The former owners moved out of state, and this was all staging furniture. So, I just bought it all."

"Just like that."

He walks behind the island in the kitchen and starts pulling bowls out of the fridge.

"Like I said, I got lucky." He sets a skillet on the gas stovetop and turns on the burner, then dumps some ground beef into the pan and starts to stir. "Not to mention, money talks, sweetheart. I made a pitcher of margaritas if you want one. I also bought that wine you like, if you'd rather have that."

I sit on a stool and stare at him. Am I dreaming? Archer is in Bandon. He bought a house and is making me tacos.

What alternate universe am I living in?

Whatever it is, I don't want to leave.

"I'll have a margarita. I wouldn't want them to go to waste."

"Good idea." He fills two glasses and clinks his to mine. "Cheers."

"Cheers."

He takes a platter out of a cupboard. Who knew serving implements would be part of the staging items included in the house? As he begins to pile stuff on it, the smells coming at me are amazing and make my stomach growl. I didn't realize I was so hungry.

"Let's take this all out onto the deck and watch the sunset while we gorge ourselves on guacamole," he suggests.

I haven't had a better offer in years. I hop up and help him gather all of the food and our drinks, and we make our way onto the deck, where a small table and chairs are set up, just big enough for dinner for two.

"I admit, this is pretty great," I say as I dip a chip in the guac and shove it into my face as I look out to the sea that's as calm as it gets tonight.

"The view or the food?"

"Both." I watch him as he chews and swallows, his Adam's apple bobbing with the motion. "You're stubborn, you know that?"

"Hi pot, I'm kettle."

"Archer, you *bought a house*. And not just any home. You bought this insanely big house. You could have stayed at the resort for a hell of a lot less."

"I'm more comfortable here," he says with a shrug. "Besides, I've lived in a *lot* of hotels lately, traveling all over the country, trying to track you down. I'd rather have a home base for a while. And, after I'm done here, I can lease this place out and make some money. Flip it when the value goes up."

"How long did it take you to find me?"

"A few months."

I feel my eyes go wide.

"I couldn't just look for you every minute of every day. I had to go back to Seattle for blocks of time so I could work, be with my family, that sort of thing. But when I could get away, I returned to the search."

"Why now?"

"Because Anastasia screwed up and let it slip that she hears from you now and then. I didn't want to talk about it. But then she messed up more by admitting that she knew why you ghosted me after we got married. After that, I became a man obsessed. I had to find you. I mean, I took one night to get stinking drunk and sing bad Irish songs in Kane's brother's bar, but then I got down to business."

"You sang Irish songs?"

His lips twitch. "Not well."

"I wish there was a video of that."

"No, you don't. Trust me."

"I still can't believe that after all this time, you came to find me."

"You *married* me," he says, his voice suddenly heavy with impatience. "I vowed to love you for better or worse. And you up and broke it off so suddenly that you made my head spin. And you wouldn't talk to me. We were together for two years, attached at the hip, and then one day, you were just gone."

"I was trying to protect you."

He growls, and I reach over to lay my hand on his arm.

"Listen to me. You don't understand because I never talked about it much. I just wanted to be a normal girl with you. I didn't want to be the princess. Different. Being with you, with your family, was the most incredible experience of my life."

"So you left me?"

"You're not listening." I want to smack him. "I never told my family I was with you. Not after I tried, and my father told me to break it off. I knew it was too risky."

"Elena." He sits back and stares at me in surprise.

"You weren't from the right pedigree. You certainly weren't who my father would have chosen for me. So, I had to keep it all a secret. I stupidly thought that if we got married, if I went to them and said it was already done, there wouldn't be anything they could do about it. I figured they'd just have to get used to it."

He pinches the bridge of his nose. "Christ."

"My father was insanely pissed," I continue, flinching at the memory of my father's face when I told him. "I'd seen him angry before, of course. He was a scary man, especially when he was mad. But I'd *never* seen him like that." I shudder at the memory of those days. Of the beating, the whipping.

The branding.

"What did your mother think?" he asks, pulling me out of the horrible memories.

I frown. "It didn't matter what she thought. My father was the boss. And not just of the household, Archer, he was a mob boss. An insanely powerful man. If he wanted you dead, he would have done it in a heartbeat and wouldn't have lost a moment of sleep over it."

He finishes his fifth taco and pushes his plate away, then takes a sip of his drink.

"Did he still punish you?"

You have no idea.

I shrug a shoulder and look out at the water. Gulls fly overhead, and the bottom of the sun is just starting to kiss the top of the horizon. The sky is a riot of color, like a fresh bruise. Like the ones I wore around my eyes for days.

"Did he punish you?" he asks again.

I take a deep breath and let it out slowly. "Making me lose you was the worst of it."

Emotional pain is always worse than physical.

"What else did that fucker do?"

His voice is hard now. I glance back at him and let my eyes roam over his face, his eyes and nose, full mouth. Yes, losing Archer was the worst thing that ever happened to me in my life.

"It doesn't matter."

"It does to me."

I stand and walk to the railing and watch people walking on the sand below. Archer joins me. He's close but doesn't touch me.

"There's a code in the family. They don't physically hurt women. Punishments are psychological, and there were plenty of those over the years. I was usually a good girl, so the punishments were always small. But this was a pretty big deal, and I pushed him past his patience."

"What did he do?"

"Archer, it was a long time ago." And something I don't like to think about. Because when I do, I can feel the whip. I can smell my dad's cologne. I remember the helplessness I felt as I hung by my hands, and the despair when I realized that my relationship with Archer was over.

But that was long ago, and I have no plans to rehash it.

He takes my shoulders in his hands and nudges my chin up to look me in the eyes. I don't want to tell him. It'll make him feel guilty and hurt all over again.

"I don't want to talk about it right now."

"Will you ever want to talk about it?" He steps back and shakes his head in disappointment. "We can't build a relationship on lies."

He tosses my own words from the beach the other day back at me.

"I'm not lying to you. I'm telling you, point-blank, that I don't want

75

to talk about the shitty past. Can't we just enjoy this sunset and each other's company for a while? Can't we simply live in the here and now?"

He sighs, and his eyes soften. "For now. But not forever, Elena. I deserve the answers to my questions."

DESPITE THE FRUSTRATING CONVERSATION EARLIER, the evening has been wonderful. An incredible sunset and even better conversation made the time fly.

If he asks me to stay tonight, I don't know if I'll be able to say no.

It feels too good being with him like this, in this amazing house. I could almost let myself daydream for a moment that this is *our* house. That we're married and living our life like ordinary people. The way it should be. The way it was *supposed* to be.

But that's silly, and I learned long ago that such daydreams are a waste of time and energy.

"What are you thinking about?" Archer asks after slipping the last dish into the dishwasher and snapping it shut.

"That I'm glad I came here tonight," I reply.

"I am, too. You look good, sitting here in my kitchen."

"You don't look so bad yourself."

His impossibly blue eyes narrow, the way they always did when he was feeling particularly sexy. I don't have to be a mind reader to know he wants me. The feeling is entirely mutual.

Maybe staying isn't such a bad idea.

"I should probably get you home," he says, surprising me.

"Oh. Right. Yeah, I should go."

He rounds the island and wraps one arm around my waist. His lips are inches from mine as he leans in.

"I want you to stay," he whispers. "Make no mistake, I want it more than I've wanted anything in my life. But it's too soon, and you have to work early tomorrow. When I have you, I don't want time constraints, and I don't want secrets between us."

Well, then.

I lick my lips and nod, watching his mouth as it pulls up in that cocky grin that always puts a knot in my stomach.

Archer reluctantly pulls away, and we make our way to his car in the garage.

The drive to my cottage is quick and silent, as both of us are lost in our thoughts. I'm suddenly bone tired. I feel like I could sleep for a week.

What is it about this man that exhausts me? And he hasn't even kissed me! Not really, anyway. The brushes of lips over breakfast and before he left don't exactly count.

"I like these seats," I murmur as I shimmy down into the warmth of the leather. "So comfortable."

"Don't fall asleep on me, sweetheart. We're almost there."

I smile and close my eyes, enjoying the warmth, darkness, and the sounds around me.

I feel him turn down my road, and then into my driveway.

"Thanks for the ride." I open my eyes and turn to find Archer watching me with a serious expression. "What's wrong?"

"I missed you, E. More than I even realized."

I reach for his hand and pull his palm against my cheek. "I missed you, too."

I kiss his skin, and then the moment is gone. Archer climbs out of the car and walks around to help me out. With our hands linked, he walks me to the door. The night has come awake around us with singing night birds and the buzz of insects. Even from this distance, I can smell the sea. The last of my summer geraniums are starting to wither.

"Do you want to come in?" I ask.

"Yes." He sighs and cages me in against the still-closed door. "So, I'd better not."

His eyes drop to my lips, and before I can say anything else, he cups my face and neck in both of his hands and lowers his head to mine, covering my mouth in the sweetest kiss I've had in more than a decade.

One hand slips down my shoulder, my arm, and lands on my hip. His fingers tighten, just enough to let me know he's there.

I can't help myself. I step into him, pressing closer, and surrender to the kiss. I want to lose myself in him. I want to remember what it feels like to be with Archer in this way. There's absolutely nothing better in the world than when this man focuses his whole attention on me as if I'm the only one in the world.

With a growl, he nips at the corner of my mouth and teases me with his tongue. But that's as deep as he takes it, and he backs away far too soon.

"You're as sweet as you ever were," he whispers against my lips. "Maybe sweeter, and I didn't think that was possible."

I swallow hard and, without giving myself time to overthink it, I wrap my arms around his middle and hug him close. This man was once my husband. He's meant more to me than anyone else in my life besides my grandmother.

And he's here.

And despite his words to the contrary, he's not leaving.

This could be catastrophic for both of us.

"Stop thinking so hard," he murmurs against my hair. "No one knows where I am. You're safe. *We're* safe, E. I promise."

God, I want to believe him.

He tips up my chin, and I stare into his gorgeous eyes.

"Trust me?" he asks.

"I've always trusted you," is my immediate response. It's true. Trust was never our issue. "But I don't know how you can trust *me* after everything that happened before."

"Stop beating yourself up, okay? I'll be just down the street a ways if you need me. And I'll see you very soon."

"How soon?"

"Tomorrow, most likely."

"Are you going to make a nuisance of yourself?"

"Oh, yeah." He laughs and kisses me squarely on the mouth, then steps off the porch. "You're gonna be sick of me before long."

I unlock and open the door, watching as Archer walks backwards to his car.

"I still think this is a bad idea."

"I told you, stop thinking. Sleep well, babe."

And with that, he gets into his car and drives away. But this time, I don't have a pit in my stomach at the idea of never seeing him again.

No, now I'm filled with anticipation, wondering how I'm supposed to wait until tomorrow to see Archer. How am I supposed to sleep with the taste of him on my lips, and the thought of having his hands on me racing through my mind?

Yes, I want him, maybe even more than I ever did before. I'm no longer a girl wearing rose-colored glasses and telling myself lies of happily ever after.

I'm a grown woman, quickly falling in love once more with a man I've been tied to nearly all of my adult life. Being with him could literally be fatal for both of us.

This is a bad, bad idea.

CHAPTER
EIGHT
~CARMINE~

I had no idea that my grandmother was a hoarder. Admittedly, I didn't spend a lot of time in her home as an adult. As children, my brothers and I, along with Elena, spent weeks here in the summer, playing and exploring the big house on the cliffs. Nothing was off-limits to us.

Our grandmother doted on us the way any normal grandparent does.

The only difference was, ours was the matriarch of a mafia empire.

No big deal.

Cannonballs in the pool. Ice cream in the gazebo. Treasure hunts in the attic that spans the entire house, the space filled with antiques and trunks full of old things.

We loved being here together, where we could do as we pleased and be indulged by a loving grandmother.

I miss her already. I was at her bedside when she died, the only one in the room when she whispered her secret to me.

"Elena," she said, *making me sigh.*

"She's not here, Grams."

"Helped her," she said and then coughed. *"Helped her get away."*

My eyes narrowed.

80

"Is she alive, Grams?"

"Hidden," she confirmed. "Find her before your father. Keep her safe."

And when I was carrying her casket at the church and looked up and saw the two different-colored eyes staring back at me, I *knew*. I knew it was Elena. She could wear any disguise in the world, and I'd still know her.

She was like a sister to me.

Of course, I had to tell my father that she's alive. If he found out I'd kept something that huge from him...well, I wouldn't like to know what the punishment for that might be.

But I played stupid about the rest of it. Grams knew that Elena was in danger, and I would find her and do everything in my power to keep her safe.

Now, to figure out where the fuck she is.

I've had a pit in my stomach for days. Rocco was right in the elevator. There would be a punishment for her staying away from the family so long. For disregarding her place in the hierarchy.

The thought of it makes me sick.

I slam a desk drawer shut in disgust.

"I've been through here," I mumble, wiping my hand down my mouth. I've been over every inch of Grams' office.

There's nothing here.

On a hunch, I run my hand under the pen drawer and find a button. When I push it, an invisible drawer on the side springs free.

"Son of a bitch."

I look over my shoulder, even though I know for a fact I'm here alone. It's two in the morning. Rocco left several hours ago.

The drawer is deep and filled to the brim. I feel like a kid again, hunting for treasures in the attic as I start pulling things out and setting them on the desk before me.

A flash drive. That goes directly into my pocket. I'll look at it later from the safety and privacy of my own home.

A notebook full of nothing but numbers. No notes to explain what they mean, just rows and rows of digits. Could they be phone numbers? Bank accounts? I have no fucking clue.

I set it aside.

There's some jewelry, birth and death certificates. It seems Grams liked this hidden desk drawer for important things rather than an actual safe.

Which was empty, by the way.

A scrap of paper at the bottom of the drawer catches my eye.

I sit back and hold it up in the light.

Bingo.

I found her.

CHAPTER

NINE

~ARCHER~

"How was your day?"

I can't stop staring at her. We're in her little cottage, and she's gathering her things, a light sweater and her purse, almost ready to go out on our date. She's in a barely-there yellow sundress, perfect for the warm, late-summer evening. Her dark hair is loose and falls in waves down her back.

Southern Oregon is in the midst of an Indian summer. Or so I've been told at least six times today from various locals around town.

"Busy, but really good," she says with a smile. "We finally hired an extra person at the refuge, so I get tomorrow off. It'll be the first day off I've had in months, at least one that wasn't because of a funeral."

"Spend it with me," I say immediately and smile down at her when her eyes jump up to mine. "Pack an overnight bag and spend the night at my place tonight. Tomorrow, we'll goof off together."

"I should get some things done. I have laundry and bills to pay. I was thinking about—"

"Please."

She sighs as if she's waging war inside herself, and then she turns without a word and walks upstairs to her bedroom.

When she's out of eyesight, I pump my fist in the air in celebration.

"I saw that," she calls down, making me laugh.

"You didn't see anything."

Less than three minutes later, she returns with the same overnight bag she took with her to Seattle. I toss it into the back seat of my car, get her settled, and pull out of her driveway.

"Where are we going?" she asks. "And am I dressed appropriately?"

"You're gorgeous." I head toward town. "I thought we'd do something tonight that we used to do back in the day."

She quirks a brow at me. "Did you?"

I feel my lips twitch. "Easy, tiger. For starters, we're going to a high school football game. It *is* Friday night, after all."

Earlier, I researched where the game is being held so it would be easy to find. I pull into a packed parking lot once we arrive.

"Small towns *love* their Friday night football games," I say as I cut the engine and turn to smile at my girl. She's not smiling in return. "What's wrong? You used to love football."

"I still like it."

"My cousin Will will be thrilled to hear that."

She rolls her eyes. "I just don't usually come to these kinds of things. I try to blend, remember?"

"You're a member of this community. Going to a game isn't going to make you stand out like a sore thumb. Come on, it'll be fun. They have hotdogs, and I'm starving. Aren't you hungry?"

"For hotdogs?"

"They might have soft pretzels. Or nachos."

I waggle my eyebrows and get out of the car, then walk around to open her door and take her hand to help her up.

"So, it's a fancy date, then," she says while batting her eyelashes. "You shouldn't have."

"We spent many a Friday night at the football field when we were younger," I remind her as I link my fingers with hers and follow the crowd walking toward the gate.

"Yeah, because you were on the team, and I was a cheerleader. Attendance was required. Also, we were in *high school.* Here, we don't even know the kids playing." She stops short and blinks rapidly.

"What's wrong?" I look in the direction she's staring, but I don't see anything out of the ordinary. "What is it?"

"Nothing." She shakes her head and then smiles up at me. "I thought I saw something. Anyway, we're no longer *required* to come to high school games."

"Hey, it's football." I wink down at her, determined to have a good time tonight. "No pro teams in southern Oregon."

"True."

"Next!" a mom yells out. She's wearing a Bandon Tigers sweatshirt, a pin on her chest with a photo of a player, and gold and black paint on her face. My guess is she's the president of the PTA. "What can I getcha?"

"Four hotdogs for me," I reply and then look down at El—Ally. "You?"

"*Four?*" she asks and then shakes her head. "I'll have one hotdog and a Coke."

"Oh, a Coke for me, too."

The lady nods, shouts our hotdog order at the other mother filling those requests, and before long, we're paid up and walking away with our food.

The lights are bright overhead, and the sun is starting to set. The cheerleaders are at their post on the sideline, just inside a wooden fence, smiling for the crowd.

As we walk past, I feel Ally move closer to me. I glance down in time to see her narrowing her eyes at the girls.

"What's up?"

"Nothing."

We climb the bleachers and find a good spot, right in the middle of the crowd.

"For real, what happened?"

Ally takes a bite of her dog and shrugs a shoulder. "They were checking you out."

"They're like...sixteen."

She shrugs again.

"I don't go for jailbait, babe."

"You did once." Her voice is cool and matter-of-fact, and I can't help but bust up laughing.

"Yeah, over *you*. And if I recall correctly, I was also jailbait at the time, so it doesn't count."

She laughs now, and I finish off one dog in two bites, then start on the next.

"You know, this isn't a contest," she says, watching me. "You can chew it."

"I am."

"How can you afford to feed yourself?"

"Good thing I'm rich." I wink at her before taking a sip from the straw in my Coke. The game is about to start. A woman climbs the bleachers and sits next to me with a smile.

"Is this seat taken?"

"No, ma'am."

She lays a blanket on the bench, sits, then spreads another blanket over her lap like it's blizzarding out.

"Do you have a son playing?" she asks me.

"No, just here to enjoy the game. You?"

"That one." She points to the field. "Number two."

"Quarterback," I say with a nod. "Very nice."

"And that cheerleader," she continues, pointing to a blond girl in the middle, "is my daughter."

"Double the reason to be here," I say with a nod. "That's great."

"They're good kids," she says, watching her daughter as she laughs with a friend. "I'm a single mom, so it hasn't always been easy, but I have no complaints when it comes to them."

"That's great," I say again.

"So, not married, then?" she asks, looking at my ring finger. "Sorry, I'm Bea."

"Hi, Bea. No, I'm not married, but I'm here with my—" My what? Girlfriend? Ex-wife?

"I'm Ally," Ally says, reaching around me to offer her hand for Bea to shake. "And I can hear you."

"Oh, I was just making conversation," Bea says, clearly flustered. "I certainly didn't mean any offense."

"Of course," Ally says with a nod and sits back, mumbling under her breath, "Home-wrecker."

I lean over to whisper in her ear. "Your green eye is especially green tonight, sweetheart."

"Your blue eyes are both about to be black," she says with a saccharine-sweet smile. "Must you flirt with anything in a skirt?"

"To be fair, she's not wearing a skirt. And I wasn't flirting. I was *talking*."

"Hmph."

"You know, your jealous side always did turn me on. Seems nothing's changed in that regard."

Her eyes are pinned to the field, but her lips turn up in a half-smile. This is a conversation we would have had before. Teasing and easy. She's not easily swayed to jealousy, so I know she's just giving me shit— the way she always did.

Falling into an easy cadence with her is as simple as breathing.

The game is underway, Bea keeps to herself now, and I spend the next two hours cheering for a team that isn't mine, in a town that isn't mine, next to the woman that *is* mine.

"Come on, ref, put your glasses on!" Ally yells, almost coming off her seat. "What a jerk."

I grin down at her. "I knew you'd enjoy yourself."

"I'd enjoy it more if that ref knew what a decent call is." She shakes her head in disgust. "He's not a great banker, either."

"Excuse me?"

"The ref. He works at the bank."

"Small towns," I murmur with a smile, enjoying myself. She's getting so worked up by the game, it's hilarious to watch. "You would love watching Will play."

"I've been," she says and sends me a sly smile. It fills my heart to know that she's still interested in my family after everything that went down between us. They loved her and were upset when we broke up. "I drove to San Francisco to watch him a couple of years ago. I always liked your family."

"I know." I swallow and watch the quarterback throw the ball. "They liked you, too. Still do."

She nods. "Anyway, it was fun to drive down for a couple of days and watch him play. He used to remind me of you."

"Because of the amount of food we ate?"

"That," she says, "and your personalities. You're both easygoing, funny. Kind of cocky."

"Hey, I'm not cocky."

She laughs and shakes her head. "Have you met you? You're completely cocky. But not in an asshole kind of way."

"Uh, thanks?"

She takes my hand in hers, smiles, and then resumes watching the game. I want to cover my heart with my hand and sigh.

I have it bad. Real bad. I don't know how we're going to make this work, but there is no other choice. Because I'm not leaving Bandon without her. Next week or next month, I don't care when.

"You put in a hot tub?" she asks as she stares dumbfounded at the bubbling tub out on the deck. We stepped out to listen to the surf below. "That was fast."

"I work fast," I reply. "It seemed like a good investment. Who wouldn't like to sit out here in that tub, watching the ocean? If I end up using this place as a vacation rental, it'll help lure in vacationers."

"I would rent it," she says and dips her hand in the water. "Is it all ready to go?"

"Yep."

"I'll be right back."

She turns and disappears into the house. I want to go after her, but my phone rings.

"Hi, Stasia," I say.

"How's it going?"

"Great."

"Are you with her?"

"Yes."

She huffs on the other end of the line. "Gee, you're so talkative. Tell me things, Archer. Where are you? What did she say when she saw you?

What are you doing now? When are you coming back to Seattle? Are you an item again?"

"Christ, do you ever stop talking?"

"I need information. You've been very tight-lipped. So, where did you find her?"

"I'm not telling you that."

She pauses. I can just see her face in my head, her brow furrowed in a frown.

"Why ever not?"

"Because she doesn't want anyone to know where she is."

"Well, you have to tell me *something*."

"No, I don't."

"What if something happens to you? What if something happens here, and I need to send for you?"

"Send for me? What is this, sixteen-sixty? I have a phone. Call me."

"Archer Steven Montgomery."

"That's not going to work, and you know it."

She sighs dramatically, and I can hear a deep voice in the background.

"He won't tell me where they are."

"Is that Kane?"

"Of course, it's Kane."

"Tell him to rein in his wife."

I grin and wait for the sputtering and spitting to come. I'd never have the balls to say that in person, she'd slice me in two, but from this safe distance, I can't help it.

"Have you lost your bloody *mind*?" she screeches, making me laugh loudly.

"You deserved it," I remind her. "We're safe, we're fine, and that's all you're going to get out of me."

"Stop hassling your brother," I hear Kane say.

"Listen to your husband, the way a good wife should."

"I'm going to slash all your tires when you get home."

"Goody. See you."

I hang up as Elena walks out of the glass doors, wearing nothing but a towel.

At least, I think it's nothing but a towel.

"Turn around," she instructs me.

"Hell, no."

She tilts her head to the side and raises a brow. "Do it, Arch."

I sigh and turn my back on her. "Fine."

I hear something fall to the deck, the water sloshing, and then, "Okay. I'm in."

I turn to see her submerged to her neck. She pinned her hair up, and she's resting against the headrest.

"This is divine."

My tongue is stuck to the roof of my mouth. She shifts, exposing the tops of her breasts, and I feel my cock harden in response.

"You should join me. I won't look while you strip down."

I blink, giving it more thought than I ever figured I would. I want to jump right in and take her, right here and now. The image of us naked and slick, making love in that water is at the forefront of my mind.

But I didn't plan to take it there tonight. I mean, I *want* to. But I won't until she can be open and honest with me about all aspects of her life, not just her body.

"Archer."

"Yeah?"

"Get in the water. Before I'm a prune."

I don't ask her to turn away. I strip out of my clothes and sink into the water. I sit across from her, keeping my gaze steady on hers.

"Who were you chatting on the phone with?" she asks. A droplet of water drips down the side of her neck and runs down her chest to the bubbling surface.

I can't take my eyes off the wet path that droplet took.

I've never been jealous of water before in my life. I guess there's a first time for everything.

"Arch?"

"Sorry?"

She grins. "Phone call?"

"Anastasia."

All humor leaves her face as she stares at me from across the tub. "Are you kidding me?"

"She's my sister."

"Did she ask where you are?"

"Of course, she did."

"Shit."

"That doesn't mean I told her. Elena, I have to have contact with my family. It's my *family*."

"How could I be so stupid?" she mutters.

"Whoa. Hold up. Neither of us is stupid. But you're the one hiding, not me. If I don't stay in contact with my siblings, they'll put an all-points bulletin out on me, and all of the Pacific Northwest will be looking. I didn't give her any information."

"Someone can trace your cell phone. Why do you think I don't have one?"

"I turned off the GPS on my phone. I did it the minute I left Washington. But if the mere thought of me talking to the people who love me the most pisses you off, we need to figure this out now. I'll call in Caleb or Matt or *someone* to help. You can't just hide here forever."

"Stop it," she says, shooting daggers at me with her eyes. "You don't dictate how this goes, Archer. I've been doing this for a *long* time. You're right, I can't tell you not to speak with your sisters. That's not fair. But I won't sit here and be a sitting duck either."

"I'm telling you, you're safe."

"And I'm telling *you*, you don't know what you're talking about."

She stands in the dark and climbs out of the water, grabs the towel off the deck, and stomps inside. I hurry after her.

She slams the bathroom door shut and locks it before I can fling it open behind her.

"Open the door." My voice is way calmer than I feel. "Elena, you have to know that I'd *never* put you at risk, and neither would my family. We're not stupid, and we're not careless."

"You don't get it," she says when she steps out of the bathroom, clad in her dress once more.

"Then tell me." I don't let her rush away. I cage her in against the wall and tip her chin up so I can look in her eyes. "*Talk* to me, Elena."

"It would be easier if we just had sex and went our separate ways."

"I'm not sleeping with you."

That catches her attention.

"Well, that's a small blow to my ego, but I'll get over it." She moves to pull away from me, but I easily hold her in place.

"I'm not going to be intimate with you until you're willing to fully open up to me. I told you that already. Not until it's more than just this incredible chemistry between us. It's true intimacy. You're not just some girl I met at the gym, or the bar, or wherever. It's *you*, damn it. I need to know what happened twelve years ago. I *need* to know what they did to you."

She closes her eyes in defeat and leans her forehead against my chest.

"Archer."

My hands glide up and down her arms.

"Come on." She looks up at me now with clear, determined eyes. "Let's go outside."

"I'll pour us some wine on the way."

"We're going to need it."

CHAPTER
TEN
~ELENA~

I haven't gone back to that day in my head in years. The memory of the physical pain has lessened with time, and I always chalked it up to a lesson.

Once Archer has the wine poured, we take our glasses out into the dark evening. He covers the tub, and we sit in the plush chairs, facing the sea.

It's choppier out there tonight, just like the emotions boiling inside of me.

"I'm not sure where to start," I admit after I take my first sip of wine.

"The beginning is always a good place."

"Before I do, I need you to remember that this is the *past*, Arch. It can't be changed, and I'm fine now."

He blows out a breath. "Not ominous at all."

I lick my lips. "I was so happy that day you dropped me off at the house. The weekend in Idaho when we eloped was the best of my life, and I was riding high on that adrenaline. I didn't think anything could touch me. I figured I'd make my announcement, pack my things, and call you to come and get me."

"That was the plan," he agrees.

I sip my wine and lick my lips. "My father was...livid. I'd never seen him like that before. He reminded me of my place in the family and then dragged me up to my bedroom."

I methodically explain the next twenty-four hours to him. From the moment my father tied me up, to the phone call where I lied to Archer and broke off our relationship.

When I finish, he doesn't say a word. He simply stands and walks to the railing of the deck and stares out at the beach. The anger rolls off him in waves. His fingers white-knuckle the railing, and the veins in his forearms are corded and popping out. For me, it's old news, but for Archer...it's happening here and now. All I want to do is soothe him.

"I know it's hard to hear."

"Stop." He turns back to me and shakes his head. "It's not hard. It's fucking unbelievable. Inconceivable. Evil. Terrifying. I could go on."

"I get the idea."

He crosses to me and squats in front of me, his hands on the arms of the chair. He's not touching me.

"I want to see the scars."

"Archer..." I look at him and shake my head. "I don't know, I—"

"Elena." He grabs my hand, squeezing it tightly. "I need this. You were the love of my life, and I dropped you off and left you there."

"Don't try to take the blame. This is all on him."

"Please."

Without hesitation, I raise the skirt of my dress high on my thigh, where the *W* is branded on my skin.

"That son of a bitch." His voice is rough with emotion, but his fingers are careful as he lightly traces the scar. He leans in and gently lays his lips on the wound and kisses me there. "And your back?"

I stand to show him, but a light from the neighbor's house comes on.

"Inside," Archer says. "And don't let me forget to have a privacy screen installed."

He leads me through the house to his bedroom, turns on the side-light next to the bed, and then turns back to me.

"Are you sure?"

"I'm going to kiss every inch of your amazing body before too much longer, so I'll see them eventually. But I want you to show me."

I turn my back to him and let the dress fall around my ankles, then pull my hair over one shoulder, exposing my back.

"Christ."

I know what it looks like. That many lashes leave a hell of a mess on a person's skin.

"How many?"

"Archer—"

"How fucking many?" he demands. His voice, still raw, isn't raised, but that doesn't make it any less powerful.

"Twenty."

I expect him to kiss them. Touch them. But he surprises me by simply wrapping his arms around my chest from behind and burying his face against my neck. *This* is what I needed all those years ago. *These* are the arms I needed around me, to reassure me, to hold me.

And we were both robbed of it. We lost so much time. We lost each other.

"Oh, baby. I'm so sorry I wasn't there. I'm so sorry I didn't fucking kill him myself."

"You were safe, and that's all that mattered to me," I insist, turning in his arms so I can see his handsome face, memorizing every line all over again. "This isn't your fault. You didn't do anything wrong."

"I failed you," he whispers. "I shouldn't have left you alone that day. I should have insisted that I go in with you to face him together."

"You wouldn't be standing here now if you had," I remind him. "And that would have destroyed me. I did what I had to do. And I'd do it again in a heartbeat if it meant keeping you whole."

He tips his forehead against mine.

"That's the whole story. You know everything now, Archer. My family is more ruthless than you could ever imagine. Every cliché, every rumor you've ever heard about the mafia is true, and in some cases, worse. They kill people, they run drugs. They hide money. They're bullies. But if you're part of the family, you're in for life. There's no leaving."

"You left," he reminds me.

"I escaped. And only because my parents were murdered, and my

95

grandmother was worried that I would be the next target. I got lucky. But I don't know how long this is going to last for me."

"I won't let anyone touch you ever again," he pledges and brushes his lips over my chin, then up to my lips. "I'll keep you safe, Elena. I swear it."

"I've missed you so much," I admit. My heart rips open wide and feels so full of joy that he's here. "It terrifies me that you insist on staying, but God, it's so good to feel you. To talk to you."

"I told you, I'm not going anywhere."

His fingers draw light circles over my back, making my nipples tighten in anticipation of receiving the same attention. I push my hands up into his hair and hold on as he takes the kiss deeper and guides me back to his massive bed. He lowers me and then covers me with his hard body. He's familiar and new at the same time, filling my senses in new and exciting ways.

Archer and I were together sexually when we were young. Still, it didn't happen often, and only in the last few months of us being together. I was a good Catholic girl, and I was young. Archer was patient, and when we did finally have sex, it was sweet and loving. Innocent.

And usually, it was quick. Not because he had no stamina, but because of our schedules and our families. Getting caught was always a concern.

So, taking our time to truly explore each other never happened until our wedding night.

Three days later, it was over.

"Stop thinking so hard." His voice is rough with lust as he kisses down my neck. "Say the word, and this ends."

"Definitely don't stop," I reply with a grin and then sigh when his hand glides behind my knee and begins to make small, soft circles that trail up the inside of my thigh, making my pussy tighten in joy. "Oh, man, that feels good."

"Your skin is so fucking soft." His fingertip brushes over the *W,* and he pauses. "Look down, E."

"Huh?" I open my eyes and find him staring down at me with those gorgeous blue eyes.

"Look down," he repeats and glances down to my thigh, where he's tracing the *W* on my skin. "When we look down like this, it doesn't look like a *W* at all. It looks like an—"

"*M*," I say with him and feel the last knot in my stomach break free.

"Montgomery," he says, his grin cocky, and then kisses me once more before moving those talented fingers in toward the part of me that's been longing for him for a dozen years. "Ah, baby."

I gasp as his finger slips inside, and when he pushes a second one in with it, I feel the orgasm gather at the base of my spine.

"Archer."

"Yes, sweetheart. Let go. I'm right here."

I fall apart, my back arches, my toes curl. And he's there, murmuring sweet words and caressing my neck with his lips as I float back to Earth.

"I don't have condoms," he admits with a growl. "And trust me when I say, I want to punch myself in the face for not getting some."

I laugh and shake my head. "I've been on the pill for years."

His eyes light up again. "Yeah?"

"Oh, yeah. We're good."

He links our fingers and presses them into the mattress near my head. "Are you sure?"

"Archer, I'm gonna need you to get a move on here."

His lips twitch as he fumbles with his clothes. Then he's braced over me once more, kissing me softly and thoroughly as he pushes in gently, inch by inch, until he's fully seated inside me.

"Christ Jesus, Elena. How is it better than I remember?"

"Because it's now." I lift my legs higher on his hips, opening myself to him even more. "And because it's right."

———

I don't even know how much sex I've had with Archer over the past few days. I'm quite sure it's more than all of the times we did it put together when we were young.

Maybe we're making up for lost time.

Or maybe we're creating memories to hold on to when he's gone, and I'm left alone again.

I frown at the thought. Of course, this isn't forever. It can't be. But I've resigned myself to simply enjoying every minute that I'm given.

I didn't stay with him last night. I was with him Friday and Saturday night, and I decided I needed a night away. Mostly, I was being stubborn and stupid because I was lonely when I woke up this morning.

And maybe a little moody.

Even my car didn't want to start. Probably because I didn't drive it all weekend.

But we're on the road now, on the way to work. Getting back to some normalcy will be good for me.

Run-down car, awesome job, Ally. That's who I am.

I nod and square my shoulders, but then my car decides to throw a temper tantrum. It sputters and dies. I'm lucky I can at least steer it to the side of the road.

"Well, shit." I lay my forehead on the wheel and contemplate my options.

It's early in the morning. The only people I know who are awake are my coworkers, who are currently *working*.

They won't be able to help.

And Lindsey is most likely at the spa already, getting ready for her first client at eight.

I pop the lever under the steering wheel and step out of the vehicle, lift the hood, and stare down at what looks like a heap of garbage to me. I don't have the first clue what any of this is, how it works, or how to fix it.

And I don't own a cell phone.

I blow out a long breath and look up and down the road. It's empty at this time of day.

"I just *had* to move to a small town," I mutter as I walk back to the driver's side door. But before I can open it, a familiar vehicle pulls up behind me. "Archer?"

He steps out, shuts his door, and walks toward me with a frown. "What's wrong?"

"I have no idea. It died." I kick the tire and then curse myself as pain shoots through my toes. "Pile of junk."

"Did you call a tow?"

"No phone."

"Right." He pulls his cell out of his pocket and taps the screen, then places a call. "Hi, I need a tow truck."

His eyes are on mine as he tells the person on the other line where we are, what kind of car it is, and then hangs up.

"Thirty minutes," he says.

"You don't have to wait. I'm sure they'll give me a ride to work. I'll have to figure out how to rent a car around here."

"Why? You have me." He leans a hip against my car and looks mildly annoyed.

"Yes, because I'm sure you want to be at my beck and call, driving me all over town. You're not a chauffeur."

"You go to work, and you go home. It's really not a big deal. I'm sure they'll have this fixed in a couple of days. No need to waste money on a rental."

"Really? *You're* going to tell me what I should and shouldn't waste my money on, mister I bought a whole *house* so I could *date*?"

"That's completely different."

I roll my eyes and lean on my car, my arms crossed over my chest.

"Oh, can I borrow your phone to call my job and let them know I'll be late?"

He passes me the mobile and waits while I do just that.

"Hey, Chad, it's Ally. I'm going to be late. My car broke down."

"No problem. Be safe."

"Thanks."

I hang up and pass the phone back to Archer.

"Appreciate it."

"I didn't like sleeping without you last night," he says and links his fingers with mine, then pulls my hand up to his lips. I was trying so hard to put a little distance between us, to not let myself go all mushy when it comes to him, and then he does stuff like this. "I didn't sleep well at all. So, I was going to fetch your breakfast."

"Do you mean you were going to get *yourself* some breakfast and get me some at the same time?"

"Well, sure." He smiles down at me. "A man has to eat."

I laugh and lean my cheek on his biceps, relieved that he was here to help me this morning. His muscle feels firm and warm against my cheek. "Thank you."

"Come stay with me for a while."

My head whips up. I stare at him as if he just asked me to jump off a bridge.

My stomach flutters as if he did just that.

"What?"

"You heard me."

"Why would I do that?"

He shrugs a shoulder. "Because I'm irresistible? Because you can't stand being away from me? Because I'll cook you all the tacos you want and rub your feet and eat your—"

"Point taken."

He gives me a wicked grin, and I feel it all the way to my center.

"I have a home," I reply slowly.

"Well, you don't have a car for a few days."

"We don't know that. Let's find out what the garage says."

"Two weeks."

I stare in shock at the man with *Lee* written on his coveralls.

"Excuse me?"

"It'll take two weeks," he repeats. "That part isn't one we keep in stock, and I'm backed up since my nephew up and left town with the girl he knocked up this past spring. So, unfortunately, your car is gonna have to wait."

I sigh deeply.

"That's if you want to fix it," he continues.

"Why wouldn't I want to fix it?"

Lee looks down at the paper on his counter. "Well, it has almost three hundred thousand miles on it. This week it's the fuel pump, but next week, it'll be the alternator or something else. It's lived its life."

"I'm not putting my car to sleep," I mutter. "Please, fix it."

"Yes, ma'am."

I give him my information, grab his card so I can call him later, and walk out with Archer. He was unusually quiet the entire time we were in there.

"Just say it."

"You need a new car, babe."

"That one will be just fine."

He shakes his head. "If you're worried about standing out, just buy another used car. It doesn't have to be fancy, but it does have to be reliable. You don't carry a phone. I found you on a deserted road, alone, at oh-dark-thirty. It's not safe."

"This one will be fine," I repeat. I know I'm being stubborn. I don't care. "Thanks for the ride to work."

"What time should I pick you up?"

I start to tell him *no thanks*, but when he looks at me, his eyes tell me he's at the end of his patience with me today.

And I'm too tired to argue.

"Two should be fine."

"Two, it is."

I nod and sit back in the warm leather seat. Being driven in this luxurious car for a couple of weeks won't be a hardship. We're passing through the heart of town when I see the same black Mercedes SUV that I saw in the parking lot of the football game the other night.

Black with tinted windows and black rims. Just like my father used to drive. What is a car that cost that much money doing in Bandon, Oregon?

Is it the family? Are they here, looking for me? Or is it just a coincidence? This *is* a resort town, and people come to visit from all over.

That's the logical answer. But I don't like it.

"AND THEN WE got new mountain lion cub triplets," I say as Archer drives me home from work. "They can't be more than three weeks old. Absolutely adorable. We don't know where their mama is. Probably poached."

I feel the heat creep up my face. Whenever an animal is lost to the greed of humans, it pisses me right off.

"Why people feel the need to illegally kill animals is beyond me. There are seasons for hunting, for the love of Moses. But we'll take care of them. The goal is to release them back into the wild."

"That's pretty incredible," he says with a nod. "I'm glad it turned out to be a good day. Now, about moving in with me."

"It feels silly to do that."

"Why?"

"Because I have a home."

"Yes, but if I'm going to be your chauffeur, it makes sense that you base out of my place until the car is fixed."

"It's not that I don't enjoy being with you, or even *want* to be with you. I hope you know that."

"But?"

"But it feels fast, and it feels like I'm taking advantage of you."

"You're not. There, we solved that problem."

Okay, he does make a good point. And, frankly, I missed him last night. And didn't I decide that I was going to enjoy every minute with him that I could get?

"You're awfully sure of yourself."

"I'm just positive that I want to be with you. If you'd rather I move into the cottage, I can do that. I don't mind."

"It seems like a waste to not stay in that gorgeous beach house," I reply.

He pulls into my driveway as I bust up laughing. But the laughter dies when I see my front door standing wide-open.

"I'm going to assume you closed that when you left this morning."

"I always double-check the locks," I confirm as dread spreads through me. "They found me. Oh, God, they found me."

"Don't jump to conclusions. And stay put." He pulls out his phone and dials 911. His hand reaches for mine as he waits for someone to answer. "We believe we have a break-in."

He rattles off my name and address, and within five minutes, the cops show up.

There's been no movement inside.

I get out of the car, but the officers motion for me to stand back.

"We're going to do a sweep, make sure no one is in there. Then we'll get your statement, miss."

"Of course."

Archer moves up beside me and wraps his arm around my shoulders as we watch the cops go inside and around to the back of the house. Less than two minutes later, they reappear, holstering their weapons.

"There's no one here, but someone definitely ransacked the place."

Bile rises in my throat.

"Can I go in?"

"Yes, ma'am. We need you to tell us if anything is missing."

There's only one thing of value in there.

I run inside and up to my bedroom, wanting to sob at the sight of my little cottage. I hurry to the dresser, open the bottom drawer, and breathe a sigh of relief when I see the photo of my grandmother, exactly where I put it days ago.

Whoever was here, they didn't find it.

But the rest of my place is in shambles. Furniture turned upside down, cabinets open, drawer contents spilled. It's a disaster.

And it's going to take days to clean it up.

"I don't know if anything's been taken," I say when I step back outside. "It's too much of a mess to know off-hand."

The officer nods and passes me a card. "Call me anytime if you discover anything's gone. We've had a string of auto theft in the area, and my guess is they're getting braver. Especially since your place is secluded."

He nods, shakes Archer's hand, and then both officers leave.

"I'm going to throw up."

"Hey, hey, hey," Archer says, rubbing a big circle over my back. "It's going to be okay."

"I have a bad feeling, Arch. I think it's the family."

"We don't know that. You heard him, it's probably kids. You need to gather up a few things and come home with me. I have a state-of-the-art security system, and no one even knows I'm here."

I nod in agreement. "Thank you. I think I'll take you up on your offer."

"Come on. Let's get you home."

CHAPTER
ELEVEN
~ARCHER~

S he's been sitting on the balcony with her knees drawn up to her chest, watching the sea, since we got home two hours ago. She's hardly said a word. Her dark hair blows around her face in the breeze, and her expression is sober.

But I can see it in her gorgeous, unusual eyes.

She's scared.

And that pisses me right the fuck off.

"Here's some tea." I set it on the wide armrest of the chair and sit next to her.

"I'm not sick," she reminds me and tries to offer me a smile.

"It's just tea, E." I can't help but touch her. Maybe I need the reassurance as much as she does. I reach out to link my fingers with hers and give them a squeeze. "You heard the officer. It's probably kids."

She doesn't touch the mug. Doesn't tear her eyes away from the water. But her fingers tremble in mine.

"I have a bad feeling," she says as she takes a deep breath and lets it out slowly. "A very bad feeling."

"Hey." I pull her out of her chair and settle her in my lap, kiss her temple, and cuddle her close. "You're safe here, E."

She doesn't reply. She just leans her head on my shoulder and continues watching the water.

"What would you normally do after work?" I ask.

"Run errands, maybe go to lunch with Lindsey. Perhaps try to get a walk in at the beach."

"You should take that walk. It'll help."

She looks at me now and then kisses my cheek. "Do you mind if I go alone?"

I don't want to admit that I'd prefer that she go alone. I have some things to do, and I'd rather she wasn't here when I do them.

"I don't mind at all. Enjoy your walk."

She stands and takes a sip of her now-cold tea. "Thanks for this, too."

"You're welcome."

"I won't be long."

"Take all the time you need."

She doesn't have to go back inside to get shoes or a jacket. She just jogs down the staircase that leads to the sand and takes off to the south, toward the rocks we ran to together.

I take a moment to watch her, and then I walk inside to my office, sit at the computer, and make a phone call.

"This is Montgomery."

"This is also Montgomery," I reply to my cousin, Matt. "Bad time?"

"I'm home today," he replies. "What's going on?"

"Is your line secure?"

He's quiet on the other end for a moment. I hear him walking, then the sound of a door closing.

"How secure do you need, Archer?"

I pinch the bridge of my nose, already regretting this call. Still, I trust my relatives implicitly, and I need information. It's handy having a police detective in the family.

"Arch?"

"Yeah." I clear my throat. "I need some information, and I can't tell you why I need it."

"That's not really how this works."

"I know. Matt, I found Elena. Let's just say what I need to know

105

involves her family, and if they were to find out that I was looking, or trace me to where we are, it could be incredibly dangerous for her."

"What do you want to know?"

"I need to know what their movements have been. Specifically, if they've traveled out of state. And if so, where."

"Archer, traveling isn't against the law."

"But you could look, without alerting them."

"I'll see what I can do. Archer, be careful. This family isn't warm and fuzzy. They're ruthless. And they're sneaky as fuck. Maybe you should leave Elena where you found her and get on with your life away from the damn mafia."

"If it was Nic, would you walk away?"

He sighs hard on the other end of the line. "No. I wouldn't."

"Didn't think so."

"I'll let you know what we find, but it'll be a few days. I want to make sure we do this right, and on the down-low, so low that no one can detect it. If it's done any other way, it could put my men's lives at risk. I'm not willing to do that, not even for you."

"I wouldn't ask you to. Thanks."

"Why now, Arch? What happened?"

I don't know how much I should tell him. The less he knows, the better. "Someone broke into Elena's house this morning. Ransacked it. Local cops think it was kids, but I want to make sure there's no chance that her family is in town."

"Understood. I'll look into it. Be careful."

He hangs up, and I sit back in my chair, staring out at the water. Elena would be livid if she knew what I just did. But I have to know, and I trust Matt a hell of a lot more than I put faith in the cops here.

"I'm finally getting spaghetti out of you."

I lean my shoulder against the fridge and watch as Elena chops up an onion to add to the ground meat sizzling on the stovetop.

"I figure since you're driving me all over, and letting me stay here, it's the least I can do."

"You don't have to repay me," I reply and watch as she dumps the onion in with the meat. "You'd do the same for me."

"Maybe." She shrugs and then grins at me. "Okay, probably."

"Are we having garlic bread with that?"

"Of course. And Caesar salad."

"You're a goddess."

She barks out a laugh and stirs the pan. "The old cliché of charming a man through his stomach sure is true with you."

She adds sauce and seasonings. Garlic. Gives it another stir, then covers the deep pan.

"It needs to simmer for a bit," she says.

"Good."

I move in fast, turn her to the wall, and pin her there as my mouth ravages hers. The desire, the all-encompassing need for her never ends. No matter how many times I have her, it doesn't appease the fire I feel for her.

Her mouth is eager under mine, matching me nip for nip. Her hands are in my hair, fisting and then combing, then clenching again.

I move in closer, glide my hands down her sides to her ass and then lift her. She wraps those gorgeous legs around my hips, and I grind against her, making us both moan in pleasure.

"Need you," I whisper against her lips. I push her hands over her head and pin them there while I continue kissing her senseless.

"No."

"Yes."

"No, Archer." She wiggles out of my grasp and pushes against my shoulders. "Let go."

I set her down and blink rapidly as she hurries away from me across the kitchen and wraps her arms around her middle.

"Whoa, what just happened?"

She clamps her eyes shut and whispers, "Shit."

"I'm gonna need you to talk to me, babe." I carefully step toward her. "If some asshole hurt you—"

"No, it's nothing like that." She shakes her head and pushes her fingers through her hair in agitation. "It's just the whole having my hands pinned above my head thing. It gave me a bad moment. And I know that's not fair to you."

"What a mean son of a bitch," I growl as frustration and rage fill me all over again.

"Without question," she agrees.

"I wish he hadn't died," I admit and prowl around the living space. "Because I'd like to rip him limb from limb until there's nothing left of him. What right did he have to treat you like that? You're his *daughter*."

"I was his possession," I remind him. "And, yes, he was mean. Ruthless. Feared. And my mother? Well, I don't know if she was worn down so far by that time that she had no fight left in her, or if she really didn't care about me at all. I don't remember ever receiving a kind word or affection from either of them.

"But if someone else tried to mess with me? They were dealt with. So while they didn't love me and couldn't be bothered with me most of the time, if push came to shove, they had my back."

"Out of principle, but not because they loved you." Anger rages inside me. Elena is sweet and kind. She always has been. How could they *not* love her? "Obviously, because he tortured you for marrying someone you loved."

"To them, obligation and love were the same thing." She huffs out a breath and walks to me. "I'm not afraid of you, Archer. I don't think you're going to hurt me. I just had a bad moment when you had my hands over my head. It was a gut reaction that had nothing at all to do with you."

"I want to hurt them for hurting you," I admit softly and finally reach out to drag my fingertips down her cheek. "I want them all to pay."

"They did."

"All of them."

She shakes her head. "My cousins, my uncle, they were always great. I don't know how my father had so little emotion in him, but his brother-in-law, my aunt's husband, was always loving and fun. He has a great sense of humor, and he was always fair. I loved him. I grew up with his three sons as if they were my brothers. They didn't do anything wrong."

YOU BELONG WITH ME

"And yet, you're running from them."

She frowns and looks down. "Because I have to. Even if they love me. And I, them. The fact that I fled the family doesn't change. There will be hell to pay if they ever find me. The punishment won't go unfulfilled."

"And what do you think that punishment will be?"

"Death."

"You already said they don't physically harm the women in the family."

"Not my death." She swallows hard. "Yours."

"They don't know that I'm here."

"It doesn't matter. They know that, no matter what over the years, you've been the one thing in this life that means the most to me. Father made me leave you and promise never to pursue you again. And he swore, that you—your life—would always be the thing the family held over my head for the rest of *my* life. Or yours."

"So, I'm the pawn used to hurt you."

"If you want to put it like that."

"That's not okay with me. I'm a grown man, and I can fight my own battles."

"Not against them." She sits, her face lined with worry. "You can't win against them, Archer. But they don't matter as long as they don't know where I am."

I pull her to me and wrap my arms around her, holding her close. "They won't find you."

"Enough of this," she says and pulls back to smile up at me. "I have dinner to finish. You haven't eaten in about three hours. You must be starving."

I smile for her benefit. "I'm withering away over here because some-one's holding out with her spaghetti."

She laughs, plants a kiss on my chin, and walks away.

"This will be ready in fifteen minutes."

I don't have the heart to tell her that I'm not hungry. For the first time since I can remember, it's not food that I want at all.

It's revenge.

CHAPTER

TWELVE

~CARMINE~

I haven't seen her yet.

But I know she's here.

"Can I get you another glass, sir?"

The waiter smiles, gesturing at the glass of wine I've been sipping for over an hour. I shake my head.

"No, thank you."

"Dessert, then? We have a delightful lemon cream cake with strawberry compote, or the house tiramisu, which is always a favorite."

I haven't had a good tiramisu since I was in Italy last year. My sweet tooth wants to beg for a slice.

But I have a job to do, and indulging in sugar isn't part of it.

"I'll just take the check, thanks."

"Of course, sir." He pulls a leather folder out of his pocket and lays it discreetly on the tablecloth. "Whenever you're ready."

He walks away from the table, and I sip what's left of my wine. I know Elena's here. I can feel it in my bones.

But I haven't seen her yet.

It's only a matter of time.

A text pings through on my phone.

Shane: *Any luck?*

Me: *Not yet. With no name to go by, it's not easy to ask around. I'll give it one more night, and then I'll start showing her photo around town, see if that turns anything up.*

Shane: *She might not be there. This could be a waste of time.*

Me: *She's here.*

Shane: *How do you know?*

Me: *Call it a hunch. I'll be in touch tomorrow.*

I slip enough cash for the bill and a substantial tip in with the check and slide it away from me. I take one last sip of my wine and stand to go back to the hotel for the night when a woman with dark hair and the right height walks into the restaurant. I can't see her face because she's walking away from me, but I'd swear it's Elena.

Same shape. Same hair. Even the gait of her walk is the same.

My blood hammers through my veins as I walk toward her. She's with a man, about the same height as my six feet, his hand resting on the small of her back as he escorts her to their table.

The host seats them, her back still to me, of course, and then passes them menus. I wait for him to leave and approach, catching the man's eye.

I ignore him and look down into blue eyes.

Not green and brown.

Blue.

"Can we help you?" the man asks.

"My apologies," I say, shaking my head as I glance down at the woman who is most definitely *not* my cousin. "I thought you were someone I know. Enjoy your evening."

Fuck.

I walk out of the restaurant and turn toward the hotel. The town is so small, there's no need to drive anywhere. I thought finding Elena would be easy in such a tiny community. But after two days of looking, that's proving to be false.

And every minute that I don't find her only irritates me more.

It's past time for my cousin to come home and claim her rightful place with the family.

Whether she wants to or not.

CHAPTER
THIRTEEN
~ELENA~

The window's open. I can hear the water churning below and the seagulls' calls as they fly overhead, searching for breakfast.

I reach my arms over my head and push against Archer's tufted headboard, stretching sleep away. I'm quickly getting accustomed to these Saturday mornings off work. It never really bothered me to work every day, but sleeping in once in a while has its perks.

One of the benefits is morning sex. But when I roll toward Archer's side of the bed, I'm met with cool sheets instead of his warm body.

I open my eyes and sit up, pushing my hair back to glance around the spacious bedroom then out to the deck.

He's not there either.

I pad naked into the bathroom, and once I've brushed my teeth and used the facilities, I pull on a pair of shorts and a T-shirt then go in search of Archer.

There's still time for a morning romp.

I grin at the thought. When we were younger, morning sex wasn't something we could indulge in. We never lived together, despite being legally married for just shy of a week.

But now, sex is on the table any time of day, and in the four days I've been staying here, we've taken advantage often.

It hasn't quenched my thirst for him. If anything, the regular sexcapades have only made me want more.

I've turned into a wanton woman. Well, where Archer's concerned anyway.

I swing by the kitchen that's quickly become my favorite room in the house, aside from the perfect balcony where I sit and watch the ocean, and fill a glass of water.

I can hear thumping coming from downstairs, so I follow the noise.

I turn a corner, and there he is, in the workout room, punching a bag that hangs from the ceiling. He's shirtless, wearing only a pair of grey sweatpants that look as if they've been through war. At some point, he cut them off just above the knee. The drawstring is pulled and tied, keeping them low on his hips.

That V that women go on and on about? Yeah, it's there. Along with a six-pack that would make the gods weep.

I lean against the doorjamb and sip my water as I watch him beat the shit out of that bag. I wonder who he's picturing in his head as he throws the punches.

Whoever it is, he's cleaning their clock.

I'd ask him, but he has earbuds in. So I settle in to watch.

He stops punching and, to my amazement, immediately falls down into the push-up position, easily pumping out twenty reps as if it's nothing at all. He's breathing hard and sweating like crazy, but his body moves with such fluidity that he makes it look easy.

His muscles bulge as he moves from push-ups to a hanging bar, where he executes ten pull-ups and then turns back to the bag.

Jesus.

Who knew? I mean, his incredible body is obvious. I've been with him, naked, several times now. I've touched him everywhere. I *know* what he looks like.

But watching him go through the motions that help to keep him in stellar shape does things to my already overstimulated libido.

So, I set the water on the hardwood floor just inside the door and strip out of my clothes. The motion must catch his eye because he turns my way, breathing hard, sweaty. His eyes narrow on me.

He pulls the buds out of his ears and tosses them aside just before I dash to him and jump against him, wrapping my legs around his waist as I clamp my mouth to his.

"Whoa," he says in surprise and stumbles back, but catches himself and sits on a bench with me situated on his thighs. "Good morning."

"Fuck me." I bite his bottom lip and scoot back on his legs to tug at the drawstring of his sweats. "Right now."

"Never was good at telling you no." He grins and helps me work his shorts down his hips. When he springs free, I pump him twice with my fist before rising up and lowering myself over him, making us both moan in delight. "Jesus, babe."

"So hot," I chant as I ride him, fast and hard. "So fucking hot."

I'm clenching around his hard length. I can feel the orgasm building in me, the power that flows whenever we're together like this. I don't want to slow down. I don't want to stop.

I want to make him lose his mind.

He pushes a hand between us and presses his thumb against my clit. I can't hold back any longer. I explode around him, crying out as I shiver and grind down. To my delight, he pulls me against him hard and comes, as well.

We're a panting, writhing heap.

It's fucking glorious.

"Hi," he says and kisses my collarbone.

"Hi, yourself."

"What happened?"

"Saw you working out."

His bright blue eyes fly to mine. "That's it?"

"That's all it takes, champ."

His lips twitch as I pull away and stand, freeing him from the bench. "And why is that?"

"Do you need me to stroke your ego?"

"You already did that." He tugs up his shorts and ties the drawstring.

"Okay, look." I pull my T-shirt on and prop my hands on my hips. "You've always been hot. Like, stupid hot. You were so good-looking that it was almost unfair."

"Keep going." He grins, his arms crossed over his chest, clearly delighted by this conversation.

"Somehow, you're better-looking now than you ever were. And I don't know how that's possible. Like, did you sell your soul to the devil or something?"

"No."

"I'm not complaining. I want you to know that this is *not* me complaining, not in the least. But I don't understand it. It's a mystery. Anyway, you've only managed to improve with age, and then I came down here looking for you and found you doing"—I wave my arms around—"this."

"What?"

"Punching the hell out of that bag, and push-ups like they're your job. And *that*." I point at the pull-up bar. "With your back muscles flexing and everything."

"So, you like it when I work out."

He tips his head to the side, watching me.

"Yeah." I swallow hard and nod once. "Yeah, I do."

"Good to know." He grabs a towel off a shelf and wipes down his face and neck. "I've been training pretty hard with Ben in Seattle. It's how I'm able to eat pretty much what I want and not gain a gut."

"Who's Ben?"

I watch his Adam's apple bob as he takes a drink of water.

Damn, I have it bad.

"You've been gone a long time," he says, but there's no censure in his voice. "I'll give you the CliffsNotes version. My cousin Jules married Nate. Nate's dad owned a gym in downtown Seattle, but he recently retired, and Ben bought it. Ben is Matt's wife's best friend."

I blink at him, not following at all.

"I'm gonna need a diagram. I think your family tree is more confusing than mine."

"There are days I need a diagram, too."

"Well, whoever Ben is, I like him."

"I CAN'T BELIEVE you've never been here," Archer says later that evening. We're sitting in the dining room at the resort's restaurant. It sits on the cliffs, looking out over the Pacific Ocean. We have a window seat where we can watch the birds and sea life below.

"I came to the resort for a massage a few years ago," I reply and sip my crisp white wine. "That's how I met Lindsey. But I've never had a reason to come up for anything else. Certainly not a fancy dinner."

"The steak's good."

I grin. "My salmon was great, too."

"I know." He eyes the last of my apple pie. "I stole a bite when you went to the restroom. Are you going to finish that?"

"Yes." I eat the pie and watch as his eyes round and then look sad. "Aw, poor guy."

"It's okay, I'll take some home for later."

We don't hurry. When more wine is offered, we accept it and linger over the candlelight and conversation.

"How are your parents?" I ask, realizing that I haven't inquired about them before this.

"Good," he says. "Dad had a heart attack last year. Gave us a scare. But he's recovered, and Mom has him eating mostly rabbit food, much to his dismay."

"I always liked them," I murmur. "I'm glad that everyone is doing so well and that your dad recovered from his heart attack."

I regret not being there for Archer during what I know was probably a terrifying time.

"Why did you sell your fishing boat?"

He sips his wine. "I was offered a *lot* of money from one of the bigger operations. I was sick of spending the majority of the year at sea, away from the family. It was time to be a land dweller, and real estate always interested me."

"We used to spend hours driving past places for sale," I say, remembering back. "And going on that Parade of Homes, daydreaming our way through gorgeous places."

"I still do that," he says. "I love what I do now. It's not nearly as smelly, the income is steadier, and I'm around for the family whenever they need me."

"You always did take care of everyone around you, Archer. Even me." I finish my wine. "You're still taking care of me, it seems."

He looks like he's about to say something, but we're interrupted.

"Hey, guys." Lindsey grins as she approaches the table. "I didn't expect to see you here."

"I could say the same about you," I reply. "You don't usually work this late."

"I had a late client, and then I had some inventory to do. Being the boss sucks sometimes." Her gaze shifts between Archer and me, but I don't offer any information.

I know I'll get drilled later.

"So," Lindsey says, "Archer didn't leave town, after all."

"Nope," he says with his charming grin. "Ally decided she wanted me to stick around for a while."

"He's like the plague," I reply. "He just never goes away."

Lindsey laughs. "Must be nice, having someone so handsome sticking close."

"Don't make his head any bigger than it already is."

Lindsey's cell rings, and she checks it. "Sorry, have to take this. Have a nice dinner."

She waves and hurries away to take her call.

"She'll insist on lunch soon so she can ask all the nosy questions that friends do." I watch as Archer signs his name on the receipt. "Which is fine. She's a good friend."

"I'm glad you have someone here. I hate the thought of you being alone."

"I have Lindsey and my coworkers, who are all great. I have a fulfilling life here, Arch. I'm not sad or bored."

"I'm glad."

The waiter brings out to-go boxes full of desserts, and we stand to leave. As we walk out the door to the parking lot, Archer's phone rings.

"Hello? Yes, she's right here."

He passes the cell to me, just as a car catches my eye. It's the black SUV. A man is in the driver's seat, but the windows are tinted enough that I can't see his face.

And the license plate is from Washington.

My stomach jumps into my throat.

"Ally?"

I look up at Archer. "Yeah?"

"Phone's for you."

"Oh, right." I take it from him and fumble with it before pressing it to my ear. "This is Ally."

"This is detective Garcia. I wanted to update you on the case. We arrested two suspects today. When we found your iPad in the backpack of one of the boys, they confessed to the break-in and robbery of your house."

"Wow." I blink at Archer as he holds the car door open for me. "Thank you so much. I didn't even realize my iPad was missing."

"It had your name on it," he says. "Inside the cover."

"That's mine. I appreciate your work on this, detective."

"You can pick up the iPad at the station anytime."

"Thank you."

I hang up and sit in the car, then pass Archer his phone.

"Good news?" he asks.

"It was kids, after all." I fill him in on what the detective told me. "So, yeah, good news."

"That's great."

He starts the car and pulls out of the parking space. The SUV is gone.

Part of me knows I'm being ridiculous. This is a *resort*. People vacation here from all over the place, including Washington. In fact, it's *likely* someone from Washington would come here because it's within driving distance. It's probably a family who came down for a long weekend at the beach.

That's what common sense tells me.

It's most likely *not* someone from my family in their typical mafia-style vehicle, looking for me.

The odds of that are incredibly slim.

But the odds aren't zero, either. And my gut says something's coming.

My instincts are rarely wrong.

Summers at Grandma's are the best. I get to come here with my cousins—Carmine, Shane, and Rocco—and we can do whatever we want for two whole months.

The servants keep our pantry stocked with our favorite snacks. The tree-house has been mended and remodeled over the spring, ready for us to wreak havoc in it, pretending to be pirates or knights of the round table.

We can play down at the beach during low tide, searching for treasures.

And in the evenings, we have movies and popcorn until we fall asleep.

We look forward to it more than Christmas. More than anything.

"Come on, Elena," Carmine calls, gesturing for me to follow him. Carmine is the oldest—and the smartest. I love all of my cousins, but Carmine is my favorite. He lets me tag along almost anywhere.

The other boys get tired of me.

Carmine never does.

"Where are we going?"

"It's a surprise," he says and stops to wait for me to catch up. He takes my hand and leads me down a path in the woods next to Grandma's house. "You know I'd never let anything bad happen."

"I know, but what if there are bears? Or tigers?"

"Tigers don't live in North America," he says and holds a branch out of my way so it doesn't smack me in the face. "But if we see a bear, I'll fight him off."

I laugh at him. "Right. Like you could fight a bear."

"Hey, I've been working out." He flexes, showing me his fourteen-year-old muscles. "And no matter what, I'll always keep you safe, Elena. The family won't let anything happen to you."

"My father might," I admit in a small voice. "He's not very nice."

"Does he hit you?"

"No." I shake my head and shiver when the sun slips behind a cloud, making the woods cold. "No, he just says mean things sometimes."

"My dad says your dad's an asshole," Carmine admits. "I overheard him. At least you can always come here with us. And you can be away from there for a couple of months."

"This is the best time ever," I agree. "I'm getting tired. Where are we going?"

"Almost there."

His hand tightens around mine as he leads me into a clearing. Suddenly, I'm not a child anymore. I'm a woman.

And in the clearing is scaffolding with a hanging rope.

Archer stands behind the rope with his hands tied behind his back.

"What's going on?" *I demand, staring up at Carmine.* "What are you doing?"

"He's taking your punishment," *Carmine says grimly, staring up at Archer.* "For running from us. For staying away."

"Grandma—"

"Is dead," *Carmine says, cutting me off.* "She can't protect you anymore."

I stare in horror at the man I love. His blue eyes are full of sorrow as he mouths, I love you.

I love you, too, *I mouth back.*

"Please don't do this, Carmine."

"It's already done."

He flicks his hand, and suddenly, Archer's neck is in the noose, and he's hanging, jerking about.

"NOOOOO! No no no no!"

I run toward him, but it's pitch-black now, and I'm falling. Falling and falling. Into what, I don't know.

"Archer!"

"He's not here," *Carmine whispers in my ear.* "He can't save you, Elena. Only we can. Only the family can help you."

"The family is a disease," *I stammer as I cry out.* "And I want nothing to do with it."

I sit up, dripping with sweat. Cool air blows in through the window and across my skin.

"Baby," Archer says, kissing my cheek. "It's okay. It was only a dream. You're safe."

"I need some water."

"I'll get it."

"It's okay." I kiss his cheek and then hurry from the bed, anxious to get out of the bedroom and away from Archer. "I'll be right back."

I snag my robe off a chair as I walk out to the kitchen. I pull it around me, tighten the belt, and rather than stop at the sink, I keep walking out to the deck to lean on the railing of the balcony.

I can't see the water. There's no moon tonight.

But I can hear it, and it soothes me.

I take several deep breaths, willing my heart to calm down. Archer was right, it was only a dream. He's alive and well, and so am I.

Everything's fine.

I hear the door behind me, but I don't turn to him. He slips his arms around my waist from behind and kisses the top of my head.

"Wanna talk it out?"

"No." I turn and bury my face in his chest as I wrap my arms around him, holding on with all my might. "I just need you to hold me. Out here, like this."

"For as long as you need, sweetheart."

FOURTEEN

~ELENA~

Margie, my boss at the wildlife sanctuary, is never at work when I am. She comes in to relieve me, working the swing shift.

But when I'm only halfway through my day, the woman comes walking into the nursery, dressed for work.

"Am I being fired?" I ask, wondering what in the world she's doing here.

"Hardly," Margie says with a laugh. "I just got this place fully staffed, and you're a dream. You'd better not be going anywhere."

"Then why are you here?"

She smiles in a way I've never seen before, confusing me more. "I'm giving you the next four days off."

I blink, sure I've heard her wrong. "Why?"

"Now that, I can't say. But from right now until Tuesday morning, you're off. With pay, I might add."

"Did I win the lottery?" I wonder, glancing around. "Hit my head on something hard? Is this dementia, and I just don't know it?"

"Follow me," she says, laughing at me. She leads me to our locker room where we keep our personal things and clean clothes.

Baby animals love to pee, poop, and throw up on people.

I stop short and frown. "What are you doing here?"

Archer grins that cocky, self-assured smile that never fails to hit me square in the gut.

"It's a surprise."

I inhale sharply, remembering those were the same words Carmine used in my dream last night.

"What kind of surprise?"

"This is where I go," Margie says and winks at me. "Have a great time."

She leaves the room, and I turn back to Archer.

"What's going on?"

"We're getting out of here for a few days. Away from Oregon and all of the ghosts that haunt you here. We need a vacation, babe."

"So you just arranged it with my boss?"

He rocks back on his heels. "I did."

I feel the smile slide slowly over my lips. No one's ever done something like this for me before. Maybe he's right. Perhaps a little holiday is exactly what we need.

"Where are we going?"

"That, my beautiful travel companion, is a surprise. But I already packed your bags, and Lindsey is going to keep an eye on your house. We're good to go."

"Wow. So, you're just whisking me away right this minute?"

"I can't figure out if you're excited or mildly pissed."

"I'm not pissed," I say with a shake of the head. "And depending on where we're going, I might be excited. So, tell me."

He moves in, wraps those ridiculously strong arms around me, and kisses me until I'm breathless.

"I'm not spilling the beans," he whispers against my lips. "And we'd better go before we miss our flight."

"Do I get to double-check your packing skills?" I ask as he guides me out of the building to his car.

"Nope."

He tucks me inside the vehicle and walks around to the driver's side, then climbs in and leans over to kiss me again.

This one makes my toes curl.

"What if I need something you forgot?"

"There are stores where we're going," he says as he drives away from the sanctuary, and away from Bandon. "Don't worry, I've got you."

"You brought me to the boonies," I say seven hours later. We landed in a remote part of Montana, although I would guess that all parts of Montana are remote. Archer rented a Jeep Wrangler, and the late summer weather is nice enough to take the top off.

Mountains rise up all around us, the trees covered in varying shades of yellow and green leaves, contrasting beautifully with the deeper shades of the evergreens.

"Cunningham Falls," I read as we drive into a small town nestled next to the mountains. "How in the world did you find this?"

"Some of my family has talked about coming here to visit," he says casually. He's in ripped jeans, a black T-shirt, and aviator sunglasses. The wind blows through his dark hair, and he hasn't shaved in a couple of days, leaving a little scruff on his face.

He's damn hot.

"And before you yell at me," he continues, "no, I didn't call anyone and tell them this is where I am. I made all of the arrangements myself. Literally *no one* knows where we are. I told Margie I was just taking you away for a few days. No details."

He grins and pulls my hand up to his lips, nibbling on my knuckles.

"You went to a lot of trouble."

"It's no trouble to spoil you a bit," he says. "I wanted to be able to do this for you for as long as I can remember. But we were in school, and I was poor. Now, I'm not."

I sigh, feeling the weight of my situation lift from my shoulders for the first time in *years*. We're hidden, alone, and in this beautiful place for several days.

"I don't remember the last time I could really relax," I reveal and tip my face back to soak in the warm sun. "And I have to admit, it feels amazing. How did you know this is what I needed?"

I open my eyes in time to see him send me a look that says, *really?*

"You're coiled so tight, always worrying, always afraid that you'll be found. I can give you a few days of letting go of that worry." He drives us through a cute little town filled with shops and restaurants and then heads out of town and up a mountain road.

"We're not staying in town?"

"No, ma'am. This is a ski resort town. We're staying up on the mountain. I've been told the views are incredible and that where we're staying is world-class."

"Well, I can't wait to see it."

I don't have to wait long. After a couple of turns off the main road that leads to a small ski village, Archer parks beneath what appears to be... "Treehouses?"

"Luxury treehouses," he says with a grin.

"Welcome!" We turn and look up to see a pretty blond woman waving from a deck above us. "I'm Jenna."

Archer waves, and we grab our bags out of the back seat and climb a staircase to one of the three treehouses. Jenna waits for us at the top of the stairs.

"I'm so glad you made it safely," she says. "I have you in the Ponderosa, which is on the end here. You'll have views of the ski run, the village, and after sunset, you can see lights from the town below.

"But the best part is at night. There's so little light noise here that you'll be able to see the stars in a way you never have before. The weather's been great too, so the show will be spectacular."

"Sounds awesome," Archer says and smiles down at me.

"Anyway, I'm babbling," Jenna says with a laugh as she unlocks the unit and leads us inside. "Sorry, it's been a long day. My number is here on the counter, along with the Wi-Fi information and anything else you might need to know. There are no other guests in the other two units right now, so you have the place all to yourself."

"We love the sound of that," Archer says.

I can't stop staring at the gorgeousness of this place. The furniture is simple but inviting. The kitchen has blue cabinets, and the backsplash is in the shape of mountains. The beds look soft and cozy, and Jenna wasn't kidding about the views.

"This is stunning," I say at last.

"Thank you," Jenna says. "It's been a labor of love, that's for sure. You guys make yourselves at home and let me know if you need anything."

"Food," Archer says immediately. "We've been traveling all day, and I'm starving."

"He would be starving if we hadn't been traveling all day," I inform her, making her laugh.

"I have two brothers and a husband, I get it," Jenna says. "My favorite restaurant in town is Ciao. It's the best Italian food I've ever had."

"Perfect," Archer says.

"I'm going to freshen up," I say and smile at Jenna. "Thank you for your hospitality."

I walk through the master bedroom that's on the main floor and into a bathroom that makes my girlie-girl heart sigh in pleasure. The bathtub is deep and inviting. The separate shower is big enough for a party of six. And the décor of this place is absolutely on point. I'd call it rustic chic. Perfect for the mountains, but not *too* rustic.

I open my bag and am pleasantly surprised to see that it looks as if Archer thought of just about everything.

Except pajamas.

I smirk and unpack, choose a red summer dress to change into for dinner, and sweep a little makeup on my face before returning to the living room.

"I think I'm starving, too," I say when I join Archer, who's checking out the provisions in the kitchen. He glances up at me, and his jaw drops.

"Fuck me, you're gorgeous."

Every girl should have a man in their life that looks at her the way Archer's looking at me right now.

"You're not so bad yourself."

He walks around the kitchen counter and frames my face in his big hands as he kisses me, lightly at first as if he's memorizing the shape of my lips, and then he sinks into me, enjoying me. My head spins, and my fingers dive into his thick hair. But before I know it, he comes up for air.

"If I don't stop now, we won't eat, and I need my strength so I can do a hell of a lot more than this later."

"I like that strategy." I nip at his lips once more and then pull out of his arms. "Let's eat."

JENNA DIDN'T STEER us wrong.

"Okay, this is pretty great," I say after we order our food and have a chance to soak in the atmosphere. Our waitress wrote her name on the white paper on our table with an orange crayon. She just delivered wine and the best garlic bread I've ever had in my *life*. "If we had this in Bandon, I'd weigh four hundred pounds. And I haven't even had the entrée yet."

"This bread," he says with half a piece in his mouth. "I could die."

I love that we can sit here and enjoy ourselves, and I don't have to worry about being recognized by anyone. I don't have to even think about what my name is or if I'm in danger here. I can just be myself, a woman in love with this incredible man who brought me here on a surprise vacation.

And, yes, I'm in love with him. I can't deny it. He was wonderful when he was twenty, but he's absolutely marvelous now. I don't know how this will all shake out, but I'm going to enjoy him for as long as it lasts.

We've both earned it.

"You're gorgeous in red," he says before shoving more bread into his mouth. He doesn't eat like a Neanderthal, but he definitely enjoys his food. And I can't blame him. "You should wear it more often."

"So noted."

Our food is delivered, and the aroma of red sauce hits my nose and makes me want to moan in delight.

"We might have to move here," Archer says grimly after taking his first bite. "I don't know if I can live without this now that I know it's here."

"Okay, now you're just being dramatic." But I take my first bite, and my shoulders sag. "You're right. We're moving here."

THE SUN HAS GONE DOWN by the time we leave Ciao, our bellies full of the most amazing food. The tiramisu we ordered was the best I've ever had, and I'm Italian.

"I wonder why I didn't think to move here when I was looking at places to go," I say after I boost myself up into the Jeep. "It's kind of perfect."

"Because you love the ocean," Archer says as he starts the vehicle and pulls out of our parking spot to head toward the treehouse. "But now that we know this is here, we'll visit often."

"Deal." I settle back in the seat with a smile when a vehicle catches my eye. I freeze.

Late-model black SUV with tinted windows.

What in the actual hell?

My heart kicks up, and I want to panic. Did someone follow us here?

But I take a deep breath and force myself to push it aside.

No one followed us. No one knows we're here.

Am I always going to react this way whenever I see a black SUV? Maybe. But I need to learn to trust myself, and Archer.

We're safe.

The drive up the mountain is a little nerve-wracking in the dark, but we're soon back at the treehouse. A note is taped to the door.

I pluck it off and carry it in with us.

I hope you enjoyed dinner! There's a little something fun waiting for you out on the deck. Have a wonderful weekend,

Jenna

"The suspense is killing me." I walk over to the sliding glass door and pull it open, then smile when I see the hot tub open, and a standing ice bucket with champagne nestled inside. There is a small table beside the bucket with two flutes and a bowl of fresh strawberries. "I wonder if all of Jenna's guests get the royal treatment."

"I wouldn't know," Archer says casually as he strips out of his clothes and sinks into the tub.

"Uh, you're naked," I remind him.

YOU BELONG WITH ME

"And I hope you'll join me," he says.

"We're outside. I'm not exactly an exhibitionist."

"There's no one here," he reminds me. "We're all alone. So, get naked and come in."

How can I resist him? I don't want to. I quickly shed my dress and slip into the water. Archer pours the champagne, passes me a glass, and before I can take a sip, he proposes a toast.

"To us, making new memories together."

"To new memories." I sip the bubbly and sit back in the tub with a happy sigh. "I'm travel weary. It wasn't easy to get here from Bandon. But man, was it worth it."

"I'm glad you think so," he says and looks up. "I don't think I've ever seen so many stars."

I follow his gaze and feel my eyes round.

"Wow. Jenna wasn't lying about this either."

It seems like the stars are so close, we could just reach out and touch them. The blanket of black is bigger than I've ever seen it before, with millions of stars winking at us.

"Jesus, it's beautiful," I whisper.

"Magnificent," he says, but when I glance his way, he's staring at me, not the stars above.

"You always were a charmer."

"I'm not trying to charm you." He sets his glass aside. "I'm only being honest. You're unbelievable, and I'm so fucking grateful that I found you."

He pulls me closer to him as the water bubbles around us, sending up steam and a cocoon of intimacy we've rarely shared before.

He leans in and presses his lips to the apple of my cheek. "I can't leave you. Not now that I've found you, Elena. I'd regret it for the rest of my life if I walked away from you, not after everything we've shared."

I want to protest, but I can't because the thought of losing him again sends absolute panic through me.

I shift, straddle him, and with my pussy pressed against the length of his cock, I cup his face and kiss him like I'm starved for it. His hands grip the globes of my ass, and he holds on tightly as I explore his mouth.

The timer on the tub ends, extinguishing the bubbles, but the night around us sings, just like the blood pumping through my veins as I take the kiss from hot to inferno in the blink of an eye.

I move back and forth along his length. I want nothing more than for him to slide inside of me and take us over, right here and now.

What sounds like footsteps or limbs breaking pulls us out of our reverie, and the next thing I know, Archer pushes me away from him, his jaw hard and his eyes shining.

"It's just an animal or something," I say, moving back in, but he shakes his head, and I hear two people whispering.

"People going for a walk," he murmurs. Before I know it, he's standing, holding me up in the cool air. My skin is hot, not just because of the warm water but because my blood is moving fast through my veins. He easily maneuvers us out of the tub and into the house.

"We're dripping all over the floor."

"I don't care," he says and carries me through the house to the master bedroom.

"We can't lie on the bed all wet like this," I insist.

"No problem." He bypasses the bed and sets me down on a chaise lounge that sits by the big windows that overlook the resort. He pushes the blinds so the moonlight still shines in, but no one below can see inside.

The moon is full, casting a glow over us. The droplets on our skin are starting to dry.

He stops kissing me and just pulls me to him, hugging me tightly.

"I said, don't stop," I mutter against his chest.

"I need to slow down," he replies and kisses the top of my head. "I want to savor every inch of you."

Before I can reply, he urges me back against the soft cushion of the chaise. I expect him to kiss me, but instead, he reaches for the pins holding my hair and pulls them out one by one until the long locks spill over my shoulders.

"I always loved your hair. You used to wear it shorter."

"I never have time to get it cut," I admit. "And I dye it darker myself. Just in case."

"I like it," he says and leans in to lightly kiss my lips. "I'm going to make you forget your own name tonight, Elena."

"Who's Elena?"

His lips, pressed to my neck, curve. "Exactly."

And here, in the moonlight, we rediscover each other all over again. His hands are bold and warm as they travel over my body. I can't help but arch into his touch and sigh every time he finds a sensitive spot on my flesh.

Every time is like the first time with him. It's the most incredible thing I've ever experienced.

"So responsive," he whispers before pulling a nipple into his mouth. He tugs gently and then scrapes his teeth over the nub. "So delicious."

"Killing me," I mutter as his hand roams down my belly to the promised land.

"You're slick." His voice is tight now as his fingers dance between my folds, sending me into a frenzy. "God, babe, you make me crazy."

"Archer." I can't breathe. I can't think. I can only feel this need inside, building until it feels like it's going to drown me. "Now, Archer."

He drops to his knees beside me, opens my legs, and replaces his fingers with his mouth. I almost jack knife off the chaise and come so fast and hard, I see stars.

He sets my leg on his shoulder and feasts on me. There's no other word for it. He gorges himself like a man starved, and it's so damn good, I think I might die from it.

When his hand glides down my leg and brushes over the scar on my thigh, he stills. When his eyes capture mine, they're slits.

"I'm okay," I assure him and push my fingers through his thick hair. "I'm more than okay. It's an *M*, remember?"

He doesn't say a word as he stands, lifts me, and turns to the bed.

"Damn right, it's a fucking *M*."

I lift a brow. "Possessive, are we?"

"That hasn't changed, sweetheart."

But everything else has changed. His body, his voice, even the way he looks at me. He isn't a young adult anymore.

He's a man. A sexy, funny, irresistible male.

And he's kissing his way up my torso. His hands are in my hair, his elbows planted on the bed at my shoulders as he rubs his nose over mine, and his cock nudges its way inside me.

"Fucking hell." He shudders. "Ah, babe, you're incredible."

"It's us," I say and feel another orgasm gather. "It's us."

CHAPTER

FIFTEEN

~CARMINE~

"Excuse me." I motion for the bartender's attention and offer her a nod when she looks my way.

"What can I get you?" she asks.

I've been through more wineries and vineyards today than I care to remember, showing Elena's photo to everyone.

So far, no luck.

"I was wondering if you know this woman." I pull the picture out of my breast pocket and hold it out for her to see. "She's my cousin, and I'm looking for her."

She frowns. "Oh, sure. This is Paige. Paige Williams, right?"

Jackpot. I smile and nod as if I knew that was her name all along.

"Paige is a sweet girl. But she moved away some time ago."

And just like that, my joy falls flat.

"Moved away?"

"Yeah, it was the oddest thing. She'd been working here for a couple of years. Never missed a day of work. And then, one day, she just up and left."

"Do you know where she went?"

"Sorry, no. Never heard from her again." She looks me in the eyes. "If she's your cousin, why don't you know where she is?"

"She's been estranged from the family. Our grandmother recently died, and she's entitled to an inheritance. I'm just trying to locate her."

"Oh." Her shoulders loosen. "Well, I hope you find her. Sorry to hear about your grandmother. I should get back to work."

She walks away, and I tuck the photo back into my jacket and walk outside. Anger and frustration bubble up inside me. I just spent three days here, and it was all a waste of time.

I get into the car and immediately call my brother.

"She's not here, Shane." I fill him in on what the bartender said. "I was so sure. This was the only clue in Grams' house."

"I have a theory," Shane says. "I think we've been attacking this from the wrong angle."

I narrow my eyes. "Go on."

"What was the most important thing in Elena's life?"

"Just spit it out, Shane."

"Archer, Carmine. Archer was the most important."

"Uncle Vinnie put a stop to that."

"Do you really think they stayed apart all these years? If you were in love with someone so deeply that you were willing to go against a family like ours to be with her, would you stay away?"

"If Pop threatened to kill her? Yeah, I'd stay away. But it's an interesting theory. The only problem is, Archer's in Seattle."

"Not lately, he hasn't been."

My hand tightens on the steering wheel. "Keep talking."

"We're not sure where he went, but he's been out of the area for a while. I think it's worth looking into."

"You're the tracker in the family," I say, hope taking root in my belly. "Get looking."

CHAPTER

SIXTEEN

~ARCHER~

My eyes are blurry. If I didn't know better, I'd think I was coming off a bender with a hangover the size of Canada.

But, no. I didn't even finish that one glass of champagne last night.

I did, however, stay up most of the night making love with Elena. We might have snagged two total hours of sleep.

I'm not complaining. I waited a dozen years for this. Every minute with her is a gift.

I send up a silent thank you when I spot the Keurig on the countertop with a round carousel of different varieties of coffee pods.

I open a cabinet in search of mugs and lift a brow when I see Jenna's collection.

"How's that coffee coming?" Elena asks as she pads up behind me and wraps her arms around my stomach, pressing a kiss to my shoulder.

"It's just getting started. Do you want *I'm no cactus expert, but I know a prick when I see one* or *Please cancel my subscription to your issues?*"

"Huh?" She leans around me to see what I'm looking at and lets out a laugh. "Oh, these are awesome. I have some funny mugs, but this collection is impressive."

"I think I'm gonna use *Hustle Juice*," I say, pulling the mug down.

"I love this one," she says, pointing to a mug on the second shelf. "*I think I've seized the wrong day.* Hilarious. Oh! *I don't like morning people. Or mornings. Or people.* This one is for me today."

"You like me," I reply with a sleepy grin as I pull that mug down and place it under the coffee machine, slip a pod in, and press brew. "According to last night, you like me *a lot.*"

"I like you and maybe four other people," she says and leans back against the counter as we wait for our coffee. She's in the black T-shirt I wore yesterday. Her hair is down and tumbled from a night of my fingers diving through it. Her legs are bare, along with her pink-colored toes.

Those fascinating eyes are heavy-lidded and full of satisfaction as she watches me.

"What are we doing today?" she asks.

"I thought we could go for a hike, if you're up for it."

"Are there bears here?"

"Possibly." I pour cream into her coffee and pass her the mug. "But I have bear spray, and there are enough people on these trails that I would be surprised if the bears hang out here. They're deeper in the woods."

"You hope," she mutters. "Because the one who runs the slowest is the bear food, and I can outrun you, my friend."

"Then you have nothing to worry about." I doctor up my coffee and kiss her lips lightly before walking past her and out to the deck where the hot tub and refreshments from last night are still on display. "I guess this sort of went to waste, huh?"

"No, it didn't," Elena says as she walks out behind me. "It did exactly what Jenna intended for it to do. It was romantic and sexy, and led to a fun-filled night."

After I close the lid on the tub, I sit on one of the deck chairs and tug Elena into my lap, careful not to spill our coffees.

"You're right." I nuzzle her ear and grin when I feel her shiver. "Are you cold?"

"It's a little brisk this morning," she says but then chuckles. "But, no. It's just you. Isn't it crazy?"

"What's that?" I brush my fingers through her hair, watching the dark strands as they fall over her shoulder.

"When we were young, we had pretty good chemistry. I was young and very naive, but I knew it."

"You weren't stupid."

"I guess it's interesting to me that, all these years later, the chemistry just picked up where it left off. Except now, it's in overdrive."

"The heart knows what it wants, E, no matter how old it is."

She doesn't say anything for a long moment, she just sips her coffee and watches the birds fly between the trees. The mountain is waking up around us.

"It's going to be a great day for a hike," she says at last, signaling that our deep conversation is tabled for now.

Which is fine with me. We have plenty of time to pick it up again later.

"So, LET ME GET THIS STRAIGHT," she says an hour later when we're on our way up the trail that leads to the summit of Whitetail Mountain. "We have to hike *up*, and then we ride the chairlift down?"

"That's right."

"Why don't we ride up and hike down?"

"Because it'll be more satisfying to be able to say you slayed this mountain. It's only four miles."

"Straight up," she murmurs, but then stops to catch her breath and looks out at the view of the valley below. "Wow. The views up here are gorgeous."

"It's just going to get better the higher we go."

She sets off again, a few steps ahead of me. She may complain about the hike, but she's doing an awesome job of keeping a regular pace, stopping to drink her water, and catch her breath.

"You're a pro at this," I say.

"Hardly. But it is really pretty up here. Please tell me I'll be rewarded with something at the top."

"I've been told the view is incredible, and there's a restaurant where we can grab lunch."

"Awesome."

We pass several people along the way and encounter others who are on their way down.

No ride on the chair lift for them, I guess.

It takes us less than two hours to reach the summit, and we are not disappointed by the views when we get there.

"Holy shit," she breathes, her hands on her hips as she looks at the mountain range surrounding us. "I think we can see all the way to Canada from here."

"We can," I confirm. "I did some research before I booked the trip. Canada is due north. And to the east is Glacier National Park."

She just stares in awe at the snow-tipped peaks and the vastness of the trees and mountains in front of us.

When we turn around, we can see the valley below, with Cunningham Falls nestled against the mountain, right next to a large lake.

"This is seriously cool," she says. "It's also a good thing that I'm not afraid of heights. Are you going to feed me now?"

"That's usually my line." I take her hand and lead her to the summit house, the building that holds not only the restaurant but also a bar and a gift shop.

We place an order and choose a table inside to take a break from being in the sunshine, sitting next to the windows that look out to the mountains.

"We didn't see even one bear," Elena says as she adjusts her ponytail and takes in our surroundings.

"Told you."

"And how did you get me hiking shoes? In my size. On such short notice?"

"I called Jenna last night," I reply. "Gave her your size and told her what I had planned for today."

"You're just full of surprises," Elena says with a grin and leans back when our food is delivered. "Don't touch my onion rings."

"I wouldn't dream of it."

She narrows her eyes at me as she takes a bite of her burger and then sighs in delight. "So good. I was starving."

"Hiking a mountain will do that to you."

Watching Elena eat is one of my favorite things to do. She enjoys every bite, and she isn't afraid to order exactly what she wants.

We don't say much as we inhale our food, and then make our way out to the chair lift to ride back down to the village.

"Oh my God," she breathes as we come over the side of the mountain and see the view spread out before us. "I don't know if I've ever seen anything quite like this."

"Now I know why the family loves it so much," I agree. "Maybe we'll have to buy a place here."

"You mean *you*."

I glance down at her and see she's shaking her head.

"You mean *you'll* have to buy a place here. I can't buy anything."

I sigh and wrap my arm around her shoulders. "Elena. You're a part of my life again, and I have no intention of letting you go. Ever. Whether you're Ally or Elena or another name, I don't care. I plan to live a life with you."

"Why?" Her voice is quiet. She stares straight ahead, but I don't know if she sees the magnificent view in front of her or if she's lost in her mind and the memories there. "Why would you risk everything for me?"

I tip up her chin so I can see her eyes.

"Because I'm in love with you. I've been in love with you for the better part of fifteen years, E. You're it for me. So, I'm going to do whatever the fuck I have to do so I can be with you."

Her chin wobbles, tearing me apart.

"Ah, baby. Don't cry."

"This could be so dangerous for you."

"*Not* being with you is dangerous for me." I kiss her forehead. "We don't have to have the answers today. We'll take it day by day and figure it out."

"You make it sound so simple."

"It doesn't have to be complicated." I kiss her temple and breathe her in. "I love you, E."

"I love you, too. I always have, Archer."

I want to shout from the mountaintop in joy.

Instead, I kiss her until my head swims.

We reach the bottom of the lift and walk the half-mile to the treehouse.

"I need a shower," Elena announces when we walk into the cool rental. Thank God for air conditioning on warm days like today.

"Go ahead," I say. "I'm going to grab some water. I'll be behind you."

She nods and walks into the master suite. I do fetch the water, but I also make a call for dinner reservations.

When I walk into the bathroom, the mirror is steamed up. I strip out of my sweaty clothes and cast them aside.

"I didn't figure you'd want a super-hot shower after that hike."

I open the glass door and grin when she turns a soapy head my way.

"The breeze on the way down was cool," she says. "What are you doing?"

"I'm gonna check you over for ticks."

She scrunches up her nose. "That's disgusting. You didn't say anything about ticks."

"Don't worry, I'm here to save the day." I reach up and help her rinse her hair. "Have I mentioned how much I like your hair?"

"Once or twice." She lets her arms fall to her sides and leans into my hands as I massage her scalp and rinse the soap away. "That's nice."

It's about to get better.

When her hair is free of shampoo, I let my hands roam over her slick, wet skin. The scars on her back and thigh ignite the anger in my belly, but I take a deep breath, content to know that she's safe with me now.

No one will ever touch her again.

My fingers glide up between her thighs, and she sighs as she braces her hands on my shoulders.

"I don't think I have ticks there," she says.

"I'm just being thorough." I pick her up and slip inside her easily, as if she were made just for me.

Because she fucking was.

I brace her against the tile wall and fuck her hard and fast until we're both spent and weak.

"Water seems to be our thing," she says when I've set her back on her feet. "Good to know."

I smirk and stick my head under the spray of water. "Everywhere is our thing, babe."

"True." She smacks my ass with a loud *thwack*. "I'm getting out of here before you attack me again."

"You're not going to wash my hair for me?"

"You're a big boy," she says with a shrug. "You've got this."

OUR TIME in Montana was over too fast. Next time, we'll stay a minimum of two weeks.

I've already begun looking at some property there. Real estate is like a drug for me. An expensive addiction, yes, but it can also be quite profitable, and if what I've seen so far about the market in Cunningham Falls is true, an investor can't go wrong by buying some property there.

I've just sent off an email to an agent there when my phone rings.

"Hey, Matt."

"This a good time?" he asks, which is code for *are you alone*?

"It is." I sit back in my desk chair and watch the waves beyond the windows of my office. "What's up?"

"There's been some movement," he says. "Mostly in California."

I feel my stomach ease when he doesn't include Oregon.

"You know, it would be easier for me to know what I'm looking for if I knew where in the hell *you* are."

I drag my hand down my face in agitation. I *want* to confide in Matt. But Elena would flip her shit, and I promised her I wouldn't tell a soul.

"I can't," I say at last.

"Archer, I can't protect you like this."

"I'm not asking you to," I reply. "But thanks for having the inclination."

"You're my family, and if you're messed up with this mob family, you could be in serious danger. I can't ignore it."

"I'm not asking you to do that either. Listen, I made a promise that I wouldn't say anything to anyone about this. I've already done too much by calling you in the first place, but I needed the intel."

"I'll continue feeding you information as I get it. Is there a specific part of the country I should be keeping a close eye on?"

"Matt—"

"You can't tell me. Right." He sighs heavily. "This is fucking frustrating, Archer."

"I know. I don't disagree."

"How long?"

"I don't know that either. Could be weeks. Could be longer."

I don't want to tell him that it could be years. I don't want to admit that even to myself.

"If you need help, at any time, you call me. I can have law enforcement engaged at a moment's notice, anywhere on this globe, Arch. I fucking mean it. Don't hesitate."

"Thank you."

"Don't fucking thank me. This is what family does. We protect each other. Watch your back. I'll be in touch."

I hang up and stand to walk to the windows.

This is what family does. We protect each other. We ask how we can help. We don't fucking whip and brand those we love.

I wish Elena could know what the love of family really means. That she wasn't afraid and running.

But I'm determined to give her that safety.

I just have to figure out *how*.

CHAPTER
SEVENTEEN
~CARMINE~

I didn't plan to go back to Seattle emptyhanded. I'd thought to have Elena with me, this whole mystery solved.

I don't like being wrong.

I wait on the plane, ready to go home, as the crew goes through their final checks. Using the family jet is convenient since it's available whenever I want, and I don't have to adhere to the schedules of commercial flights. I'm anxious to get back to Seattle to continue the search for my cousin.

I won't rest until she's home.

"We're ready for you, sir."

I nod at the pilot as my phone rings.

"Don't take off yet. I need to take this call."

"Yes, sir."

He disappears into the cockpit as I answer.

"Give me good news."

"Found him," Shane says into my ear, coming across as pleased with himself. Shane has always been the quiet one, the least emotive, but he sounds downright chipper right now. "He covered his tracks fairly well for a nobody. But I'm no amateur."

"Where is he?"

"Oregon," Shane replies. "Rocco and I are headed there now. I'll text you the exact location and meet you in a few hours."

"Good work," I say as my stomach clenches in anticipation. "Get me that info, and I'll see you soon."

I hang up and buzz the pilot.

"We've had a change of plans."

———

THREE HOURS LATER, and my brothers and I are in a booth at a diner in Bandon, Oregon.

"Why don't we just go get her?" Rocco asks.

"Because we don't know for sure that she's with him," I reply. "This could be another wild goose chase. Maybe Archer just happened to buy an investment property here."

"I have a feeling," Shane says, slowly shaking his head. "I feel it in my gut. She's here."

"We need to stake out his house," Rocco says. "We'll see who goes in and comes out."

"Agreed," I reply. "And there's no time like the present. Let's do this."

I throw some bills on the table to cover our coffee, and we file out to the rented SUV parked at the curb.

My adrenaline is up as Rocco follows the GPS to the house on the shoreline. We park down the road so we can still see the driveway but also remain inconspicuous.

"No one's coming in or out without us knowing," Rocco says as he cuts the engine, and we settle in to wait.

Some stakeouts take minutes. Others, days. We have no way of even knowing if Archer's in residence right now.

If all of this is for nothing, I'm going to be royally fucking pissed.

But less than an hour later, a white Audi pulls out of the driveway.

"Let's go."

CHAPTER
EIGHTEEN
~ELENA~

"I can't believe you got me a cake." I shake my head at Margie as I bite into my second piece of the chocolate deliciousness. Between this and the donuts I had for breakfast, I'm on a serious sugar high. I really need to give up sugar. I just wish it wasn't so delicious. "You didn't have to do all of this."

"We're happy you're here with us," she says and taps her plastic solo cup to mine before taking a sip of her cola. "Besides, six years as an employee is something to celebrate. As you know, it's not easy to keep loyal employees around here."

"Hey," Chad says with a frown. "I'm only six months behind Ally."

"And you'll get a cake, too," Margie says with a wink. "Thanks for staying a little late so we could celebrate."

"Thanks for the celebration," I reply happily. "It was a nice surprise."

I finish my cake and lean over to hug Margie.

"Also? All those people who quit didn't have the chops for this job. Taking care of baby animals isn't all snuggles and cute photos. It's hard when they die, and when they're sick. It's not a reflection on you, Margie."

"I know. Sucks, though. I sure appreciate you and Chad for stepping up in such a big way over the past year. I don't know what I would have done without you."

"You'd have been on a lot of medication," Chad says with a laugh. "To stop from going crazy."

"You're not wrong."

"Ally's right," Beverly, the new girl, says after setting down a tiny bear cub that was found on someone's back porch. "It's not easy. I know I haven't been here long, but there were moments when I thought I wasn't cut out for this."

"Please don't tell me you're quitting," Margie says, her face transforming into panic.

"No," Beverly says. "I'm not quitting. But the first couple of weeks were rough. So, I also have to give props to Chad and Ally for being here so long."

"I've wanted to do this job since I was a little girl," I admit.

Margie's eyes light up at something behind me, and I turn to see Archer walking toward me. "I like him."

"Me, too."

He's tanned and wind-blown and everything I've ever wanted in my life. And he's finally mine. He loves me, and he's sticking.

I think it's crazy, and I don't know how we'll work it all out, but I'm here for it.

A woman would be stupid to turn Archer Montgomery down. And I'm no fool.

"You're having a party without me?" Archer asks, his blue eyes intent on the cake, making me laugh. "With food?"

"You'll have to take a piece to go," I inform him. "My car is ready to be picked up. Finally."

"You don't like my car?" Archer's already stuffed one piece of the cake into his mouth and grabbed another for the road.

"I like it fine, but I need my own set of wheels. So, let's go get it."

Margie laughs, waving us off. "See you tomorrow, kiddo."

"Have a good night." We walk out to Archer's Audi. I'm in an *incredible* mood. I feel like I have the best life in the whole world. "They surprised me because I've officially been at the job for six years."

"Very nice," he says and leans over to kiss me. "They're good people."

"Yeah, I think so, too. I'm excited to get my car back. And then I have plans to have drinks with Lindsey later this afternoon after she gets off work. We're just going to the bar at the resort, keeping it simple, but it'll be good to see her. We haven't had any girl time in a long while."

"I love it when you're in a good mood," he says as he kisses my fingers, driving toward the auto shop.

"It's been a wonderful couple of weeks," I say and roll the window down so the breeze can flow through my hair. "I have no complaints."

"I couldn't agree more," he says as he parks in front of the garage. I feel like I'm almost bouncing as we walk inside, and the smell of motor oil and rubber tires hits me.

"Hey, Ally," Lee says with a wave from behind the counter. "We've finally got you all fixed up. Sorry it took so long. We've been pretty swamped."

"No worries. It all worked out." I lean on the counter and smile at the older man. "How much do I owe you?"

He gives me the figure, and I whistle.

"Wow. It was really broken."

"I warned you it would be better to scrap it," Lee says.

"This should get me through for another year." My voice sounds more confident than I feel, and by the look on Lee's face, he also has his doubts.

"I can point you in the direction of an honest used car person when you're ready," Lee says as he passes me my receipt.

"Thanks. For everything. Have a great weekend."

I wave, and with my keys in hand, turn to Archer.

"I'll follow you home?"

"Sounds good, babe." He leans down to kiss me lightly, smacks me playfully on the ass, and we go our separate ways to our vehicles.

Yes, it's a damn good day.

I adjust my seat and mirror, roll down the windows to clear out some of the mustiness from it sitting so long, and start the engine.

It fires up and purrs like a kitten.

Okay, it sputters a bit, but it's running, and that's the most important thing.

Archer pulls out ahead of me, and when I'm behind him, we take off toward his house. I can't help but turn the radio up and sing along with the Journey song wailing through the speakers.

I have a few hours before I'm due to meet with Lindsey. I can either jump on Archer and have my way with him for a while, or head over to my cottage and start cleaning up the remnants of that fiasco.

I just haven't had it in me since the robbery to go in and start dealing with the mess. It's going to take several days. And now that it's been defiled so badly, it's lost its luster for me. I know I'll eventually have to go back and make it my home again, but for now, I'm procrastinating.

Not to mention, I'm in a fantastic mood, and I don't want to ruin it.

So, jumping Archer's bones, it is.

I smirk as I pull in behind Archer in his driveway. Movement in my rearview catches my attention, and I frown when I see a black SUV pull in behind me.

No.

My good mood evaporates, replaced by swift, all-consuming fear.

I step out of my car, just as my cousin Rocco climbs out of the driver's seat of the SUV. But he smiles at me, and that loosens the knot in my stomach, just a smidge.

Then my cousin Shane gets out of the back seat, and when his eyes lock on mine, he winks.

Okay, maybe this won't be so bad.

But then Carmine gets out of the SUV, and the fury on his face has my stomach clenching all over again.

"You have exactly fifteen seconds to get the fuck off my property," Archer says from behind me. He plants his hands on my shoulders, and I watch in horror as Carmine pulls a gun from under his jacket and points it at us.

"Wrong," Carmine says. His jaw is tight, and his brown eyes are locked on mine, his expression filled with hurt and anger and more that I can't read. I want to hug them all. I've missed them. And I'm terrified of what's about to come next. "You're both going to get in the car."

"No," I say immediately and step in front of Archer, shielding him.

"You're coming with us, or I'll kill him here and now. And trust me, Elena, I have no problems doing exactly that."

"He has nothing to do with this," I insist.

"Uh, yeah, babe, I do," Archer says and kisses my hair. "I go where you go."

"No." I turn and stare up into his eyes. "*No.* You can't save me from this."

"I told you," he says, "I'm in for the long haul, no matter how it shakes out. I'm not leaving you to fend for yourself. I'll never do that to you."

"It's too dangerous."

"As entertaining as this lover's spat is," Shane says, "we have things to do. Get in the fucking car. Both of you."

I press my lips together and will myself not to cry. This is it. This is the moment when my life is being torn away from me. The moment when everything I've worked so hard for over the years is just *gone.*

"Hey." I turn at the sound of Rocco's voice. He's standing closer now, and his voice is softer than Carmine's. "We really do need to go, Elena. Once we get where we're going, we can talk, okay?"

"You have to promise me you won't hurt him."

"You know I can't do that," Rocco replies. "Come on. We'll figure this out."

Archer takes my hand in his and leads me to the black SUV.

We have no choice.

I DON'T KNOW how much time passes. No more than a few hours, I'd guess. We flew in the family's plane to Seattle and are holed up in an apartment in the heart of downtown.

"I thought for sure you'd take us to Uncle Carlo's office," I say to Carmine, who's currently pacing the floor.

"Why would we do that?"

"Because he's the boss."

His eyes narrow into slits. "So you have been paying attention to the family all these years."

"I had to keep tabs on things. I'm not stupid, Carmine."

His hands slide into his pockets, and he doesn't look away from me when he says to the others, "Give Elena and I some time alone."

"You heard the man," Rocco says, nudging Archer out of the room.

"I stay wherever she is," Archer insists.

"He won't hurt me," I say. "He's mad at me, but I'm safe with him, Arch. I promise."

Archer squeezes my shoulder and then leaves the room with my cousins, and Carmine and I are left alone.

God, how I've missed this man. He was basically a brother to me my whole life. He was my protector. My confidante. My best friend.

"What—?" I begin, but he cuts me off with one look.

"What the fuck were you *thinking*?" he demands.

"At what point, Carmine? When my parents were brutally murdered, and I was afraid I was next?"

"We would have protected you," he says, pacing the room again. "*I* would have protected you."

"How? They managed to kill my father, and as much of a bastard as he was, he wasn't stupid. He couldn't protect himself or my mother. I was a sitting duck, and Grandma knew it. So, she got me out of there and told me to wait for her to send for me. Which she never did."

"Un-fucking-believable," he growls and pushes his hand through his dark hair. "Do you realize that we thought you were dead? The three of us *mourned* you."

"I'm sorry." My voice is soft as I think of these three men that I love so much hurting over the thought of losing me. "I'm so sorry that it had to be that way."

"It *didn't* have to be that way. After everything I've been through in my life, I've never felt this betrayed, Elena. And I didn't expect that treachery to come from *you*, someone I trusted with my life."

"It's not like I deliberately did anything to you," I say in my defense. "I had to disappear. And for eight years, I've been safely hidden away, living my life. I will *not* apologize for loving that life, Carmine."

"So, you go away, and you live your fun life away from the family for eight fucking years. None of us knows. And then one day, you attend a funeral, and we find out about it, and we're supposed to just leave you be?"

"So you did recognize me."

"I'd know you anywhere," he says. "Not only did you betray me by leaving, but now I have to punish you, Elena. I have to hurt you, the one person in this world that I *never* want to hurt. All because you couldn't be loyal to the family."

"I DIDN'T CHOOSE THIS FAMILY!" I yell, surprising us both. "I don't want any part of this life, Carmine. And I'm sorry if that hurts your feelings because I love you so much, but the mafia life isn't something I want."

"That's not how this works, and you know it." He paces away and then comes back to me again. "You don't get to fucking choose."

"Now you sound like my father."

"Your father was a pitiful excuse for a human being. He was a horrible boss, and a deplorable husband and father. But in this, he wasn't wrong, Elena. You don't walk away from this family, or from this life. Gram gave you an eight-year vacation, and that's over. It's time to get back to real life and accept the consequences of your actions.

"But I'll tell you this: no matter how much you hate the fact that you're part of this family, you can either make it work for you or against you. That's something you never understood."

"It's always against me if I can't be with the man I love, Carmine."

"That's another thing," he says and shoves his hands into his pockets. "You didn't trust *me* enough to let me know that you were okay, that you were hiding, but you've been shacking up with Archer all this time?"

I shake my head. "You obviously haven't been watching me for long. Archer found *me* about a month ago."

"And you just fell right back into bed with him."

I feel the blood drain out of my face and then surge back into my veins with fury.

"Let me be clear, Carmine. We didn't split up because we fell out of love. We split because my father beat the shit out of me and threatened to kill him if I didn't break it off."

Carmine's eyes turn sober.

"He *hurt you*?"

151

I turn and lift my shirt and hear Carmine's quick gasp from behind me.

"He tortured me for days, then showed me a live feed of Archer and his sister, with one of his goons ready to fucking kill them both. I wasn't given a choice. Because I don't have the right to choose, remember?"

"You never told me that he did that to you. You *know* that goes against what we believe in."

"And you know that he didn't give a shit about me. He just wanted to control me. In any way he could. So, yeah, when Grandma gave me the option to run away, I grabbed onto it with both hands, and I never looked back. No matter how much I missed you and Shane and Rocco. Because any family who would do *this* to me is one I want no part of."

"Well, you're back now," he says, and then his shoulders sag in defeat. "Fuck, Elena. I'm sorry I couldn't protect you from that piece of shit. I'm sorry that he ever laid hands on you. I would have been there—"

"You were hardly more than a kid yourself, with no clout in the family yet, Carmine. There was nothing you could have done."

I feel the tears threatening.

"I know you're angry and hurt, but I did miss you. All three of you. And I wondered about you often. When I came home for Grandma's funeral, I wanted nothing more than to hug you. I walked right past you. I knew I shouldn't have gone at all, but I loved her so much. I had to thank her for saving my life."

He turns to look out the window.

"A part of me died when you left," he admits, his voice quiet again. "I think the *good* parts of me died."

"That's not true." He turns back to me with tormented eyes, and I can't hold back any longer. I walk to him and wrap my arms around him, holding on tight. Slowly, he returns the hug, and we stay that way for several long moments. "You're a good man, Carmine."

"No. I'm not, Elena. I can't be given the line of work I'm in. But I love you, and I'll do what I can to protect you."

I pull back to look up into his handsome face.

"What will Uncle Carlo do?"

He sighs. "I don't know."

CHAPTER
NINETEEN
~ARCHER~

I'd consider this apartment beautiful if I weren't being held in it against my will. Actually, that's not correct. I'm here willingly because they have the love of my life, and I'll do whatever needs to be done to keep her safe. Leaving her alone with Carmine was like tearing a limb from my body. Everything in me screamed not to let her out of my sight.

But she was so calm about it, so sure that she was safe with the man. Not to mention, I didn't exactly have a choice with Rocco holding a gun to my side.

"So, you're the infamous Archer," Rocco says after leading me into the master suite from the living room, where Carmine is having words with Elena right now.

"And you three are the cousins."

This room doesn't have a bed in it. Instead, it's set up as an office. A large desk fills the middle of the room with several computers, a printer, and more paperwork than I would expect on the surface. Then again, I have no idea how much paperwork it takes to run a mafia family. There's a chair behind the desk, two in front of it, and a small couch off to the side.

It looks like the Martinellis have set this place up as some kind of home base so they don't have to use their private homes or offices for the dirtier jobs.

If I wasn't so fucking pissed, I'd be impressed.

"We should probably tie him up," Rocco says to Shane, but I scoff and shake my head, getting their attention.

"Why?" I hold my hands out at my sides. "We're here willingly. I'm not going anywhere unless it's with Elena. I won't run."

Shane watches me with calm, cool, blue eyes. All three men have an air of danger around them. On a normal day, I would avoid fucking with them.

This isn't a typical day.

"What's he doing to her in there?" I ask, pacing to the door to try to hear anything, and then turning back to them. "No offense, but I don't trust any of you."

"He won't hurt her," Shane says. He stands by the windows, his arms crossed over his chest. All three were wearing suits, but they've since shed their jackets and rolled the sleeves of their white shirts up to their elbows. All of the brothers are tall and broad with dark hair. Carmine's and Rocco's eyes are dark, while Shane's are blue.

"You, on the other hand," Rocco adds, "might want to worry about your own skin."

"What are you going to do to me?" I lean my shoulder against the wall, facing them. "Skin me alive? Shoot me in the knees? Cut off my fingers at the knuckles? Will I be swimming with the fishes?"

"None of that today," Shane says. "But Pop will want to meet you sooner or later, and then it'll get interesting."

My phone, which they confiscated right away and set on the desk in the middle of the room, lights up.

"Your phone's been blowing up all day," Shane says, peering down at the screen. "Who's Lindsey? Are you two-timing my cousin?"

I laugh. "No. That's Elena's best friend. She has my number because Elena doesn't have a cell phone. They were supposed to have drinks today. She's probably wondering where Elena is, and why she's been stood up."

The screen lights up again. If they plan to monitor my phone all day, it'll be a full-time job. It never stops.

"And Matt?"

"My cousin." I see Shane's eyes shift to Rocco. "But you already know that. Your family dug up everything there is to know about mine *years* ago. So, you know who they are. When they can't reach me, they'll start a search, and it won't be a tiny neighborhood watch."

"Oh, look at that," Shane says, his voice as dry as the desert as he throws my phone on the floor and smashes it with the heel of his boot. "I've just run out of fucks. It doesn't matter to me who your family is. You're dealing with *my* family now, Montgomery."

"You should have just stayed away from her," Rocco says, joining the conversation. "If you'd minded your own business, life would be so much easier for you."

"She *is* my business."

"How long have you been shacked up together? Since she left eight years ago?"

I frown. They obviously don't know as much as they want me to think they do.

"I found her a month ago," I reply. "I was done being without her."

"Maybe it wasn't explained to you the way it should have been," Shane says as he walks away from the window. "It's not just about Elena. It's about the *family*. Her father forbade your relationship because you don't come from the right pedigree. She was supposed to marry someone in another mafia family, to tie the two together and strengthen us as a whole."

"She's a woman, not a business merger."

"She's both," Rocco says. "And she was the only child of the boss. Because she's female, the Watkins name ends with her."

"How are you related?" I ask, truly curious.

"Elena's father and our mother are siblings," Shane says. "Our mother married Pop, bringing in the Martinellis to the family. The connection between the Wakinses and the Martinellis goes back generations. Sometimes, it was good. And other times not so good. Our parents' marriage smoothed the relationship, and made the Watkinses stronger than they ever were without us."

"And that was the goal with Elena," Rocco continues. "She was

155

betrothed to a member of the Russian mafia, but that didn't work out for...various reasons."

"What reasons?"

"Those aren't important," Shane replies. "What *is* important is that you understand why you'll never marry Elena, and why you can't be a member of this family. If you're brought in, your loyalties have to change immediately. Family first."

"And he means the mafia family," Rocco clarifies. "Not your family, or Elena. The organization as a whole."

"Your family, the people you care about and come from, will no longer exist in your world. You'll be completely consumed by the Martinellis and their needs."

Bull. Shit.

"I can see that doesn't sit well," Shane says. "And it shouldn't. We're not a normal situation. Unless you're born and bred into it, it seems wrong. But it's not. It's just...different."

"Killing and blackmailing aren't wrong?" I ask.

Rocco cracks his knuckles. "They probably deserved to get dead."

I shake my head and turn back to the door, wondering what's happening in the living room.

"You're not going to talk me out of what I want, gentlemen."

"So, you're willing to risk your family, your business, *everything* for Elena? You'd choose her over those you love the most? Because that's what it boils down to, Archer." Shane tilts his head to the side, watching me carefully. "What are you willing to do? What are you willing to give up for the woman you say you love?"

"God, I'm so tired," Elena says. It's twenty-four hours later, and nothing has changed. We're in the same apartment, wearing the same clothes, stuck with the same people.

The difference there is, the cousins have taken turns sleeping.

We aren't allowed to do that.

"I don't understand this particular form of psychological warfare," I say, keeping my voice mild when I feel anything but. I long to stand

and pace the room, punch a wall. *Anything.* "You keep us awake for what?"

"Mental exhaustion is just one way to wear a person down," Elena says with a sigh and leans her head on my shoulder. We're curled up on the couch together while Carmine and Shane work on laptops at the dining room table. "It's an old trick. Guys, just let me nap."

"No," Carmine says as he continues tapping on the keyboard of his laptop.

"What do you want?" I ask, still mindful to keep my voice calm. "Are you wearing us down to talk about something? Do I have information you need? What's the end goal here?"

Carmine looks up from his computer. "We want you to willfully leave Elena be. To agree to disappear from her life forever."

"No."

Elena stiffens beside me. "Are you fucking serious?" she demands. "*That's* what this is about?"

"What did you think it was about?" Shane asks.

"I thought you were just holding us here and being jerks until Uncle Carlo decided to stop by."

"That's only part of it," Carmine says. "The *end goal,* as Archer put it, is for him to leave permanently."

"Not going to happen."

"No?"

"No."

Carmine sits back in his chair and sighs. "I get it, Archer. Elena's easy to love. She always has been. But don't do this to yourself. You won't win."

Oh, yeah, motherfucker? Try me.

Carmine stands and, with his computer, walks to us, sitting on the arm of the sofa as he taps some keys.

A photo comes up of Rocco squatting next to two little girls at a park, and I feel my blood run cold.

"Who's that?" Elena asks.

"My cousin's daughters."

I'm going to rip your damn eyeballs out of your skull.

"Seems your cousins drop their kids off at birthday parties and just leave." Carmine clicks his tongue. "That's not very safe. Anyone could just walk right up to little Olivia and Stella here and snatch them away. Look at how they're laughing at what Rocco's telling them."

"When was this?" Elena asks.

"This afternoon," Carmine says as if he's talking about what kind of flowers he plans to plant in his garden this year. "Oh, look at this one. It really is fun to look at photos of your family."

He taps the arrow key, and a new picture fills the screen.

"Anastasia, isn't it?" he asks. "She's beautiful."

If you touch a hair on her head, they will never find your fucking body.

"Looks like she's leaving a women's health clinic. Did you know she's pregnant?"

What? I have to fight not to blink quickly or stand and demand to leave so I can call her. Pregnant? That news is amazing and fantastic.

And I'll murder these assholes myself if they touch her.

"Oh, my God," Elena whispers, gripping onto my arm. "Carmine, no."

"It would be a shame, wouldn't it, if Anastasia was in a horrible car accident and they both died?"

You. Mother. Fucker.

But my expression is impassive when he looks down into my face.

"Carmine, this is *insane*. Since when do we threaten the lives of innocent people?"

"Since always," he says, not even sparing her a glance. "You've just been very sheltered, Elena."

"No," she says and stands to pace, stopping by Shane. "Stop this."

"Don't you have anything to say?" Carmine asks me.

"What do you want me to say?"

He shuts the computer with an angry snap and paces away from me. "Don't you give a shit about your family, Archer?"

"You haven't been *listening* to me," I reply as I stand and prop my hands on my hips. "They aren't some small, meek people in the middle of nowhere that you can bully. If you do this, if you hurt anyone I love, you have no idea the wrath they will unleash on you. On all of you. You think the fucking mafia is scary? Try fucking with the Montgomerys. We have deep contacts with law enforcement, with the military. Hell, the

O'Callaghans may have ties with the Irish Mafia, for all we know. The connections and money my family has are endless, and they will *end you* if you hurt us."

Shane laughs, surprising Elena. "I have to respect your arrogance, Montgomery. You're foolish, but you're confident."

"Nothing I've said is a lie," I reply.

"Archer," Carmine begins and walks to me, putting his nose only inches from mine. "We know everything there is to know about you and your *connections*. Do I look concerned?"

"You should be."

"No, my friend." He shakes his head. "*You* should be worried. Because that wrath you speak of? It's about to rain down in ways you've never dreamed of."

"I'm not your friend." I stare at him, unblinking. "Bring it."

LESS THAN AN HOUR LATER, Rocco returns to the apartment with an older man that looks just like him. With his dark hair slicked back, dressed in a dark suit with a dark shirt, and the signature mafioso ring on his right little finger, this man screams *mafia boss*.

I glance down and see Elena shrink against me as if she's a scared little girl afraid of the bogeyman.

And that pisses me right off, igniting more anger in me than I've felt even in the time we've been here. Even after Carmine threatened my family.

"Uncle Carlo," Elena says and lifts her chin, but she doesn't pull away from me.

The man stops in front of us. His face is stern, but his dark eyes soften as he stares at the woman he hasn't seen in many years.

"Little one," he says and immediately tugs Elena into his arms for a firm hug. "Oh, how I've missed you, sweet girl."

In her shock, she doesn't hug him back right away, but then her arms encircle him, and she holds on tightly.

"Are you surprised?" he asks when he finally pushes her away.

"Shocked," she admits.

"Oh, don't get me wrong. We'll be having a stern conversation before the night is out, but for right this minute, I want to look at you. You're a beautiful woman, Elena. And a smart one."

He pats her cheek and then walks away without even acknowledging that I'm standing here.

"Maybe too smart," he continues. "However, you underestimated me. You see, Elena, I've known where you were since the minute you left Seattle eight years ago."

Elena's eyes grow wide, and Carmine rounds on his father.

"What the fuck are you talking about?" Carmine demands. "You *knew*? Why would you send us off on some wild goose chase if you already knew where she was? I just wasted weeks of my life."

Carlo is impassive as he stares at his eldest son. "Because, my dear boy, you have to earn my trust back."

He dismisses Carmine and turns back to Elena.

"You know there's a price to pay for deserting the family the way you did."

"Grandma sent me away," Elena replies. "For my own safety."

"That wasn't her call to make," he says easily. "She wasn't in a position to make those decisions. Do you think the men she called to help with your arrangements didn't immediately report back to *me*? They were my employees, not hers."

"Then if you knew where I was, why didn't you come for me before now?" Elena asks.

"Because I didn't have a need for you. You were safe, and I kept an eye on you."

She narrows her eyes. "I've seen black SUVs around town, but I always brushed them off."

Carlo smiles. "See? I told you, you're a smart girl. We kept tabs on you, watched out for you. That break-in you had a few weeks ago was unfortunate. I suppose boys will be boys."

"Holy shit," Elena whispers.

"So, yes. I knew you were safe, and I didn't need you, so I left you be. You'd endured enough at the hands of your father, piece of shit that he was."

On that, we could agree.

"So, why now?" Elena asks. "What do you need from me now?"

"Why, nothing. But you came to the funeral. Mistake number one." He strides across the room and sits on a stool by the kitchen island, leaning an elbow on it as he turns to us conversationally. "I knew the minute you left Bandon with your little friend here."

His eyes turn to me.

"And I'll get to you in a moment. I was surprised when I didn't see you in the crowd at the church, but I was busy mourning my mother-in-law and seeing to the service. I would have left things alone and let you return to Bandon and live your life for a while.

"But Carmine recognized you."

Carmine shakes his head and rubs his hand over his mouth in frustration. He's seething. All three brothers look as if they're ready to kill their father themselves.

"So," he continues, "I couldn't very well brush it off, could I? And, I'll be honest, it didn't sit well with me when I found out that Archer had found you."

He turns to me now, his eyes cool.

"You've been an issue for my family for way too long, Mr. Montgomery."

"Uncle Carlo—"

"But I'll expand on that in a moment. First, there are consequences for what you did, Elena. A price to pay for leaving and for doing so much in your power to stay gone, as if you don't want any part of us at all."

"I don't," she says and crosses her arms over her chest.

"Well, I'm sorry to hear that. Now—"

"I'll take her punishment," Carmine says. "It's my fault that she's here. I'll take it."

Carlo takes a deep breath. "Noble. But no, that's not possible. You know that's not how this works. You have to dole out the punishment, my boy."

"You won't touch her," I say, speaking for the first time since he walked into the room. "*I'll* take her punishment."

"Brave," Carlo says, his eyes brightening as he thinks it over. "And this becomes an all new ballgame.

"No." Elena takes my hand in hers. "Archer, no."

"I accept," Carlo says, watching Elena. "But you won't get off scot-free, little one. No, your punishment is that you have to watch. Every moment. Every single thing that's done, you'll watch, and you won't beg for it to stop."

"Uncle Carlo—"

"It's settled." He motions to his sons. "Clear the room and tie him up, then we'll get started. There's no time like the present."

CHAPTER
TWENTY
~ELENA~

No. No no no no no. This is my worst nightmare come to life. I watch in horror as Rocco and Carmine move the furniture to the edges of the room, and then Shane places a kitchen chair in the middle.

"Have a seat," Carmine says, gesturing to the chair.

"No. Please, no." I grab onto Archer's arm, but he turns to me, frames my face in that special way he does, and smiles down at me.

"Hey, it's okay, E. Everything's going to be okay." He kisses me softly and then turns away, sitting in the chair. Before Rocco can even start tying his hands down at his sides, securing them to the legs of the chair, Shane hauls off and punches Archer in the face.

"Jesus," I mutter and crush my fist to my mouth.

"It'll be over before you know it," Uncle Carlo says with a wink. "Now, I won't tie you up unless you do something stupid like run in there and get yourself hurt. Stay on this stool."

I can't move. I *want* to. Everything in me screams to run to him, to cover him with my body so I can absorb the beating and not him.

But if I do, I'll only make things worse for him.

So, I stay put and feel my eyes glaze over as Rocco pulls a bullwhip out of a gym bag.

"No," Carmine says, glancing at me. "Not the whip."

"Why the fuck not?" Rocco asks.

"Show them," Carmine demands. I shake my head no, but he advances on me, spins me around, and pulls up the back of my shirt.

"What the fuck is this?" Uncle Carlo exclaims. "Did this prick do this to you?"

"Of course, not," I growl, turning to my uncle with a glare. "My *father* did it."

He sputters, and his face flushes with fury as I yank my shirt down and turn back around. His jaw tightens, and he merely nods at my cousins.

Rocco tosses the whip aside but pulls a hammer out of the bag instead. Archer's eyes don't leave mine as Rocco rears his arm back and brings the hammer down on Archer's hand, smashing it against the leg of the chair.

"Motherfucker," Archer growls, his body shaking in pain and anger, but he still doesn't look away from me. It's as if he's soaking in *my* strength, my love for him, to use as a shield against what's about to come.

The three of them take turns, punching and kicking him until he's a bloody, swollen mess, breathing hard and sweating profusely.

I glare at all three of my cousins, silently damning them to hell for putting Archer through this insane pain.

But Archer doesn't cry out again. He winces, but he never once begged for the torture to stop. Archer pants hard, his tanned skin streaked with his blood and sweat. His head begins to fall forward in exhaustion.

"Well. Now he's ready," Uncle Carlo says with a smile. "Untie him and let's see what he has left in him. If he fights back and manages to survive the beating, I'll let him live."

"You'll do better than that," Archer says with a growly voice. "You'll let me marry Elena."

Uncle Carlo's face transforms from agreeable to rage in an instant.

"Who do you think you are to tell me what I'll agree to?"

"I'm taking her punishment for leaving eight years ago," Archer continues, not retreating from my uncle in the least. "If I win this fight, you'll give us your blessing to marry. This is more than a decade in the making, Carlo, and you know it. We've earned it."

I'm watching Archer's face as he struggles to breathe through the pain, blood dripping down his cheek from the side of his swollen eye. His dark hair is wet with sweat, and his naked torso gleams in the light from the setting sun behind him.

"Let's see if you win first," Uncle Carlo sneers and nods at my cousin Shane to untie Archer.

We're surrounded by my family, all of them hell-bent on torturing Archer. On keeping us apart.

But after more than ten years, I'm done being without him.

While the cousins untie him, Archer's gaze never leaves mine.

I love you, he mouths.

I love you, too, I mouth back.

Finally, his hands are free, and he pushes to his feet.

"Rocco," Uncle Carlo says. "Take care of him."

The three gang up on him, but when Carmine and Shane hold his arms so Rocco can punch him, Archer uses the two brothers as leverage to kick up his legs and knock Rocco out.

My cousin falls in a heap on the floor, unconscious.

I feel Uncle Carlo shift next to me, and we watch silently as Shane throws a punch. Archer deflects, captures Shane's hand, and while bending it back until there's a loud *snap*, Archer punches the heel of his injured hand into Shane's nose, sending him falling to the floor, as well.

"Maybe we underestimated you," Carmine says, wiping at the sweat dripping from his forehead.

"In more ways than you realize." Archer's voice is hard and gravelly, filled with determination and grit. Hope fills my belly when Carmine moves to punch Archer, but he deflects. Archer is going to win this! We're going to leave here and be together.

But Carmine rounds on Archer and tags him from behind. He wraps his arm around Archer's neck and holds him in a headlock. Both men grunt from the exertion, their skin red. Archer's face is turning purple. My God, I want to run to him, help him. Carmine could kill him!

"Don't." That's all Uncle Carlo says.

And then I watch in fascination as Carmine leans in and whispers something in Archer's ear.

We can't hear what is said, but the next thing I know, Archer grips the arm around his throat with his good hand and pulls down hard, then flings his head back and connects with Carmine's nose, sending blood spraying everywhere as Carmine falls to the floor.

Archer stands in the middle of the room, chest heaving, eye swollen shut, and covered in blood. But his eyes are on me as he says, "I win."

I wait. I want to beg Uncle Carlo to do the right thing. I *know* that he's a good man deep down. I felt the love he had for me when he wrapped me in his arms.

Uncle Carlo rubs his hand over his chin and watches Archer thoughtfully, ignoring the groans coming from his sons on the floor.

"Carmine was right, we did underestimate you. I'll concede that you won."

"I'm taking Elena, and we're leaving. We're *leaving*. She won't ever see you again."

"I won't agree to that," Uncle Carlo replies. "You know that's not possible. She can never leave. It's been a hard lesson to learn."

He turns his eyes to me.

"I'll allow you to marry, if that's what she wants."

My heart soars. Is this really happening? But then the reality of it hits me right between the eyes.

"I can't." I turn to Archer. "I can't let you get sucked into this. Maybe we can run and hide again."

"We're done running," Archer says and hobbles to me, wrapping his arm around my shoulder. "No more hiding. No more. There's not much I can do for you, Carlo."

"You'd be surprised," my uncle replies with a thin smile. "I'll approve of this match, with the understanding that if and when I need you, I'll call on you, and you'll answer. If you hide from me, we'll find you. And it won't end as well as it did for you today."

"I told you," Archer says, "I'm done hiding. But I have a condition of my own."

My uncle's eyes narrow, but he doesn't say anything as Archer continues.

"You'll leave *my* family alone. They have no part in this, and you'll never hold them over my head again. My family is as important to me as yours is to you, Carlo."

He waits for a heartbeat, and then Uncle Carlo nods once. "Agreed."

Without another word, Archer and I walk to the door. I glance back at my cousins on the floor, but Uncle Carlo is already on the phone, calling in the medical team that he keeps on the payroll to help.

"Where are we going?" I ask once the elevator doors close, and Archer leans heavily on the wall. "My God, you can hardly stand."

"Get me home."

"I'm going to get you to a hospital, that's where I'm taking you."

"No." He shakes his head and then grimaces. "Home. I'll make some calls."

"Archer—"

"For once, just do as you're told, Elena."

I want to yell at him and maybe smack him for having the audacity to speak to me like that, but I can't argue because he just leans his head on mine and sighs.

"I love you, babe. Was worried I might not walk out of there."

"I love you, too."

WE'RE at Archer's house in West Seattle, and he's been in and out of consciousness.

I don't know what to do, so I call Anastasia from Archer's landline.

"I need your help," I say immediately and tell her about Archer's condition. "He won't let me take him to the hospital. I'm worried his hand is broken, and I think he might have a concussion. What am I going to do?"

"Sit tight," she says brusquely. "I'll be there with a doctor in less than thirty minutes."

She hangs up, and I run a washcloth under ice-cold water, then press it to Archer's forehead. He's burning up.

"I called your sister," I say softly. "I'm so worried. Why won't you go to the hospital?"

"Too many questions," he mutters. "I'll heal. Had worse."

"Yeah, right." But he's done what he likely intended and made me smile. "She said she'll be here in a few with a doctor."

"Jase," he says. "Lia's brother-in-law. Surgeon."

"Good." I dab at his wounds with the rag. He needs more attention than I can give him here with no supplies.

He's just drifted off again when the doorbell rings. I sprint downstairs and fling open the door, relieved to see Anastasia and a man holding a medical bag.

"Where is he?"

"In the bedroom."

They both step inside, and Jase takes off up the stairs.

"That's Jase," Anastasia says before pulling me in for a massive hug. "He's a doctor."

"Archer told me." I hug her back, just as fiercely. "Hi."

"Oh my God, it's so good to see you. I was afraid I'd never see you again."

"I know." I pull back and take her in. "Wow. You're not a kid anymore."

"Neither are you." She smiles and we walk to the couch, where we sit and hold each other's hands. "What happened?"

"So much." Everything pours out of me. Archer finding me. Falling back in love with him. Getting caught in Bandon and being hauled back here. Everything that happened over the past two days. "I'm so sorry. He's broken and hurting up there because of *me*. And that's the last thing I ever wanted to happen, Stasia. It's why I broke it off all those years ago because I was afraid of exactly this happening. They could have killed him."

"But they didn't," she says, covering my hand with her own. "And he's strong. Besides, now you can be together without hiding."

"I don't know." I shake my head slowly. "I've been thinking about it since we left the apartment. Uncle Carlo said we could be together, but only if Archer agreed to be a part of the family and do whatever needs to be done when Uncle Carlo needs him. I can't ask that of him. I don't want him to get swept up in my family. I think it's best if I make sure Archer's well, and then I leave again."

Anastasia's eyes are narrowed as she listens, and then she blows out a gusty breath.

"Have you lost your fucking mind?" she demands. "First of all, if you run again, he'll just find you. Or I will and beat the snot out of you. Second of all, if you break my brother's heart again, I'll still beat the snot out of you."

"You've become very violent since I last saw you."

"You mess with my brother, and you bet your ass, sister. You weren't there to pick up the pieces after you broke up with him before. I was. It was horrible. And then when he found out *why* you ended it, and went on a bender, singing songs in my husband's family's bar? Yeah, it wasn't pretty."

"He told me. I wish I'd seen the singing part."

"No, you don't. It was embarrassing as hell. *Then* he was like a man possessed. Whenever he had a spare minute, he was searching for you. He loves you *so much* he risked his life today to be with you. And you're ready to walk away from that? Jesus, Elena, I hate to ask just what your standards are in men if this isn't good enough for you."

"I feel guilty. I feel like I'm asking too much of him."

"Do you think my brother does anything he doesn't want to do? He's as stubborn as they come. And he wants *you*. Any way he can get you. Why don't you hold on to that? Why don't you believe in the love you have with Archer and be grateful for it? Live your life, *Elena*. Not Ally. Live Elena's life, and be happy. Every day. If your family kicks up some drama here and there, you'll deal with it. But living in *what-ifs* and trying to stay ten steps ahead of a possibility that might not ever happen is no way to survive."

I swallow hard and brush at the tears falling on my cheeks.

"You're right."

"Of course, I'm right."

We turn as Jase comes walking down the stairs.

"How is he?"

"Someone beat the shit out of him," Jase says. "I'm Jase, by the way."

"Elena." I shake his hand. "Does he have a concussion?"

"A slight one," he confirms. "You'll want to wake him every two hours and check the dilation of his pupils. I cleaned up the wounds, and the dressings will need to be changed daily. I'd like to have that hand x-rayed. And I think there may be some fractured ribs, as well."

"Jesus," Anastasia says. "How many were there?"

"Three against one," I reply, my voice grim. "Meds?"

"Ibuprofen every four hours as needed. If he needs anything stronger, let me know, and I'll write a script. He needs rest, so don't let him decide to run a marathon this weekend."

I smile. "I won't. Thank you very much."

"Call me if you need anything." Jase passes me his card. "My cell number is on there."

"You can call me, too. And tell my brother to call me tomorrow when he's up to it," Stasia says.

"I will. Thank you both. You didn't have to do this."

"This is what family does," Jase says with a wink.

When they're both gone, and Jase has given me more instructions for ice, rest, and elevation, I check on Archer. He's sound asleep, so I take a quick shower to get the last forty-eight hours off me and find a T-shirt of Archer's to slip into.

When I return to his bedside, he's still sleeping, breathing slow and steady. It's not time to wake him up yet, so I just slip into bed next to him with my head propped on my elbow and lay on my side to watch him.

I almost lost him tonight. They might have killed him. I don't believe my cousins wanted that, but what they want doesn't always matter.

As I well know.

Archer's legs become restless, and he moans in his sleep. I brush my fingers through his hair, still stained with blood, and murmur to him.

"It's okay, my love. You're okay. No one's going to hurt you."

He opens the one eye that's not swollen and turns to me. "Thought you were a dream."

"No, I'm right here."

"We won," he says before his eye drifts shut again.

"Yes, we did."

"Worth it."

"Babe, can I ask a question?"

He reaches out to take my hand in his good one and brings it to his lips, pressing a kiss to the pads of my fingers.

"Anything."

"When you were fighting, what did Carmine whisper to you?"

His lips twitch, and that eye opens again. "*You'd better win this, motherfucker.*"

I blink in surprise. "That's what he said?"

"Yeah. I don't think your cousins are bad people, babe. I think the mafia is fucked-up."

"You're right about that." I want to skootch in and cuddle him, but I'm afraid of hurting him, so I lean over and kiss his cheek. "How do you feel?"

"Like someone hit me with a bus."

"Close enough. I have a confession." I lick my lips, watching this strong man before me. This guy that I love so much. "I almost ran again. Because the thought of you being caught up with my family is almost too much for me to bear."

"I'd find you."

I smile, remembering what Anastasia said. "I know. And I had to remind myself that you were right. We're done hiding. I'm going to live every day, one day at a time, with you. Grateful. Because we've earned our life together, Archer. It's been a long time coming."

"I'm glad you finally figured it out," he says, his voice more slurred. "So tired. Gonna sleep, okay?"

"Sleep. We have all the time in the world to be philosophical."

"'kay."

His breathing evens out, and I know he's sleeping once more.

TWENTY-ONE

~CARMINE~

I'm sitting in the screened-in porch of my home, waiting for my brothers to arrive. It's a rainy day in the Pacific Northwest, mirroring my mood perfectly. In the week since we found Elena and all three of us took a beating from Archer, I've been planning.

Calculating.

I'm almost ready to set my scheme into motion, but I want to run my thoughts by Shane and Rocco. I'll need their help if this idea is going to be a success.

"Hello?" Shane calls from inside the house.

"Out here," I call back. I'm in gym shorts and a sweatshirt. No shoes. My third cup of coffee sits on the table next to me.

It's barely eight in the morning.

"It's fucking early," Rocco mutters as he walks out onto the porch with Shane, both holding steaming mugs of coffee from my kitchen.

"Help yourselves."

"We did," Shane says and sits opposite me. Rocco stands with his shoulder against the railing and sips his brew.

Both of my brothers have black eyes, faded from purple to a sickly green now.

I know my face doesn't look any better.

"He really fucked you guys up," I mention casually and cross an ankle over the opposite knee.

"Looked in a mirror today?" Rocco asks.

"He gave as good as he got," Shane adds. "It doesn't feel good, but I have to respect that. He'll protect Elena."

I nod in agreement. "Which leads me to why I asked you to come over here. I've been thinking."

"Whenever you start thinking, I get my ass kicked," Rocco mutters, glowering into his half-empty mug.

I ignore him.

"We've known for a while now who is responsible for Uncle Vinnie's death. It's time we did something about that."

"Why now?" Shane asks.

"A few reasons. Elena's home, so it's time to close that circle completely. Avenging her parents' deaths will do that."

"And?" Rocco asks.

This is the sticky part for me. The bit that leaves a sour taste in my mouth.

"I have to earn Pop's trust, remember?"

Shane's eyes narrow. "Pop was being a dick when he said that."

"He knew where Elena was, and he lied about it and then sent us all on a wild goose chase. It fucking pisses me off. I'm too old to play these games with him. So, I'm going to settle the score all around."

"How?" Rocco asks.

I reach for a photo lying next to my coffee mug, flip it over, and toss it back on the table. Both of my brothers lean in to get a look at the tall, willowy blonde in the picture. She's wearing sunglasses and a short skirt. Her hair is long and straight, and her lips are painted a bold red.

"Nadia Tarenkov" Shane asks with a raised eyebrow. "You're going to infiltrate the Tarenkov family through the boss's daughter?"

"Balls of fucking steel," Rocco mutters as a slow smile spreads over my face.

"What's the saying about revenge?"

"*Revenge is but a small circle?*" Shane asks.

"*Dead men tell no tales,*" Rocco adds.

I laugh and shake my head, lifting the photo of Nadia and studying it.

"I was thinking more along the lines of *paybacks are a bitch.*"

CHAPTER
TWENTY-TWO

~ELENA~

"Your breakfast, my lady." Archer steps onto the deck at his beach house in Bandon, his arms laden with pancakes and all the fixings.

Including bacon. I think the man keeps the pork industry in business all on his own.

"You didn't have to make breakfast," I say as I accept the plate and set it on the arm of the chair next to me, already salivating at the smell of the deliciousness before me. "But I'm grateful."

"We worked up an appetite last night," he says with a wink and takes a huge bite of his pancakes. "We need the calories."

I watch him as I eat, relieved to see that the bruises have faded away. Unless you look closely, you'd never know that he'd been beaten so badly just two weeks ago. Archer kept his word, he healed from the injuries quickly. I had to order, bribe, and beg him to stay in bed longer than two days so he'd heal faster, though.

"I missed it here," I say as I take a deep breath and enjoy the salty air. The water's a little choppy this morning, and birds fly over the waves in search of their breakfast. "We got lucky with the weather this weekend."

"I watched the weather app last week, and it looked like a few storms blew through Bandon. They got it worse here than in Seattle."

I nod and chew my bacon. "I'm going to really miss living here."

He frowns at me. "We own property here."

"Speaking of which, I need to get my cottage cleaned up and ready to put on the market."

"Are you sure you want to do that? You could rent it out. You don't have to sell it."

"I don't know how often I'll be in town, and I don't want to hassle with a rental company. Plus, since it got ransacked, it just doesn't feel like home anymore. It's time to sell and turn the page on that chapter. Are you going to keep this place?"

He swallows and turns to me fully now. "Elena, are you under the impression that we'll go back to Seattle and never come back here?"

I frown, hating the idea of never returning to Bandon. "With your work in Seattle, I just assumed we'd be there most of the time."

"You know I run my own company," he says. "I work just fine from here, and I can do that from time to time. I have no intention of selling this house. I love it here. But most importantly, *you* love it here. So, we'll come whenever you want."

The love is swift and all-consuming, filling me so full, it feels like light will start shooting out of my fingertips any second.

"You're awfully good to me," I say. "I'd like that. I have a busy day ahead. In addition to starting on the cottage, I have to go to the animal refuge and see Margie and Chad. And I'm having drinks with Lindsey this afternoon."

"You finally get your happy-hour time," he says with a grin.

"Yeah. I know they've all been worried and confused. It's time I come clean about everything. I'll miss that job."

"There are animal rescues in and around Seattle," he says. "I'm sure one of them would be happy to welcome you on staff. And like I said, we'll be back to visit. You're not saying goodbye forever like you did in California."

"You're right. I guess it's just an old habit. It's amazing, isn't it? How much can change in six weeks? My life is completely different. For the better."

"Same here," he says. "I'm relieved it's over. That you've come to an understanding with your family, and we can get on with our lives. It's past time."

"It's because of you that it happened," I reply. "I owe you so much."

"You don't owe me anything, Elena. I'd do anything to keep you safe and make sure you're happy."

"These pancakes are a good start." I grin and don't react when the phone buzzing starts.

"That's yours, babe."

"Oh, right."

When Archer replaced his phone, he got me one, as well. It's the first cell I've owned in almost ten years, and I'm not used to listening for it.

I scowl at the name on the screen.

"Hello?"

"Good morning," Uncle Carlo says. "How are you today, little one?"

"I'm fine." The food I just ate sits like lead in my stomach. "What's up?"

"I need to see you in my office as soon as possible."

I close my eyes and feel despair creep through me. "Already? Uncle Carlo, we just arrived back in Bandon, and we're seeing to a few things here. You need us for something so soon?"

"No, you misunderstand," he says. "I'm not calling you because I need something from you or Archer. I need to see you because we need to discuss your parents' estate. It's been sitting for eight years. And added to that is your inheritance from your grandmother."

"Oh." I blink and look over at Archer, who watches intently. "Honestly, I don't want anything from my parents. I don't care what you do with it."

"I can't do anything with it."

I laugh at that. "Of course, you can."

Uncle Carlo chuckles with me. "Elena, I know you didn't have a close relationship with your parents. But this all belongs to *you*. Real estate, investments, money, jewelry. The value is in the eight figures."

My mouth goes dry, and my tongue sticks to the roof of my mouth as I stare at Archer in shock. I had no idea my parents were worth so much.

"Elena?"

"I'm here."

"You were their only child, and everything was left to you in their will. It's gone through probate, and as the executor, I've been managing it. But it's time for you to take it all over. Now, I honestly don't care what you decide to do with it all, but don't be foolish and turn it down just because your parents failed you. Make it work for you. And if you need advice, I'm always happy to help. But you're a smart woman, Elena."

"Let me do some thinking. I'll be sure to call you when we're back in Seattle. It'll probably be a week or two."

"That's perfect. Travel safe."

He hangs up, and I open and close my mouth like a fish out of water.

"He said—"

"I heard," Archer says. "You're an incredibly wealthy woman, Elena."

My shoulders sag. "I already was, actually. But this is...unexpected. I guess it never occurred to me to think about what happened with their estate after they died. I left less than forty-eight hours after their deaths and figured anything they had would have been absorbed by the family."

"You assumed wrong," Archer says and reaches over to take my hand. "But don't worry. I'm not just after you because I'm hot for your money."

I chuckle and then start to laugh, the kind of laugh that grabs hold of you, where you're helpless to stop it.

When I finally take a deep breath, tears are running down my face. My stomach muscles ache. My face is frozen in a most unattractive expression, I'm sure. But I don't care. That felt damn good.

"ALLY!" Lindsey rushes to me across the lobby of the resort and pulls me in for a tight hug. "I don't know what the hell's been going on, but you've got some 'splaining to do."

"I know." I hug her and then step back. "But first thing's first. My name isn't Ally. It's Elena."

Lindsey frowns and then takes my hand and leads me toward the bar. "I think we need drinks before you say any more."

"Good idea."

We choose a booth in the corner where we'll have some privacy, and once our martinis are sitting in front of us, Lindsey takes a breath.

"Okay. Start from the beginning."

And so, I do. It feels amazing to finally be able to tell my best friend everything, from being with Archer in high school to our separation, then about my parents' deaths, and everything that happened after.

"How didn't I recognize you?" she wonders as she takes the last sip of her drink. "I used to *love* watching the gossip on your family."

"I was never in the spotlight much. I'm an introvert by nature, and I always stayed out of trouble."

"Well, it makes sense."

"What does?"

"That day at the diner when your grandmother's death was on the news, and you flew out of there like a bat out of hell. And Archer—who I like, by the way. He's nice, and he's *hot.*"

"I know." I grin, enjoying being with my friend again. "I'm sorry I had to lie to you for so long."

"I'm just sorry that you had to at all. But I'm so glad that it's over for you. Have you already talked to your job?"

"Yeah, I was just there. Margie cried." I feel my eyes fill with tears at the mention of it. "She'd been worried, and she's sad that I have to quit. Archer and I will live in Seattle full-time, but we're keeping his house here. So, you're not getting rid of me. I'll be back to visit and check in on you."

"Damn straight, I'm not losing you," she says. "I'll come visit up there, too. I love the city and don't get to shop nearly often enough. I have a ton of vacation time coming."

"We can meet up in Portland sometimes, too," I suggest.

"Absolutely." She signals to the bartender that we want two more drinks. "What are you going to do with your house?"

"Sell it."

Her eyes get big. "Really? Would you be willing to sell it to me?"

I tilt my head to the side. "I didn't know you were looking to buy a house."

"I wasn't, but I *love* your place. It's so cute and close enough to the water that you can walk to the beach, but not *too* close to make it worth millions." She grins happily and then deflates. "Wait. Unless you are planning to sell it for millions."

"No." I nod at the bartender when he delivers our drinks. He doesn't even look my way. He only has eyes for Lindsey. But she doesn't spare him a glance. When he walks away and is out of earshot, I pounce. "What's going on there?"

"What? Nothing. I don't know what you mean."

She sips her drink, trying to be nonchalant.

"Bullshit. Spill it."

"There's nothing to spill."

I sit back in the booth and cross my arms over my chest, giving her the *liar, liar, pants on fire* look.

"Okay." She leans in and holds her hand up to the side of her face in case he can hear us from fifty feet away. "I slept with him last weekend. I was lonely and feeling a little needy and totally did him. And now, *he's* the needy one."

I press my lips together, trying not to laugh. "He's pretty hot. Was the sex bad?"

"No, it was good."

"Then why are you ignoring him?"

"Because he failed to mention to me until *after* I'd had my third orgasm that he's *married.*"

I gasp and glare at the douche canoe behind the bar. He glances our way, and I flip him off.

"*Ally!*"

"Elena," I reply. "And I'm not sorry. Cheating asshole."

"I already sent an email to his wife just before I met with you today. So, his home life is about to *really* suck."

"He deserves it. I hope she chops off his balls. What a jerk."

"Oh, he's totally a jerk. He didn't understand why I was so pissed-off. He said the relationship sucks, and they're probably going to get divorced anyway, so what did it matter? I did manage to slam his fingers in the door when I left, and he tried to run after me."

"Attagirl." I clink my glass to hers.

"Okay, I have a question," she says, already changing the subject. "Like I said before, your family has always been interesting to me. But what's Rocco like? He's always so stern and mysterious in photos."

I swallow quickly before I blow vodka out of my nostrils. "*Rocco?*"

"Yeah. He's totally hot. Come on, help a girl out."

"No." I shake my head vigorously. "Just, no. Absolutely not."

"You're no fun," she says. "But maybe I'll meet him someday."

"Maybe you'll stay away from him," I say, all-business now. "I'm telling you, Lindsey, my family isn't one you want to get all tangled up in."

"I mean, getting tangled with him sounds kind of fun."

"You're incorrigible."

"I do try."

THE SUN IS JUST STARTING to set when I pull into the driveway of the beach house. I'm exhausted. Between the manual labor of cleaning my cottage and the emotional strain of seeing my coworkers and Lindsey, it's been a hell of a day.

I'd love nothing more than to get in the hot tub with Archer for a long soak, watch some trashy TV, and then maybe go to bed early.

Yep, it's a wild Friday night for me.

I park in the garage next to Archer's Audi and walk through the mudroom to the kitchen. It occurs to me that I spent all morning at the cottage and didn't feel a connection to the place at all. And I lived there for six years. Yet as I walk into this beach house, it feels like home. I'd like to think it's because of the man waiting for me here. Home is wherever Archer is.

There are a dozen red roses in a gorgeous blue vase on the counter with a note.

E-

I'm down on the beach. Join me. Grab a sweater, it's getting cold.

-A

I guess the soak will come later. I can't resist a sunset stroll on the beach with the hottest man alive.

I smile when I see one of Archer's sweatshirts lying by the sliding glass door. I throw it on and walk down the steps to the sand below.

When I catch sight of Archer and the scene before him, I stop short.

I <3 U has been drawn in the sand, but the heart is made out of lit candles in hurricane glasses. My heart soars because as cheesy as it is, it's exactly like a night twelve years ago in Seattle.

Which tells me he's about to ask me a very important question.

"It's déjà vu, right?" Archer asks as I approach. He stands in the middle of the candle heart, wearing cargo shorts, a green T-shirt, and the biggest smile ever. He holds out a hand for me, and I take it, joining him.

"It was cheesy back then," I say with a laugh. "And it's a little cheesy now. But maybe the sweetest thing I've ever seen."

His incredible blue eyes turn sober as, with his gaze pinned to mine, he lowers himself to one knee and pulls out a gorgeous ring from his pocket.

"The first time I did this, I thought my love for you couldn't be stronger. That I'd never love you more than I did in that moment. But I was wrong, Elena. I love you more now than ever before, and you're still the woman I want to spend the rest of my life with. I don't want to miss out on one more day with you. I want to grow old with you, have babies and grandchildren, and give you everything you could ever need or want. I tried to live without you, but I was just a shell of myself without you by my side. So, I'm asking you, right here and now, to make me the happiest man in the world and be my wife. Marry me."

I sink to my knees in the sand in front of him and frame his face with my hands.

"I never stopped loving you, Archer. I know, deep in my heart, that we were always meant to be together. It would be my honor to be your wife."

I can't look away from him as he slips the ring onto my finger and then slides his hands into my hair as he kisses me like never before. As if his life depends on it.

He stands and pulls me to my feet and then slings me over his shoulder, carrying me up to the house.

"Hey!"

He slaps my ass, making me bark out a laugh.

"I can walk," I remind him, but take a moment to admire the ring on my finger. The round stone is massive and set classically. It'll be beautiful with any style of wedding band.

"Not fast enough," he says as he runs, with me still on his shoulder, up the steps to the house. He doesn't pause until we're in the bedroom, and he dumps me on the bed.

"Well, that was romantic."

He laughs and joins me, covering me with his strong form. "I suddenly had the urge to have you in my bed. Naked. Writhing. Unable to control yourself."

"Romantic *and* humble? I hit the jackpot."

He kisses me again, and his hands are swift and sure as they strip me bare. He really is talented at unfastening a bra with one hand.

His lips clamp over a nipple as I open for him, hitching my legs around his hips in invitation.

But he doesn't slide home. No, he takes his time, tickling me with his fingers, making sure I'm slick and ready. And only when I *am* writhing beneath him does he bury himself, balls-deep, as he lovingly cradles my head in his hands.

"I've loved you my whole life," he says. "And I can't wait to finally build a life with you."

I gasp as he presses the root of his cock against my clit. I tighten around him, making him swear under his breath. My hands clench his ass, holding him to me tightly. We're as entangled, emotionally and physically, as we've ever been. It's intoxicating. Addicting. And I don't have to give him up, now or ever.

"It's about damn time."

EPILOGUE

TWO MONTHS LATER

~Archer~

"So, you're getting hitched." My cousin Matt, along with Luke Williams and Shawn O'Callaghan, stand with me at the O'Callaghan Museum of Glass, all holding pints of Guinness as we watch some of the ladies dancing to the music the DJ plays for us.

Anastasia and Kane insisted on hosting our engagement party here at the museum. Elena was hesitant because having a party like this meant we'd be obligated to invite her family, but the Martinellis seem to be having a good time, mingling with the Montgomerys. Despite several members of my family being part of law enforcement.

I know Carlo and the cousins won't try anything shady on a night meant to celebrate Elena. They love her too much for that.

And Carlo and I have had several private conversations, and he's assured me that he respects me too much to go against his word of not doing my family harm.

As shady as Carlo can be, I trust that he'll keep his promise.

"He can't keep his eyes off her," Shawn says. "I'd say it's a damn good thing he's marrying her."

"She's the best thing in the world," I confirm. Luke grins as he watches his wife, Natalie, dancing.

"I understand completely," he says. A woman walking nearby catches his eye, and he motions for her to join us. "This is perfect timing. Shawn, I'd like to introduce you to N—"

"Lexi Perry," the woman interrupts, shaking her head slightly at Luke and giving Shawn her attention. Shawn's eyes light up at the sight of the beautiful redhead.

"I asked Ms. Perry to come to town on business, and thought it was rude of me to leave her alone in the city this evening," Luke continues. "So, I invited her here. After checking with our hosts, of course."

"It's a pleasure to meet you," I say with a nod. "Welcome."

"Congratulations," she replies and shakes my hand. "I was hesitant to crash the party, but Natalie and Luke assured me it would be okay. And I have to say, your family is incredibly welcoming."

"We always have room for more," I reply. "What do you do, Lexi?"

"I'm a writer."

I feel Shawn stiffen beside me. "Oh? Shawn's also a writer. What do you write?"

"Novels," she says and turns to Shawn, but he holds up a hand, stopping her.

"I'm not here to entertain any new projects tonight," he says.

Lexi's face goes from friendly to cold in a heartbeat. Luke sighs. I can feel in my gut that something just went very wrong.

"That's convenient," Lexi replies. "I'm not here to pitch a project to you, Mr. O'Callaghan. I know who you are, but it's not terribly important to me. I do fine all on my own. Have a good night, gentlemen."

She nods and walks away in her tight black cocktail dress and mile-high shoes.

"So, that was Nora Perry," Luke says, sipping his drink. Shawn's face whips around to stare at Luke.

"She said her name was Lexi."

"Nora is her pen name," Luke says and slaps Shawn on the shoulder. "You just managed to insult the woman you'll be working with starting on Monday." Luke turns to me. "Congratulations again, Archer. Elena is beautiful and lovely, and we can't wait for the wedding. Now, if you'll excuse me."

He walks away, leaving Matt and I with a stunned Shawn.

"So, you're gonna be working with her, huh?" Matt asks.

"Buggering hell," Shawn growls, the Irish accent kicking up with agitation as he stomps off in the direction Lexi headed.

Matt and I laugh as we watch him leave, and then he takes a sip of his beer.

"I've been pretty pissed at you, man," he says.

"Why's that?"

"Jase told me how beat up you were when he came to clean you up. You should have fucking called me."

"They broke my phone," I say. Our eyes scan the crowd as we talk. "And you and I both know I had to handle that myself. I needed to end it once and for all."

"Could have died."

"I didn't."

But, God, it felt like I might have when I was in the thick of it.

"I don't like that their family is going to be tied to ours."

"I've already handled that, as well."

He watches me for a long moment. "I'll still keep my eyes open."

"I'd expect nothing less."

"Is she worth it?"

"And more." I tap my glass to his. "She's worth everything."

The End

If you're interested in learning more about the Martinelli family, the With Me In Seattle MAFIA is coming in 2021, beginning with Carmine and Nadia's story, *Underboss*. And I have a sneak peek, just for you! Keep reading...

UNDERBOSS

A WITH ME IN SEATTLE MAFIA NOVEL

Underboss
A With Me In Seattle MAFIA Novel
By
Kristen Proby

UNDERBOSS

A With Me In Seattle MAFIA Novel

Kristen Proby

PROLOGUE

~NADIA~

I *hate* these parties. Papa says I have to be here because it's a family duty, and I'm expected to be on my best behavior. Behave like a lady. Be alert, kind, passive.

I'm always alert.

I don't think I'm always kind, but I wouldn't say I'm mean, either. I mean, the other girls at the private school my parents send me to all seem to like me. I'm not like that mean girl, Shannon, who makes fun of the girls who haven't gotten their boobs yet.

I don't have boobs yet, either.

But I can't wait for the day I get them. Then maybe I won't hate coming to these stupid weddings the family is obligated to attend. They're so *boring*. But, someday, my boobs will grow, and the boys won't ignore me anymore.

No one will ignore me.

But back to my behavior. I'm not passive. And I'm not meek, even though I'm sure my father would prefer that I was. I talk too much. I ask too many questions. But I want to know everything there is to know about my family and the business we're in.

I take a sip of my Shirley Temple and scan the crowd. My parents are laughing with a bunch of other people—all old, like them. Papa puffs on a cigar. He doesn't usually smoke, but Mama doesn't mind if he does at events like this, in celebration.

The bride, in her white dress with its puffy sleeves, twirls around the dance floor with the groom, who doesn't look nearly as nervous as he did at the ceremony.

I thought he might pass out. He was green and shiny, and someone had to pass him a tissue to clean up the sweat on his forehead.

It was awesome.

I've seen most of these people before—usually at other weddings or funerals. I've heard Papa and Mama talk about the *families* and how it's important to maintain peace during these functions.

Whatever that means.

My big brother, Alex, is off chasing after some girl. I saw him looking her over with hungry eyes, giving her the kind of once-over he seems to do more often now that he's sixteen.

It's gross.

And when I told him so, he said I was just a baby and that I'd never understand.

But I'm not a baby. I'll be thirteen next month, after all. I'm practically a grown-up.

I blow out a breath, and when my eyes land on *him*, I feel my stomach clench. I haven't seen him before. He looks about Alex's age. Tall with dark hair and brown eyes. And he's laughing at something another boy said.

The guy looks as if he could be the dark-haired one's brother.

I smooth my hands down my red dress, square my shoulders, and walk over to him.

"Hi. I'm Nadia," I say and look all three of them in the eyes as I hold my chin high and wish I had bigger boobs. "I don't think I've met you before."

They turn quiet and look at me as if I'm a science experiment.

"Carmine," the most handsome one says. "And this is Shane and Rocco. My brothers."

"*Rocco?*" I snort. "Did your mother not like you very much?"

"It's a nickname," Rocco says with a shrug. "I like it better than Rafe."

"You're wrong." I prop a hand on my hip. "Rafe is much better. I want to talk to you."

I point at Carmine and then take his hand in mine, pulling him away from the others. We walk past the food table loaded down with shrimp and crab and then move around a corner where we can have some privacy.

"Are you always this forward?" Carmine asks.

"Sure. What's the point in being anything else?"

His brown eyes narrow, and he looks me up and down. Once again, I'm reminded that I'm sorely lacking in the boob department.

I should have stuffed this stupid bra with something to make me look...*fuller*.

"What did you want to talk about?" he asks.

"I don't want to talk. I want to do this." Before he can reply, I boost myself up onto my toes and press my mouth to his. He squeaks in surprise, but he doesn't pull away.

I drop back onto my heels and stare up at him. Holy shit, for a first kiss, that was fun.

Really fun.

And he didn't even use any tongue.

"Look, Nadia—"

"Gotta go."

I turn and hurry away, suddenly embarrassed and not sure what to say. I just wanted to kiss him. To see what it was like.

And now, I know.

It was freaking awesome.

I smack into a hard chest. When I look up, my eyes meet my father's.

"What are you up to, little one?" he asks.

"Nothing." I shake my head. "I was just—"

"Do you know who that is?" he interrupts. Of course, he knows. He *always* knows. It's so annoying.

"Who?"

"That boy you were with."

I shrug a shoulder. "Carmine."

"Carmine *Martinelli*." I feel my eyes round. I've heard my father talk about that family before. "I want you to stay away from him. And his brothers. Is that understood?"

When his voice takes on that edge, I know he's not to be questioned. "Yes, sir."

"Good. Now, come on. They're cutting the cake."

I follow my father but glance back to find Carmine leaning his shoulder against the wall, watching me. A slow smile spreads over his face.

It's too bad he's off-limits.

CHAPTER
ONE
~CARMINE~

"When will you be back?"

I sip my whiskey and gaze out the window of the family's private jet, waiting for the pilot to get the go-ahead to take off.

"Depends on how this goes." I cross one foot over the opposite knee. "If it goes well, I don't know. If she tells me to go fuck myself, I'll be back tomorrow."

My younger brother, Shane, snickers on his side of the call. "From what I know of Nadia, she'll tell you to fuck off either way."

"True." I feel my lips twitch just as the pilot's voice comes over the speakers.

"We're cleared for takeoff, sir."

I push a button next to my seat. "Excellent."

"Have a safe trip," Shane says. "Keep me posted."

"Talk soon." I hit end on the screen and blow out a breath. No detail *hasn't* been scrutinized or picked apart. Nadia already knows me. There isn't anything I can do about that.

But she doesn't know what I have up my sleeve, and that's in my favor.

Now, I just have to get down to Miami—literally on the other side of

195

the country from my home in Seattle—and make her fall in love with me.

I blow out a breath and tip my head back against the fine leather seat.

Piece of cake.

IN OPULENCE AND LUXURY, the resort rivals any in any major city of the world. I've stayed in some impressive places, from Monte Carlo to the Maldives, and The Island Resort ranks right up there.

I'll be in the lap of luxury over the next few hours to days, and that doesn't disappoint.

I checked in, settled into my suite, and now I'm on the hunt for my prey.

I don't have to go far to find her.

I keep people on my payroll to give me the information I need the second I ask for it, and they've been on their toes when it comes to keeping track of the Bratva princess.

I walk through the resort spa to the private pool with its white chaise lounges, and sure enough, there she is, soaking up the sun in a pitiful excuse for a black bikini.

It's hardly more than two scraps of fabric, but it showcases Nadia's slim, tanned body to perfection.

At some point, she cut her blond hair into a short style that complements her stunning face nicely. I always forget how gorgeous she is until we're face to face, and it hits me like a punch to the gut.

"Is this seat taken?"

"No," she says without cracking open an eye. She looks serene. Relaxed. Almost as if she's about to fall asleep. She looks like the spoiled daughter of a powerful man.

Which is exactly what she is.

It's a comfortable eighty-two degrees outside as I lower myself onto the chair and stare at the Atlantic Ocean beyond the pool. I take a deep breath of salty air and turn to the woman next to me.

"It's a nice day, isn't it, Nadia?"

The use of her name has her slowly turning her head against the chair. She lowers her Chanel sunglasses down to the tip of her nose and takes me in from head to toe with those blue eyes.

"Carmine." My name sounds like acid on her tongue. "Fancy meeting you here."

"Funny coincidence, isn't it?" I grin and take the fresh glass of whiskey delivered by the waiter. "How's the family?"

Her eyes are cool as she sits up and sips the iced drink at her elbow. The glass is sweaty as though it's been sitting for a long while, ignored. I can't help but watch her plump lips wrap around the straw.

With long, willowy limbs, full lips, ice-blue eyes, and light-colored hair, Nadia is a beautiful woman.

She's also a very dangerous one.

"Everyone is fine. Thank you for asking." She sets the glass aside. "And yours?"

"Oh, they're doing well. What brings you to Miami?"

"Vacation."

"Well, who can blame you? I'm here on a little holiday myself. It's still too cold in Seattle. I needed some sunshine."

"And you've found it."

I nod once, watching her. She looks relaxed. Calm. As if she doesn't have a care in the world. Then again, what could she possibly have to worry about?

Aside from me, anyway.

Because I'm about to chew her up and spit her out.

If I didn't hate her family so deeply, I might pity her.

"Do you have dinner plans?"

Her eyebrows climb in surprise. "Are you asking me out on a date, Carmine Martinelli?"

"A dinner among friends," I reply and shrug a shoulder as if it's the most natural thing in the world. "Our families are very old friends."

Two opposing mob families are hardly buddies.

"Right." She smiles now, and I can admit, my stomach clenches in response. Yes, Nadia is breathtaking.

Fucking her won't be a hardship.

"I'm quite sure I can change my plans. What did you have in mind?"

"Something simple. Quiet so I can talk with you. Catch up. Meet me in the lobby at seven?"

"I'll be there."

I stand to leave, but before I can, her quiet voice calls me back.

"You look better than I remember," she says with a half-smile as her eyes travel down my torso to my swim-trunks-covered dick and back up again. "You grew up well."

"I could say the same for you." I nod and turn to leave, then toss over my shoulder, "Don't be late."

SHE STRIDES into the lobby at three minutes after seven, wearing a long, black gown with a dip in front that falls almost to her navel, displaying her cleavage. She's in shimmering silver shoes and carries a small clutch in her hand.

I don't doubt that she has a small pistol strapped to her inner thigh.

"You're late." I lean in to kiss her cheek.

"Am I?" She smiles coolly. "Well, I never was good at taking orders. I'm starved."

"Excellent. We're staying here for dinner."

I lead her into the hotel's steakhouse. The hostess shows us to our table, discreetly located in a quiet corner of the restaurant so we can be alone.

Once the wine has been poured and our appetizers and entrées ordered, Nadia sits back and studies me over the candles on the table set for two. She swirls the wine in her glass. Her mind is clearly whirling.

"What is it?" I ask her.

"How did you know I was here?" She doesn't miss a beat, and she's not coy.

Nadia is a clever woman.

I don't falter as I set my wine glass on the table. "I didn't. It was a happy coincidence."

"Bullshit."

I quirk a brow. "I'm a lot of things, Nadia, but I'm not a liar."

She sneers into her wine glass. "Right. The Martinellis are known for being upstanding citizens."

I laugh and then shrug as if to say: "*What can you do?*"

"I'm not here on behalf of the family. I'm here for some peace and quiet. And I ran into a beautiful woman that I happen to admire and find appealing. It's really that simple."

"Handsome *and* charming," she murmurs. "What a lovely surprise, indeed."

Dinner is lively. We talk about people we both know. We flirt and laugh. And we both drink a little too much wine.

So much that two hours later, once we've consumed the food, and I've paid the hefty check, I don't bother asking her where her room is. I simply take her up to mine.

"Are you planning to seduce me, Carmine?"

"Yes." The answer is simple. And it might be the first truth I've spoken since I saw her at the pool.

"Excellent."

"WHERE ARE YOU GOING?" I catch Nadia's hand in mine and tug her onto my lap as she walks past me to the balcony.

"I need to make a call." Her voice is smooth as silk as she leans in and presses her lips to mine. She takes it further than just a peck, and just when I'm about to grab hold of her and tumble her onto the bed, she pulls away. Wearing nothing but the hotel robe, she saunters through the open glass door to the balcony beyond.

We moved from Miami to St. Petersburg last week. I rented a sexy little car, and we road-tripped across the state and up the west coast of Florida with the top down, enjoying each other's company and the views.

Now, we're checked into the Don Cesar resort, settled in another top-floor suite with magnificent views and top-notch service.

I watch Nadia pace the patio for several moments, her phone pressed to her ear, and then decide to get in a quick shower. We might actually leave the hotel today and do something besides each other.

KRISTEN PROBY

I've spent the past two weeks with her, and I know our time together is running short. Aside from every inch of her delectable little body, I haven't learned anything about her family's secrets. She's a tight-lipped woman.

It's frustrating as fuck.

And, I can admit with reluctance, admirable.

I just finish washing my hair and turn off the water when she opens the bathroom door and grins when I step out of the glassed-in stall.

"Did your call go well?"

"Not exactly." The smile falls from her face, and her lips turn into a pout.

"What's wrong?"

"Nothing's *wrong,* exactly. I just won't be able to go home tomorrow as I originally planned. It looks like I need to book a room at the Ritz in Paris."

I dry my legs and wrap the towel around my hips. "Why Paris?"

"Paris is always a good idea, Carmine." She laughs and boosts herself up onto the countertop. "My house is being remodeled, and it won't be ready for at least six more months. So, I'll be living out of hotels for a while. And why not do that in my favorite city in the world? I'll shop and take in some culture."

"Come stay with me in Seattle."

The offer is past my lips before I even realize what in the hell I'm suggesting.

"That's ludicrous."

"Why?" I frame her face in my hands and brush my lips across hers. "Why is it ridiculous that I want to spend more time with you? Your home is unavailable, but mine is just sitting there."

"I've never really spent much time in your city," she says hesitantly as if she's actually considering it.

"I'd love to show you Seattle."

She sighs softly and rubs her nose over mine. "Are you sure about this? When your family finds out that you're practically living with a Tarenkov—"

"Let me deal with my family, darling. I'll make some calls right now so the condo is ready."

200

"You live in a condo?" She tips her head to the side.

"Yes, why?"

"You just strike me as a house man. A big, fancy one."

I have a fancy house, but you won't be living in it with me.

"Well, it's a big, fancy condo in the heart of downtown Seattle. Penthouse. So, I'm not exactly slumming it."

Her lips twitch.

"When would you like to go?" I ask as I bring up my assistant's contact on my phone. "Tonight?"

"Tomorrow," she says as she jumps off the counter and tugs my towel away. "I have plans for you today."

I pull the belt of her robe free and feel my dick harden at the sight of her small, firm breasts, already puckered and ready for my mouth. She lets the terrycloth drop to the floor, and when I simply reach out and plant my fingertip against her hard clit, she gasps.

Her body is responsive. And as much as I hate myself for it, I can't get enough of her.

I lift her and carry her back to the bedroom, where we tumble over already-mussed linens. She rolls on top of me, straddles my thighs, and tugs the skin of my neck between her teeth.

The bite stings, but only briefly before she licks me there, humming in delight.

I drag my fingertips up and down her calves. She's so fucking soft, so smooth. *Everywhere.*

"I'm going to ride you hard and fast," she mutters.

"No."

Her blue eyes meet mine in surprise.

"It's not going to be fast."

In one quick move, I have Nadia pinned under me.

"I'm going to take my time with you for the rest of the day. I'm going to make you moan, sigh, and forget your fucking name."

Her pupils dilate, and her breaths come faster with lust and anticipation.

I kiss my way down her torso and then nudge my shoulders between her legs, spreading her wide. I feast until she's a writhing mass of lust, and my cock pulses with need.

I almost forget to reach for the condom but remember to sheath myself just before I plunge inside her. And then I still.

"Move," she insists, but I only grin down at her.

"Is this what you want?" Very slowly, I pull back, letting the rim of my dick glide against the walls of her womanhood. I'm not disappointed when she moans in delight.

"Faster."

"No."

I kiss her lips and slowly slide back in, torturing us both.

"You're not in charge right now, Nadia."

She whimpers, and I pull out again, then slam into her, making her gasp and open her eyes in surprise.

"Jesus, Carmine."

"No, darling. Just Carmine."

I take her on the ride of her life, moving effortlessly from slow and easy to fast and frenzied. Finally, when we're both sweaty and gasping, I let her fall over the edge into oblivion.

Enjoying Nadia has been a pleasure. Making her fall in love with me...seemingly effortless. If her last name weren't Tarenkov, I might let myself feel something for her other than simple desire.

But that's not the case. Because hatred has a pulse, and I have a job to do.

"WELL, you weren't kidding when you said it was fancy," Nadia says the next afternoon as we step off the private elevator into the penthouse. The truth is, the family owns the entire building. We use the apartments on the lower floors for many different things, such as offices and torture space. The penthouse is a luxury condo that we keep for guests—or for times like these when someone in the family needs to use it. "Look at this view!"

She hurries over to the heavy glass doors and opens them to the balcony. Puget Sound spreads out before us in all her glory, the blue water dotted with sailboats and ferries.

"You definitely can't beat the view."

I walk up behind her, rest my hands on the railing on either side of her, and kiss her smooth neck just below her golden hairline.

Nadia's short hair is sleek and sexy. Just as alluring as the long hair she's been known for.

"What made you decide to cut your hair?" I ask.

"I didn't." She turns in my arms and leans her elbows on the railing as she stares up at me. A slight breeze blows around us. "It was cut for me."

"By?"

She shrugs. "Doesn't matter."

I catch her face in my hand. "Who cut your hair, Nadia?"

She licks her lips. "I honestly don't know. I was ambushed. They cut it, broke a rib, and then disappeared. That's why I was in Miami. I needed to get away."

"Why hasn't your family tracked down who did that to you?"

As much as I hate the Tarenkovs, my blood boils at the thought of anyone laying a hand on this woman.

We don't hurt women. Ever.

"Because they don't know. I didn't tell them."

"Nadia—"

"Don't lecture me."

"Your father and brother need to know so they can protect you."

"*I* can protect myself."

"I don't doubt that for a moment. But someone was able to get to you. Why your hair?"

"I'm known for it. It's just hair, Carmine. It'll grow back. It was the broken rib that really pissed me off. Couldn't breathe right for a month. Now, let's drop it."

"For now. But we'll circle back to it. Now, would you like the grand tour of your new abode?"

"Hell, yes."

CHAPTER

TWO

~CARMINE~

Three Months Later...

"I love you." The lie rolls off my tongue easier than the first time I said it, just a few weeks ago. Nadia and I have become inseparable since she moved in with me. We fuck. We laugh. We eat. And then we fuck some more.

I know her body better than I know mine. Every curve, every erotic inch that makes her writhe in ecstasy.

But it's a shot to my ego and my pride that I still don't know her mind. Nadia is good at keeping her thoughts close to her chest and only sharing bits and pieces of information. But she's loosened up considerably, and our time together has been fun.

So much so that I enjoy having her in my house.

No, not *mine*. I won't have the daughter of the man I hate most in the world living in my home. But she doesn't know that.

I press a kiss to her nape as she fusses with an earring, and then she smiles at me in the mirror.

"I love you, too, darling," she says. Her eyes go wide as I slip the diamond necklace around her neck from behind and fasten it with nimble fingers. "Oh my God, Carmine."

Her hand moves to touch the ice that glitters in the mirror.

"Later, when I make love to you, you'll wear this and nothing else."

Her gaze flies to mine, and she smiles quickly before turning to launch herself into my arms.

"You know I love gifts," she says against my mouth.

"And I love giving them to you." Nadia is spoiled. Selfish. Indulgent —all of the things I expected of her.

It's a pity that she didn't prove me wrong. Part of me wanted to respect her. To discover that she's nothing like the rest of her family.

But that didn't happen. Don't get me wrong, Nadia's been fun, but she's the typical, overindulged daughter of a powerful man; a woman used to getting her way.

She playfully tugs on my lower lip with her teeth, then walks across the room to open her Hermes bag, moving a few small things over to her tiny clutch.

"I hope nothing horrible happens today," she says with a sigh. "It's Annika's wedding day. She deserves to have a happy day without any mafia shenanigans thrown in for good measure."

"Weddings, like funerals, are truce days. You know that." I fasten my cufflinks, the ones with the rubies that Nadia got me for my birthday last month. "Everyone will be on their best behavior."

We've been in Denver for three days, preparing for Nadia's cousin's wedding. Annika's groom, Richard Donaldson, has no ties to any mafia family, and that's the way Annika wanted it. Rumor has it that her family isn't thrilled, but they're permitting the union.

Reluctantly.

My family flew in yesterday. Nadia and I had dinner with my parents, Shane, Rocco, and my cousin, Elena, and her husband, Archer. Elena was raised like my sister. When someone murdered her parents, I took it upon myself to see to avenging their deaths.

Nadia's family *will* pay.

But not today.

Three other family organizations will also attend Annika and Rich's wedding. But there's an unwritten rule for weddings and funerals of mafia families. No violence. No retribution is to be dispensed on those days. They're days of celebration. Community. If beefs or scores need to be settled, it's for another time and place.

We may be brutal, but we *can* be respectful.

"My brother flies in this morning." Nadia checks her lipstick in a handheld mirror, and I school my features.

Alexander Tarenkov will die at my hand. Not today, but one day soon. For his many transgressions.

"I was surprised he didn't come sooner."

"He was in Europe," she says with a shrug. "Doing what, I have no idea. You know he doesn't say much to me."

I smile as she takes one last look in the mirror. "Are you ready, sweetheart?"

"Ready."

―――――

"A TOAST," Igor Tarenkov says as he raises his glass and gets the attention of the roughly three hundred people at the reception. "To my niece, Annika. My little firefly. You make a lovely bride, my darling. And to Richard. If you fail to take care of my girl, you'll swim with the fishes. Cheers."

We laugh and raise our glasses as Igor sits at the table with his brother—Annika's dad—and Richard's parents, who look a little worse for wear.

"I don't think Rich's parents are used to people like us," I murmur to Nadia, who chuckles and sips her champagne.

"You'd be right. Annika said they're doctors from the suburbs."

"Just like her," I point out as the bride approaches our table.

"I'm so happy to see you," Annika says to Nadia as she leans in to kiss her cousin's cheek. "Are you all having a good time?"

"What's not to like?" Rocco asks.

"Hello, Rafe."

My brother's expression turns to a scowl. "I've told you a million times to call me Rocco."

"I will never do that," Annika replies with a straight face. "Your name is *Rafe*. That's what your mother calls you."

"You're not my mother," my brother reminds her.

"Isn't that fortunate?" Annika replies without missing a beat.

I always liked Annika. Like my cousin Elena, Annika has no interest in the family business. She's a doctor with a business in Denver. Her new husband, Rich, is also a physician.

They'll live a quiet life, making a good living from their jobs, even if Igor uses them from time to time to clean up a mess or two.

Having a doctor in the family is incredibly helpful.

Rocco narrows his eyes on Annika, but she just smiles at us. "Oh, I want you to meet someone. Ivie, come here."

I recognize the maid of honor as she hurries over to our table and offers us all a smile.

"Everyone, this is my best friend since we were six. Ivie Roberts."

"Hi." Ivie waves and flashes a shy smile. She's pretty but not beautiful. Not extraordinary like the other women in the room. "It's nice to meet you."

"The pleasure is all mine," Shane says as he takes her hand and kisses her knuckles. "You're lovely, aren't you?"

Rocco and I share a surprised look.

"Oh, it's just the dress," Ivie says, glancing down at the blood-red gown that fits her curvy body like a glove.

"No, I think it's the woman wearing it."

"How charming," Nadia says. "Ladies, let's make a trip to the champagne table."

Nadia loops her arms through Annika's and Ivie's and leads them away. Ivie glances back and gives Shane a sassy wink.

"Really?" I say to Shane, who just stares back at me blankly.

"What?"

"What do you mean *what*?" Rocco says with a laugh. "You were totally mooning over that girl. And she's not your type. She's not *any* of our types."

"What does that mean?" Elena demands, and Archer suddenly seems fascinated with the silverware on the table.

Smart man.

"She's fucking amazing," Shane replies with a scowl. "Did you *see* her?"

"Yeah." I nod slowly. "We saw her."

Without another word, Shane stands and goes in search of the woman, and Rocco lets out a laugh.

"What's wrong with her?" Elena demands again. "She's pretty."

"She's not ugly," I agree. "But she's hardly Shane's type. He goes for the cold, supermodel types."

"Like Nadia?" Elena asks with a cocked brow.

My eyes narrow on her. I don't know why I suddenly feel so defensive of the Bratva princess. I can't stand her.

"You don't understand." The words are clipped. Short.

But Elena doesn't back down.

"You know how I feel about this."

She thinks my mission's futile—is sure that Nadia doesn't have the answers, and that I'm wasting my time.

I think she's wrong.

"Let's dance," Nadia says, suddenly at my side. I take her hand, kiss the palm, and stand at her request.

"That would be a pleasure."

She leads me out to the dance floor. As the Goo Goo Dolls sing *Iris*, I pull Nadia to me, flush against me, and we move around the space.

Her lean body is a temptation that I never stop longing for. It'll be a pity that I won't get to fuck her anymore once all of this is said and done. I don't know that I've met a woman I've been so sexually compatible with before. I may not find one ever again.

The fire in her eyes as she gazes up at me tells me that she's just as fired up as I am.

Without another word, I take her hand and lead her off the floor, down a hallway, and to an empty storeroom that must be used as a maid's closet for the hotel.

I lock the door behind us and yank her against me.

"Did you do that on purpose?" I growl against her neck. "Seduce me on the dance floor so I'd be hard and wanting you?"

"Maybe." Her voice is breathy as her hands immediately reach for my slacks, pulling them open so she can plunge her hand inside to cup me. "Probably."

"Fucking hell." I turn and pin her against a shelving wall of folded sheets. I gather her skirt in my hands until it's up around her waist and then grin when I find her bare.

"I love it when you go without panties, babe."

"I know." She bites my earlobe. "Now, fuck me, Carmine."

She doesn't have to ask me twice. I retrieve the condom from my suit pocket, and when I plunge into her, I'm like a wild animal, unable to stop myself from fucking her hard and fast, punishing us both with the crazy rhythm I set.

"God, yes," she sobs and lets her head fall back against the sheets. "Fuck, yes."

It's over as quickly as it began. Once I dispose of the condom and we right ourselves, I open the door so we can return to the party.

Pandemonium hits.

"Oh, shit, what happened?" Nadia says as she hurries to the dance floor where a crowd has gathered. I follow.

We push our way to the front in time to see Armando, one of my father's men, seizing on the floor. He's foaming at the mouth, his face beet-red, eyes bulging.

"He's been poisoned," I mutter as I stare down at the man.

"I'll call the police," someone offers, but they're quickly taken aside.

We don't call the authorities.

And the fact that this was done *here*, with a mix of families and civilians, makes my blood boil.

I march over to Nadia's father's table, where my dad is already standing, his expression mutinous.

"That drink was meant for *me*," Pop says. "Armondo grabbed it by accident. We laughed about it, and then I flagged down the waiter for another. Moments after drinking it, that"—he gestures to the floor—"happened."

"Are you implying that I ordered your murder at my niece's wedding?" Igor asks, his tone mild. "I'm not the only boss here, Carlo."

"Yours is the only family the Martinellis have an issue with," Pop replies.

Shane and Rocco stand beside me, all of us behind our father. Nadia and her brother, Alexander, stand behind their father.

My gaze holds Nadia's.

"I don't know what you're talking about," Igor says. "I've never done anything to you or your family."

"You had my sister killed," Pop immediately replies.

"I always liked Claudia," Igor says and drums his fingers on the table. "Vinnie, not so much. He was a pitiful excuse for a man and certainly had no business being the boss of your organization. But I suppose that's none of my business."

"So you killed him," Pop says.

"I certainly did not," Igor says and leans forward. "No one in my organization is responsible for Vinnie's or Claudia's deaths. If I was, I would take responsibility for it."

My father nearly vibrates with his fury.

"What good would that do me?" Igor continues. "The Bratva is successful, thriving, without the need for war. Just because I thought Vinnie was a worthless piece of shit doesn't mean I ordered his death. And I certainly wouldn't give the order to have you, my *friend*, Carlo, killed at my firefly's wedding."

"Then what the fuck is going on?" I demand and scan the crowd. Someone took Armondo's body away and cleaned up the floor. The guests murmur quietly. The DJ started the music again.

Only at a mafia wedding could someone get murdered and have the party carry on as if nothing at all happened.

"Clearly, someone has it out for our families," Igor says. "Nadia."

Nadia places her hand on her father's shoulder. "Yes, Papa?"

"I'm assigning this to you."

"Carmine will help you," Pop agrees, and I feel my back straighten.

"I don't need to involve Nadia in this."

"I've just involved her," Igor says. "You've been playing house for weeks, and nothing has come of it so far. Let's change tactics."

My eyes move to Nadia's, and right before me, the warmth I've seen in those blue orbs freezes.

"Did you honestly think I was in love with you?" She smirks. "Grow up, Carmine."

I should have seen it. I should have known that she was double-crossing me. Maybe I did. Perhaps I ignored it.

I'm a fucking idiot.

"It's decided," Pop says. "You two will hunt down those responsible for what's happened here today. And for my sister's death."

With the wave of a hand, we're dismissed. Before Nadia can run away, I corner her and turn her to me.

"What?" She glares up at me.

"What was the end game?" I ask, my voice hard as stone.

"I didn't have one. Yet." Her gaze falls to where my hand rests on her arm. "I didn't give you permission to touch me."

I feel the smile slowly spread over my lips. "So, it's true what they say? You're nothing but an ice princess."

She doesn't even flinch. "And you'd do well to remember that. I don't want your help with this."

"You have it anyway."

"I said—"

"Do you think I give two fucks what you said?" I lean in to her. "We work together. Starting now. No more show. No more lies."

"No more sex."

I chuckle. "Darling, you couldn't keep your hands off me if you tried."

"Watch me."

CHAPTER

THREE

~NADIA~

"What are you doing here?" Papa asks as I walk into his Denver office. He frowns and sets a pen on the notebook he was scribbling notes in. "You're supposed to be in Seattle with Carmine."

"I'm not going to Washington." I pace to the window and stare down at Coors Field, downtown Denver, and the mountains beyond. I have to admit, it's a beautiful city. Once you get past the high altitude, it's one of my favorite places. But I'm not here to admire the scenery.

"Carmine is in Seattle," Papa reminds me.

"I believe so."

"So, I'll ask again, what are you doing here?"

"I don't need to be with Carmine," I say and watch as a crane works on a skyscraper. "I can work just fine without him. Better, actually."

"You're supposed to be working together."

"Now that the charade is over, there's no need."

"That's not your decision to make."

His stern voice has me turning to look at him.

"We don't trust each other." I cross to my father. "For good reason. The Martinellis think we had their family members killed."

"We didn't."

212

"You and I know that, but convincing them is another matter entirely. And why would he work with me anyway?"

"Because he's been ordered to do so."

I roll my eyes and then sigh as I sit in the chair opposite my father.

"You've worked hard for your entire adult life to be taken seriously in this family," Papa says thoughtfully. "You don't question orders. Why now?"

"Alex wouldn't want to work with him, either."

"Did you fall in love with him?"

I scowl at the absurdity of the suggestion. "Absolutely not. He's a liar—and not a particularly good one. And he's a Martinelli."

"He's also young and handsome."

And excellent in bed, but I'm sure my father doesn't want to know that.

"I'm not young and stupid," I remind him. "I just didn't see the value in following him to Seattle when what we're looking for most likely isn't there."

"It's a place to start," he replies and waves me off. "Get up there. *Today*, little one. And keep me apprised of the situation."

"Yes, sir."

I stand and turn to leave.

"Nadia?"

"Yes?" I spin back to him.

"I love you."

I smile and blow him a kiss. "I love you, too, Papa."

There's a car in his circular driveway. I don't think the older Cadillac belongs to Carmine.

I park behind it just as the front door opens, and Carmine steps out with another man. The unknown person nods and then gets into his vehicle and drives away.

I slam the door of my rented Lexus and send Carmine a sassy grin as I climb the steps of his house.

"I knew you were the big, fancy house type."

"How did you find out where I live?" he asks by way of greeting.

"Oh, Carmine." I pat his cheek and breeze right past him and inside, not bothering to wait for an invitation. "Don't insult either of us by asking stupid questions. You knew plenty about me before you found me in Miami. And I know more about you than you'd probably be comfortable with."

"I just have one question," he says as he follows me into his living room. "Is your house really being remodeled?"

I cross to the mantel and run the pad of my finger over a little owl statue there. "I don't have a house. If you'd done more research, you'd know that."

"Maybe you live in a house owned by your father," he suggests.

"I bounce from place to place," I say without elaborating. I walk over to a painting and touch the name of the artist. "You have a lot of expensive knickknacks."

"Are you going to simply walk through my house and touch everything?" I notice his teeth are clenched, his hands fisted. It fills my heart with glee.

Pissing him off is a pleasure.

"Maybe." I smirk and wander into the kitchen. "I'm starved. I couldn't stomach the crap they served on the plane. I know you have a private jet, but I went ahead and jumped on a commercial flight this morning. Even first class turned my stomach."

I open his fridge and take inventory of the contents. I pull out a cheese and cracker tray and dig in.

"This salami is fantastic. Where did you find it?"

"You'd have to ask the caterer." He leans his hip against the island and crosses his arms over his impressive chest.

Carmine Martinelli is the male version of beautiful. He looks like a fallen angel. With that thick, dark hair, those deep brown eyes, and full lips that could turn a girl inside out, he's an impressive specimen.

No, I didn't fall in love with him.

But I enjoyed him. Every chance I got.

"You look well," I say and pop a cracker into my mouth. "But you have some bags under your eyes. Not sleeping well?"

There are no bags. He looks fucking magnificent. But seeing the spark of annoyance flicker in his eyes is worth the dig.

214

"What do you want, Nadia?"

"We're working together, remember?" I shrug a shoulder and open a jar of green olives. I didn't lie about being hungry. I'm suddenly starving.

"Given that I haven't heard a peep from you since the wedding, I figured you'd blown that off."

"A peep?" I snicker and chew on another olive. "You're cute, Carmine."

He huffs out a breath of annoyance.

I love ruffling his feathers.

"Anyway, I thought I'd come to Seattle and see you. Find out what you know."

"I'm working on some leads."

I nod slowly. "What kind of leads?"

"Rumors. Making calls."

"The mafia is good at keeping secrets, aren't they?" I shake my head and close the food containers back up, then return it all to the fridge. "Bastards put a lot of bullshit in this world, but when it comes to covering their tracks, they're damn good at it."

"What do *you* know?" he asks.

"I did get a call when I got off the plane," I admit and walk over to him. I brush my finger down the buttons of his white shirt. "I always did like looking at you in these white button-downs."

He catches my hand in his and pushes me away.

"What did the caller say?"

The rebuff hurts my feelings more than expected—and more than it should. But I keep my face schooled in the sneer I've worn since I arrived.

"A new chemical's being passed around," I say casually. "It's lethal. Highly addictive. And in large quantities, can cause seizures and foaming at the mouth."

"Who—?"

"I'm not going to tell you that," I say smoothly. "And you know it. That's all I know for now. I really should go. I'll be in touch."

I march away from him before I do something monumentally stupid, like strip him naked and suck his cock.

Carmine has a grade-A penis.

And it's off-limits.

"Have a good day."

"Wait," he says as he hurries after me. "Where are you staying?"

"Oh, don't worry. I'll be around."

"Nadia."

"Goodbye, Carmine."

I hop in the car and zoom away from his house.

I'm not good at emotions. I'm excellent at keeping myself aloof. Cold, even. I don't mind being called the ice princess at all. Because when emotions get tangled up in business, you die.

And I'm not ready to meet Satan yet. Or, should I say, he's not ready for me?

I don't like that I feel things when I'm around Carmine. It's purely physical.

"Yeah, keep telling yourself that," I mutter as I drive toward the freeway.

I knew the several months I spent with Carmine were a lie. He didn't love me, and I certainly didn't love him. We were merely playing house. Manipulating each other.

But we also had fun. We laughed a lot. We got along well. And the sex...

Well, let's not go there.

I enjoy him. And that's the part that annoys the hell out of me. Because he's a Martinelli, and my father told me when I was thirteen that anyone with that name was off-limits.

Nothing has changed in that regard.

So, I'll do as my father asked and keep an eye on Carmine, but I'll also keep my distance.

For my fucking sanity.

Because I'm going to be the next boss. My brother doesn't have the chops—he's too selfish, too immature.

I can't stand him.

I'm the one who studied at my father's knee since I was a child. I'm the one who pays attention and does as she's told.

And I'm often overlooked because I'm a woman.

But that won't stop me.

I'll do my job here and continue proving to my father that *I'm* the one who should step up after he's gone.

THE HOTEL just wasn't cutting it. Too many people were in and out. Too many eyes. I know that Carmine has eyes on me, but I was making it too easy on him.

So, I checked out two days ago and secured a vacation rental by owner, a VRBO, instead. I used my father's assistant to make the reservation, so my name's nowhere on the application.

I like being anonymous. Carmine wasn't wrong. My family owns the condo I live in just outside of Atlanta, and my name isn't on that one either. I don't want anyone to trace me back to any holdings. I want to be mysterious.

It's hard for the bad guys to find you if they can't figure out where you live.

Not that they didn't find me anyway, I muse, rubbing a hand over the rib that still sometimes gives me fits.

I haven't heard anything on the drug thing for days. I'm basically just sitting in Seattle, twiddling my thumbs. I could do this from *anywhere*.

But Papa wants me here.

I blow out a breath and shut my laptop. I've been calling in favors and making calls, and I'm going nowhere fast. It's like I'm two inches away from getting the information I need, but then it gets tugged just out of my reach.

It doesn't help that I don't know exactly what I'm looking *for*. The simple news of a new drug doesn't give me much to go on. That happens every day in every city, and my family isn't into the drug-dealing scene.

Maybe our fathers have us on a wild goose chase, just to see if they can pull the strings and have us follow along like good little puppets.

I wouldn't put it past them.

I need some air, so I slide my feet into my running shoes, grab my windbreaker, and set off on a jog.

This little neighborhood near the water is beautiful. Full of older homes, it's clearly an established neighborhood with low crime and little drama.

I would generally think of it as boring.

My pace is steady as I climb the first hill. Seattle is nothing if not hilly, but it makes for a good workout so I'm not complaining.

I just hit my stride when something sails over my head, and someone lifts me from behind.

"Let go of me, you asshole!" I'm kicking and flailing about, but it's no use. I can't see who grabbed me.

So I go limp. Deadweight.

The man holding me grunts with the effort it takes to hold me, but throws me onto a seat of a vehicle. And then we're moving.

"Who the fuck are you?" I demand.

No one replies.

I know there are at least two of them. The one who grabbed me and the other who's driving.

Fuck, this isn't good.

They could kill me and dump me. My father would rain hell down on them, but they could still do it.

The vehicle—van?—parks, and I'm jerked out and taken down what feels like a series of hallways. Finally, they dump me onto a chair and tie my hands behind my back.

"What the fuck?" I ask—and am punched in the jaw.

I see stars. My mouth throbs.

"You're asking a lot of questions."

I frantically search my brain to place the voice. Have I heard it before? It doesn't sound familiar.

"And that pisses you off," I guess.

Someone punches me again, in the left eye this time.

"We're going to teach you to keep your questions to yourself, bitch."

The beating is ruthless. By the time they dump me on some random sidewalk in downtown Seattle, I'm bloody, bruised, and quite sure my right shoulder is dislocated.

It's hard to breathe.

I pull the bag off my head but can't see out of my left eye. What I can see is clouded and red because of the blood in my right eye.

Christ, I don't know what to do.

I can't go to the hospital. And I'm never stepping foot in that VRBO again.

How did they find me?

I'm going to pass out, and I don't want to do that here, so I stumble to my feet and look around. I'm in an industrial area. People walk about, but they don't look my way.

It's as if women are dumped, bloody and broken, every fucking day.

Whoever grabbed me didn't take my phone, so I pull it out of the sleeve in my leggings and punch in the address for the condo that Carmine and I lived in for several months. I know his family owns the building, and no one lives in the penthouse full time.

I'll crash there until I figure out what to do.

According to my cell, I'm only a couple of blocks away. I hobble toward the building, having to stop and lean on the concrete to catch my breath a few times.

Did they break another goddamn rib?

It takes five times longer than it should to reach Carmine's building. I'm ecstatic to discover that my codes still work on the door and the private elevator that leads up to the penthouse.

When the apartment doors open, I step in and lean against the wall as I listen for any movement inside.

There's nothing.

It doesn't appear as if anyone's been here since Carmine and I were here before leaving for Denver last week.

Has it really only been a week?

The red roses Carmine got me are still on the sofa table, wilting. A pair of my heels lay on the floor next to the kitchen island.

This is the only safe place for me in the city. I need to call my father, but that will have to come later. I'm not even sure what my name is right now.

The adrenaline of the attack is wearing off, and I know I'm going to be sick. Nausea roils my stomach, and dizziness fills my head. I just want to *sleep*. I probably shouldn't. I most likely have a concussion, but I'll be fine.

Everything will be fine.

God, I hurt. More than I ever have in my life.

I swing by the kitchen to grab a bucket from under the sink in case I do throw up, and then stumble to the couch in the living room. The sofa is huge, deep, and so comfortable that Carmine and I took many an afternoon nap here, tangled up with each other.

We also fucked like rabbits on it, but I'll think about that later.

The moment I lie down, I feel exhaustion overtake me. But the rest is fitful—I can't get comfortable. I can't catch my breath.

I really should call an ambulance. My father would *not* be pleased, but I'm alone, and something is very wrong.

I feel the anxiety building in my stomach. I reach for my phone, only to discover that I set it on the counter in the kitchen.

I want to cry.

Everything screams in agony.

And, suddenly, someone looms over me.

CHAPTER

FOUR

~CARMINE~

I'm in the middle of my second set of pull-ups when my phone rings.

I ignore it.

I've been pissed for days. Does Nadia think she can just waltz into my home, taunt me, and then breeze out again? That she can smirk at me and act as if I haven't had her in every position imaginable? That I don't affect her at all?

I won't admit to anyone that she got under my skin.

But goddamn it, she did.

My phone rings again. When I drop to the floor, I accept the call.

"What?"

"I'm sorry to interrupt you, sir. You need to come to the penthouse."

I narrow my eyes. "What happened?"

"Nadia's here, sir. And she's going to need you."

"I'll be there in thirty."

I end the call and, without another thought, hurry to grab my keys and wallet, then get into my car and peel out of the driveway, headed toward the freeway.

I like living away from the areas where we conduct business. I like keeping things separate. My grandmother taught me the importance of that.

But in times like these, it's a royal pain in the ass.

Thanks to traffic on the freeway, I make it to the building in twenty-six minutes, park in my reserved space, and take the private elevator up to the penthouse.

What in the hell is Nadia doing back here? Gathering the things she left behind when we went to Denver? That made sense.

But when I step off the elevator, I instinctively know that something is very wrong.

The space is still. The blinds are still closed, so it's mostly dark inside.

I flip on a hallway light to illuminate the area and see Nadia's blond head on the couch.

She's lying down.

And when I approach her, every drop of blood in my veins boils.

"Don't hurt me," she moans. "Can't."

"Nadia." I squat next to her and take in her bruised and bloodied face. "It's Carmine. I'm not going to hurt you."

"Carmine?" She lets out a small gasp through cut and bloody lips. "Didn't know where to go."

"You came to the right place. No one will think to search for you here. I have to call my people to come in and take care of you."

"No."

"Yes." I kiss her bloody hand. "I'll take care of this."

I pull out my phone and call our medical team. After they assure me that they're only minutes away, I hang up and hurry into the bathroom where I wet a washcloth and return to start cleaning her face as best I can so I can see the extent of her injuries.

"Hurts."

"I know." My voice is clipped, even to my ears. It takes everything in me to be gentle.

All I want to do is get my hands on the piece of shit who did this and make them pay. Painfully. Slowly.

Horrifically.

The elevator slides open, and the three men we employ to handle our medical needs come marching in.

"Christ," Malloy says with a hiss. "What did you do to her?"

"If you want to keep your job, you'll never ask that again," I bark as I step back and let them take over. At first, Nadia recoils from their touch, but with some soothing murmurs, she finally relaxes and lets the men examine her.

"I can't tell if her vision's been affected in this eye," Malloy says grimly. "It's swollen shut. I'll need to take another look in a few days."

He stands and pulls me aside as the other two continue working their magic with gauze and antiseptic.

"I've never suggested this before, and I know it's not how we do things..." Malloy begins and then props his hands on his hips. "But she needs to be in the hospital, Carmine."

I shake my head, but Malloy continues.

"She's been beaten so severely; I don't know if she has internal bleeding or a punctured lung. Her shoulder may be dislocated, and we might have to reset it. I recommend leaving the room for that one."

"I won't go."

He swallows and shakes his head. "Whoever did this was obviously given an order to fuck her up and leave her just this side of dead. And that's what they did. I have no idea how she even got herself up here."

"Because she's stubborn and damn smart. I'm not taking her to the hospital."

"Sir—"

"No. We'll take care of her here. Do your damn job, Malloy."

His mouth flattens into a line, and then he nods once. "I'm going to give you a list of things to watch for. If even *one* of them shows up, you need to call an ambulance right away. I mean it."

It's brutal standing back and watching them care for her. I feel helpless. She screams when they move her shoulder, but it's not dislocated —just wrenched badly. She whimpers when they poke and prod to see if anything is broken.

They hook her up to an IV and start pumping her full of antibiotics and morphine to help with the pain. Before long, she's settled back on the big couch with fresh dressings, a blanket, and orders to stay and rest for at least a week.

I'll personally see to it that she fucking obeys that order.

After my men leave, I return to her and gently brush her hair off her face.

"Sorry," she murmurs drunkenly.

"For what?"

"You're mad."

I sigh and lean over to press my lips to her forehead. "Not at you. When I find out who did this, I'll kill them."

"Get in line."

"Do you know who it was?"

She licks her swollen lips. "No. Couldn't see. Water?"

"Of course."

I hurry to the kitchen and fill a glass with crushed ice, and then bring it back to her.

"Here, suck on this."

"Mm." She sucks greedily on a chunk. "Nice."

"I'll be right here, Nadia. I'm not going anywhere. You sleep now and get healed up so you can kick some ass."

"Yeah." She sighs but reaches for my hand. "Stay."

"I told you, I'm here. I promise, I won't go."

"'Kay."

She slips into sleep, and I pull my hand down my face.

What the fuck? An hour ago, I wanted to spank her ass. Now, I want to protect her, fight for her. Keep her safe.

Because the truth is, she *has* gotten under my skin. That doesn't mean I trust her, but she didn't deserve this.

"KING ME."

Nadia scowls down at the checkerboard. "You're cheating."

"Negative." I stand and walk into the kitchen to get more chips.

We've been in the penthouse for five days. She slept the first three away, allowing her body to heal.

And now she's up and showered, her arm in a sling, scowling at me over a checkerboard.

"Is there any queso left?"

"No, you ate it all last night. At least your appetite is back."

"Yeah, well, I like food. You know that."

I grin, thinking back on all of the fun meals we'd had together. "I do. Watching you eat isn't a hardship. Where have you been staying? I'll have someone go and gather your things. Bring them here."

"I can go get my stuff soon enough."

"Why won't you tell me?"

"You probably already know."

I do. But she doesn't need to know that.

"Nadia, I think we're in the truce zone here. Think of this like a wedding or a funeral."

"Yeah, well, it almost *was* my funeral. And I don't know that it wasn't *you* who ordered this to be done to me," she blurts and stands to walk to the window. "You got here awfully fast after it happened."

I have to shove my hands into my pockets. Just six months ago, I would have said that nothing this woman could say or do could hurt me.

But things have changed.

And it seems she *can* hurt me.

That's unsettling and something to think about later.

She turns at my silence. The bruises on her face are beginning to fade from black to a sickly purple.

"You won't deny it?" she demands.

"I don't know how your family does things," I begin slowly, "but in *my* family, I've been taught to *never* hurt women. Physical punishment is not tolerated when it comes to women. Ever, under any circumstances."

I remember the day my cousin Elena first showed me the scars on her body she'd sustained at the hands of her father, my uncle. More anger seethes through me.

"Maybe not everyone in your family feels that way."

"They do." Agitated, I pace the floor. "I can say, without a shadow of a doubt, that my family is not responsible for this."

225

"Maybe one of your brothers—"

"IT WASN'T US!" I shout at her and then swear under my breath. "For fuck's sake, Nadia, no. I may not know what to feel when I'm around you, but I know that I wouldn't hurt you. No one in my family would hurt you. *You* haven't done anything to my family or me."

"Except make you think I'd fallen in love with you. Fucked your brains out. Moved in with you."

"Good sex isn't worth maiming over."

She shakes her head.

"I'm not convinced that your family isn't responsible for my aunt's and uncle's murders. And if they are, they *will* pay. I guarantee you that."

"If my father gave that order, he would cop to it," she says with a sigh. "I admit, I don't know every single order he's given, but he's not one to kill and then deny or deflect. He takes ownership of his decisions without regret. If he was behind those murders, he'd say so."

I can tell she believes what she's telling me.

"But, at the end of the day, we don't trust each other," she continues.

"Do you remember what happened when I found you here?"

"You were *so* pissed at me," she says.

"No." I cross to her, needing to touch her. "I told you then, and I meant it. I wasn't angry with you. I was livid that someone —*any*one—had put their hands on you this way. The fury was, and still is, a breathing thing inside me. I would have been upset to see any woman hurt like this, but the fact that it was *you* made it so much worse. So, no, we may not fully trust each other, but damn it, I care about what happens to you. I don't want to see *anything* happen to you. And we've been given orders to work *together*. To figure this mess out and get it resolved. I don't know what's happening now, with the murder at the wedding and your attack. I don't know if it has anything to do with my aunt and uncle, but I need to find out. I have connections that you don't and vice versa. We're stronger in this together. So, until we resolve this, you're stuck with me."

Her blue eyes slide to mine. "What do you mean?"

"You'll be staying with *me.* I can't protect you the way we've been doing things, obviously."

"I don't need—"

"Just stop talking." In exasperation, I march away from her. "Yes, you're strong and badass, and you can take care of yourself. But right now, people want to hurt you, and I'm partly responsible for that. There's a team of people here to help keep us safe. And goddamn it, that's what you're going to let me do."

"So, I'm being held hostage?"

I grunt but can't help but start laughing. "Yes. Clearly, this luxury penthouse is a horrible situation. I feel for you, Nadia. But keep a stiff upper lip. Suck it up and deal with it."

She snorts. "No sex. I mean it."

"I'm not in the habit of forcing unwilling women to fuck me."

Her face sobers at the steel in my voice. "I didn't mean to insinuate that you'd rape me."

"I need some fresh air."

She nods and glances at her phone when it rings.

"Not gonna answer?"

"I have no intention of speaking to my father. At least for a few more days."

I narrow my eyes. "Why haven't you told him about this?"

"Because. And the reasons are none of your business."

"If you confide in him, you could live wherever the fuck you want. He'd send protection, *and* he'd start his own hunt for the bastards who touched you. Nadia—"

"You have the luxury of trusting your family," she interrupts. "It's not something we share."

I step back, surprised. "You don't trust your family? When it comes to the business we're in, trusting them is of the utmost importance."

"My father, yes. I know he loves me and would do anything to protect me." She swallows hard. "But I don't trust my brother at all."

That's something we can agree on. Alexander Tarenkov is a slimy piece of shit, and it would make my black heart happy to tear him limb from limb with my bare hands.

"Why?"

"Alex is a selfish man," she says simply. "Only concerned with himself and how to manipulate every situation to his advantage. He'd make a horrible boss. The family, the *organization*, would collapse within a year. I don't know what shady deals he has going on the down-low, but I'd guess there are a few of them. No. I shouldn't be telling you any of this."

With a sigh, she lowers herself to the couch.

"I hate your brother with every fiber of my being." My voice is flat as I sit across from her. "There's nothing honorable about him."

"I know."

"Do you think he's behind everything that's going on?"

"No." She smirks. "He's a pussy. He doesn't have the balls to kill anyone. Alex is self-serving, yes, but he's also content to ride just under the radar. I do think he's laundering money that he's hiding from Papa. And when he's found out? Well, let's just say it won't go over well.

"But killing another family's boss? Possibly starting a war? No. He's not smart enough for that."

Unfortunately, I agree with her. He's slimy to the core but also as weak as they come.

And not especially intelligent.

"So, in the meantime, you've been attacked twice, and your father has no idea."

"He'll be angry," she admits. "But until I figure out who's behind it and everything else, I'll keep it to myself. Besides, what's done is done. He can't undo it."

"If I kept something like this from my father, he'd be *livid*."

"You're lucky," she says. "That your family is so close. That it's your safe haven."

"You need that, too. Our business is too lonely to be alone, Nadia."

"I'm not alone. I'm being held hostage, remember? So, what now? What's our next move?"

"We're staying here for another week."

She scowls, but I hold up my hand to stop her from saying anything more.

"You're healing, but you're still fragile. When we get out of here, I need to make sure that you're well and capable of having my back.

We're likely going to get into a couple of sticky situations. As long as you're feeling up to it, we'll go to New York next week."

"Have you called the Sergis?"

"I'll call Billy when I have a solid date." No mob family travels to another family's territory without alerting them and asking for permission. It's a code we all live by and respect.

So, the fact that someone was in Seattle to hurt Nadia only intensifies my anger.

No one should have been here.

"They hate me there."

"*Hate* is a strong word," I remind her.

"And accurate."

"You'll be with me."

"What if they hate you, too?"

I smile thinly. "They don't."

CHAPTER

FIVE

~NADIA~

"I'm bored out of my *mind*." I pace the penthouse in front of the windows. "It's been two damn weeks. I feel great. I can even cover what's left of the bruises with makeup, and you'd never know they're there."

Carmine lounges on the couch, reading something on his iPad.

"What are you doing?"

"Reading stock reports." He sips his coffee. "How are your investments doing?"

I cock my head to the side. "Are you some kind of financial advisor?"

His grin is wide and toothy—and cockier than any one man has a right to be.

"I have a master's in finance," he says. "I guess you could say that I'm a financial advisor."

"To your family," I finish for him. "You help them hide money."

There's that smile again. "I assure you, everything I offer is legal."

"Bullshit."

"So, I'll ask again. How are your investments?"

He's evading.

"I don't have any."

His brow knits. "*None?*"

"No."

"Nadia, you're pushing thirty. You should have a Roth IRA, at the very least. You should have stocks. I know you're set to inherit more money than the net worth of several countries, but—"

"Carmine. I don't want to talk about finances. I want to get the hell out of here."

He sighs. "Let's go for a walk."

"Anything." I bounce into the bedroom to snatch up the new shoes I ordered a few days ago. Since blood now covered the running shoes I had on the day I was attacked, I needed new ones.

When I'm dressed and ready to go, Carmine sets his iPad aside, and we step into the elevator.

"We should head to New York tomorrow," I say as we ride down to the ground floor.

"It's Friday, Nadia. Let's go Monday."

"Because the mafia takes weekends off?" I roll my eyes. "You're stalling."

"I told you before; I want to make sure you're healthy."

"I feel great." It's not a complete lie. Aside from a little ache in my shoulder when I raise my arm above my head, and the vision in my left eye still being a little blurry, I feel pretty good. The doctor said I might not get my sight back all the way, though.

That pissed me right off.

But I'm not dead, and that's something.

"I saw you wince this morning when you reached for a mug in the cabinet."

"You're watching me like a fucking mother hen." I scowl as we step outside and then stop to take a deep breath. "I love summer."

"Seattle is nice in the summer," he says. "Less rain, more sun. Not too hot, thanks to the Sound."

"It's a beautiful day." I tip my head up to the sky.

"You might want to pay attention, so you don't faceplant on the concrete."

I laugh and glance up at him. "You would probably catch me."

"Maybe."

These past two weeks have shown me that I can let my guard down around Carmine. Now that it's just *us*—no pretenses, no blatant lies or games—I actually trust that he won't hurt me.

Not intentionally, anyway.

He's the only person in the world that I *can* trust right now, and I just hope that he doesn't do something stupid to betray that faith.

"What's that place?" I ask, pointing across the street. "It looks like a coffee shop. Cherry Street Coffee House. How did I not know that was here all the time we've lived here?"

"I don't think I've been in there," he says. "Do you want some coffee?"

"Yes. An iced Americano sounds awesome right now. Let's do it."

We watch for traffic and then hustle across the street. The café is so cute, and it smells *amazing* when we walk inside.

I order my iced coffee and throw caution to the wind, including an orange and cranberry scone. Carmine gets the same. Before long, we're walking out of the shop again, loaded down with our treats.

"This is the best day I've had in two weeks."

Carmine laughs. "If I'd known that all it took for you to have the best day ever is a coffee and a scone, I would have done this sooner."

"Now we know. This could be a new daily occurrence."

"I overheard the barista telling someone that they have killer cinnamon rolls." Carmine shrugs as he takes a bite of his scone. "Maybe we'll have to check it out for breakfast."

"God, yes." I sip my coffee in happiness. "It feels good to finally feel semi-normal, you know?"

"I imagine that it does," he replies. "And it's good to see you looking like yourself again."

"I think that—*whoa!*"

My toe catches on an uneven part of the sidewalk, and I pitch forward. My coffee flies, and before my face can hit the ground, Carmine's arm wraps around my waist, and he catches me.

It all happened so fast, yet at the same time, it seemed to be in slow motion.

Especially the part where my almost-full coffee fell and splashed *everywhere.*

"Sonofabitch," I growl. "I was enjoying that."

"You can have mine." Carmine makes sure I'm standing upright and offers me his cup, but I shake my head.

"No, you enjoy it. I still have my scone."

"We'll share," he says, and then his eyes narrow on my face. "What hurts?"

I don't want to tell him. I don't want to say it out loud because then it'll be true.

"I'm fine."

His finger gently taps under my chin, and he makes me look him in the eyes.

"Don't fucking lie to me, Nadia."

"My shoulder." I sigh in exasperation. "I wrenched it a bit when my arm flailed. But it'll be fine. I'll just ice it and take an Advil when we get back. It'll be just fine."

He sighs and offers me a sip of his coffee, which I accept.

"Let's head back."

I'm tired. I didn't expect our walk to exhaust me as much as it did. Maybe it was the almost-fall that did me in.

The return trip is more subdued. We're quiet as we sip Carmine's coffee and eat our scones. When we get up to the penthouse, Carmine orders me to sit on the sofa.

"I'm getting you some ice," he informs me. His tone says he's not to be argued with.

I'm not really interested in arguing anyway.

The ice pack feels good on my sore shoulder. "Why don't you sit with me, and we'll put a movie on?"

He nods, turns on the TV, and passes me the remote. Then he sits next to me with his iPad in his lap.

He often works as I watch television. I won't admit it out loud, but I enjoy just being with him.

And that's stupid. But it is what it is.

"How about *Thor*?" I ask. "The third one. It's the funniest."

"I'm game."

I turn it on and then lean my head on Carmine's strong shoulder. Thor and Hulk are in an arena, about to battle it out as my eyes slip closed, and I fall asleep.

"Wake up, pretty girl."

I take a deep breath and crack open one eye. It's still dark outside. "Jesus, what time is it?"

"Five," he says. He's already fully dressed in a dark suit, no tie. "I told the pilot we'd be in our seats no later than six-thirty."

"Here's your hat. What's your hurry?" I bury my face in my pillow.

"We'll lose three hours to the time change, and I want to see Mick and Billy this afternoon."

Just the mention of the Sergi family makes me groan.

It's been five days since we took our walk, and I almost fell. My shoulder seems to have recovered, and Carmine called Billy Sergi, the second in command there, last night.

They granted him access to the city.

Of course, Carmine didn't say anything about having *me* with him.

I drag my ass out of bed and stumble into the bathroom. After I've done my business and am in the steamy shower, Carmine magically appears with a cup of coffee.

"You're a god," I say as I take the mug and sip the hot brew. "Thanks."

"You're welcome. Be ready in twenty."

He marches out again, but not before his eyes wander over my naked body.

Carmine hasn't made any moves on me in the weeks we were at the penthouse. He's kept things completely platonic.

And I know that it was *my* insistence that ensured we didn't have sex.

Sex muddies the waters. Clouds judgment.

And sex with Carmine is so fucking good, I would be a quivering pile of sexual need twenty-four-seven if we started something physical.

But damn, I miss the sex. And judging by the look in Carmine's eyes when he walked away, he does, too.

I let the hot water and caffeine wake me up, and thirty minutes later —much to his annoyance—I'm ready to go.

"It's a good thing I packed last night," I say. "Or I would have been late."

His brow lifts, and I can't help but laugh.

I'm back in business-mode, dressed in black slacks, a white silk shirt, and a red scarf. Tall, black Louboutin heels complete the outfit, and when I stand next to Carmine, I'm only a few inches shorter than he is.

"Those shoes do things to me," he mutters.

"I know." I tuck my makeup bag under my arm and follow him into the elevator. When we reach the garage, the driver meets us and tucks our bags into the trunk.

Because it's so early, traffic to the airfield isn't crazy. We don't go to SeaTac. Instead, we're driven to Boeing Field, where many private planes come and go.

The driver parks near the Martinelli jet, and before long, we're tucked safely inside, coffee at our elbows, and a flight attendant at our beck and call.

I don't like the way she ogles Carmine.

Not that he's *mine*. He's not. But I still don't like it.

"Have you fucked her?" I ask quietly.

He frowns down at me. "Who?"

"Her." I don't look up at the flight attendant.

"Look at me."

I don't do as he asks. I won't look at him and show him the vulnerability in my eyes. It pisses me off that it's there in the first place.

"Nadia."

"Forget I asked. Let's talk about how high-maintenance you are, Carmine. Why can't we just take a commercial flight to New York? First class is pretty swanky these days."

"Your father has a jet."

"Yeah, for *him* to use. The only time I'm on it is if I'm traveling with him. I'm okay with a normal flight."

"Must I remind you that you're carrying a ten-thousand-dollar handbag?"

I glance down at my Birkin and smile. "I never forget about my bag.

But it was a gift. And a one-time purchase. It doesn't cost me anything to maintain it."

"You're decked out in luxury brands from head to toe, Nadia. You live well. I won't apologize for doing the same. We all have things we're willing to splurge on. This is one of mine. I fund every flight I take on this jet. Not the family. And because I've been savvy with my money, I can afford the luxury."

"Hey, I'm not irresponsible with my money." I poke him in the side. "I just don't have a fancy portfolio."

"I'm going to help you with that."

"Why would you do that?"

"Because it's important to have investments. It only adds to your independence. And after what you told me about your lack of trust with your family, I think it's imperative that you're dependent on them as little as possible."

I stare at him, my mouth agape. "You're *worried* about me."

He rolls his eyes. "Don't be silly."

"You *like* me," I continue, teasing him. "I think you *like me,* like me, Carmine Martinelli. What will people say?"

"Stop talking."

"The next thing you know, you'll be pledging your undying love and proposing. I don't want to have babies, Carmine. I'm telling you that now—"

The next thing I know, I'm trapped against the back of the seat, and he's kissing the hell out of me. This isn't a playful peck to get me to stop talking. It's passionate, full of frustration and lust, and I hear the moan coming out of my throat as I sink my fingers into his dark hair and hang on tight as he takes me on an erotic ride.

"That'll teach you to shut up when I tell you to," he mutters against my lips as the plane taxis down the runway. "And the answer to your question is, no. I've never fucked her."

I clear my throat as he backs away and returns to his seat, settles in.

"It's none of my business."

"Keep telling yourself that, sweetheart."

"Maybe I should stay here."

We've been in the suite at the Four Seasons for an hour. The space is decorated in black and white, all modern and clean and completely sterile.

It's beautiful, most likely costs a small fortune, and is not my style *at all*.

But I'd rather stay here than head into the lion's den.

"You're not staying here, Nadia."

"I told you before...the Sergi family doesn't like me, Carmine."

That's putting it mildly.

"What did you do, kill one of them?"

"No. I was supposed to marry Billy but I threw a fit, and my father told them never mind. It pissed them off. You know how it is when a family is supposed to marry into another."

"Elena was supposed to marry Alex," he says dryly. "She dodged that bullet."

"Exactly. I dodged the same one. And they're just not happy about it. They don't trust us now."

"When did this happen?"

"Six years ago."

He whistles between his teeth. "That's a long time, Nadia. If all's been quiet since then, I'd think they've moved on and have other things to be mad about."

"Yeah, well, you'd think." I bite my lip. "Still, I'll just hang out here and wait for you."

"No, you'll come with me. But I suggest you change out of those heels."

I shake my head, resigned to my fate. "They're a weapon if I need them. And I can run in them as easily as I can in my sneakers. I also have a concealed sidearm on me."

"Where?"

I smirk. "I'm not telling you that."

He saunters over to me. "Maybe I'll find it for myself later."

"You can try."

His jaw tightens as he looks me over with hungry eyes, but he only swallows and turns away.

"Let's go. The sooner we do this, the quicker we can start asking questions in other areas of the city. This is a courtesy call to say hello and let them know what we're up to."

"Great."

The Sergi's headquarters is located in downtown Manhattan, right in the middle of all the action. The building looks innocent enough.

But I would bet every cent I have in the bank—which is more than Carmine expects, and that I invested just fine, thank you very much—that the things that happen in this building would turn Carmine's hair white.

I take a deep breath as he holds the door for me. We're shown into an office where Billy and his father Mick sit.

Mick's the boss.

Billy does his bidding.

It's all very customary as far as mafia families go.

"It's good to see you, Mick," Carmine says. But, suddenly, Mick flies to his feet, and guns are drawn, all pointed our way.

"What the fuck is she doing here?"

CHAPTER
SIX
~CARMINE~

"Whoa, whoa, whoa." I hold up my hands and slide to my left, closer to Nadia. Jesus, she wasn't kidding.

They really don't like her.

"You didn't say anything about that bitch being here," Mick sneers.

"She's with me," I say quickly. "Our families are working together because we've recently come under attack. I'm here because we need your help."

Mick's eyes narrow, but he signals for his goons to put away their weapons.

"What's going on?" Mick asks.

Billy hasn't said a word. He only glares at Nadia as we step forward into the luxurious office and sit across from Mick.

I briefly fill the boss in on the attempt on my father's life at the wedding in Denver, the subsequent attack on Nadia, and then remind him of my aunt's and uncle's murders long ago.

"Do you honestly think Vinnie's murder is tied to this now?" Mick asks, doubt hanging heavily in his voice.

"I don't know, but I'm going to find out," I reply. "I need to ask around the city, find out what your men know about the attempt on my father's life—and Nadia's for that matter."

"The Martinellis and the Tarenkovs are working together," Mick mutters and shakes his head. "Fascinating. Well, you can ask around, but no one will tell you anything. Even if they do know what's going on. This isn't your territory."

"Then what do you suggest?"

"Go home," he says bluntly.

"Not without answers."

Mick blows out a long breath. "We should have had this conversation over the phone. If you'd given me a heads-up, I could have asked around before you got here."

"There's a lot to be said for looking into a man's eyes when you talk to him." I clear my throat. "Mick, *you* aren't behind this, are you?"

"No." His lips flatten into a hard line. "It's true, there is no love lost between our family and the Tarenkovs, but my beef isn't worth a war. And Carlo and I have always had an agreeable relationship. But, if you'll give me a couple of days, I'll ask around. On the down-low. I don't think it's wise to bring a lot of attention to this. It might escalate the situation or make those responsible go into hiding. And then you'll never get your answers."

I nod in agreement. He hasn't said anything that I didn't already take into consideration.

"It looks like Nadia and I will spend a few days in your beautiful city. Take in the sights. Maybe see a show."

"Enjoy your vacation," Mick advises. "I'll be in touch when I know something."

"Thank you." We rise and start to leave, but turn back at Mick's voice.

"The next time you request entry into my city, you'd better be fucking honest about who you're bringing with you. I don't like surprises."

"Understood."

"I've heard great things about this show." Nadia walks out of the walk-in closet off our suite's bedroom and holds the necklace I gave her in Denver out to me. "Will you please fasten this?"

"Of course." I slip the diamonds and platinum around her slim neck and fasten it under her hairline, then kiss the ball of her shoulder. I notice she doesn't have any earrings in. "You're damn beautiful, Nadia."

She grins at me and then does a little spin in her red dress, showing it off. "Thanks. I'm glad I brought this along, just in case. And you look pretty damn good yourself in that suit."

I adjust the knot of my tie and then hold my hand out for hers. "Shall we?"

"Let me just grab my clutch." She rushes to the bed and slips a tube of lipstick into her bag, then takes my proffered hand. "Let's go watch a Broadway show."

The truth is, Nadia takes my breath away. She handled herself well at Mick's office today, knowing when to stay quiet and let me do the talking. She's intelligent. And she's sexy as fuck.

I shouldn't have kissed her on the plane this morning. I was only trying to shut her up, but all I did was remind myself how good we are together in bed.

How much I want her.

How I never *stopped* wanting her.

And she's made it clear that a physical relationship is out of the question.

I'm a damn fool. I need to keep my hands to myself and keep my focus on the task at hand.

She's a colleague who has become a friend. That's all.

But when we step into the elevator, and she leans her head on my shoulder as we watch the floors tick down, all I want to do is pull her to me and kiss her breathless.

Instead, I turn my lips down and kiss the top of her head.

"Tell me about this show." *Before I take you back upstairs and fuck you into next week.*

"The lead actress is London Watson. She's a *huge* name in theater, and she wrote this show a couple of years ago. Still stars in it. I'm excited to finally see it."

"Sounds great."

We walk through the hotel lobby and see our car is waiting. The ride through Manhattan is slow, as always, but before long, the driver drops us off in front of the theater. I bought us VIP tickets, so we bypass the line and are immediately shown to our seats.

"That's Paul Rudd," Nadia whispers and nods to the man several seats down. "Holy shit, I love *Ant-Man*."

"Tell him so. We have a few minutes before the show starts."

She bites her lip and then shrugs her shoulder and stands to approach the actor. Paul smiles up at her, then stands to talk to her. I can't hear everything that's said, but there are smiles, a couple of laughs, and then Nadia returns to me.

"Oh my God," she says. "He's so nice."

"He looked like a good guy."

She grins. "This is a fun day. Well, aside from having guns pointed at my face, of course."

"Yeah, that was a little intense."

"But the rest of it has been better than expected."

"I'm glad."

She links her arm through mine and leans on me. Nadia has become more and more physically affectionate over the past few weeks, at least since we started staying at the penthouse again.

I don't mind the affection.

But damn if it doesn't make me want more.

"You really do look nice in this suit," she says casually. "I don't think I've seen it before."

"I'm sure you have."

"No, this one is navy. You usually wear black."

I glance down at her. "You pay attention to the color of my suits?"

"You usually wear black," she says again. "I like this on you."

The lights flicker, signaling the start of the show. Through the entire three hours, Nadia touches me—holds my hand, leans her head on my shoulder, smiles up at me.

She's flirting with me.

Blatantly.

Boldly.

Either she's trying to seduce me, or she's playing a game. And I have no patience for that. She has me tied in knots, my dick semi-hard as we leave the theater.

"London was *amazing*," she gushes as we get into the waiting car. "She's so talented. I absolutely loved it. Man, I'm starving."

She grins over at me.

"Are you hungry?"

"Hmm."

She frowns. "You don't know if you're hungry?"

"I could use something." I turn my head and watch Manhattan pass us by. The traffic is no less frantic at midnight than it was close to four hours ago.

"Let's just order in at the hotel," she suggests. "We can get comfortable and eat all the food. That sounds awesome."

I nod. When the car stops in front of the Four Seasons, a bellman opens our door. I climb out first, then turn to offer Nadia my hand to help her out of the vehicle.

She's in another pair of those mile-high heels she loves. The kind that look damn hot over my shoulders as I fuck her into oblivion.

I remember very well.

"New York just energizes me," she says when we step into the elevator. "Don't you love this city?"

"You're talkative tonight," is my only reply.

"It's New York," she says. "Like I said, it energizes me. I don't come here often enough. For obvious reasons."

She slides her hand into mine, and I glance down at her.

"Why are you flirting with me so hard tonight?"

Her smile doesn't dim, but the light in her blue eyes sparks. "Oh, so you *did* notice?"

"Hard not to." I lead her out of the elevator and down the long hallway to the presidential suite, then unlock the door and walk inside. "You've turned it up."

"Turned what up?"

"The flirting." I turn and look at her as I loosen my tie. She drops her bag onto a table and crosses her arms over her chest. "What's going on?"

"I like flirting with you." She moves to me and brushes my hands out of the way so she can unbutton my shirt. "I like *being* with you."

"You set the rules hard and fast from the beginning of this, Nadia. No sex. I've upheld my end of that bargain."

"I know." There's no flirtation in her voice now as her eyes find mine. "And I also know that it's unfair and just plain ridiculous to muddy the waters. To change the rules."

"But I have a feeling you're going to do just that."

"We're good together," she says at last. "I thought I could turn that piece off. That I could ignore it. But damn it, the truth is, we *are* good together. And we'll be working together for God knows how long."

"Are you saying that you want to reintroduce sex into our dynamic?"

"Well, that just sounds like a business merger." She rises onto her tiptoes and barely skims her lips over mine. "And there's nothing sexy about a business merger. What you and I do to each other is fucking sexy, Carmine."

I sigh, wanting nothing more in this moment than *her*. And in about six seconds, I'm going to have her.

But we need to get something straight first.

"There's no pretense here, Nadia. No act."

"It's just you and me, who we *really* are, enjoying each other, Carmine. I know that."

"Good."

I don't waste any time. I lift her against me and hurry to the bedroom. "If anything hurts—"

"Trust me, this doesn't hurt."

I grin and set her on her feet next to the bed. "Leave the shoes on."

Her eyes are full of pure female satisfaction as she reaches behind her and unzips the dress, letting it pool around her ankles.

"Leave the necklace on, too."

"Any other requests?"

I laugh and urge her back onto the bed. "No. Let me do the rest." I take her right foot in my hand and kiss her ankle bone, right above the shoe. "Do you have any idea what these fucking shoes do to me?"

"Why do you think I wear them?"

She leans back on her hands, watching me as I kiss up her leg, then spread her wide and lick a wet trail from her inner thigh to the pink lips of her glistening pussy.

"You were always good at this."

She sighs and lays back on the mountain of pillows as I take her on the ride of her life—all with my mouth. I lick and suck, then lick some more. I vary the pressure and speed, and when I push two fingers inside of her, she comes apart spectacularly.

"Good girl," I murmur as I kiss up her flat stomach to her breasts. "I love your tits. You know that, right?"

"They never grew in."

"Excuse me?"

She laughs and brushes her hand through my hair. "When I was young, I was desperate for them to grow so boys would notice me. Much to my dismay, they stayed small."

"I see zero things wrong with these." I brush my tongue over a hard peek and then kiss her neck passionately.

I fumble in the bedside drawer, find a little packet, and make quick work of protecting us. But before I can slide home, she pushes me onto my back and straddles my hips.

She always loved this position the best, and she'll get no complaints from me.

She rides me hard and fast and reaches back to cup my already-tight balls.

"Fuck, Nadia."

"Yes, fuck Nadia," she agrees and clenches her core around me.

I don't want to come yet, so I grip her hips in my hands, lift her, then shift our position so I'm behind her. Then, I push back inside. Her round ass is in the air, and I give it a loud smack as I fuck her from behind.

"God, Carmine." She clenches the bedsheets in her fists and pushes back against me. "Yes."

Three more hard thrusts are all it takes to have us both coming apart at the seams, crying out in ecstasy.

"Oh, God, I love this."

She's wearing a white hotel robe and nothing else, and we're sitting on the terrace, a large tray of food on the table between us as she eats her weight in shrimp cocktail.

"I mean, just look at the lights."

The New York lights are stunning. We're not far from the World Trade Center memorial and can even see the lights of it from here.

"It's a beautiful place," I agree and reach for a taco. Tacos aren't on the menu, but they made them for me tonight. "If you love it here so much, why don't you live here?"

"Because I'm a Tarenkov," she reminds me. "There's no way the Sergis would allow that. Especially Billy. That little worm."

She sips her chocolate shake and scowls.

"He did seem a bit angry with you today."

She laughs at that and then switches from her shrimp to the dessert she ordered: crème brûlée.

"He's a baby. Worse than Alex," she says as an afterthought. "I would keep an apartment here in a heartbeat, but it's not possible because of the family drama. The Sergis don't trust us, and we don't trust them either, truth be told. But once a year, I do come shopping. I send Mick an email, and he always replies cordially, giving me a four-day pass to spend some time here. It's the best four days of my year."

"This is still a free country, Nadia."

She turns sad, blue eyes up at me. "Come on, Carmine. You know that isn't true for people like us. Never has been. Men who claim to love us dictate our lives, but they wouldn't hesitate to use us for personal gain if they saw the need arise. It's a game we play every damn day of our lives."

She eats more of her dessert.

"But you know what? I don't want to talk about that."

"What do you want to talk about?"

"I don't want to chat at all. I want to lick what's left of this crème brûlée off your penis."

My eyebrows climb at the suggestion. "I'm not saying no."

"I didn't think you would."

246

CHAPTER

SEVEN

~NADIA~

I wake up in the center of maybe the biggest bed on Earth, all of the blankets rumpled and in a pile in the middle, with me draped around them like the big spoon.

Carmine, however, is nowhere to be found.

I sit up and rub the sleep from my eyes. I'm sure I have mascara shadows under my lashes because I didn't bother washing my face before Carmine carried me in here and had his way with me.

I grin and stand, feeling the pull of tender muscles. The soreness feels good, though, not at all like it did as I recovered from the attack. I feel good and sexed.

I pad naked into the living space to see if Carmine is reading the news on his iPad, but he's not out here, either. So, I walk into the half-bath in the hall, use the restroom, and then find the white robe on the floor where Carmine let it fall, wrapping it around myself.

I journey back through the bedroom to the master bath and lean on the doorjamb with a grin.

Lounging in the white porcelain soaking tub is Carmine, up to his neck in sudsy water. He's laid his head back, and his eyes are closed.

I cross to him and let my robe fall to the floor.

"Don't you smell nice?" I murmur. He opens his eyes. They immediately warm, then travel the length of me. "Looks like there's room for two."

"Why don't we find out?"

I grin and climb into the hot water, straddling his hips and rubbing myself against him playfully. "I didn't peg you as a bath guy."

"It feels good to soak now and then."

I sniff the air. "Is that rose oil, I smell?"

"What's wrong with a little rose oil?"

I lean over to bite his neck. "Like I said yesterday, you're just a little high-maintenance."

"I like luxurious things," he says, but his voice doesn't sound defensive. He's simply stating a fact. "Whether that's a private jet or a soak in a tub the size of Manhattan, it doesn't matter."

I push my wet hand through his hair. "I just like to give you shit."

"If you keep rubbing yourself on me like that, I'll give you something, too."

"Oh?" I cock an eyebrow and grind on him. "Like this?"

"You're a vixen," he mutters. "And it would take a saint to resist you."

"I have it on good authority that you're no saint."

He laughs and glides his hands up my thighs to my waist and then around to my ass, cupping the globes and lifting me gently so he can urge his cock inside of me.

"No condom," he growls.

"Still on the pill." My voice is raspy. The water sloshes around us as I start to move. God, I love this position. The head of his dick glides perfectly over my most sensitive places, sending thrilling shockwaves through me.

I never last long when I ride him, and with the water caressing my ass, my sides, and my lower back, I come faster than ever, crying out with each wave that hits me.

"Again," he orders. "Look at me."

His brown eyes are hot as he works me harder and faster. He's sitting up now, guiding me, pushing me until we both succumb to a climax that has us shivering and panting.

"Well, okay then." I swallow hard. "Good morning."

"Yes, it is." He nuzzles my breasts, then leans back against the tub once more. "What shall we do today?"

"Are you kidding me? I'm in New York. I want to go shopping."

His grin is wide and full of humor.

"I was hoping you'd say that."

I stand and carefully step out of the tub. I don't want to fall on my ass, and we spilled a lot of water during our fun time.

"I need a shower, but I'll be ready in an hour."

"I'll order up breakfast," he says as he climbs out of the tub.

"It's handy having you around, Carmine."

He grins, winks at me, and then leaves the bathroom.

Jesus, Mary, and Joseph, that man is sexy. I start the shower, and when the water is the right temperature, I step in and get busy washing my face.

I'm in a damn good mood. Maybe the best I've been in for months. Maybe ever. I'm in my favorite city, with someone I enjoy, and I'm going to spend an obscene amount of money.

"Breakfast will be here in twenty," Carmine calls out.

"Sounds good," I yell back.

Yeah, it's damn convenient having that man around.

"THE BAG you just bought looks like the one you already have."

We're eating pizza and sitting by a fountain. The boutiques will deliver our new things to the Four Seasons for us so we don't have to walk around Manhattan loaded down with bags.

"Uh, excuse me Mr. I-just-bought-a-ten-thousand-dollar-watch-that-looks-just-like-the-one-I'm-currently-wearing."

He stops mid-chew and narrows his eyes at me. "It looks nothing like this watch."

"And my new bag looks nothing like the others I have." I shrug a shoulder. "Besides, it's a new style this season. And it's going to look *so* cute with jeans and a sweater."

"I want to look at shoes at Bergdorf."

I grin at him. "I can live with that."

We finish our pizza and walk down the street to the old store, wandering through. Browsing. When we find the men's shoes, Carmine studies some Louboutins that have me salivating.

He's not the only one who appreciates luxury.

"You could wear those with any and all of your suits."

He nods and wanders down the table, picking up a pair of sneakers. Carmine flags down a salesperson and asks to try them on in his size.

"Sneakers?"

"I do wear casual clothes."

I take in his khaki slacks and light blue button-down. "When?"

"I brought out a couple of sizes because you just never know how Louboutins will fit," the salesman says as he returns and sets the boxes at Carmine's feet.

After twenty minutes—and six pairs—Carmine chooses two, and then we're off to find the women's shoe section, just one floor up.

"I need more heels like I need a hole in the head," I mutter as I brush my index finger over a pair of glossy patent leather Chanel heels. "But damn if they're not beautiful."

I try on Dior, Choo, and Hermes, and settle on a pair of Dior sling-backs, Hermes sneakers, and the *cutest* Valentino flip-flops.

Again, they'll deliver everything to our room, so we leave the store and start walking down Fifth, hand in hand, enjoying the afternoon sun.

"I did a lot of damage today," I say with a happy sigh. "But it's so fun. Nothing compares to shopping in New York. Well, aside from Paris. Paris is the mecca, of course. But New York ranks up there. I could have spent all day in the Hermes boutique and bought scarves and all kinds of fun little things. But I won't wear them often, so I need to be strong and cut myself off."

"I enjoy watching you shop. You touch everything."

"I'm a texture girl. I like to feel the leathers, the silks, and cashmeres. It *feels* pretty, you know?"

"Just one of the reasons I enjoy touching you."

I laugh, but when I look up at him, he's staring down at me, and he is *not* laughing. "You're charming, you know that?"

"I'm just telling the truth. I hope you like tea."

"Tea?"

He nods and leads me to the doorway of the Tiffany & Co. We get in the elevator and ride it to the fourth floor, and then he leads me to the Blue Box Café.

"Oh, I've never eaten there."

"We're having afternoon tea," he informs me with a smile.

"Fancy."

A regal woman with perfectly coifed, sable hair greets us. She takes Carmine's name and checks her reservation list, then leads us to our table and sets Tiffany-blue menus in front of us.

"We're having the afternoon tea," Carmine informs her.

"Of course." She nods and backs away. What seems like only moments later, a waiter wheels a cart to our table, piled high with finger foods and hot, steeping tea.

The waiter explains everything on the tray, pours us each a cup, and then leaves us to our own devices.

"I'm sort of shocked," I admit as I reach for a scone, break it in half, and spread real, whipped butter on it.

"At what?"

"This is the last thing I would have expected from you."

"We've had plenty of meals together."

"I meant the *tea*." I chuckle and take a bite of my scone, then close my eyes in happiness. "This is delicious."

"We'd already had lunch, but I wanted to do something different for you."

"This is different. And fun. And fancy."

I watch as his brows knit together.

"It's okay, Carmine. I like the fancy side of you."

We try the finger sandwiches, some fruit, and spend an hour simply enjoying each other's company.

"This place is just so beautiful." I look over at the wall with an enormous clock on it. The wall itself looks as if it's made of gray and Tiffany-blue granite. "And the food was great."

I yawn and cover my mouth with my napkin.

"Am I boring you?" he asks.

"No. Definitely, not." I laugh and run my fingers through my hair. "I think all the walking and shopping is finally catching up with me. Maybe it's time to head back and catch a nap."

"We have one more stop to make first."

I tilt my head. "Where?"

"It isn't far."

He pays the check and then pulls me through the restaurant and back into the elevator, but rather than leave the store, he leads me to a waiting salesperson.

"Hello, sir," the man says with a slight bow. "I'm Dennis. I'll be happy to work with you today."

I frown at Carmine. "Looking for another watch?"

"Earrings," he says as Dennis starts to pull velvet boxes out of the glass cases and sets them on the counter. "You weren't wearing any earrings when we went to the theater last night."

I stare up at him. "Seriously?"

He quirks a brow. "I'm quite sure Dennis would be rather upset if I were kidding." He turns to the other man. "Did you see the necklace?"

"My necklace?"

Dennis nods. "I received your text with the photo. It's a stunning piece, and I'm sure we have earrings here that will match it nicely."

"You want me to pick out earrings to match my necklace?"

I stare at him, blinking slowly, dumbfounded.

"That's why we're here," he says.

"You don't have to do that."

"Give us a moment," he says, and Dennis discretely walks away so we can talk in private.

"Carmine, you don't have to buy me gifts."

"I don't have to do much of anything," he says. "I *want* to do this for you. They'll look beautiful."

"You gave me a lot of gifts when we were fake-dating." I chew my lower lip.

"We're not fake anything now," he says smoothly and reaches out to brush his thumb across the apple of my cheek. "I enjoy you, Nadia. More than I anticipated. And I'd like to buy you something beautiful to remember our time in New York. No strings attached."

What if I'm starting to wish for strings?

My heart flutters. What the fuck is wrong with me?

Carmine signals for Dennis to rejoin us, and I turn to the several velvet trays with a sigh.

I know as soon as my eyes land on them.

They're understated, which works well because the necklace is anything but. These earrings won't overshadow the diamonds around my neck but will add just a bit of sparkle to my ears.

"These."

Dennis offers them to me, along with a mirror, and I fasten them onto my lobes, then tilt my head side to side, admiring them.

"Would you like to look at the chandeliers?" Dennis asks, pointing to a gorgeous pair of diamond earrings that probably cost about the same as a small suburban home.

"No, thanks." I turn to Carmine. His lips are tipped up in a small smile. "These will go perfectly."

"I think you're right."

He reaches out and touches my ear with his finger. "Discreet, but beautiful."

"And the necklace is still the centerpiece."

"No." He steps into me and lowers his lips to my ear. "*You're* the centerpiece, sweetheart. The jewelry is just frosting."

He turns back to Dennis.

"We'll take them."

"Excellent, sir."

Dennis is all smiles as he sees to the bill, and I can't stop hearing the last words from Carmine in my head.

The rest is just frosting.

Has anyone taken the time to see me for *me*? To see past the designer clothes and accessories to the woman beneath? I feel like I've been constantly trying to prove to my father, my brother, and everyone in our family that I'm smart enough and damn savvy enough to take over the organization one day.

But they always dismiss me.

Not Carmine. He respects my opinions and listens to me when I talk. He acknowledges that I enjoy pretty things but also knows that it's just the surface.

That what's beneath is so much more.

"Ready?" he asks with a smile.

"Yes." I look in the mirror once more, happy to wear the earrings out of the store. "You know, I hope you realize that when I give you shit for being a diva, I don't really mean it."

He glances at me as we walk through the store. "You've never called me a *diva*."

"Not in those words, exactly."

"Does it truly bother you that I like the finer things? Does it emasculate me in your eyes?"

"No." Visions of Carmine and I in bed swim in my head. Of him working out. Of all the ways that he shows, every day, that he's a *man*. One I'm incredibly attracted to. "Not at all."

"Good, because I plan to take you back to the hotel and fuck you blind."

My mouth opens and closes. I'm not sure what in the hell to say to that.

But when we step outside, four men suddenly surround us, all with weapons drawn.

"The boss wants to see you. Get in the car."

I sigh and frown at all four of them. "What in the hell is it with the Sergi organization and guns? Can't you just ask a girl nicely?"

"Let's go," the goon says, ignoring my statement altogether. "You can complain about how we do things to the boss."

CHAPTER
EIGHT
~CARMINE~

"You do realize that it's not necessary to hold us at gunpoint to get us into your office." My voice is dry as I sit across from Mick and narrow my eyes at him. "We're happy to come in willingly." Mick smiles, but his eyes aren't full of humor.

"I have no idea what you're talking about."

I just stare back at him until he looks down at the papers on his desk. "I've done some asking around, some talking, and I'm afraid I don't know much more than you do."

"But you know something."

Mick leans back in his chair and folds his beefy hands over his impressive stomach. When you think of the stereotypical mob boss, Mick is the image that comes to most minds. He's a big man—in both stature and weight. He's imposing.

"Turns out, someone approached one of my men about selling something new here in the city."

I sit forward. "A new drug?"

"Yeah, but I don't know who did the approaching. Or what kind of drug."

I scowl. "Come on, Mick, you know everything that goes on in New York."

The other man's eyes flash with anger. "I thought I did. And trust me when I say that I'd be happy to drag my man in here to interrogate him myself."

"Then do it."

"He's fucking dead."

"Goddamn it." I rub my hand over my mouth. "How did he die?"

"I was at that wedding," Mick reminds me. "My man has been dead for a few days, but it looks like he met the same fate your father's man did."

"Poison," Nadia murmurs beside me. "Are they trying to sell poison? Why would anyone take it if the result is death?"

"I don't think it's the poison they want to sell," Mick says. "There've been rumblings of something new on the streets. Something damn powerful, addictive, and cheap to make."

"Hell, you just described meth," Carmine says.

"I'm not a fan of drugs," Mick replies. "I know some of my guys sell a little here and there, but that's not my game. And they know it. My hunch is that my guy told the stranger no, and that answer wasn't the right one. I have no way of knowing who it was that approached him."

"His cell?" I ask, already knowing the answer.

"Gone." Mick hisses out a breath. "Listen, this doesn't sit well with me, either. Someone came, unannounced, into my city and killed my man. I'm damn pissed."

"I know the feeling." I stare at Mick. "What now?"

"I'll keep asking," Mick says. "You keep me posted, as well. Some-one's going to pay for this."

"On that, we can agree. I'll keep you informed when and if we find anything. I appreciate you working with us on this, rather than against us."

"It seems someone has decided to wage war with several organiza-tions," Mick says thoughtfully. "They're either very brave or out of their fucking minds."

"Maybe both," Nadia adds, and Mick's eyes slide over to her for the first time.

"We'll stay in touch," Mick says again, dismissing us.

"Thanks for your time." We stand, and before I can walk away, Mick says my name.

"Carmine. Watch your back. This has *conspiracy* written all over it."

"Same to you."

"I GUESS THIS WAS A WASTED TRIP," Nadia says as she flops onto the sofa in our suite.

"Not at all."

I sit next to her and lift her feet into my lap. "We had a good few days here. And although it's not the information we were hoping for, we at least know it's not Mick."

"He could be lying."

I stare at her pink-tipped toes as I push my thumb into the arch of her foot. "I don't think so. He's pissed."

"What now?"

I've been running that question through my mind since we left Mick's office. "I think we need to go back to the city where this all started."

"Denver."

I nod and reach out to brush her hair behind her ear just as my phone rings.

"Hi, Shane."

"Hey, what did you find out from Mick?"

I relay the information and hear my brother curse on the other end of the line. "Yeah, that was my thought, exactly."

"This is a game for someone," Shane says. "They're fucking playing with us. But why? What's the end game?"

"That's the million-dollar question," I reply. "Nadia and I are headed to Denver first thing in the morning. I think we need to do some digging there."

"Denver is supposed to be neutral ground for all of the families," Shane reminds me.

"Yeah, well, that went in the toilet when someone tried to kill Pop."

"I'll meet you there," Shane says. "See you at the office."

"See you."

I hang up and turn to Nadia, who's watching me closely.

"Shane's going to meet us in Denver. He's been at his place in the mountains for the past couple of weeks, doing some digging of his own."

"Why does he have a place in Colorado?"

I tilt my head to the side. "Why shouldn't he?"

"Denver is neutral ground. We all have offices there, but no one lives there."

"Your cousin and her husband do," I remind her. "Just because your father isn't based there full time doesn't mean he doesn't have connections to the city. Besides, Shane doesn't live *in* Denver. He lives in a small mountain town called Victor, several hours outside the city."

"Shane's been there this whole time?"

I narrow my eyes at her. "He's a grown man and can live anywhere he likes, Nadia. Shane likes solitude. The mountains suit him. And he's within driving distance to several airports and can get in and out easily."

"Hmm," is all she says as the doorbell rings. "Oh, I bet that's our stuff."

She hurries to the door, and sure enough, it's the bellman with all of our purchases on a cart. He unloads them onto the dining table big enough to seat eight, then leaves. Nadia is all smiles as she starts digging into bags and boxes wrapped with ribbon.

"I'm *so* glad I got these shoes," she says as she slips out of her sneakers and tries on her new Dior heels."

"What's your problem with my brothers?" I ask while she's in a good mood and on a new shoe high.

"I don't know them well," she replies. "Oh, I forgot about this jacket. I know it's summer, but it'll be perfect for fall."

"But you don't like Shane having property in Colorado."

She shrugs a shoulder as she checks out her new purchase in a full-length mirror. "It's just all suspect. Shane has a place near Denver. This mess started in Denver."

"Your cousin lives in Colorado," I remind her once more. "All of the families have offices there. Just because Shane spends more time there than most doesn't make him the cause of all of this."

"I know." She sighs and turns back to me. "And I also know that you care about him, and you'd defend him to the ground."

"Every fucking day," I agree, frustration a bubble in my throat. "If we're all going to be judged by our taste in real estate, Annika and her husband could be the cause of all this, too. The first attack happened at their wedding, after all."

"Oh, come on." She turns to me as she lets the jacket fall off her arms and catches it with her fingers. "Rich is an ear, nose, and throat doctor. He's no mobster. And he certainly isn't a drug dealer."

"Annika?"

Her eyes flash in temper and annoyance.

Good, we're on equal footing.

"Annika has worked her ass off to stay out of the family business. She wants no part of it. None of it. She's a damn good doctor. Hell, *I'm* more likely to be the one behind this than she is."

I cock a brow.

"No. It's not me."

"Well, it's not me, either. At least, we've established that. Let's get to Denver in the morning. We can plan what happens next then."

She blows out a breath and reaches for her Chanel shopping bag. "Okay. In the meantime, I'm going to play with my new goodies."

"Play away, sweetheart."

"Rocco." I smile at my brother as Nadia and I walk into our Denver offices. "I wasn't expecting to see you here."

"Shane called me last night. I want in on the fun." He nods at Nadia. "Hi."

"Hello. *Rafe.*"

My brother rolls his eyes. I don't know why he doesn't care for his given name, but he's always insisted that people call him Rocco, ever since he was a kid.

Of course, Mom refuses to call him anything but Rafe. She named him after one of her favorite characters in a romance novel.

Maybe *that's* why he doesn't like it.

"I have something," Shane says as he hurries through the door. "And let me just say, it wasn't easy to get."

"What is it?" I ask as he sits at the desk and opens his laptop, then starts tapping the keys.

"The waiter from the wedding." Shane's brow furrows as he searches the screen. "No one knew who he was. I asked the catering company. They had no record of him. I had to bust into the security camera logs at the resort. And let me just tell you, their security is buttoned down *tight*. Took me several days to crack the code.

"But once I did, I was able to find some footage of our man. Here." He points to the screen. "See him? He's floating through the crowd a bit."

"It's grainy and in black and white," I say, squinting to see better.

"Yeah, their security is the bomb, but the video quality sucks. I cleaned it up a bit."

He points to the bigger monitor on the desk, and Rocco, Nadia, and I shift our attention there.

"Carmine and Nadia sneak off," Shane says with a cheeky smile. "You look a little intense there, brother."

I was. I wanted to fuck Nadia like I'd never wanted anything else in my whole damn life. And if memory serves, it was some pretty damn good sex.

Nadia glances up at me with a smirk.

"Okay. Here." Shane points to the screen. "See, he's setting the glass for Pop on the table."

"And looking around while he does it," Nadia adds. "That's definitely shady."

"None of us noticed," Rocco says. "We were all too busy partying."

"Our guards were down because it was supposed to be neutral territory," I say, thinking it over. "Not just in Denver, but at the wedding. We all had our guards down."

"Before Pop can take a sip, Armando takes the glass by accident. He's laughing with someone and just picks it up and drinks."

I watch as Armando does just that. Pop looks over and scowls for a second, then shrugs and laughs, signaling for a waiter to order a fresh drink.

"I'm going to speed this up a bit because it takes a couple of minutes for the poison to kick in." Shane hits a button, and the video runs faster. Then he slows it down, and Armando's face changes. He reaches for his throat, his eyes bulge, and the next thing we see, he's flailing about and ends up in the middle of the dance floor, seizing.

"That's enough," I say, but Shane shakes his head.

"Watch here." He points again. "There's our man. He takes a picture of the scene and then slips back into the crowd. And he doesn't come back. He ducks out."

"You said you found out who he is?" I ask, seeing red.

"Sean Brown," Shane says. "At least, that's the name he's gone by for a while. I found him doing a search for his image. He's also gone by Clark Brown and Rudy Brown."

"Why all the names?" Nadia wants to know.

"He's been in and out of jail," Shane says. "I assume he changes his name so he can get jobs. Have a clean record."

"He's anything but clean. Fuck, he's a contract killer."

"Looks like it," Shane agrees. "I have an address."

"What are we doing sitting here, then?" Rocco pulls his nine-millimeter out of his shoulder holster and checks the magazine. I do the same, and I notice Nadia pulling her small piece from her Hermes bag, checking it, as well.

I laugh.

"What?" she says.

"You carry a concealed in an eleven-thousand-dollar handbag?"

She grins. "Doesn't everyone?"

———

"WE DON'T KILL HIM." My voice is firm with the order. "We question him."

"Maybe break his arm," Rocco says with a shrug as we climb the steps to the upstairs apartment. Sean—or whatever his name is—

lives on the second floor of a rundown building in a shitty part of town.

I raise my fist to knock on the door, but it's ajar.

"Not a good sign," Shane murmurs as he pulls his weapon. We all follow suit, and I nudge the door open with my toe. We soundlessly hurry inside.

But we don't have to go far.

"Fucking hell," I mutter and stare up at the man who used to be Sean as he swings from a noose tied to a beam in the ceiling.

"Shit." Nadia circles around him. "He's been up there a while."

His face is purple, eyes bulged, and the rope cut the hell out of his neck. The smell of decay is overwhelming.

"There's a note," Rocco says and begins to read aloud.

I can't live with what I did. I've done some fucked-up things but killing ain't one of them.

"That's it," Rocco says.

"Well, damn." I rub my hand over my face and listen as Shane murmurs into his phone. He's calling in a cleanup crew.

The cops won't find Sean.

He won't be found at all.

And we're at another dead end, literally. Back to square one. Which royally pisses me off.

"Look for a phone," I say, already headed back to the one and only bedroom in the flop. His phone is on a charger by the bed, so I pocket it. Shane can dig into it when we get back to the office.

I rummage through drawers but don't find anything else when Nadia pokes her head in.

"You'll want to see this."

I follow her to the bathroom and snarl. "Jesus fucking Christ, this is disgusting."

"Yeah, our boy didn't know what a toilet brush is. But that's not what I wanted to show you." She opens the medicine cabinet. "Look at these."

Bags and bags of little blue pills.

"I'll give you two guesses what these are," she says.

"Given that none of us are pharmacists, it could be anything. Maybe Sean had an Aleve habit."

Nadia rolls her eyes. "Right. It's an anti-inflammatory. That's why he had like five thousand of them in this cabinet."

"We'll take them," Shane says. "Crew's on the way. Let's bail."

We take the bags of pills with us, and I skirt by the body still hanging in the living room.

"He looks like a baby."

"Twenty-two," Shane confirms. "Still wet behind the ears."

"Seasoned enough to kill," I remind him. "I'd hardly call him innocent."

CHAPTER
NINE
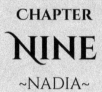
~NADIA~

I'm fucking tired.

It's late. Carmine and I left New York before the sun came up this morning, and we've been working hard all day.

Carmine's still at the office with his brothers, but I bailed. I need to sleep. I have to get my mind off drugs and death for a few hours.

I need a break.

I fill the tub in the master bathroom of the beautiful Airbnb Carmine rented and add some bath salts to the water. Before I can strip down and sink in, my phone rings.

Why would Alex be calling me this late?

It's midnight in Atlanta.

"Is Papa okay?" I ask in way of greeting.

"As far as I know," he says. "Can't a guy just call his sister to check in?"

"Not usually. No." I lean my butt on the counter and stare at the water in the tub, wondering what he wants. "What's up?"

"I'm wondering how you're doing. Found anything yet?"

"Not really. We're back in Denver."

"Yes, I heard."

My eyes narrow. "How?"

"We have eyes everywhere, Nadia. You know that. You're still with Carmine."

"Yes."

"Are you still fucking him?"

I don't even know this man anymore. When we were kids, we were close. I adored him. But the older he got, the colder he became.

"You realize you basically just called me a whore?"

"Answer the question, Nadia."

"No, Alexander. I won't. Because I'm a grown woman, on a job given to me by the boss, who doesn't happen to be *you*."

"You're such a bitch. Just tell me what's going on there. Keep me in the damn loop. I can't help if I don't know what's happening."

"I don't want or need any help from you," I counter. "I never have before, and I definitely don't need you now. Just keep your nose and your fingers out of this."

"Nadia—"

I hang up before he can say more.

The water has grown cold, so I drain it and think about starting over. But I'm too tired, and I've lost interest.

Instead, I start the shower and get in, quickly washing the day away, and then step into leggings and a sweatshirt.

I stop by the kitchen and pour a glass of Cabernet, then scoop up my laptop and walk into the living room.

The sofa faces a wall of windows. It's dark now, but during the day, you can see the mountains to the west.

Carmine has a thing for beautiful views.

I've just opened the laptop and started going through some unanswered emails when Carmine walks through the front door, also looking tired.

But my eyes zero in on the box in his right hand.

"Is that what I think it is?"

He sets the container on the kitchen island, tosses his keys next to it, and glances at me. "I thought you'd enjoy some donuts for breakfast."

"I'd enjoy some donuts *now*."

I laugh and launch off the sofa with renewed energy at the promise of sugar but stop short when I get a good look at Carmine.

"What's wrong?"

He shakes his head and walks to the fridge, pulls out a bottle of beer I didn't know we had, and takes a long pull from the bottle.

"Did something else happen?"

"No." He swallows another sip and then sits on one of the stools. "It really shouldn't be this hard. I feel like I'm on another wild goose chase, just missing the mark by an inch. It's damn frustrating."

"I know. But we'll figure it out. People are loyal, but I've also found that they like to run their mouths. Someone will fuck up and say something they shouldn't, and we'll find them."

"It's odd for a family to target another and not be bold about it. To stand up and say, '*Yeah, motherfucker, I did this. And I'll do it again.*'"

"The mafia has arrogance down to a science," I agree with a laugh.

"Well, they're not copping to anything now."

I open the box and immediately salivate at the sight of a maple bar. I grab for it like a kid starved to within an inch of her life.

"These are my favorite donuts in the city." I wander over and sit on the couch, chewing happily. "Oh, by the way, we're having dinner at Annika and Rich's place tomorrow."

"We are?" he asks.

"Yep. She called earlier. Your brothers are also invited."

He nods and then wanders to me, leaning in to take a bite of my donut.

"Hey, get your own."

"No." He takes my hand, pulls me to my feet, and leads me to the bedroom. "Now, I want to taste you. You're much more delicious than any donut."

"Lead the way."

Annika and Rich's home in the Cherry Creek neighborhood of Denver is beautiful. It's an upscale area that professional sports players, celebrities, and the wealthy in general call home.

And I can see why. In addition to a nice golf course with a country club, there is excellent shopping, restaurants, and bars. If I lived in Denver, this is where I'd buy a house.

"Hi, you guys," Annika says with a wide smile as she opens the front door and gestures for us to come inside. "I'm so excited to see you all."

"You're gorgeous," I say as I lean in to kiss my cousin's cheek. But when I pull back, I can see the tension around her gorgeous blue eyes. I narrow mine, but she shakes her head quickly, sending me a silent message that now isn't the time for that conversation.

She greets Carmine and Shane, and when she reaches Rafe, she pauses. "Hi, Rafe."

"Annika." He kisses her cheek, as well, but the look he gives her is anything but friendly.

It's intimate.

How did I miss *that*?

"Come on in, everyone. Dinner's almost ready. Ivie's checking on it right now."

"Ivie's here?" Shane asks, his interests piqued.

"I thought it would be fun if she joined," Annika replies as we all take seats around the large living room. The house is traditional, all of the rooms separate—no open-concept here.

But it's beautifully decorated, and I know that Annika invested a lot of time making this house a home for Richard and her.

"Where's your husband?" I ask, but before she can answer, the man does.

"Sorry, everyone," Rich says as he hurries into the room from the back patio. "I had to take a call."

Rich is tall, slender, and utterly *boring*.

I don't know what Annika sees in him. Sure, he's smart and comes from a good family, but he's as dry as a corpse that's been left out in the sun for a year.

I bet he only likes to fuck in the dark, under the covers, after a shower.

I wrinkle my nose at the thought and then smile when Rich turns his attention on me.

"Hello, Nadia."

"Hi, Rich. Thanks for having us over for dinner."

"Oh, it's our pleasure. Annika should get to see her family from time to time."

What the hell does that mean?

Before I can ask him, Ivie comes bustling out of the kitchen and almost falls on her face.

Poor Ivie. She's such a klutz.

"Whoa," she says with a laugh.

"Easy there." Shane immediately jumps up to help her. He takes her hand, kisses it, and leads her over to the sofa.

"Oh, thanks. I'm good. Just clumsy. Annika and I decided to make lasagna with garlic bread and salad. It's just about done."

I notice Carmine and Rafe share a look.

There is so much happening here, all unspoken, and all I can do is watch in fascination. There's trouble in paradise with my cousin and her husband. Shane wants to get into Ivie's pants. And Rafe and Carmine clearly find it all comical.

This is the best entertainment I've had in years.

"I'm starved," Annika says with a grin. "Let's eat."

"Not too much pasta for you, darling," Rich says as he pats her shoulder. "Why don't you stick with the salad?"

"Why don't you let your wife eat whatever the fuck she wants since she's a grown woman and everything?" I turn to Rich with a toothy, humorless smile.

It's not returned.

And I give zero fucks.

He simply sits at the table, and we start passing around dishes, filling our plates as Annika pours the wine.

When she reaches Rafe's glass, he shakes his head, and she moves on to the next.

But the glare Rafe aims at Rich would make most men piss their pants.

"How are things at the clinic?" I ask Ivie.

"Great," she says with a nod. "We're busier than ever right now."

"What kind of clinic do you run?" Carmine asks.

"We have a medi-spa," she replies easily. "We offer services from simple facials to botox to reconstructive surgery."

"Plastic surgery?" Shane says.

"Sort of, yes," Ivie says.

"There's a lot of botox happening in this city," Annika says with a wink. "And thank goodness."

"I was thinking of coming in to see you," I say, pointing to the crows' feet around my eyes. "I have a few lines I'd like to take care of."

"You don't have wrinkles," Carmine says, staring down at me in surprise.

"Yeah, I do."

"I can fix you right up," Annika assures me. "And I'd love to spend some time with you."

"Can you fit her into your already busy schedule?" Rich asks, his voice hard.

What the fuck is up with him?

"I always have time for Nadia," she replies. Her voice is just as hard as her husband's. Rich's jaw clenches.

Yeah, I'd say the honeymoon is over there.

And I definitely need to talk to her. Soon. Find out what in the hell is going on. Annika has always been my best friend. My confidante. Sure, I've been busy since the wedding, but that's no excuse.

Whatever she's going through, she won't face it alone.

"Oh, my God, this is so good." I bite into a piece of hot, crusty bread. "Seriously, A, you're an amazing cook."

"Ivie and I did it together," she says with a smile and gazes longingly at the bread. "I'm glad you like it."

"Here, try it." I pass her the basket, and she shrugs, takes a piece, and then passes it back.

Rich isn't happy. The dick. And that only makes me want to offer her another chunk.

I *despise* men who try to control their wives like this.

Carmine and Rafe chat about stocks, and I tune them out because it's all Greek to me.

Shane flirts shamelessly with Ivie, making her blush like crazy, which I think is absolutely adorable. Ivie's shy, a little clumsy—or a lot, depending on the day—and while she's pretty, no one would call her a beauty queen. She's the perfect epitome of the girl next door.

But she's smart and funny, loyal, and also one of my best friends.

I turn my attention to Rich, who's shoveling food into his mouth and doing his best to ignore his wife, who I see is drinking wine like a fish.

And Annika doesn't drink.

I'm going to get to the bottom of this.

"I'm going to put more bread in the oven," she says and stands from the table, pushing her way through the swinging door to the kitchen.

"I'll go see if she needs help," Rafe says and follows her.

Rich just rolls his eyes.

"I need to use the restroom. Is it just around the corner there, Rich?"

He nods and points to the hallway on the other side of the kitchen. There's another entrance to the kitchen on that side, so I stop and lean against the wall, just out of sight, listening to the conversation happening within.

"I've got this," Annika says.

"I can help. Jesus, A, what's wrong?"

"Nothing." I can picture the fake smile on her beautiful face. "Everything's great."

"Bullshit." Rafe lowers his voice now. "You look miserable."

"I—" There's no sound for a moment. "You shouldn't be in here."

"You never should have married that asshole," Rafe says. "You know it should have been me."

"And your father said no," she reminds him, and I stumble back in surprise. Annika wanted to marry Rafe Martinelli? Why would Carlo say no? Our families aren't enemies.

"Yeah, well, your uncle didn't like the idea, either."

Papa knew?

I scowl.

Why am I always the last to know about this stuff? And why didn't Annika confide in me?

I know it's not all about me, but it hurts my stupid feelings.

"Let's get this out to the table."

"Annika."

"Rafe, I can't do this. I'm a married woman whether I like it or not."

"And I'd say that you don't like it very much right now."

"That doesn't matter."

"Oh, yes, it does."

"I'm not talking about this anymore."

I walk around the corner in time to see Annika and Rafe coming out the other door, Rafe carrying the bread for the table.

I look at Rich. He doesn't even raise his eyes from his plate.

I feel like I've just entered an alternate universe.

"Shane got Ivie's number tonight," I inform Carmine as he unlocks the door of the Airbnb.

"I saw," he says and shakes his head. "I don't get it."

"Get what?"

"Nothing."

"No, you started it. What, exactly, don't you get?"

"Look, if I answer you, I'm going to sound like a huge asshole."

I cross my arms over my chest, raise a brow, and wait.

Carmine sighs painfully, pushes his hand through his hair, and then shrugs. "Okay. I like her. She seems like a nice woman."

"But?"

"But she's just not Shane's type."

"And what type is that, exactly?"

"You know..."—he gestures to me, waving his hand up and down—"he usually goes for the supermodel types."

"You do realize that even supermodels don't look like that in real life, right?"

"You do," he says without even thinking twice, and I have to blink at him.

Then I laugh.

"No, I don't. I think you're a little biased. Which is sweet. Ivie's awesome. She's funny and smart. And, yes, she's pretty. Shane isn't good enough for *her*."

"I told you I'd sound like a jackass."

"Sometimes the person we fall in love with isn't what we expect."

"He's not in love with her."

"Not yet." I kick off my shoes and walk over to the freezer, grabbing a tub of ice cream. "Something else happened tonight."

"What's that?"

"Did you see how unhappy Annika looked?"

"I saw that she and Rich are most likely fighting," he says. "It doesn't take a professional to see that. He's a douche."

"He didn't used to be." I shove a spoonful of Chunky Monkey into my mouth. "When they were dating, he was sweet. Laid-back. Even a little bit beta."

"*Beta*? What the hell does that mean?"

"You know, not alpha. Not in your face, or the one to put his foot down about things."

"So...soft."

"A little."

"I'm no beta."

I laugh again and wipe ice cream off my chin. "No, you're alpha all the way. I don't like that things seem to be changing for her so soon after their wedding. She looked sad and *scared*."

"Do you think he hurts her?"

Carmine's eyes darken. I know this is a sore spot for him.

And it's something I respect.

"I don't know." It's an honest answer. "But you can bet that I'm going to ask her. I didn't like that he told her what she could and couldn't eat."

"I caught that," Carmine says. "And he didn't like your response."

"How many fucks do you think I give about that?"

"Less than none."

"You'd be right. Oh, and there was something else."

He opens his mouth for a bite of my ice cream.

"I listened in on a conversation between Annika and Rafe in the kitchen."

"Busy little thing, weren't you?"

I ignore that and keep talking. "Did you know that your brother and Annika had a thing going? That they wanted to marry, but our fathers wouldn't allow it?"

Carmine's face blanks in surprise, and then he blinks rapidly.

"No fucking way."

"I heard it with my own two ears."

"He would have told me."

"And I would have said that she would have told *me*. But here we are, neither of us in the loop, and I know what I heard in that kitchen. He said that it should have been him. And she reminded him that your father said no."

Carmine swears under his breath. "Jesus. Why didn't he say something?"

"I think it's time I catch up with Annika for lunch. Just us girls. We have a lot of talking to do."

CHAPTER

TEN

~NADIA~

I'm loaded down with greasy burgers, fries, and shakes from another of my favorites here in Denver. Yes, I'm going to gain sixty-five pounds if I keep this up, but there's a method to my calorie-filled madness.

This is Annika's favorite meal in the whole world. And if I want to get information out of her, it won't hurt to feed her something extra delicious.

I walk into the medi-spa and smile at Ivie behind the front desk.

"Hey," she says with a bright smile. "You're right on time. The last patient just left, and Annika and I are officially free."

She clicks the mouse on the computer, then hurries over and locks the door.

"Annika is in her office, but we can have lunch in the conference room."

"Perfect. I brought a *ton* of food."

"You always were my favorite," Ivie says as she winks and knocks on Annika's door. "Nadia's here with food. Come join us."

"I'll be right there," Annika calls back.

"She's been in a mood today," Ivie says as she opens the door to the conference room. I set the bags of food on the table. "I've hardly seen her at all, and when I asked her what was going on, she blew me off. Very *not* like her. So, I'm glad you're here. Between the two of us, we'll get it out of her."

"I have plenty to get out of her," I reply and then sigh. "I hate feeling so disengaged from you guys. I miss you."

"You're here. We talk and hear from you. But we miss you, too. We need to be better about seeing each other more often."

"Agreed. I wonder what's going on with Annika." But I know. It's that asshole, Rich.

Ivie and I unpack the bags, and I just start to suck on the straw of my vanilla shake when Annika walks in.

I immediately know that something isn't right.

She doesn't look up as she sits in one of the comfortable chairs and starts unwrapping her burger.

"Thanks for lunch," she says.

"Look at me," I order her.

"Don't be silly—"

"Look at me, A."

She looks up, and I want to punch the wall. "What the hell happened?"

"What do you mean?"

Ivie leans in to examine Annika's face. "How did I miss it? Annika, you have a black eye. You tried to cover it up, but holy shit. What's going on?"

"Oh, it's nothing." Annika tries to laugh and pops a fry into her mouth. "I tripped while walking down the stairs, and—"

"No." My voice is hard and low and leaves no room for argument. "What. Happened. To you?"

With her eyes still trained on her fries, she shrugs a shoulder.

"I've been begging you to talk to me for days," Ivie says. Her voice shakes with emotion. "You can trust us. You know that."

"You're the only two I *can* trust," Annika whispers.

"Tell us the truth. Let us help." I reach over and take her hand in mine.

"I don't know who he is anymore," she begins. "As soon as we got married, everything changed. It was like a switch flipped, and he went from being a fun, laid-back man to the devil himself."

She rubs her forehead in agitation.

"Suddenly, he wants to control *everything*. Even what I eat. When he said last night that I should stick with salad, in front of all of you, I wanted the floor to open up and swallow me. I was *so* embarrassed."

"He said that you should get to see your family once in a while," I prompt her. "What was that about?"

"I've been telling him for weeks that I wanted to go see you or invite you here, and he kept telling me no. No way. He's systematically cut me off from my parents, from everyone I love—except for Ivie because we work together."

"Just let him try to cut me off from you," Ivie says with fire in her voice. "I'll cut his fucking balls off first."

"Down, girl." I smile at an irate Ivie. "Clearly, Rich can't get rid of us. We're here to stay. This all started after the wedding?"

"On the wedding night," she confirms. "We went to the honeymoon suite, and I took a bite of some cake—we had so much wedding cake left —and he took it away from me and tossed it in the trash. Said I'd never eat that garbage again. That I was too fat."

I've never experienced rage so swift and all-encompassing. I wish he was here right now so I could bloody his damn face.

"Since then, he's counted every calorie. I have to keep a log of what I eat and give it to him at the end of the day. If he thinks I'm lying, well..."

She stops talking, and Ivie and I share a look.

"He what, Annika?"

She simply points to her eye.

"He's been hitting you this whole time?" Ivie demands.

"Not often, but more than once is too many times."

"Why didn't you tell us?" I ask. "Why didn't you say something?"

"If I tell, the family will kill him."

"So?"

Annika shakes her head. "I don't want him *dead*. I just don't want him. But I'm married to him now. I'm just...stuck."

"Bullshit."

"No way."

Ivie and I speak in unison.

"Divorce *is* an option," I say. "My father will absolutely approve of that, especially when I tell him about the abuse."

"You can't." Annika grabs onto me, her movements desperate. "You can't tell. You have to promise me that you won't tell *anyone.*"

"Annika—"

"Promise," she continues. "I don't want them to hurt him."

"And why not?" I stand and pace the room, so frustrated that I don't know what to do with myself. "Annika, he's hurting you. Daily. Why shouldn't the family take care of it? Even if it's not death, he should be ostracized. He can go fend for himself. There's no place for him here."

"I agree," Ivie says. "You're not this woman. You're not a punching bag. No one is, and you have the resources to get out of this."

Annika sighs and rests her face in her hands.

"I can't leave him. Not yet."

"What else is happening that you're not telling us?"

"I think he's involved in something bad. I don't know what, but I have to keep an eye on him for a little while longer."

"To what end? I refuse to let you get killed over this, Annika." Ivie stands and leans over toward her friend. "You don't have anything to prove."

"I just need a little time," Annika insists.

I want to rail at her, and I can see that Ivie feels the same. But my cousin has dug her heels in.

"If he hits you again, you fucking call me." My voice is ice. "You call me, and I'll come get you."

"Okay."

I want to ask about Rafe. I want to convince her to leave that pitiful excuse for a man *today.*

But she's had enough.

Ivie and I share a long look. The silent message is clear.

We'll watch, and we'll protect her.

Two hours later, I can't get to Carmine fast enough. But on my way to the Marinelli office, I call my brother.

"Thought you didn't want my help," he says, and I roll my eyes.

"Don't be a baby. I have a question. When Annika started dating Rich, and when he proposed, did the family do a standard background check on him?"

"Yeah, I ran it myself. He's so clean; he's boring. And his family is the same. Why?"

"I just left Annika."

I hesitate. I don't trust Alex with much, but he and Annika were close when we were younger. I think he'd want to know about this.

"Let's just say that Rich isn't the happy-go-lucky guy we all thought he was."

"What does that mean? Is he hurting her?"

I sigh. "I was at their house for dinner last night, and he was a major ass. The way he spoke to her, the way he looked at her, it was *not* good. And today, she had a black eye."

"What the fuck?"

"It just doesn't make any sense, so I wanted to reach out and ask if you'd run the background. I should have known that it was done, but I needed to double-check."

"If he's a con man, it slipped past me."

That wouldn't surprise me. Alex is lazy, and if Papa gave him the task of running the check, it wouldn't shock me if he just looked at the surface and then let it go.

Except this is *Annika.* And Alex has always had a soft spot for our cousin.

"What are you going to do now?" he asks.

"She asked me not to do anything for a little while, so I'll just be here in case she needs me."

That's not the whole truth, but he doesn't need to know the rest.

"Keep me posted, please," he says, his voice softening. "If this continues, we'll take care of it."

"Yeah. We will. Okay, I'll let you know if anything else happens."

He clicks off without saying goodbye, and I hurry into the office to see the three Martinelli brothers all huddled around computers.

They are a sight to behold. Carmine and Shane are both tall, dark, and handsome, with chocolate eyes. Rafe is on the lighter side with blue eyes, but there's no mistaking them for siblings. And just walking into this room would send a normal woman's blood pressure into the stroke-zone.

"I might have something," I say as I walk into the room. All three heads come up to look at me.

"Hello," Carmine says as he stands and pulls me to him for a kiss. Right there, in front of the others. "I haven't seen you all day."

"Don't get mushy in front of your brothers."

"I'll get mushy wherever I damn well please."

I laugh as Shane clears his throat.

"Stop pawing at her and let the woman talk."

"Yeah." I slap at Carmine's shoulder as I pull away. "Stop pawing at me."

"You didn't seem to mind last night."

"Really?" Rafe demands.

"Fine." Carmine lets me go, and I push my hair away from my face.

"Okay, so last night, something seemed very *off* with Annika."

"Clearly, she and the new husband are having issues," Shane says with a nod. "You could cut the tension with a fucking knife."

"Definitely," I agree. "And he just wasn't acting like himself. That jerk isn't the guy we all knew before the wedding."

My eyes are on Rafe as I speak. His face is rigid, and he clenches his jaw as I keep talking.

"So, today, I decided to go see her, take her lunch, and do some digging. After all, Annika and Ivie are my two closest friends in the world, and if Annika is hurting, I want to know why. And I want to make someone pay.

"When I got there, I discovered that she had a black eye."

"What the fuck?" Rafe asks as he comes out of his seat. "The bastard hit her?"

"Yeah." My voice quiets. "He did. And he's done more than that."

I relay what happened during my lunch with my friends. When I finish, all three men are pacing the office, each with mutiny written all over his handsome face.

"I'll fucking kill him with my bare hands," Rafe growls, but I shake my head.

"She wants time. And here's the part that doesn't add up, though I didn't say anything to her at the time. She thinks he's up to something."

"Up to what?" Carmine asks.

"She didn't say, but my alarm bells went off like crazy. I asked Alex if the family did a standard background check before the wedding, and he said that he did it. But my brother is lazy, and I know he didn't dive very deep. He couldn't have."

"I can go so deep, Richard will feel me in his kidneys," Shane says, reaching for the computer. His fingers fly over the keyboard. "Yeah, this first pass is pretty standard. Credit score is seven-fifty. No jail. Really nothing to report at all."

"That's too tidy," Rafe says, his face still set in hard lines. "That reeks of cover-up."

"Agreed. It would be easier if I had fingerprints."

"Be right back." I turn to leave, but Carmine stops me.

"You're not going by yourself."

"Well, then get a move on, and let's go. I'll call Annika from the car. She can meet us there. Let's nail this whole mess on this slimeball."

Carmine and I hurry to his rental. I barely have time to fasten my seatbelt before he's peeling out of the parking lot and merging onto the freeway.

"How could my family let this happen?" I wonder out loud. "How the fuck did Rich make his slimy way into my family and start killing people? And why would he do it at his own wedding?"

"Smoke and mirrors," Carmine says. "If it happened at the wedding, he'd be the last person anyone would look at. Son of a *bitch*."

"Why does a random doctor from Denver want to kill your father?" I wonder out loud. "It doesn't make any sense."

"Shane's still digging. I don't buy this whole boring suburban doctor bit. He's hiding something, and we'll find out what it is. In the meantime, we need to get those prints, and we need to make sure Annika is safe. I don't like her being there with him."

"I don't, either." I shake my head and watch the city zoom by. "It was all I could do not to kidnap her and make her come with me. I don't want that asshole anywhere near her, ever again."

I'm just about to call Annika when my phone rings in my hand. "Hey, I was just going to call you."

"I need you." Annika breathes hard in my ear. She sounds panicked.

"What's wrong?"

"I need you to come to my house."

"Carmine and I are headed there now. That's why I was going to call. Are you hurt?"

"No, but if he gets here before you, I will be. Hurry. Please, hurry."

She hangs up, and Carmine steps on the gas.

"You heard?"

"Yeah." The set of his mouth is grim. "I don't know what I expected when we came to Denver, but this isn't it."

"No. It's not."

I want to thank him. His family is under no obligation to help with this. But I've learned one thing in the months I've known him: Carmine is a man of honor.

All the Martinellis are.

They may be part of a mob family, but they do what's right. And my instincts weren't wrong when I decided to start trusting him.

He's become much more than just a job to me. There are feelings in play that I haven't taken the time to dissect, to just *be* with and figure out.

There just hasn't been time. I need to do some sorting, determine where my head and heart are.

But for now, it's enough to be able to depend on him—and to know that I'm safe.

Carmine drives through the open gates of Annika's drive, and when we pull up to the front door, he cuts the engine, and we're both out of the car like a shot.

Annika opens the door, her eyes wide in shock.

"What is it?"

"Oh, God."

CHAPTER
ELEVEN
~CARMINE~

"I knew it," Annika says as we hurry into the house behind her. "I knew something was wrong. I just found this."

She practically runs into an office at the end of a long hallway as if she has to get there before whatever's in there disappears.

"Is he here?" Nadia asks.

"No." Annika's voice shakes as she points to a trunk on the floor next to her husband's desk. "Look in there. Rich always tells me to stay out of this trunk, that it's none of my fucking business what's in here."

"Lovely way to talk to your wife," I mutter as I open the lid and stare down at what must be a dozen sandwich bags full of pills, a bundle of hundred-dollar bills, and a piece of paper.

"It's an address," Annika says when I pick up the paper. I open it, and sure enough, it's an address.

449 Oak Ave. 4pm

"He's a fucking drug dealer." Annika sits on the arm of a sofa and stares blindly ahead. "He's dealing. I want no part of this. I've worked damn hard to stay *out* of the illegal scene, Nadia. You know I have."

"I know."

"Where is he?" I ask as I turn to look at the two women. "Where is he right now?"

"His office, I would guess," Annika replies. "And if you're going there, I'm going with you because I want to give him a piece of my damn mind."

RICHARD'S OFFICE is across town, so it takes us a good thirty minutes to get there.

I don't know what kind of pills are in those packages, but I have a feeling it's the same drug that killed Armando at the wedding. I took a bag and the computer mouse from the desk to give to Shane for prints.

The three of us march through the medical plaza and up a flight of stairs.

"His office isn't attached to the clinic," Annika says, pointing to a door next to the clinic. "He likes having a separate entrance."

"How convenient," I mutter and knock once before turning the knob. To my surprise, it isn't locked.

"Well, shit," Nadia murmurs as she holds Annika back. "No, baby. No, you don't want to see this."

"Yes, I do." Annika forces her way through, and all three of us stare at Richard, slumped over his desk, white foam coming from his mouth. "Oh, Jesus."

"Keep her back," I say to Nadia. She nods, and I step closer to the desk. More of the same pills are in piles on the top as if he'd been counting them out to go into bags. Could he have accidentally taken one and killed himself?

Or did he do it on purpose?

Without touching the body, I search the space. I see no note, and nothing seems out of place.

I reach into his pockets and find his phone and wallet.

"Do you know the code to the phone?" I ask Annika.

She just blinks, staring at her husband.

"Annika."

"No. He wouldn't tell me."

"Can I take it to Shane?"

I just keep adding things to my brother's to-do list.

"Yes. My God, he's dead."

"We're going to leave everything exactly as it is," I say and take her arms in my hands. "We're going to sneak out of here like we were never here, and then we're going to call the police."

"Carmine," Nadia says in surprise.

"I could call the cleanup crew, but if I do, he'll go missing. His family will look for him. If we call the police, it'll be wrapped up as a drug situation gone wrong, and Rich's family can bury him."

"And I can play the part of the devastated newlywed," Annika says bitterly.

"It's your call," I tell her. "How do you want to play it? Either way, you have to lie."

"Call the cops. His family will know that he was a drug dealer and a piece of shit. And they can bury him. But I won't act the part of the devastated widow. He didn't earn that."

"Okay, let's go. When we get to your house, you can call the office and ask them to get Rich from his office."

She nods, and we leave the way we came.

"I HAVE prints and drugs for you." I toss both items on the desk as Shane looks up in surprise.

"Where'd you find drugs?"

I fill him in on everything that happened over the past few hours.

"So, the fucker's dead?" Shane shakes his head. "Well, without the prints, I can tell you that I found quite a bit that piece of garbage, Alex, missed. Rich never went to college. It was all a front. And he didn't work at that clinic. He rented the office next door and pretended to go there to *work* every day."

"Holy shit."

"I'm still digging into some stuff, but these prints will help. If my suspicions are right, Rich was behind everything all along. He tried to kill Pop, he sent out the feelers to New York, and when that fell through, he had that kid killed."

"But why? It just doesn't make sense." I shake my head, perplexed. "Why start wars with the mafia when he just came into the family?"

"Good question. Maybe he thought he was proving his worth to Nadia's dad so he could start working more intensely for the family. Who knows? How's Annika holding up?"

"She's damn pissed off."

"Yeah, I would be, too."

"Nadia stayed at the office with her. The police are probably there by now."

My brother's brow lifts. "Police?"

I tell him the plan and remind him that we have a few contacts in the Denver PD to make things go down the way we want them to.

"Looks like we have our man," Shane says. "Right here in Denver, all this time."

"It's a hell of a thing," I agree. "I wish he'd been alive when I found him. I'd have liked to break his fingers and then shove a pill down his throat myself."

"Are you sure it was self-inflicted?"

I shrug. "My gut says so. I think he poisoned himself by accident because he was an arrogant idiot. He was counting pills on his desk. No gloves."

Shane clicks his tongue. "All he had to do was lick his finger or something, and it would all be over."

"My thoughts exactly."

"So, what now?"

I shake my head. "I'm not entirely sure. I still have questions. Why would he have Nadia attacked?"

"Because she was digging around, and he didn't want her finding him out."

"You're right. It makes sense."

"I'm still going to keep digging on him. I want to know more, but I have a few other jobs coming up, so it'll take some time."

"He's dead. I'd say there's no hurry. Where's Rocco?"

"He got called back to Seattle. He's probably in the air by now."

I nod. "Thank you. For all of your help. You didn't have to."

"It's what family does," he reminds me. "Now, I'm going to load up and get back to my place in the mountains. The city gives me hives."

I laugh as Shane closes his computer and shoves it into his bag. He's a recluse, through and through.

"I'll lock up behind you."

"Want me to call Pop?"

"Nah, I'll do that, too."

It's late when Nadia finally walks into the Airbnb. She texted a while ago to tell me she was on her way.

Just from her text alone, I could tell she was exhausted.

And sad for Annika.

Nadia may do her best to hide things behind her hard exterior, but she's full of love and compassion, especially for those she loves.

She shuts the door behind her, then turns. Her eyes widen as she takes in the room. I've lit several dozen candles, and I have food waiting in the oven. But first, I'm going to pamper her a bit.

"Follow me." I take her hand in mine and kiss it, then lead her back to the bathroom, where a hot bath waits for her.

"Roses in the bath?"

"That's right."

She doesn't say a word as I help her out of her black shirt and blue jeans. When she's naked, I keep her steady as she steps into the bath.

"I didn't even realize I needed this."

"I did." I kiss the top of her head and let her soak. The wine I bought —Nadia's favorite—is chilled and ready, so I pop the cork and fill a glass. "Sip this while you soak. Just sip it. I don't want you to get drunk on me."

"What did I do to deserve this five-star treatment?"

I squat next to her and tuck her short, blond hair behind her ear. "We've been so caught up in things since we got here that I haven't done enough things like this."

"Is this goodbye?"

The question is a whisper.

"What do you mean?"

"Now that we know who was behind the murder, there's no need to work together anymore."

I lick my lips and watch her face intently. "Is that what you want? To go our separate ways?"

"It's the way it is. We did our parts. It's done. Now, we move on."

I nod and stand, walking out of the bathroom. She didn't answer the question. She didn't say that parting is what she wants.

It's definitely *not* what I want.

I pull out the steaks, potatoes, and salad, get everything plated and ready to eat, then walk back in to check on Nadia.

She's not in the bath.

She's in the bedroom, packing her bag, wearing nothing but a robe.

Excellent.

"What are you doing?"

"Packing, obviously."

I nod once. "Why don't you eat before you do that? I have dinner ready."

"I'm not hungry."

"Just humor me."

I take her hand once more and tug her behind me to the kitchen, where our food awaits. She sniffs and then softens.

"You know I can't resist steak."

"I know." I hold a chair for her, then sit next to her and start cutting into my ribeye. "How is Annika tonight?"

"She was sleeping when I left. We went through some things in Rich's office, but then the police came, and then his family. It was just a mess. I got everyone but Ivie out, fed her, and then poured her into bed. Ivie's staying the night with her."

"She'll have a rough few weeks, but then she'll be able to move on with her life."

"I know. How do you move on from that, though?" She takes a bite of salad, seeming to think it over. "She was convinced that she knew him, was head over heels in love with him, and it turns out he was scamming her the whole time. How do you ever let yourself trust again? Fall in love again?"

"I think it takes a lot of time and healing." I pass her a hot roll. "She may need some therapy. Does your family have access to a psychologist?"

"Yes, my father has one on staff. She'll have a lot of support and anything she might need available to her, of course. I just feel for her."

"You love her." I take her hand in mine and squeeze.

"Yeah, and I can count on one hand the number of people who mean something to me in this world, and she's in the top three."

"Who are the other two?"

She frowns, pulls her hand out of mine, and returns her attention to eating. "How are Shane and Rafe?"

"Shane's back at his place in the mountains, and Rocco was pulled to something in Seattle."

"I can't believe you guys still call him Rocco."

I shrug a shoulder, watching her eat. Her lean throat moves as she swallows her food, her eyes heavy with fatigue.

She's magnificent.

And after tonight, she'll know without a shadow of a doubt that I do *not* want to say goodbye.

"I'm thinking Paris," I say, earning a surprised glance.

"For what?"

"For our first stop." I eat some potatoes. "A week at the Ritz would be nice. And then I think we should spend another week in the south of France, on the beach. There's a lovely resort there that I'll arrange."

"Did you hit your head today?" she demands.

"Not to my knowledge, no."

She takes another bite of steak and watches me. "So, you're going to take a several-week vacation in Europe? Awesome. Have fun."

"Not me." I wipe my mouth on a napkin. "*We.*"

"Who's we?"

"You, my lovely Nadia. And me. Us."

"But I thought you said—"

"I didn't say anything. I asked you if it was what *you* wanted, and you didn't answer the damn question."

"Okay, fine. I don't want to say goodbye. Is that what you want to hear?"

"Yes, actually. It is."

"But I don't see an alternative. I live in Atlanta. You live in Seattle. We're not working together anymore."

"The last time I checked, we're both adults."

"You know that it doesn't matter for us. Our lives aren't ours, Carmine."

"Do you really think our fathers will lose their damn minds if we spend some time together on vacation? I think they have enough to worry about."

She doesn't respond to that.

"So, we'll spend some time in Paris, and then in Cannes. We'll shop, we'll eat, and we'll explore. And I'll make love to you day and night, damn it. I'm going to soak you into every pore of my body. When it's all over, you'll be sick of me."

"Doubtful," she whispers.

"Sweetheart, don't cry."

"I'm not crying. There's an onion in my salad."

I scoop her into my lap and kiss her softly. "Let's enjoy each other for a while. No pretenses, and no tracking down murdering assholes."

"I should stay here for a couple of days to make sure Annika's okay."

"Of course." I kiss her once more. "We'll stay here for as long as you need."

"Carmine."

"Hmm?" I kiss down her neck, unable to resist her.

"I'm not going to fall in love with you."

I can't help but smile against her skin. She's everything I've ever wanted. She's my match in every way. And my opposite.

"No, there will be none of that."

But there already is. And we both know it. We're just too fucking stubborn to admit it.

CHAPTER
TWELVE
~NADIA~

"He's in the ground, and it's time to move on."

Annika rakes her hand through her long, blond hair and blows out a shaky breath. She's sitting on the couch, her feet tucked under her, still in her black mourning dress.

Ivie sits next to me. Now that the guests have gone and it's just the three of us, we've kicked off our shoes.

"I didn't think his mom would ever leave," I say, staring down into my wine. "She just kept going room to room, loading up everything she could into her arms like she was on a game show or something."

"I don't even care." Annika turns tired eyes to me. "She can have it all."

"And she'll take it." Ivie's voice is heavy with bitterness. And I can't blame her. "She has no right to any of it. You're his wife."

"Do you think I want it?" Annika demands. "I couldn't care less about the clock he bought in Germany or any of the other *fancy* knick-knacks he had lying around. I'd just sell or donate it all anyway. There are some papers that I need to go through myself, and I have my things, of course, but I can't get out of here soon enough."

"Did you say that the realtor is coming tomorrow?"

Annika nods. "I don't know when I'll be able to put the house on the market, but as soon as the lawyer gives me the go-ahead, I'll list it and find something else."

"You should buy one of those fun little condos downtown," Ivie suggests. "Right in the heart of the hustle and bustle. You can shop, eat, go to shows or games."

"I don't even know if I want to stay in Denver," she admits softly.

"What about Seattle?" Annika's mouth firms at my suggestion. "It's a great city, and I'm sure the Martinellis would give you the green light to live there."

"No."

I sigh and tip back my head. I'm done beating around the bush on this one.

"What in the hell is up with you and Rafe?"

Annika blinks rapidly, and Ivie scowls, first at me and then at our friend.

"I don't know what you mean."

"Oh, yeah, you do. I overheard you two in the kitchen when we were all here for dinner."

"It's not polite to eavesdrop, you know."

"Yeah, well, I'm not sorry."

"Wait." Ivie shakes her head and sits forward. "I'm missing something. Annika had something going with *Rafe*?"

"It was years ago," Annika says with a sigh. "We were kids. We'd see each other at things like weddings and such, and we both went to college at Duke."

"Rafe went to college at Duke?" Ivie asks, clearly impressed. "Wow."

"There's chemistry there," Annika whispers. "And, yeah, we saw each other for a while. But you guys, we're in mob families. Opposing ones. My parents would have thrown a fit."

I frown, thinking it over. "We aren't exactly at war with the Martinellis."

"But we're not on the best of terms, either. The betrothal between Alex and Elena fell through, and then they assumed our family had killed theirs for years. All of that happened at the same time. So you can't tell me that they would have welcomed my affair with Rafe with open arms."

I nod and shrug a shoulder. "Okay, so the timing was bad. But we're on better terms now. And if Rafe's who you want, I think you could make that happen."

"I don't want Rafe or anyone else involved in the organization." Annika's voice is clipped. "I never have. I thought I'd found a nice, settled, professional, and we'd live a boring, happy life in the suburbs. Look where that got me."

"It makes sense that you're not exactly ready to get back on the horse, so to speak, right away," Ivie says. "There's no rush."

"I don't know how I can ever trust anyone again," Annika says. "And while I do trust Rafe, I know that he's not the one for me. Not for the long haul."

"Why didn't you tell me that you had a thing going with him?" I ask her.

"Honestly, it was kind of fun to have a secret fling with someone I shouldn't. It felt taboo and reckless. But then I fell in love with him." She whispers the last three words, and I can't help but cross to her and hold her hand.

What is it about the Martinelli brothers?

"But it was a long time ago, and my life has changed. And I still don't want to be involved in the family business. He's neck-deep in it. It wouldn't work."

"I understand what you mean."

"Now, you tell us about Carmine," Ivie says with a smile. "Come on, spill it."

I don't want to hold back, so I tell them everything, from my father asking me to keep an eye on Carmine, to him *finding* me at the resort in Miami, and everything that went down since then.

It just feels so damn good to tell someone I trust what's going on.

"And now he's going to take you to France?"

I nod, thinking it over. "I should talk to Papa before he goes back to Atlanta. Make sure he doesn't have a problem with it."

"How does it feel to be in love with Carmine?" Annika asks.

"I'm not in love with him." I shake my head and stand to pace. "I mean, I *like* him. We have a good time together. The sex is *crazy*. And over the past few months, I've grown to trust him—which surprised me the most."

"But you don't love him." Ivie's tongue is in her cheek, and I glare at her.

"No. I don't love him."

Even I hear the lie.

"We're enjoying each other."

"Enjoy away," Annika says. "You've earned it."

"Right. I discovered that your husband was a killer and a drug dealer. I don't feel like I've earned a posh European vacation."

"I discovered it," she reminds me. "It's not your fault that I fell in love with a liar. Now, you can stop babysitting me because I'm a damn strong woman who can figure this out. And I have Ivie here. Go have crazy amazing French sex."

I giggle. "Is French sex different from regular sex?"

"Go find out," Ivie says. "We've got things handled here. I'll keep Rich's mom under control."

"Oh." I turn to her and prop my hands on my hips. "Did Shane ever call you?"

"Yeah." A smile covers her pretty face. "We've talked a bit. All on the phone. He's...interesting. Intense. Sexy as all get-out."

"What is it about the Martinelli brothers?" I voice the question this time, and we all giggle. "They're too sexy for their own good."

"I'm glad I caught you." I walk into my father's office, shut the door, and walk around the desk to hug him. "How are you, Papa?"

"I'm always better when my daughter comes to see me." He grins and kisses my cheek. "What are you up to, little one?"

"I just wanted to talk to you before you went back to Atlanta." I sit on the desk next to him and let my feet dangle, the way I've done since I was a small girl. "I haven't spent much time with you in a while."

"You've been busy," he says, leaning back in his wide leather chair. "I hope you're planning to take some time off now."

"Actually, that's what I wanted to talk to you about." I clear my throat. "Carmine invited me to go to France with him for a couple of weeks."

Something sparks in my father's eyes, but then he blinks, and it's gone.

"And did you accept?"

"Yes, but I thought I should run it by you, in case it's something you'd rather I not do."

"You're an adult, Nadia. You can spend time with whomever you choose."

My eyes find his. "You know that isn't true."

Papa takes a long, deep breath. "It's true. There are men that I would not be okay with you spending time with. Like Billy Sergi."

"*I'd* not be okay if I spent time with him." I wrinkle my nose. "The little worm."

"I hope you enjoy yourselves," Papa says. "There's a restaurant on the Seine that I highly recommend."

"Thank you." I bend down and kiss his cheek again. "I miss you, Papa. When I get back, let's spend a weekend together."

"I'd love nothing more, little one. Be safe. Tell Carmine I'll break both his legs if even a hair is disturbed on my precious daughter's head."

I laugh, but I know the threat is real. "No need to be violent. I'd better go pack. I think we're leaving this evening."

"Nadia."

I turn back to him with raised brows. "Yes, Papa."

"I love you."

"I love you, too."

"I think that's it." I walk through the Airbnb, making sure that I didn't forget anything. "I brought more than I thought."

"We shopped in New York," Carmine reminds me as he sets our suitcases by the front door.

"Ah, yes, how could I forget New York?"

He catches my hand and pulls me against him, then nibbles the side of my mouth. I immediately turn to mushy goo.

This man is potent.

"We're trying to leave," I remind him. "Not get naked again."

"I'll get you naked on the plane."

He lets go, and I stare after him. "On the *plane*? But we won't be alone."

"Close enough. And I have a very discreet staff."

And with that, he walks out the door, pulling two of the suitcases behind him, a backpack slung over his broad shoulder.

It's unfair that simply toting luggage is sexy on this man.

I grab my smaller bag, my handbag, and one last roller suitcase and let the door close behind me.

Our time in Denver is over. Now, we're on to France.

Denver International Airport is quite far from the city, so I sit back, expecting at least a forty-five-minute drive, but the driver leaves the freeway sooner than expected and takes us to a smaller airfield closer to the city.

"This is easier," Carmine says simply. He's holding my hand, softly rubbing his thumb over my knuckles.

Now that our attention has turned from finding a killer to just enjoying each other, he's much more physically affectionate than he was. And that's saying something because Carmine's always been handsy.

Not that I'm complaining. A girl could do far worse than having Carmine Martinelli's hands on her.

I'm not typically an affectionate woman, but with Carmine, the rules seem to fly out the window.

"This plane is bigger." I glance at Carmine. "You have *two* private jets?"

"No." He leans over and kisses my nose. "We have two private jets and a helicopter. Rocco flies the 'copter. I usually prefer the smaller plane, but this one is more appropriate for trans-Atlantic travel."

"Oh, right. Yes, it's better for *trans-Atlantic travel.*" I press my lips together so I don't laugh. I love teasing him. "You're so fancy."

"And you've just earned your first spanking."

He doesn't even look at me. Doesn't smile. He just steps out of the car and offers me his hand.

I don't bother sputtering a protest.

The ground crew is already loading our luggage onto the plane. We're greeted at the top of the stairs by a man in his fifties, wearing a simple black suit and a red tie. His hair is silver, threaded through with just a few dark strands, and he has a bushy mustache over his top lip.

He looks like someone's grandfather.

"Good evening, Mr. Martinelli. Ms. Tarenkov. It's a pleasure to have you aboard tonight. Please, make yourselves comfortable."

"Thank you, Charles," Carmine says with a nod. "Please let the pilot know that we're ready whenever he's given the okay to take off."

"Of course, sir."

I smile at the polite Charles and follow Carmine down a short hallway to a lounge area on the plane. There are cream-colored leather couches, a faux fireplace with a television hung above it, and a wet bar.

"We'll spend most of the next nine hours or so in here, but there's a bedroom back there." He points and then leads me farther back on the plane to show me a small bedroom with a king-sized bed and little else. "In case you want to sleep. Or...other things."

"I liked the couches," I reply and turn on my heel to return to the lounge. I sit, fasten my seatbelt, and pull my iPad out of my bag.

Carmine sits across from me just as Charles returns with a tray in his hands.

"What can I get you to drink?"

"Just water for me," Carmine says.

"A Coke would be lovely."

Charles nods regally and turns to the wet bar to fetch us our drinks. Carmine holds my gaze with his as Charles fills glasses, delivers them to us, and then walks back to the galley.

"I could have gotten this myself if I'd known it was right there."

"Charles enjoys his job," Carmine replies. "We have lots of food aboard, as well, and he'll serve us dinner. And breakfast in the morning."

"Just like first class."

"Admit it. This is much better than first class."

I smirk into my glass. "It's a small step up."

Carmine's brown eyes are full of humor when Charles returns with menus so we can choose our entrées for dinner, and then the plane begins to move.

Within just a few minutes, we're airborne.

Once we've reached cruising altitude, Carmine unclips his seatbelt and moves over next to me. But rather than kiss me, or hold me against him, he simply holds out his hand.

"Give me your foot."

"Which one?"

"You choose."

I raise my left foot, and he starts to knead my arch with his thumb. I moan and lean my head back, closing my eyes as I enjoy the best foot rub of my life.

"You're good with your hands."

"I'm good with a lot of things," he reminds me. "I plan to spend the next nine hours reminding you."

"I'm so glad I'm getting a refresher course." I snort. "I think I've forgotten everything."

"You're extra sassy tonight."

I don't lift my head off the seat, but I turn to look at him. "I'm sorry. I don't mean to be difficult."

"I'm not complaining. You were tense in Denver. Worried. And as soon as we got on this plane, it was as though a huge weight was lifted."

"That's how it felt." I sigh, letting the tension from the last couple of weeks go. "I'm glad it's over. Still, I hurt for Annika. But we had a great talk last night, and I know she's going to be okay."

"She's going to be amazing. And now it's time for you to rest, relax, and let me take care of you for a while."

"I'm perfectly capable—"

He covers my mouth with his, playfully at first, but then it turns intense, and all I can do is grip onto him and return the kiss.

Finally, he pulls away and kisses my chin lightly. "Just enjoy, Nadia. For once in your life, don't overthink it."

"You talked me into it."

CHAPTER
THIRTEEN
~CARMINE~

"You could shop anywhere in Paris," I say to Nadia as she leads me down a little cobblestone street tucked back in a corner off the left bank of the Seine in Paris. "And this is where you want to go?"

"Yes." She tugs on my hand and smiles at me. We arrived in Paris yesterday morning and spent the day in our suite at the Ritz, sleeping and fucking, recovering from jet lag.

This morning, she was ready to explore the city.

After I had my way with her in the shower.

"There's a little shop tucked away back here," she says as we stroll along the uneven sidewalk. "And it's the best. Just wait until you see it."

There are many *little shops* along this street, all selling different things—clothes, jewelry, art. But the store she stops at has me scratching my head.

"This?"

"Yep." She climbs the three uneven steps and tries the knob, but it's locked. "Jean Luc must be on a break. Oh, there he is."

She grins as an older man with little hair, wrinkled, leathery skin, and what's left of a cigarette burning in his mouth walks up with a frown.

298

"I only come for you," he says gruffly.

They don't hug or even exchange pleasantries, but he unlocks the door, and Nadia steps inside with an excited flourish.

I'm even more confused when I follow her.

The store is no bigger than my bathroom at home, and every surface is covered with things. If I were a claustrophobic man, I'd turn around and leave.

But I'm far too fascinated to leave now.

"Oh, Jean Luc, you never disappoint."

The man simply sits on a stool behind a tiny glass counter and watches Nadia. "I have a new Chanel. Vintage from 1968."

"Let me see it."

He reaches under the counter, pulls the signature black bag out, tugs a handbag free, and sets it on the glass.

"Oh, she's pretty. And the leather has really stood up well."

"It was hardly used, in all these years," Jean Luc replies. "I know you're fond of Chanel."

"Who isn't?" She grins. "I'll be hitting up Angelina tomorrow."

"Such a tourist trap now." He clicks his tongue.

"Yes, but *she* went there. Every day," Nadia reminds him. "And I do enjoy that hot chocolate."

"Who does not enjoy a cup of *le chocolat chaud* now and again?" he says, and unless I'm seeing things, he actually smiles at her. "Eight thousand."

Nadia's brows climb. "That's a little steep."

I want to interject. Eight thousand euros for a *used* handbag?

Jean Luc shakes his head and gives her a morose look as if she's physically hurting him. "Seven, then."

"Five," she counters.

"Nadia, you pain me. You can't find vintage like this, in this condition. I could sell to many others for more than five."

"Then sell it to them." She shrugs a shoulder as if it makes no difference to her, and Jean Luc sighs heavily.

"Six, and no less."

"I can live with six." She nods happily. "Done. Now, do you have a black Hermes Kelly?"

Jean Luc's eyes narrow for a moment as if he's pondering the question, but something tells me the man knows exactly what he has.

"For you? I will show you this."

He walks to a cupboard and pulls out another handbag, setting it on the glass next to the Chanel. A black handbag with a top handle and a gold clasp.

"Oh, she's beautiful. What year?"

"2004," he says. "Also, never used. Sat on a closet shelf for years."

He pulls out a pair of gloves before opening the bag and then showing it off to Nadia.

I'm lost. Who is Kelly, and why does she have a handbag named after her? I start to ask when Jean Luc tells her the price.

My eyes widen at the five figures that just came out of his mouth.

But Nadia doesn't even blink as she looks it over.

"Not even a scratch on the hardware," she murmurs. Her hands lovingly caress the leather as if she's touching a lover.

As if she's touching *me*.

"Jean Luc, you just sold yourself a Kelly. I'll take both."

"I have new jewelry," he begins, but Nadia shakes her head with a laugh.

"I'm going to stop while I'm ahead. But thank you. And thank you for opening your shop just for me. On a *Tuesday* morning."

"The French don't keep American hours," he reminds her, but his eyes are full of humor. "Who is your man?"

"I'm sorry, I got so excited, I completely lost my manners. Jean Luc, this is Carmine."

I shake the other man's hand, surprised by his firm grip. "It's nice to meet you."

"And you. Coming to Paris to fall in love is always a good idea."

This makes Nadia blink rapidly and seems to catch her off guard.

"Paris is called the city of love for a reason, no?" he continues as he gets the two new purchases ready for Nadia to take with her. "I thought Nadia would never find her man, but I see I was wrong. You've been coming to see me for how long now? Six years?"

"About that," she says quietly, clearly uncomfortable, but I step forward and take her hand in mine, giving it a squeeze.

"Six years, she always comes alone. Such a beautiful woman. I think she should be with someone. Not me. I am too old. But someone."

He takes her credit card and expertly uses the new machine discreetly tucked to the side.

"So I'm happy you called and came in today and brought your Carmine." He passes the card back and asks her to sign the slip. "I will worry less."

"Jean Luc, you're the sweetest." Nadia leans over and kisses his cheek. "You don't have to worry about me. I'm perfectly fine."

With fondness, he tucks an extra little box into Nadia's bag and walks us to the door.

"Enjoy your time in Paris. You're welcome to come see me anytime."

"My credit card is already weeping," Nadia says playfully. "But you know I'll come see you every time I'm here. Take care, Jean Luc."

He waves us off, and we stroll away. I take the bag to carry and lean over to kiss her temple.

"That made you uncomfortable."

"I've never known that man to talk so much," she says. "He's always so quiet. I assumed he didn't speak English well. Then, I bring you with me, and he's Chatty Charlie. It's just weird."

"No, weird is paying what you just did on used purses."

She gives me the side-eye and then raises her chin defiantly. "You just don't understand."

"Then explain it to me. I'd love to see what you do when you look at those bags."

"Okay." She nods and then offers me a grin. "I'm getting hungry. Let's go to Café Flore for lunch. We can chat about it there. It's not far."

"You've spent a lot of time in Paris," I comment as we make our way to the café.

"I wasn't lying when I told you that it's my favorite city. When I don't have anywhere to be, I come here. I roam the streets, wander the museums, you name it."

"And meet interesting Frenchmen who sell you old accessories."

She smirks as we cross the street to the café. We're seated, and to my utter shock, Nadia orders our lunch in perfect French.

"What?" she says when she turns back to me.

"You speak French?"

"Yeah, but don't tell Jean Luc. I like him thinking I don't so I can pretend not to understand when he tries to upsell me." She winks and takes a sip of her coffee, but her face sobers as I continue watching her. "What is it?"

"There are moments I realize that I don't know nearly enough about you." I reach over and take her hand. "I thought I'd already learned so much, but I realize that I've only scratched the surface with you, Nadia."

"Well, we spent the better part of three months lying to each other," she reminds me. "Then, we had a job to do."

"That's not a good excuse."

"It works both ways, you know. I don't know much about you, either."

"Then, for the next two weeks, we're going to do exactly that. Learn about each other. So, tell me about the bags."

She shimmies in her seat. "My favorite topic."

"What was it about these two bags that you loved?"

"It's two very different reasons. We'll start with the Chanel. Coco Chanel lived here in Paris, at the Ritz, actually, but she also had an apartment above her boutique. She didn't sleep there. She gave parties and worked there. I've never been upstairs, but I've been on *the* stairs, and it's a trip, let me tell you. Anyway, she went to a little café near the Louvre called Angelina. Every single day. She sat at the same table and always ordered the hot chocolate. It's a short walk from the Ritz. We'll go. You'll never feel the same about hot chocolate again. And I think Chanel's quality is insanely good, especially the vintage pieces. And because this bag was made before her death, she may have held it herself. I love the history of it, and it's always in style."

"Fair enough. And the other?"

"That was Grace Kelly's favorite handbag. Hence the name, the Kelly."

"Ah, makes sense now."

She smiles and leans back as our lunch is served. Once the waiter bustles away, she eats a fry and then keeps talking.

"These bags are made by hand, here in France, by artisans. Each one takes a lot of hours to make..."

I sit and watch her perfect face as she talks, using her hands for emphasis, explaining in detail how every product makes its way to a storefront.

Her enthusiasm is contagious. I don't need a bag, but she has me ready to run out and buy the first one I see.

"And here I thought you were all about the family," I reply when her story winds down.

"I am." She takes a bite of her sandwich. "It's always the priority and will be until the day I die. But this is a fun hobby."

"An expensive one."

"Says the man who bought a ten-thousand-dollar watch in New York."

"It wasn't secondhand."

Her laughter is a drug.

"Have you spent much time in Paris?" she asks.

"Not as much as you," I reply. "And I've only really seen the most touristy of places."

"Then we'll avoid those." She chews thoughtfully. "Will you think I'm weird if I suggest a cemetery?"

"Are you planning to kill me, then?"

"No. I've heard about a really beautiful cemetery here in Paris. If you're up for it, we could go check it out this week. The weather's beautiful."

"I'm game."

"Bet you never thought you'd be hanging out with me in a cemetery, did you?"

"Honestly, I never thought I'd be with you at all." I push my finished plate aside.

"Same." She rests her chin in her hand. "I told my father about us coming here."

I raise a brow in surprise. "And what did he say?"

"He didn't seem to care in the least."

"And if he did?"

She sighs and glances down at her empty cup of coffee. "If he'd been angry or forbade it, I wouldn't be here." Her eyes find mine again, and I see the heaviness in them. "We have responsibilities, Carmine. To our fathers. I love him. I respect him. And, at the end of the day, I guess I'm trying to prove something to him. So, as much as I wish I could say that I'd tell him I'm a big girl who can call her own shots, I know that's not the case."

"I understand." It sits like a lead ball in my stomach, but I do understand. Because I'd do the same thing.

I, too, had a conversation with my father before we came to Paris. And if he'd been unhappy with it, well, I'd be in Seattle.

Alone.

"Do you ever wish we weren't...?" She waves her hand in the air, not finishing the sentence.

"Intelligent? Wonderful? Wealthy? Witty?"

"Part of the organization, you moron," she interrupts with a laugh. "And, I should add, modest."

"No." I reach for the check and put my credit card in the leather folder. "I don't wish that. Do you?"

"No. I'm not like Annika. She hates it. Wants to be as far removed from it as she can. But I always found it fascinating."

"Maybe it ties in with your love of history," I suggest, and she nods.

"I think so. Our family goes back generations. To Russia. I used to love sitting on my father's knee and listening to him tell stories from his childhood about his parents—and theirs. My family has been in our line of business for hundreds of years."

"That's something we have in common." I sign the check and reach for Nadia's bags. "Let's go back to the hotel."

"I could use a little rest."

WE'VE JUST REACHED our suite when I get a call from Rocco.

"Isn't it the middle of the night there?" I ask.

"Early morning," he replies. "Just giving you a heads-up. Someone broke into Gram's house last night."

I narrow my eyes and watch as Nadia sets her new bags in the closet, then starts taking her clothes off. "What the fuck?"

"What is it?" she asks, but I hold up my hand.

"The alarm went off at about two this morning," he continues. "Our security was there within ten minutes, and the cops came five minutes later. A window was broken. I don't know what they took. If anything. They didn't make much of a mess."

"I wonder if they were looking for something specific."

"If they were, they found it and bailed. No prints. They took out the cameras."

"Damn it."

"Yeah, I know. We're locking it down, and I'm going to live there for a while. It's not good that it's been sitting empty for this long. We need to sell it, Carmine."

"And do what with all of her shit?" I rub a hand over my face. "I'll be home in a couple of weeks. Let me know if this happens again."

"Will do. Have a good vacation."

He clicks off, and I turn to find Nadia watching me with concern. "What happened?"

"My grandmother passed away last year."

"I remember. We went to the funeral."

I nod and recall seeing her at the church. "Her house has been sitting pretty much empty since she died. I went through a lot of stuff because I was trying to find Elena, which is another story. But aside from that, there's ten thousand square feet and sixty year's-worth of shit to sort through."

"And someone broke in."

"Yeah. We shouldn't have left it that long. Rocco's gonna stay there for a while."

"It was probably a professional. Someone who staked it out and knew that it was empty."

"Most likely," I agree and push my finger into the waistband of her jeans. "Now, let's forget about the goings-on more than an ocean away."

"What do you have in mind?"

CHAPTER
FOURTEEN
~NADIA~

"I want to be with you," he murmurs as those talented lips take a slow journey down my neck to my shoulder. His hands skim down my arms, over my naked torso, and down to my ass, still covered in denim.

He squeezes, and my core clenches in response. But before I can say anything, his hands grip my thighs, and he lifts me like I weigh nothing. I wrap my legs around his waist, and he carries me to the dining room table.

"I want to kiss you." He unfastens my jeans, and I lift my ass so he can guide them over my hips and down my legs.

The underwear follows, and I'm left lying naked and spread wide for him.

I expect him to dive right in, wrap his lips around me and take me for one hell of a ride.

But to my surprise, that's not what he does at all.

His fingertips barely brush my skin, sending goosebumps all over me.

"You're so fucking soft," he whispers before kissing my inner thigh. "So damn responsive. God, you're getting wetter by the second."

"Come on, Carmine. You're killing me here."

He just shakes his head and continues taunting me, teasing me. His touch is gentle, his kisses wet and carefully placed over my already heated skin.

I arch my back, wanting nothing more than to have him fuck me hard on this table. What's with the gentle shit?

Sex is impatient. Fast and dirty.

It's not *this*.

"Carmine," I breathe when his fingers brush over my most intimate lips. "Jesus, don't be such a tease."

He chuckles and licks up my stomach to my navel and then farther to the underside of my small breasts.

Who knew that little spot was so damn sensitive?

"You're killing me."

"Just relax," he croons. His voice is thick and sounds like melted chocolate. Full of lazy lust and affection, and it does something to me.

Something I don't recognize—or particularly feel comfortable with.

My throat closes, and my core clenches when his lips drag up over one already perky nipple. I don't know what this is. My already raw emotions are even more on the surface, and I don't like it. I don't want to feel vulnerable with him.

"Damn it, Carmine, you're going too slow. Just fuck me already!"

He stills, pulls his hands back, and raises his head to look down at me. "That's not what I'm doing here, Nadia."

"What *are* you doing?"

My breasts rise and fall with my breaths, coming faster now. What is all of this *emotion*?

"I don't have to spell it out for you."

"Yeah, I think you do. You have me tied in knots here. Just *do* it already. What's wrong with you?"

His eyes narrow, and if I'm not mistaken, he looks hurt. But before I can say anything, he quickly unfastens his slacks and pushes into me, hard.

"Is this what you want?" he demands and then slams into me again. And again. "You just want me to fuck you?"

I grip onto the edge of the table and hold on tight, but he suddenly stops and swears under his breath.

"Goddamn it."

"Carmine."

"Just give me a second." He shakes his head, and I can see despair there. Confusion. So, I sit up and take his face in my hands. "A few months ago, I would have simply fucked you until you walked wrong and been content with that. But that's not where we are anymore, Nadia."

I frown as he kisses the palm of my hand. "Carmine, we're enjoying each other. Having a good time together."

"Yeah, we are, but it's more than that. And if you say it's not, that you don't have any feelings for me beyond that, you're lying."

I bite my lip and feel my eyes fill. And that just pisses me off.

"Don't cry, baby."

"I'm not." I clear my throat.

"I can't just fuck you and then go on with my day. Not anymore. I feel more than that, and I'll be damned if I continue denying it—if that's what you're asking me to do."

"I don't know what I'm asking."

"Why is this so hard for you?" He brushes his thumb over my lower lip, his eyes following the movement.

I *want* to give in to my feelings for him. I *want* to fall in love with him.

"Of course, I have feelings for you. Maybe tender sex just isn't my thing."

"You're not a great liar."

"I'm an amazing liar," I disagree and narrow my eyes. "But maybe I'm not lying about that."

"You are. Tell me why you don't want to be vulnerable with me like this. Jesus, Nadia, we've been honest with each other about so many things over the past few months. We've seen a lot and been through more. Why does this level of intimacy scare you?"

I shake my head. I don't want to admit that I'm scared, and I hate him for putting me in this position. Why can't we go back to it being simple?

Why do I find it so hard to do this?

"What if I get my heart set on something that isn't possible?"

There. I said it out loud.

The look in Carmine's brown eyes softens, and he tips his forehead against mine. "We don't know that it's impossible."

"We don't know that it's not," I say and hear the tremble in my voice. "Falling in love with you, *really* falling in love, was never part of the plan."

"No. It wasn't." He kisses me gently. "I hated your guts for a long, long time, Nadia. I wanted to make you hurt. Wanted to make your whole family pay."

I frown. "Well, that's one way to make me feel all warm and fuzzy."

"Smartass." He smiles and kisses my nose. "But then I spent time with you, learned who you are. And I know that not only are you not the one I should hate, but I respect the hell out of you. You're going to make one hell of a Bratva boss one day."

My mouth just opens and closes in surprise. I've never felt more naked. Exposed. Not just physically but emotionally, as well.

He's still inside me, and he just stripped my emotions bare.

"I want that," I whisper.

"I know. And you deserve it. But even more than that, I've grown quite fond of the woman you are. One who enjoys sweets and can kick ass. Who isn't afraid to ask for help when she needs it. A woman who spends more money than some people make in a year on a used handbag."

"You really need to get over that."

He laughs and finally starts to move, slowly, in and out of me.

"You're everything," he says. It sounds so simple but carries *so* much weight. And all I can do is show him how I feel because I can't say the words.

I just can't.

I brush my fingers through his hair and kiss his shoulder as he slowly makes love to me. And after I have the craziest climax of my life, he carries me to the bedroom.

"We aren't done yet."

"You may not be, pal, but I'm exhausted."

He chuckles and kisses my cheek. "We'll wake you up again."

Okay, so there's something to be said for making love.

I've never done it before.

I feel energized the next morning. Satisfied. And oddly...sentimental.

I'm not an overly romantic girl. Damn him for digging his way under my skin when I wasn't looking and making me get all used to him.

"Here we are," Carmine says as our taxi stops next to the entrance of the cemetery. He takes my hand, and we walk over to the towering iron gates.

"This place is huge," I say as I look at a map. "We might be here awhile."

"We have all day."

We walk inside, up a short hill, and then all I can do is stand and gape. The cemetery is enormous. The headstones are old and different, and I can't wait to check them all out.

"Let's go this way and then check out the mausoleums last," I suggest.

"Lead the way," he says, gesturing with his arm. He's dressed casually today in a black T-shirt and cargo shorts, and he makes my mouth water.

How can a man look like that in a shirt and have it be legal?

I have no idea.

I'm in a simple red sundress today because it's summer in Paris and it's warm. Thankfully, I also have a good-sized crossbody bag that holds my concealed carry, and I have a smaller piece tied to my thigh.

Yes, we're on vacation, but you can never be too careful. I saw Carmine slip his handgun into a holster in the waistband of his shorts, above his impressive ass.

"It just goes on and on," I say and point out a statue. "That headstone looks like a woman weeping, and she's holding the hand of someone in a jail cell."

"This whole place is a work of art," he says.

"I hope this isn't boring for you."

"Not at all." He takes my hand in his and kisses my knuckles. "It's fascinating. And I'm with you. How could I be bored?"

"Good point." I wink at him and then glance over my shoulder. It looks like someone is watching us.

I do a double-take, and the person is gone.

Huh. I must just be on edge today. My emotions are all over the place, and I'm keyed up. That's all.

Nothing to worry about.

"Okay, this is...interesting." I stop next to a large concrete casket covered in moss. But coming out of the top are two arms with the hands touching, as if two people are buried here, holding hands even in death.

"I don't think I want to be buried like that," Carmine says thoughtfully.

"You don't think it's romantic?"

He glances down at me. "Do you?"

"I don't know. It's kind of macabre, but it's also kind of sweet."

We wander around some more and see the graves of Chopin, Oscar Wilde, and other artists. The memorials are absolutely stunning.

Then we turn a corner, and behind a chain-link fence is the grave of Jim Morrison.

"It's a shame they had to close it off because of vandals," I say. "But still cool to see."

"Do you like The Doors?"

"Sure." I shrug and glance back.

The same man is there again.

"I think—"

"Yep, I saw him. We'll find a more private spot and confront him."

I nod and, hand in hand, we walk down a road in the cemetery that looks as if it belongs in New Orleans with beautiful aboveground mausoleums.

"These are beautiful."

"It's amazing how different every part of the cemetery is."

"I agree."

I glance back but don't see the man following us any longer. But just as we turn a corner, he walks out from behind a crypt, a knife in his hand.

"Get in here," he hisses. "Now. Don't make a scene."

Carmine squeezes my hand, and we follow him into an open mausoleum. We slip inside, and he shuts the door.

"Who the hell are you?" Carmine asks, but the man strikes out with the knife, and I take out his knee.

He crumples to the ground, but he lashes out with the blade again.

Carmine punches him, then picks him up and holds him by the collar. "Who the fuck are you?"

"You're going to die today," the man growls, but before he can wave the knife again, I bend his hand back and take it from him, then press my gun to his head.

"Answer the damn question."

His eyes jitter back and forth between Carmine and me.

"You're not exactly discreet," Carmine says, his voice perfectly calm but hard as stone. "Either you wanted us to see you, or you're shitty at this job."

"Fuck you."

"I don't think so." Carmine knees him in the stomach, sending him to the ground once more, wheezing. We circle him slowly.

"Who sent you?"

"I'm not telling you *shit*."

I smile sweetly and squat next to him. "Oh, yeah, you are. Because if you don't, you won't leave this place alive. You'll spend all of eternity here with the..."—I check the name on the crypt next to me—"the Bettencourts. I'm sure they're nice people. And there's plenty of room here for you. You like to snuggle with corpses, don't you? I mean, they've been here since..."

I recheck the tomb.

"Since 1928. They're probably nice and decayed by now."

He looks green; like he's about to throw up.

"I won't ask nicely again," Carmine says.

"Richard hired me to follow you," he snaps. "I've been tailing you since you were in Denver. I'm just supposed to keep an eye on you and report back."

My gaze flies to Carmine's, and I stand to talk to him.

"How does he not know that Rich is dead?" I murmur.

312

Carmine shakes his head and then looks down at the man and curses. "Are you..."—he waves his hands around—"*crying*?"

The man is just sitting there, weeping.

"There's no crying in the mafia."

"Why are you quoting movie lines?"

He turns to me. "Because there's no crying. He's crying."

"Yes, I know."

We both turn back to him and swear.

"Fucking hell."

He's already seizing, foaming at the mouth. "He took a pill."

"He'd rather die than give information," Carmine agrees, and we watch until he stops jerking.

"What now? We can't leave him like this. Someone will find him. A groundskeeper or someone."

"We do what you suggested. Open that crypt and put him in there with the nice Battencourts."

I raise a brow. "Ew."

"I'll do it."

"No, I'll help." First, I poke my head out the door to make sure we haven't drawn a crowd. That would be uncomfortable.

But no one is even about.

"It's clear."

Carmine nods and opens the tomb. We both look down at the man.

"Wow, he looks good for being dead for almost one hundred years."

"The embalming did its job," Carmine agrees. "Nice suit, too."

"Well, this is a nice mausoleum. They had money." We turn back to our stiff. Carmine grabs his shoulders, and I take his feet, and we maneuver him into the burial chamber. "He just fits."

"No one will find him for a long time." We close the lid and have to push down for it to settle. "If ever."

"I don't get it." I straighten my dress and return my gun to its leg holster. Carmine picks up the knife and wipes it free of prints, then opens the other crypt. I walk over to look. "His wife."

"She doesn't look as good as he does."

The skin on her face is mostly gone, leaving her teeth showing. I check the date.

"She's been dead twenty years longer. They didn't embalm then."

He tosses the knife in with her and closes the top.

"You know the most interesting things, sweetheart. You were saying?"

"I don't get it," I continue. "He didn't know that Rich was dead. It wasn't a secret. You and I were at the funeral. If he was following us like he said, he would have seen us there."

"Maybe he was off work that day," Carmine says with a shrug and walks over to the door. "I don't really care. He's not following us now."

He opens the metal gate, and we step out, much to the surprise of a young couple currently walking around through the cemetery.

"Oops." I grin and wipe my mouth, then wink up at Carmine. "Finally checked that one off the bucket list."

Carmine laughs and pulls me away, just as the young woman gasps.

"Never a dull moment with you, is there?"

"Nope. And you're welcome."

CHAPTER

FIFTEEN
~CARMINE~

"You really should come in with me," Nadia says as she treads water in the crystal-blue pool. We've been at the resort in Cannes, on the French Riviera, for five days. We went from sightseeing and walking all over Paris to lazy days by the pool and eating all of the food in sight.

It's all about balance.

"I'm happy to sit here and watch," I reply. Nadia just shakes her head and starts swimming back and forth. We're not alone here at the pool since it's open to all resort visitors. But because it's the middle of the week, it's not overly crowded, either.

I'm sitting on a lounge chair, similar to the one that Nadia was sitting in that day that I found her in Miami all those months ago.

But so much has changed since then.

Finished with swimming, she moves over to the infinity wall and stares out at the water beyond.

The view here is stunning. We've spent quite a bit of time on the balcony of our penthouse suite, enjoying the sunsets.

It won't be long before we're back home, immersed in all of the responsibility that comes with our lives.

But for now, we're simply enjoying our vacation. Together.

KRISTEN PROBY

I take a sip of the fruity drink that Nadia ordered for me and watch as the woman turns from her view and gives me a smile as she swims through the water.

Her eyes widen in surprise, and I lean forward, wondering if she needs my help.

"Oh, crap," she mutters, and as she walks up the steps and out of the pool, her bikini top is in her hands.

And her breasts are bare and on display.

"You'd best cover yourself."

"The damn clasp broke," she says. "And I liked this suit. Oh, well, I brought another one."

"Put something on, Nadia."

She looks up and frowns. "We're in *France*. Trust me, no one cares that I'm topless."

"I care."

She tips her head to the side. "Seriously, it's no big deal, Carmine."

"Put something on, or we'll go to the room."

She simply sits on the chair, leans back, and tips her face up to the sun, her small breasts out for everyone to see.

"No."

I press my lips together in frustration. "Nadia."

"Carmine," she says lazily and reaches for her drink. "I'm a grown woman. It's not illegal to be topless poolside in France. So, I'm going to sit here. Topless."

"For fuck's sake." I grab her black cover-up, toss it over her, and lift her into my arms. I don't miss the man across the pool, watching us.

He'll be dealt with later.

"What in the hell are you doing?"

I don't answer. I simply carry her to the elevator, and when we reach the top floor, I stride into our room.

She's glaring at me now.

I couldn't care less.

"You're such a fucking caveman," she growls. "I didn't do anything wrong, Carmine."

"Stop talking." I set her on the floor and then pin her against the wall. I take her hands in mine and lift them over her head with one of

316

mine. With the other, I worry a nipple between my fingers. "If you think I'll sit back and let you sit out there on display, for everyone to see, you're sorely mistaken."

"*Let* me—"

"I said, stop talking." I drag my nose over the shell of her ear, breathing her in. My fingers pinch the nipple, just a little harder. "This, right here, is mine. Only for *me* to see."

She whimpers when I move over to the other side and pay that nipple the same attention.

"No one gets the pleasure of seeing this but me."

"Caveman," she whispers, but I can tell the anger has left her, replaced by pure, unadulterated lust.

I make quick work of her bikini bottoms and my shorts, and with her hands still pinned over her head, I boost her up and slip right inside of her.

"This is what happens when you defy me, Nadia. You piss me off and make me want to claim what's mine."

"Oh, my God."

"Look at me."

With her blue eyes on fire and pinned to mine, I work her hard, making her come fast. With the second orgasm, I follow her over and lean my forehead against her shoulder as I release her hands, and she wraps her arms around my neck.

I can't breathe.

And I can't let her go.

"Jesus, you do shit to me," I mutter.

"Same." She swallows hard and looks at me as I pull my face back. "It really bothered you, I guess."

"I wasn't playing."

Her mouth quirks into a grin. "I can see that. Fine, I'll wear the suit. But I could say the same."

"I'd look awful in a bikini top."

She smirks. "Do you think I didn't see the waitress flirting with you when she delivered your drinks? Or how the other women watch you when you walk across the pool area, wearing nothing but your shorts?"

"And how do they look at me?"

"Like they want to eat you alive. And I can't blame them." Her hands glide down my chest. "You're a sexy man, Carmine. You have muscles for days. Combine that with this smooth olive skin and that sexy face of yours, and well, you turn heads."

"Thanks for feeding my ego."

"I'm not. It's just how it is. But I don't wrap you in a towel and pull you out of there."

"I didn't like it," I repeat. "And I won't apologize for it. If you want me to wear a T-shirt at the pool, I'll do that."

"Well, that makes me just sound dumb."

"No." I grin and kiss her chin, then set her on her feet. "It makes you sound possessive, and that doesn't bother me so much."

"I'm going back down." She pads over to the dresser and pulls out a clean swimsuit. When she's dressed, she turns back to me. "Are you going to join me?"

"Yes. Would a tank top be too revealing?"

She laughs now and shakes her head. "You don't have to wear anything."

I slip the tank over my head and shrug. "If it makes you more comfortable, it doesn't bother me."

"We're sappy. You know that, right?"

"Darling, what a sweet thing to say."

THE CASINO IS loud and bustling around me. I'm seated at a high-roller blackjack table, sipping whiskey and watching Nadia from several yards away.

She's at a poker table, pouting because she just lost five thousand dollars.

"Well, poo," she huffs and gives the man beside her a forlorn look. "I'm really bad at this, aren't I?"

I ask the dealer to hit me and hold at nineteen.

"I've seen worse," her companion says. "Let's try this, shall we?"

His hand is on the small of her back and drifts down to her ass as he leans in to help her with her next hand.

My stomach twists.

He's going to lose that hand. And I'm not talking about the cards.

I win at nineteen and rake in twenty grand in chips as the asshole laughs and nuzzles Nadia's nose.

I sip my whiskey and act disinterested.

She loses again.

"That wasn't quite as bad," he tells her and moves in closer. "Now, for this hand, we'll do things a little differently."

I'm dealt a four of clubs and a queen of hearts. I tell the dealer to hit me and draw the six of diamonds.

I hold, and the dealer goes down the line of other players.

Nadia wins her hand and claps her hands joyfully, then kisses the man on the cheek.

That earns her ass a nice squeeze.

Fucking hell, how long do I have to watch this shit?

Finally, she whispers in his ear, and he rewards her with a wide smile and a nod of acceptance.

They leave the poker table.

I fold my cards, take my chips, and follow them.

"Are you on a good floor?" she asks, loud enough for me to hear her.

"The twelfth is nice and quiet," he assures her as they get into an elevator.

I take a different one and count my lucky stars when I get off just after them and follow them down the hall. He opens their door, and I hurry up, then push my way inside before he can shut it behind them.

"Hey, what's the big deal?"

"We could ask you the same thing," Nadia says, not smiling and flirting now.

He tries to act as if he doesn't know what she's talking about, but the longer we just stare at him, our weapons drawn, he loses the fight. He finally blows out a breath and holds up his hands in surrender.

"I guess you caught me."

"You've been following us for days," I reply. "And you're not very good at it. Just like your associate in Paris. Who's dead, by the way."

He narrows his eyes and then shrugs a shoulder. "He was a shitty operative."

"So are you."

This gets his temper up. "No. I'm not."

"We saw you," I repeat. "And what was that show downstairs? Did you think you could just flirt with her, and she'd jump right into bed with you?"

"And why not?" he asks, his voice bold. "We've all heard the stories about Nadia Tarenkov, fucking anyone who offers."

Without hesitation, I hit him across the face with the butt of my sidearm, drawing blood.

"Wait. Are you *in love* with her?" He laughs and doesn't bother to wipe at the blood on his face. "That's not even funny. It's sad. Pathetic, really. She'll just double-cross you, man. That's what she does."

"Shut the fuck up." Nadia kicks over the desk chair and forces him down into it, and I pull the twine out of my pocket and secure his hands behind his back.

"Why are you following us?" Nadia asks him.

"I don't have to tell you shit. Go ahead and kill me. You're going to anyway."

He's not wrong.

"Rich has been dead for weeks. Why are you still doing his bidding?" I ask.

He scoffs. "You think this came from *Richard*? Come on, Carmine, you weren't born last night. Pull your dick out of your brain and think about it. This comes from way higher up than Richard. That dude was a piece of shit. A total pussy."

"You know, I don't disagree with you," Nadia says as she walks around him. "But I never understood why men like to compare weakness to female genitalia."

She reaches down and grips his dick in a firm fist, making him yell in rage.

"When it's your *dick* that's so weak. So, the truth is, Richard was a dick."

Then she looks up at me and laughs. "Dick is short for Richard."

"Makes perfect sense, then," I agree.

She lets him go and walks over to me, urging me to the side so she can speak to me privately.

"Could it be true that Richard was working for someone else?"

"It could be, but Shane dug around on him and didn't find anything. He was going to keep delving into it in his free time. I'll have to call him and see if he found anything new."

"Yeah, let's do that. Ah!"

The asshole has Nadia pinned to the wall, his hands around her neck in a flash. I have no idea how he got out of the restraints.

"Let her go." I press the business end of my sidearm against the side of his head, but he doesn't let up on his grip. Nadia's face is already turning purple. "I said, fucking let her go."

No response.

I glance at Nadia and see that she won't last much longer.

So I squeeze the trigger and kill the son of a bitch.

"Jesus," she wheezes as he slumps to the floor, and she can breathe again. "Fuck."

"Hey, look at me."

She does as I ask. Her eyes are red. Her throat will be bruised.

I aim and shoot him once again.

"He's dead, Carmine."

"I thought he'd let go when I had the gun to his head."

"He was cocky and arrogant," she says when she finally catches her breath. She pulls an unopened bottle of water out of the fridge, but I shake my head no.

"Don't drink that. We don't know that he didn't poison everything in here."

"You're right. Christ." She drops the bottle to the carpet. "Who's going to clean up this mess?"

My smile is humorless as I pull my phone out of my pocket and tap a series of numbers, then send the text through.

"It'll be handled."

She just stares at me. "In *France*?"

"Anywhere." My answer is simple. "Your family would do the same."

She nods and pushes her hand through her hair. "You're right. I'm just rattled. I'm not used to being choked out like that. I guess it's safe to say that breathplay isn't my jam."

"No." I lean in and press a kiss to her neck where the bruises are already starting to form. "We won't be exploring that. There are too many other ways to bring pleasure. Let's go."

I don't spare the goon on the floor a glance as I open the door and lead her out, keeping an eye on our surroundings in case there's someone else lying in wait.

But as we leave the casino, we're alone. Once in the car on the way to the hotel, she leans her head on my shoulder.

"We need to go home," she murmurs.

"Agreed." I kiss the top of her head. "Vacation is over. We'll fly out tonight."

"Good. Are we going to Seattle?"

"Yes. Unless there was somewhere else you wanted to go?"

"No, Seattle works. I'll need to call my father when we land. I need to fill him in on what's going on."

"I think we should have a meeting with both of our fathers. Do you think yours would come to Seattle?"

She thinks it over. "If your father sends the invitation, I'm sure he will."

"I'll get that ball rolling. We thought what was happening in Denver died with Richard."

"We were wrong." She yawns. "We were very wrong."

And I'm furious.

No one will ever touch her like that again.

"I shouldn't have paused in shooting him," I say when we're in the elevator headed up to our room. "I hate myself for it."

"He might have stopped," she says. "Hey. I'm here, and I'm fine. We're going to figure out who's behind this, and we're going to kill *them*. No hesitation. No second chances."

"No. No hesitation." I pull her to me when we close the door to our suite and hold her close. We're rocking back and forth, clinging to each other, when my phone rings.

I don't let her go as I bring it to my ear. "Yes."

"The plane will be ready within the hour."

"Excellent."

I click off and tip her chin up with my finger.

"Let's go home, babe."

CHAPTER

SIXTEEN

~NADIA~

" T hat's your grandmother's house?"

Carmine cuts the car's engine, and we sit in silence, staring at the enormous brownstone home just outside of Seattle, still perfectly manicured and maintained.

"It is." He sighs and then turns to me. "My brothers, Elena, and I practically grew up here. Especially in the summers. The house sits on roughly twenty acres of land. More than sixty years ago, when my grandfather bought the property, he got it for a steal."

I raise a brow, and he laughs.

"No, he didn't *steal* it. But he got a great deal on it. Today, it's worth well into the eight figures."

"I bet someone would love to buy it, divvy up the land into smaller parcels, build, and sell. Make it a nice little neighborhood near the water."

"I'm sure they would. And they'd make a good deal of money off it. But that's not going to happen."

"So, you're just hanging onto it for what? Sentimental value?" I shake my head and get out of the car. "Carmine, this property is prime real estate to make your family money."

"We have plenty of money," he reminds me. "And we're making more every day. Now, let's go find Rocco and see what's going on."

He slips his hand into mine and leads me through an arched, double door entrance and into a grand foyer with a split staircase.

It's a stunningly beautiful home. And it suits what I know of Carmine's grandmother, the matriarch of their mafioso family.

"He's probably in the kitchen," Carmine says and leads me through rooms full of old furniture, artwork, and windows that offer a view of the water.

"I see why you have a thing for beautiful views."

He smiles. "I learned from her."

We walk past a dining room and into the kitchen, where sure enough, Rafe leans on the counter, tapping keys on his laptop as he munches on a sandwich.

"Hey," he says and looks up at us. "Jesus, you look like shit. Aren't you supposed to come home from vacation looking all bright-eyed and bushy-tailed?"

"What the fuck does that even mean?" Carmine asks with a laugh. "We came straight here from the airport."

"Ah. Jet lag. So, I hear you had some fun being tailed over there."

"You heard right," I reply and open the fridge, starving. "You have cream cheese. Do you have bagels?"

"Sure. Here you go."

He opens a cupboard, and I have my pick of everything, cheese, or plain.

I always go for the cheese.

"Want one?" I ask Carmine.

"Sure. I'll do it. You're exhausted. Here." He takes over, and I point to the cheese, then settle back to chat with Rafe.

"And you had a break-in here," I reply, to which Rafe nods.

"Yeah. Fucker got inside by breaking one of the big picture windows in the library. I had them repaired yesterday."

"But not with the original glass," Carmine says with frustration.

"No," Rafe agrees, then turns to me to explain. "Ninety percent of the glass in this house is original. It was built in 1909. Gram was particularly fond of the glass."

"I'm sorry. That sucks. What did they take?"

"As far as we can tell, nothing." He blows out a disgusted breath and paces the kitchen. "I've been through every room. Aside from the window, *nothing* was moved. It doesn't make any sense."

"Unless they were looking for something or *someone* who wasn't here," Carmine replies as he sets a plate full of bagel goodness in front of me and then sits next to me with a plate of his own.

"I thought of that," Rafe says. "Since it's not been a secret that the house has been empty, I'd say it was some*thing* they were looking for."

"If it was a run-of-the-mill thief," I say, licking cream cheese off my finger. "He could have been looking for jewelry, artwork, antiques. But I saw a lot of priceless art and antiques on our way through when we arrived."

"And nothing is missing," Rafe says. "Father took all of the jewelry and any money Gram had lying around here home with him a few days after she died."

"So, someone broke in and was disappointed at the lack of loot," Carmine says with a shrug. "We'll ramp up the security, especially if you don't want to keep living out here."

"I don't really mind it," Rafe says, thinking it over. "It's just so damn far out of the city. By the way, I checked your house the other day. Nothing's going on there."

"We'll head over after we finish here," Carmine says. "But thanks for checking. I have around-the-clock security."

I finish my bagel and sigh in happiness. "Thanks for the carbs."

"You're welcome. Have you heard from Annika?"

I wondered if he'd bring up my cousin. Part of me wanted him to so I could drill him.

But the man standing across from me just looks...miserable.

"Yeah, we text just about every day."

"How is she?"

I tip my head to the side. "Why don't you ask her?"

"I have. She doesn't fucking reply." He drags his hands over his face in agitation. "She's cut me out entirely, and it's more frustrating than I can tell you."

"She's getting by," is all I say, but when he just stares at me, I continue, carefully choosing my words. "She feels foolish. And she's mad."

Rafe nods, and Carmine reaches over to squeeze my hand.

"If you talk to her, just tell her to text me back."

I laugh and then shrug when Rafe sends me a look that's likely made plenty of men piss their pants.

"I'll mention it. But Annika is her own woman, Rafe. And she wants *nothing* to do with the mafia. She's never made that a secret."

"I can't be held responsible for the family I was born into." The frustration rolls over his face as he shakes his head. "And neither can she. She has to stop punishing us both for it."

"Is that what she's doing?" I wonder. "Or is she simply trying to live a simple life?"

"She's stubborn as hell, that's what she is," Rafe says.

"On that, we can agree. I'll pass along your message." I turn to Carmine, who's remained quiet as he listened to the exchange between Rafe and me. "What time are we meeting with our dads?"

He checks the time and then stands. "In a few hours."

"You're meeting with Pop *and* Igor?" Rafe asks with surprise.

"Yes. We need to talk about the men who followed us in France," Carmine says. "And I want to do it in a secure place. Over the phone or internet won't cut it. You're welcome to join us. Is Shane still in Colorado?"

"I'm not sure where he is," Rafe says. "He said something about a job in Colombia."

I raise a brow. "What, exactly, does Shane do for a living?"

"That, we can't tell you," Carmine says but takes the sting out of the statement with a kiss to my head. "Let's go home and freshen up for our meeting. Rocco, we're meeting at three, at the downtown building."

"In the office?" he asks.

Carmine nods and sets our dishes in the dishwasher, then leads me out of the kitchen and toward the front door.

I want to ask for a tour of the magnificent house, but I know that we don't have time. And, at the end of the day, no matter how close Carmine and I have gotten, I'm still a member of the Tarenkov family.

There will always be a line. And taking me on a tour of the Martinelli matriarch's house might be crossing it.

We're quiet in the car. So much so that I close my eyes and rest. Neither of us slept on the flight here. We even went and laid on the bed, snuggled up, but couldn't doze off.

We didn't talk, simply lay there. Restless. Uncertain.

Pissed off.

Someone's still after us, and we don't know who. Not to mention, I didn't like leaving bodies behind in Europe. It was supposed to be a *vacation*. We weren't supposed to have to kill anyone or constantly look over our shoulders.

Not that the looking behind you ever entirely goes away, even when you feel absolutely safe.

Because the truth is, being in the mafia means you're *never* truly safe.

I open my eyes when Carmine stops the car and then frown.

"We're not going to the penthouse?"

"No," he says and turns to me. "I want you here. In my home."

"I don't understand."

"When I first brought you to Seattle months ago, I didn't want you here because I didn't trust you. And I was with you for other reasons. It was all a farce. The penthouse was neutral territory, so to speak. But that's all changed."

He takes my hand and threads his fingers through mine.

"I want you here, in my house. Not the penthouse."

"But all of my things—"

"Have been moved here," he finishes with a small smile. "Come on, let me show you."

He hurries out of the car, then comes to the passenger side and opens my door.

"You were here once," he says as he pulls me up out of the car and leads me to the door. "And I certainly didn't trust you then, either. It irritated the hell out of me that you found me here."

"Oh, that was certainly the point," I reply with a laugh. "I wanted to frustrate you that day."

"You succeeded. But today, I'm inviting you."

"So, this is your home. And I see that it's not far from your grandmother's."

"No." He unlocks and pushes open the door and then leads me inside. "I loved spending time with her there. And I came to learn that I liked keeping my personal time separate from work. I like our building downtown, don't get me wrong. But it's not home."

I take in the expansive living space with new eyes. The style is *very* different from the home we just left, but it's no less opulent or beautiful.

"The kitchen is gorgeous," I say as we walk through it. "I enjoyed going through your fridge while you fumed."

He chuckles and leads me past, showing me guest rooms, a workout space, an office, and finally, his master bedroom.

It's big, but he's a big man, so it suits him. "More views," I muse and walk to the door that leads out to a patio and a lush garden.

The master bathroom and drool-worthy walk-in closet are nothing less than what I'd expect of a man like Carmine, someone who definitely enjoys all of the finer things in life. It doesn't escape me that all of my clothes and personal things are in the closet, hung neatly.

"You have a lovely home," I say as he pulls me to him. My voice is sincere. It *is* lovely. "And it suits you."

"Thank you."

"You weren't kidding. All of my things are in that sexy-as-fuck closet. My shampoo is even in the shower."

"We won't be living at the penthouse," he confirms. "I hope that doesn't upset you."

Upset me? No. But I'd be lying if I said I wasn't a little confused as to where this was going.

Then again, maybe I'm just overthinking things. It doesn't have to *go* anywhere.

He kisses me, long and slow, as we stand in the middle of his bedroom. "We have time for a nap."

I smile at the suggestion. "Do we have time for more than a nap?"

His brown eyes narrow with lusty mischief. "Oh, yeah. We can manage that."

THE DRIVE into the city doesn't take long. With an hour of sleep and a round of lazy sex behind us, I feel surprisingly rejuvenated.

And I'm excited to see my father.

I've been in constant contact with him since the incident at the casino in Cannes. He accepted Carlo's invitation to meet in Seattle—much to my surprise and delight.

Carmine parks in the underground lot of his building. Rather than hitting the button for the penthouse in the elevator, he pushes the one for the tenth floor.

I raise a brow.

"This is the office."

"Your father's office?"

"No." He shakes his head. "That's on the twentieth floor. Don't worry, you'll see. It's more comfortable. Less imposing."

When we arrive at what used to be a condo but is now a beautiful office space, I see that he's right.

Rather than a large desk where an authority figure might sit, there are sofas, tables, and workspaces throughout. Someone stocked the kitchen with everything a person could ever need or want.

The decorations, in muted colors, are perfect for making someone feel comfortable and at ease.

Less than a minute after we arrive, Carlo walks in with Rafe right behind him.

His face lifts into a smile as he shakes Carmine's hand. "Welcome home, son. Hello, Nadia. You look lovely."

"Thank you."

"Of course, she does. She's the spitting image of her mother," my papa says from the doorway. "Hello, little one."

"Papa!" I run over and kiss him on the cheek, then take his hand and lead him into the room. "I'm so happy to see you. Thank you for coming all this way."

"For you, I would fly to the end of the world." He cups my face and gives me a wink, then turns to Carlo and his sons. "Hello, my friend. Thank you for inviting me into your city."

"Thank you for coming," Carlo says as the two men shake hands.

"My son made it clear that what he and Nadia have to tell us is very important."

"It is," I assure them both as we all take seats. I glance at Carmine, giving him a silent nod to go ahead.

"As you all know, Nadia and I were vacationing in Europe. A little holiday after discovering that Richard was responsible for killing Armando and several others. We thought the situation was settled with Rich's death."

He glances at me, and I pick up the story.

"However, while we were in Paris and strolling through a cemetery, we discovered we were being followed."

I recount the incident with the man in the mausoleum and how we handled it.

Carlo laughs, much to my surprise.

"I apologize. I know it's not a funny situation, but you hid the body in a crypt? That's just priceless."

My father chuckles with him, and I continue.

"A couple of days later, we moved on to Cannes, and within about forty-eight hours, we picked up on another tail. He was at the pool when we were there. At the same restaurants as ours. You get the idea."

I glance at Carmine, and he continues.

"We devised a scheme to catch him. And we did. But this time, when we told him that Rich was dead and asked why he was following us, he said that Rich wasn't the one who gave the orders. That it went *much higher than that.*"

Papa and Carlo share a glance.

"Do you know what that means?" I ask.

"It means this goes deeper than we thought," Papa says with a long sigh. "And someone tried to kill my daughter. Whoever is behind this will die."

"Who was Rich working for?" Carlo wonders aloud.

"We're going to fucking find out," Rafe says.

CHAPTER
SEVENTEEN
~CARMINE~

"For a doctor, your husband sure kept a lot of files at home," Nadia says to Annika. We're in Annika's home, in various areas of Rich's old office, poring over paperwork. He had tons of files, and every piece of paper has to be looked at.

"He wasn't a fucking doctor," Annika snaps back. She's sitting cross-legged on the couch, her dead husband's laptop in front of her as she tries to break the passcode. She sighs and leans her head back on the sofa. "Sorry. I don't mean to sound like a bitch. I wish I could figure out this password."

"For *not* a doctor, there sure are a lot of patient notes here," I muse as I open another file and frown down at medical information on someone named Samantha Briggs. "I would think it's illegal to have patient information at home."

"It is," Annika assures me. "It's also illegal to pose as a doctor when you aren't. I'm so fucking mad at him." She stands and paces the office. "I wish he was alive so I could punch him in that smug face and then kill him myself."

"While I understand—and agree with—the sentiment," Nadia says, "that won't help us today."

"I don't even know what we're looking for," I reply and toss a file on the growing stack.

"Sorry I'm late," Ivie says as she hurries into the office, then promptly stubs her toe on the doorjamb. "Ouch! Son of a bitch."

"I swear, you need to wear Bubble Wrap," Nadia says, shaking her head. "Are you okay?"

"Yeah. That hurt." Ivie sits and rubs her toes. "I tried to get here sooner, but traffic was a bitch. So, how can I help? What can I do? Annika filled me in on the whole mystery at hand."

I turn to Annika and raise a brow, but the woman only shrugs. "She's my best friend, Carmine."

"I'm totally trustworthy," Ivie assures me. "I can help you look through the house or something, but I likely won't know what I'm looking for."

"That makes four of us," Nadia says. "None of us knows what we're looking for, but we'll know it when we see it."

"Something out of the ordinary," I reply. "Names, numbers, notes that are vague or even incriminating. That would be convenient."

"I'm trying to get into his computer, but the fucker locked it down pretty solid," Annika adds.

"How about this?" Ivie says. "I'll make you all a late lunch and help out wherever I can."

"I need a break from this," Annika says and tosses the computer onto the cushion beside her. "I'll help you, Ivie. We'll be back in a few with sustenance. Maybe I'll be more productive if I'm not hangry."

The two women leave the room, arm in arm, and Nadia sighs across from me.

"I guess it's a good sign that she's hungry," she says, still staring at the doorway. "She looks a little better than she did when we left here a few weeks ago."

I want to disagree. I think Annika looks horrible. The anger and hatred are festering inside of her. She has dark circles under her eyes, and she's lost a lot of weight in a very short time.

But I don't say any of that because Nadia is worried enough, and we have plenty on our plates.

"Carmine."

"Yes, sweetheart?"

"We're not going to find anything in these medical records. I don't even know why he has them here or what he used them for. But this isn't the answer."

"I agree." I rub my hand down my face. "I've been trying to reach my brother to see if he's had time to tinker some more. I'd like to have Rich's phone here so I can do some digging, but I can't reach Shane. He won't answer his damn phone."

"Maybe he's still out of the country," she suggests.

"It would help if he'd answer and tell me that."

Annika and Ivie return with a tray full of sandwiches and chips, soda, and water.

"I'm starving," Annika says, taking a sandwich and some chips for herself. "Eat up. There's more in the kitchen if you're still hungry."

"This is enough for an army," Nadia says and bites into a sandwich.

I try to call my brother again, but it goes straight to his voicemail.

"Son of a bitch," I mutter and then pin Ivie with a stare. She blinks and looks behind her.

"What?"

"I know you talk to my brother. Have you heard from him?"

"Shane?"

"Yes, Shane. Where the fuck is he?"

"I don't know." She shrugs and then says it again. "Honest, Carmine, I don't know. I haven't heard from him in a few days. He said he had some work to do and that he'd be in touch. Not to worry."

"Yeah. That sounds like him."

I bite into a turkey on rye and look around the room.

Nadia and I have been back in Denver for three days, and we haven't learned anything that we didn't already know when we arrived.

It's damn frustrating.

"If you hear from him, tell him to call me."

"I can do that."

"So, um, Annika," Nadia begins and smiles at her cousin, "Rafe asked about you the other day."

Annika doesn't even pause in the fast consumption of her chips. "Okay?"

"I told him to ask you, but he said you don't reply to his texts or calls."

"No." She slips another chip into her mouth. "I don't."

Nadia sighs and watches her cousin in exasperation. "Are you ever going to?"

Annika chews her bite, swallows, then looks at Nadia and says, "No."

"Why not?" Ivie asks. "He's a good guy, A."

"This is nobody's business," Annika replies and reaches for another bag of chips. "I'm just not going to, okay? I'm sorry, Carmine. I don't mean to insult you or anything."

"Rafe's an idiot," I reply happily. "I wouldn't reply, either."

"He's not an idiot," she says softly. "He's brilliant and kind and all of the good things that Rich wasn't."

She sets the unopened bag down.

"Then I'll ask again." Nadia's voice is gentle. "Why won't you answer him?"

I figure this must be what it's like to be a fly on the wall during a girls' night. I don't think I want to repeat the experience.

"Because I'm broken, and Rafe is way too good for me."

"That's a pile of bullshit," Nadia says simply. "You're not broken, and *no one* is too good for you, Annika Tarenkov. You're hurting, and you need time to heal. You'll get there."

Annika shrugs a shoulder and reaches for the laptop.

"Let's just get back to work and get this over with."

Time drags. Several hours and two sandwiches later, we're still at square one.

"I officially hate paper," I announce as I push the last folder aside. "And I know too much about all of these people's medical histories."

"Let's call it a day," Nadia suggests. "We can start again tomorrow with fresh eyes. Maybe we'll go to Rich's office."

"It's empty," Annika replies. "I went there to clean it out shortly after you left for Europe, but someone beat me to it. The only thing left was the desk."

"What?" I stare at her, dumbfounded. "Why didn't you say anything?"

"Because you were in France, on vacation. And, frankly, I didn't care. It was one less thing I had to deal with. Somebody did me a favor."

"He wouldn't have kept something incriminating there," Ivie says, shaking her head. "It wasn't secure, and he wasn't there all the time. If there's something that can help point to who's behind all of this, I think it'll be here. Rich was cocky. Arrogant. He felt safe here. Knew that no one would mess with him here."

"You're right," Annika agrees. "And I was *not* allowed to be in here. Especially when he was gone. If there's something to find, it's here."

"We need to stop for today," Nadia announces. "We're all moody and tired. We've been at it since sunrise. We need to get some rest and start again tomorrow, like I said."

I watch Nadia. She looks exhausted. We haven't stopped moving since France. There's been little time to rest and get over the jet lag.

She's not wrong. We do need to rest.

"You're right. We're probably missing something because we don't have our wits about us. Let's pick it up in the morning."

"Thank God." Annika closes the laptop. "I've tried every combination of words and numbers I can think of."

"If Shane would answer his phone, he could get into it without breaking a sweat. I'll keep trying him."

"I will, too," Ivie adds and reaches for her cell.

"It's settled then," Nadia says and stands to stretch. "We'll come back tomorrow."

"I NEEDED to get out of there," Nadia confesses when we pull into the driveway of our rental. "I love my cousin, you know I do, but she was irritating the shit out of me today."

"She's angry."

"She's being a brat," she counters. "And that's not like her. She won't talk to me. All she wants to do is brood and sulk, and it's irritating as fuck."

"Not everyone knows how to handle their emotions after a powerful loss like that."

"I know. And I'm sympathetic. She lost who she *thought* was her husband, the life she imagined they'd build together before he even died. And then he was just...gone. She couldn't confront him. She must have so many emotions going on, and I feel for her. But her attitude is shitty, and I needed a break."

"Fair enough." I park and lock my car, and we walk inside the house. It's the same one we used when we were here a few weeks ago. It's starting to feel like a home away from home.

I wonder if the owners would consider selling it? It would be convenient to have a piece of property here in the neutral city of Denver.

I'll have to make some inquiries.

"I'm taking a shower," Nadia announces, and already has her shirt over her head as she saunters down the hall to the master, her ass swaying in that way that never fails to kick me in the stomach with lust.

I want her.

I always want her.

I've fallen in love with her.

I follow after her and hear the water turn on in the shower. Deciding to leave her alone to wash off the frustration of the day, I light a few candles and then go to the kitchen to arrange some fruit, cheese, and crackers on a tray. It's not fancy, but it'll be a nice snack.

I set the platter next to the bed and turn to find Nadia standing in the doorway, towel-drying her hair.

She's naked and still damp from the shower. I can't wait to get my hands on her.

"Is that for me?"

"It seems that most of what I do these days is for you," I reply as I cross to her and cup her face in my hands. "Better?"

"Yeah, that felt good."

I kiss her lips tenderly. "Come, relax. Have a snack."

"I can think of something I'd like to snack on." Her lips curl up into a flirty smile, and she drops her hair towel to the floor, then reaches for my jeans.

"And what would that be?" The question is playful. "A card game, perhaps?"

"I'd kill you at poker."

"I've seen you play poker," I remind her.

"That was an act. I could have cleaned up on that table."

"Darling, you're just full of surprises."

She yanks my shirt over my head and tosses it to the floor, and then she's on me, raw need pouring from every pore of her body. We stumble to the bed, fall in a clumsy heap, and then it's all groping hands and laughter as we fumble our way to each other.

She's out of breath when I pin her beneath me, but her blue eyes are wild and locked on mine as I nudge her thighs apart with mine and drive home.

I gasp as she moans.

I *need* her the way I need air. I can't be gentle as pure desire fuels me, pushing and pulling, driving us both to the ultimate destination of eruption.

"Christ Jesus," she moans. Her back arches, and she clenches around me, then lets go.

I can't keep my hands off her breasts, my mouth away from her neck, and move up to her lips as I press on, still chasing the all-encompassing need to claim her. To show her how much I *need* her.

Finally, with my jaw clenched and my eyes shut, I fall over the edge and collapse on top of her, heaving and tingling.

I feel fingertips roaming over my spine and shift my face from the pillow to her neck.

"You're the best part of my life. Don't ever forget that."

Those fingertips still for just a moment but then begin moving again.

"I won't forget," she promises. "But you're going to have to move because I can't breathe."

I find the strength to roll to the side and smile over at her. "Sorry."

"It's okay. I'm mostly numb anyway." She giggles and reaches for a strawberry. "And I'm *so* hungry. Why am I so hungry?"

"You've been eating like a mouse since France."

"No, I haven't."

337

"Yes. You have."

She watches me and reaches for some cheese, then sits up to eat. "I've just had a lot on my mind, you know?"

"I do. And so do I. Don't worry, I'll keep an eye on you and make sure you eat."

"It's handy having you around."

"I'm glad you think so. Because I'd like to stick around for a long while. When all of this is done, I want you to move in with me."

She frowns. "Aren't I basically already moved in?"

"I want to make it official. I want to move all of your things to Seattle."

She swallows her cheese and watches me with those stunning eyes of hers. "To your house?"

"Yes. To my house. If you hate it, I'll sell it, and we'll buy something else."

She stands and reaches for her robe, wraps it around her, and turns back to me. "You'd sell your house for me if I didn't like it?"

Why do I feel like that's a trick question? "Of course, I would. I want to make a life with you, Nadia. I want you to live where you're comfortable and happy."

"In Seattle."

I see where this is going.

I tug on a pair of shorts and stand across the bed from her, my hands in my pockets.

"Yes, I'd like to live in Seattle. Is that a problem for you?"

"I don't know." She moves a piece of wet hair off her cheek. "It's not something I've considered before. Seattle is off-limits because our families—"

"Our families are fine. If you don't like Seattle, don't want to make a home there—"

"I didn't say that." She hurries around the bed and takes my hand in hers, then kisses my chin. "I'm overthinking it. I like Seattle, Carmine. And I like your house. I mean, it could use a woman's touch here and there..."

Hope spreads through my belly.

"It could. You're right. Do you know of a woman who might want to add her touch?"

She smiles and tips her face to mine. "I just might. I'll put out some feelers."

"You're a sassy one."

"And you get to live with me. Lucky man."

Yes. Yes, I am a lucky man.

EIGHTEEN

~CARMINE~

I slept like the dead. I don't remember the last time I slept that hard.

I roll over and look at my watch.

9:30 a.m.

I sit up and scowl.

Nine-thirty? What in the actual fuck?

Nadia's already up. I don't know why she didn't wake me. It's completely uncharacteristic of me to sleep past seven.

I drag my hand down my face, then reach for my shorts. Jesus, jet lag is a motherfucker.

I pad into the kitchen and narrow my eyes. The whole house is still.

Where's Nadia?

Just as my phone rings in my hand, I notice the note on the counter.

C-

Ran out for donuts and coffee. You're so sleepy! Be back soon.

XO,

N

"Yeah?" I say without looking at the name on the display.

"You need to come up to Victor."

"Shane? What the fuck, Shane? I've been trying to reach you for days. Why don't you ever answer your goddamn phone?"

"I have a life, brother. But never mind that now. I need you to come up to my place to look at some stuff. Rocco's on his way to get you. Should be there any minute. I've been calling you for a few hours."

"I overslept." I sigh and scratch my scalp. "Christ, I haven't even had any coffee yet."

"I have plenty. Get your ass ready to go when Rocco gets there. Oh, and, Carmine, come without the girl."

"Why?"

"Just don't bring her. This is as confidential as it gets."

He ends the call, and I hurry back to the bedroom to get dressed and pull myself together. I usually trim the scruff on my face in the mornings, but there's no time for that today. I clean up a bit, comb my hair, and walk back out to the kitchen.

I look up to see Nadia coming through the door, juggling a box of her favorite donuts and a tray of coffees.

I rush over to help her, gratefully lift a coffee from the tray, and take a long sip.

"God bless you."

"Are you okay? You have sleep marks all over your face."

"I slept hard."

"Yeah, you did." Nadia lifts the lid of the box and sniffs the treats inside. "I bought too many, but I couldn't help myself."

"Thanks for going out to get this." I take her shoulders in my hands and kiss her. "I have to go."

"Huh? Where are we going?"

I kiss her forehead so I can stall and figure out a lie to use. I haven't had to lie to Nadia in months, and it leaves a sour taste in my mouth.

"I have to meet with my brothers. Some business that isn't tied to what we've been working on."

She nods and takes a bite out of a maple bar. "Okay. Are you sure you don't want me to go with you? We could go straight to Annika's from there."

There's a knock on the door.

"That's my brother. You know what? You take the car. I'll meet you there."

"Okay." She frowns, watching me. "Are you sure everything's okay?"

"As far as I know, everything's fine."

Rocco walks into the house and grins. "Mornin'."

"Hi, Rafe," Nadia says. "I didn't get enough coffee for you, but you're welcome to take a donut or two. Actually, here. You might have just saved my life. I'll take two, and you guys take the rest. Now I won't eat them all myself."

"Nice. Thanks."

I take the box and kiss her again. "Thanks. I'll see you later."

"See you later," she says cheerfully as I close the door behind me and follow Rocco to his car.

"What the fuck is going on?" I demand when I climb into the rental.

"No idea," he says and stuffs half the donut into his mouth. After he swallows, he continues. "Got a call from Shane. Thirty minutes later, I was in the chopper headed here."

"Where's it parked?"

"Not far. We'll be at Shane's in an hour."

I feel sick after lying to Nadia.

We arrive at an airstrip where the chopper is waiting for us. Rocco and I climb in, buckle up, and he checks gauges and flips switches. When we have our headsets on, we take off.

The air over the high Rockies is choppy, so the ride is rough, but it doesn't take long before we land about a hundred yards from Shane's house on his property near Victor, Colorado.

As an old mining town in the mountains, Victor used to host more than a hundred thousand people. But now that most of the gold is gone, aside from the last few plots that large corporations own, the town has shrunk to just a couple of hundred people.

Just the way Shane likes it.

How he can live at ten thousand feet, in the middle of nowhere, I have no idea. The air is thin as hell, and it always takes me a day or two to get used to being up this high.

Rocco cuts the engine, and we get out of the helicopter and jog to the house where Shane's standing just outside his door, arms folded across his chest.

"Saved you a donut," Rocco says as he passes the box to Shane. "Your favorite."

"*One?*"

"Better than none," Rocco replies and shrugs as we follow our brother into the big farmhouse.

Shane's property is a fortress. Sitting on a few hundred acres, it's surrounded by state-of-the-art security with cameras and alarms. He has all kinds of toys, weapons, and other equipment that I probably don't want to know about, in addition to the helipad.

He leads us through a honey oak kitchen and the dining and living spaces, which all look completely normal. Fancy, but normal.

Then, he passes through a doorway and procedes down a long flight of stairs. When he flips on the lights, we're no longer in a simple farmhouse.

We're in a headquarters.

Machines beep and computers cover several desks. There are phones, screens, maps.

It's all very James Bond.

Or, Shane Martinelli.

"I got home a couple of days ago and was finally able to start digging into that slimeball, Richard," he begins with a donut in his mouth. "It was right there, in front of our faces the whole goddamn time."

"What was?" I demand.

"Let me start at the beginning." He flips on a screen, and it fills with a photo of Richard. "This asshole isn't Richard Donaldson at all. It's a cover. One that was well crafted, by the way. But it was thin. They didn't add layers, so I didn't have to dig far to discover that he's a phony. If Alex Tarenkov had done his job, it would have been harder to find. But, more on that in a minute."

He clicks a button, and data starts scrolling across the screen.

"Dimitri Lebedev." I turn to Shane in shock. "He's Russian?"

"Oh, he definitely is. But he was born in New York City in 1987. His parents were KGB spies in the seventies and early eighties and came to the US for asylum. The fucking government gave it to them in exchange for some information. You know, we were dealing with the Cold War at that time, and I'm sure they had plenty of secrets to share.

"So, our boy Dimitri was raised here in the US. Went to college at NYU. Smart kid, majored in PoliSci. Guess who his roommate was?"

Rocco and I stare at him. "Who?"

"Alexander Tarenkov."

Shane clicks some keys and some photos of the two men show up on the screen.

"Motherfucker," I mutter.

"So, these two were buddies in college. How Annika didn't know that, I have no idea. Because from what I've heard, Annika and Alex always got along well. Maybe Alex wasn't the type to bring his bestie from college home for the holidays. Maybe he knew if he brought Dimitri around his father, there would be trouble given that Dimitri's parents were KGB agents and all. But that's all speculation."

"We'll have to ask him," Rocco says.

"Wait a minute. If these are his parents"—I point to the couple on the screen—"who were the people at the wedding who claimed to be Rich's family?"

We all look at each other, and then Shane shrugs. "They were hired to act the part. This whole thing was a cover. But not for Dimitri."

"For Alex," Rocco finishes.

"Bingo. Whatever this jerk's into, it goes deep, and it's been going on for a long time. He had one arrest in college for dealing, but it was just some weed. Those records were buried. I assume thanks to his father."

"But the Tarenkovs don't deal," I say, shaking my head. "Nadia told me herself that drugs aren't their game."

"And I buy that," Shane says, continuing. "Igor has always been adamant that their family isn't into the drug game. But that doesn't mean that *Alex* isn't."

"I need to ask Nadia—"

"Look, I know you're in love with her. Jesus, it's all over your face. But you need to tread carefully here," Shane interrupts, turning to me. "Because I have reason to believe that she's in on it with him."

No. Absolutely not. Everything in me wants to rail at him in anger, punch him in the fucking face for even *suggesting* that the woman I love is connected to this.

But I don't.

I wait.

Shane clicks more keys, and the photos on the monitor shift to ones of Nadia and Alex.

"These were taken just six months ago in Atlanta," Shane says.

The two of them are walking down the street together, laughing.

"The Tarenkovs are based in Atlanta," I remind him, but my gut is still in knots. Nadia hates her brother.

So why then is she in all of these photos with him, looking as close as two siblings can be?

"The point is, we don't *know*, Carmine. She could be playing you. She could be double-crossing you."

I remember what the goon in Cannes said: *"She'll just double-cross you, man. That's what she does."*

Fuck, has Nadia been playing me this whole time? I've been falling in love with her, and she's been playing me?

"Take me back." I march toward the steps, my heart pounding. I need to get to Nadia. I need to look her in the eyes when I confront her about this. "Right now, Rocco."

"We're all going," Shane says, shutting down the equipment in a rush and then running after us. "Goddamn it, slow down. I have to lock up."

"This place is a fucking fortress. No one even knows it's here."

"I know," he mutters before we all jog out to the waiting helicopter.

"I'm going in alone." Rocco doesn't even pull into the driveway, he just pulls up to the curb. "I'll come to the office after I'm done confronting her."

"Are you sure she's here?" Shane asks.

"The car's still in the drive," I say with a nod. "She's here. I'll see you in a bit. Go see if you can find out where Alex is."

Rocco drives away as I walk up to the house. Jesus, am I completely blind when it comes to Nadia? I didn't go into this with the intention of falling in love with her. My guard was up, I was careful. Watchful.

I reach for the handle, but movement through the window in the door catches my eye, and I stop.

"Fuck me," I whisper. Nadia is sitting on the couch, her back to me. And Alex, that son of a bitch, is pacing the living room, talking and gesturing with his hands.

Shane was right. The evidence is right here in front of me. Nadia didn't expect me back for hours, so Alex came over, and they're having a meeting in the house I'm paying for.

I pull my phone out of my pocket and call Shane.

"Yeah?"

"You need to come back here. Alex and Nadia are both here. I haven't gone in yet. I want backup. I know how badass she can be."

"On our way."

I shove my phone back into my pocket and decide to walk around the house to get a better view. We'll have to surprise them. Alex is weak and small, but Nadia is excellent at both hand-to-hand combat and with her weapon.

I ease my way around the opposite side of the room and peek my head around the window. Alex is standing in front of Nadia, his arms still flailing about.

And when he steps away, my blood turns to ice.

Nadia's hands are tied in front of her. Both eyes are blackened. Her shirt is ripped, probably from a struggle, and there's a gash in her shoulder with blood running down her chest.

The son of a bitch *hurt* her.

Nadia's eyes roam away from her brother and meet mine. They widen in surprise for a moment, and then she recovers. She watches Alex, who's still on a tirade, and then gives me a shake of the head.

It's barely noticeable, in case Alex sees her, but it's there.

She doesn't want me to come in.

Well, she's going to be very disappointed.

I hurry back around the house just in time to see my brothers hurrying up the driveway.

"He beat her up," I say quickly and bring them both up to speed. "She's not in on it, and he's going to kill her."

"No." Rocco takes out his sidearm and disengages the safety. "He isn't. How do you want to do this?"

"There are two entrances, aside from the garage." I point to the front door and then gesture to the side of the house. "Both are within his line of sight, so when we go in, we go in firing. But you have to be careful. Nadia's tied up on the couch."

"Rocco and I are going in on the side," Shane says, cool as a cucumber as he thinks it through. "Carmine, you go in through the front door as if you're just coming home and don't know what's going on. Play stupid with him for a bit. We need to catch him off guard."

"And if he just draws a weapon and shoots me?"

Shane smiles. "Duck."

"That's not helpful." I tap my piece at my ankle and the one at my back. "He's yelling. I'd say he's telling her everything he's done."

"Alex *would* brag," Rocco says. "He'll want to tell her everything before he kills her."

"I'm using that to my advantage," I say and walk to the door. "Get in position. I'm going in."

Without another word, I open the door.

"Hey, babe, I'm home! I hope there are still some donuts left. I'm starving. The gym was pretty empty today, so—"

I come up short when Alex points a gun in my face.

"Hey, hey, hey, what's going on? Nadia?"

"Hello, *darling*," Alex says with a sneer. "Go sit with her. This works out well. I can kill you both at the same time."

CHAPTER
NINETEEN
~NADIA~

N o. All I can think is *no*.

Alex is going to kill me.

And now, he's going to kill Carmine, too.

"Let Carmine go," I say through throbbing lips. "This is between you and me."

Instead of answering, Alex slaps me and then lowers his face to mine and sneers. "Papa didn't teach you to keep your cunt mouth shut, so I'm going to do it. Don't you fucking talk unless I tell you to."

"Why'd you do it?" Carmine asks calmly as he sits next to me. "Why'd you enlist Rich and go about this whole dramatic game?"

"Game?" Alex turns on Carmine but doesn't hit him. No, he's too much of a pussy to hit a man stronger than he is. "This isn't a game. This is brilliant. I was just telling little sis here all about it, but I'll explain it to you, too. She'll just have to hear it twice. But you don't mind, do you, sis?"

I shake my head no. From the corner of my eye, I see Carmine slip his phone out of his pocket. He taps on the screen, but I can't see what he's doing.

Hell, *he* can't see what he's doing.

"Papa is too set in his ways," Alex begins. "He's weak. He thinks we should respect the old ways of doing things. And because of that short-sightedness, he's missing out on a lot of money. I'm not willing to do that."

"You're not rich enough?" Carmine asks.

"Fuck, no. Who's *rich enough*? There's no such thing, you dumbass. Drugs. Drugs are where it's at. And when you have a new brew, all the better."

"That *new brew* you have kills people," Carmine says. "That doesn't make for repeat customers."

"That's not what we were selling." Alex laughs. "That was just to get people out of our way. The stuff we sell is the best high you can have. It's better than coke, better than meth or anything else. People will be *begging* me for it. They'll pay anything at all for it."

"What is it?" Carmine asks.

"It's a synthetic. You don't have to sniff it or shoot it. You pop the pill, and in twenty minutes, you're on the best ride of your life. I call it Hades."

"How original," Carmine says calmly. "So, you went to some of Sergi's people in New York, and they turned you down."

"Weak assholes," he says with the shake of his head. "They didn't want to do anything unless they ran it by Mick first. And I couldn't allow that."

"Why not?"

"Because this is *my* fucking operation," Alex yells and drives his finger into his chest. "Mine. Not theirs. And if they want to try to bring anyone higher up in, they get dead."

"So, what about Richard? Or should I say, *Dimitri?*"

What? Who in the hell is Dimitri?

Alex's smile falls, and he wipes his mouth with the back of his hand before smiling again, but I can tell he's nervous now.

"I figured you'd find out about that sooner or later," Alex says. "It was so pitifully easy. With his background, he was just itching to get into something on the down-low. Something big. It was his idea to marry into the family. I thought he should marry Nadia." He turns to me, and I want to throw up. "But he had a thing for Annika. He said Annika was weaker and would be easier to fool. And I hate to admit it, but he was right. She fell for the whole sappy I-love-you act—hook, line, and sinker. I mean, he actually got her to *marry* him! Women are so stupid. So easily manipulated. They're fucking worthless."

He turns to me and raises his hand, but Carmine stops him. He's up in a flash and has Alex's wrist in his fist.

"If you touch her one more time, I'll rip your goddamn arm off."

Alex shoves away like a pouty child. "Don't touch me. Don't fucking touch me."

He reaches for his gun, but it's gone.

"Looking for this?" Carmine holds it up, and Alex's face goes white.

Oh my God. We're going to live through this.

We're going to live through this.

Carmine throws the gun across the room and turns to me.

"Don't—" I begin, but it's too late. Alex hits Carmine over the head with the tray that was on the coffee table. Carmine turns and backhands Alex, but then, to both of our surprise, Alex retaliates.

Carmine takes as many hits as he dishes out. I rush across the room and retrieve the gun, my hands still tied with the twine Alex brought with him. Still, I'm able to point it down at my brother, who's now bleeding from the nose.

"Freeze."

Suddenly, Rafe and Shane run into the room, their weapons drawn, and Alex sags against the hardwood in defeat.

"Fuck," he says and then coughs and looks at me. "I will kill you. It may not be today, but it's going to happen. My men should have done it in France, but they were too weak. I knew I should have done it myself. And I will. Every minute of your life, you'd better sleep with one eye open and watch your back."

I look at Carmine. "Did you record everything he said earlier?"

He grabs his phone and nods. "It's on here. But I learned everything from Shane. That's where I was this morning."

I look over at Shane as Alex starts to moan and whine. "Do you have all of the evidence my father will need to prove that my brother was behind everything?"

"I do," Shane says with a solemn nod.

350

With the gun still in my hand, I look down at my brother, and I squeeze the trigger, killing him instantly.

"Call the cleanup team." I drop the gun and let Carmine fold me into his arms. I ache all over from the beating Alex gave me, and my heart hurts, too.

"Shh." Carmine rocks me back and forth. "I'm so sorry, baby."

"He was an ass. A complete ass. But he was also my brother. And there was a time that I loved him."

"I know." He kisses the top of my head. "Come on. Let's get you cleaned up."

"We've got this," Shane says, but before we can leave the room, he kisses my cheek. "You did the right thing."

"Sometimes, the right thing really sucks."

"I know."

"Don't worry about this," Rafe says kindly.

"I have to call my father. There's different protocol here."

"I know," Rafe says. "Don't worry."

Carmine leads me to the bathroom off the master, closes the door, and I fall into his arms, sobbing like I never have before.

"I'm a monster." I pull back, just out of his grasp. "Jesus, Carmine, I'm a monster. I killed my brother."

Without a word, he takes my shoulders and turns me to look into the mirror, pressed close behind me.

"Look at yourself."

My eyes are swollen and blackened. My lips are puffy and split. I have a cut on my shoulder from the kitchen knife.

"He knocked on the door about thirty minutes after you left," I begin and swallow hard. "Of course, I let him in. Turned my back. And he started in on me. He had a baseball bat. I couldn't react. Couldn't defend myself."

"He was a coward."

"He told me that he was behind all of the killings. Said that he was going to kill me, then Papa. That he'd be the boss. Said he'd turn our family into a drug lord empire—exactly what Papa doesn't want."

"And he was going to continue hunting you, would try to end your life, Nadia," he reminds me. "That wasn't an empty threat. If I hadn't arrived when I did, you'd probably be dead now. Can you look us both in the eyes and say that what you did was wrong?"

"No." I shake my head slowly. "I don't think it was wrong. Because he would have killed you, too, and I couldn't live—"

I turn back into his arms. "I couldn't live with myself if he hurt you, Carmine. I love you so much, I can't bear the thought. Oh my God, what would I do without you?"

He tips my chin up with his finger. "Do you mind saying that again?"

"What would I do without you?" I sniff, more tears falling at the thought of Carmine being gone.

"Not that part, baby."

"I love you, Carmine. I don't know how it happened or when. We went from being enemies to *this*. But I do. I love you so much it hurts. I really thought you'd come into this house and find me dead. That alone almost broke me. But then when I thought that he might kill *you*, as well, I just... You are the best part of my life."

"I think that's my line." His lips touch the side of mine, ever so gently so he doesn't hurt me. "I love you, too. With all of my heart and soul. You are meant to be with me. I feel that in my heart."

"I do, too." I snuggle into him for just a moment. "We'd better get me cleaned up so I can face my father. I don't know what he'll do."

"He'll love you," he says simply. "And he'll grieve."

"Yeah." I nod as Carmine reaches for a washrag. "We'll both do that."

Six of us sit in my father's living room in Atlanta. Carmine and his brothers flew me here this afternoon, and their father, Carlo, met us.

We didn't meet at an office.

We came to Igor Tarenkov's home.

"Your mother is lying down after taking a sedative," Papa says as he reaches for me. His eyes are shadowed and sad, but he touches me with tenderness. "How do you feel, little one?"

"A bit sore. It's not as bad as it was in Seattle when I got—" I stop talking at my father's furious look and swallow hard. "Oh, I guess I forgot to tell you about that."

"I suggest you tell me now."

I look over at Carmine, who's sitting next to his father. All four men are imposing. Carmine nods. "It's time, sweetheart."

So, I take a deep breath and tell them all about getting attacked in Seattle, and how Carmine and his people helped me get well.

"But that wasn't the first time."

I tell him everything, going back to when I was jumped in Atlanta, and my hair was cut.

"It seems your brother has been terrorizing you for a long time," Papa says quietly. "I'm sorry. I'm sorry that I never saw it. I should have known."

"He was good at covering his tracks," I remind him. "Papa, I understand if you don't want to see me again. If this is goodbye—"

"What kind of nonsense is this?"

"I killed your son." I bury my face in my hands and weep. "I murdered my brother in cold blood, and I would do it again. What kind of daughter does that make me? What kind of boss would I make?"

"No one asked for my opinion," Carlo says, catching my attention, "but I'm going to give it anyway. You would make an excellent leader, my dear. Because you did what you had to do to keep the rest of your family and those you care about safe. Your brother was the bad seed. And I hope I'm not speaking out of turn when I say we all saw that."

"You're not," Papa says. "I will grieve for the son I had and the man I needed him to be. But the punishment fit the crime here, Nadia. Don't torture yourself. You were defending yourself. And me."

Relief floods me. "Thank you."

"I'm sorry for the way this ended," Carlo says to my father. "If there is anything my family can do for you, we are always at your disposal."

"Thank you, old friend," Papa says. "And likewise."

"We still haven't figured out who killed Elena's parents," Rafe points out. "That goes back farther than Alex."

"That's something we'll keep digging into," Shane agrees. "We'll find them."

"I have something to say," Carmine says. "Mr. Tarenkov, I'd like to ask for your permission to marry your daughter."

My eyes fly to Carmine's in surprise.

Our fathers share a smile.

"Well, it's about damn time, my boy," Papa says. "Carlo and I have been throwing you at each other for years."

"I thought they'd never come to their senses," Carlo says with a laugh. "A couple of stubborn children we have here, Igor."

"Wait. You *wanted* us to marry?" Carmine asks.

"Of course. Why do you think we've allowed you to spend so much time together?" My father winks at me. *Winks!* I don't think I've ever seen him wink a day in his life.

"How do you like that?" Shane says with a laugh. "Pop's a matchmaker."

The brothers both laugh as Carmine crosses to me with humor in his chocolate brown eyes.

He lowers to one knee.

"Will you marry me, Nadia, and be the best part of my life until I'm no longer on this Earth?"

"Let me think about it." I grin as he digs into his pocket and comes out with a rock the size of a baby's fist. "Geez, Carmine. Did you have to get something so fancy?"

"Yes." He slips it onto my finger and then kisses my knuckles. "I'm going to give you everything you've ever dreamed of."

"I believe you." He kisses me carefully.

"Is that a yes?"

"That's a hell yes."

EPILOGUE
~IVIE~

It's been a long-ass day at the clinic. Annika took off for home about an hour ago, but I decided to stay and clean up a bit. Annika just hasn't been herself over the past month or so, not since her husband died.

I'm worried about her.

So, if I can stay late at work, make sure everything is perfect for her here and take some of the burdens off her, I'll gladly do it.

Annika is my best friend. She's the only person in the world who knows my deepest secrets. And I'll do whatever it takes to help her.

I hear the bell on the front door and hurry out to tell whoever it is that we're closed.

But when I get there, I stop cold.

"Hello, Ivie." He flips the lock on the door, and I dial Annika's number and leave my phone on the desk so she can hear everything. I hope with all my might that she answers. "Or should I say, *Laryssa*?"

I shake my head. "I'm sorry, I don't know a Laryssa. I'm Ivie. And we're closed for the day. But if you'd like to make an appointment, I can help you with that."

"You know, I thought for a long time that your father was an imbecile. Stupid. He didn't cover his tracks well."

I just raise my chin, determined not to let him see my fear.

"But you're different. You covered your tracks *very* well. And I know that you couldn't have done that alone. Which tells me that your father isn't as stupid as I thought."

"I don't know what you could possibly want from me. I'm just living my life."

"And a nice life it is," he says. "Good for you, Laryssa. I couldn't make your father pay for his sins when he was alive—and we both know that those sins were many. But now I've found you."

I shake my head as he walks around the counter.

"Now, don't do something silly like try to get away. You're coming with me. And you're going to pay for the sins of your father."

He jabs a syringe into my arm, and I immediately feel...heavy.

"There, now. Come along, Laryssa. We have plenty of work to do."

Don't miss HEADHUNTER, the next book in the With Me In Seattle MAFIA series! You can get it here: www. kristenprobyauthor.com/headhunter

And here is a sneak peek at Headhunter:

HEADHUNTER

A WITH ME IN SEATTLE MAFIA NOVEL

Headhunter
A With Me In Seattle MAFIA Novel
By

Kristen Proby

For my husband, and his family, for introducing me to Victor, Colorado. I took liberties for this story, of course. But the heart of the town is here. I love you.

PROLOGUE

~IVIE~

"I'm not doing this for you anymore." I glare at my father and raise my chin, trying to appear way more confident than I feel.

My stomach pitches when he slowly turns to glare at me with cold, blue eyes. The same eyes that look back at me in the mirror.

But I'm nothing like the man who sired me. And I never will be.

Without another word, he turns back to the task at hand, making an egg sandwich. Our apartment is small and in a dirty little neighborhood in the Bronx. He says it helps us blend in, that no one will pay us any mind here.

In reality, he spends money as quickly as it lands in his pocket, and this is all he can afford.

I turn sixteen this summer, and he's already made it clear that I'll be quitting school and taking a full-time job.

What I want doesn't matter. It never has with this man.

"Did you hear me?" I demand.

"I hear nothing important." His voice is calm, thick with that Bulgarian accent that I hate so much.

"I'm serious. I'm not doing your bidding anymore. If I get caught, I'll go to *jail*."

"You are too young for jail."

"No." I shake my head and plant my hands on my hips. "I'm not too young. They'll send me to juvie. Either way, I'll be locked up, and I'm not doing that for you. This is ridiculous. Why can't you be a normal father instead of gambling and selling fake jewelry? Why don't you just get a real job so we can live a normal life?"

Without a look, he spins and backhands me, sending me sprawling on the floor. My cheek sings in pain, and I see stars as he leans over so close that his nose nudges mine.

"You are my *property*," he growls. "You are nothing but a female. And you'll do exactly as I say, *when* I say. If you try to defy me again, I'll sell you to the many men who have already asked for your body."

I gasp and stare up at him in utter shock and revulsion. "You *wouldn't*."

"Yes." He stands and straightens his crisp, white shirt. "I would. Do not test me again, Laryssa."

The knock on the door is sharp, startling us both.

"I know you're in there, Pavlov," a man yells through the door, and all the blood drains from my father's face.

"How?" he whispers and then turns to me. "Hide me, daughter."

I shake my head, only enraging him further. He raises a hand, but before he can hit me for a second time, someone busts the door open, and three men walk inside.

"Did you think you could steal from us and get away with it?" The biggest one reaches for my father and pushes him against the wall.

This is it. This is my chance.

I scurry into my little bedroom and grab the bag I always keep packed—always ready to run if the opportunity arises.

I won't get another chance like this.

"No, I wouldn't steal from you. I just had to earn the money to repay you."

Another man punches him in the face as I slip out the front door and make a run for it.

My heart hammers in my chest. I can't hear the street noises through the rush of blood in my head and over my loud, panting breaths.

I have exactly four hundred and thirty-two dollars, some clothing, and my mother's wedding ring.

And a new freedom.

Because I'm *never* going back to live with a man who makes me do the things my father does.

I'll die first.

CHAPTER
ONE
~SHANE~

"Take the shot."

The voice is calm in my ear, coming from several thousand miles away in a secure office at the White House.

I'm lying on my stomach on a rooftop, my sights trained on the target, but people keep walking in front of him.

"Not clear," I whisper and swear when the target walks into another room.

"It's taken three weeks for you to find him," the president reminds me. "Take him out. *Now.*"

Yeah, yeah. I don't need her to remind me how long I searched for this asshole. And as soon as he moves a little to the left...

I squeeze the trigger, and less than a second later, the target falls.

"Mission accomplished," I say and move quickly to the stairwell that leads to a waiting car below.

In less than three minutes, I'm safely away from the scene and headed to the airport.

"Good work," she says into my ear. "Now, get yourself home. The plane's waiting for you."

"Thank you, Madame President."

I nod to the driver, my partner for this operation, and he steps on the gas to get us to the airfield quicker.

Suddenly, the front window explodes, a bullet hitting the driver squarely in the forehead, killing him instantly.

"Miller's down," I say with a calm I don't feel as I reach over to take the wheel. I maneuver him out of the seat and manage to step on the gas, winding my way through the foreign city.

If I'm caught, I'll also be killed.

And I'm not ready to die today.

Only one car is following me, and it doesn't take me long to lose them.

"Your transport has been compromised," I hear in my ear. "The crew was killed. I need you to disappear for a couple of days. Lay low and await further instructions."

"Abandoning me in a foreign country wasn't part of the deal."

"We're not abandoning you," the president replies. "We'll get you out."

"See that you do."

"WE EXPECTED you home a few days ago," my brother, Carmine, says as I walk into his office at our family's base of operations in Seattle, Washington. Rocco, my other brother, stares out the window but turns to look at me as I move farther in.

"Yeah, well, I got hung up."

I won't mention that I spent two nights curled up under a box, waiting for the US government to get me out of enemy territory after I assassinated one of the bad guys.

My brothers aren't allowed to know any of that.

It's better this way. The less they know, the less likely they could be killed for having the knowledge.

"Have I missed anything important?"

"Wedding plans," Rocco volunteers and then smiles at our brother sweetly. "I mean, it was a rough few days there, deciding between lilacs and freesia. And then there was the matter of the cake flavors."

My gaze bounces between Rocco—who's clearly getting a huge kick out of razzing our big brother—and Carmine, whose mouth firms into a hard line.

"He's the groom," I say simply and cross to the small kitchenette to see what kind of food we have stashed away in the fridge.

I'm fucking starving.

"I never pegged Nadia as the type to get all swept up in the fancy wedding deal," Rocco says thoughtfully.

"She's a woman," Carmine reminds him. "And big weddings are the mafia's way. You know that."

"So, which was it? Lilacs or freesia?" I ask as I return to the desk with a half-eaten sub sandwich and a bag of nacho chips.

"Both," Carmine says with a shrug. "She couldn't decide, so we went with both."

"As one does," Rocco says with a wink.

The door bursts open, and the bride-to-be herself hurries inside, her eyes wide with an emotion I rarely see on my brother's fiancée.

Fear.

"Carmine," she says as she hurries over. "I have Annika on the phone. She needs our help."

"Put her on speaker," I say, and we all lean in to hear what Nadia's cousin has to say.

"Okay, they can all hear you," Nadia says as she plants her hands on the desk. "Tell them *exactly* what you just told me."

"It's Ivie," Annika says, immediately getting my full and undivided attention. "She's been taken."

"Taken by *who*?" I ask, keeping my voice calm but feeling my blood erupt through my veins with a surge of new adrenaline.

"I don't know," she says and sniffs. "I got a call from her, but I was about to get in the shower, so I let it go to voicemail."

She sniffs again, frustrating me.

Just fucking *tell me*.

"I remembered it the next morning, *this* morning, so I listened to it. Oh my God, you guys. She's been taken. She was trying to get me to pick up, to listen, and help her. And I failed her horribly. I need you. Is Shane there?"

369

"I'm here."

"Thank God. Please, we need your help."

We all look at Rocco, who's already pulling his phone out of his pocket.

"The plane will be ready when we get to the airport."

"I THOUGHT Annika was going to tell me that this was all connected to Rich," Nadia says, shaking her head as the plane lands in Denver. "That there was more information or that someone else was dead. *Something*. I didn't expect her to tell me that Ivie had been taken."

I swallow hard, fear a very real and icy demon settling in my stomach.

I don't fear much. But Ivie and I have become friends over the past several months, and if my life weren't well and truly a shitshow, I'd take it much, much further with her.

If anyone touches a hair on her gorgeous head, I'll fucking skin them alive.

"Rich's organization fell," Carmine reminds his fiancée.

"We don't know that now," Nadia says, shaking her head. "Maybe this is tied to that. Maybe someone thinks they can get something out of Annika, or punish her by taking Ivie."

"We don't know what's going on," I remind everyone. "Let's get to Annika's place and figure things out."

My mind is racing. I haven't slept in seventy-two hours, and aside from the stale sandwich, I haven't eaten.

And I don't give a shit.

I need to find Ivie. Make sure she's safe and whole.

Annika's house is an hour from the airfield.

"You should sleep," Nadia says to me, her voice soothing. "I can see that whatever job you were on took a toll. You need rest if you're going to help Ivie."

"I'm fine."

"You're not fine," she counters, and I *barely* stop myself from rolling my eyes at her.

370

Nadia is a fierce woman. I don't need her to kick my ass over an eye roll.

"I'm *fine*," I repeat and narrow my eyes at her.

"What is it with the Martinelli brothers and being so fucking stubborn?" she asks as she turns back in her seat and scowls out the windshield.

"It's just part of our charm," Carmine says, but Nadia shakes her head.

"No, actually, it's not charming. It's dumb. He's going to hurt himself if he keeps overworking like that."

As if I have a choice. I can't exactly tell her that I sleep when the fucking *president* says I can.

So, I just grunt and watch Denver whiz by outside the window. The few hours it took to get here is, unfortunately, valuable time wasted. Time that I could have spent trying to find Ivie.

Jesus, where is she? What are they doing to her? And *who the fuck* are *they*?

"Almost there," Rocco mutters and sends me a sympathetic smile.

I know my brothers are aware of the massive crush I have on Ivie. I've never had a *crush* on anyone in my fucking life. But I saw her once, and that was all it took.

I know that Rocco and Carmine don't understand my attraction. That's because she's a little awkward and has a classic, girl-next-door look about her that I find absolutely hot as hell. She's not the type that would usually turn my head, and my siblings know it.

In the past, that may have been true.

But Ivie attracts me in every damn way. She's funny and sweet. *So* damn sweet. We've spent a little time on the phone, talking. I'm not much of a talker, but it comes so easily with Ivie.

How my brothers *don't* see the amazing woman she is, is beyond me.

I know that a relationship—hell, a *future*—with Ivie is out of the question for someone like me. My job consumes my life, and what's left over belongs to my family. Between the government and the mafia, I've killed more than any one man should. My time doesn't belong to me.

But if things were different, if I were free to be my own man, I would scoop Ivie up and make her mine in a heartbeat.

"She looks worse than the day she found out that Rich was a lying asshole," Nadia says as we pull into Annika's drive and see the woman standing in the doorway, waiting for us.

Her eyes are red-rimmed from crying, her nose chapped from wiping it too much. And when Nadia hurries to her and engulfs Annika in a hug, the other woman falls apart once more.

"Let's go inside," Carmine says, urging the women into the house and to the living room.

When Annika's seated and wiping her wet eyes, Carmine speaks again.

"Now, tell us again *exactly* what happened."

"Okay." Annika takes a long, deep breath and then tells us again about seeing the call from Ivie, but how she let it go to voicemail because she was getting into the shower and how she didn't remember about the call until this morning.

"So I finally listened to the message, and my blood ran cold."

"Play it," I say, sitting next to her as she pulls it up on her phone, taps the screen, and it starts to play.

"I'm sorry, I don't know a Laryssa. I'm Ivie. And we're closed for the day. But if you'd like to make an appointment, I can help you with that."

"You know, I thought for a long time that your father was an imbecile. Stupid. He didn't cover his tracks well. But you're different. You covered your tracks very well. And I know that you couldn't have done that alone. Which tells me that your father isn't as stupid as I thought."

"I don't know what you could possibly want from me. I'm just living my life."

"And a nice life it is," the man says. *"Good for you, Laryssa. I couldn't make your father pay for his sins when he was alive—and we both know that those sins were many. But now I've found you. Now, don't do something silly like try to get away. You're coming with me. And you're going to pay for the sins of your father."*

There's a pause.

"There, now. Come along, Laryssa. We have plenty of work to do."

"After that, it's dead air for a couple of minutes, and then it ends," Annika says, locking her phone.

"Do you recognize his voice?" I ask her.

"No. I didn't recognize his face, either."

My head whips up. "You saw his face?"

"Yes, we have security cameras at the spa, of course. I looked at the footage, but I don't know who he is."

"I can find out," I reply. "I'll need to see it."

Annika nods, but Carmine shakes his head.

"He kept calling her Laryssa. That's not her name. Could she be a victim of mistaken identity?"

"No," Annika says softly and then stands to pace the room. "I can't believe I'm about to tell you this, but she's in danger, and you *have* to know."

My hands curl into fists.

"Know what?" I demand.

"Ivie's real name is Laryssa Pavlov. Her father was a Bulgarian asshole, but she escaped him when she was young. Made a new life for herself—one she could be proud of."

I can't believe what I'm hearing. After all the hours Ivie and I spent talking, she never told me any of this.

"So, this guy really is trying to punish her for her father's sins," Rocco says, blowing out a breath.

My brother's eyes haven't left Annika. It's no surprise he doesn't give me a hard time about Ivie. He, too, longs for someone he can't have.

It's a shitty situation to be in.

"What was her father's name?"

"Ivan. Ivan Pavlov," Annika says. "I can't tell you much about her past. She told me the story in confidence, but this definitely has something to do with her father."

"Get me that footage so I can find this motherfucker and get Ivie home where she belongs."

"Of course," Annika says, reaching for her laptop.

"I need to transfer this file to my system," I inform her, already tapping the keys on her computer. "I can find out who he is by running the face through some software and a database I have."

My hands fly over the keyboard, and then I reach into my bag for my laptop and get to work again, fingers flying.

When the screen simply says *Searching...* for what feels like a fucking year, I want to punch my hand through a wall.

But, finally, an image and bio appear on the screen.

"Boris Nicolov, fifty-eight. Bulgarian. Last known address is in New York. Looks like I'm going to the east coast."

I stand, and Rocco joins me. "Maybe you should do some more digging before you head off on a wild goose chase."

I push my brother against the wall and get up in his face.

"Get the fuck out of my way."

"Hey." His hands come up in surrender. "I'm not *in* your way. I'm just, you know, trying to be the voice of reason."

"Either you'll help me, or I'll do this without you."

"You know we'll help," Nadia says.

"I'll inform the Sergi family that we'll be on their turf for this," Carmine adds, referencing another mafia family. No one just shows up on another family's turf. You always let them know in advance.

"I didn't even think of that," I mutter and rub my hand down my face. "Thanks. Let's do this."

"Keep me posted," Annika says as she hurries behind us to the door. "I guess I could have shown you all of this while you were still in Seattle."

"It's better in person," I reply and then reach back to squeeze her hand. "And this way, we're closer to New York than we were a few hours ago."

She offers me a watery smile, and Nadia, Carmine, and I all hurry back to the car.

Rocco hangs back to say something to Annika that has her tearing up again, then he jumps in the car with us, and we're off to the airfield.

"What did you say to her?" I ask quietly.

"It doesn't matter."

TWO

~IVIE~

My head is pounding. I can't see well because my eyes are blurry from the multiple slaps across the face that this asshole seems to enjoy handing out.

I don't know where I am. After he plunged the needle into my arm at the clinic, I blacked out. This room is dark, with no windows. And I'm sitting in a chair, my hands tied behind my back, just like the James Bond movies.

"You're going to tell me," he says. His voice has remained calm the entire time. How long has it been? It feels like weeks.

"I've told you over and over again, I *don't know*."

"I don't believe you." His lips spread into a thin line. "My associates and I will be *very* disappointed if you don't tell me where he hid the money. And they'll be here soon."

"My father couldn't keep a dollar in his pocket," I reply. "He spent money, his or anyone else's, as soon as it landed in his hand. If he had your money, I'm sure he spent it long before he died and went to hell."

His eyes narrow. "You didn't like your father."

"Of course, I didn't. He was a pitiful excuse for a human being, and I ran away the first opportunity I got. And let me just say, at fifteen, it wasn't like I could hide easily. But he also never came looking, so there was no love lost, was there?"

I firm my lips and blink the tears from my eyes. Not from crying. No, this asshole isn't going to make me blubber like a baby. The water is from that last slap.

The man has a hell of a right arm.

He sighs and shakes his head.

"It's too much money for you not to know where it is," he insists. "So, we're going to have to get a little rougher."

He reaches over to a table and retrieves a pair of needle-nose pliers and bolt cutters.

"It would be a shame to start removing fingers from those dainty little hands."

"I. Don't. Know. Anything."

"I. Don't. Fucking. Believe. You."

He leans in and almost touches my nose with his. I can see light flecks of gold in his green eyes. And something starts to spread through me.

Not just anger. Not just fear and frustration.

Determination.

"I'm going to take off your fingers and then your toes. And if that still doesn't make you talk, I'm going to poke those pretty blue eyes out."

"There's one thing you didn't think of," I reply evenly. His eyes narrow just a bit, and I smile widely. "You forgot to tie my feet."

And with that, I pull my knees to my chest and kick out with all my might, plowing the soles of my feet right into this asshole's gut, sending him flying backward.

His arms flail, and he trips on a broken floorboard.

And then, as if in slow motion, he hits his head on the corner of a table and falls to the ground, blood gushing from his head.

His eyes are empty.

He's not breathing.

"Oh my God," I whisper, staring at him in horror. "Oh, shit. Shit shit shit. I *killed* him."

I look around at the plain walls and the single door behind me that must lead to the outside.

But I can't move. My hands are not tied to the chair, they're tethered to the floor, the rope through a metal ring. So it's not even like I can scooch my way over to the door and make noise.

I'm *stuck*.

I knew I was going to die in this room. Even if I'd told him what he wanted to know, even if I *could*, he would have killed me as soon as I did. I knew I wasn't leaving here alive.

But now I have to die by starvation and without water? I would have rather he put a bullet in my head.

I sigh and stare at the man. I don't know him. I have no idea what his name is, or how he knew my father. Obviously, my father double-crossed him on some deal. He mentioned his *colleagues*.

Who are they?

I don't even know how long my father's been dead. When this guy told me that he couldn't make my dad pay before he died, it was the first I'd heard of his demise.

I'm not surprised. He would have only been in his mid-to-late fifties, but he'd lived a hard, dangerous life.

For me, he died when I was fifteen, and I ran out of that horrible place in New York.

"I'm going to have to sit here and watch him decompose," I whisper in horror. "He's going to smell and get disgusting. Jesus, why do I have to be so clumsy? Leave it to me to send his head into the corner of a table just right."

I try to stand and attempt to work my way around so I can untie my hands, but I only succeed in almost dislocating my shoulder.

That won't help anything.

"Did he say his associates would be here soon? Oh, hell, I *am* going to die here. They're going to kill me."

I bite my lip. My heart starts to race. I haven't had a panic attack in a long time, but I'm on the verge now.

I'm stuck with a corpse, and bad men are on their way to kill me.

I'm a sitting duck.

"I didn't even get to tell Annika that I love her," I wail, feeling horribly sorry for myself. "Or have sex with Shane. Or even just spend time with him! I'm halfway to falling in love with him already, and now I'll never get to finish. I won't get to see the sun or eat raspberries in ice cream or go to the ocean."

Now, tears well up in my eyes. I thought I was safe. My cover was iron-clad. How did this asshole find me?

I hear rustling on the other side of the door and freeze.

This is it. This is how it ends.

But I won't go down without a fight, damn it.

I hear the door open, and then everything happens so fast. I lash out, kicking and yelling.

"I won't make this easy on you, motherfucker! You may kill me, but I'll kick your ass first."

"Hey, hey, hey." The voice is soothing, and when I open the eyes I didn't realize I'd closed, I see Shane standing in front of me, then kneeling to look me in the eyes. "It's us."

"Us?"

I glance around to see Shane's brothers and Nadia, one of my very best friends in the world.

Carmine squats next to *him*, checking for a pulse. "Dead."

"You killed him?" Nadia asks as Shane gently rubs his fingers through my hair, and Rafe works on the ropes.

"Yeah. My clumsiness paid off." I tell them how it happened. "But we have to get out of here. He said he had associates on their way here. That's who I thought you were."

"In and out," Shane says, seeming to remind them all of their mission. "We deal with the rest later."

"What's the rest?"

"Plane's ready," Rafe says with a nod. Suddenly, my hands are free, and Shane lifts me into his arms.

"We're getting you out of here, little dove."

I lay my head on his shoulder, suddenly so tired I can't keep my eyes open. I feel weird. Dizzy.

And then I feel nothing at all.

"WAKE UP, SWEET GIRL," Shane croons in my ear. I feel like I must be in heaven. Surely, I've died, and heaven is a place where Shane's voice wraps around me and makes me feel safe. "Come on, Ivie, I need you to open those gorgeous eyes for me."

My eyes flutter open, and I see Shane leaning over me, smiling down at me softly.

"There you are," he says. "You scared me for a minute there."

"I'm in a bed." I frown and glance around. "Are we *flying*?"

"Yes, we're flying back to Denver."

"Wait." I sit up and press my hand to my head. "Weren't we already in Denver?"

Shane sits next to me, takes my hand, and then kisses my fingers, making my stomach jump.

"What do you remember?"

"I remember being taken out of the clinic. I was drugged. Then I woke up in a shitty room and got beat up a bit. Ended up killing my captor *on accident*, and then you arrived."

"I suppose that's the CliffsNotes version," he murmurs. "Honey, he took you to New York. We found you in a basement in Queens."

I blink, completely baffled. "I was passed out that long? I wonder what he drugged me with?"

"As do I," Shane says, examining me. "Does anything hurt?"

"I'm a little stiff and sore from having my hands tied behind me for so long, but other than that, I'll live."

"When I saw his handprint on your cheek, I wanted to kill him myself," he admits. His voice is mild, but by the look in his eyes, I can see that he means every word.

"I kicked him," I say, thinking it over. "He was up in my face, trying to intimidate me, and I just brought my feet up and kicked him in the gut, hard. He jerked back, tripped, and then fell against the table."

"That was too good of a death for him."

I blow out a sigh. "Yeah, well, it was fast. I don't know who the hell he was."

"I do," Shane says. "We'll talk about it all when we get to my place."

"*Your* place?"

He just looks at me with those gorgeous brown eyes that always seem to hypnotize me.

"Shane, I have to work. Annika needs me. Oh my God, Annika!"

"We've already told her that we found you safe and sound," he assures me. "We'll stop and see her before we go to my place in the mountains."

"Shane, I can't go with you to the mountains."

"And I can't let you go home," he says. "Not until we have a full picture of what's going on here. I'm going to keep you safe, no matter what. A little time away from work won't hurt anyone."

"I don't—"

"I'm not asking," he says, his voice sharp, and I gape up at him.

"I was just kidnapped once. I won't do it again, Shane. I care about you, and I enjoy being with you, but I'll live my life under *my* terms."

He rubs his hand over his lips in agitation. "I'm just trying to keep you safe."

My head is throbbing. "I don't want to have our first fight on this plane."

His expression softens, and then he chuckles. "Fair enough. Have you eaten?"

"My captor didn't offer me room service."

"Let's go eat something," he suggests and reaches out for my hand. He leads me into a different part of the plane where the others are seated. Carmine and Nadia are curled up on a loveseat, looking at an iPad. Rafe is staring out the window. All their heads come up when they hear us enter.

"How are you feeling, sugar?" Nadia asks, rushing over to hug me.

"I'll be okay. I'm hungry."

"I have a tray ready for you, miss." I look up at the formal voice and blink at the older gentleman who's smiling kindly at me. "I'm Charles, and I'm happy to help you today."

"Thank you." I glance up at Shane, but he just nods and gestures for me to sit at a table. Within a few seconds, Charles sets a charcuterie board full of cheeses, meats, nuts, and olives in front of me, and I immediately dig in. "This is awesome."

"What would you like to drink, miss?" the attendant asks.

"Water, please."

He nods and turns to fetch my drink. Shane sits opposite me, watching me wolf down the food.

"Want a cashew?" I ask him, holding out the nut.

"No, you eat," he says.

"How long has it been?" I ask, suddenly not sure how long the jerk had me. "Since I left the clinic?"

"About twenty-four hours," Rafe says.

"This is pathetic," I reply with a laugh. "I just ate twenty-four hours ago and I'm starving. I can't even consider this a fast."

"Killing people burns a lot of calories," Nadia says.

"And so does adrenaline," Carmine adds.

"True. And probably the drugs. What a crazy turn of events. So much for living a boring life."

"I have questions." I look up at Shane's statement, and my stomach tenses. "Questions I need answers to so I can do my job here and protect you."

"I'm not your job."

His jaw clenches. "Yes. You are."

"No. I'm not." I eat a grape and consider him. "Don't get me wrong. You'll never know how much I appreciate all of you for saving me. I shudder to think what might have happened to me if you hadn't come to find me. I would have died. Whether that was a long, slow death with a corpse decaying next to me, or a quick one when the other bad guys got there, I don't know. But I wouldn't have lived through it. So, I owe you a huge debt of gratitude that I can never repay."

"You don't *owe* us anything," Nadia says. "This is what family does."

"We rescue each other from kidnappers?" I ask, suddenly feeling emotional. Annika and Nadia are the only family I've ever really had.

"Among other things," Nadia says with a wink.

"I'll answer your questions," I say with a sigh. "But can I please eat this delicious cheese and get some rest first?"

"I don't see why not," Shane replies, seemingly placated for now. I need to think about how much I'm going to tell him.

It's not that I don't trust him. It's that I'm embarrassed. Of what and who I come from. Of what I had to do as a child. And I've always hoped that my past was so far in the rearview that it was forgotten.

Over.

But now, out of the blue, it's front and center. Exactly where I never wanted it to be.

But, worst of all, I'm afraid that when I tell Shane the whole truth, his feelings for me, whatever they may be, will change. He'll lose that spark of interest in his eyes whenever he sees me. He'll want nothing to do with me.

And that will hurt most of all. Because even though we don't know each other all that well yet, he's come to mean a lot to me.

"Looks like we're landing," Rafe says as the plane starts its descent. "We'll be at Annika's in about an hour or so."

CHAPTER
THREE
~SHANE~

"You really should go with him," Annika insists for the third time, but Ivie just shakes her head stubbornly.

"I'm needed *here*," she says. "I have a job and a life to see to. I can't let them win."

"Staying *safe*," I insist through gritted teeth, "isn't letting anyone win. It's being smart."

"I'm not trying to be difficult," Ivie says with a long sigh. "Honestly, I'm not. But I almost lost this life, and I love it. I've worked hard for it. And, damn it, I want to get back to living it."

"Nothing says that you won't be back at it in just a few days," Carmine points out. "In the meantime, hang out with Shane until all of this can get resolved."

Ivie firms her lips, and I decide that I'd like to tie her up and carry her to my place myself.

But I don't think she'd like that either.

"Fine. If you won't go, I'll stay." I stand and shove my hand through my hair. "I'll stay with you."

"Shane—"

"Did you really think that after what happened to you over the past twenty-four hours that I'd just walk away?" The outburst is unusual for me, but I can't hold it in any longer. "Because the answer to that is fuck no. You come with me, or I stay with you. That's the way it's going to be. You choose."

Her little chin comes up, and she meets my eyes. "Fine. I have a spare bedroom."

"Fine."

"I think you're both tired," Nadia says and pats Ivie on the shoulder. "Go get some rest. Fight in the morning."

"Good idea," Annika agrees. "I'm so, *so* relieved that you're home. And I'm sorry that I let you down."

"Stop apologizing," Ivie insists. "You didn't know. I'm just glad you listened to the message and sent the cavalry in to save me."

"Oh, this is Uncle Igor," Annika says as her phone rings. "He's been worried sick. Hello, Uncle. Yes, she's here. She's safe. The Martinellis are with her. I'll let her know."

"Your family is the best," Ivie whispers.

"They love you," Nadia says with a shrug. "Was Papa angry?"

"Livid," Annika confirms. "And very concerned. We all have been. We're just relieved that she's safe."

Tired hugs are exchanged. Once outside, I pull Rocco and Carmine aside.

"I would rather be at my place. I can protect her better there."

"I know," Carmine says. "We're going to stick close for a few days, just in case."

"I'll be around, as well," Rocco says and gestures to the two additional vehicles on the street. "I had these delivered. Figured we'd go our separate ways."

"Appreciate it," I reply with a nod. "I'll let you know if anything comes up."

"Same here," Carmine says, and the three of us go to our separate vehicles to drive away.

"How did these cars get here?" Ivie asks after she buckles up.

"Rocco had them delivered."

She frowns at me as I back out of the driveway. "How?"

"We have people, Ivie. In every major city of this country, and several around the world. All we have to do is make a phone call, and certain things happen."

She chews her lip and then frowns when she realizes that I'm headed right for her house.

"How do you know where I live?"

"I dropped you off there one night, remember?"

"I'm surprised *you* remember."

I have an excellent memory when it comes to things I want.

"Are you mad at me for not going with you?" she asks.

"Yes." The answer is short and simple. "I'm frustrated because it would be easier to keep you safe at my home. I feel blind this way. But I'm not going to force you to do anything you don't want to do, so we'll try it your way."

She blows out a raspberry through her lips and then lets out a gasp of surprise when I turn into her driveway.

"My door is open," she says. "I know I didn't leave it like that when I left for work yesterday."

"Stay here. Lock the doors."

I jump out of the car and immediately pull my sidearm from its holster. Before rushing inside, I make a quick loop around the house to see if I can detect any movement.

From out here, it looks empty.

When I make my way back to the front door, I ease it open farther and step inside, raising my weapon when a figure walks across the living room and snaps on the light.

"For fuck's sake, Ivie, I told you to wait outside."

But she's not listening to me. Her eyes are trained on the destruction in her home. The place has been ransacked, turned over and destroyed.

"Oh my God," she breathes.

"Stay with me," I order her, my voice sharp. "Do you hear me? Ivie."

"I hear you." She slips her hand into mine, and I lead her through the house, to each room, with my weapon drawn in case anyone is still here.

"We're alone," I say at last when we're standing in her bedroom.

She slips her hand from mine and hurries over to her closet. I follow her over and see her stumble over clothes, then peel back the carpet in a corner, open a hidden spot on the floor, and pull out a small box.

"They didn't take it," she breathes in relief. "My mother's wedding ring. It's the only thing I have from her, and I could never replace it."

She hugs the box to her chest and allows her gaze to roam over the mess.

"I guess you're getting your way," she says at last.

"It's not a competition." I take her hand and pull her to her feet. "Honey, I just want you to be as safe as possible."

"Well, it doesn't look like that'll be here. I'll try to pull some things together and be ready in a few minutes."

I nod and step out of the room so I can text my brothers, letting them know about the change of plans. I also call my father to keep him posted. We've been feeding him information since all of this began.

When these assholes took Ivie, they pissed off two powerful mafia families in the process.

They're fucked.

"I'm ready." Ivie has a small suitcase that's seen better days, a tote filled to the brim, and a purse, which she retrieved from Annika earlier. "The bastards ruined my Louis Vuitton handbag. It was a gift."

"It can be replaced."

"Do you know how much those things cost?" she demands. "Anyway. It's just a purse. But it pissed me off. I'm taking the few valuable things I have with me, some clothes and toiletries, and that's about it."

"That's all you'll need," I assure her. I can feel the sadness and despair radiating off her as we walk through her little house to the front door. She locks it as I put her bags in the car, and then we're off again. "We have a bit of a drive ahead of us."

She just nods and stares out the window. So, I decide to let her be. A lot has happened. She's exhausted.

My questions can be answered tomorrow.

"So, you live way out here in the middle of nowhere," she says when I turn onto my dirt road.

I let my caretaker know that I was on my way, and the make and model of the car we're in, so the gate automatically swings open at our arrival.

I imagine Curt is sitting in his little cabin, watching the monitor.

"Yes. I do."

It's dark now. I think this has been the longest damn day of my life. We're quiet, as we were the entire drive, as I navigate the Lexus past the helicopter landing pad, my shooting range, a barn, and an underground bunker—all of which is out of view in the darkness.

I pull up to my house and cut the engine. Several lights are on, also thanks to Curt.

"Is someone else here?" she asks, then turns to me with wide eyes. "Oh my God, do you have a girlfriend?"

"No. No girlfriend."

"Why are the lights on?"

"I have a friend who lives in a cabin here on the property," I begin as I open my door, then hurry around to open hers. I take her hand and help her out of the car. "He's an old Army buddy. He likes to be alone, and he's damn good at his job. So it works well for both of us. You might meet him."

She nods and follows me up the stairs to my back door. I set her bags down and open the door, then gesture her inside.

This entrance leads right into my kitchen. "When I built this house, I wanted it to look like an old farmhouse. To blend in and look rustic at the base of the mountain."

"I love it," she breathes, looking around with tired, sapphire eyes. "It's modern and beautiful, but also has that old-fashioned vibe to it."

"Bingo. Come on, it's not a huge place. I'll show you around. This is the living area. TV and all that jazz. There's a sunroom over there, but I've never gotten around to furnishing it."

I swing into the guest room and set her bags on the floor, switching on the light. "This is your room. Make yourself at home. There's a bathroom through that door. Walk-in closet here. When the sun's up, you'll have a great view of the mountains."

"Thank you." She runs her fingertips over the comforter on the queen-sized bed. "Where will you be?"

"Down here," I reply and take her hand, leading her just down the hall to my bedroom. "This is my room. Nothing too fancy, but it's home."

She takes in my king-sized bed and the chair in the corner.

"I have another bathroom through there. If you go up the stairs by the front door, there's a loft and another guest room. If you'd rather have that one—"

"No, the one you've given me is great." She offers me a forced smile. "It'll be perfect."

Seeing her like this, distant and sad, tears at my heart, so I pull her to me and wrap my arms around her. I bury my lips in her hair and kiss her gently.

"Besides the obvious, tell me why you're miserable."

"Because you don't want me here, and I feel like I'm crashing into your life, and—"

"Whoa." I pull back and stare down at her. "I'm the one who *told* you that you'd be better off coming here with me."

"Only because you're feeling overprotective," she insists. "I'm just a burden, and I hate that."

"Let's get something straight." I tip up her chin, making her look me in the eyes. "I don't do much that I don't want to in this life. If I didn't want to be with you, I'd have put you in a safe house and staffed it with security. I want you here, Ivie. Hell, we're friends. We've spent time together. And God knows I think you're the sexiest damn thing I've ever seen in my life."

She lets out a snort, and I narrow my eyes.

"Is something I said funny?"

"You don't have to lay it on so thick."

I don't reply. I simply step into her and lay my lips on hers. Gently. As far as first kisses go, it's not the way I'd planned to do it, but it works. She tastes like sin, and the little noise she makes in the back of her throat as she melts against me would make a weaker man lose control.

But I end the kiss and smile down at her.

"Does that feel like you're a burden?"

She shakes her head.

"You're here because I care about you, I want you safe, and I'm the only one I trust to do that correctly. I get the bonus of having you with me pretty much nonstop for the foreseeable future."

"Thank you," she whispers.

"Are you hungry?"

"Yes, actually."

"Good. Me, too. I'll fix us something."

I lead her back out to the kitchen and get her settled on a stool while I set about making us a couple of omelets. Nothing fancy but full of veggies and nutrients to get us through until morning.

"So, was it your caretaker who stocked your kitchen for you?"

"Yeah. Curt keeps this place running when I'm gone. I haven't been here in..." I stop, lean on the counter and think about it. "Fuck, I haven't been home in two weeks."

"Where were you?"

There's no way I'll ever tell Ivie about the horrors I see when I'm out on a mission. So I just smile at her and shrug a shoulder. "Here and there."

"I have questions," she murmurs.

"That makes two of us."

She swallows hard and then nods. "We'll talk tomorrow, okay?"

"That works for me. I haven't slept in at least three days, and you look like you're ready to drop."

"I don't remember ever being this tired before," she admits.

"Are you finished there?" I gesture to her half-eaten plate.

"Yeah, I'm done."

I clear our dishes and then kiss Ivie's forehead. "Let's go to bed, then."

I escort her to her door, and after she closes it, I pad to another room that I didn't show her. This isn't as big as the operation I have in the basement, but it's a convenient space where I have monitors set up to show me the security cameras around the property.

With roughly a thousand acres, there's a lot of ground to cover. I shuffle through the live feeds, satisfied that everything looks calm tonight. After I send a note of thanks to Curt, I shut down everything and head to bed.

But at least an hour later, after a shower and some reading, I can't get comfortable. It's not like me to toss and turn like this after an exhausting operation like the one I just finished. Add to it the adrenaline of looking for Ivie, and my body is just about ready to quit on me.

But I can't get comfortable. I wonder how she's doing down the hall. Was she able to settle in and get comfortable? Is she having nightmares after her ordeal?

Does she need anything?

I'm just about to get up and go check on her when there's a light knock on my door.

"Come in."

The door slowly opens, and there's Ivie, standing in the moonlight.

"Can I sleep in that chair?" she asks, pointing to the chair in the corner of the room.

"No." I shift to the side and peel back the covers. "You can come sleep here."

"Really?"

"Come on, honey."

She closes the door behind her and turns to walk my way. Suddenly, she trips and lands on the bed, hard.

"Sorry, I didn't see the floor there."

I chuckle and tuck her in next to me, spoon up behind her, and breathe her in. She, too, had a shower, and her hair smells amazing.

But I don't want to ravage her. I want to *hold* her. Another new emotion for me.

"You're naked," she says, glancing over her shoulder at me.

"Yes, ma'am. Do you want me to put something on?" I kiss her hair, still breathing her in.

"No, it's okay. Just another surprise, that's all. I was scared," she admits with a whisper.

"No need to be," I whisper back. "I'm right here. I've got you. Just sleep, baby."

CHAPTER
FOUR
~IVIE~

I hurt. My neck is sore, my ribs ache, and I feel like I got hit by a bus.

And then the events of the past few days come into my mind, and I sigh, even before opening my eyes.

No wonder I ache.

But then last night comes into focus, and I can't help but smile. I was so scared in that bedroom by myself. I'm in a strange place, in the middle of the woods, and people are trying to kill me.

At least, I think they are.

I didn't want to be alone. And Shane didn't turn me away. Instead, he welcomed me into his bed, wrapped his big, strong arms around me, and held me all night. Naked.

So, so naked.

When I woke up in the middle of the night with a jolt from a nightmare, he soothed me until we both fell back to sleep.

I can't remember the last time I felt this protected.

Have I ever been?

I shift a bit and realize that Shane's hand landed on my left breast in his slumber.

I glance down, and sure enough... His huge hand rests over my breast, and I look up in surprise.

Damn, he has big hands. I'm a well-endowed girl in the boob department, but his hand completely covers me.

I blink rapidly. I wonder if that means he's *big* in other areas.

I can't hold the snort in, but then try to cover it up with a fake sneeze.

"Go back to sleep." Shane's voice is deep and gravelly, and he shifts, dragging his hand down my breast to my ribs as if we do this every morning.

"I'm asleep."

"Then why are you talking to me?"

I grin and turn to glance at him but end up hitting him in the chin with the ball of my shoulder.

"Ouch."

"Sorry." I wiggle around until I'm facing him but cover my mouth with the blanket—because, morning breath. "So sorry."

"You don't sound sorry."

I just smile from behind the blanket. Shane opens an eye and then chuckles. "How are you this morning?"

"Oh, I hurt everywhere."

"Wait. What?" He sits up, pulling the blanket from my mouth. It pools at his waist.

Jesus, his chest and abs are sculpted.

"Wow," I whisper, wanting to reach out and touch him.

"What do you mean you hurt everywhere?"

"Calm down." I slowly sit up beside him and wince with the effort. "He kicked me in the ribs a couple of times so they're a bit sore today. And I have a headache. Probably from being slapped."

"I want to fucking kill him." The words are said with perfect calm, just as matter-of-factly as if he were giving me a weather report.

"I got to do that," I reply. "It was an accident, but I can't say that I'm sorry. Does that make me a bad person?"

"No." He shuffles to the opposite side of the bed, and I see a glimpse of his tight, bare ass before he slips on his jeans and turns to me with them still unfastened. His dark hair is rumpled from sleep. His eyes not quite awake. And seeing him like this does things to me.

Sexy things.

I clear my throat and look away.

"I have to unpack," I say and stand to escape the room.

"Wait."

I turn back to him and see he's gazing at me with a lazy grin. "I'm going to eventually tumble you into this bed and have my way with you, Ivie. But not while you're hurting, and not until I've had time to kiss the hell out of you first."

What in the hell am I supposed to say to that?

I start to speak, but it just comes out as a squeak, so I clear my throat and just say, "Okay."

"You unpack. I'll make breakfast. Do you like French toast?"

So much for going gluten-free. "I love it."

"Excellent." He pulls a black T-shirt over his head, covering up all that glorious, tanned skin and those abs, so I turn to go unpack. "Ivie?"

"Yeah?" I turn back to see his hot, dark eyes roaming up and down my body.

"Nice night thing."

I glance down at my simple red sleep shirt. It says *Knocked Out* on the front. There's nothing particularly sexy or interesting about it.

"Huh?"

He just grins, and his eyes fall level with my butt. I realize that it barely covers my round ass.

He's been staring at my black panties and bare cheeks.

So, with a sassy turn, I let him enjoy the show.

Shane's laughter follows me down the hall to the room that he offered me last night. I like Shane's home. It's simple. The kitchen is glorious, and I would love to work some magic in there. I love the farmhouse vibe.

Joanna Gaines would be proud.

But it's evident that a bachelor lives here. There are no little touches like pretty towels, decorative rugs, or pieces of artwork hung here and there.

As wonderful as this place is now, it could be truly beautiful.

But it's clean, it's safe, and for now, that's all I really need.

I start by unpacking my tote bag. I have all of my bathroom supplies in here, so I just take it with me to the restroom and unpack my razor, special hair mask, and other shower needs. I used my shampoo and conditioner last night but didn't bother to unpack the rest.

I set up the sink with my favorite soap, toothbrush, and toothpaste, and all of my skin-care bottles—which is more than most people use, but I work at a medi-spa. Having flawless skin is important and healthy.

I toss the empty tote into the closet and move onto the suitcase.

I've had this thing for as long as I can remember. It's the same one I had when I fled my father's house all those years ago. I've added other luggage here and there over the years, but this one belonged to my mother, so I'll likely keep it until it's nothing but rags.

I tuck my jeans into an empty drawer in the dresser and hang my shirts in the closet, then stow my undies and bras in another drawer. I only brought a couple of pairs of shoes and lay them in the bottom of the closet.

When the suitcase is empty, I zip it shut, pick it up to stow it away, and hear a rattle.

"Did a button fall off of something? That would be my luck," I mutter as I unzip it and glance inside.

But I don't see anything.

I pick it up and shake it.

Still rattling.

The lining of the bag has several tears.

"Something must have slipped through." I unzip the liner and reach my hand in, feeling around. When I come up with a small, black flash drive, I scowl.

"Oh."

"I'm telling you, I don't want to."

"I do not care what you want, Laryssa." Father just flicks his wrist as if he's batting at an annoying fly. "You'll do as I say without question."

I want to stomp my feet. I want to yell at him and tear my hair out in frustration. Why won't he listen to me? Why is he so awful?

I'm so sick and tired of being his errand girl. Of going into scary places

394

with mean people and men who like to cop a feel as I walk past them, just to drop off these stupid things.

How important can this be, anyway?

I turn and stomp away, pissed and hurt that my father can't show me even an ounce of kindness.

Rather than take this where he wants me to, I reach into my tiny closet for Mommy's suitcase and tuck it away inside. I don't want to go to that place again.

It smells, and the men look at me in weird ways that make me feel dirty.

I'm not going.

Father won't know. It's not like he'll ever find out that I didn't take it.

I secure it back in the closet and then slip my feet into my shoes, making a hasty escape out of the dirty little house we live in. I'll go down to the diner where they're nice to me and let me eat all of the ice cream I want.

I shake my head and stare down at the flash drive in my hand.

"Shane!" I run out of the bedroom to the kitchen, where Shane's just plating up our breakfast.

"You're just in time." He smiles as he glances up, but when he sees my face, the smile fades. "What's wrong?"

"This." I hold it up and stare at him in horror. "I think this could be something."

"What kind of something, Ivie?"

I swallow hard and wish with all my might that we didn't have to have the conversation about to come.

"I guess it's time to talk," I say.

"Okay. Am I about to lose my appetite?"

"Maybe. I don't know." I set the flash drive on the counter, unable to hold it anymore. "My birth name is Laryssa Pavlov. My father worked with some kind of government intelligence agency in Bulgaria, and when I was very small, we moved to the US. I don't remember being in Bulgaria. My mother died when I was four. My father raised me, so to speak."

I sit and stare at the French toast and then decide...*fuck it.* I'm hungry. I'm going to eat. So, I start slathering it in butter and syrup and keep talking.

"I don't honestly know what he was into. I was his minion. Not his daughter." I take a bite of bread and sigh in happiness. "He made me run errands for him in New York. I had to deliver things, usually like *that*"—I point at the flash drive with my fork—"to men who were creepy and handsy."

"Handsy?"

I look up at him. "They liked to look, and they liked to grope. And my father didn't give a shit. Anyway, I was fifteen, and I hated him with every fiber of my being. I hated having to do his bidding. I didn't know what he was into, but I knew it was illegal, and if I got caught, I could get into trouble. So, I told him, flat-out, that I wasn't going to do it anymore."

"And how did that go over?"

"Not well." I shrug and take another bite. "He hit me. Threatened to pimp me out to the creepy dudes who liked to look. And then these guys came banging on the door and started to beat *him* up pretty bad.

"I'd already packed my bag, ready to run as soon as I had the chance. And what better opportunity than when he was getting the shit kicked out of him? So, I grabbed my suitcase, the one currently in your closet, and I ran. I never saw him again."

His eyes narrow on me as he, too, eats his breakfast. "Where did you get that?" He points at the flash drive.

"I'd forgotten that I'd hidden it a couple of weeks before I ran away. He wanted me to deliver it to one of those places, and I was just so *sick* of it, Shane. It was awful. So, instead, I hid it away in my mom's suitcase. I hid it in the interior lining, you know?"

He nods, and I keep going.

"I forgot about it. For all these years. Just now, after I finished unpacking, I heard the rattle and found it."

"What's on it?"

"Your guess is as good as mine."

With our plates empty, Shane retrieves the drive and takes my hand. "Let's go."

He keys in a code on a locked door and leads me down a long stairway. When we reach the basement, he turns on the light, and all I can do is stare.

Monitors fill one wall. There are computers, printers, maps, papers...

all spread out around the room. It looks like a command center, and as I stare at Shane now, as he punches at a keyboard, and some of the monitors come to life, I realize that's exactly what it is.

A command center.

"Are you James Bond?"

His fingers stop tapping, and he turns to me with a slow smile. "I'm better than him, honey. Come here."

I join him at the desk, leaning over his shoulder as he slips the flash drive into a slot and what looks like gibberish fills a screen.

"What is that?" I wonder aloud as I stare at it. "It looks like some kind of weird hieroglyphics."

"Whatever's on here is encrypted."

He's still typing, but even I can see that he's going about it the wrong way.

"You're doing it wrong."

His sexy dark brow quirks above his eye. "Excuse me?"

"May I?"

"By all means." He scoots the chair back and tugs me into his lap, and for half a second, I'm not sure what I'm supposed to be doing. Shane's nose nuzzles my ear.

"Well?"

"Well, what?"

He chuckles. "You asked for the control, Ivie."

I love that he calls me Ivie. That everything I told him in the kitchen doesn't seem to bother him in the least.

I get to work, tapping keys, trying to break the fail-safe on this thing.

"I was something of a hacker in college," I mutter as I meet a wall, curse, and then keep going. "I was already using Ivie as my name, but I had to make it legal without people asking a bunch of questions or requesting birth certificates."

"So you learned to *hack*?"

"I'm a bit of a nerd." I shrug and try to ignore his fingers doing delicious things to my back. "There. It's searching for it now."

I lean back into him as the computer does its thing and turn my face up to his.

"You're the sexiest nerd I've ever seen in my life."

I grin. "I'm not sexy or beautiful. I know it, and it's okay. I'm passable at best when I'm all gussied up."

"Who told you that?"

"No one needed to." *My father hammered home every damn day that I was a disappointment in the looks department.* "I can see myself in the mirror."

"Then you're looking at the wrong damn thing." He kisses my jawline while his hands roam over my ribs. "From the minute I saw you at Annika's wedding, I couldn't take my eyes off you. You're addictive, Ivie."

I want to snort. I want to laugh. This is a joke, right? Because no one's ever called me *addictive*. Pretty? Sure. You look nice? Occasionally. But never this.

However, based on the way he's touching me, I'd say he's not joking.

He cups my face and turns me to him. His lips are gentle on mine as they linger, tasting me, teasing the corner of my mouth until my nipples stand at attention.

He takes the kiss deeper, my fingers diving into his hair, and we're consumed by each other when the beeping starts.

"It's done," I whisper against his lips.

"Damn it," he replies, making me laugh.

When I turn back to the screen, I scowl. "This is just more gibberish."

"It's a language," Shane says.

"Oh, good. We can just plug it into Google Translate and call it a day." Shane stares at me as if I just suggested we jump into shark-infested waters. "What?"

"We absolutely can *not* use Google for this. Whoever's looking for this would be here in an hour. Now it's your turn to sit back and let me work my magic."

"Have at it."

I watch as he taps the keys, copies and pastes, then hits enter and waits.

"Did that just happen?"

"Fuck."

CHAPTER
FIVE
~SHANE~

"Did that just erase itself?" Ivie demands, panic laced through her sexy voice.

"It seems so."

"Damn it." She reaches out to start working on the keyboard again, but I stop her. "Maybe I can get it back."

"If we keep trying, it'll corrupt itself, and we won't get anything at all."

"Then what are we supposed to do?"

"I'm calling a friend." I pull my phone out of my pocket, tap the screen, and then reach out and push my fingers through Ivie's hair as I wait for him to answer.

"Cox."

"I need your help." I give him a brief report on what we have going on. "The sooner, the better."

"Yeah, I can look at it. Just send it through. I'll get to it later today."

"No, I need you to come here. I'm not sending this out anywhere."

There's a brief pause. "Are you in Colorado?"

"At the ranch," I confirm and wink at a waiting Ivie. "The sooner you can get here, the better. Wait, are you out of the country?"

"No, I'm in Seattle. I can be there later this afternoon."

"I owe you one."

"You owe me about a dozen."

He clicks off, and I methodically shut down the system and pull the drive out of the slot.

"So, who is Cox?" Ivie asks.

"Cameron Cox is a friend. An old Army buddy and the best computer genius in the country—maybe in the world. I've been on missions with him all over the globe. I'd trust him with my life, or yours."

"And he's based in Seattle?"

"On an island not far from the city," I confirm. "His family is there. He'll be here later today."

"And he's just going to drop everything and come here? Just like that?"

I lean back in the chair and watch her. I do enjoy looking at her. The way her hair falls around her face. I want to kiss the little beauty mark next to her eye.

"Cox and I have been through hell and back together. If you get a call asking for help, you help."

She nods, thinking it over. "If Annika or Nadia needed me, I'd be there in a heartbeat."

"Exactly."

"So, you were in the Army?" She follows me up the stairs, and I lock the door behind us. I've never had anyone break into my place, but if they did, that room is the last place I'd want an intruder.

"For a few years."

"But you still work for the government?"

I like Ivie. My feelings for her are strong, more intense than I've ever had for a woman before. And I trust her. That's not the issue. But most of what I do can't be talked about with anyone. Even if we were married, I couldn't tell her.

"I do work for the government here and there." We walk into the kitchen, and I set our dishes in the dishwasher.

"What kind of work?"

I sigh and lean on my hands. "I don't want to lie to you or mislead you. If you were anyone else, I'd say none of your damn business and go about my day, but you're not anyone else. I can't tell you what I do. Everything I do is classified. Locked up so tightly, only the president herself knows all the details."

Ivie's eyes widen in surprise. "So, you're a mobster *and* a government operative?" She swallows hard and sits on a stool.

"Okay, talk to me."

"You're exactly the type of man I've avoided all my life. All I ever wanted was a nice, simple life. Nothing illegal going on, nothing to be afraid of. And I had that—until yesterday. I always saw myself with someone boring like an accountant or a small-business owner. Or just something *safe*."

"You can still have those things." The words are out of my mouth before I can stop them. Ivie's mouth closes, and her brow furrows.

Jesus, I'm a grade-A asshole.

"Of course." She offers me a polite, fake smile. "I'll just be in my room."

"Ivie."

"I'm fine." That smile disappears as she turns to leave.

"Stop, damn it."

But she doesn't. She flees into the guest room and shuts the door, but I open it and walk right in after her.

"Ivie."

"I'm not upset," she says, but tears swim in her eyes, breaking my heart in two. "Really. You haven't made me any promises. I was silly to think that just because we talked a lot, and you flirted with me, and are so hell-bent on protecting me that this could go anywhere."

"You're not silly." I shove my hands into my pockets because I don't know what else to do with them. "You're not silly at all. I'm an asshole for chasing after you when I knew good and well that I could never have you."

She scowls at me now, and I don't even flinch because I deserve it.

"I'm right here," she says, spreading her arms wide. "I'm not married. And I'm not saying no. So why can't you have me?"

"Didn't you hear me out there? I can *never* tell you about my job, Ivie. Ever. I'll be out there in the world doing some really shady shit that you can never know about. And you said yourself that you don't want that kind of life. You want a stable one. And while I could always provide for you financially—"

"I don't want your money."

"—I can't promise you that I'll always come home from every mission alive."

She swallows hard. "So, what, you've just been playing with me for these months? Was I just something fun to do when you're not off doing God knows what, God knows where?"

"No." I push my hands through my hair, pissed at myself. "I told you earlier, you're addictive. I *hate* not being able to speak to you when I'm gone. And hearing your voice or seeing you is what I look forward to the most when I come back."

She shakes her head and crosses her arms over her chest. "I don't believe you. Shane, *I'm* not the girl who guys fall for like that. I'm the one they play with. Ask out on a dare. Laugh at me because I'm good with computers and am a little clumsy. I'm not Nadia or Annika."

"Stop it with this." Unable to hold myself back, I cross to her and take her shoulders in my hands, mindful that she's still sore from yesterday. "If that happened to you, it's because boys are fucked-up in the head. It had nothing to do with *you*."

"Look." She shrugs out of my hold. "You don't owe me anything. It was only some harmless flirting. I get it. I'm a big girl, and you've just made it perfectly clear where we stand. Understood."

"Fuck." I drag my hands down my face in frustration. I *want* her. I want every inch of her, for today and for the rest of my fucking life. And that makes me the biggest, most selfish jerk in the world because this can't work. "Ivie, you're a beautiful woman. You're funny and smart, and your clumsiness makes you all the more fun. I think you're amazing."

"But you don't want me." She nods and motions for me to leave. "You can go."

"No, damn it." I advance on her and pull her against me, fold my lips over hers and take her. This kiss is desperate, full of fire and frustration. After a long moment, her hands fist in my shirt at my sides, and she holds on as I take us both on a ride. "I want you. I want you so badly it's fucking killing me."

"I'm *right here*." A soft sob escapes her throat as I kiss my way down to her collarbone. "Wait."

She takes my face in her hands and looks deeply into my eyes.

"You're afraid."

I start to deny it, but she holds me tighter.

"You are. Why are you scared?"

I tip my forehead to hers and let out a long, even breath.

I'm afraid of falling in love with you and then leaving you here alone.

But I can't say that. I just can't. Not right now.

"I'm afraid of a lot of things," I say at last and brush my fingertips down her cheek. "You being hurt is at the top of the list."

Her eyes clear, and all of the anger and confusion from a moment ago just evaporates. What's left nearly takes my breath away.

"Don't fall in love with me, little dove."

"No. That would be ridiculous." Her lips twitch into a small smile. "Are we done fighting now?"

"I feel like that's a trick question."

"Looks like we are. Let's get out of this house. Show me around. I just have to change my clothes. Can we walk the ranch, or will we be in the car?"

I know what she's doing, and it won't work. But I don't want to see the happiness in her eyes disappear.

"We can walk it."

"Well, it's a good thing I brought some sneakers. I'll be ready in ten."

"WHY DO YOU HAVE A BUNKER?"

We're standing at the opening, staring down into the black hole.

"Are you a prepper?" she asks before I can reply to the first question.

"I'm the king of preppers," I say with a laugh. "I'm always prepared for anything."

"I see that." She glances around. "Like the nuclear apocalypse."

"Hey, you never know, right?"

She narrows her eyes at me. "If there's a nuclear apocalypse, I don't want to survive it. Do you know how horrible it would be? *Horrible.* That's a solid 'no, thanks' for me."

I laugh and tuck her hair behind her ear. "This isn't here for that. If someone ever breached my property, and all hell broke loose, this is the most secure place on the ranch."

Her eyes go wide, and she looks down again. "Jesus, Shane. You're intense."

"You have no idea."

I look up at the sound of an engine, just in time to see Curt making his way over to us on an ATV.

"Hey, boss," he says when he cuts the engine. "Welcome home."

"Thanks. This is Ivie. Ivie, this is Curt."

"Ma'am." Curt offers her a nod. "Everything okay at the house?"

"It's great. Cox is coming this afternoon."

"He called me," Curt confirms. "He should arrive around oh-sixteen-hundred. Been quiet around here while you were gone."

"We like it quiet."

"So, Curt, how long have you lived here?" Ivie asks, trying to make conversation.

"Oh, going on about eight years or so now, I guess."

"Nice. And where are you from originally?"

Curt smiles politely but checks his watch. "I have some things to see to. Nice to meet you, ma'am."

He nods and takes off to the other side of the ranch.

"What did I say?"

"He doesn't like to talk about himself much."

"He's much younger than I expected," she admits. "You said he doesn't like to be around people?"

"No. He saw some bad things in action and has some pretty severe PTSD. He does better being a little isolated. The ranch suits him."

"Poor guy," she murmurs. "Okay, do I get to see this super-safe bunker?"

"Sure."

I lead her down the stairs to the large room below. I flip on lights and step to the side so she can look around.

"Holy shit, Shane. This is huge."

"Yeah." I grin and take it all in. "Tunnels run throughout the ranch. There's one to my house, Curt's cabin, the barn, and the helipad. All hidden from view, of course."

"Why are you showing me this?"

"I don't know, I think it's pretty cool."

She laughs and leads me through two bedrooms, a bathroom, and the kitchen. "It *is* cool. Is this your toy? Like, some guys get expensive cars, and others like boats, but you have a crazy bunker?"

"Something like that, I guess."

She grins. "You really are 007."

I chuckle as she steps to me and drags her hands up my arms to my shoulders. Ivie's never been the aggressor, so I wait to see what she's got on her mind.

Those hands climb into my hair, and with her breasts pressed against me, she offers me her lips.

I won't turn down an offer this gorgeous.

This time, the kiss is sweet and slow but no less full of passion. I boost her up so she can wrap her legs around my waist and carry her to the wall so I can let my hands do a little wandering over her gorgeous curves.

She bites my bottom lip, making my already-hard dick jump in surprise.

"God, you're something." I nibble my way down her neck, enjoying the scent of lemons on her skin. "I want to fucking consume you."

"Three months of foreplay is a long time," she says and hums in satisfaction when my lips return to hers.

Barely holding myself in check, I yank her shirt out of her jeans and let my hand roam over the warm, smooth skin of her side and stomach before cupping her firm breast.

She arches into my hand in invitation.

"Find a bed," she instructs me. "We need more room, Shane. Somewhere softer."

"Right. A bed."

I carry her through a door to a small bedroom and tumble us both onto the unused mattress. No one has ever stayed down here.

Which means, we'll be christening this room.

I take the tab of her jeans in my teeth and yank the button free, and just as I start to urge them down her hips, my phone beeps.

"Damn it," I growl and look at the message. "I'm getting really sick and tired of being interrupted by technology."

"What is it?" Her voice is breathless, and her eyes are on fire.

"Cameron just landed."

"Oh, he has at least an hour until he's here, right?"

"No, sweetheart." I cover her again and kiss her softly. "He just landed on the helipad."

"Well, damn."

"Don't worry." I kiss her once more and then help us both to our feet. "The first time I have you isn't going to be in my bunker. It's going to be in *my* bed, where I can take my time and memorize every gorgeous inch of you."

"I'm going to hold you to that, Shane Martinelli."

I laugh and help her right herself. When we're both put back together, I kiss her temple. "Let's go put Cameron to work, shall we?"

"Oh, absolutely. I can't wait to see what he does to bring that thing back to life."

"He has tricks and secrets. He'll get it figured out, and then we'll know what your father was doing."

"I'm not sure I want to know."

"There's no going back now."

CHAPTER
SIX
~IVIE~

"Nice to meet you," I say to a tall, dark, and ridiculously handsome Cameron Cox as the three of us walk from the helipad where Cameron just jumped out of a helicopter and to the house. "Is the pilot just going to wait there?"

"That's his job," Cameron says with a smile. "He'll be fine."

So, I guess he's not planning to stay, then.

"I didn't know helicopters could fly that far."

"We just had to stop in Boise to fuel up," Cameron replies as Shane opens the back door of the house, and we file inside. "So, your phone call was mysterious this morning."

"I'm hoping you can help us solve something." Shane unlocks the door to the basement, and we all go down the stairs.

Cameron has clearly been here before.

"Ivie has a flash drive that she needs to be able to read, and it's encrypted. When we tried to decode it, it wiped itself."

Cameron's eyebrows climb in surprise. "Interesting. Okay, let me see what I can do."

He sits behind the computer, and as it boots up, he slips black-rimmed glasses onto his nose and gets to work.

"Someone worked really hard to make sure this didn't get into the wrong hands," Cameron murmurs. "You have no idea what's on it?"

"None," I reply and watch in fascination as his fingers fly across the keys. When he taps out a series of numbers and letters in a formula I recognize, my eyebrows climb. "Oh, I never thought to do that."

"Why would you?" Cameron asks.

"Ivie's something of a computer hacker," Shane says with a proud grin. "It's a sight to behold."

"Really?" Cameron smiles at me. "That's pretty cool."

"How are things with that woman you were telling me about?" Shane asks him, making conversation. "Maggie?"

"Slow," Cameron mutters with a frown. "If anyone in the world is more stubborn than Mary Margaret O'Callaghan, I haven't met them. But I'm working on it. Okay, I've got it back."

"That was fast. Holy crap," I mutter.

"I'm good, sweetheart." He looks up at the screen. "Would you like me to translate this for you?"

"Absolutely." I drop into a chair beside him as he continues tapping the keyboard. Finally, words written in English fill the screen.

"Whoa," Cameron breathes. "This is some deep shit."

He clicks through some files and then turns to Shane.

"What is it?" Shane asks.

Cameron glances at me, but Shane just shakes his head. "It's *her* drive, man. She should know what it says."

Cameron blows out a breath and then starts in. "Okay, so this is all about a dude named Ivan Pavlov. I've heard of him. He died about a decade ago, in a really, *really* gnarly way. Anyway, this guy was a true piece of shit."

He stands to pace the room, and Shane and I turn to watch him. Shane's standing, his arms crossed over his chest. And all I can do is sit and listen to every single word.

"He was a European operative in the nineties. Ruthless. This man killed hundreds if not thousands of men, women, and children. Here."

He moves back to the computer and taps some keys. Suddenly, a folder with photographs opens.

"All of these photos are of people he killed, supposedly under the direction of his government. Although many think he was a mercenary and not tied to the government at all. Anyway, all of these people are dead because of him.

"Then, about twenty-five years ago or so, he got in with some extra-bad people. He pissed them off. Big time. And they said the only way to get back into their good graces—i.e., not get dead—was for him to kill his own family."

I feel Shane's eyes shift to me, but I can't take my eyes off of Cameron. How did I not know *any* of this?

He taps the keys, then stands to pace once more. Suddenly, I'm staring at a photo of my mother.

Murdered.

"He killed the wife," Cameron continues. "And as you can see, he wasn't nice about it. But I heard that he spared the kid because he decided he could get them—I don't know if it was a boy or a girl—to do his bidding. No one suspects a kid getting in and out of places. After he came to the US, Pavlov was mostly into selling information. As far as I know, he didn't kill here in the States like he did in Europe. Maybe he was getting older and wanted a new gig, who knows?"

"How do you know all of this?" Shane asks.

"I had to research him right before he died." Cameron turns to look at Shane. "I was on a team that had been given the order to find and terminate him, but someone beat us to it. It looks to me like every single sin this guy ever committed is documented on this drive, along with what looks like account numbers. Now, *my* question is, why do *you* have it?"

I can't stop staring at my mother. In the photo, her throat is slashed, her mouth open, her eyes staring in shock.

He killed her.

"They're my parents," I manage to say and then turn to look Cameron in the eyes. "I was the kid. And, yes, he used me. Ruthlessly. But I got away from the son of a bitch." I feel my blood boiling, running through my veins faster than ever before. And then I can't stand it anymore. I can't stay here.

I stand and flee, running up the stairs and through the house, then out the back door, just in time to lose whatever's in my stomach in the bushes beside the porch.

Someone comes up beside me, rubbing my back and holding my hair out of the way.

When it seems I have nothing left in me, I straighten, and Shane pulls me to him for a tight hug.

I don't even know how to process what I just saw. How do I deal with this?

"Hey, man, I have to get back to Seattle."

I clear my throat and turn to Cameron. "Thank you. Really. I appreciate your help. I'm going to let you two say goodbye. I'll be inside."

Cameron nods, and I hurry into the house and to the guest room, making a beeline for the bathroom so I can brush my teeth and wash my face.

But when I'm done, the anger and grief swamp me again.

My poor mama. My God, why did he do that to her?

"HERE, DRINK THIS," Shane says as he sets a cup of tea near my elbow. After Cameron left, Shane came inside, built a fire in the woodstove, and then set to work making me some tea. I just wrapped myself in a blanket and sat by the fire, staring at the pretty, orange flames.

"How could I not know?" I wonder aloud before taking a sip of the tea. "All of these years, I never knew the cause of my mother's death. He just came home one day and said she was dead and wasn't coming back."

I shake my head and wipe at a tear.

"I knew he was bad. I guess I didn't want to see that he was pure evil. He must have had that drive and wanted me to take it to someone to decrypt it for him. I don't know how he got it."

"But you never delivered it where he wanted it to go?"

"No." I shake my head and sip the tea. "I was so over it at that point, I hid it instead. I don't know why he would even have that. Basically, his resume of all the killing he did. Why would he have that?"

"I don't know how it came to be in his possession," Shane says, thinking it over. "Maybe they used it to blackmail him. If it got into the wrong hands, he could have been arrested and prosecuted. Maybe even deported to Bulgaria and executed."

"Oh my God," I gasp and stare at Shane in horror. "I should have called the police. All I did was run away. I should have called the police. It didn't even occur to me. How could I be so stupid?"

"Stop." Shane stands and joins me on the couch, pulling me to him. "You were a child."

"I was never really a child."

"Yes, you were. Despite what he made you do, you were still young, Ivie. You were just trying to survive. And I'd say you did a damn good job of that."

"He killed my mama." I feel the tears falling again and lean my head on his shoulder. "She was a good person. So funny. And she made the best breads and desserts. She would let me help her in the kitchen. Because *he* was gone so much, it was mostly just the two of us, hanging out together. We were already in the US when she died. She told me once that she was afraid of New York. It was so big, so noisy, and she didn't know the language very well."

"Do you speak Bulgarian?" he asks as he kisses my forehead.

"Not anymore. I did when I was very small but I don't remember it. I did everything I could to forget that life and to make this new one—one that doesn't embarrass me. I shouldn't just sit here and babble about my mother. She's been gone for a really long time."

"Yes, but for you, the wound is new again," he says. His voice is gentle and sexy at the same time. "You can talk about her. It's not like we have anywhere to be. I'd like to hear anything you want to say."

I kiss his cheek and smile up at him. "Thank you for always being so kind to me."

He wipes a tear from my cheek, and I think of my mother again.

"She was tall. Taller than my father. I must get my height from him, given how short I am." I smile a little as I think of her. "And she loved to dance."

For a long while, I just sit by the fire with this man I've come to care for, telling him the few stories I remember of my mother.

"I wish I knew more, but he never wanted to speak of her after she died."

I swallow and then something occurs to me.

"If those people want the drive, let's just give it to them, Shane. They'll have what they want. Although, at this point, I'm not sure it matters because he's dead and gone. I can just get on with my life."

He shifts and then shakes his head. "It's really not that simple."

"Why not?"

"After you came inside, Cameron and I had a minute to talk. He finished the story."

My stomach fills with dread. "What is it?"

"Well, there's no easy way to say this, so I'm just going to tell you. There's a bounty on your head, Ivie. One million dollars for your capture —dead or alive."

"The *police* want me dead?"

"No, baby, not the police. Those bad guys Cameron told us about. They're still pissed at your father. And it's not just one group. Apparently, this goes deep. The man who took you the other day has likely been looking for you for a very long time. He was going to kill you and collect the money. Just as any of them would."

"*Why?*" And then that man's words come back to me. "To pay for the sins of my father."

"These guys have a long memory," Shane says quietly. "They're worse than the mafia, and that's saying a lot given what my family is capable of. I'd like to know what your father did to them to make them this angry."

"I have no idea. He might have killed someone he wasn't supposed to or stole from someone and really pissed them off. He couldn't hang on to money to save his life. Who knows?"

"Well, one thing I do know is that we're staying here for a while. We're safest here. I'm going to start doing some digging, and Cameron said he'd do some on his end, as well. I'm supposed to meet up with him in Denver in a week."

"You don't pass information via the internet." It's not a question.

"No. Not this kind. It's too sensitive. He'll bring anything he uncovers with him next week. In the meantime, I'll put out the word that my associates should keep their eyes and ears open, and I'll work on the secure network downstairs."

"I can probably help with that."

"If I need you, I'll let you know. But I want your fingers out of this as much as possible."

"So, what? I'm just supposed to *sit* here for God knows how long?" I stare at him with disgust. "I'm not good at being idle, Shane."

"You won't be. We're going to start some lessons."

"What kind?"

"I'm going to teach you to shoot. We'll go over hand-to-hand. You're going to learn to defend yourself if anything like this were to happen again."

"Have you *met* me? I'm the clumsiest person on Earth. I have no business holding a gun."

"You're going to shake that and get used to it. You're going to be so good by the time I'm done with you, being clumsy won't even be a thought in your beautiful head."

I blink up at him. "Really?"

"Really. You'll never be taken by surprise like that again."

"You're intense. I kind of like it."

"For today, just relax. Take a nap if you want. I'm going to start making those calls."

"A nap actually sounds really nice." I stand and stretch. "I'll go lie down."

I walk to the guest room, but Shane calls out my name.

"You won't be sleeping in there. You'll sleep with me. Go have a nap in my room."

I grin at him, but he's already looking down at his phone. So, I change course, shuck my jeans and socks, maneuver my way out of my bra, and then climb under the cool, crisp sheets.

His bed is comfortable, and my eyes are heavy from all of the crying.

Finally, I fall asleep.

No! Don't you dare do that!

"Shut up." Father slaps me aside and turns to Shane, who's kneeling on the floor. My father fists Shane's hair and pulls his head back, ready to slice his throat with a knife.

"No!" I try to run at him again, but my feet won't move. I can't get to him. Oh my God, I can't move! "Don't kill him! Please, don't. No."

"Shh." Shane cradles me to him. "Just a dream, baby."

"He was going to kill you." I grip onto him tightly and bury my face against his chest. "Oh, God, he was going to kill you. Just like he did my mama."

"I'm right here, and he's long-dead, Ivie. He can't hurt me."

I can't stop the tears. They just keep coming. For my poor mama and the thought of losing Shane in the same way.

"He can't hurt me," he says again and kisses the top of my head.

"But he keeps hurting me," I whisper and shake my head in despair. "He keeps hurting me."

CHAPTER

SEVEN

~SHANE~

"You have a shooting range."

It's the following morning, and I'm pleased to see that the shadows have cleared from Ivie's eyes this morning. After a quick breakfast, I brought the sexiest woman alive to my own private little playground, out here in the middle of nowhere.

It's a bit overkill, as Carmine would say. But it keeps me in top form. I have to practice and work on my skills so I don't get killed on the job.

"Yes, I do." I press my palm to a plate to unlock the door with my print, and the door slides open. I flip a switch, and lights illuminate the massive area that I carved into the side of the mountain.

"Holy shit, Shane, this is some crazy high-tech stuff," she says. "I thought this only existed in movies."

"If you have the money and know the right people, it's out there."

"And you know the right people. You're a little scary. Also, this was just a door in the side of a hill," she reminds me.

"Actually, once upon a time, this was a gold mine. Gold is huge up here in the mountains, and just about five miles that way,"—I point to the west—"is a mine that yields several million dollars in gold every day. This particular shaft has been abandoned for a hundred years at least. When I bought the property, I knew it would be the perfect place to hollow out and put in my shooting range."

"Of course." She nods, then glances around with her hands on her hips. "That's what I would think when I see an abandoned mine. *Let's make it into a super-secret, high-tech shooting range.*"

"Precisely." I laugh at her sarcasm and pull her to me for a quick kiss, then lead her to another door before I decide to press her against the wall and take her right there in the side of a mountain. "Lay your hand right here."

She frowns but does as I ask. I tap on the screen of my phone, recording her palm print into the security system. When the light blinks green, another door slides open.

"You have access to this door now," I say as more lights flip on and we step inside.

"Holy. Shit." She stops and turns in a circle, taking in the weapons lining the walls around us. I'm fully equipped with everything a person could ever need—especially if they're going to war. "It's an arsenal."

"Yes." I take a deep breath as she turns back to me and stares up at me with confused blue eyes.

"Who the hell are you, Shane?"

"It's better if you don't know the answer to that." I take her hand and walk her to the back of the vault where the bulk of my handguns are stored behind glass in a case mounted to the wall. The ammunition is kept beneath the case in a stainless-steel cabinet. "We're starting out small and easy. This is a .22 pistol. It won't have much kickback, and it will fit easily in your hands."

I take the weapon from behind the glass and offer it to her.

"Shane—"

"It's not loaded yet. I want you to hold it. Get a feel for the weight of it, how it feels in your palm. A weapon should be an extension of your hand. It's a tool."

She does as I ask, careful not to point the barrel at herself or me.

"This isn't your first rodeo." My voice is full of surprise as I watch her hold the weapon with the hands of someone who's done it many times before.

"I took a class once," she says softly. "But it made me nervous because I *am* so clumsy. I always worried that I'd hurt someone."

"You didn't have confidence," I reply and retrieve two boxes of ammo for the gun, then take her hand and lead her to the firing range. "Which tells me that whomever you took the class from was shitty at their job."

"Maybe. I was one of about twenty students."

"I'm not shitty at this," I inform her as I set up a target, then flip a switch and send the paper with its black outline down the lane about twenty yards. "In fact, it might be one of the things I'm best at. And we can practice as long as it takes to get you comfortable. I want this to be as easy as breathing for you."

"We could be here a while," she says with a laugh.

"I have time." I kiss her cheek, then reach for two sets of eye and ear protection. "Okay, we're going to start simple. Are you ready?"

"As I'll ever be."

"For this round, I'll load and get you ready to go. But after this, you'll do it. We'll also practice doing it quickly. The bad guys won't wait for you to load a gun."

"I feel like I'm in boot camp," she mutters, making me laugh.

"Nah. We're much more friendly here." I load the magazine with rounds of ammo, clip it into the gun, and pass it to Ivie. "Here we go."

I step back to watch her first, to see how much she already knows. Her stance is excellent, feet spread shoulder-width apart, her hands wrapped around the gun, her shoulders down.

Damn, she looks like a fucking pro.

When she empties the magazine, she turns to me.

"I don't buy that you didn't do well in that class."

She shrugs a shoulder. "I didn't say I didn't do well. I just didn't feel comfortable."

"Okay, let's build that confidence."

"How do you feel?" I ask her after we lock up the range and head toward the barn.

"I'm okay," she says.

"Does anything hurt?"

"My hands are tired. Who knew that squeezing a trigger that much could wear out your hands?"

I knew. But I keep the thought to myself.

"We have one more stop this morning."

"Are we feeding animals?" she asks as I park by the barn.

"No. I don't have much for animals here. Just some elk, deer, and the occasional mountain lion or bear." I wink at her, and we walk toward the barn door, which is also secured with a palm plate.

"It feels like your security might be overkill."

I turn and look at her, then bust up laughing. "That's exactly what Carmine says."

"Your brother's not wrong."

"The security is necessary. And right now, I'm damn glad I have it to keep *you* safe. Come on."

We walk inside, and I'm pleased to see that Curt is already here.

I converted the barn into a massive gym about five years ago. On this floor, we have a sparring ring and weights. The second floor has treadmills, ellipticals, rowing machines, and bikes.

"You don't do anything half-assed, do you?" Ivie asks, turning to me.

"No, ma'am. What's the point in that? Or the fun?" I cross to Curt, who's already dressed in a simple T-shirt and gym shorts. "Thanks for doing this."

"Hey, I just work here," he says with a half-smile.

"What are we doing?" Ivie asks, her brow raised.

"Sparring."

She coughs in surprise and then stares at the two of us. "The two of you are going to beat each other up? Why do I have to be here for this?"

"No, honey. You and Curt are going to spar. I'm going to coach you."

She looks back and forth between us. "You're insane."

"That may be true, but it doesn't change things. Now, let's step into the ring."

"No." Ivie crosses her arms over her chest. "I'm not *hitting* anyone."

"Let me ask you something." I don't walk to her, just stand my ground and fist my hands at my sides. "If you'd had some self-defense training, would that asshole have been able to take you out of the office like that? Would he have been able to stick that syringe into you and just walk you out of there?"

"I don't—"

"No. The answer to that is *no*. Now, we're going to make sure that no one has the opportunity to do that again, Ivie. And this is part of that."

"I don't want to punch Curt. He's too nice for that."

"No," Curt says with a shake of his head. "I'm not. I probably have it coming, Miss Ivie."

"You're Southern," she says. "Where are—?"

"Let's do this," Curt interrupts and walks into the ring, deflating Ivie's sails.

"I'm going to break through that wall he's got up," she says to me as she stomps past. "Mark my words."

I just shake my head and follow behind her, enjoying the way her hips sway when she's riled up.

Ivie certainly has less experience with hand-to-hand than she does firing a gun. We spend an hour just going over the basics.

She's sweaty and panting when I give her the order to go ahead and punch Curt in the face.

"No." She turns to me in horror. "I'm not going to actually punch him."

"Yes, you are."

"It's okay," Curt assures her. "You can't hurt me."

Ivie's eyes narrow at the challenge, and I see determination fill them as she takes the stance we've been teaching her, stomps on his foot, then follows through with a right hook to the jaw, sending Curt back on his ass.

"Oh, yeah?" Ivie asks, staring down at him.

"Okay, I was wrong." He cradles his jaw in his hand and shifts it back and forth. "That hurt. Nice one, Miss Ivie."

"Thanks." She grins and offers her hand to help him off the floor.

But Curt doesn't like to be touched, so he just shakes his head and climbs to his feet unassisted.

"One more time," Curt says.

"I really don't want to hit you again," Ivie says and turns pleading eyes to me. "Don't make me."

"You're too nice," Curt says and approaches her from behind. Wrapping his arm around her neck, Ivie immediately slips into defensive mode. She slips out of his hold, knees him in the balls, and jams the heel of her hand into his nose, making it bleed. "Never mind. Not too nice."

"Oh, God." Ivie covers her face with her hands. "I'm so sorry."

"You did exactly what you were supposed to do," Curt says and dabs at his nose. "I provoked you on purpose. A few more lessons, and you'll be able to kick both our asses with a blindfold on."

Ivie's smile is wide and proud. "Yeah?"

"Yeah," Curt replies. "Good job."

"Why won't Curt talk about himself?" Ivie asks when we walk into the house, and I start making us sandwiches for a late lunch.

"I told you, he has some baggage. He doesn't like to be around people."

"He can't be more than thirty-five," she says.

"What does his age have to do with anything?"

She shrugs and bites into a potato chip. "I don't know. It just seems sad. He's so young."

I stop opening the mayo and slowly turn to her. "Ivie, are you telling me that you have a crush on my ranch manager?"

She scowls and then laughs. "No. No, *he's* not the one I have a crush on at all. I just feel bad for him because he seems kind. And he's young and handsome and—"

"If you keep singing Curt's praises, I'll fire him."

She laughs in earnest and crosses over to me. She wraps her arms around my middle and lays her cheek on my chest. "I just like him. And maybe I feel bad for him."

"Don't." I kiss the top of her head. "He's where he wants to be, doing what he loves."

She sighs and then tips her face up to mine. "I'm glad you're his friend. I'm hungry."

"If you stop singing Curt's praises, I'll finish making lunch."

She grins. "Deal."

She pulls another handful of chips out of the bag and munches happily as she watches me build sandwiches.

"Are we ever going to have sex?"

The turkey falls out of my hand and onto the counter as I spin and stare at her. "What?"

"Sex. You and me. Is it ever going to happen, or are we just going to flirt and kiss and drive me crazy forever? I just want to know so I can plan accordingly."

"What if the answer is no sex?"

She shrugs. "Then I need to order a vibrator or something because a girl can't be with a sexy guy like you forever and not touch the goods. Is that how it's going to be?"

"Fuck, no." I shake my head and return to the sandwiches. "You were a little upset last night, Ivie. And we had things to do this morning."

"So, you're a planner when it comes to sex."

I cut the sandwiches and deliver them to the breakfast bar. She immediately digs into hers as if we're discussing the stock market. I take a bite, as well.

"I didn't say that."

"You just said—"

"I know what I said. And it didn't include *plans* for sex. It just wasn't...shit, I don't know. I want you so badly that I ache with it. I've wanted you naked and under me the minute I saw you at Annika's wedding, for Christ's sake. Keeping my hands to myself has been the hardest thing I've ever done."

"Cool. Let's not do that anymore, okay?"

"Do what?"

"Keep our hands to ourselves. I'm sleeping in *your* bed. I haven't told you no, and I don't plan to. I'm on the pill, I'm healthy, and I want you, Shane. I'm not playing games here. This also isn't a Stockholm syndrome thing. I'd want you under *any* circumstance. So now you know."

"Are you about done with that sandwich?"

She grins and sets it on the plate. "Yeah."

"Good."

I circle the breakfast bar and take her face in my hands, staring down into her fierce, blue eyes. "If there's anything you *don't* like, you need to tell me."

"I'm not shy, and I don't think you could do much that I won't like."

"Jesus, I don't deserve you." I kiss her long and hard and then take her hands and pull her quickly through the house to my bedroom. I close and lock the door.

"Expecting someone?" she asks.

"I'm not taking any damn chances." I shuck my boots and yank my shirt over my head. "Now that I have you here, right where I want you, I'm not taking any chances that someone could fuck this up."

"Good plan." She smiles and pulls the band out of her ponytail, setting her hair free, letting it tumble around her shoulders. Then, she calmly pulls her pink shirt over her head and lets it fall to the floor. With her eyes on mine, she unclasps her bra from the front and drops it with the shirt.

I swallow hard. Jesus fucking Christ, she's gorgeous. Those full breasts that I can't wait to get my hands on are on full display, her nipples already tight and begging for my lips.

When she reaches for the waistband of her yoga pants, I shake my head once and then step forward.

"Let me," I whisper as I take her hand in mine and draw it up to my lips. "Let me unwrap the rest of you. I'm going to worship every damn inch of your gorgeous body."

"It's good, then, that I have lots of extra inches for you to enjoy." Her lips twitch, in both humor and a little insecurity.

"Every bit of you is stunning. And I'm going to show you, slowly and methodically, just how much I want you. All of you. Every bit."

"Oh, that sounds like a good idea."

CHAPTER
EIGHT
~IVIE~

Has anyone ever looked at me the way Shane's gazing at me right now? Like he wants to eat me with a spoon?

No. The answer to that would be a resounding *no.*

"Are you getting nervous on me?" he asks as he slowly crosses to me and hooks his finger into the waistband of my yoga pants.

"No, why do you ask?"

"Because I can see your pulse throbbing, right here." He leans in and ever-so-gently lays his lips over the tender flesh of my neck. If I wasn't already turned on, which I definitely am, that would have done the trick. He's warm, and when my hands glide up his bare arms, he's smooth and firm. And I get to touch him. Do whatever I want to and with him.

Good God, am I dreaming?

"It's not because I'm nervous." I swallow hard and let my eyes drift closed as pure sensation floats through me.

"No?"

I slowly shake my head and then smile when his lips drift up to my jawline and over to my lips.

This kiss isn't light, playful, or comforting.

It's slow and hot. Arousing. All-encompassing.

"Never met anyone quite like you," he whispers as his hands slip into my pants, and he slowly pushes them over my hips. He makes a sweet, slow journey down my torso with his lips, planting hot kisses as he guides my pants down my legs.

When I'm standing before him in nothing but my neon green panties, he kisses me over the small scrap of material, right on my pubis.

My sharp inhale of breath has his gaze flying up to mine, and with an amused grin, he stands, takes my hand, and leads me to the bed.

Shane's eyes are soft and so full of lust, it makes me want to look behind myself to make sure it's *me* he's gazing at.

The thought makes me laugh a little.

"Is this funny?"

"No."

With his hands framing my face, he urges me onto the mattress and rolls me to the middle of the bed where he can cover me and keep kissing me.

"What made you smile?"

"Just a stupid thought."

"None of your thoughts are stupid, Ivie."

I love that he calls me Ivie. That it seemingly never even occurred to him to use my given name when he learned the truth about me.

"Just trust me on this," I assure him and push my fingers through his dark hair. "You still have your pants on."

His lips twitch. "What are you going to do about it?"

I bite my lip, considering, then push against his shoulder and urge him back, reversing our positions.

I've never been quite so bold in all my life, but it's exhilarating to be the one in control—if only for a few moments.

Rather than tug his jeans open with my hands, I kiss down the hard ridges of his abs, nuzzle his navel, and grip the denim with my teeth, pulling the top button free. All five open easily, and I'm not even a little surprised to find him naked underneath.

"I guess that answers that question."

"Which one is that?" He gently pushes his fingers through my hair.

"Boxers or briefs?"

He snorts out a laugh but smothers it when I urge his jeans over his hips and plant a kiss on his cock, right under his sensitive tip. Shane's hips jerk in surprise. When his jeans are long gone, I don't give him time to retake control.

I take his cock in my hand and wrap my lips around the tip, enjoying myself.

He's rock-hard, and if the way he moves beneath me, and the moans of delight coming from his lips are to be believed, he's enjoying my efforts immensely.

"Jesus H., Ivie, where did you learn to do that?"

Satisfaction bubbles through me, but suddenly, he rears up, takes my shoulders in his hands, and pushes me back onto the bed.

"Hey, I was having fun."

"Too much fun. I'm not going to come in your mouth the first time. We're going to make this last a bit."

"Okay, I'll do it again later."

He laughs and kisses me hard. "Do you have any idea how fucking beautiful you are?"

I raise a brow. "I'm glad you think so."

I'm not stupid. I know I'm not a beauty queen. I'm passable at best. But it fills my heart with joy that this sexy-as-hell man thinks I'm attractive.

His lips are everywhere. His movements are suddenly more urgent as if he just can't hold himself back any longer.

And I don't want him to. I want Shane to lose himself in me. In *us*. I don't think he lets himself just *feel* very often. The fact that he's doing so with me is both humbling and arousing.

He doesn't guide my underwear down my legs.

No, he just rips them off.

I blink at him in surprise.

"They were in my way." With that simple statement, he nudges my legs apart with his shoulders and settles in between them.

But he doesn't lower his mouth to me.

He *pets* me.

His fingers linger over my lips, then glide up to my clit, barely pass over it, and then move back down again.

My hips surge.

"Lord, have mercy," I mutter as my back arches. "Shane."

"Yes, baby?"

"Shane."

"I'm right here."

"More."

He kisses the inside of my thigh. "What do you need? Tell me."

"More," I repeat and reach blindly to grip the sheets.

"More of this?" His touch is firmer now, but it's not his fingers I want. "Or this?" He gently circles my hard clit—electricity shooting through me. "What do you want?"

"You." The word is a plea. My God, I feel like I'm about to burst from wanting him. "Your mouth."

"Good girl. Watch this."

I open my eyes and watch as he lowers his head to lick me. Then, he starts doing magical things that I can't even comprehend as my head falls back against the pillow, and he treats my body to a smorgasbord of sensation.

I can't hold back. I couldn't if I wanted to. Falling over the crest of oblivion is as natural as water rushing over a waterfall.

And when I begin to surface, I feel those magical lips on my thighs, then up my belly. When he buries his face against my neck and takes a long, deep breath, I wrap myself around him, arms and legs enfolding him, needing him close.

"I'm clean, too," he whispers against my ear. "I'd never put you at risk."

"I know."

And with that invitation, with his face close to mine, and our bodies twined together, he slowly slips inside me, filling me completely.

"Christ," he mutters, his voice hoarse. "Christ, Ivie."

I stroke his back, his hand slipping beneath me to cup my ass as he begins to move. He does so slowly at first and then with vigor, the push and pull driving us both over that cliff and into the abyss beyond.

When the room quiets, and we're tangled together, both catching our breath, I smile and drag my foot up his calf. "I've been waiting for that for months. I didn't think you'd ever want to do me."

He snorts. "You have such a fun way with words." He turns his head to press a kiss to my cheek. "I've enjoyed getting to know you. It's unexpected and not typical for me, but the learning-you parts, the *foreplay* as you put it, has been as fun as the sex itself. And given that I can't feel my legs and am eighty-percent sure I had a stroke when I came, that's saying something."

I can't help the giggle that comes out of me, and I drag my fingertips down his cheek.

I'm in love with him. I've been falling for weeks. Every time he called me, each time we flirted during a meal or just exchanged looks from across a room, led to this.

Shane Martinelli is everything I've ever hoped to find in a man. Not because he completes me or anything cliché like that, but because he's simply...*him.* I know he thinks we can't have anything permanent because of his dangerous job.

But maybe he'll come around. Perhaps he'll see how good we are together and change his mind.

I CAN'T SLEEP. I've never had insomnia issues before, and after a rigorous afternoon of sex, some delicious food, and even *more* sex, you'd think I'd be comatose.

Shane's sleeping soundly next to me, his breaths even as the light of the moon filters through the window.

I envy him. I'm restless, so rather than toss and turn next to him, potentially waking him, I slip from the bed and wrap up in one of his flannel shirts. I'm able to get out the door without a sound and decide I'd like to sit outside.

We're headed solidly into fall, and evenings are cool here in the mountains, so I grab a blanket off the couch on my way to the back door.

It's a clear night. With no light noise from any city, it's *dark,* aside from the light of the moon, and I can see more stars than I ever have in my life.

If I'm not mistaken, I can see Venus. I bundle the blanket around me and take a long, deep breath of crisp, fresh air.

I see why Shane loves it out here. The air is clean, and no one's around.

I would never have thought I'd enjoy the quiet like this, but it's peaceful.

A coyote howls in the distance. A light breeze blows through, rustling the bushes beside the back porch.

I can see Curt's little cabin off in the distance. The lights are on, and there's a small trail of smoke coming from a chimney. I can't help but wonder what kind of horrors that man has seen in his life to make him want to exile himself out here with no interaction with anyone except Shane. Did the two of them serve together? Did they see the same horrors? Neither seems eager to discuss it.

But I'm nosy, and I'm curious.

An owl—at least, I think it's an owl—flies overhead, making me smile. It may be quiet, but it's not boring out here, even at night.

I don't know exactly what has me so restless tonight. "I'm just silly."

"Hoo. Hoo."

I glance up. Yep, it's an owl.

"I am," I reply with a smile. "I should be fast asleep, and you should be out hunting for your breakfast."

"Hoo. Hoo."

"Exactly."

Suddenly, there's a commotion behind me, and Shane comes running out the back door, yelling my name.

"Ivie! Ivie!"

"Hey, I'm right here." I stand, letting the blanket fall. "Shane, I'm right here."

He's panting and out of breath as his chin falls to his chest in relief, and then he takes my shoulders in his hands. "Don't ever fucking do that again."

"Do what? I couldn't sleep so I came out to look at the stars."

"You can't just leave while I'm asleep and not tell me where you're going."

"Yes. I can."

He shakes his head and paces away from me as if he's completely frustrated. "No, Ivie. There are people out there looking for you. People who want you *killed*. And it's my goddamn job to keep you safe. I can't do that when I don't know where you are."

"Where am I going to go?" I demand and prop my hands on my hips, staring at him. "You're overreacting, Shane. I couldn't sleep so I came out to talk to that owl that just flew off. I didn't sneak out to go to a party."

"I'm not overreacting." He shakes his head and then rubs the back of his neck in agitation. "I woke up, and you were gone. Not in the bathroom, not grabbing something in the kitchen. *Gone.* I have top-of-the-line security here. If anyone breached the perimeter, I have alarms that would go off. But what if someone managed to slip through and get you?"

"Hey, they didn't." I walk toward him, but he won't let me touch him. "Shane, I literally just wanted some fresh air."

"Just wake me up and tell me next time." He blows out a breath.

"You're scared." I blink at him in surprise.

"Of course, I am." He rubs his hand over his mouth. "You'll never know what it felt like to hear that you'd been taken. To watch the footage on Annika's tape. To know that someone had you and I wasn't there to get you."

"But you did get me."

He shakes his head. "You don't get it."

"Okay, tell me."

He rubs his neck again. This time, I don't let him back away. I wrap my arms around him and press my cheek to his chest.

"Tell me." My voice is quiet now.

"If something happened to you, I don't know that I would ever get over it." He presses his lips to my head. "You are important, Ivie. I won't ever let someone get to you again. If you want fresh air, we'll get fresh air. But I need to *know*."

"Okay." I rub his back in soothing circles. "I'm sorry that I scared you. I just wanted to let you sleep."

"When all of this is over, you can let me sleep."

Is he still going to be around when all this is finished?

429

It's a question I'm not brave enough to ask. Not yet.

"So, if I want to go for a walk on your property, I have to ask for permission?"

"Either Curt or I will go with you."

"Okay." I kiss his chest and pull back to look up at him. "I have to use the bathroom. Do you want to go with me to that, too?"

His lips twitch as his eyes narrow into slits. "Wouldn't bother me a bit."

I scowl. "Ew. It would bother *me*. You aren't allowed in the bathroom. That's where I draw the line."

"We all have one," he says simply. "Do you still want to sit out here?"

"The owl and I are done talking." I reach down for the blanket. "We can go in. I'm sorry you ended up waking up anyway."

"I'm not. You scared ten years off my life, and I have a feeling it's going to be a short one as it is."

I stop and stare up at him. "Don't say stuff like that." He shrugs and moves to walk inside, but I stop him. "Seriously. Don't. You hate the idea of something happening to me, and the same goes for me, Shane. It's not funny."

"No." He kisses my nose and then takes the blanket to carry. "You're right, it's not funny. Let's go get some rest."

"Holy crap, I'm sweaty," Ivie says as we hop off the ATV and walk toward the house. "That was quite a workout."

"You did more than I expected." I take her hand and smile down at her, proud of her. She kicked ass today. Literally. "I think Curt will need a long soak in a hot bath. It's a good thing I provide him with excellent health insurance."

"I don't like hitting him," she says softly. "I'm not a violent person like my father was."

"I know." We stop on the porch, in the same place we stood last night, and I kiss her forehead. "But you have to practice. You didn't hit him much. I'm just teasing you."

"I don't like hitting at all. And carrying a gun around in my pants isn't my favorite thing, either."

"It won't be forever. Just until we get this mess all figured out."

She sighs and then nods. "I don't mean to complain. Thank you for everything you're doing for me. I'm gonna go hop in the shower and get this ick off me."

"Enjoy it. I'll be in in just a bit."

She walks into the house, and I pull my phone out of my pocket. I dial Carmine's number and wait for him to answer.

"Yo," he says in greeting.

"How are things there?" I ask, getting straight to the point.

"Quiet. Rocco and I are in the office, and we were just saying that it's been very quiet. No chatter."

"That's not typical." I lean on the railing and watch a herd of elk make their way into my pasture about a hundred yards away. "I don't like it when it's quiet."

"I know. The ears on the ground say the same thing. No chatter, pretty mellow right now."

"That means something's going to happen."

"We agree," Rocco says, clearly on speakerphone. "You're right to stay there for now. It's likely the safest place."

"Agreed," I say with a sigh. Not because I don't like being on my ranch. Quite the opposite. It's the safest place for us, and it's where I feel the most comfortable. But I don't like this quiet. Feeling on edge, like the other shoe is about to drop. "I'm waiting for more info from Cox, and I have some feelers out, but I'm trying to be inconspicuous. It takes time."

"If you need us, we can be there in a couple of hours. Or you can always come here if need be," Carmine reminds me. "I know you don't think it's as safe as the ranch, but we can lock it down when we need to."

"I know. Thanks. I'll check in tomorrow."

"Over and out," Rocco says, cutting off the call.

Like I said, I don't like it when there's no chatter. It's like when a person has a toddler, and quiet means chaos.

For now, all I can do is what I'm already doing. So, I walk inside, expecting Ivie to be out of the shower by now.

But when I come around the corner, I hear her talking to someone. I slow down, listening.

"I will fuck you up. That's right, I said it. You don't want a piece of me. Oh, does that make you nervous? What are you going to do about it?"

I inch forward, wanting to get a glimpse of what's going on without being seen. If someone's in there with her, I'll kill them.

I pull my sidearm from the holster at my back and continue inching forward.

"Are you looking at me?"

I peer around the door and feel every muscle loosen in relief. Ivie's standing in front of the mirror in just her blue jeans and black bra, her pistol tucked into her jeans at the small of her back. She quickly whips it out and points it at herself in the mirror.

"Are you fucking looking at *me*?" she demands and narrows her eyes at herself, leaning forward. "Yeah, that's what I thought."

Then she holsters her weapon again.

I have to clamp my hand over my mouth so I don't bust up laughing. I wouldn't miss this show for the world.

She starts to walk away, then turns back quickly, drawing the weapon once more.

"Don't piss me off, asshole."

I can't help it anymore. I can't hold in the laughter. Ivie stills, and I see her cringe in the mirror as I walk up behind her and rest my hands on her shoulders, looking her reflection in the eyes.

"You're kind of scary."

She presses her lips into a line as her cheeks bloom into a bright pink. I want to kiss the hell out of her.

"I didn't know you were there."

"Obviously." I grin and kiss her neck where it meets her shoulder. "You do a great DeNiro impression."

"You weren't supposed to see that. Besides, you're the one who literally just told me that I need to practice drawing my weapon."

"I did, you're completely right." I can't keep my hands off her. She's simply irresistible. She spins to face me, and our lips meet in a kiss that starts sweet but quickly escalates to hot and needy.

"I'm too sweaty for sex," she informs me but doesn't push me away when I free her of her bra and let it fall to the floor.

"You're just going to get sweaty again."

"It's different," she insists and presses her hands to my chest. "Seriously, I need to wash up."

"Okay." I kiss her once more, then back up. "I'll help."

She quirks a brow. "Will you?"

"I'm an excellent back-washer," I inform her, keeping my expression perfectly serious. "I've been told that I should go into business for myself, washing backs."

"Told by whom?" She quirks a brow, purses her lips, and I know this is a trap.

Well, shit.

"Uh..."

She laughs and slips around me to start the water in the shower. "Relax, Shane. You're no virgin. Neither am I, actually."

I frown. I don't like the thought of Ivie having had sex with anyone but me. I know the way she sounds, the way her fists clench in the sheets—or my hair. The way she tastes.

And the fact that *anyone* in the past or the future would have the same knowledge fills me with an all-consuming rage.

"Why do you look like that?" she asks.

"Like what?"

"Like you want to punch a wall."

I make myself grin and then shrug. "I couldn't tell you."

She doesn't smile back. She just blinks at me, and then, before stepping into the shower, hits me with, "Don't lie to me again, Martinelli."

I catch her elbow before she can step into the shower. "I don't like the thought of other men having been with you."

She nods once. "That's better. And I don't like the idea of you washing someone else's back. But, we're both old enough to know that we've been with other people. That doesn't mean I'm sleeping with anyone else now. And for as long as you're having sex with *me*, I'd ask for the same consideration."

I love the fire in her blue eyes. She's staking a claim, here and now. And as much as I've told myself over and over again that this can't go anywhere, that even though I'm completely wrapped up in her, she can never really be mine, I can't help but feel my gut clench, and my heart pound in response to her possessiveness.

"Baby, I can't *see* anyone but you." I cup her cheek and bend down to kiss her softly. "Now, let's get in this shower before we waste all the hot water."

"Do these still hurt?" I brush my fingertips over her damp skin where the bruises over her ribs have turned from black to green. I reach for some arnica and rub it gently over the wounded area.

"No, they're just ugly now," she says and then sighs at my touch. "You're good with your hands. And now I can vouch for the back-washing praise. You're hired."

I grin as I turn to wash my hands, and Ivie pulls her clothes on.

"Shane?"

"Yeah."

"I'm bored." She leans on the vanity and crosses her arms over her chest. "I'm getting cabin fever."

I walk into the closet to put on clean clothes, and Ivie follows me.

"Let's go somewhere."

"No."

"*Shane.*" It's not a whine, but it's damn close. "We've been in this house for almost a week. And while I love your ranch, I need to see something else."

"And you will. As soon as—"

"As soon as we figure this out," she finishes for me. "Let's just go for a drive. Just a short one where I can see different trees. Your windows are tinted, and no one's up here anyway. We're in the middle of nowhere."

I should stick to my guns and say no, but she's been restless all morning, and I know she's not a loner like I am.

"We could drive into town and get lunch at the best deli I've ever been to," I offer. "But you have to stay in the car when I pick it up."

"Deal." She hops and claps her hands in excitement. "Perfect."

"I'll call ahead and order," I mutter. "But don't get used to this."

"Of course." She crosses her heart and holds her fingers up like she's a Boy Scout. "Scouts' honor."

"You were never a Boy Scout."

She giggles. "Well, no. But I promise. Thank you. I'm going to grab my shoes."

She runs out, and I send a text to Curt, filling him in. Then I call the deli to place an order. Ten minutes later, we're in my SUV and headed into town, which is only about twenty minutes away.

"The trees are turning," she murmurs. "I bet it's gorgeous up here in the fall."

"Another week, and it'll be breathtaking."

She bites her lip, and I reach out to take her hand. "We might still be here."

She nods.

"You're always welcome here, Ivie, whether assholes are chasing you or not."

That makes her smile, and she glances my way. "Is there a private spot where you can pull over?"

"Do you have to pee or something?"

She just smiles again, so I pull over to the side of the road. "This is private. It's still my property."

"Geez, Shane, how much land did you buy?"

"A thousand acres."

She blinks over at me in surprise. Once I've put the vehicle in park, she unbuckles her belt and leans over the center console.

Her hands dive for my jeans.

"Here?" My voice is high and breaks as if I'm a fifteen-year-old kid.

"Here." But she doesn't climb on top of me, she takes my cock in her hand, jacks me twice, and then sinks that sweet mouth of hers over the head. I'm immediately lost to her.

"Fucking hell, Ivie."

The woman is a master with her mouth and with her hands.

I push the seat back so she has more room, and so I can lean back a bit and enjoy the ride. She never fails to surprise me. And just now, as she cups my balls and sucks gently, I see stars.

"Jesus." It's a prayer and a curse, and before I can stop myself, I'm coming. I watch as Ivie laps up every drop, then sits back, buckles her belt, and wipes her mouth.

"Well, that was fun."

I bark out a laugh as I tuck myself away. "What did I do to deserve that?"

"You're taking me for a drive," she says simply. "And I appreciate it."

"You're easy to please, sweetheart."

"Not really." She shrugs as I put the vehicle in gear and start once more toward town. "But you're irresistible."

My eyes narrow into slits as we get closer to town. I survey the streets, looking for anything out of place, but it looks the same as it always does. Like it's something out of the Old West.

"Wow, it's like a time capsule," she says, echoing my thoughts.

"It was a booming gold town about a hundred years ago," I inform her. "When it seemed that most of the gold had been mined, people left to find other claims. Some stayed. There's always been working mines here, but it slowed down considerably. The downtown area looks pretty much the same as it did back in the old days. The buildings have withstood the test of time."

"It's very cool," she says. "I'd love to wander around and take it all in."

"Another time. I promise. Today, I'm anxious to grab lunch and get back to the ranch."

"I understand." I glance over when she lays her hand on my arm. "Honest, I do."

"Good." I park right in front of the deli. "Lock these doors. Do you have your weapon?"

"Of course."

"Keep it handy. Keep your eyes open. Don't look at your phone or fall asleep."

"You'll be gone for all of thirty seconds," she reminds me.

"Sometimes, that's all it takes." I lean over and kiss her cheek. "Do as I say."

"Yes, sir."

I hop out of the car and nod in satisfaction when I hear the snick of the locks. Ivie isn't careless, and I know she'll do as I ask.

"Well, good morning, handsome."

Mrs. Ullrich is sixty-five if she's a day, and she's a hopeless flirt. She's also been married for forty-seven years and has eight children, some of whom are my age.

"Hey there, Mrs. Ullrich. Do you have those sandwiches for me?"

"Right here." She fetches a brown paper bag from a shelf. "I added it to your tab."

"Thanks. Appreciate it." I toss a five-dollar bill into the tip jar and turn to leave. "Have a good day, ma'am."

"You, too, you handsome devil," she calls after me, making me grin.

I haven't exactly become a member of the community. I'm not one to attend town hall meetings and get acquainted with my neighbors.

But there's value in knowing who's here, who I should watch out for, and letting the community know that I'm not someone to be wary of.

I'm an outsider. I know that. But I keep to myself, and I don't make trouble. In return, the townspeople have been cordial, and I trust that I'm safe here.

Which is more important now than ever before.

When I walk out of the deli, I feel my blood fucking boil.

"In the car," I bark to Ivie, who's standing on the sidewalk, covered in puppies. "Now."

She smiles at the teenager who's walking them, gives one a kiss on the head, and then climbs in next to me.

"Don't yell at me, Shane. They're *puppies.*"

"I don't care if they were the cutest puppies on the planet—"

"Which they were."

"I told you to stay put. What if there had been a sniper in one of these buildings?"

She stares at me as I pull onto the road and head back toward home.

"You're being ridiculous."

"No, I'm not."

"There are no *snipers.*"

"That you know of."

"For God's sake, Shane, I was out of the car for less than fifteen seconds. I wanted to pet a puppy."

"Fifteen seconds is all they need. Trust me. We won't be leaving the ranch again."

"So now I'm being punished? I'm taking that blowjob back."

I want to laugh. But I'm too fucking mad.

CHAPTER
TEN
~IVIE~

"I'm going to—" Shane begins when we pull up to the house, but I put my hand up, stopping him from speaking further.

"I don't care what you're going to do. I'm not speaking to you right now."

I shove out of the SUV and hurry into the house. I hear him behind me, and I remember that I'm starving, so I whirl back and reach for the bag in his hands.

"Which one is mine?"

He doesn't reply, so I glance up at him and cock a brow.

"Shane?"

"Now you're speaking to me?"

I just narrow my eyes menacingly, and he's smart enough to sigh and hang his head. "They're the same."

I fetch one of the sandwiches from the bag and turn to march away once more, headed for the guest room, where I shut and lock the door behind me.

I'm adult enough to restrain myself from *slamming* the door. Barely.

"He drives me fucking crazy," I mutter as I unwrap the sandwich and pull my phone out of my purse to video call my best friend, Annika.

I've been friends with the gorgeous doctor for more years than I can count, and she knows *everything* there is to know about me.

She'll talk me down from the ledge.

"Hey, friend," she says with a bright smile. I prop the phone on the desk so I can see her, and vice versa, and still eat my lunch.

"I'm going to be eating in your ear."

"I'll join you. I just made some leftover lasagna for lunch."

"Lasagna leftovers are the *best*."

"Hell yes, they are," she agrees and takes a bite. "I'm so happy you called. I haven't heard from you since you went up to Shane's place."

"Oh, I'll likely get into trouble for this call, but I just don't give a shit. He made me mad, and I want to vent."

"Tell me everything." She wipes her mouth with a napkin. "And I do mean *everything*."

"He's mad at me because I got out of the car when we went to the deli to pick up lunch."

"Why would he get mad?"

"He's totally overprotective," I say, getting riled up. "I mean, I know he's just trying to protect me, but I was out of the car for less than a minute, petting puppies. *Puppies,* Annika. And he flew off the handle and said I could have been taken out by a sniper."

She frowns as she chews on some bread. "Do they have a lot of snipers in the mountains?"

"Right? That was my thought. I highly doubt it. But he was pissed off, and that made me mad. So, here we are. I told him I was taking the blowjob back."

Annika coughs and has to take a drink of her water. "Wait. What? *Blowjob?* Ivie Jordan, you're not telling me everything. Stop babbling about snipers and get to the good stuff. You know I'm living vicariously through you."

"You don't have to," I remind her. "Rafe—"

"We're not talking about Rafe. We're talking about you and blowjobs. Spill it. Right now."

"Oh, we're sleeping together."

I feel the smile spread slowly over my face.

"*Ivie.*"

"Okay, so you know we've been flirting for months and talking a ton. There's some serious attraction there. Not just on *my* part, which is still kind of a mystery to me. I mean, have you seen him? What does he see in me?"

"Ask me that again, and you'll no longer be my best friend." She narrows her eyes at me. "There are a million reasons to love you, and I'll send you an essay on the subject later. Tell me more."

"Well, the chemistry is off the charts. There has been sex. Like, really good sex. I finally know what all the fuss is about. I mean, I'm not a virgin, but I'm the girl boys had sex with on a dare or because they were drunk. And it's not like it was a fantastic time for me. But Shane takes his time and pretty much worships every inch of my body."

"You bitch."

I laugh, and Annika joins me.

"You know I love you and mean that in the nicest way possible."

"Of course." I take a bite and think about the frustrating man in question. "The Martinelli brothers are ridiculously sexy. Like, their gene pool must be made of gold."

"You're not kidding. Hotter than hot. And for a long time, my family didn't mesh well with theirs, but with Nadia and Carmine marrying soon, things have mellowed out. Which makes me happy."

"I like Carmine for Nadia."

Nadia is my other best friend. The three of us have been tight for a long time, and I'm so happy for her, that she found love with Carmine—even if he was the last person in the world anyone thought she'd end up with.

"But let's not talk about them. Let's talk about you," Annika suggests. "What else is going on? I miss you. I can't wait for this whole mess to be resolved so you can come home."

"Me, too." I sigh and roll my empty sandwich wrapper into a ball, tossing it into a nearby trash can. "It's really pretty up here, I have to admit. I can see why Shane likes it. But it's so far away from everything. So isolated."

"I assume that was the point of it," she says.

"A fortress in the mountains. Well, if that's what he was going for, that's what he got. The house is really nice. And he has a bunch of other buildings on the property. And a farmhand. Is that what it's called?"

Annika giggles. "Is the farmhand hot?"

"Actually, yeah. Kinda. He's the strong, silent type. Doesn't say much, but he's nice."

"Maybe I should make a trip to the ranch," Annika says, waggling her eyebrows.

"You have no idea how much I would *love* that."

"Ivie," Shane calls through the door. "Who are you talking to?"

I roll my eyes and move to the door, then unlock it to open it just a crack. "None of your business."

"Are you on your *cell phone?*" He stares at me like I've lost all my marbles.

"Of course, I am. I'm talking to Annika, and—"

"Not anymore, you're not. Sorry, Annika, I'm hanging up on you."

He ends the FaceTime call and rounds on me.

"I know you did *not* just hang up on my best friend."

"Why would you call her in the first place?"

"Because she's my best friend, and you're being a dick, and I needed to vent about *you!*" I shout in his face. "That's what girls do, Shane. We vent when the guy we're sleeping with is being a douche canoe."

"You can't call out on your phone," he says and props his hands on his hips. "Anyone who's looking for you, who knows your number, can trace it here."

"You never told me that."

"You're a smart woman," he replies. "I would think you'd just know it."

I laugh and pace the room. "I'm not into espionage or finding people, Shane. How would I know that? It's something from movies."

"No, it's very real. This isn't a funny situation."

"You're right." I sober and face him. "There's nothing funny about it. Your behavior over the past hour has been disrespectful and just shitty all around."

"*My* behavior?" he demands. "Mine?"

"Yes, yours."

"Ivie, you were careless."

442

"How do you know?" I prop my hands on my hips. "You just made a split-second decision that I was being careless, but you didn't ask me anything. You assumed that I was stupid, and you punished me for it."

"Okay. Tell me what you were doing."

I just stare at him, still fuming.

"Please."

"The young boy who was walking those puppies fell. He was being pulled, and he wasn't strong enough to hold onto them. He fell right next to your car. I surveyed the area, knew that I had my weapon on me, and decided to get out and help him right himself. It took ten seconds. Then you walked outside and threw a fit."

"I did not—"

"Oh, yes, you did. I'm not a child. I chose to help the boy after I weighed the situation. I didn't feel like I was in danger. Especially knowing that you'd return any second."

"I told you to stay in the car."

"And I'm sure you're used to people following your orders."

"To the letter," he agrees.

"I'm not your subordinate." I raise my chin. "You're teaching me to defend myself. I'm not an idiot, and I won't be treated like one."

"That's not—"

Before he can finish the sentence, a loud beeping starts, and he holds up his hand to shush me, then cocks his ear, listening.

"Fuck," he mutters and runs out of the room. I'm right on his heels as he opens the door of the 007 room downstairs as I've come to think of it, and we hurry down the stairs. He flicks a switch, and all of the monitors on one wall come to life.

"These are cameras showing the whole property," I mutter.

"Someone breached the perimeter," he says grimly and presses his phone to his ear. "Yeah, I hear it. I'm looking at the monitors, but I don't see anything. The alarm was tripped in quadrant forty-two. Okay. Yeah, I'll go check, too. You take the south and east sides, I'll take north and west, and we'll cover quadrants forty through forty-five. They can't have gotten far. Report back. Out."

He turns to me, his eyes flat and cold, and his voice is hard. "I need you to stay *here*. Do not go upstairs. Do not leave this room. I'll lock it on my way out. It's bomb-proof, fireproof, and impossible to get into if you don't know the code."

"Shane—"

"I don't know who's on my property, but they're about to get a rude awakening. Stay, Ivie. Keep your weapon on you, in case."

"I won't leave."

He nods once and starts to leave, but then he turns back to me and kisses me hard. He releases me as quickly as he grabbed me, takes the stairs two at a time, and then he's gone. The locks snick into place, and I'm left alone. To worry.

I turn back to the monitors. I see Shane exiting the back door, his weapon drawn as he takes off at a run.

Movement catches my eye on another monitor. It's Curt, also hurrying from his cabin, weapon drawn.

Jesus, it feels like something out of a mystery novel.

I wish I had sound.

I narrow my eyes as Curt and Shane come in and out of range of the different cameras. Each monitor is labeled with a number.

"Shane said quadrant forty-two," I mutter, looking at the corresponding screen. I walk to it, looking for switches. "Nothing."

Curt and Shane continue coming and going, making their way through the thirties until they're in the quadrants in question.

I tap a couple of keys on a keyboard and pray with all my might that I don't fuck something up.

Suddenly, I can hear what's happening.

"Jackpot," I murmur, pleased that I haven't lost my touch when it comes to electronics.

"Nothing," I hear Curt say as he meets Shane in quadrant forty-four.

But then I see something in quadrant thirty-eight. I pick up the phone I grabbed on our way down here and text Shane.

Me: *Q38. Man with rifle.*

Shane looks at the smartwatch on his wrist, then crouches and gestures to Curt. I can't hear what he whispers to the other man, but they move fast and sleek from the monitor, through the others, making their way to the intruder.

"Oh, God," I whisper as I clasp my hands and press them to my chest. "Be careful. Who the hell is that?"

For two men crouched so low to the ground, they move fast. Suddenly, they're coming at the stranger from opposite sides.

"Stop right there," Shane commands, pointing his weapon at the man. "Drop the rifle."

"Hey," the guy says and raises his hands, slowly lowering his gun to the ground. "I'm not looking for any trouble."

"What *are* you looking for?" Shane asks as Curt retrieves the weapon and walks with it out of range of the stranger.

"Elk," the man says. "I'm just hunting elk."

"You're doing it on private property," Shane informs him. "*My* private property."

"I didn't realize I left state land."

"Bullshit," Curt mutters. "There are signs everywhere, asshole."

"Not to mention, I don't know of anyone around here who would shoot an elk with an assault weapon." Shane steps closer and pushes his pistol into the other man's face. "Who do you work for?"

"I'm just hunting elk." But the other man doesn't blink. Doesn't even look scared.

I'm terrified, and I'm safe in this room.

"Who sent you?" Curt asks and relieves the man of his wallet. "And is your last name really Sugarbaker?"

"Sugarbaker?" Shane smirks, but the man moves quickly, takes Shane's pistol, and rounds on Curt when he advances. There's a fight, a gunshot, and the camera goes dark.

"Oh, God." I tap keys frantically, but I can't get the feed or the sound back. They're just *gone.*

"No. Don't do this to me, Shane. Move into the range of another camera."

But they don't. In fact, systematically, every monitor goes dark.

Minutes that feel like hours tick by, but there's nothing.

Absolutely nothing.

Until the sound of another gunshot comes through another monitor. I don't see anything, but I hear the shot.

Jesus, is Shane hurt? Is Curt injured?

How can I be expected to just sit here and *wait*?

I try to call Shane's phone, but there's no reply.

"He told me to *stay*," I remind myself. "He'll be pissed if I don't."

I chew my lip.

"But he could be hurt. Oh, God, did more men show up? How long am I supposed to wait here? What if they're both bleeding out there somewhere?"

I can't just sit here on my hands. I *can't*.

I check my weapon and keep it in my hand as I climb the steps to the first floor. I put my hand on the knob and take a long, deep breath.

He's going to be *so mad*.

But I need to know that he's okay.

I bite my lip and turn the knob. When I open the door, I come face-to-face with Shane himself. He's bleeding. And he's *so pissed*.

"What in the fucking hell are you doing?"

CHAPTER
ELEVEN
~IVIE~

"Oh, my God." I collapse against him and hold onto him. "Where are you bleeding? Who was that creep? What happened to him? Is Curt okay? I was worried sick, Shane. All the monitors went blank, and I didn't know if you were the one who got shot. I didn't know what to do. I couldn't just stay down there by myself; I was going crazy."

"You were supposed to stay put."

I lean back to look up at him, relieved when there's no fury in his gorgeous brown eyes. "But what if you were dying?"

"Then you still stay put. There's nothing you can do if that's the case." He wipes a tear I didn't even know was there from under my eye. He doesn't look nearly as mad as I expected him to be. "Come on."

"Where are we going?"

"My bedroom. I need to clean up, and we need to talk about you following orders."

I sigh, in both relief and defeat, but follow him down the hall to his bedroom and through to the bathroom. He strips out of his shirt, and I gasp at the hole in his arm.

"You were shot!"

"Yeah, it stings like a bitch. Just grazed me, but those hurt worse than the alternative, if you want to know the truth."

I just stand and stare at him. "Shane."

He glances up at me as he pulls supplies from a medicine cabinet.

"You were *shot*."

"It's not the first time. Probably not the last. It's not too bad."

I shake my head and cross to him, pushing his hands aside as I begin to dress the wound. "Tell me everything."

"In a second. I don't want to fight about this anymore, Ivie. I'm not trying to control you or be a douche canoe, as you put it. I'm trying to keep you alive. And if you don't follow my orders to the letter, you put yourself at risk."

"I won't apologize for needing to know if you're dead or alive." I look him in the eyes and lean in to kiss his cheek. "I was so scared." My voice is a whisper. "I knew I'd be okay because you're here. And even if that asshole had killed you, you'd probably find a way to be a ghost and kick his ass if he tried to put his hands on me. You'll protect me no matter what, Shane. I needed to know if you were okay."

"I'm okay." He tips his forehead against mine. "I had a bad minute when he fought back. You said the screens went black?"

"Yeah, he must have shot the camera. They all went out. But not before I saw him struggle with you, take your gun, and then it went off. I was a mess of nerves."

"I was afraid that would happen to the monitors. The fucker who wired them did it wrong. I'll look at them."

"Forget the monitors. How was he able to surprise you like that?"

"We were laughing at his last name. I didn't expect him to fight back, honestly. And that's my fault. I know better than to let my guard down for even a second. We recovered quickly, but the damage was done. It was a stupid mistake, and one I don't plan to repeat."

"Is Curt okay?"

"Yes."

"Is the other guy dead?"

Shane's eyes are calm. And cold. "Yes."

I swallow hard and resume dressing his wound, keeping my fingers gentle. "Did you kill him?"

He takes my hand and kisses my knuckles. "I didn't have to."

"Curt killed him?"

"He self-terminated," he replies. "I don't know who he was. Curt's running him right now. We found his vehicle on the road where he breached the property. Got a name and some info on him, but I've never heard of him before."

"He was here for me."

Shane's hand tightens on mine. "He never admitted to that, but I'm pretty sure he was. He could have been sent in to assassinate me. We'll know after Curt gets more info."

"You?" I scowl at him. "Why would anyone want to kill you?"

There's no humor in his laugh. "I've committed dozens, if not hundreds of sins in my lifetime, Ivie."

"We all have."

He cups my face gently. "Not like me. I belong to a very small club, honey."

"So, you're never safe."

"I wouldn't say that."

"I wish you'd tell me more. Help me understand you. I just want to know you, Shane."

"You do know me. In all the ways that matter. Now, get this sewn up before I bleed out."

"I don't think you're going to bleed out. You don't even need stitches." But I reach for the antiseptic and dab at the wound. "You took his gun away. How did he kill himself?"

"He had a blade. Cut his own throat."

I still and stare down at him with my mouth agape. "Jesus."

"That's what I thought."

"What did you do with his body?"

He kisses the inside of my wrist. "It won't be found. Well, animals might get him, but that's it. The body, and the vehicle, are long gone."

"So, I shouldn't ask questions."

"You can ask them. I don't know how much I'll tell you, though. The less you know, the better."

I don't necessarily agree with that, but I keep my opinion to myself and cover the injury. After I put the supplies away, I turn to walk out of the bathroom, but Shane snags my wrist and tugs me back into his arms.

"I'm sorry I was gruff with you," he says against my hair. I melt against him, soaking in his warmth and strength. "I need to keep you safe. Not because you're a job to me, Ivie. But because if anything were to ever happen to you, I don't think I would survive it."

My heart might explode from the admission. I glance up at him, but before I can say anything, Shane crushes his mouth to mine and lifts me, carrying me to the bed.

"The thought of you being hurt out there was pure torture," I admit against his lips as he tugs my shirt out of my jeans. "I know I should have stayed. But I couldn't *see* you. I heard the gunshot, and I didn't know. Shane—"

"I know." He gently covers my mouth with his. "I know, baby."

The room is hushed and dim with the blinds closed as, without a word, we undress and come together once more. Our touches are just a little more reverent. Our kisses linger, and each breath, each moment is more beautiful than the last.

We tumble over the linens, and when we join, I gasp and then moan as he begins to move, thrusting in just the right rhythm to make my body sing in pleasure.

His fingers lace with mine, and he pins my hands above my head.

"You're gorgeous," he mutters before nibbling on my lips. "You're *everything.*"

I tilt my hips, meeting every thrust, then tighten around him as the orgasm moves through me, taking me by surprise.

"That's it," he whispers. "Let go, baby."

"Shane."

His body clenches above mine, and his hands tighten on mine as he lets himself go.

And later, when we're lying together in the waning light of the afternoon, he turns to me for more.

"Brutus Sugarbaker," Curt says with a shrug. We're all sitting in the 007 room, eating pizza and staring at the monitor. Brutus's face fills the screen. It looks like a mugshot. "Forty-seven. From Atlanta."

"What was he doing in the middle of Colorado?" Shane wants to know.

"Not hunting elk," I murmur and take a bite of pepperoni. "He wasn't dressed like a hunter. If he was trying to blend in as someone from here, a hunter, he didn't do a good job of it."

"Hardly," Curt agrees. "However, I did a *lot* of digging, and I can't trace him back to any syndicate. He doesn't work for the government. He doesn't seem to belong to anyone. He was born and raised in Georgia, not far from Atlanta."

"Family?" I ask.

"A wife and three kids." I frown, but Curt keeps talking. "On the surface. It's a cover. I dug a little deeper. His name is Art Fink. How he came up with Sugarbaker, I don't know."

"*Designing Women*, of course." Both men turn and stare at me. "The TV show from the eighties. Come on, surely you've heard of it. I mean, I was hardly *born* in the eighties, but even I know about it. It's a classic."

"Nope," Curt says, but I do get a half-smile out of him, and I consider that a win. "However, just because I uncovered his legal name, doesn't mean I found much of anything else. No marriage on file. No kids. Also, like Brutus Sugarbaker, no ties to any organization. Just the vehicle registration, the one he had with him. No mortgage. No credit history."

"How can he have no credit history?" I demand. "Surely, he can't be a ghost. Is this another false name?"

"I found the birth certificate," Curt replies.

"Did you find what he does for a living?" Shane asks.

"No."

Shane blows out a breath. "So, we still don't know who, exactly, he was trying to find. He could have been here for Ivie or me."

"Or me, really," Curt says philosophically. "God knows I've pissed people off over the years."

"No way," I say, shaking my head. "You're too sweet and quiet."

"Keep flirting with Curt, and I'll break his legs," Shane snarls.

Now Curt does smile, showing off straight, white teeth. "Fooled you, have I?"

"No." I shake my head and reach for another slice of the delicious pizza. "I know shitty people when I see them. Trust me, I've seen my fair share, especially when I was younger. I've seen the worst of the worst. The scariest. You're not that, Curt."

"Hmm," is all he says in reply. "Well, whoever this Fink asshole was, he won't be bothering us again. What I want to know is, who sent him, and who was he supposed to report back to?"

"The million-dollar question," Shane agrees. "He worked for someone, and they'll be looking for him. Did you find anything on his phone?"

"Nope. He had no email loaded on it, no text messages. It was wiped clean. No calls, in or out."

"On the *phone*," I say, thinking it over.

"That's right."

"But not on the number itself. Gimme." I motion for Curt to hand over the cell, which he does. I open it and frown when I see it's locked.

"I have the—" Curt begins, but I cut him off with a sharp shake of my head and tap the screen.

"These are easy to break open," I say and smile when the screen opens. "Ah, you're right. It looks like it's straight from the factory. No apps, no messages. No call log. However, I can get the number off of it and do a little hacking on the computer."

I find the phone number and sit at the computer. I crack my knuckles, shift my head back and forth, and then get down to business. My fingers fly across the keyboard as I search the number, find the carrier, and hack into their system.

"Jesus," Curt mutters in surprise. "You're in their server."

"Yeah, we're going to find out who this jerk talked to. This is a burner phone, but I can still find out what calls came in and out, and we can search those numbers, trace them back to their owners. He wasn't speaking to everyone on burner phones. That's impossible. And it's a mistake that's going to help us."

I type furiously, excited at the idea of helping, of getting to the bottom of this.

"I know solving this won't solve *everything*, but it's a start. Okay, he called four people. Write these numbers down."

Shane pulls out a notepad and pen and scribbles furiously.

"How am I supposed to read this?" I demand when I glance down. "Are you sure you're not a doctor with that chicken scratch?"

"Who owns the numbers?" he asks.

"Okay, this first one is owned by an Oliver Freemont. Lives in New York."

"Got it," Shane says, still scribbling. "No idea who that is. The next?"

"Give me a second." This one doesn't want to give so easily. "It could be another burner phone. It's under some layers, which is unusual. I've got it. Billy Sergi."

"What?" Shane demands. "Look again."

"It's registered to a Billy Sergi."

"Motherfucker son of a bitch."

"Who's Billy Sergi?" I ask in confusion, but Shane shakes his head.

"Who else, Ivie?" he asks.

I move on to the third number. "This one *is* a burner phone. No specific owner. Working on the fourth now."

I keep typing. When I sit back, I stare at the monitor in disbelief.

"Well?" Shane demands.

"There's no possible way, Shane. It has to be a mistake."

"Who is it registered to?"

I turn my gaze up to his and shake my head. I don't believe it. I *can't* believe it.

Rather than ask me again, Shane leans over to look over my shoulder. When he sees the name on the screen, he swears under his breath.

"That's impossible."

I stand and pace the room. "Well, I guess we know who he was here to find."

"There's a mistake," Shane insists and starts typing on another screen. "This is a cover for someone else, to throw us for a loop."

Well, if that's what someone's trying to do, it's working. Because my head is spinning. I can't breathe.

"Hey," Curt says and taps Shane on the shoulder. "Your girl's panicking."

"How can this be?" I wonder aloud and continue pacing the room until I run into a brick wall of a chest. Shane's arms close around me in comfort. "He's dead."

"It's meant to fuck with you," Shane assures me. "And you're letting it."

I pull back to stare up at him. "Wouldn't you?"

"It would throw me, yes. But keep your wits about you, sweetheart. This isn't real. It's smoke and mirrors. And if the person I think is behind this is truly responsible, it fits his M.O. perfectly."

"Who?"

"Sergi," he says simply. "And if he's responsible, I'm going to be fucking pissed off."

I pull out of Shane's arms and return to the computer.

"I'm going to keep digging because there has to be a mistake," I say as my fingers start to fly over the keyboard once more. But no matter where I dig, no matter where I look, I keep getting the same result.

And I can't accept that.

Because the owner that keeps popping up on the screen is my father, and he's been dead for more than a decade.

CHAPTER
TWELVE
~SHANE~

I vie's skin is soft where I kiss her, right next to her eyebrow, and then I silently back out of the room. She's sleeping peacefully, which is exactly what she needs after the mind fuck that she went through in my office.

I close the door behind me and walk out to the living room, where Curt sits, waiting for me.

"She's finally asleep." I pour myself two fingers of whiskey and do the same for Curt. After passing him the glass, I collapse into my favorite leather chair. "This whole thing is fucking nuts."

"I've seen some shit, you know I have." Curt sips his whiskey. "But I don't know if I've ever seen anything like this before."

"Yeah, it's not typical, that's for sure."

I stare at my friend, lost in thought. I saw all of what Curt did—and plenty more since. Curt was on my squad. Was the best assassin I've ever worked with.

He's quick, stealthy, and ruthless. When he needed to leave, to disappear, I knew I had to have him here on the ranch. I'd trust no one more to make sure things run smoothly here when I'm gone.

And I'm gone plenty.

"You know you should leave," he says, surprising me.

"I live here."

He shakes his head and then pins me with that intense stare he gets when he knows things are about to go to hell.

"Take her out of here. If that idiot found her, it's only a matter of time before someone else does."

I blow out a breath and then take another sip of whiskey. "Even if they do find her, I can protect her here better than anywhere else. I know every inch of this land like the back of my hand. And so do you. We can take on an army here if we need to."

"I think it's the wrong move, but you're the boss."

"We keep our eyes open and remain on high alert for the foreseeable future." I lean forward, my elbows resting on my knees, and stare into my glass. "I know that this isn't what you signed on for, man. If you want to go somewhere and lay low until this all blows over, I won't be angry or think any differently of you."

He swallows the rest of his whiskey and sets the glass down without a sound. "I'm not afraid. What happened today didn't give me any bad moments. I thought it might, but I slipped back into the job, you know?"

"Yeah." I nod once. "I know."

"But I came here so I wouldn't have to do that anymore. I know you think it was cowardly of me—"

"Hold up." I raise a hand and scowl at my friend. "You're no coward. You did what you had to do to survive, Curt. You did more on the job than anyone else has. It was too big an ask, and it was wrong."

"It was the motherfucking *job*," he insists. "And it sucked, but it was just the job. And maybe because of that, I can't do it anymore. But I won't leave this land. I won't run away and hide. If they're brave enough to come here and fuck with us, we'll show them just how stupid they are."

I nod grimly. "Damn right. But this isn't your fight."

"It's yours, and that makes it mine."

He says it so simply. As if there's no other way of doing things. As if it's as easy as breathing.

"You'd do the same for me," he continues.

"Without hesitation."

His lips twitch.

"So, you're not leaving, then?"

"Not yet." I shake my head and rub my hand over my lips in agitation. "But I need to call my brothers and Cox. I need to know what the fuck is going on. If that piece of shit Billy Sergi is behind this, I'll kill him myself."

"And start a war in the process," Curt adds, knowing very well that the Sergi family is a force to be reckoned with. The mafia family is based in New York, and our families don't always see eye-to-eye.

I wouldn't put this past them.

"If they're trying to kill Ivie, it won't be a war. I'll end them."

Curt stares at me for a moment and then mutters, *"Fuck,"* under his breath before scrubbing his hands over his face.

"Sure you don't want to go lay low somewhere for a while?" I ask.

There's no humor in his laugh. "Oh yeah, I do. But I won't. We'll finish this. I'm going to go secure that fence line and make sure the alarms are set. I don't want any more surprises."

"Great. I'm going to make some calls. I'll be sticking close to the house while Ivie sleeps."

He nods and stands, but then turns back to me. "You're in love with her."

It's not a question.

"I know that it can't go anywhere." I sigh again. "But, yeah. She's incredible."

"Does she know? What you do?"

"No. And she won't."

"Shane—"

"The less she knows, the better."

"I'm just going to say this, as your friend. She's a smart girl. She's not weak. And she deserves to know the truth so she can make the decision for herself. It's not your place to decide for her."

"I'm protecting her."

"Did she ask you to?" He raises a brow, and with that, he walks out of the house.

It's damn annoying to have people in my life who are so fucking smart—and stick their noses into my business.

I reach for my phone and start with Cox.

"Yeah, yeah, I'm working on it," he says by way of greeting.

"Work faster," I suggest and fill him in on what happened today.

"If I move any faster, I'll raise flags, and people will start asking questions," he says, frustration heavy in his voice. "Jesus, Shane, what did this girl do?"

"Nothing. That's just it. This is all about her father. And it's pissing me the fuck off."

"Yeah, well, I'm moving as fast as I can without putting everyone at risk, but I should hear back from the one contact I've reached out to tomorrow morning."

"Meet me in Denver at noon tomorrow."

He blows out a breath. "No pressure or anything."

"Oh, there's plenty of fucking pressure. I'm going to call my brothers and ask them to meet us there because this goes deeper than I thought. I don't want to talk about it over the phone."

"Yeah, okay. I'll see you tomorrow. You're annoying, you know that?"

I grin. "Yeah. I know. Thanks for noticing."

I hang up and immediately dial Carmine's number.

"Yo," he says, his usual greeting. He only does it with Rocco and me because it always made us laugh as kids.

Old habits die hard.

"I need you guys closer," I say and explain again what happened today. "I have details that I can't talk about on the phone. Cox is meeting me in Denver at noon."

"We'll head that way tonight. Nadia wants to do some shopping for the wedding anyway."

"I'm so glad I could accommodate your fiancée's shopping needs."

"I heard that," Nadia says into my ear. "And thanks. I can kick ass *and* shop."

"Who says I need you to help me kick ass?"

She laughs. "You three wouldn't know how to kick ass without me, Shane."

"We did just fine for a long time without you," I remind her.

"Okay, kids," Carmine interrupts. "We'll see you tomorrow. Noon."

He clicks off, and I feel marginally better after some light verbal sparring with Nadia and knowing that I'll have my brothers nearby in just a few hours.

I know that I *can* do this without them. But I don't have to. And that feels damn good.

"Hey."

My head whips up at the sound of Ivie's voice. She's standing at the edge of the room, her hair tousled from sleep. She's chewing her lip as if she's not sure what to do.

"Come here." I hold out my hand for her, and when she crosses to me, I tug her into my lap where I can cuddle her. "How do you feel?"

"Drowsy. I woke up and didn't know what year it was." She smiles softly. "But it was also refreshing."

"Good. You needed it."

She plays with the button on my Henley and rests her cheek on my shoulder. "What have you been up to?"

"Making calls, talking with Curt. The usual."

"I don't think today was *usual*."

"No, you're right. It wasn't. I can honestly say that I haven't had any excitement out here since I built the ranch."

"And yet, it's built to be a fortress."

"Came in handy today." I kiss her forehead. I can't keep my lips or my hands to myself. She's a fucking siren.

"So, what's the latest?"

I don't want to give her too much information because I want to *protect* her, but then Curt's words come back to my mind, and I decide to take them to heart.

Because he's right. She's intelligent and capable. And maybe I'm doing her a disservice by keeping the details from her.

At least where this current situation is concerned.

"I'm headed into Denver tomorrow morning," I begin and tell her about meeting with Cameron and my family. "We're going to come up with more answers and a plan for moving forward."

"What time do we leave?" she asks.

"*We* aren't going. I am."

Ivie scowls. "You're killing me here, Shane. I *need* to go with you, for my mental health."

"And I *need* you to stay here, for your physical safety. I won't risk taking you into the city. You'll stay here with Curt."

"Great, so I have a babysitter." She pouts, and I can't resist taking her mouth with mine, nibbling that plump lower lip.

"He's not a babysitter. He's a companion. Don't flirt with him."

She grins at that, which was exactly my intention. "I could use that time to try to get more information out of him. I'm determined to be his friend."

"Good luck with that. I'll be back tomorrow afternoon. It'll be a quick trip."

"Okay." She sighs. "This all sucks balls."

I can't help myself. I wrap my arms around her and hold her tightly against me. "Yeah, it does."

"I mean, I thought I'd get to spend time with you and get to know you better under much different circumstances. I didn't think we'd be forced into it."

I scowl. "I don't think that we're being *forced* into anything."

"Aren't we? I'm not allowed to leave. You have to stay here to protect me. Feels pretty forced. And I'm not complaining, I'm just saying it's not a fun way to start seeing a guy. Pretty unconventional, actually."

"Well, I never was the traditional type, I guess."

She laughs and then sighs. "So, what do you want to do this evening?"

I raise a brow, thinking it over. "You seem to be feeling better."

"I'm just fine, thank you for asking."

I stand with her still in my arms and walk through the living room, down the hall to my bedroom.

"Do you want to take another nap?" I love this playful side of her.

"That's not what I had in mind, actually." I set her gently on the bed and climb on next to her, my head braced in my hand and the other one gliding down her torso. She's wearing an orange tank and black shorts.

No bra, as evidenced by her tightening nipples.

"Do you want to talk some more?" she asks, all innocence.

"Yeah, I want to talk."

She glances up in surprise. "Okay, what do you want to talk about?"

"How fucking sexy you are," I reply as my hand glides up her smooth stomach, under the tank top that was clearly designed to drive a man out of his fucking mind.

"That's not a fun conversation."

"I think you're wrong." I scoot down to kiss the skin I just uncovered. "I think it's the best conversation ever. And it's going to take us a while to go through all of the talking points."

"Did you make a PowerPoint presentation?"

I chuckle as I unearth one perfect breast. "I should. Maybe I will, actually. I'll have to include photos. So, I should probably take some pictures of your perfect body."

"A: My body isn't perfect by any stretch of the imagination. And B: No one, and I do mean *no one,* will ever take naked photos of me. It would ruin my political career."

I snort and then look at her in surprise. "You want to be a politician?"

"Of course, not. But if I did, it would ruin it. So, no photos."

"I guess that means I'll just have to commit everything to memory." I pluck the nipple with my lips, enjoying the way her back arches at my touch. "Like that?"

"Yeah. I like that."

"There's much more where that came from."

"Are you going to tell me or show me?"

"Both." I surprise her by flipping her over onto her belly and then cup her round ass in my hands. "You have a stellar ass, Ivie. You've just gotta love any god you pray to for making an ass like this."

"You're crazy." She giggles and then sighs when I slip my fingers up the hem of the leg of her shorts and graze her most intimate lips. "How do you do this to me when I'm still fully clothed?"

"Talent." I kiss the small of her back. "I don't mean to brag, but I'm a dedicated worker. I take my job of making you feel fucking amazing very seriously."

"Holy shit, Shane."

"What's up, Ivie?" I can't help but grin when she pushes that ass off the bed in the best fucking invitation I've ever had.

"Oh my God." Her hands fist in the bedsheets, and I know she's close. I haven't even pushed a finger inside her yet. I've only teased.

Her responsiveness is the most arousing thing I've ever seen in my life. I can't get enough of her. I want to explore her, to just submerge myself in her for about a year.

And it still wouldn't be enough.

"You're almost there," I murmur and kiss up her spine as my fingers continue playing her like an instrument.

There are no more words coming out of her now. No, it's just moans and gasps, and when I finally slide a finger through the wetness and inside of her, she bucks and then falls apart.

When she's finished quaking, I turn her to face me and kiss the hell out of her.

"Small talk is over," I inform her with a grin and pull my shirt over my head. "Let's get to the good stuff."

"Oh. Right. Okay." She licks her lips. "Let's get to the good stuff."

THIRTEEN

~IVIE~

"You *have* to talk to me," I inform Curt as we sit in the barn, out of breath from sparring.

Shane being gone doesn't mean I get to be lazy. No, Curt informed me right away that we'd be working out most of the morning, which I don't mind. It keeps my mind occupied and off the scarier things.

Like men trying to kill me.

"About what?" he asks and takes a sip of water.

"Everything. I don't know anything about you, and I've been beating you up for *days*."

"I don't think you've beaten me up," he says with a frown. "I've let you get some punches in. To teach you."

"Right." I smirk and take a sip of water and then square my shoulders, determined to crack through his hard shell. "Let me just ask ten questions."

"That's a lot of questions," he says. "A lot."

"I have a hundred, so it's not really that much. Deal?"

He sighs and stares at me with guarded eyes. "I reserve the right to say, '*no comment.*'"

"Of course, I'm not a monster." I toss a sweatshirt over my shoulders to keep from getting chilled. "Okay, first question. What's your favorite meal to eat for dinner?"

He blinks, surprised. I want to laugh, but I don't. Does he think I'm going to start with the hard questions first? This isn't my first rodeo.

"Spaghetti, I guess. Because it's easy to make. I heat up a jar of sauce and cook some noodles."

I scrunch up my nose. "Ew. If that's your favorite, I will blow your mind with my spaghetti. I'll make it this week. Okay, question two. How old are you?"

"Thirty-four."

"Wow, you don't look thirty-four. I would have said late twenties."

"I feel eighty," he mutters, only intensifying my curiosity.

"What's your dream car?"

He grins, a full-on grin, and I'm struck by how handsome he is. I mean, he's not hotter than Shane, but he's a good-looking guy.

"1964 ½ Mustang convertible in cherry red."

I blink at him. "That's pretty specific. And...*old*."

"They're harder to find than they used to be, but it's a honey of a car. Purrs like a kitten."

"I'm going to take your word for it. I was never really a car person. I don't like to drive."

He frowns over at me. "You don't like to drive? Why not?"

"Well, because I'm super clumsy for one. I trip over my own feet. I warned Shane that I wouldn't be good with a loaded weapon or with sparring because I'd end up killing someone."

"You just need some confidence," Curt insists, and it makes me smile because it's exactly what Shane said. "When you have the confidence in your weapon, and it's an extension of *you*, you won't be clumsy with it."

"I'm getting better," I admit with a nod, wanting to keep the conversation moving. This is the most I've heard Curt speak since I got here. "But driving unnerves me because what if I don't see something that I should, or...I don't know? Anything could happen. I don't want to hurt anyone. I have a car, but I only drive to work and back home. That's really it."

"At least in Denver, there's a public transpo system."

"Exactly." I smile at him. "Are you originally from the city?"

"No. Small town in North Carolina, near the ocean."

"Oh, nice. I haven't been to either of the Carolinas, but I hear they're beautiful."

"Yeah, it's pretty nice over there."

I nod. "Is your family still there?"

"Some of them, yeah."

"Cool. That's something I always missed, you know? I just had my dad when I was little, and he was no prize, as you know. No siblings or extended family to speak of, at least in the US. I don't know if there was or is family in Bulgaria. He never spoke of it. So, I always felt like I didn't have roots."

"You've set down roots in Denver," he points out. "You have Annika and Nadia and their family."

"That's true." I smile as I think about it. "You're right. I guess family doesn't always mean being tied by blood."

"No, it doesn't."

"What did you do before you came to the ranch?"

He clams up now and shakes his head. "I think we should get over to the shooting range for some practice."

"You said I could ask ten questions. That was only, like, six."

He pushes his hand through his hair in agitation. "I worked with Shane in the military."

"Oh, wow. Thank you for your service."

He just gives me a stiff nod, and I decide to change course. "Do you have a girlfriend?"

"No." He snorts and shakes his head, his shoulders loosen. "Do you see any women out here? Besides you?"

"I'm sure there are single girls in town somewhere. Or maybe a long-distance relationship. There are options."

"I'm kind of a loner, Ivie."

"Yeah, Shane mentioned that. Why is that?"

"Because I'm an introvert." He swallows hard. "And I'm not good with people."

"Well, I think you're just fine. But I get it. People can suck. You should see some of the patients that come into our clinic. Annika and I run a medi-spa. She's the doctor, and I'm the office manager. There are days that my eyes hurt from all the eye-rolls behind patients' backs."

His lips twitch. "Do you guys do nose jobs and stuff?"

"She can, but mostly we do botox, fillers, peels, that sort of thing. Annika is an amazing doctor. I think she should work in a reconstructive surgery practice. Help women who have lost their breasts to cancer or burn victims. She's really good. But her family was old-fashioned and didn't think she should do that."

"So, they're misogynistic, then."

I blink rapidly, thinking it over. "I guess so, actually. Her father and her uncle love her to distraction, but she's in a mafia family, and what they say goes. Not to mention, she's sometimes on call to help them out when someone's been hurt, and they don't want to involve a hospital."

Curt nods. "Yeah, the Martinellis have that, too. It's an...interesting way of life."

"I hate it," I admit. "And I'm on the outside, looking in. Even though Annika's family treats me like I'm one of theirs, I don't have the same responsibilities that she does because I'm *not* blood. And I'm relieved. I had to do a lot for my father when I was young that no person should have to do. He wasn't technically part of any mafia organization, but he was dangerous and mean. And I always swore that I'd never get involved with anyone like that again."

"What happened?"

I glance at him, suddenly wondering how we turned the tables to questions about *me*.

"I met Annika in college. We didn't know anything about each other at all. But one night, we got drunk in our dorm room. And Annika started telling me about how her uncle was a boss and detailing the whole damn family tree. I was so surprised because she is just a normal girl, with an abnormal family. So, I felt comfortable telling her about me. And when we were done and had sobered up a bit, we knew that we would be friends for life. Because of shared experiences, and because we can trust each other."

"Honestly, that's very similar to my friendship with Shane," Curt says, surprising me. "We have shared experiences that most don't have. The trust is rock solid, and I would do anything for him."

I smile over at him. "See, this isn't hard."

"What?"

"Talking."

"I'm not used to it. It's outside my comfort zone."

"Usually, the best things in life are those outside our comfort zones."

Curt smirks and then glances down at his buzzing phone. "That's Shane. He's on his way back. Should be here in a couple of hours, at the most."

"Cool. Okay, let's go shoot some targets. I'm going to pretend they're that asshole from yesterday and teach him a lesson."

"You're a little scary sometimes. You know that, right?"

"Me?" I laugh as we lock up the barn and get in the ATV to drive over to the shooting range. "Nah. I'm a pussy cat. But that guy pissed me off. He could have hurt one of you. Or killed you."

"He didn't." Curt parks in front of the door in the side of the mountain, and we jump out. He places his hand on the palm plate, and once we're inside, he locks us in as I open the vault.

"I want to use something bigger today."

Curt arches a brow. "Feeling brave, are you?"

"I've been using this small 9mm. Shane upgraded me to it a few days ago. And I'm sure it's appropriate for me, but I want to try something a little...beefier."

"The sidearm that Shane assigned to you *is* perfect for you, and I'll tell you why. It's slim and perfect for the size of your hands. It's easy for you to manipulated and control. But it's a 9mm so the bullets are lethal. You have a lot of power in that weapon. If you start shooting something bigger, you run the risk of hurting yourself because it'll be more difficult to handle. And if you were ever confronted, it could be easier for the assailant to get it away from you.

"So, this is what you should master. Personally, I think you should carry two of them. One at the small of your back, and a clutch piece on your ankle."

"Wow. You really know this stuff."

"It was my job for a long time. And, no, I'm not going to talk about it."

"Killjoy."

He laughs at that and hangs a target for me, then sends it down the lane.

"Okay, using the weapon assigned to you, let's see what you've got."

"I can admit when I'm wrong," I say as I finish reloading my weapon and tuck it into the small of my back. "You're right, this is the right size for me."

"It's good that we had you try a couple of others. You never know when you might have to pick up a discarded weapon and use it."

"I don't plan to go to war."

"No one does." He smiles thinly. "You'll be prepared for anything. That's not a bad thing."

"No, I suppose not."

We've just started to shut down the range when sirens start.

"Fuck," Curt says sharply and opens his phone. "We've been breached again."

"Oh, my God. Maybe it's Shane."

"Not Shane." His face is grim as he looks up at me. "There are several men, all in military gear. I'm not going to lie to you, Ivie. This isn't good. I want you to go through that door and take the tunnel to the bunker."

"I can help you."

"No." He shakes his head in frustration as he hurries back into the vault. I'm on his heels as he takes weapons out of cases, loads them, and stuffs his pockets with ammo. He tucks a knife into his pants, a small pistol at his ankle. He looks like Rambo. "You absolutely cannot. You're trained to protect yourself, not infiltrate. So, listen to me very carefully. You take that tunnel to the bunker, and you sit tight. You do *not* come out until someone comes for you."

"But—"

He's looking down at his phone as he types furiously. "I've just alerted Shane. I hope he's not out there in this mess. I mean it, Ivie. Stay in the bunker until someone comes to you. If it's a bad guy, you shoot them. Do you understand? Don't hesitate."

"I won't." I hurry to him and hug him hard. Curt stiffens. "Be smart out there."

"Get to the bunker," he says again, and then he's gone. The door locks behind him, and I take a second to breathe long and deep.

Curt's out there, but he's armed to the gills.

I have two sidearms on me, and I open the vault to get more ammo, lock it behind me, and then do as I'm told and hurry through the tunnel.

Shane was smart enough to show me a map of the tunnel system down here and insisted I study it.

I'm so glad he did because it's not just one tunnel. I remember him telling me that there are tunnels to the main house, Curt's cabin, and the barn.

But I stay to the right, remembering the map, and am suddenly at a door. I open it, lights automatically come on, and I'm in the bunker.

I lock the door behind me and check the locks to the outside, and then I immediately look around for monitors.

Shane wouldn't hole up down here without being able to see what's happening above. I find a bathroom, the two bedrooms, and then stare at a small door that looks like it goes to a tiny closet.

"You disguised it." My heart is hammering when I open the narrow door and grin. I flip the lights on and sigh in relief.

It's a smaller version of the 007 room. I flip on computers and monitors and sigh in relief when the same cameras come to life.

"Oh, fuck." I lean in, watching in horror as at least a dozen men walk through the property, all on different monitors. "They've spread out. My God, it looks like an army."

It's not. A dozen men do not make an army, but it looks damn scary to me.

"There's Curt." I cover my mouth with my hand and watch as Curt sneaks up behind a man dressed in all black. With the swipe of an arm, he cuts the man's throat wide-open as if he's cutting through warm butter. I gasp and watch as the dead man falls at Curt's feet, and then Curt narrows his eyes and looks to his right.

Another man with an automatic weapon makes his way toward Curt, but Curt's too fast. He raises his hand and throws the knife, hitting the man square in the forehead.

"Christ." I have to turn away, unable to watch it. Curt's a trained killer. It's obvious in every move he makes that this is what he was taught to do. I don't know how to reconcile the man I was chatting with in the barn with this assassin.

I check the time. Shane should be back anytime. I hope Curt's message reached him, and he doesn't walk into this without being warned.

My God, they could kill him.

And it would all be my fault.

Why did he bring me here? Why did he put himself and Curt at risk?

Sure, we flirted a lot over the past few months, but it's not like he *owes* me anything. And now his property and his friend are at risk.

He is at risk.

Because of me.

If something happens to him, I'll never forgive myself.

CHAPTER

FOURTEEN

~SHANE~

"It's a party," Cameron says when my brothers and Nadia file into the office in downtown Denver. "I should have brought chips or something."

"Good to see you," Carmine says, shaking his hand.

"I wish it were under better circumstances," Cameron replies. When we're all seated around the room, me behind the desk, Rocco standing to my left, and Nadia and Carmine on the couch, Cameron gives his report.

"As far as I can tell, the Sergis were behind yesterday's attempt at a raid," Cameron says, making Carmine swear ripely. "I was able to do some digging and found ten-thousand dollars deposited into the asshole's account. I suspect it was just a scouting mission. If they were serious about getting in and grabbing Ivie, there would have been more than just one guy there."

"I thought the same," I add with a nod. "Why would Billy start a war with the Tarenkovs?"

"Because he's a piece of shit," Nadia says coldly. "He has to know that Ivie is one of ours. He's not stupid, and he was at Annika's wedding earlier this year. Not to mention, he has a grudge against me."

"The Sergis love money," Rocco adds.

"They have plenty of fucking money," I remind him.

"Come on, man," Rocco says. "You know he heard that there was a bounty on Ivie's head, dead or alive, and figured he'd cash in on the payday."

"A million dollars," I mutter, shaking my head. "He's willing to start a war over a measly million dollars. They're worth a hundred times that much."

"Billy's not particularly smart," Carmine adds. "I wonder if his father knows what his son's up to."

"I'm going to kill him."

All of the eyes in the room fly to me. Cameron scowls. "Shane—"

"I'm going to tie him up and disembowel him. Slowly. The son of a bitch will pay for this."

"There's more." Cameron stands to pace the office. "You said that Ivie kept coming up with her father's name as one of the owners of the phone numbers yesterday."

"What?" Carmine demands. "I thought he was long dead."

"We all did," I confirm, and can see from the look on Cameron's face that the man is very much alive.

"It was a cover," Cam says and blows out a breath. "If anyone finds out that I came into this information, my family and those closest to me could be at risk. The O'Callaghans can't be touched for this."

"They'll be protected," I assure him. "You all will."

"I'm trying to get the fuck out of this life," Cox reminds me and then shakes his head in disgust. "Okay, so about a dozen years ago, maybe a little more, a lot of people wanted Pavlov dead. He was a piece of shit, a bad businessman, and liked to borrow money that he never repaid. We won't even get into his lack of parenting skills.

"Anyway, I was part of a taskforce back then that was trying to find his whereabouts so we could get in, assassinate him, and get out."

"The government wanted him gone?" Rocco asks, surprised.

"Oh, yeah. He was a Bulgarian operative. It's all just a mess, and the world was better off without him. Anyway, before my team could get in and take care of him, someone supposedly beat us to it. Killed him. We saw a video of it, for fuck's sake. They hung him.

"We closed the case and forgot about it. Wrote it off. We had other

472

missions to worry about, and while Pavlov was a pain in the ass, he was small potatoes compared to some of the things we do."

"But?" I ask.

"I made some calls, started asking around. Discretely. Called in some favors. It was a cover. Pavlov wasn't hanged that day. It was a guy who looked a lot like him. Turns out, Pavlov has been living in Dallas for at least a decade, still doing his shady shit but on a smaller scale."

"Who was behind this?" I demand, seeing red.

"Sergi." Cameron blows out a breath. "Pavlov was working on his turf. But Sergi didn't want him dead because Pavlov knew too many people, kept too many secrets. He needed him alive, just in case. So, he staged the murder, hid Pavlov away, and no one was the wiser.

"But, about a year ago, Pavlov fucked up again and pissed off some people. The wrong people. In Dallas. Who is the Dallas syndicate?"

"It used to be the Carlitos," Carmine says thoughtfully. "But the boss died twenty years ago, and no one was interested in taking over."

"Apparently, that changed, too," Cox replies. "A kid by the name of Benji Carlito has decided to take up the reins. He's twenty-four."

"Grandson," I murmur, remembering stories from my father. "He was the boss's grandson."

"And he has a taste for the mob," Cox says. "I don't know who Pavlov pissed off, but it filtered to Carlito, and that is what spurred the search for Ivie. They thought they could hurt the old man if they got their hands on his daughter."

"Little do they know that Pavlov doesn't give two fucks about Ivie," Nadia says, fury shooting from her gorgeous blue eyes.

"Are Carlito and Sergi working together?" I wonder aloud. "I want to know *exactly* what Billy knows. That piece of shit."

I want to punch something. Hard.

"Okay, we're going to go about this methodically." Rocco turns from the window where he's been taking it all in. "I'm headed to Dallas in the morning."

"Nadia and I will go to New York," Carmine says. "I already have a rapport with Billy. And I can just tell him that Nadia wants to shop for the wedding. I had good dealings with him just a couple of months ago."

"Good." I tap my fingers on the desk. "I'm not going to just sit on the ranch anymore. It's not safe. I should have left last night, but I didn't have this information yet."

"Leaving is a good idea," Cameron says with a nod. "Get her to Seattle."

"He's right." Carmine stands. "Take her to Gram's house. The security is brand new, the house is secluded, and it's not under your name. Not to mention, it has the safe room in the basement."

I nod, thinking it over. "It's the best solution. We'll be ready to go by this evening."

"I'll fly you over before I go to Dallas," Rocco says. "It's not exactly on my way, but I'd like to be the pilot for that trip."

"Appreciate it."

"I'm done," Cameron says, regret in his eyes. "I can't do any more for you. I'm sorry. I'm breaking free of this life because I want a family of my own. I want Mary Margaret. And I want to make sure she's safe."

"You've done more than enough." I shake my friend's hand. "Thank you. I want an invitation to the wedding."

"I have to talk her into marrying me first." He grins. "You'll get one. You all will. Good luck, and be careful."

He waves and shuts the door behind him, leaving me alone with my family.

"I'm fucking pissed," I growl.

"Are you angry because they're threatening *someone* or because they're trying to kill the woman you love?" Carmine wonders.

"I won't deny it. I love her. I won't let them hurt her. And I'm going to kill them all."

Carmine nods. Rocco cracks his knuckles.

"We'll help," Nadia says as she stands. "It's time we teach the Sergis a lesson."

I TEXTED Curt when I left Denver to let him know I'd be back home shortly. I hit some fucking traffic just outside of the city, which lost me about thirty minutes, but I'm now getting close to the ranch.

Cell service is spotty on this section of road, but suddenly a text comes through from Curt.

Curt: *12 to 20 operatives. Breached from the west.*

"Fuck. Fuck, fuck, fuck." I hit the steering wheel. I should have listened to Curt and my gut last night and gotten the hell out of there.

Instead, Ivie and Curt are both in harm's way.

I slow the vehicle and snarl when I see four Jeeps pulled into the bushes on the edge of my property.

I pull in behind them, arm myself with a knife and two pistols, and make a mental note of where I have weapons hidden on the property. No one, not even Curt, knows that I've got at least ten stashes of weapons placed strategically.

I ease out of my vehicle and silently creep up on a man who's standing by the Jeep in front. He's looking at his phone.

He's an idiot. These people need to hire better lookouts.

I easily sneak up on him and slit his throat, then let him fall to the ground.

One down. I have no idea when Curt sent that text since I'm often in dead zones between Denver and the ranch. I don't know if he's already taken out a good portion of the men, if they've killed him, or even if they've reached Ivie.

Fuck, I'm going in blind.

I take a deep breath and walk, low and fast, through the invisible fence and up a short hill to survey the scene.

I see two men, pacing back and forth, each armed with automatic weapons. These two have more training, watching the area around them closely.

I pull my sidearm from its holster, screw on the silencer, and shoot them both in the forehead before they can blink.

Three down.

I hurry over to the bodies, relieve them of their weapons, and crouch, listening.

I hear voices to the east but no gunfire. No struggles.

Staying close to the ground, I hurry on. When I see the door to the bunker, I blow out a breath of relief when I see the discreet green light level with the ground.

That means someone is inside. Safe. It hasn't been breached. Praying that it's Ivie in there, I continue, moving toward the house, and see movement on my right.

It's Curt, cutting a man's throat very much the same way I just did back at the Jeeps.

I start to wave him down, but he sees movement and throws the knife, hitting another man square in the forehead, killing him instantly.

I don't ever want to be on Curt's bad side.

I issue the low whistle we used to use back in the day and nod when Curt's gaze finds mine. I see his shoulders relax, and then he starts giving me hand signals.

Eight more men on the property. Four at the house, four at the barn.

I nod and silently give him directions to go to the barn, indicating I'll take the house.

He nods in affirmation, and we set off to find our targets. I crouch in the long grass and quickly type out a message to Rocco.

Me: *Infiltrated. Need the chopper to get out ASAP.*

I don't wait for a reply as I hurry to the house. I don't see any movement outside, so I press my back against the wall and ease over to look in a window.

Two men in the kitchen.

I keep going around the house, looking in the windows. The basement door is still secure. That's a good sign.

I move to the side door, near a sunroom that I've never furnished, and see two more men about to come outside.

So, I wait for them. Let them come to me. If I can eliminate them without using a firearm, all the better. I don't want to alert the two inside.

With my back to the side of the house, I wait while the two come through the squeaky screen door, and when they come around the corner, I spring into action. The first one gets his neck broken, and then I spin and wrap my legs around the other's neck, taking him to the ground. I fling my arm back and stab him in the neck.

Seven down. There are two more here, and four with Curt.

I slink into the house, silently moving through the rooms, my weapon drawn.

HEADHUNTER

Both of the remaining men are bent over the basement door lock, trying to disarm it and get inside.

Morons.

I'm able to sidle up behind them and look down at the doorknob.

"How's it going?" I ask, surprising them.

Before they can draw their weapons, I have them both on the ground, dead.

No blood.

That would be messy to clean up.

I check for pulses before opening the basement door and slinking down the stairs to look at the monitors. I check the bunker first.

Ivie's there, watching the other wall of monitors. Good, she's safe.

Then I check the barn. I count three dead bodies. None of them are Curt, but I can't locate him. After scanning the rest of the screens, I don't see any other men on the property.

Just Curt and one remaining asshole.

I shut it all down, hurry up the stairs, lock the door behind me, and am out of the house and running to the barn within seconds.

When I reach the building, I stop to listen.

I hear a scuffle coming from the side of the structure.

I run toward it, my weapon drawn once again, and find Curt punching the fuck out of a man. He has blood coming from his nose, but he's spouting profanities.

"Don't kill him," I instruct in a firm, cold voice. Curt immediately stops punching but holds the asshole against the building.

"Who do you work for?" I demand.

The piece of shit spits in my face.

"That's not the answer I wanted. Curt?"

Curt takes his knife and slices off the man's ear, making him squeal like a pig.

"Now, let's try that again. Who do you work for?"

"You're just going to kill me." He's not wrong. "I'm not telling you shit."

"All of your comrades are dead. All of them. Now, we can make this easy on you, and I can kill you fast—you won't feel anything. *If* you answer the question. If you don't, I can make your last few minutes as

477

miserable and painful as anyone has ever been through. It's up to you."

His eyes fill with tears, his lip quivers.

"Billy Sergi."

"Not his father?"

"I take my orders from Billy."

I nod thoughtfully. "Is anyone else on their way?"

"He hired us to handle it. We're military-trained. How you two killed us all, I'll never know."

"Whoever trained you should be ashamed." I push my face close to his. "I'm going to be the one to end you. And Billy. And anyone else who tries to kill her."

And with that, I press the barrel of my sidearm against his temple and pull the trigger.

CHAPTER
FIFTEEN
~IVIE~

"What is taking them so long?" I pull at my hair and pace the dark bunker. I've never been more relieved in my life as I was when Shane came on camera. And then, when he and Curt systematically killed every single one of those men, all I could do was watch with my jaw dropped.

I have *so* many questions for the man I've completely fallen in love with.

But first, I need him to come get me. I promised that I wouldn't leave this bunker until someone came to get me.

So, where the fuck are they?

I hurry back to look at the monitors and almost squeal in delight when I see Shane walking toward the bunker door.

I run to the stairs, and when he opens the door, I launch myself into his arms and hold on tight.

"Oh, God. Oh, God. You're okay."

"I'm okay." His arms tighten around me. "You stayed put."

"I'm not stupid." I cup his face in my hands and kiss him hard. "Shit, that was scary. Is Curt okay?"

"He's fine."

I glance over Shane's shoulder at the sound of Curt's voice.

"I have so many questions," I reply.

"No time," Shane says and sets me on the floor. "We all need to pack a bag and be ready to leave in ten minutes. Rocco's on the way with the chopper."

I'm relieved. I want to get the hell out of here.

"I should stay." Curt hooks his thumbs in his jeans and shakes his head. "Someone needs to be here to make sure everything's okay."

"It's not safe," Shane says, his voice leaving no room for argument. "You're coming with us."

"Shane—"

"I mean it. I need you with us, not here like a sitting duck. We're headed to Seattle. When everything is over, we'll come back."

"Let's just hope there's something to come back to," Curt mutters but hurries away without more argument.

"Come on. Let's grab what you need and get out of here."

"You'll get no complaint from me," I reply and have to hurry to keep up with Shane's long strides. I'm short, and I don't run—unless something's chasing me.

And right now, something is definitely chasing me.

"Shane, I want to talk."

"We'll have plenty of time in Seattle," he assures me and seems to move faster as we approach the house. "There are bodies inside, baby. I'm sorry. I don't have time to clean them up."

"I'll be okay." I take a deep breath. "Are you just going to leave them here?"

"A cleanup crew will come in later today and get rid of them."

I stop and stare at him. "A *cleanup* crew?"

"That's right. Now, hurry up and grab what you need. I'm headed down to close up the basement."

"Want me to grab some stuff for you, too?"

"That would be great."

He pats my ass, and then he's stomping down the stairs, and I'm running to the bedroom.

I find my mama's suitcase, and it only takes a few seconds to throw my clothes inside. Then I make a quick run through the bathroom to gather my things and Shane's, too.

By the time he rushes into the bedroom, I have our bags packed.

"You're fast," he says.

"This isn't the first time I've had to do this."

I can hear the helicopter as Shane tips up my chin. "I know. I'm sorry, honey."

"Let's get out of here."

I refuse to look at the men dead on the floor as we run out of the house and join Curt at the helicopter.

Rafe doesn't bother jumping out. We all climb in, put headsets on, and buckle up.

"Ready?" Rafe's voice says in my ear. Shane and Curt give him a thumbs up, and I follow suit, and then we're rising above the Earth, and my stomach does a flip.

I hate rides. I usually get sick. But all I can think about is getting out of here.

I see bodies scattered on the earth. And then I just see trees as Rocco picks up speed, and we're suddenly flying over the mountains.

"The plane is ready in Denver," Rafe says. "We'll leave as soon as we get there and set out for Seattle."

"Can I see Annika?" I ask, speaking for the first time. "She'll worry, and I'm not allowed to call her."

"Don't worry," Shane says, taking my hand. "We'll figure out a way for you to speak with her."

I nod, bite my lip, and look out the window, doing my best not to cry. Now that the adrenaline is wearing off, I just want to sob.

And maybe sleep for a week.

Shane puts his hand on my thigh and gives it a squeeze, but I can't look over at him.

He's safe.

Curt's fine.

We got out.

But, damn, I'm still so scared. And what if we get to Seattle, and it doesn't stop? We can't run forever. I can't ask these people to keep putting their lives on hold and continue putting themselves at risk.

Something has to give.

I have to talk to Shane about all of this. I need to know more about him. I need more, period. He must have more information after speaking with Cameron earlier today.

Was that just today? It feels like a million years ago.

Denver comes into view, and soon, we're descending to a helipad.

"I thought we were going to the airport?" I ask, confused.

"This is a smaller airfield. For private aircraft," Rafe says and makes the landing look *so* easy. The hatch opens, and we hustle out of the chopper and hurry over to the waiting plane.

When I climb the stairs and duck inside, I'm shocked to find Carmine, Nadia, and *Annika* already seated.

"Oh, my God. What are you doing here?"

"Rafe seems to think I'm in danger," she says as I cross the space and sit next to her. Rafe, who's just come in behind me, scowls at my best friend.

"You *are* in danger," he says. "She was taken from *your* clinic. She's *your* best friend. I don't need one of these assholes coming in to try and get information from you. You're coming with us, where we can keep you safe."

Annika blows out a breath, rolls her eyes, and turns to me.

"See what I've been dealing with? And that was all over the phone. Now that he's here in person, he'll just glare at me all day."

I feel my eyes fill with tears. I didn't know until this moment how badly I needed my best friends.

Nadia sits on my other side and takes my hand, and I lay my head on Annika's shoulder.

The tears come now. Big, hot tears that I've been holding inside. They just burst out of me, and all I can do is hang onto my friends for dear life.

They know me, inside and out. They know *everything*.

And they love me.

When the tears have dried up, and all I can do is sit and rest, someone offers me a glass of water.

"Remember Charles?" Shane says from across the aisle, watching me with sober brown eyes.

"You need some water, miss," Charles says. "And I'm happy to bring you anything else you might need."

"I could go for some pizza," I mutter. "And chocolate ice cream."

"We'll make sure you get that when we get settled." Nadia pats my arm.

"Can I offer you some cheese and crackers? Some fruit?" Charles asks.

"That would be nice." I nod and sit up straight, pushing my hair back over my shoulders. "Sorry, everyone. The day just caught up to me."

"No apologies necessary," Carmine says. "You've had a hell of a day."

"All I did was sit in a bunker and watch Shane and Curt—" I shake my head. "I didn't do much."

"You kept yourself safe," Nadia says and kisses my cheek. "That's a lot."

"YOUR GRANDMOTHER HAD A BEAUTIFUL HOUSE," I say three hours later after we've landed in Seattle and made our way to the mansion we'd be staying in for the foreseeable future. It's a fortress of a house, which I would expect from the Martinellis.

A massive manor in the middle of manicured lawns with fountains and shrubberies. It was a bit intimidating when we drove up.

Then slipped over into ridiculously intimidating when we walked through the door. I've only seen tapestries in movies. The antiques are incredible. And yet, despite the grandeur of the home, it's incredibly modern and comfortable.

"Gram liked nice things," Shane says as he leads me on a tour through the home. "But she also liked to be comfortable, so she managed to keep it updated. The kitchen is less than five years old."

I nod and then follow Shane up a flight of stairs.

"All of the bedrooms are on this floor. Eight of them altogether."

"Geez."

He grins at me. "I know. It's a lot. Our room is at the end, with the pond out back. You can see where our treehouse is, and the view is especially pretty in the morning."

I don't say much when he opens the door, and I follow him in. The bed looks comfortable. And expensive.

The attached bathroom boasts a tub big enough to swim in.

I'll be more than comfortable here.

"This is great. Thank you."

"Okay, I've had it." He closes the door and pulls me into his arms, holding me tightly. "You're quiet, your eyes are haunted, and you're scaring me. What are you thinking?"

I want to cry again. "I don't know. It's just a lot, you know?"

"I know." He kisses my head. "I'm so sorry, babe. This is a safe place."

"We thought the ranch was safe." I swallow hard and back out of his arms. "I think I should look at going out on my own."

His eyes flash, and he starts to shake his head, but I hold up a hand.

"Hear me out. They're finding me because they know I'm with *you*. With the Martinellis and the Tarenkovs. They'll keep tracking down you and your family, Annika, to find me. That's not fair to anyone, Shane. It's not right."

"Ivie."

"I've disappeared before," I remind him. "And I was a lot younger with little education. Now, I can hack into anything, change my name again, and start over. I can go anywhere. I'm smarter, and I have a little money saved up to get started."

"No."

I pace away from him, my mind forming around the idea.

"I mean, I'll miss you all. Never seeing Annika and Nadia again might kill me, but if it keeps you all safe, it's the right thing to do."

"No."

"Shane, be reasonable."

"You going out on your own with some idiotic idea of keeping *us* safe is not being reasonable, Ivie. It's fucking stupid."

"I am *not* stupid."

"I didn't think so either until about thirty seconds ago. I don't need you to keep me safe."

"Yeah, I saw that on the monitors."

That makes his jaw clench, and his eyes narrow.

"Who *are* you? I keep asking and asking, and you always blow me off. If you don't want anything to do with me, fine. You don't need to tell me. But we're *sleeping* together, Shane, and you can't convince me that it's just sex. It's not. So, don't even try to say it is."

"It's not just sex," he mutters and rubs his hand over the back of his neck.

"Then I need you to *talk* to me. Because I feel that you care about me, and I sure as hell care about you. Jesus, I *need* you all to stay safe. I don't know everything that's happening, and that means that I'm scared and frustrated, and you're asking me to just blindly trust that you have everything under control."

"I *do* have everything under control. Why can't you just trust me on this and let me do my damn job?"

"Because I don't know what your job is!" I round on him, aggravation coming out of every pore on my body. "I don't know what Cameron said. I don't know *anything* except that I watched you and Curt systematically assassinate at least a dozen men today, men who were after *me*. And now you're trying to just tuck me away in this beautiful ivory tower while the menfolk take on the bad guys."

He sighs. "What do you want to know?"

"Everything!" I push my hair off my face. "I want to know everything. I think I have the right to that, Shane."

"Okay." He blows out a breath. "Curt and I *are* trained assassins. We kill people for a living for the US government. Well, he used to. He's retired."

"But you're not."

His eyes are cold and level with mine. "No. I'm not. And I can't tell you more because it's classified."

"Who do you kill?"

"Whomever they tell me to."

I swallow hard. "What did Cameron say?"

"The Sergis are behind this. The last guy we killed at the ranch confirmed he was working for them. Carmine and Nadia are planning to go to New York, where the Sergi family is based, to do some digging."

"That's it?"

He nods. "Yes."

"And now I'm just supposed to sit here and wait again?"

"I don't know what else you'd like to do. You're definitely not going to New York."

"I don't want to go to that godforsaken city ever again." I sink onto the side of the bed, suddenly bone-tired. "At least if I left, went out on my own, I'd have something to *do* and it would keep you safe."

"I'm not the one in danger," he reminds me, and the scene from just a few hours ago clearly comes to mind.

"I beg to differ."

"If you left, I would find you. And not in a creepy serial killer way."

That makes me smile, but I bite my lip, trying to stay serious.

"I didn't intend for you to come to mean so much to me, Ivie, but you do. You matter. You matter more than anything else in my life, and you going anywhere that I can't find you isn't an option for me. I know it's fast and that we have a lot to talk through when we get this all figured out. But I'm not letting you leave me."

He gently drags a fingertip down my cheek.

"I need this to be over." My voice is a hoarse whisper. "It's too much. I don't deserve this, Shane."

"I know." He pulls me into his strong arms and holds on tight. "I know. We're going to figure it out. Together."

I nod and take a deep breath. "Do you think the pizza is here yet?"

"Let's go find out."

CHAPTER
SIXTEEN
~SHANE~

"You look really good for a girl who survived a war zone this afternoon," Annika says to Ivie, who's sitting beside me in the family room, balancing a plate of pizza on her lap. "How are you holding up, honey?"

"I'm fine." Ivie sighs and takes another bite of Hawaiian pizza. "I feel like it was all a movie and that it didn't really happen. But it did."

"And now it's over," I assure her, but want to wince when she looks up at me with wide, blue eyes.

"No, it's not over."

"It will be," Nadia assures her. "Sooner than later, even if I have to kill every one of them myself."

"Let's talk about something less violent," Annika suggests, making the rest of us laugh. "I've been thinking about getting a puppy."

"What kind?" Ivie asks, sitting forward. "I want one, too. Let's get siblings from the same litter, and they can be besties."

"Oh my gosh, *yes*," Annika agrees with excitement. "I was thinking a Shih Tzu. Or a Bichon. You know, something small and cute."

"A chick dog," Rocco says with a smirk.

"It's a *small* dog," Annika says and sends my brother a glare.

"Because I don't have time to exercise a big dog, and a small dog can go to the office with me. Why do you care, anyway?"

"I literally said three words," Rocco says.

"Well, maybe you shouldn't say any words at all, Rafe Martinelli."

"Rocco," he corrects her, and Carmine and I share a look. He'll never win this battle with these women. Never.

"I will not call you *Rocco*," Annika reminds him. "Your mother named you Rafe. Your name is *Rafe*."

"Seriously, dude, Rafe is so much better," Nadia says. "I've never understood the Rocco thing."

"It's *my* name, and I can decide what I want people to call me," my brother says. "If you call me Rafe, I won't reply."

"Fine," Annika says. "I don't want to talk to you anyway so that works just fine."

"Why are you so difficult?" Rocco demands.

"You two are so cute," Ivie says with a dreamy look on her face. "The way you tease and flirt is adorable. Why don't you just go ahead and start making out, right here."

Both Rocco and Annika glare at Ivie, which only makes us all laugh harder. These two have been fighting whatever is between them for years. And they hid it. I was shocked to discover earlier this year that they'd had a secret relationship years before. I've asked Rocco to tell me about it, but he just clams up.

He won't speak of it.

It's baffling.

"Yes, my annoyance is cute," Annika says, sarcasm dripping from every word.

"It is," Ivie insists. "If you didn't give a shit, you'd ignore him. But you do give a shit. And I don't know why you're fighting it so damn hard. But that's none of my business. I guess I was just reminded today how short life can be. And what's the point of denying what you love? What you enjoy?"

"This is getting *really* philosophical," Nadia says as she rises to her feet and wanders into the kitchen, then opens the freezer to find the ice cream. "I'm scooping up ice cream for this talk. And pouring wine. Wine and ice cream."

"I'll pour the whiskey," I offer and pour myself, Curt, and each of my brothers three fingers. Curt's sitting at the edge of the room, looking uncomfortable. Which isn't unusual when he's in a room full of people.

But he knows my family.

"Drink this." I pass him the glass and pat his shoulder. "You more than earned it today."

"I won't turn it down," he says and takes a sip. "I think I'll turn in, man. Helluva day. And I need to look over the cameras at the ranch, make sure everything is as it should be."

"Appreciate it. Let me know if you need anything. Otherwise, I'll plan to meet with you at oh-eight-hundred."

"I'll be there." He stands with his glass, nods at everyone in the room, and starts to leave, but Ivie calls out to him.

"Curt!" She jumps off the couch and hurries across the room, throwing her arms around him. "Thank you. Thank you so *much*."

"Hey." He pats her back uncomfortably and looks at me with panic in his eyes. "Don't cry."

"You saved me," she says and sniffs loudly. "And I just think you're wonderful."

"Uh, you're pretty great yourself."

I move in to rescue him, and he passes a weepy Ivie over to me. She buries her face against my chest, and I wrap my arms around her.

"Goodnight, everyone," Curt says and leaves the room.

"I know I sound stupid," Ivie says as she pulls back and wipes her eyes. "But when it all started to go down, we didn't know where Shane was, and Curt was with me. We'd just finished target practice in the firing range and were putting things away, cleaning up, when the alarms went off. Thank *God* that's where we were so he could grab weapons. I took some, too, and he made me go through the tunnel to the bunker and wait. Made me promise not to come out, under any circumstances."

She sits on the couch again and wipes her eyes. Annika passes her some tissues.

"I know you wanted to talk about less violent things—"

"It's okay," Annika assures her before I can. "Talk it out, honey."

Ivie nods. "I found the monitors in the bunker, and I could watch what was happening on the property. It was *so* crazy. Scary as hell. And then I saw Shane, and for a second, I was relieved that he was there to help, but also so fucking terrified that one of those bastards would h-h-hurt him."

I take her hand, link my fingers with hers, and raise her hand to my mouth.

"But they didn't get hurt. They saved me. And now I'm here, in Seattle, eating ice cream and pizza with my favorite people."

"I'm touched," Rocco says, making her grin.

"You're one of my favorite people, too, *Rafe*."

My brother scowls. "I can't win with these women."

"Get used to it," Carmine suggests, earning a glare from his fiancée. "I mean that in the nicest way possible, of course."

"Sure, you do." Nadia stands and stretches. "We should go home where I can punish you for that. Let these guys get some rest."

"You're not staying here?" Ivie asks.

"Our house isn't far away," Nadia assures her. "I'll be back in the morning. I'm bringing breakfast. Then Carmine and I are headed to New York for a few days."

"I don't like it," Ivie says, blowing out a breath.

"Don't worry. We'll be fine." Nadia hugs Ivie close. "I'll see you in the morning."

Carmine and Nadia say their goodbyes, but Rocco hangs back.

"I'm staying," he says simply and looks at Annika. "My room is next to yours. If you need *anything*, just let me know."

"I—" Annika begins, but Rocco cuts her off.

"Don't argue, just say 'okay.'"

"Okay," she replies. "Thanks."

He nods and walks out of the room.

"He really does worry about you," I say to Annika.

"I know." She sighs and offers me a small smile. "I've worked really hard for a while now to distance myself from him and my feelings for him. Old habits die hard. I'm going up, too. But I suspect I'll be back for another glass of wine."

"Take the bottle," Ivie suggests. "I'll sneak over and drink it with you."

"You don't have to sneak." I grin at her.

"Even better."

———

"WE HAVEN'T HEARD ANYTHING."

Ivie and I are walking across the grass of my grandmother's property. It's been three days since we arrived. Carmine and Nadia are wrapping things up in New York, and Rocco is on his way back from Texas. He left yesterday morning.

He didn't want to be away from Annika for too long.

Even though the woman pretends that she can't stand the sight of him.

"Everyone will be back by morning," I assure Ivie.

"But I don't know what they found. Where did Rafe go, anyway?"

"He just had some work to do, some things to see to. I suspect we'll have information from all of them tomorrow."

"I hope so. We've been here for three days, and nothing is happening. It's quiet. Which I'm not complaining about because I've been up close and personal with the alternative and I'll take quiet over that every time. But I don't trust it."

I don't either. There hasn't been any chatter, nothing to report. It's too quiet again.

I don't like it.

"Let's enjoy the sunshine today and worry about the rest when the others get here tomorrow," I suggest.

"You're right. It's a nice day. Tomorrow is Annika's birthday, and I haven't had time to get her anything."

"I'm quite sure she understands."

Ivie smiles. "You're right. I'll figure something out for her. It's pretty out here. You said you spent a good portion of your childhood here?"

"Yes. This was my father's parents' home. We came here every summer, along with our cousin, Elena. Ran wild all over this property. Swam in the pond, played in the gazebo. Gram had that treehouse built when Carmine was about eight."

I point to the treehouse ahead. I'm taking her there. It's private, and

I plan to talk to her. Tell her how I feel—how much I love her, and that I want to make this work between us. She's right, life is short, too damn short, and I'm going to hold onto her for as long as I possibly can.

"I can picture it," she says with a smile. "It's a great property for kids."

"And Gram spoiled us rotten. She had a firm hand, and we didn't get anything by her, but she gave us just about anything we wanted. The entire top floor of the house is an attic, and we loved to play up there. She never threw anything away."

"I bet it's a treasure trove."

"It is. She's been gone more than a year now, and we haven't had time to go through everything yet. But she'd be happy that we're using the house."

"And your parents? Are they close by?"

"Yes. Actually, my father will be here tomorrow to meet with my brothers and me. My mom might come with him. You'll get to meet them."

"I've met them," she says with a soft smile. "At Annika's wedding. I've seen them from afar here and there over the years."

I look down at her in surprise. "I don't remember meeting you before that wedding."

"I don't think we met. Not formally, anyway. I was just around now and then at parties the families were invited to."

"No way. I would have noticed you."

"No, you wouldn't." Ivie shakes her head and then laughs. "I'm not the type of girl that men notice, Shane."

"We've been over this. I think you're hot. So, if you were around, I would have noticed."

She smiles up at me as we approach the treehouse. "Well, we're here now, and that's all that really matters."

"I'm excited to show this to you. I'll go first and make sure it's still sound."

"Please don't fall through rotted wood," she says and watches as I climb the ladder. When I arrive at the top, I'm pleased to see that everything is as sound as it was the day it was built, almost thirty years ago.

"It's good." I look down at her. "Come on up."

"Are you sure?"

"Totally sure. Solid as a rock."

She climbs up the rungs and takes my proffered hand to pull herself up to the platform.

"It's bigger than it looks," she says.

"That's what she said."

She frowns at me, slaps my arm, and then giggles. "Okay, that was funny. But seriously, it's really spacious up here."

"We used to have furniture and all kinds of crap, but it got thrown away a long time ago. It was just a squirrel magnet and would have rotted this place quick. So, it's just sitting here empty."

"I like it." She paces around the space, walks to a window and looks out over the green grass, the pond, and the house. "You got to grow up here."

"Yeah. Pretty great, huh?"

"Pretty great." She nods and turns to me. "How many girls have you brought up here over the years?"

I grin and rub my chin as if giving it a lot of thought. "Man, at least... one. Just you."

She cocks a brow, and her eyes shine in approval. "I think we should have sex. Right here."

And just like that, all of my thoughts of romantic words and confessions flee my brain, and my cock is fully alert.

"Is that right?"

She nods and backs away from the window, pulling her skirt up around her hips, then letting her panties fall to the floor. "Yeah. I'm not gonna get naked because I don't want splinters in my back."

"Good plan, babe." I unzip my pants and cross to her, pinning her against the wall as I take my time kissing the ball of her shoulder, then up her neck to nibble on her earlobe.

"I don't want it to be slow." Her breath is airy now and catches when my fingers slide up the inside of her thigh to her wet center. "I want you to fuck me, right here, against the wall of your treehouse."

"It would be rude of me to tell you no."

She laughs, and then I boost her up, her legs encircling my hips as I drive into her, making us both gasp. Her mouth gapes as I sit there, buried deep, staring into her eyes.

"Mine," I whisper.

"Yours." She clenches. "Move, Shane. Fuck me."

I tip my brow to hers and can't resist her. My hips move faster and faster. With the way I'm pounding into her, it's a damn good thing this thing is sturdy, or we'd be on the ground, twenty feet below.

Her fists clench in my hair, and she moans, long and low, as she comes around me. The ripples are fierce and nearly coax an orgasm from me.

My God, I'm lost in her. In every way.

And I'm never letting her go.

"Again." I pull out, set her feet on the floor, and turn her away from me. "Grab the wall and hold on."

I easily slide back inside and take us both on another ride. Her round ass is perfect in my hands as I take her from behind. I grip the hair on the back of her head and push us both harder, faster than before.

The second orgasm is more powerful than the first, and when we've finally caught our breath, all I can do is pull her to me and hold on.

"I should have had a bed brought up here."

She chuckles against my chest. "That wouldn't have been obvious at all."

"Who cares what anyone thinks?" I tip her chin up and kiss her long and slow.

"I couldn't agree more."

CHAPTER

SEVENTEEN

~IVIE~

"This is the *best* way to spend a birthday," Annika says with a long, luxurious sigh. We're lounging in a massive sunroom, with a water fountain trickling not far away. The lounge chairs are plush and comfortable enough to fall asleep in. And all three of us, Nadia, Annika, and me, are being pampered. "I can't believe you brought the spa here."

"We can't go to the spa," Nadia says and sips her mimosa, "so why not bring them to us? Oh, here, I chose the red polish for my toes."

Nadia passes her nail tech the polish and then grins over at me.

I don't remember the last time I felt this *relaxed*. My toes are freshly painted pink, I've had a massage and a facial, and just finished eating the *best* salad I've ever had in my life. And now I'm sitting with my best friends, drinking mimosas. It feels like the old times.

"I want to marry that masseuse," Annika says with a wink. "He had *very* good hands."

"Raul is amazing," the nail tech says with a grin. "And is my husband."

"You're a lucky woman." Annika laughs.

"I think Rafe would be unhappy if you married the masseuse," I say and slide a sly look over at my best friend. "I noticed he went directly to your room when he got back last night."

Annika shifts in her seat and reaches to refill her glass. "He was just checking in."

"Are you ever going to give him a chance?" Nadia demands. "You're not married anymore. I know Rich has only been dead for, like, three months, but there's no love lost there."

The nail tech clears her throat and tightens the lid on her portable caddy. "Ladies, I think we're done here. It was a pleasure to meet you all."

"Thank you," we all say in unison. Nadia and the woman exchange a couple of words about the bill, and then we're alone in the sunroom. "I think I might have scared her when I mentioned that your husband is dead."

"I thought she was going to choke." I shake my head and then giggle. "Anyway, the point is still valid. Rich was a grade-A dick, and he's gone. There's no reason you can't start something with Rafe."

"Rafe isn't meant for me," Annika insists.

"You're so fucking stubborn." I sit up and turn to face my friend. "It's not every day that a girl meets a guy who looks at her the way Rafe looks at you."

"Oh, you mean the way Shane looks at *you*?" Annika counters. "Tell us what's going on there."

"You're changing the subject."

Nadia and Annika just lean in closer, waiting for me to answer.

"Fine. Shane is awesome. The sex is off the charts. He's attentive and sweet, and sometimes maddening. But, hey, who isn't, right?"

"Carmine drives me up the fucking wall," Nadia agrees. "Have you said the L-word yet?"

"No." I sigh and stand to pace the room, but when I almost trip and fall into the fountain, I return to my chair where it's safe. "There are...issues."

"Honey, you don't get past the age of sixteen and not have issues," Annika reminds me. "I mean, I know that yours are heavier than most, but you've come a long way since that girl in New York."

"Not just my stuff—of which there is legion—but he has stuff, too.

And I don't think Shane is convinced that he *deserves* to have someone in his life long-term, you know? He's told me a bit of what his job is, and that coupled with his family and all of those responsibilities...I think he's resigned to being alone. And that's sad."

"You're in love with him." Annika's statement leaves no room for argument. And I don't want to deny it.

"I am." I prop my chin in my hand and sigh. "I mean, have you seen his muscles? And that smile? And when he gets really intense, his brown eyes get this edge to them that makes me want to just *bite* him."

"Carmine has the same eyes," Nadia says with a nod.

"So does Rafe, except his are blue." Annika blinks when we just stare at her. "What? They're brothers."

"Anyway, we'll figure it out, one way or the other. I just hope I don't end up with a broken heart because that will suck."

"If he breaks your heart, I'll break his kneecaps," Nadia says.

"You're scary sometimes." I pour more mimosas for all of us. "Sometimes, like now, it's easy to forget that you're a badass bratva princess."

"Honey, I'm a queen." Nadia's grin is sassy and confident.

"I want to be Nadia when I grow up," I declare as I raise my glass to my lips. "Now, tell us about the wedding plans."

"We're going to have it here. At this house."

"Oh, that's a great idea," Annika says. "The grounds are just gorgeous."

"Yeah, and Carmine was really close with his grandmother, so I think it's a nice tribute to her." Nadia shrugs a shoulder. "My father is fine with it, which kind of surprised me given that our families haven't always been besties, but things are better now."

"Do you have a dress?" I ask. "I hate that this whole mess has happened while you're planning, and that I haven't been able to go with you."

"Neither of us has," Annika says. "I'm sorry."

"Actually, I have twenty dresses arriving here from New York in about an hour. I need help. So, they're coming to us."

"God, it's good to be rich." I sit back and grin at my friend. "You lucky bitch."

"It has its perks." Nadia raises her glass. "Oh, and Carmine's mom is coming to help. My mom will join us via FaceTime."

"Well, let's go get ready, then."

"Darling!" Flavia Martinelli bursts into the massive room that's been converted into a dressing room, her arms outstretched. She engulfs Nadia in a big hug. "You're as gorgeous as ever. I'm so grateful that you invited me here today to see the dresses."

The Martinelli matriarch is tall, slender, and shrewd. Carlo married an attractive and clever woman, who raised three boys, is submerged in her community, and keeps an eye on the who's who of Seattle's elite.

She's known for being a force to be reckoned with. She's always been kind to me, and I have to admit, I admire her for her style, and her sense of humor.

Then again, I suspect one would need to have one to be a boss's wife.

"Hello, girls," she says, turning to Annika and me. "I haven't had a girls' day in...I can't even remember. I'm always surrounded by men."

"Good-looking men at that," Annika reminds her.

"Well, that doesn't hurt, now does it?" Flavia winks and accepts a glass of champagne. "Oh, how lovely. I'm so excited. Get your gorgeous body into a dress, Nadia."

"Okay. First, let me get my mom on the computer."

"Oh, how wonderful," Flavia says and claps her hands. "Katya and I spoke just last night about wedding plans. We're just beside ourselves with excitement."

I sit back and watch as Nadia gets her mother on screen, and Flavia and Annika share a smile.

And I can't help but grieve, for just a moment.

I won't ever have this moment with my mother. Someone stole that from me. And I can't make the person who took her from me pay for that sin. I can't help but feel a little envious that Nadia has this with her mom.

Of course, I'm also excited for her. And when Katya sees me, she grins and waves.

"Hello, Ivie, my darling girl. You look just as beautiful as can be."

"Thank you, Mrs. Tarenkov."

"I'm here, too," Annika says, waving to her. "Hello, Aunt Katya."

"Oh, Annika, you're as lovely as always. Who else is there?"

"It's me, Katie dear." Flavia smiles at the computer. "I wish you were here with us."

"Well, give me just a minute."

Suddenly, the door opens, and Katya walks into the room, opens her arms wide, and starts to laugh.

"Did you think I'd watch this on a small, pitiful screen?"

"Mama!" Nadia rushes over and hugs her mother. The room erupts into chaos as we all shriek and laugh and hug each other in delight.

Carmine pokes his head in the doorway, grinning. "Surprise."

"I love you." Nadia crushes her mouth to his. "Now, get out of here. You can't see any of this. It's for girls only."

"I'll have food sent up in about thirty minutes. Have fun, ladies."

He shuts the door behind him, and we all settle in for the fashion show.

"Oh, this is just the best day," Flavia says as she clasps Katya's hands. "How lovely."

Before long, Nadia walks into the room wearing a long column of white. It hugs her curves, has just a hint of lace, and is absolutely gorgeous.

She steps up onto the pedestal that the fashion house brought with them as a woman named Lydia fluffs the trumpet skirt.

"Now, that is gorgeous," Annika breathes. "The back is *stunning.*"

I tilt my head, not convinced that it's the right one.

"Oh, Flavia," Katya says. "Can you imagine the pretty grandchildren we'll get?"

"Mom." Nadia rolls her eyes. "I'm not having babies."

"Nonsense." Katya brushes the comment away with the flip of her hand. "Turn this way, please. What do you think?"

"It's not me," Nadia replies. It's pretty, but I don't like the lace. No lace."

"Okay, let's try again." Lydia smiles and gestures for Nadia to follow her to the changing room.

Two hours, ten dresses, three glasses of champagne, and six finger sandwiches later, Nadia has tears in her eyes as she stares at herself in the mirror.

"Oh, darling," Flavia breathes. "Carmine will lose his ever-loving mind."

"He'll pass right out," I agree.

"I met him at a wedding," Nadia whispers. "When I was twelve. And I thought he was the most handsome man I'd ever seen in my life. And now I'm *marrying* him."

Katya rests her hands on her daughter's shoulders and looks at her in the mirror. The two look so much alike with their fair hair and skin and big, blue eyes.

"You're a vision," Katya says. "Your father will blubber like a baby."

"I've never seen Papa cry."

"Well, you will on your wedding day. Is this the one?"

"Yeah, it's no contest. Now, I'd better get it off before I rip it or spill something on it."

"Such a wonderful choice," Lydia says, nodding in approval. "And this one is on the less-expensive side at only twenty-two thousand dollars."

I blink, sure I've heard her wrong. She added a zero in there somewhere. Right?

But Nadia just nods once, and says, "I'll take it."

I LOVE them all so much, but I need a few minutes of quiet. And I want to see Shane. I haven't seen him hardly at all today, and the fact that I'm having withdrawal is just another clue that I'm totally head-over-heels for the man.

I feel fantastic. My body is loose and relaxed, and I haven't laughed with my friends so much in years. Things are finally starting to look up.

I am just about to turn the corner into the kitchen when I hear Shane's voice and stay out of sight, frowning.

"I still can't believe the son of a bitch is alive."

"I remember when he was supposedly killed." That voice is Igor Tarenkov. "Many people wanted him dead."

"Yeah, Pavlov was a real piece of work," Carlo Martinelli says. "He was on all of the families' radars. He was mostly harmless but completely untrustworthy. He was a thief and didn't even have enough honor to protect his wife and child."

"I've known that Ivie was his daughter since the day Annika brought her home from college," Igor says, surprising me. I didn't know that he knew. "I likely knew before Annika did. Ivie is a good girl. She couldn't be more different than the man who sired her. She certainly doesn't know that the man lives."

I cover my mouth, suppressing the sound of my surprised gasp. My father *is* alive? How? I saw him hanging for myself. We were so sure that the phone number we found was a cover.

Without giving it another thought, I storm into the kitchen, every nerve ending in my body radiating anger and frustration.

"What did you say?" I stare at Shane, my hands on my hips.

"Ivie, we're in a meeting—"

I step forward until I'm toe-to-toe with him. "*What* did you just say?"

"I like her," Carlo says, but I don't look his way.

"Your father is alive," Shane says.

"And how long have you known that little piece of information, Shane?"

He doesn't even have the decency to look ashamed.

"A few days."

"A *few* days? Did you know the day we arrived here and we talked? When you fucking *swore* to me that you didn't know more?"

His nostrils flare, and I already know the answer.

"Yes. I knew then."

"I can't *believe* this. I trusted you. All of you. And you withheld this from me? What possible reason could there be for that, knowing what that monster did to me?"

"We were gathering information, little one," Igor says, and I turn to him. His eyes are full of compassion, and it's almost my undoing.

But I firm my lower lip and look around the room at a group of men I thought were being honest with me—and just feel complete betrayal.

Especially from Shane.

"Tell me more."

"I saw him with my own eyes. He goes by the name of James Peterson now," Rocco adds. "I sat in front of his house in a suburb outside of Dallas for an hour. No one came or went, but I added a camera to his mailbox, pointed at the house, just in case something interesting happens."

"Like what?" I ask.

"*Anything*," Carmine replies. "We don't know enough about him at this point to know who he's involved with or how he's been spending the past dozen years."

My father is *alive*.

That piece of shit is still allowed to breathe?

No.

"You should have told me." I glare at the man I love and turn to run out of the kitchen.

I'm too angry to stay. I'll end up saying something I regret. Instead, I run up to my bedroom and pace for a moment, and then make a snap decision.

I'm going to go find that asshole and kill him myself. This is what I've been training for, isn't it?

I quickly grab my laptop and purse and hurry down the stairs and out the front door, but stop short when I see the security guard named Peter blocking my way.

"Miss?"

"Oh, hi." I offer him a charming smile. "I was hoping I would run into you. Shane told me to find you and ask you to drive me to the airport."

He narrows his eyes. I'd better talk fast if I'm going to make him believe me.

"He's currently in a meeting with his father and the others and can't be interrupted. He said you'd take care of me."

"He said no such thing."

My eyes close at the hard voice behind me. *Shit.*

EIGHTEEN

~SHANE~

"What do you think you're doing?" I demand when I get Ivie back inside. She's quivering with anger, and frankly, I'm just as pissed.

"I'm going to Dallas. To kill my father."

I blink at her and then shake my head. "Like hell, you are."

"Like hell, I'm *not*." She narrows those spectacular eyes on me. "You've been training me for weeks. Do you think I'm not capable of this?"

"I think you're perfectly capable, Ivie. What I won't allow is having you sneak out of here to go there *alone*."

"Oh, you won't *allow* me?" She drops her bag to the floor and crosses her arms over her chest. "Because I'm what, your *child*?"

"Now you're just pissing me off for the sake of pissing me off."

"No, I'm being an adult woman who doesn't need your permission for anything, Shane. You're not my father or my husband."

We'll be rectifying that little detail as soon as possible. But now isn't the time or place to propose.

She'd tell me to shove the ring up my ass.

"Now, excuse me. I need to go call a cab."

503

"No, damn it." I take her arm but quickly let go when she swings around and punches me in the jaw, just the way we taught her. "Hell."

"I'm not playing around, Shane."

"Obviously. Fine, but you're not going alone."

She starts to argue, but I've had about enough of this bullshit.

"Stop talking for two fucking minutes." I pace in a circle, frustration pulsing through me. "We'll go to Dallas, but you won't go by yourself. If you think I'd be okay with that, in any universe, you don't know me at all."

"You're right. I thought I knew you, but all you do is fucking *lie to me.*"

"Stop it. I didn't tell you because I didn't know if it was fucking true. You wondered, as well when we saw his name tied to those phone records. I wasn't going to tell you something that would change your entire world off hearsay, Ivie. We needed eyes on him. Confirmation. And *then* I was going to tell you. Today. I needed the intel from Rocco."

"I should have been in on the information from the get-go. And then, if it wasn't true, I should have known that, too. I'm not some damsel in distress here, Shane. Now, get me to Dallas, or I'll go myself."

I want to shake her. I want her to just *listen* and try to see this from my perspective, but she's too angry.

It'll have to wait.

"We'll leave in an hour."

She turns on her heel and walks away, and I return to the kitchen, where everyone is still waiting.

"Looks like we're headed to Dallas," is all I say.

"I really like her, son," Pop says with a grin. "Keep that one."

NINETY MINUTES LATER, we're all on the jet, headed for Dallas. Even Pop and Igor decided to join.

They don't usually go into the field anymore—haven't for many years—but they wanted to come along. They'll visit a friend in Dallas while we find Pavlov.

"Do you realize what you're about to do?" I ask Ivie, who's sitting across from me. Her gaze flies to mine and holds steady.

Good girl.

"Yes."

"He isn't a stranger," I remind her, aware that all eyes are on us. Nadia watches with concern and reaches out to pat Ivie on the shoulder.

"No, he's a monster," Ivie says in a firm voice. "And he killed my mother. I've seen the photos of what he did to her. To save his own ass. And I remember, in vivid detail, the things he made me do on his behalf. He doesn't deserve to live."

I sigh and realize that I won't be able to talk her out of this. But she won't go alone.

"Blood isn't always family," Igor says, looking intently at Ivie. "Sometimes, what's born into a family is not the same. Does not belong."

I glance at Nadia, knowing full well that Igor is speaking of his son.

"And there are other times when family has no blood tie at all, and that's what we have with you, Ivie. You are one of us, and we will do everything in our power, which is considerable, to keep you safe and make sure you have your revenge."

Ivie blinks quickly, soaking in his words.

"Now, you said earlier that you thought you could trust these men, and I'm here to assure you that you *can*. But you already know that. Your anger is warranted, but make sure you focus it on the appropriate target. Shane was doing what he thought was right. Because he cares for you and doesn't want you hurt."

"I know," she whispers and blows out a breath then looks up at me. Everything we've been through together flows between us. We're going to be okay. "I know that."

"Good."

"One more thing," Nadia adds. "Don't hesitate. If you do, you won't go through with it, and you could be hurt. If your intention is to kill, don't pause. He may be an old man, but he could be dangerous. Keep your mind clear. Don't let him surprise you. I made that mistake, and it almost cost Carmine and me our lives."

Ivie nods in agreement.

We spend the rest of the flight in relative quiet. We check weapons for the fifth time, just in case. With a face made of stone, Ivie tucks her sidearm into the holster at the small of her back after checking the magazine.

She's not shaky. She's not upset.

She's on a mission.

I glance at Curt and see him nod. He's thinking the same thing I am. She needs this. No matter how much I want to protect her from it, to shelter her, she needs it.

And we'll be here for her through it.

Shortly after landing in Dallas, we climb into a large, black SUV, and Rocco drives us to a suburb, while a guard drives my father and Igor to another location.

They didn't tell us where they were going, just that they had someone to pay a visit to.

I hope they're not going to see the Dallas syndicate without us. I know that our fathers are powerful men, but they shouldn't go in alone. This isn't the time.

But I'm not the boss. They are. And what they say goes. I have to block that out, secure in the knowledge that they're not currently in danger, and focus entirely on Ivie and the mission ahead.

"That's his," Rocco says, pointing to a small house as we drive past. The curtains are drawn in the front, but not the sides. The blue paint is peeling as if the person living there hasn't had the money or inclination to keep it painted.

"Bastard is living better than he ever did when I was a kid," Ivie mutters. "Why aren't you stopping?"

"Because we need to make sure nothing is going on," I reply and take her hand in mine. To my relief, she doesn't pull away. "Rocco will circle the block, just to be sure that everything is calm, and then we'll park a few houses down so we don't draw attention."

"Right." She blows out a breath. "Sorry, I'm impatient. And I'm so damn *mad*."

"Impatience will get you killed," Curt says from behind her. "Slow your body down, Ivie. Take a deep breath, then another. Calm your mind. If you rush, if you let your anger lead, you'll fail."

"I won't fail," she vows softly and follows Curt's orders by taking a deep breath.

When we've parked several houses down from Pavlov, I reach for the door handle, but Ivie stops me.

"I'm going in alone."

"Ivie—"

"I know you want to protect me." She takes my hand and gazes up at me with those intense blue eyes. "I know that. It's who you are, Shane, and I appreciate you so much. I appreciate everything you've done for me. But like I said earlier, I'm no damsel in distress here. *You* made sure of that. I've been training for this for weeks, and I didn't even realize it. I need time with him. I have things to say."

"You have fifteen minutes," I reply reluctantly. "And then we're coming in. This isn't up for negotiation."

"I'd take that offer," Carmine says. "It's the best you'll get from us."

"Okay, I'll see you soon." She nods once and then, without hesitation, steps from the vehicle, looks both ways, and crosses the street. She walks up the sidewalk and then up the steps to the front porch.

She doesn't bother knocking, just walks right inside. My gut twists.

"Jesus." I pull my hand down my face in frustration. "I never would have thought I'd let her do this."

"She needs it," Curt says. "And I know how she feels."

After everything Curt's been through, he would understand perfectly.

"Yeah, well, she's not a trained operative."

"But she's trained with her weapon and hand-to-hand. Her father is an old man now. She can protect herself."

"It's different when it's blood," Nadia says, her voice hollow as she stares at the door Ivie just walked through.

Nadia killed her brother earlier this year after discovering he was behind a plot to double-cross his family.

I can't imagine the bad moments she's had since then, even knowing that what she did was the right thing.

Carmine wraps his arm around her shoulders and whispers something in her ear.

We're quiet for a long moment, and then Rocco says quietly, "Is the hair standing up on anyone else's neck?"

"Something isn't right," Carmine agrees.

The air is too still.

It's too quiet.

"Let's go." I pull my weapon from its holster. "Nadia and Carmine, take the right side of the house. Curt and I will take the left. Rocco—"

"I'm going *up*," my brother says with a hard voice.

We can't see the roof of the house from here. I don't know how Rocco intends to do what he has planned, but he's more than capable.

With weapons drawn, we move silently across the street to the house. My heart is pounding harder than it ever has on any other mission. I'm usually like stone, perfectly calm. But I've never faced the possibility of losing someone I love on a mission before. This is new territory.

I don't plan to ever repeat it.

I just keep silently berating myself for letting her go in alone. I should be in there with her. I should be by her side.

But then Curt's words come into my head. If I let the frustration, the *fear*, take over, I'll lose. I have to remain focused and steady. For her sake and that of everyone here.

We're a team, and we have a fucking job to do.

As soon as Curt and I walk around the house's left corner, we come face-to-face with two armed men dressed in black.

We silently neutralize them and keep walking, leaving the bodies where they fell.

How did we not see them from the front? Were they hiding?

What the hell is happening here?

We slip around the corner to the back yard in time to see Carmine and Nadia kill two men. Curt and I take care of two more headed their way.

"Six?" I ask.

"Eight," Carmine replies.

"Twelve," Rocco says as he jumps down from above.

"Jesus," I whisper and immediately move to the back door.

"There are men inside," Carmine says grimly. "I counted two in the kitchen. I saw three people in the living room, but that doesn't mean there aren't more."

"There's no one upstairs," Rocco adds. "It's clear."

We kill two more in the kitchen.

Fourteen men.

I motion for the others to stop and be silent, and I quickly look around the corner where I hear a man speaking rapidly in a foreign language.

There is no one else in the house that I can see. Just Ivie, her father, and the other man yelling at them.

"Bulgarian," Nadia whispers in my ear.

I turn to look at the others and point to myself.

I go in first.

They nod once.

But when I turn back around, all hell has already broken loose.

CHAPTER
NINETEEN
~IVIE~

O nce across the street from Shane and the others, I snap my
spine straight and clear my throat.

No hesitation. No nerves.

This is a long time coming, and I'm going to take advantage of it. It's an opportunity I never thought to get. Just hours ago, I was thinking that I'd never have my mama with me to fluff my dress and giggle with my friends before I got married.

And it's *his* fault.

I get to make him pay.

But before I do, I have a lot to say to the man I thought was dead. I won't waste the moment.

I climb the small house's rickety steps. He lives in a beautiful neighborhood, but his home is starting to crumble. It doesn't surprise me. I wonder if the neighbors are pissed that he's bringing their property values down.

Without knocking, I turn the doorknob, surprised to find it unlocked. I walk right in.

The space smells of him—tobacco and stale onions. I would never forget that smell. The air carries a light haze from cigarettes. There's a TV on upstairs.

The furniture is old and has holes in the cushions. A photo of my mother on the wall has me seeing red.

How *dare* he?

"Hello?"

The man who sired me walks into the living room and stops cold, staring at me with surprised eyes.

"Have a seat," I tell him with a hard voice.

"Laryssa."

"Does not exist," I reply calmly. "Sit the fuck down, Pavlov."

His face turns red, and his eyes narrow. "You will not speak to me like that."

"Oh, I'm gonna speak to you any way I see fit, you piece of trash. If you don't want to sit, that's fine. You can hear me just fine while standing."

"How did you find me?"

"It doesn't matter. I am going to do the talking, and I want the damn *truth*. Why did you kill my mother?"

He glances toward the photo on the wall.

"No, don't you dare look at her. Why did you kill her? Cut her throat?"

"Because I was given an order to," he says simply.

I stare at him, unblinking. This man that scared me so badly as a child, who hurt me on a whim, looks so old and frail now. I'm as tall as he is. His face is wrinkled, his eyes dull. He's lost most of his dark hair.

He's a shell of the man he once was.

"You were supposed to die," he continues. His voice still carries the thick Bulgarian accent from my youth. "I spared you."

"So I could do your dirty work." I shake my head and prop my hands on my hips. "So I could steal and deliver shit that you didn't want to be caught with. You spared me so gross, old men could ogle me—a *child*—and give you what you wanted."

"And it worked. We were a good team, you and me, Laryssa."

"I said Laryssa doesn't fucking exist. I killed her and created someone new. Someone who doesn't carry your name, who has nothing at all to do with you. And I've done a damn good job of making a nice life for myself."

"In the mafia," he says with a nasty sneer. "How appropriate."

"So you knew where I was, after all. And you never came after me."

"You started to have a mouth on you. I knew that you didn't always deliver what I sent you to do, and that no matter how much I punished you, you wouldn't fall in line. Just like your mother. It angered me when you ran away, but I had other problems to see to. Worrying about where you ended up was not a priority."

I wanted the truth, and he was giving it to me.

There was a time when his words would have hurt me.

But not now.

"You're a worthless piece of garbage," I inform him.

"The apple doesn't fall far from the tree, Laryssa."

I snarl, but then Igor's words come back to me. *Family isn't always blood.*

"I was never your daughter in any way that mattered. I was a tool. And I got out. I'm *nothing* like you."

"Aren't you? Are you telling me then that you're not here to kill me?"

"Oh, I'm going to kill you," I agree. "But not because I'm the same as you. No, I'm going to kill you because you slit my mother's throat and left me motherless."

"She was nothing."

"Is that why you still have her photo hanging on your wall? Because she was nothing?"

He narrows his eyes, and his hands fist at his sides.

"I did not realize you'd let your daughter speak to you in such a disrespectful way."

We turn as a man walks into the room from what must be the kitchen, gun in hand. He's tall and lean with round, wire-rimmed glasses. He looks like Doc from *Back to the Future.*

And his accent is the same as my father's.

"Both of you, sit," he instructs us, pointing to the two chairs facing an empty television. I eye him, considering whether I can fight him for the gun, but he steps forward. "I said, sit."

Pavlov sits, glaring at the man, and I sit next to him.

"I am Elian Pavlov."

I scowl. "Pavlov?"

"That's right. I'm your father's brother. Your uncle. We're just a big, happy family."

"I'll break out the photo albums. Oh, wait, we don't have any. Because we aren't a family."

Elian doesn't smile. "Your father's past transgressions when he was still living in our homeland have caught up with him."

"The transgressions from after he left Bulgaria have caught up with him, too."

Suddenly, Elian starts speaking rapidly in Bulgarian and pacing the room as if a switch was flipped and something I said—or didn't say—set off his temper.

"What are you saying?"

He doesn't reply, just keeps going, pointing at me and then my father.

"What the fuck are you saying? I don't speak Bulgarian!"

He stops and stares at Ivan. "You did not teach her?"

"He taught me how to be a son of a bitch, and that about covers it."

"He is saying—" my father begins, but I cut him off by holding up my hand.

"No. I've said all I need to say to you, and I don't want to hear another word from your lying mouth. You,"—I point to my uncle—"you talk."

He pushes his face close to mine. "You may speak to your father like that, but I won't allow it."

I raise an eyebrow. "I don't fucking *know* you. And, frankly, I don't care who you are."

I have no idea where this bravado is coming from, aside from the fact that I'm damn sick and tired of the men in my family being assholes.

Elian backhands me with the butt of his sidearm, making me see stars.

"You will speak with respect, the way a woman should."

I glare at him.

My father shifts next to me.

And then I look at them, back and forth, as the situation starts to make sense.

"Have you been here this whole time?" I ask Elian.

"Of course."

"You followed us."

He smiles thinly. "You're smarter than you look."

"There's a mole." I shake my head. "There's a mole in the Martinellis' organization."

"I've been watching you for a long time, Laryssa," Elian says and then laughs. "I mean...Ivie. We finally had you in our grasp in New York, but you managed to wiggle your way out of that."

"You were behind the kidnapping."

"No," my father says as he stands next to his brother. "I was."

My mouth drops open. I stare at the two men and then narrow my eyes as pieces start to click into place. "Are you *twins*?"

"Triplets, actually," Elian says. "Our brother was hanged just over twelve years ago."

I blink rapidly as the last of the puzzle fits together. "You killed your brother to hide your death, and then you let the Sergis hide you?"

"We used their money," my father says. "Let them think they were the ones I was funneling information to. Let them believe they were in charge."

"They were not," Elian adds.

"What do I have to do with any of this?"

"You took the drive," Ivan says with the shake of his head. "When you ran away, you took the information with you."

"For fuck's sake." I sigh and shake my head slowly. "Something I didn't even remember I had until two weeks ago is the reason you've wanted me dead?"

"Not dead, necessarily," Elian says. "Just found. All this time, if you'd done what you were instructed to do in the first place, you could have gone on living your life, none the wiser. But you didn't. Where is it?"

"I don't know."

"Liar," Ivan says and reaches for me, but I duck out of his grasp and move quickly away. "Where is it?"

"I certainly don't have it on me," I reply and evade him again.

Both Elian and Ivan start speaking in rapid Bulgarian, and I can't understand them again.

Why didn't I stay brushed up on the language?

"Stop moving."

I look at Elian, his words spoken in English, and stare down the barrel of his weapon.

Before he can pull the trigger, a knife appears at this throat and slices deep, spattering blood everywhere.

"Jesus."

My father is holding the knife and staring at me with hollow, dead eyes.

Shane bursts into the room, his weapon drawn, but I shake my head.

This is *my* fight.

"Tell me where the drive is, Laryssa."

"I told you." I stomp his foot, ram my knee into his crotch, and grab the knife from his hand, then drive it right into his heart. As his mouth gapes, and his eyes bulge, I lean into him. "My name is *Ivie.*"

As he gurgles, I pull out the knife and rest the blade against his throat.

"And this is for my mama."

Without hesitation, I slice from left to right and let him fall, next to his brother.

The blood is revolting. It covers *everything.* Me, the floor, the walls, and the furniture.

But I ignore it and walk to the wall to pluck the photo of my mother from the nail. I use my sleeve to wipe blood spatter from the glass.

"I'm taking you with me." I kiss her and then turn to Shane. "Get me the hell out of here."

"On it, baby." He nods to the others, who flank me, and helps me out of the house and to the vehicle.

"I'm calling in cleanup," Carmine says as we get settled in the vehicle, and he takes out his phone.

Rafe fires up the car, and we pull away from the curb and head back the way we came.

"Plane's ready," Rafe says.

"There were two of him," Shane says, turning to me.

"His brother." I tell them everything that happened after I walked into the house. "He had *two* brothers that I didn't even know about."

"None of us did," Shane says. "It didn't come up in the research."

"They framed the Sergis," Nadia says in surprise. "My God, who the fuck are they?"

"Bulgarian operatives," Curt says, getting all our attention. "I recognized Elian's name. But Pavlov is a common Bulgarian name, so I didn't link him with Ivan. I've never seen a photo of him. He was a slimy, sneaky son of a bitch. He was on every hit list in the fucking world."

"Well, he was hit." My hands have started to shake. "By his own brother."

"Are you hurt?" Shane asks me. "Tell me all this blood is theirs."

"It's theirs." I swallow hard and feel sick to my stomach. *Oh God, do not get sick here. Hold on.* "I need a shower."

"We have one on the plane," Rafe says as he changes lanes. "I'll have you there in ten minutes."

It takes eight.

Shane helps me up the stairs where Igor and Carlo are waiting for us.

"Oh, little one," Igor says, but I hold up my hand.

"Not yet." I look up at him with pleading eyes. "I need to clean up and gather myself."

"Of course." Carlo points to the back of the plane. "Everything you need is back there, Ivie. Make yourself at home."

"I'm coming with you," Shane says, and I don't argue. I *need* him now—more than I ever have before.

I manage to hold myself together while he starts the shower and helps me out of my ruined clothes.

"There isn't enough room in there for both of us," he says grimly.

"I'm shocked we're in a plane," I say. "It's huge."

"There's soap, shampoo, and anything else you need." He opens the glass door for me, but before I can step inside, he cups my face in his hands and kisses me gently. "Take your time, love. We won't take off until you're ready."

516

"Thank you." It's a whisper. I climb into the shower and let the hot water beat on me, just soaking in the warmth.

I'm so cold. I can't stop shaking.

Maybe this is shock.

Finally, I reach for the soap and start washing up. My hair is next. When I'm as clean as I can get, and as warm as I'm *going* to get for now, I open the shower door.

Shane is waiting with a big, fluffy towel.

"Come here."

I step out to him, and he wraps me in that terrycloth and pulls me to him. I lose control and cling to him as I start sobbing. I've always thought that people who wail when they cry are just dramatic, but I get it now as I bawl against the strongest man I've ever met.

The man I love with all my heart and soul.

And grieve once more for the mother I loved so much, and the father I hated with everything in me.

When I've quieted to soft hiccups, Shane finishes drying me and wraps me in a white robe, then leads me out of the bathroom and into the bedroom with a queen-sized bed.

He pushes a button and speaks into a microphone.

"She's out of the shower, and we're safe in the bedroom. You're cleared for takeoff."

Shane pulls back the crisp, white linens, and we lie down, tangled in each other, just clinging to one another as we hear the engines come to life and feel the plane start making its way down the runway.

When we're airborne, and my tears have stopped flowing, Shane turns my chin his way.

"I'm so proud of you, sweetheart."

My chin wobbles, but I lick my lips and rub his nose with mine. "I wasn't scared. I was just...mad. And when I killed him, I wasn't sorry."

"Yeah. I get that."

"Does that make me an evil person?" I wonder aloud. "Does it make me like *him* that I was able to end his life with no remorse?"

"No." His voice is firm as he urges me to look him in the eyes. "You're not evil, Ivie, you're human. It's over now. He's gone, and he can't hurt you ever again. We'll do some more digging to make sure that it ends with Ivan and Elian. I suspect it does, but we'll cross every *t* and dot every *i*, just to be sure."

I nod and blow out a breath. "It's over."

"Yes."

My breath hitches. "Curt can go home, where he's happiest."

His lips twitch. "I'm so happy to hear that you're worried about Curt."

"What will you do?" I ask.

Shane's eyes sober. His hand cups my cheek again, and just when I think he's going to kiss me, he says, "I love you, Ivie. I love you more than I ever thought I could love someone. You've wound your way inside me, and I can't let you go.

"So, to answer your question, I'm going to talk to the people I work for and set new parameters there. Because I refuse to ever leave you alone. I will *not* put myself into a position that might mean I never come home to you."

A tear falls down my cheek, but it's not because of my father. It's from the hope that's just set up residence in my belly.

"I love you, too."

"Good." He grins and kisses me lightly but then pulls back again. "I'm glad to hear that, sweetheart because I'd like to ask you a serious question now. I'd get on one knee, but this feels a little more intimate, and pretty much perfect for us since we haven't done anything the traditional way since the day I met you."

I bite my lip, waiting.

"Marry me, Ivie. Make me the luckiest man in the world. I know that my family is a lot to take on, and as crazy as they are, they will love and protect you until the day they die. You will never want for anything. You'll never wonder for even one moment how much I love you, how devoted I am to you. Be my wife."

"That sounded more like a command than a question."

His lips twitch. "Well, I'm used to giving orders, so..."

I laugh and wrap my arms around him. "Yes, Shane Martinelli. I'll be your wife. Under one condition."

"What's that?"

"You give me babies. I want lots of children. I might not come from the best of parents, but I know I'll be a good mom."

A slow smile spreads over his gorgeous face. "I'm on board with that. In fact—" He pushes the robe open and slides a talented hand inside. "Why don't we get a head start on that?"

"You'll get no argument from me."

"That's a first."

EPILOGUE

~ANNIKA~

One Month Later...

"It is my honor to introduce you to Mr. and Mrs. Martinelli!"

We all stand and clap as Nadia and Carmine walk into the ballroom of the Martinelli family home just outside of Seattle. She's changed into the sexier gown she bought, just for the reception.

Leave it to my cousin Nadia to be more than a little *extra* on her wedding day.

But I wouldn't have her any other way.

The weather held beautifully for the ceremony out by the pond. There were even swans swimming gracefully across the still water as Ivie and I stood by Nadia's side and watched with pride as our best friend promised to join her life with Carmine's.

I don't think there was a dry eye in the audience. Even Igor, my uncle, wiped a tear from his eye as he gave his daughter away.

The house is packed with at least three hundred guests, and likely close to that many vendors, here to make sure that Nadia's day goes off without a hitch.

And I'd say, so far, it's been absolutely perfect.

"Come dance with me."

I glance up at Rafe and feel my heart pick up speed, the way it always does when he's near. I've loved this man since I was nineteen.

And he loves me.

But we can't be together.

"Come on," he says, urging me to follow him to the floor. "It's just a dance, Annika. I'm not asking you to marry me or anything."

I frown at him but melt against him when he wraps those strong arms around me and guides me into a sweet, slow dance.

I've gotten good at saying "*no*" to Rafe.

But it feels so wonderful when I give in and say, "Yes."

I rest my cheek against his muscled chest and close my eyes, letting the music fill me. And for this moment, I almost forget that I'm damaged goods and that if Rafe ever found out what my secrets are, he'd stop asking me to let him in.

To give him a chance.

To give *us* a chance.

They all think that the worst part of me died with my husband.

But they're wrong.

When the song ends, a fast one starts, and Nadia makes me stay on the floor with her as we jam out to music from when we were young and would dance our asses off in her bedroom.

When I can barely feel my feet anymore, I wave them off and make my way to the table to change my shoes into flats—I'm a smart woman who brings appropriate footwear when I know dancing will be involved —and take a sip of water.

"Oh, honey, you look absolutely gorgeous today," Katya, Nadia's mom, says as she leans in to kiss my cheek. "Don't you think everything came together nicely?"

Katya is a typical mother, even though she's married to a billionaire and can have anything she wants with the snap of her fingers. She just wants her daughter's special day to be perfect. And she's been fretting for days.

"It's so lovely," I assure her. "You were right to go with the lilacs outside. They smelled heavenly, and added just the right pop of color."

"Oh, I'm so happy to hear you say that," she says with a whoosh of relieved breath. "I was worried that someone would be allergic. That's why we went with simple roses in here, just in case."

"You never miss a thing, Aunt Katya." I kiss her cheek. "Are you going to dance with Uncle Igor?"

She glances over to where her husband is smoking cigars with Carlo and the Sergi boss. "He'll save some dances for me. In the meantime, I'm going to let him tell tall tales with his friends and drink some whiskey."

Aunt Katya winks at me.

"The secret to being married to a man like Igor is to let him think he's always in charge, while having the backbone to steer him where he needs to go." She glances over, and I follow her gaze. She's looking at Rafe. "You remember that, my love."

"Oh, I don't think—"

"It's just a suggestion," she interrupts and then kisses me on the cheek before rushing over to chat with a table full of guests.

Everyone thinks I should be with Rafe. Even *Rafe* is convinced I should be with him.

But they're wrong.

I sigh and sit at my table, reaching for the bag beneath the table-cloth so I can change my shoes when a waiter taps my shoulder.

"Miss Annika?"

"Yes?"

"This was just delivered for you. They said it was urgent, so I brought it right over."

"Oh?" I frown at the manila envelope and nod at the young man. "Thank you."

He nods and hurries away. I glance around to make sure no one is looking over my shoulder and open the envelope.

There's a note on top.

If you do not meet our demands, we will send these to the press. Your family will be ruined. You will be ruined.

We will be in touch.

I flip the note to the back and feel my blood run cold as I stare down at the first photograph.

It's from another lifetime. When the man I married made me do things that I hated, that I was uncomfortable with. Things I'm not proud of.

My nakedness is on full display in the photo. And the next one. The third shows me doing things I'd never even *think* of doing again.

Suddenly, I feel a strong hand on my shoulder and look up into Rafe's hot blue eyes.

"What the fuck is that?"

Turn the page for a sneak peek at the final installment in the With Me In Seattle MAFIA series, Off the Record:

OFF THE RECORD

A WITH ME IN SEATTLE MAFIA NOVEL

Off the Record
A With Me In Seattle MAFIA Novel
By

Kristen Proby

OFF THE RECORD

A With Me In Seattle MAFIA Novel

Kristen Proby

Copyright © 2021 by Kristen Proby

For Chelle.
Thank you, for everything.
I couldn't do this without you.

PROLOGUE
~ANNIKA~

Rafe Martinelli. Also known as the love of my life. The man of my dreams. My one and only. I know, I'm only twenty, and my cousin Nadia would tell me that it's completely ridiculous to think that I could meet my soul mate in college when I should be out sowing my wild oats—whatever in the world that means.

I love Nadia. She's my closest friend, as well as my cousin, and she's one of a very select few who knows what it's like to live in this crazy family of ours. My roommate, Ivie, knows.

And Rafe.

Because while my uncle is the boss of one of the most prominent crime families in the country, Rafe's father is the boss of *the* biggest family on the west coast.

And our families don't like each other.

Which means that everything Rafe and I are to each other, everything we've done, and what we're about to do tonight is a secret.

Because if our families found out, we'd be in big trouble.

"Class dismissed."

I sigh in relief when my biology professor gives us the okay to leave. I gather my books and papers and rush out of the lab toward my car.

Ivie and I live in an apartment just on the edge of campus. My uncle is kind enough to pay for it. Lord knows, neither Ivie nor I could afford it.

I know, I'm a lucky girl.

My date with Rafe is in an hour. Which means, I have to take a shower and get ready to go fast because Rafe is never late.

It's just one of the million reasons I love him so much.

"Hi, friend," I announce as I rush past Ivie to my bedroom. "Can't talk. Gotta hurry."

"I'll follow you," she says and leans her shoulder against the door of my bedroom as I strip naked and make a beeline for the bathroom. "What lit a fire under your butt?"

"Date."

"With Rafe?"

"It'd better be with Rafe. He'd be pretty mad if it was with someone else."

Ivie smirks as I start the shower and throw my hair up under a shower cap. She's the only one who knows about Rafe and me. I *had* to tell her. She lives here, and I spend a lot of time with him.

"Tonight's the night," I inform her.

"Of what? Is there a new movie out?"

"No, it's *the* night."

She flings the shower curtain back and stares at me with wide, blue eyes. "You're going to *do it*?"

"Yep." I smile and shave one armpit. "I've been on the pill for a month, so we're covered there. I mean, we've literally done *everything* else. It's borderline torture. I'm so ready. He does things to me that I didn't even know were possible. The way I feel when he looks at me, let alone what happens to my skin, to my stomach when he touches me... I'm telling you, Ivie, it's incredible."

"I'm totally jealous." She pulls the curtain shut again, but I can hear her organizing things on the countertop. "Also, you're stupidly hot together. Like, you could be a celebrity couple, you're so pretty. It's like Brangelina."

I lather up one leg but pull the curtain aside so I can grin at my best friend. "You're so sweet. Thank you."

"I think you should tell your parents."

"No." I get to work shaving and shake my head, even though she can't see me. "No way. Uncle Igor would throw a fit, and I'd be in big trouble. I don't even want to think about what the punishment for this would be. And for Rafe, it would be worse. So, no. It's our secret."

"But what happens after this, Annika? I know it's exciting now, but you won't be in college forever. What then? Are you going to get married in secret and have secret babies?"

Tears want to threaten, but I swallow them and rinse my legs.

"Stop it. Tonight is going to be special, and I'm not going to think about the future and ruin it. It'll all work out. All I can do is live day to day."

I wrap the towel around me and immediately reach for my makeup bag.

"I don't agree with you, but I hope tonight is everything you want it to be." She pats me on the shoulder and leaves the bathroom, and I stare at my reflection.

"Everything's going to be just fine."

"Are you okay?"

"You've asked me that about six times." I smile at Rafe as he tucks a loose strand of hair behind my ear. The truth is, I'm sore, and it hurt way more than I thought it would, and was over pretty fast, too. But I've also never felt more connected to a person in my life as I do right now, lying in Rafe's giant bed.

"Are *you* okay?" I ask him and drag my fingertip down his nose. Rafe is a handsome man. He's tall and broad, and I know he works out almost every day. The efforts show. He has muscles on top of muscles and tanned skin. I could lick every inch of him.

And have.

"I don't think I've ever been better." His smile is soft, lazy, and a little proud. "You're amazing, babe."

I grin and rest my head on his shoulder. When I draw circles on his chest, he clasps my hand in his, kisses it, then holds it against his heart.

"I wish we could just stay right here, forever," I whisper.

"Me, too."

"What do you think will happen?"

He sighs. He knows exactly what I'm talking about.

"I don't mean to ruin this night," I rush on. "Forget I said anything."

"You didn't ruin anything," he assures me and kisses my forehead. "And the honest answer is, I don't know."

"We're meant to be together," I continue. "I mean, how else do you explain that we randomly chose the same college? And on the east coast, no less? This isn't a fluke. It's destiny. Maybe we can convince our families of that. Eventually."

"Maybe." He kisses my forehead again. "Eventually."

Two years later...

I'VE BEEN SUMMONED to my uncle's office. I don't quite know what to make of that, given that it's never happened before.

I smile at his assistant, who nods and says, "You can go on in, Annika."

"Thanks."

I push through the milky glass doors and am surprised to see not only Uncle Igor but also my father.

"Close the door, please," Uncle Igor says. He's sitting behind his enormous desk, looking more powerful than any man I've ever seen.

But he's never frightened me. He's always been loving and generous with me.

"Is something wrong?" I ask as I sit in the chair across from my uncle, next to my father.

"No. Actually, we have some good news for you. But first, I want to congratulate you on doing so well in college, my little firefly." Uncle Igor smiles proudly. "You finished your bachelors in just three years, and you're on track to finish medical school in only two years."

"That's right. And I want to thank *you* for the opportunity. I know it's not inexpensive, and I appreciate everything the family has done for me."

"I know you do. You're a good girl, Annika." Uncle Igor and my father share a look. "I wanted to let you know that you'll be moving to Denver for your residency."

I frown and shake my head. "I don't understand."

"You'll be switching schools in the fall. You'll complete your residency in Denver."

What about Rafe?

"Why? I'm doing well here, and I like this college. I have friends here."

"I know." He folds his hands on his desk. "And a boyfriend, eh?"

I blink rapidly. I *hate* lying to my family. "No, of course, not."

He tosses several photos on the desk in front of me, and I swallow hard when I see images of Rafe and me, walking hand-in-hand on campus, laughing while seated at our favorite restaurant, and kissing on a bridge where we like to take walks.

"You've never been a liar before, firefly."

I feel my father shift next to me, and tears immediately threaten.

"I don't like lying now," I confess and swallow hard.

"You know that the Martinellis are off-limits."

I clasp my hands tightly in my lap.

"Look at me," he says, but his voice is gentle, and his eyes hold compassion when I meet his. "You fancy yourself in love, do you?"

"Yes."

He nods and turns to look out the windows.

"He was sent here to follow you."

I blink, certain I've heard him wrong.

"They're keeping an eye on you and trying to get information. The fact that they'd stoop so low and use my innocent niece as a pawn is unforgivable."

"No, that's not what's happening. Rafe was surprised to see me. We didn't know we were attending the same college."

"Annika," Papa says beside me and reaches for my hand. "You know this is not possible. It's forbidden."

A tear drops onto my cheek. "I didn't mean to fall in love with him any more than I can be to blame for his family tree."

"You're smarter than this," Uncle Igor says. "And I'm ending it. Now. Your last day of class is Friday. You'll be packed up and moved by Saturday afternoon. I've already arranged for the movers. This is not up for discussion."

My world is crumbling out from under me.

"What about Ivie?"

"She'll go with you. I know she's your closest friend and your confidante. I'm not a monster."

I have to try. I have to fight for what Rafe and I have. "Please, Uncle Igor. If you could just listen. If you could maybe talk to Rafe…"

"I am not at fault here," he replies, his voice hard now. "You know what it means to be a part of this family. You *know* that the Martinellis are off-limits. You need to remember your place and be grateful that simply changing schools is your punishment for defying me."

He's all boss now. I know better than to talk back.

So, I simply nod.

"Yes, sir."

"Good. End it today. I have an apartment waiting for you and Ivie in Denver. It's in a nice part of town and is newer than the place you have here."

"Thank you." It's a whisper.

When they dismiss me, I walk on numb legs out of the office building and stand on the sidewalk in the sunshine.

My God, how will I tell him?

CHAPTER
ONE
~RAFE~

Present Day

"They *met* with him?" I demand. I shove my hands into the pockets of my tux and work at keeping my face expressionless.

We're at a wedding, for Christ's sake.

"Pop confirmed it last night," Carmine says, rocking back on his heels. "I meant to pull you both in and tell you, but things got crazy."

"It was the night before your wedding," Shane reminds him. "Of course, it's crazy. What in the hell were they thinking, going in there alone? They're too old for that shit."

I share a look with my brothers, and then we all chuckle.

"They may be older," I reply, speaking of our father and Carmine's new father-in-law, Igor Tarenkov, both bosses of two of the strongest crime families in the world, "but they're not weak. They're also smart. If they went in to talk to those in Carlito's office without us, they knew what they were doing."

"Yeah, well," Carmine says, "I wish they'd let us in on it."

"This isn't the time or place," Shane says and claps a hand on our eldest brother's shoulder. "We're here to celebrate. Go dance with your bride. I'm going to find my smokin' hot fiancée and take her for a spin around the dance floor myself. Did you see how hot she looks today?"

Carmine and I smile as Shane hurries off to find Ivie.

"She's good for him," I say, watching as our brother takes Ivie's hand, kisses it, and then pulls her onto the dance floor. "She makes him happy."

"She does." Carmine nods and then glances to our left, motioning with his head. "She seems to frustrate you."

I follow his gaze and sigh when my eyes land on Annika. My gut churns, the way it always does whenever I see the woman I've loved for almost a decade.

"She does more than that," I murmur and sip my champagne. "I want to kiss the fuck out of her and take her over my damn knee."

Carmine laughs and taps his glass to mine. "That's a woman for you. I think I'll follow our brother's lead and go find my wife."

His grin flashes over his face.

"My wife."

"You went and chained yourself to a dame for the rest of your life."

"Hell, yes. And I'd do it again in a heartbeat if it meant I could marry Nadia all over again."

"I guess you're allowed to be sappy on your wedding day. Go find your bride and dance inappropriately for a while."

"My pleasure."

Carmine saunters across the room, his eyes set on Nadia. She's a beautiful bride, and her eyes light up when she turns to see Carmine approaching.

They're both a couple of saps.

I guess I would be, too. I turn to look at Annika once more and sigh. She's as stunning as ever, with her long, blond hair falling around her in loose curls. Her makeup is flawless and more glammed-up for the occasion. The dress she's in showcases every curve to perfection, and my fingers ache with my desire to touch her.

Hell, it's not just my fingers that ache.

I've become accustomed to admiring her from afar. Keeping my distance.

Giving her space.

But my patience is running thin.

Her piece-of-shit husband has been dead for months. Nothing's standing in our way now.

Nothing except her stubbornness.

I set my empty glass on a tray and walk to where Annika is sitting, alone. She's holding an envelope, and I watch as she tears it open, quickly pages through the contents, and then runs a shaking hand through that silky hair.

I'm not at all ashamed that I look over her shoulder.

I almost wish I hadn't.

The image in her hands has my blood running cold.

"What the fuck is that?"

She jumps, puts the photo face-down on the table, and turns to me. "Oh, you startled me. It's nothing."

"I'll put up with a lot of things from you, Annika, but lying isn't one of them." I lean down, leveling my gaze with hers. "What is that?"

She swallows hard, glances down, and shoves everything back into the envelope. "Not now. Not here. It's Nadia's special day, and I won't ruin it with this. Especially not with this."

She turns embarrassed eyes up to me.

"Annika."

"Let's dance." She shoves the envelope into a bag under the table, takes my hand, and tries to pull me onto the dance floor.

But I outweigh her by at least a hundred pounds and stand my ground.

She looks up at me, sighs, then retrieves the envelope and leads me out of my grandmother's ballroom and to a nearby empty room.

"I don't want this to go *anywhere* but this room for today," she says, her voice strong, her tone saying it isn't open for discussion. "It's my best friend—my *cousin's* special day. Got it?"

I can't promise her that. But I nod. "I'll do everything I can not to ruin the day."

She blows out a breath and pulls a note out of the envelope, passing it to me.

If you do not meet our demands, we will send these to the press. Your family will be ruined. You will be ruined.

We will be in touch.

I scowl and look up at Annika. "Who the fuck sent this?"

"You know as much as I do." She shifts her feet.

"Show me the rest."

"No." She shakes her head quickly. "These are private photos, and I don't want you to see them. It's humiliating. You saw the last one."

What I thought I saw was Annika, naked, spread-eagle and tied to a bed with a group of men standing around her.

And by the look on her face, I'd say my memory isn't wrong.

I want to fucking *kill* someone.

I was her first. I knew everything about her, once upon a time.

Is this who she is now?

"I don't want to talk about it."

No. By the look on her face, I'd say that's not who she is. I have so many fucking questions.

"Here you are," Nadia says as she walks into the room, a bright smile on her face. "I thought I saw you leave. We're about to cut the cake."

The new bride stops talking and glances back and forth between us.

"What's wrong? Are you arguing again?"

"No." Annika pastes on a smile. "Of course, not. We were just talking."

"She needs to know."

The color leaves Annika's face, and Nadia turns to me, all badass now. "What the fuck is going on?"

Carmine walks in behind her and cocks a brow.

I pass them the note as Annika curses and paces away to look out the window.

"Who is this from?" Nadia asks, but Annika doesn't turn back from the window.

"We don't know," I reply softly. "There are photos, as well."

"Let me see," Nadia demands.

"No," Annika says, shaking her head. "Let's just forget this and go back to the party. We're ruining your day."

"Someone is *threatening* you," Carmine says, his voice much gentler than the look in his eyes. "Let us have the information, and if we can't handle it today, we'll tuck it away and push it aside until tomorrow."

Annika turns to him, her bottom lip trembling.

I want to pull her into my arms and assure her that everything will be okay.

But I can't.

She wouldn't welcome it, and I don't know that everything *will* be okay. I can't lie to her.

"Photos." She passes them to Nadia. "Do *not* show those to Carmine."

Nadia frowns, looks at the images, and then gasps. "*Annika.*"

"What are you guys doing in here?" Ivie asks as she and Shane walk in.

"Close and lock that door," I say to Shane, who frowns but does as I ask.

I quickly fill them in on what we know, which isn't much, and Nadia shows Ivie the photos.

"Jesus, Annika," Ivie breathes. "What in the ever-loving hell is this?"

Annika shakes her head, fights tears, and I go to her and take her hand, giving it a firm squeeze as I smile down at her.

"We're your friends and your family. You're safe here, honey."

She takes a deep breath.

"I really wish we didn't have to have this conversation right now— or ever." She licks her lips. "For now, let's just say that Richard was a son of a bitch. And after we got married, he turned into someone I didn't know. He had certain...*preferences.* If I denied him, he punished me, but also if I *agreed*—so to speak. Obviously, someone took photos, and they're trying to make a buck or two off of it. No biggie. I can afford to pay them to go away."

"Fuck that."

"No way."

"Absolutely, not."

Annika stares at all of us as we fume around her.

541

"You pay them this time, and they'll just come back for more," I inform her. "Besides, it doesn't say they want money. It doesn't specify the demands. I assume they'll be in touch again."

"I'll handle it." Her chin comes up, and she squares her shoulders. "I. Will. Handle. It. Now, I want all of you to go back to the party. Me, too, actually. I need a stiff drink."

"We're sticking close," I insist.

"Of course, you are. You're my people. Now, let's go have cake and champagne and get damn good and drunk in celebration."

We all exchange looks but nod and follow Annika back to the ballroom.

Carmine, Shane, and I hang back a bit as Ivie and Nadia flank Annika as they walk down the hall.

"We meet in the office at oh-nine-hundred," Carmine says. "All six of us. We'll figure this out."

"Copy that," I agree.

"Oh, my God, I'm hungover." Ivie walks into the office, makes a beeline for the coffee and donuts set up on the credenza, and sinks into a brown leather chair, her eyes closed. "Sugar will help."

"I feel great," Nadia says as she pours herself some coffee. "Must have been all that married sex we had all night long."

Carmine winks at his bride and takes a sip of his own coffee as Shane and Annika walk through the door.

"I found this one in the kitchen, sulking over a bowl of Cocoa Puffs."

She's still carrying the bowl.

"I'm not sulking."

"Well, you weren't smiling," Shane says and sits on the arm of Ivie's chair. "Hey, baby."

"Hey. I'm consuming all the sugar to help fight this hangover. I know better than to get drunk on champagne. It hurts."

"Drink lots of water today," Nadia advises her. "Okay, we're all here."

Carmine closes and locks the door. "I want to keep this between the six of us for a while. I don't think we need to involve the parents at this time."

"*You* don't have to be involved," Annika says. "Really, I can handle this."

"Can you?" Shane asks before I can. "Okay, what's your first move?"

"Nothing. I wait."

"Wrong," Shane replies. "We're going to question the staff. We're going to look at security disks. We're going to hunt these motherfuckers down and kill them."

"Can't I just sue them? Why do people have to die all the time?"

"Because they deserve it."

They deserve much more than just death.

And I'll be the one to hand it out.

"Nadia and Carmine are headed out on their honeymoon," Annika begins, but Nadia shakes her head.

"We're postponing, but only for a little while."

"No. No, Nadia. You deserve this break. Go on your honeymoon. I have these three looking out for me—whether I like it or not."

"Hey," Ivie says with a scowl, and I feel my lips twitch.

"Do you really think I'll just leave when this is going down?" Nadia demands. "Not a chance in hell. Besides, we'll get it wrapped up quickly, and I'll be lying on a tropical beach somewhere before I know it."

"I have a flight to catch this afternoon," Annika says, checking the time. "I'm headed back to Denver so I can get back to work."

"No."

She arches a brow at my one-word proclamation.

"Excuse me?"

"I didn't stutter. You're not taking a commercial flight."

She props her hands on her hips. "Yes, I am. I'm not like you. I don't always have to take a private jet."

"Someone is threatening you. That means you won't be on a commercial flight, Annika. When the time comes to go back to Denver, I'll fly you."

"The time is *today*," she stresses. "To. Day."

"God, you're stubborn." I push my hand through my hair and shake my head. "I'm not trying to control you or be an asshole here. I'm going to keep you safe, whether you like it or not."

"You're a caveman," she retorts.

Carmine smirks.

Shane coughs into his hand.

"Me, caveman." I thump my chest. "Me save you."

Annika just rolls her eyes.

"Ivie and I will get started on the security disks," Shane says and then smiles down at Ivie. "As soon as her head feels better."

"I need another donut." Before she can stand and retrieve it, Shane fetches it for her. "Thank you. I'll be good in a few minutes."

"I have a call in to the catering company to ask about the waiter who delivered the envelope," Carmine adds. "We'll get to the bottom of this."

"And what do I do in the meantime? Just sit around and wait?"

"You have your computer with you," Ivie points out. "You can get caught up on charting, make calls to patients, that sort of thing."

Annika blows out a breath. "Fine. I'll be in my room, working."

She stomps away, and I want to run after her. My room is next to hers, and I heard her crying all night.

It's a personal torture, knowing that she hurts, but I know she wouldn't welcome my comfort.

"If I'm going to hack into stuff, I need more coffee," Ivie says.

"No one said you had to hack anything," Shane says with a laugh. "We *own* the security footage."

"Well, where's the fun in that?"

I blink at her, then look at Nadia. "What am I missing?"

"Ivie's killer with a computer," Shane says proudly. "She can hack into anything."

"Well, that'll come in handy." I grin and grab three donuts and a full cup of coffee, then head for the door. "I'll be in *my* room, making calls and keeping an eye on Annika. Just let me know if you find anything. I'll do the same."

The others nod as I stride out of the office and head up the stairs to the bedrooms.

I know my grandmother's old home like the back of my hand. My brothers and I practically grew up here. Since she died, it feels like we've spent even more time here.

That would make Gram happy.

I stop by Annika's door and press my ear against the wood.

The water's running.

She's in the shower.

I walk into my space and shove a donut into my mouth while I boot up my computer.

CHAPTER

TWO

~ANNIKA~

No matter how much I try or how long I stand under the hot water, it won't wash away the filth I've seen or done. It won't make me feel clean.

I turn off the taps and reach for a towel, wrap my hair, and then grab another for my body.

I'm actually relieved that I don't have to go sit on a plane today. I don't have to keep my shit together. I can hide away in this pretty room.

Once I'm dry, I pull a fluffy robe around me and get into bed, pulling the covers over my head.

And feel the tears come.

I thought that with Richard gone, I'd be able to forget about all of the horrible things he did and made *me* do and move on with my life.

But he just keeps hurting me, even from the grave.

"A?"

I sigh at Nadia's knock, then fling the covers back and walk to the door. I unlock it and crack it open.

"Yeah?"

"Can I come in? I brought provisions."

"I'm coming!" Ivie hurries down the hallway, out of breath. "I have the coffee."

"Come on in." I turn away and lie on the bed once more, but don't cover my face with the blankets. "I'm not really in the mood for a party, though. And I feel *awful* about this, Nadia. You're supposed to be off on your honeymoon, having wild sex and relaxing. I didn't mean to fuck that up for you."

"I already told you," Nadia replies as she passes me a maple bar, "I'm still going, just a few days later than planned. This isn't your fault."

"Yes." I take a bite, but it just feels like cardboard in my mouth. "It is my fault."

"I personally think it's a waste of time to argue about fault," Ivie says and sits on the bench at the end of the bed, facing me. "I'm quite sure you didn't hire someone to blackmail you at Nadia's wedding."

I take another bite. "No. That would be dumb."

"Exactly." Nadia grins at me, but her blue eyes are full of worry. "Honey, let's not talk about the blackmail part because that's being handled. What I want to know is, what's in those photos? Tell me they're photoshopped and it's not you."

It would be so easy to deny it. To take that line and insist that it isn't me in the pictures.

But I don't like to lie. And I'm not good at it.

"I didn't find out until after we got married that Rich was into some really weird stuff. At least, weird to me. There are people in the lifestyle, consensually, who enjoy it. But, I'm not one of them."

"Are you telling me he *made* you do that? That's rape, Annika." Ivie scowls.

"I guess I had a choice. I could either agree to it, or he would punish me for days if I said no. Sometimes, the punishment was worse than just going along with him. I had no idea that I was being recorded."

I pace over to the windows and look out across the green, manicured grounds of the estate. The cleanup crew is here, disassembling the gorgeous wedding that took several months to plan.

"Someday, we're going to unpack all of this baggage that Dick brought into your life," Nadia says. "And the carry-on luggage that I carry because Alex had a hand in it."

"We all need therapy," Ivie adds and takes a sip of her coffee. "We're some fucked-up people."

"I think we're pretty great," I say, watching my best friends fuss over me. "We may be fucked-up in some ways, but we're awesome in plenty of others."

"Hell yes, we are," Nadia agrees. "Do you think it's smart to go back to Denver right now? We could all stay here for a little longer. It's safer. I don't like the thought of you being in that big house alone when these assholes are out there carrying a grudge."

"I'm selling the house," I announce. "It goes on the market next week. I don't want to live there. Too many memories."

I won't even get into the fact that one of the photos in that awful envelope was taken in my basement.

"I think that's a good idea," Ivie says. "It's a lot of house for one person anyway."

"I think I want a condo. Downtown. Something close to restaurants and shopping."

"Sounds perfect to me," Nadia says. "You know I love house hunting, so if you want help looking, I'm your girl."

"Count me in," Ivie agrees. "Okay, I have to go work my computer skills for my fiancé. He thinks I'm hot when I'm typing away at a keyboard. Maybe I'll wear something sexy, just to make things fun."

I laugh and reach for another donut. "Keep us posted. And maybe call a doctor because I'm pretty sure we're about to put ourselves into sugar shock with all of these donuts."

"We'll have a salad for lunch." Ivie winks and leaves the room, closing the door behind her.

"Nadia," I say when we're alone. "Are you sure I can't talk you into going on your honeymoon today as planned?"

"You're stuck with me," she says. "Someone is trying to hurt someone I love, A. What would you do?"

"The same thing," I admit. "I'd do the same damn thing."

"Exactly. So, stop worrying about me. We'll get it all figured out, bust some kneecaps, send someone swimming with the fishes, and be on our way."

I can't help the snort of laughter that escapes at that descriptive image. "You're such a mobster."

"Thanks." Nadia winks. "I have to warn you. If we can't resolve this soon, we're going to have to bring in my father."

I shake my head, but Nadia keeps talking.

"He'll be beyond pissed if we keep something big like this from him. I wanted to warn you because he'll want to see the photos."

"Jesus, Nadia, I don't want him to see that. I don't want *anyone* to see it." The tears start again. "It's so humiliating. Please, don't tell him."

"I won't. Yet. We might have this all resolved by tomorrow morning."

"I hope so."

Nadia pulls me in for a tight hug. "You're an amazing woman, A. You've been through hell and back, and yet you're thriving. I'm proud of you."

"Stop making me cry."

She laughs and kisses my cheek before pulling away. "Okay, no more being mushy. Take the day to rest. Nap. Work. Whatever. I'll keep you posted."

"Thanks."

"You have to get out of this bed."

I shift under the covers and crack an eye to find Ivie frowning down at me.

"Why?"

"Because it's been two days, and you've barely moved."

I know I'm being a coward. Weak. I should be facing this head-on, the way Ivie or Nadia would. But, damn it, I'm just so *tired*.

"Sleepy."

"Honey, you're starting to smell bad."

I crack that eye again and scowl at my best friend. "Thanks."

"Come on. Up. In the shower. I have dinner here for you, but you can't have it until you scrub up. And for the love of all that's holy, brush your teeth."

"You're really good for my ego, you know that? So much for being my best friend. I might replace you."

"Uh-huh. Right. Get in there."

She pulls me to my feet and pushes me toward the bathroom. "I'm going. God, you're bossy."

"You haven't seen anything yet, sister."

"Being in love has made you sassy, and I don't know if I like it."

"You love me. Now, go."

She closes the door behind me, and I take a second to stare at my reflection in the mirror.

She's right. This is ridiculous. And I look like hell.

So, I take my time in the shower, shave all the places I've neglected, and then brush my teeth.

When I open the bathroom door, she's set up a tray by the window, complete with a red rose in a bud vase.

"Are we on a date?" I ask her.

"Eating on a pretty table will make you feel better. It's a chicken Caeser salad with lemon on the side and a chocolate torte for dessert."

"My favorite." I sink into the chair, and my stomach growls loudly. "I'm hungry."

"I bet you are. You've hardly eaten anything since the donuts yesterday."

I take a big bite of salad and frown at Ivie. "Are you keeping track?"

"Hell, yes, I am. Someone has to. After dinner, we're having a meeting with the others."

That means I'll have to see Rafe.

And that makes me nervous under the best of circumstances. With things the way they currently are, it almost makes me lose my appetite.

"Eat."

"You know, the whole hovering and shoving food into my mouth thing isn't a good look for you."

"That's okay," she says smoothly. "You look better."

The salad is delicious. I can't stop shoveling it in.

"I'm feeling better." When the plate is empty, I shift to the chocolate and sigh in delight after the first bite. "Oh, God."

"I know, right? So good."

"You ate it, too?"

"Yes, we already had dinner. We invited you, but you didn't answer."

I sigh and lick the spoon. "I slept a lot. Sleep has always been my escape from bad things."

"I know."

"And it's time to wake up and face this." I sit back and sigh, contentedly full. "Okay, lead the way to the meeting."

Ivie raises a brow. "Are you going to wear that?"

I look down at the towel wrapped around me and laugh. "Uh, no. I guess I'd better put something on."

I grab leggings and a teal blue sweatshirt and throw my wet hair up in a messy bun. I'm no fashionista, but it's an improvement.

"Better?"

"Much. Okay, let's go."

We walk downstairs together. Everyone else is already waiting in the family room off the kitchen, dressed in casual clothes and laughing at something Carmine said.

"There she is," Nadia says with a smile. "How are you doing, sugar?"

"Better. I'm done sleeping, I think. Now it's time to kick ass."

"Good girl," Rafe murmurs as he sidles up next to me and takes my hand.

I want to pull it away.

Not because I don't want him touching me. Exactly the opposite. It feels too damn good, and I don't want to get into the habit of feeling him close.

But I'm too weak to pull back right now.

So, I give his hand a squeeze and smile at the others.

"Okay, friends, what do we know?"

"The kid who brought you the envelope was hired by the catering company to be a server. We talked to him, and he said that someone passed it to him. He can't remember who because it was busy at that time." Shane leans forward and takes Ivie's hand. "We do have footage of a car coming and going, but when Ivie ran the plates, she found it's a rental."

"So, I did some hacking," Ivie picks up. "Of course, the name of the person who rented it is John Doe."

"Seriously?" I take my hand from Rafe's, immediately feeling the

551

loss, and prop my hands on my hips. "The rental company allowed someone named *John Doe* to take their car?"

"They probably did everything online," Rafe points out. "Didn't even have to see a live person to pick it up."

"Technology doesn't always help," I mutter. "Were you able to figure out who John Doe is?"

"No." Ivie bites her lip. "Sorry, it was a dead end."

"So, we're back to square one."

"Not square one," Carmine says. "We're aware of what's happening, and we can be on the offensive. They're going to try to reach out to you again. It's just a matter of when and where."

"I'm not going to simply sit here and wait." Rafe starts to interrupt, but I shake my head. "This is ridiculous. Maybe they just wanted to scare me. Who knows? I have a life to get back to. Patients. A clinic to run. So, I'm going back to my life, and all of you should, too. While keeping an ear to the ground, of course."

"She's right," Shane says before anyone can object, surprising everyone in the room, including me. "We don't know when or if they'll contact her again. I believe they will. I think it'll be sooner than later, but not as long as she's in this fortress, and we're all on the lookout."

"See? I'm right."

"She should go back to Denver. Back to her life. We'll go with her and strategically protect her."

"Wait. That's not what I meant."

Shane shakes his head. "You need to get back to *normal*, so to speak, to make them think that you're not worried about what they'll do. But you know as well as everyone else in this room that we won't just drop you off and wish you well, Annika."

"Hell, no," Rafe agrees. "We all go."

"This is really annoying." I rub my forehead in frustration. "The most annoying part is that you're probably right."

And I don't want to admit that it makes me feel better, safer, to know that they'll all be close by. The thought of going back on my own is terrifying.

"Can we go tomorrow?" I ask.

"The plane will be ready anytime you are," Rafe assures me.

"Looks like we're going to Denver," Nadia says. "I like it there."

"Ivie and I are going to the ranch for a couple of days to check in with Curt and make sure everything is good there," Shane says. "But we can be back in Denver within an hour if something goes wrong."

"I'll be back at work with you by Monday," Ivie assures me. "Thanks for all the time off."

"You've more than earned it." It's the absolute truth. Ivie hasn't taken a vacation from being my office manager since we opened the Medi-spa's doors two years ago. "I'll check in with Deidre when we get there to make sure the office is ready to reopen next week."

"I already did," Ivie says. "She assured me that everything is good to go."

I nod and suddenly feel eighty years old. The past year has aged me. I'm exhausted.

But I'm not going to lose this fight. Someone is dicking with me, and I'm so over being the pawn in other people's games.

We're going to finish this.

And then I'm going to start rebuilding my life and live it exactly as I want.

With no excuses or apologies.

CHAPTER
THREE
~RAFE~

"Okay, so Nadia and Carmine are just a mile away," I say as I help Annika into her house with her bags. It's late in the evening. Annika wanted to come earlier in the day, but Carmine had some things to see to, and one thing led to another, so we didn't leave the city until well after dinner.

But we made it.

I follow her to her bedroom and set the suitcases on the bed so she can easily unpack them. "You're not in the master?"

"Hell, no." Her grin doesn't reach her eyes. "I'll never set foot in that room again. I'd rather not be *here*, but it's not for much longer."

She doesn't meet my gaze as she unzips one bag and starts emptying dirty laundry into a basket.

"How can I help?" Jesus, I want to touch her. I want to pull her to me and kiss the fuck out of her like I used to. It used to be that I didn't have to ask to be near her. We were like magnets; we couldn't keep our hands off of each other.

I used to know every little detail about her.

And now, she might as well be a stranger.

It makes me fucking crazy.

"Rafe, you've gone above and beyond," she says with a small sigh. "I'll set the alarm after you leave. Everything should be just fine here."

I scowl and can't hold back from reaching for her. I take her hand in mine, and she looks up in surprise.

"I'm not leaving."

"Of course, you're leaving."

"Annika, I'm here to protect you. I can't do that from some hotel room."

"Listen, Rafe, I appreciate that you want to help, but—"

"Is that what you think this is? That I'm just here to *help* like I'm some fucking Boy Scout, A?"

"You're my friend."

I push a hand through my hair and have to clench my jaw so I don't yell that I'm here because I'm in love with her.

I've been in love with her for almost a decade, goddamn it.

"Yeah. I'm your friend." I can't help that the word *friend* sounds like a dirty word. "I'm not leaving."

"Well, you know what they say? You don't have to go home, but you can't stay here."

I narrow my eyes at her, and she just cocks a hip and sets her hand on it, nothing but stubbornness and sass.

God, I want to kiss her so badly, I ache with it.

But now is not the time. I don't know when it'll *be* the time.

"Fine."

I turn and walk out of the room, down the stairs, and out the front door. I don't stop until I get to my rental car, slamming the door behind me before settling in for a long damn night in the cramped space.

Because I'm not leaving, no matter what she fucking says.

What I said the other day is completely true. I want to eat her with a damn spoon and spank her, all at the same time. She's infuriating. She always was, but now that I can't touch her, *be* with her, it's even more so.

Damn woman.

I've just reclined the seat and found an easy-listening station on the radio when Annika opens her front door, frowns and me, and comes stomping to the car.

I roll down the window.

"Problem?" I ask.

"What are you doing?"

"Listening to the radio. Keeping an eye out. You know, the usual."

She shakes her head and blinks furiously, the way she does when she's frustrated.

"Why are you out here in the car like a stalker?"

"Not a stalker. I'm on a stakeout. Since you won't let me stay in *there*,"—I gesture to the house—"I'm going to be out here instead. It's not the best of circumstances, but I have heat, and I can always order a pizza or something."

"You'll order a pizza." She laughs and shakes her head. "And what? Tell them to deliver it to the car in my driveway?"

"Sure. Is that weird?"

"Yeah, Rafe, it's weird. Just go to the hotel. I'll talk to you tomorrow."

"Like you said, I don't have to go home, but I can't stay here. Well, I'm not in there. And if you don't want me in your driveway, I can park at the curb."

She watches me for several seconds—to see if I'm bluffing, I'm sure. I'm not.

"Fine. Have it your way. Stay in the car in the driveway, Rafe. You'll last one night, and then you'll be at the hotel tomorrow night."

"Don't bet on it, sweetheart."

"Why are you so stubborn?"

"Hi, pot, I'm kettle."

She growls in frustration and marches back to the house, glaring at me over her shoulder before slamming the door shut.

I hoped she'd cave and let me back inside. Hell, I'd settle for the couch at this point.

But that's not my Annika. No, the woman has more backbone, more stubbornness in her little finger than most people have in their whole bodies.

It's one of the reasons why I love her to distraction.

A pizza doesn't sound half bad, so I make a call and entertain myself as I wait by checking in with my contacts to see if there's been any additional chatter about the current situation with Annika.

There hasn't been.

The pizza kid parks behind me, and I get out to intercept the pizza.

"Uh, hi," he says and swallows hard. "That's thirty-seven-fifty."

I pass him a fifty. "Keep the change."

"Solid. Thanks." He flashes a smile. "Are you surprising someone with pizza or something?"

"Something like that," I agree and nod when he turns to leave. Once he's gone, I take one of the two boxes, set it on the porch in front of the door, and then return to my car and open my box.

I type out a quick text to Annika.

Me: *Dinner's on the porch. Better fetch it before it goes cold.*

There's no reply, but then, I don't expect one. I'm halfway into my second slice when the door opens, and Annika stares down at the pizza box. She glances up at me, picks up the box, and takes it inside.

Pepperoni with olives is her favorite. She'll be out in no time, telling me to come inside and eat with her. There's no way she'll leave me out here all night. She may be stubborn, but she has a soft side.

And I can usually get there through her stomach.

But I finish off all but two pieces of my pie, and still no Annika.

Two hours later, when there's nothing left for me to do but sit and watch the neighborhood, she *still* hasn't said a word.

"She's seriously going to leave me out here." I shake my head and can't help but laugh. "Is it any wonder I want to spend the rest of my life with her?"

Bam! Bam! Bam!

I startle and open my eyes. Shit, I fell asleep.

"Good morning," I mutter as I roll down the window. "What time is it?"

"Six," she replies, but her mouth softens into a smile. "You really stayed out here."

"Of course." I wipe my mouth, conscious of the stubble on my face. "Last time I looked at the time, it was four-thirty. So, I wasn't out long."

"Come on, tough guy. I'll make you some coffee."

"And pancakes?"

She shakes her head, but she's laughing. "Sure, I'll make pancakes. I also have leftover pizza."

"Me, too." I grab a few things from the car. When we turn to walk back into the house, I scowl. "What the fuck is that?"

"What?" She looks up and then gasps. "Oh, God. I didn't see it when I came outside. But I was looking at you."

"Motherfucker," I growl and stomp up the steps but don't take the envelope off the door yet. I take my phone from my pocket and call Carmine. "We have another envelope. Haven't opened it yet."

"Jesus, it's six in the goddamn morning. Give us thirty and we'll be there."

He ends the call.

"I need gloves."

"Be right back," Annika says and slips through the door, avoiding the envelope like it's a snake that might strike out and bite her, then hurries back to me with a gardening glove.

"You don't have any latex gloves?" I ask, scowling at the glove in my hand.

"No, I'm out."

"This won't fit me."

"Oh. Right. You have big hands. I can get a baggie or something."

I pass the glove back to her. "It's okay. You put it on and grab the envelope."

"No."

She firms her lips and shakes her head.

"It can't hurt you."

She stares at me for a long moment. "I'm quite sure that whatever's in there will hurt me."

I blow out a breath and use the glove to take the envelope off the door, careful not to add prints to it. We'll have Shane run it later, along with whatever's inside.

He ran the last ones, but the evidence was contaminated with too many other fingerprints to find anything useful.

We move inside, close the door, and I lay the letter on the dining room table. I text Carmine and ask him to bring gloves.

"I can't believe I didn't see that when I opened the door," Annika mutters. She walks into the kitchen and gets to work making coffee. "I guess I was too focused on you."

The last words are a whisper, but I heard them.

"A—"

"I always was," she continues as if she has to fill the silence with words. "I couldn't see anything *but* you for years. Is it weird that it was the best time of my life?"

"No." I swallow and fist my hands because they itch to hold her. "It's not weird."

"It's silly," she says and then blushes a bit. "I shouldn't have said that."

"Hey, we're friends. We used to be much more than that. And you can trust me. You can say *anything* to me."

"No." She turns to me, her big, blue eyes full of tears. "I can't. I can't, Rafe."

"Sweetheart—"

"Hello?" Nadia calls out from the front door. "Where are you guys?"

"Kitchen," Annika calls back but hasn't taken her gaze away from mine. "Let's just deal with this, okay?"

"Yeah. Okay."

"I'm making coffee," Annika announces to Nadia and Carmine. "There's cream and sugar and anything else you could want around the kitchen here."

"Excellent," Nadia says as she leads Carmine into the room. Her short hair is still a little disheveled, and her face is clean of makeup, her eyes sleepy. "We came right over, but I did insist that we make a quick stop at the donut place down the street."

"God bless you," I reply and reach into the pink box for a cinnamon twist. "I think, given the turn of events, my homemade pancakes are off the table for today."

"You'll live," Annika says and sets a mug of steaming coffee in front of me.

"When and where was the package left?" Nadia asks.

"It was taped to the front door." I sigh in frustration. "I fell asleep for ninety fucking minutes, and they slipped past me. Jesus."

"Not your fault," Carmine says. "And, this is a new clue."

"I have cameras," Annika announces, surprising me.

"What?"

"I had them installed after Ivie was taken," she explains as if she's discussing new gutters or rosebushes. "There's probably something on them."

"I know we're all sleepy," Nadia says as she chomps on a maple bar, "but you should have started with that information."

"I'm tired, and I'm frustrated, and it just occurred to me." Annika shrugs and drinks her black coffee. "Should we call Shane and Ivie?"

"Already did," Carmine says. "They'll be here in about an hour. Less now."

"We'll wait, then," Annika says. "I'm not exactly in a hurry to open that envelope, and I assume Shane will want to look for fingerprints."

"That's ideal," I reply, watching her. She's fidgety. Nervous. "Honey, what are you afraid of finding in there?"

"What? Oh, I couldn't tell you."

What in the bloody hell did that piece of shit make her do? I want to ask. I want her to feel comfortable enough with me to tell me everything so I can help her. So I can make the bad memories go away and replace them with new, happy ones.

But she won't open up to me.

And it's making me damn crazy.

We've made our way through a second round of coffee when Ivie throws open the door and comes running inside, straight for Annika.

"Are you okay? What did they leave? Oh, God, I'm so sorry that I was so far away."

"Hey, it's okay." Annika hugs Ivie and pats her back in reassurance. "I'm fine. It's been really boring, actually."

"We didn't open it yet," I inform Shane. "Thought you'd like to check it out first."

"Thanks," he says with a nod and points to the envelope at the other end of the table. "That it?"

"Yeah."

My brother sets a case on the table next to it and starts fiddling with dust and brushes.

"No prints," he announces.

"Well, damn." I sigh and drain my mug, then look at Annika. "Looks like you're up, honey."

She wrinkles her nose. "I was hoping to stall a little longer."

"Let's get it over with. Then we'll know what we're dealing with," Nadia suggests. "Ivie and I are right here. We're *all* here. You're safe."

Annika nods and walks to the end of the table. She takes the envelope from Shane and breaks the seal.

"I used to love getting mail," she says conversationally. "I would wait every day for the mail carrier and hope there would be something for me. Anything at all. Even junk mail. I know it's silly, but I always looked forward to it.

"And then this happens. Now, I'll never want to check my mailbox again."

"Open it," I say, my voice calm and soft. "Let's see what we've got, then we'll look at the security video."

She nods and pulls a stack of sheets out of the large envelope. We all sit facing her so we can't see what she's looking at.

Her blue eyes shift from guarded curiosity to embarrassment to confusion. And then, just when I'm about to rush to her and take everything out of her hands so I can see, those eyes turn fierce and angry.

And I know, without a shadow of a doubt, that the game has changed for her.

She's pissed.

CHAPTER

FOUR

~ANNIKA~

With all five of them staring at me, I rip open the envelope and pull out the contents. Just like last time, there's a note on top.

Now that we have your attention, let's talk terms. We don't want money. That's too...cliché. No, Annika, we want you. Based on what we've seen you do and know you're capable of, what your tastes are, this shouldn't be a problem.

We'll be in touch very soon.

Jesus. I swallow hard and steel myself to flip to the photos.

The first is like the others. I'm tied up on a bed covered with satin sheets. I'm naked. No one else is in the photo.

I flip to another and have to bite the inside of my cheek so I don't gasp in terror. My God, how is it possible that someone took *photos* of this? Of what those men did to me?

I hurry to the next.

There's a yellow sticky note on the last one.

In case you plan to deny us, perhaps you should consider that we know what you did. What you were involved in. Drug distribution is a federal crime.

562

It's a photo of me walking out of my clinic with my briefcase, simply leaving work.

But they're implying that I knew that Richard was a drug dealer, and they're threatening to call the cops.

Fuck. That.

"What is it?" Nadia asks.

"More of the same." I sigh and stuff it all back into the envelope. "But they're more specific about what they want now."

"How much?" Carmine asks. My gaze meets his, and I shake my head.

"They don't want money."

"What in the hell *do* they want?" Rafe demands.

"Me." I toss the envelope onto the table and try to control the shaking in my hands. "Also, they're implying that I knew about Rich's drug distribution, and state that if I don't give them what they want, they'll turn me in."

"Blackmail *and* extorsion," Ivie says. "They're a bunch of over-achievers."

I grin at her. It's either that or throw something. "Clearly, they won't get *me.*"

"What, exactly," Rafe says, rage coming from him in waves, "do you mean by they want *you?*"

I lick my lips. "Sexually."

"Motherfucker son of a bitch," he growls and starts prowling my dining room. "I'm going to fucking kill them. Every one of them. Slowly."

"Let's look at your security footage," Shane suggests.

"Good idea." I walk past Rafe but stop to lay my hand on his shoulder. "It's going to be okay, you know."

"As soon as I kill the son of a bitch who's doing *that*,"—he points to the table—"yeah, it'll be fine."

I pat his shoulder, try not to acknowledge the bulging muscles under his shirt, and go to fetch my laptop.

Ivie holds her hand up for it and grins at Shane.

"I got this, babe." She opens the computer, taps the keyboard, finds my software, and narrows her eyes. "Okay, so this would have been dropped off between four-thirty and six. Let's see what we've got."

She blows out a raspberry. Shane looks over her shoulder. The rest of us just stare at her, waiting with bated breath.

"Got him." She taps a key, and we all crowd in behind Ivie to see what she found. "Look, right here at five-fifteen."

"He's in a hoodie and a mask," Nadia says.

"And stays close to the wall," Carmine adds. "We can't see enough of him to figure out who the fuck he is."

"I agree," Ivie says with a nod. "But he messed up. He runs back to his car and drives in front of the house. I can blow this up and pull the plate."

"What if it's John Doe again?" I ask.

"I have a good feeling about this one. Give me a little room and a smidge of time."

"That's code for stop crowding her," I say as we back away. "I need more coffee."

"I'll take another donut," Nadia adds and joins me in the kitchen. "Talk to me. We're alone."

"What do you want me to say?"

"Tell me how you feel, sugar." She takes my shoulders in her hands and gives me *the look*. The one she always uses when she thinks I'm not telling her everything.

"I'm pissed." I sigh and push my hand through my hair. "I'm just so *mad*, Nadia. Who the fuck is doing this, and who do they think they are, thinking they can treat me like this? I didn't do anything to anyone. I just want to live my boring life in suburbia. Mind my own business. But that just can't seem to happen, and it's driving me *crazy*."

"Well, I'm glad you're past feeling sorry for yourself and landed squarely in being angry. It's a nice change."

I narrow my eyes at her, but she just grins.

"Okay, I've got something," Ivie calls out. "The plates aren't linked to a John Doe but rather a Larry MacDonald. We have a place to start digging."

"Thank God. What do we do now?"

"We're going to the office," Shane says. "We have better equipment there. I'll do a deep-dive on this MacDonald asshole. If we're lucky, we can pay him a visit later today."

"I'll come with you," I reply.

"No." Rafe shakes his head. "We don't know who we're dealing with, and you haven't trained for this, A."

"So I just sit here and let you all do my dirty work?"

"Yes." Nadia kisses my cheek. "You're too pretty to kill people, A."

I roll my eyes and watch as they all gather their things and go, leaving Rafe and I behind.

"Aren't you going with them?"

"No." He shifts his feet. "I'm staying here with you."

"I don't need a babysitter, Rafe."

"Didn't say you did. But you need a friend."

I sigh. "Is that what you are? My friend?"

"Absolutely." He smiles that charming smile I can never say no to.

"Fine, you can stay. I have some work to do, so I'll be in my office if you need me."

"Where can I set up shop?" he asks. "Here in the dining room?"

"It's not very comfortable." I frown, taking in the formal table and stiff, high-backed chairs. "There's a desk in the guest room. It'll be more comfortable. Come on, I'll show you."

He lifts his bag off the floor and follows me up the stairs. I can feel his eyes on my ass. He always did have a thing for my behind.

"It's just a butt, Rafe."

"A grade-A one," he agrees, his voice filled with a grin.

God, I missed flirting with him.

The guest room is on the second door on the left. I open it and usher him inside.

"You can use anything you need. But really, Rafe, wouldn't you be more comfortable at the hotel?"

"Are you kidding me? You think a hotel is better than this? No." He grins and sets his bag on the bed. "Thanks for the loan. Do you mind if I borrow the shower in this attached bathroom?"

Rafe is going to be naked. In my house.

Lord have mercy.

"Of course, not."

His blue eyes sparkle as he winks at me. "Thanks."

"Okay. I have some charting to catch up on, and I need to review cases for next week. If you need anything, I'm just downstairs. Oh, and you can't stay here tonight."

"Annika."

"Nope. No way." I shake my head and turn to leave the room.

Rafe Martinelli will *not* be sleeping under my roof. No way, no how.

He's in his car again.

I pace my bedroom, sipping wine. He's just so damn stubborn, that's what it is. He thinks he has to *protect* me. But Shane and Ivie are *this* close to figuring out where all of this is coming from, and then it'll be over. Probably by tomorrow.

He doesn't have to stay.

Okay, so it feels kind of good knowing that he's right there, in the *very* slim chance that something was to happen.

"You can't let him sleep outside again." I walk through the house, set the wine on the table by the front door, tighten the belt on my robe, and walk outside.

Rafe watches as I approach his car. He rolls down the window.

"Problem?" he asks.

"Yes. You're in my driveway. I know, I can't talk you into going to the hotel. Come on. You can crash in the guest room."

"I'm fine out here, if you'd rather."

"Clearly, I don't rather." I open the door and wait while he closes everything down and snags his bag. "I can't leave you out here for another night. No matter how crazy you make me, I feel bad."

"I make you crazy?" He flashes a smile, and I have to turn away and walk to the house before I do something stupid like kiss him silly. "Tell me more about that."

"No." I hold the door for him and then close and lock it. "Want some wine?"

"Nah, I'm good."

I nod and walk into the kitchen to refill my glass, then gesture for

Rafe to join me in the family room. This is one of my favorite spaces. It's cozy with deep-cushioned couches, colorful pillows and throws, and a TV.

I sit, toss a blanket over my lap, and sip while Rafe kicks off his shoes and curls up in the couch across from me.

I'm already feeling the effects of the wine. Just a little. And that's good because I could use a little buzz tonight.

It's been a hell of a week.

"So, what's new?" I ask and get the laugh I expected. His laugh always made my stomach clench.

Nothing has changed in that department. God, he's a sight to behold. "What is it about men getting better-looking as they age?"

He tilts his head. "Did you just call me old?"

I snort and take another sip. "No. I said you're getting better-looking as you get older. There's a difference."

"I miss you," he says and rubs his hand over his face. "Do you know how hard it is to sit over here, see that you're struggling, and not hold you?"

I don't know what to say to that, so I sip my wine. The small buzz has progressed into a pleasant, bigger buzz now.

"You're a good person," I reply.

"Fuck that." He shakes his head and braces his elbows on his knees, leaning forward. "I'm not a good person, A. I've done some shitty things in this life."

"Me, too." I stare down into my glass and think about what he said earlier about being my friend. Maybe I need to talk about this. And it's not like I can be with him for the long haul, so who better to talk to? "The pictures they sent... The things that Richard made me do. It was pretty bad."

I take another drink for courage and watch as Rafe sits back again, his eyes pinned to mine, listening.

"We dated for *years* before we got married. I thought I knew him inside and out. He was smart and funny and gentle. Kind of boring, truth be told, but I was okay with boring. You know that."

He just watches, so I keep talking.

"Then we got married, and it all changed. Not overnight, either. It changed that *day*. Suddenly, the man I thought I knew was gone, replaced by this cold, mean man that I didn't recognize at all. He liked to punish me. Got off on it, I think. And he liked some weird sexual shit, Rafe. He liked to watch. And other...things. If I said no, he got angry. Furious. It wasn't just the run-of-the-mill silent treatment or yelling and then getting over it.

"No, he'd rant and rave. Lecture. Take my car away. One night, he locked me out of the house."

"He locked you out of your own house?"

"It wasn't mine. My name wasn't on it. It's only mine now because he died and left it to me. He was a horrible person. So, I learned that it was just easier to go along with what he wanted. At first, he only wanted other people to watch. That was awful. But then, it just...got worse. I'm not going to go into the details because they're embarrassing and awful. But I did those things, Rafe. Even if it made me sick. Even if I didn't want to. I still did them."

"You were terrorized," he says, his blue eyes shooting flames of anger. "Enslaved. Abused doesn't even start to cover it. Christ, A, if I'd known—"

"It's over now." I shift in my seat and frown at my empty glass. "My lips are numb. I should probably stop drinking now."

"You should go to bed."

"Yeah." I blink at him. "You're so handsome. And I'm still just as drawn to you as I was when I was nineteen. Too bad it didn't work out. Well, I'm going to bed. Make yourself at home."

I wave and wander up the stairs to my room, take the robe off, and climb into bed.

I'm just *so tired*.

But then the dreams come.

"You're going to lie on that bed and let me do whatever I want to you, Annika."

I scowl and try to keep the tears at bay. "Richard, this makes me uncomfortable."

"I don't fucking care. You're mine. That means you'll do what I say, when I say. Now, get on the bed with your ass in the air like I told you to."

I let the tears fall, but I know they won't matter. Richard never cares what I say or do, as long as he can use me the way he wants. He's awful. He's evil.

People are watching, but I close my eyes and block it out. I'm at the beach, in a chair, with the sun shining on my face.

For just a moment, I almost believe it.

But then something hits me over the butt, hard. *I cry out, but it keeps happening, over and over, making my skin sting and more tears come to my eyes.*

God, is it over yet?

But, no. No, it's not.

They take turns. Some fuck me. Others laugh. Touch. I'm nothing but a thing to them. I'm nothing.

"He'll never want you now," Richard hisses in my ear. "You're damaged goods, and Rafe will never look at you with anything but disgust. You're a slut. A whore."

"No." I clench my fists and cry out again. "No, please. Just stop. I'll be good. Just stop."

"Hey, baby. Hey. You're okay."

He pulls me to him, and I want to cling to him. To tell Rafe how much I love him. To thank him for making me feel safe.

But the words won't come, and the dreams won't stop.

CHAPTER
FIVE
~RAFE~

The screaming woke me. The whimpers tore at my heart. No man wants to hear the love of his life cry out in terror.

And now, holding her hand in the dark, I'm torn between needing to comfort her and wanting to kill someone.

I've never felt the need to murder the way I do on Annika's behalf. I'm the least violent of the three of us brothers. But she's hurting, and someone needs to pay.

The worst part is, I have a feeling that the person responsible for the anguish is already dead.

I should go back to my own bed now that she seems to be settled down, but she's so damn tempting.

Just leave her be, Martinelli.

I turn to leave, but she whimpers again, and I make the executive decision to stay. I slip between the covers and spoon her, pulling her against me as a million memories flood my mind.

I spent *years* sleeping with her just like this. Years. It's as familiar as breathing. Sometimes, we wouldn't sleep at all. We'd lie in the dark and talk and laugh. Other times, we'd make love all night long.

I miss all of it. Every minute of it. The fact that I can't be with her because of who our families are makes me rage like nothing else ever has.

"Damaged goods," she says, talking in her sleep.

"Shh." I smooth her hair away from her face and kiss her cheek. "It's okay."

"Rafe won't want me."

I blink, surprised. What the hell kind of dream is this? In what alternate universe would I ever *not* want her?

"Not good enough."

"Hey, babe. Hey." I kiss her again and brush my fingers down her cheek. She wiggles onto her back, her eyes flutter open, and she offers me a half-smile. "You're safe, Annika."

"Safe." She sighs, burrows into my shoulder, and seems to calm down.

Does she think she's not good enough for me? That *anything* she may have done in her past would make me want her any less? That I could ever fall out of love with her? For Christ's sake, I've loved her all of my adult life.

If that's the case, we need to have a serious conversation because it couldn't be further from the truth.

I've tried to tell her for years that I want her. Even when she was married to that no-good piece of trash. And I'm not proud of that. Being married is a commitment that I believe in. I don't poach on someone else's territory.

But she doesn't belong to him anymore. She never really did, given she didn't know who she was marrying.

She's *mine.*

And I'm going to do everything I can to remind her of that.

"Don't go," she whispers.

"Wild horses couldn't drag me away, sweetheart."

She falls back to sleep, more peacefully now, and I kiss her forehead and then let sleep settle around me, too. I'm exhausted.

It feels like I just closed my eyes when the house alarms start blaring shrilly through the house.

"Rafe!" Annika yells, already leaping from the bed. "Rafe!"

"I'm right here," I reply as I climb out of the other side of the bed.

She whirls around and frowns. "What are you doing *in my bed*?"

"Seriously?" I shake my head. The alarm continues going crazy. "Now isn't the time for this conversation. Do you have a weapon?"

"I have a baseball bat."

I swear under my breath. "We have some work to do. Stay here. Lock the door. I'm going to take care of this."

"Be careful," she hisses before I shut the door behind me. I don't have shoes or a shirt. No weapon on me.

Because I'm an idiot.

Or a man in love, and Annika needed me.

Either way, it's no excuse.

I rush down the hall to the guest room, and when I see that no one's in there, I grab my pistol and shove my feet into my shoes.

Then, I make my way downstairs.

If it's a random robbery, they should have been scared off by the alarm and long gone by now. If it's a mistake in the system, we can fix that.

But if it's tied to the other shit happening, someone might be inside the house.

They won't leave alive.

Suddenly, the alarm quiets, leaving me in deafening silence. I can hear Annika talking, probably to the security company.

I hear shuffling coming from Richard's old office.

"Motherfucker," I whisper and quietly make my way down the hall, peeking around the doorjamb.

I move fast, and with one strike, I have the asshole on the floor. He lashes out, a taser in his hand, but he's no match for my strength. I turn the taser on him, and while his body convulses from the jolt, I haul him into a nearby chair and press my nose to his.

"I'm going to end you, asshole."

"Rafe?"

"Shit." I don't know if anyone else is in the house.

"Do we need the police?"

"No."

Annika tells the operator that everything is fine and hangs up.

"Get in here," I command and clench my jaw when her eyes widen at the sight of the man in the chair. "I need rope."

"Uh, will my robe sash do?"

"Sure." She passes it to me, and I get the jerk's hands tied behind his back just as he starts to come to. "I'm calling Carmine and Shane. Close and lock that door. I don't know if anyone else is here, and I won't leave you."

She does as I ask as I call my brothers.

"I could sue you," the jerk in the chair says. I punch him in the face.

"I suggest you shut the fuck up."

"Sue me?" Annika demands. "*Sue* me? For what? I didn't invite you here. You're trespassing, you moron. Just what the fuck do you think you're going to sue me for?"

He doesn't answer, just keeps his face lowered toward the floor.

"Carmine and Shane will scout the outside and clear the rest of the house. They're on their way."

"It's four in the morning," she says with a frown.

"Yeah, and we have an intruder."

Annika flips on some lights and sits on the leather couch, clenching her robe around her. Less than ten minutes later, there's a knock.

"All clear," Shane calls out. I hurry over and open the door to find Shane, Ivie, Carmine, and Nadia all standing on the other side.

"It's a party," I say dryly. "And this guy crashed it."

Nadia walks over to him, takes his chin in her fingers, and raises his face to hers. "Hello there, fucker. How does it feel to know you're about to die?"

"Fuck you, bitch."

"Now, see, I don't like that word." Nadia purses her lips in a pout and then backhands him with the butt of her weapon.

"That's MacDonald," Ivie says, narrowing her eyes. "This is the idiot who left the envelope yesterday."

"Back for more?" I ask him, but Annika approaches and looks into MacDonald's face.

"You were the waiter," she says, shaking her head. "*You* were the waiter at the wedding who gave me the first envelope."

He doesn't reply. He doesn't flinch. Gives no reaction at all.

I glance at Carmine and then Shane. This isn't the first time someone infiltrated a wedding. I'm getting damn sick and tired of it.

"Who do you work for?" Annika asks.

Again, no reaction.

"Here, step back, babe." Annika does as I ask, and I plant the business end of my fist in the asshole's nose.

Blood gushes everywhere. He hisses a breath through his teeth.

"I'm about to start pulling off your fingernails," Shane says calmly as he pulls a pair of plyers out of his bag. "So, I suggest you start talking."

"Bullshit," MacDonald sneers.

Carmine unties him, holds one arm, and I take the other as Shane steps forward and plucks a nail right off his thumb.

"Son of a bitch!" MacDonald screams. "You're fucking crazy!"

"No...angry," I reply. "There's so much more that can be done to you before we let you die. You have no idea. You're going to want to talk."

"Who do you work for?" Annika asks again.

"I can't tell you that," MacDonald says, so Shane takes another nail. "I can't! If I do, they'll hurt my family."

"*We'll* hurt your family if you don't," Carmine replies. "Kind of a rock and a hard place, isn't it? If you rat them out, people get hurt. If you don't, people still get hurt. Either way, you're dead. Thing is, we're the ones dishing out the pain right now."

Shane takes another nail.

"The McCarthys," he wails.

I step back and shake my head. "The crime family in Boston?"

"Irish mafia," Carmine mutters.

"I'm just an errand-runner. I don't ask questions, and they don't tell me dick."

"Not a good place to be in, MacDonald," Nadia says. "Why Annika?"

"Like I said—" This time, Shane just breaks a finger. "Goddamn it! I don't know! I was told to deliver stuff to her."

"What were you doing inside her house tonight?" I ask. "Trying to deliver something in person?"

"No." He's weeping now. "I was supposed to take her."

"Take. Her. Where?" My face is inches from his now. His haunted eyes meet mine.

"To Boston. I overheard something about sex trafficking. They thought they could get more for her because she's willing to do... things." The last word is whispered. "That's all I know. I can take you to the boss. To Connor McCarthy. He's behind it all. Maybe you don't have to kill me if I help you out, right?"

"Wrong."

Shane pulls the wire from under his palm and wraps it around MacDonald's neck, then pulls until the life leaves the man's body before letting go.

"I'll call for cleanup," Carmine says, reaching for his phone.

"I'll make sure the jet is ready to go," I add.

"You're not going without me," Annika announces. We all turn to her. Her chest is heaving, and she looks like she wants to throw up.

She's not used to this. She's worked hard to make sure that *this* isn't part of her life.

"Every time one of these girls says that, it never turns out well," I say, shaking my head.

"If I stay here like some coward, you'll have to stay with me. To *protect* me," she points out. "Are you going to stand there and say that that idea is okay with you? That you're content to sit here with me while these four run off and kill the assholes responsible for this?"

I blow out a breath. "No. I can't say I'd be okay with it. But if that's what I have to do, then so be it."

"No." She's pacing now, absolutely pissed off. It's a sight to behold with her fiery blue eyes and mussed blond hair. "Absolutely not. If what he said is true, these fuckers thought they could *use* me. For sex. And why? Because they think I was a willing participant in *anything* that happened in those photos? Jesus, people saw me cry and beg. And no one did anything."

"Then that wasn't a reputable club, and was likely part of the sex trafficking epidemic, as well," Carmine says, fire shooting from his eyes. "Because real lifestyle clubs would never permit that. Ever."

"They're all going to pay," Annika says and turns back to me. Her mind is made up. I've never seen her this...fierce.

It's a fucking turn-on.

"I want to look them in the eyes and know that it's because they ever fucked with me that they're going to die. That they hurt *any* woman, or anyone at all for that matter, and made them do things against their will. It's going to stop. Right now."

"Looks like we're all going to Boston," Ivie says with a grin. "And we're going to kick some ass."

We've cleared out of the office where the body is, and are sitting in the living room when the call comes in from Nadia's father.

"Papa?" Nadia frowns over at Annika. "Is everything okay? What? Wait, hold on, I'm putting you on speaker."

She taps her screen.

"Okay, you're on speaker. I'm here with everyone, including Annika. There was just an...issue at her place. But it's been handled."

"Firefly? Are you safe?"

"Yes, Uncle," Annika replies. "We're all okay. What's going on with you?"

"I just got off the phone with Carlo. We just got word that Thomas Luccio, the Chicago boss, and his family were found dead late last night."

"In their home?" I ask.

"No. At the bottom of the river. Luccio, his wife, and both grown children all had cement shoes on. We don't know what the motive was or who did it, but when these things happen, we all pay attention. I want you all to keep your eyes open."

"Pop's calling me," Carmine says and leaves the room to take the call. "Yeah, we're speaking to Igor now."

"We're headed to Boston," Nadia tells her father. "We have some business to see to there. I need you to know that we'll be leaving some blood behind, Papa. The McCarthys have been fucking around with Annika, and we're going to make them pay."

He's quiet for a long moment.

"Why wasn't I apprised of this situation?"

"Because we didn't know until about twenty minutes ago that it was them. Now that it's been confirmed, we're going in."

"Understood. Do what you need to do. But get in and out quickly. The McCarthys aren't particularly powerful, but we don't need a war."

"Agreed. It'll be quiet. No mess. I love you, Papa."

"I love you, too. All of you, stay safe."

He ends the call, and Nadia tucks her phone away.

"I'm going up to get dressed. I'll be ready in thirty," Annika says. I follow her up the stairs to her room. "You don't have to babysit me while I get dressed, Rafe."

"Do you understand what's about to happen?"

"Perfectly."

"Killing a man—"

"Look. I know that I've always stayed out of the family business, and I prefer it that way. And I also know that I haven't been the strongest of the group the past few days. But, damn it, Rafe, I'm pissed. And I have Tarenkov blood running through my veins. I know exactly what this means, what I'm getting myself into, and what I'll see when we get there. I'm going all the same."

I blow out a breath as she lets the robe fall to the floor, and with her blue eyes on mine, slips out of her nightgown, unashamed of her nudity. I've seen her naked more times than I can count. I know her body better than I know mine.

But I think, in this moment, I'm seeing more than just her body. She's naked in *every* way possible.

And she's trusting me to keep her safe and to help her see this through.

I'll be damned if I fail her.

CHAPTER
SIX
~ANNIKA~

"We go in quietly," Shane says as he briefs us all on the plane, just minutes from touching down in Boston. "There's going to be security. Rocco and I will take care of them before we go into the house."

"Why don't we go to the office?" I ask.

"Because we can't guarantee that McCarthy will be there," Carmine adds.

"It'll be the middle of the day with the time difference by the time we get there," Nadia says. "We can't guarantee that he'll be home, either."

"She has a point," Rafe says. "Half of us should go to the house, the other half to the office."

"No, we need to stick together," Shane insists. "If you'd like to try the office first, we can do that. We can go in as if we just want to have a meeting with McCarthy. Make it seem like we're just a family visiting another's territory."

"I like that better," Nadia says. "It makes more sense and is way less messy."

"It's decided, then," Carmine says. They all check their weapons, even Ivie. I know that after everything she went through just a couple of months ago, she's become proficient in handling a gun as well as in hand-to-hand combat. She's a total badass.

But it's still surprising to see my best friend with a handgun.

Of course, I'm not armed. I could use one if I had to, but it's been so long that it's probably not wise for me to be armed.

"You stay with me," Rafe says quietly beside me. "You don't hesitate to move when I do. You stick with me as if you're fucking tied to me."

"Okay."

He nods as the airplane descends.

I know this is what both the Martinellis and my family do, but I've never witnessed it. It's fascinating to watch all of the people I trust more than anything transform from my easy-going, funny friends to stone-cold killers.

There's not much to say as we land. A large, black SUV waits for us near the plane. Rafe opens the front passenger-side door for me as everyone climbs in, and then Rafe joins me in the front, taking the driver's seat.

"I have it pulled up," Shane says as his phone starts giving us directions to the McCarthy office.

It takes about an hour to snake our way through traffic.

"You have to be fucking kidding me," Rafe growls as he pulls in behind an ambulance. Cops and another ambulance block the street, their lights flashing.

"What's going on?"

"I don't know." Carmine rolls down his window and waves to one of the police officers. "Hi there. We have an appointment with Mr. McCarthy in this building."

"Not today, you don't," the cop replies.

"Well, I guess we'll try to meet with him somewhere else, then."

"Nah, man. McCarthy's dead. I can't tell you more than that, except it sounds like he was into some bad shit."

"Well, damn." Carmine shakes his head. "Thanks for the information. We'll get out of your way."

Rafe puts the vehicle in reverse and, within seconds, we're driving away from the scene.

"I'm making some calls," Carmine says as he taps his phone. We listen to his side of the conversation, and when he hangs up, he drags his hand down his face. "Sounds like McCarthy has been threatening more than Annika. He was in deep with a sex trafficking ring, pissed off more people than he could count, and someone finally killed him early this morning."

"Beat us to it," Rafe says grimly. "Fucking pisses me off."

"At least, he's dead," Nadia says.

"I guess we're headed back to Denver," Ivie adds.

KNOWING that the asshole responsible for my harassment is gone and can't do it to anyone else is a relief. And yet, the trip was oddly anti-climactic.

We're in the plane again, headed back home. Ivie and Shane have their heads together at a table, talking low and intimately.

Carmine and Nadia sit on the couch across from me, both quiet. Carmine's reading on his iPad, and Nadia has her eyes closed, her head resting on her husband's shoulder.

They look cozy. Sweet.

In love.

I've had some bad moments of jealousy over the past several months when it comes to my cousin being able to marry the man she loves. After all, she fell in love with Carmine, the eldest son of Carlo Martinelli, and her father, *my* uncle, gave her his blessing to wed.

Though just over a decade ago, Uncle Igor made me leave Rafe behind because the Martinellis were not to be trusted and were off-limits for us.

Why did he make me break up with Rafe, someone I loved so much? We weren't hurting anyone. And then, so many years later, allow his daughter to marry the eldest of the Martinelli sons?

It feels...*wrong.*

I shift my gaze to Rafe, only to find him watching me with calm, blue eyes. He sips his coffee, lounging in his seat, his gray Henley shirt-sleeves pushed up on his forearms where muscles twitch and move as he takes another sip from his white mug.

I want him. I want him more than anything in the world. Always have. I was once told that it was impossible because of our family trees.

Obviously, things have changed there. Nadia has Carmine, and Ivie has Shane. It's true that Ivie isn't related to us by blood, but she's as much a part of the Tarenkov family as I am.

Holding Rafe's gaze, I take a deep breath.

Yes, I want him. And while I may be damaged goods, I have to at least try to be with him damn it.

"Thanks for the ride home," I say as I unlock the door and let us into the big, horrible house that I still live in. "I appreciate it. I'm sorry we all had to go so far just to find out that someone beat us to the punch."

"Don't be sorry," Rafe says. "Stay down here. I'm going to do a quick sweep of the house to make sure everything is secure."

"I'm sure—"

"Just please stay here," he says again and takes off up the stairs.

I blow out a breath and hurry over to the liquor cabinet, pouring myself a shot of vodka and slinging it back. I need some liquid courage for what I'm about to do. God, I'm nervous. I've always been able to say anything to Rafe. Anything at all. But something tells me he's not prepared for what's about to come out of my mouth.

"It looks like nothing has been disturbed since we left," he says as he hurries down the steps.

"Am I too damaged for you to love me?" I blurt out, needing to just get the words out of my head.

He stops cold and stares at me with wide eyes. "Excuse me?"

"You heard me. After everything that's happened, you know exactly what I went through with that idiot I refuse to name. And now that you know, are you disgusted? Does it ruin everything we might have been to each other?"

"No." He crosses to me and drags his knuckles down my cheek. "No, honey. What happened wasn't your fault. When you cried out in your sleep, and I came to your room...God, was that just last night? Anyway, when you talked in your sleep, it nearly tore my heart out. You said you were damaged goods and that I'd never love you."

"Yeah." I blow out the breath I've been holding. "That doesn't shock me."

"You're the most loveable person I've ever met, A." He leans in closer. My heart is pounding so hard I'm surprised he can't feel it.

Finally, after the longest one-point-five seconds ever, his lips meet mine in the softest, sweetest kiss of my life.

But before he can take it further, I plant my hand on his chest and push.

"Okay, I'm getting mixed signals here, Annika."

"I'm sorry." I clench my eyes shut and swallow hard. "That's not what I mean to do. It's not that I don't want you to kiss me."

"Good." He steps forward, but I put my hand up once more.

"But I can't do this here." I can't help but reach out for him. I press my palm to his chest and feel his heart beating as quickly as mine. It gives me the courage to keep talking. "This house is full of horrors that I'll never tell you about, Rafe. I just can't. I don't want those images in your mind. But at the same time, I don't want to start something new with you, something really great, while in this awful house."

"Looks like we need to go house hunting, then." His lips twitch. "Do you want to call your realtor, or do you want me to?"

"What? Like *today*?"

"No time like the present. It's only three in the afternoon. We can look at some places."

I shake my head, but his eyes are completely serious.

"You want to go house hunting. With me. Today."

"Yes."

I laugh but reach for my phone.

"Okay, let's do it."

"I WAS SO happy that you called," Noreen, my real estate agent says with a grin. "Some new condos came on the market this week. And there's a gorgeous townhouse I want to show you, as well."

"We're not in a hurry," I assure her. "So, we'll look at all of them if you have the time."

"I certainly do." Noreen winks and directs Rafe to park on the street in front of a brand-new condo building in downtown Denver. "As you can see, this is a new build. There are two and three-bedroom units with a four-bedroom penthouse unit still for sale, as well."

"I'd like to see the three-bedroom. And the penthouse."

"Perfect." She smiles widely and escorts us inside. "The three-bedroom I'm about to show you doesn't have to be the unit you go with. It's just ready for walk-throughs. There are other same-sized units with better views—for a bit higher price, of course."

"Of course." I nod and follow her inside. Denver is damn expensive. Much more so than when I first moved here for my residency. But I like it here. My business is here. So, I'll pony up a lot for a condo.

It's a good thing that godforsaken house will bring in a nice amount of money.

"It's spacious," I say as I walk through the modern kitchen, complete with the farm sink I've always wanted. "And full of light."

"Yes, these condos have been decorated beautifully," Noreen says. "I'm going to go up to the penthouse to get it ready for you. Feel free to look around."

"Thanks."

Noreen leaves, and I turn to Rafe. "Well? What do you think?"

"It's your place, A."

I shrug a shoulder and look around the room, taking in the fireplace. The balcony. "Let's look at the bedrooms. I need a guest room and an office."

I walk down one hallway and find two good-sized bedrooms, each with its own bath. Then I retrace my steps and take the other hallway, which leads to the master.

"Wow, this is bigger than I expected."

"That's what she said," Rafe murmurs as he walks up behind me, wraps his arms around my waist, and kisses my neck.

It takes me so off guard that I spin and push back.

"What are you doing?"

"Trying it out."

"Trying *what* out?"

"The bedroom." He moves to me, and his hands glide from my hips to the small of my back as he pulls me close and nibbles my ear. My God, I might just slither down into a pile of goo at this man's feet.

He was always good at this. But was he *this* good, or did I just block it out of my memory? Because holy Christ on a cracker, the man can kiss.

"Well?"

"Well, what?"

He grins. "Does it feel *right* here?"

I want to tell him that it feels right everywhere, but Noreen calls out from the kitchen before I can.

"Annika? Are you still here?"

"In the master," I call back, my eyes on Rafe's. "It's a spacious unit."

"Yes, the square footage is well worth the price tag." Noreen grins. "Shall we go up to the penthouse?"

"Sure."

We follow Noreen through the condo and into the elevator. Rafe and I are at the back of the car while Noreen pushes the button.

Rafe slips his hand into mine, laces our fingers, and gives me a squeeze.

I want to cry in relief. God, I've missed him.

Soon, we arrive on the top floor, and when the doors slide open, we follow Noreen into the space.

"Wow," I breathe as we step inside.

"It's twice the square footage as the unit you just walked through," Noreen begins.

"And twice the price," I murmur but cross to the floor-to-ceiling windows to stare at the mountains to the west. "The view is incredible."

"One of the best in the city," Noreen agrees.

I turn to Rafe, but he's not looking at the mountains. He's watching me.

"Feel free to wander around," Noreen says and sits on the sofa. "I'll just answer some emails here and give you some privacy. If you have any questions, I'm here."

"Thank you."

We walk through the spacious unit. I like the bedrooms and bathrooms. Laundry. And when I walk into the master closet, I almost have an orgasm from all of the space.

"Wow."

"They always get you with the closets," Rafe says with a grin. "It's a hell of a closet."

"You're not kidding. But, damn, the price on this place is ridiculous."

"Denver is expensive," he says.

"Yeah."

And when I walk out to the bedroom and stand at the window to take in more of the views of the mountains, he does what he did at the last place. He steps up behind me, rests his hands on my shoulders, and lowers his lips to my neck.

How is it possible that my body can spring to life with just the simplest touch from this man? It doesn't matter where we are—this or any other room. His touch will forever make me burn.

"What do you think?" he asks.

"It's not right. The house, not you."

He kisses me once more, then turns me to face him. "Are you determined to stay here in Denver?"

"My business is here." But the statement isn't firm; it's more conversational. "I'd rather not close it. I have employees I would hate to lay off."

"I understand that." He nods thoughtfully. "But a lot of things have changed for you. Have you given any thought to Seattle?"

I blink and frown. "No, honestly, I haven't. But Nadia will be there more. And probably Ivie, as well."

"You're wounding my ego, sweetheart."

I laugh. "Right. But, yes. You, too. Maybe moving to a new city and not just a new house is the fresh start I need. But my business..."

"There's no need to make any big decisions right away." He takes my face in his hands. "It's just something to think about. Talk to Ivie about it."

I love that he knows that I'll need to bounce this off my best friend. He always *knows.*

"You're right. I'm in no hurry. And I'll think about it."

CHAPTER
SEVEN
~ANNIKA~

"I can't even begin to tell you how good it feels to have a girls' night that doesn't involve the mafia," I say as I pour us each a glass of wine. We're at Nadia's place in Denver, all in our leggings and baggy shirts, hair up in knots, looking way less than glamorous but incredibly comfortable.

"Every day involves the mafia," Nadia reminds me. "But it feels good to have things wrapped up and calm for once."

"And you get to go on your honeymoon tomorrow," Ivie adds, clinking her glass to Nadia's. "There's a tropical beach with your name written all over it."

"Thank the good Lord and all of the saints," Nadia agrees and takes a sip of her wine. "I'm ready to sip fruity drinks and soak in some sunshine. And have all the honeymoon sex. I still can't believe I'm a married woman. It's absolutely ridiculous to me."

"Carmine is perfect for you," I remind her.

The grin that spreads over her face is full of satisfaction. "Yeah. He is. Okay, enough about me. How are you, honey?"

"Oh, I'm good." I wave her off, but both Ivie and Nadia narrow their eyes at me. "What? I am. I'm fine."

"Fine." Ivie nods and sips her wine. "You're fine."

"Yes. I'm fine."

"Bullshit. Spill it, Tarenkov."

I shake my head and laugh at my friends as I reknot my hair.

"Something's up with you," Ivie agrees.

"Okay." I take another sip of wine for courage. "I do have some stuff to talk through. And you guys are the only ones I can do that with."

"And we're right here," Nadia says.

"You know I'm selling the house."

"Thank God," Ivie says. "I hate that place."

"Me, too. I'm selling. Rafe and I went and looked at some condos the other day."

"You went without us?" Nadia demands. "Damn it, A, I love house hunting."

"But she went with *Rafe*," Ivie reminds her. "We would have been third wheels."

"Rafe isn't the point. I went, and nothing felt right. The thing is, I don't know if *Denver* feels right anymore. I've been here a long time, and I love it, but there's nothing here for me except the spa. And I love it, and people depend on me there, but it's just..."

"It doesn't fit anymore?" Nadia asks.

"Yeah. I think that's it. But that makes me feel so guilty because I have a staff of people who depend on me for their jobs. I can't just close it down."

"You're the boss," Ivie points out. "You can totally close it down."

"But you are my office manager."

"I am. And I like my job, but to be brutally honest, I also love working with Shane. I don't know, A, I think our lives are starting to change a bit. And it's for the better. If you offer the other employees a severance package and a letter of recommendation, they'll be fine. It's all in how you handle the situation. There are so many medi-spas here in Denver, and they're all wonderful employees. They won't have a problem finding something else."

I bite the inside of my cheek, thinking it over. "Do you really think so?"

"I do." She nods and reaches over to lay her hand over mine. "I think you're an awesome person for being worried about it. But don't over-think it. You need to do what's right for you."

"If you sell everything here and move, where do you want to go?" Nadia asks.

"Well, Rafe suggested Seattle."

My two best friends beam at me, and I feel my cheeks flush.

"So, it *is* about Rafe," Nadia says smugly.

"This part could be," I admit. "I'm a complete basket case, you guys. I have gone from thinking that I can never be with the man, that I'm not good enough, to saying '*fuck it*,' all in a matter of *hours*."

"Fuck the wine," Nadia says as she stands. "We need tequila."

She quickly returns with a full bottle, three shot glasses, and a baggie full of cut-up limes.

"Forgot the salt," she says before rushing to the kitchen to fetch the shaker.

"Mixing wine and tequila doesn't sound like a good idea," I say with a frown.

"Live a little," Nadia suggests and pours the shots. "And keep talking."

"I'm so back and forth, and it's confusing me. I mean, all we've done is kiss, but it made me feel exactly the way I did all those years ago, you know?"

"No, I don't know, because you didn't tell me about it before, remember?" Nadia takes a shot and scowls at me as she sucks on a lime. "I can't believe you didn't tell me."

"I didn't want Uncle Igor to find out," I admit quietly. "But he found out anyway, and made me break up with him. Because he was a Martinelli."

"He's still a Martinelli," Ivie points out.

"Yeah, but things have changed quite a bit from what they were a decade ago," Nadia points out. "I don't think you'll have a problem with the family this time around."

I nod, thinking it over.

"I like that he suggested Seattle," Ivie says. "Nadia and I will be there more often now, and maybe it's the right time for you to start over somewhere new."

"That's what I'm thinking." I blow out a breath. "Change is scary, you know?"

"No, it's exciting," Nadia says. "It's the chance for a fresh start, and you already have a support system there. You can always open a new spa in Seattle, or just take your time and think about what you want."

"Actually, that's a good question," Ivie adds. "What *do* you want, A? In a perfect world, what do you see happening for yourself?"

I take a shot, then suck on a lime. "I want Rafe," I admit. "God, I want him."

"Then I think you've already decided," Ivie says with a wide smile. "And I'm so excited for you, friend."

"Me, too. I have Noreen the realtor coming to the house tomorrow so we can put it on the market. I really don't want to spend any more nights there."

"Stay here," Nadia offers, gesturing to her beautiful Denver home. "Carmine and I leave tomorrow. You'll have the place to yourself."

"Really? You don't think Carmine would mind?"

"Honey, Carmine is a softy when it comes to women. All of our men are. He knows your situation. He'll be absolutely fine with you staying here."

"They're good people." I look down into my empty shot glass, and Nadia fills it back up. "The guys. They're good. And I'm really so glad they're ours. Well, I don't know for sure about Rafe being mine, but you know what I mean."

"No man looks at a woman the way Rafe looks at you and doesn't consider her his," Nadia replies, her blue eyes solemn. "And, yes, they're good. I mean, they kill people and stuff, but they're good men."

I laugh and then nod. "Good killers. I guess it's a thing."

"It's totally a thing." Nadia holds her glass up for us to clink. "To the sexy Martinelli men."

"And their gorgeous women," Ivie adds just before we all shoot the tequila.

"You know, Ivie, I love the confidence that has grown in you since you started fucking Shane," Nadia says. "It's high time you realize just how beautiful and wonderful you are."

"Thanks." She smiles shyly. "It's hard to continue thinking of your-

589

self as dowdy and as the ugly duckling when the man you love can't keep his hands off you and tells you how irresistible you are all the time."

"I like Shane a lot," I say and bring my knees up to my chest. "He's really intense and quiet, but I can see how much he loves you. And I know, without a doubt, that you're safe with him."

"We're all safe," Ivie says. "And it's a damn good feeling."

I CAN HANDLE THE HANGOVER. It's the memories that hurt.

I blow out a breath, prop my hands on my hips, and try not to think about how horribly I must smell right now. I stayed the night at Nadia's, and after she and Carmine left for their fun honeymoon this morning, I dragged my ass out of their house and over to mine so I could pack up what I want to keep.

So far, it's two boxes.

In the three hours that I've been here, I've managed to throw away a ton of crap. I've made piles of things to be donated. And all of the furniture can also be donated or sold with the house.

Thankfully, Richard and I only lived here for a few months before he died, so I don't have many years' worth of accumulation to dig through. I've managed to pack a couple of bags full of clothes to last me several weeks, all of my toiletries, and I have my briefcase full of office stuff. I can be mobile for a little while.

With my closet emptied, I make my way downstairs. I want to keep my KitchenAid mixer. It was a gift from Ivie, and I use it a lot. I like to cook. I also box up the cookware that was a wedding gift, only because it was exactly what I wanted when I registered, and it's top-of-the-line. I also throw a few knickknacks into the box, but the rest can go.

Next, I box up my library. This was my favorite room in the house, and a space that Richard never came into. He didn't like to read. It takes more than an hour to box the books because I like to look at each one and think about how much I love the stories inside.

But once the shelves are empty, I only have two rooms left to tackle, and I've been avoiding them both like the plague.

Richard's office, and the basement.

I gather up a couple of empty boxes and walk into the office first.

Thankfully, right after he died, we went through most of the paper-work left in here, and I burned it in the backyard while I guzzled down a bottle of wine. Most of what's here is just masculine furniture and some office supplies.

I start to box up some things but then stop and sit back on my haunches.

"What am I packing anything for?" I wonder aloud. "So it can sit in a storage closet until I die and become someone else's problem? That's dumb. I don't want any of this."

I leave it all in the middle of the room, set to go out in the trash. I do make sure there's nothing in there that should be shredded, but it all looks pretty harmless.

Until I cross to the safe behind a painting on the wall. I already looked inside after he died, and it was empty, but I open it one last time just to make sure I didn't overlook anything.

"Empty," I murmur, staring at the black velvet interior. But just as I'm about to turn to leave, I notice a small, black ribbon in the back corner. "I swear my life is a movie plot."

I close my eyes and pinch the bridge of my nose.

"I don't want to pull on that ribbon." I shake my head, pace the room, and then come back to the safe. "But I have to. Goddamn you, Richard."

I tug on the little strip of fabric, and a false wall gives way. Behind it is a stack of cash at least six inches thick and an envelope with my name on it.

"Fuck fuck fuck fuck fuck."

I take it all to the ugly brown couch and sit, then open the envelope. With dread hanging heavy in my belly, I begin to read.

Annika,

If you're reading this, you found the hidden compartment in the safe. You'd better hope that I'm dead. Because if not, and I find out you've been snooping, I'll kill you myself.

Now, then. In the event that I've died, there are a few things to say. First of all, our marriage is a scam. I don't love you. I find you to be the most boring and inconvenient person I've ever met in my life. You're a snooze-fest, A. But I know your heart is in the right place, and that since we've been married, I've put you in situations that you found to be...uncomfortable.

I have to put the letter down and take a deep breath so I don't rip it to shreds before I'm finished reading.

Uncomfortable? Motherfucker.

While you were a means to an end for me, I know that you entered into our marriage with the best of intentions, and that you did love me. I'm not so heartless that I don't recognize that. Because I couldn't return your love, and to thank you for your loyalty and dedication, I've stashed some money away for you. There is a quarter of a million dollars here for you. I know that's not much compared to what your family has at its disposal, but it's what I can offer you, along with the money you'll get from the sale of this horrible house.

Be well, Annika.

R

I blow out a breath, fold the note, and tuck it back into the envelope, then into my back pocket. So, he left me with a bunch of money and a lot of regret.

Generous of him, really.

I roll my eyes, take the money out of the safe, and then pause when I see a small scrap of paper.

It's just a phone number.

I tuck it away and, more than ready to be done with this room, walk out.

Now I just have to tackle the basement, which is really the root of my hate for this home, and for the man I lived with here.

But there's no way in hell that I'd allow someone else to deal with what's down there. It's too humiliating. Too horrible.

I would take a swig of liquor, but I'm still hungover from last night. Instead, I take a long drink of water and square my shoulders.

I flip on the stairway lights and feel the ball of dread grow in my stomach with each step until it feels like it might suffocate me.

When I reach the bottom and turn on the lights, it's just...empty. There's no sign that anything used to be down here at all. No wall of whips and restraints. No bed. No toys.

Nothing.

I blink, sure I'm imagining things. I haven't been down here since before Richard died. I certainly haven't let anyone else come down here.

Where did it all go?

"Annika?"

I turn and hurry up the stairs at the sound of Noreen's voice.

"Oh, there you are," she says with a smile. "What's wrong? You look like you've seen a ghost."

"Oh." I shake my head and force a smile to my lips. "Nothing. It's just already been a long day."

"I understand. Selling a house is a lot of work. And I see you've been hard at it. I'm glad we've already taken photos for the listing."

"Yeah." I cringe. "I'll get this cleaned up. I won't be living here anymore, so I wanted to clear some stuff out. I have a dumpster coming for the trash, and I'm donating a bunch of things to charity. The rest can be sold with the house if the buyer wants it."

"We can take care of that," Noreen assures me. "Do you have somewhere to go?"

"Yes, several somewheres, actually. I'll be okay."

"Good. Okay, let's do a walk-through, and I'll put the sign in the yard. It'll go up online this afternoon. It's a seller's market right now, so I don't think it'll sit for long."

"Perfect. The sooner we can sell, and I can wipe my hands of it, the better."

EIGHT
~RAFE~

"My house sold in three days."

Annika's voice in my ear is like a balm to my soul. I've been staying away, letting her sort through everything she needs to figure out. I want to be there, helping her. Hell, I want to handle everything for her and protect her from any more pain.

But I know Annika. She needs to handle this on her own.

"It actually went into a bidding war, and I got more than the asking price," she continues. "I was stunned. And then, when I had the meeting with everyone at the clinic and told them my plans, they were so sweet about it. There were some tears and hugs, but they all understood."

"I'm sure you offered them a nice severance package."

Her chuckle makes me grin. "Of course. It didn't hurt. I closed the clinic immediately and referred my existing patients to other doctors."

"You're wrapping it up quickly."

"Yeah." She's quiet for a moment.

"Did I lose you?"

"No, I—" She sighs. "Can I come see you in Seattle for a while?"

Her words come out in a quick whoosh of air, and the insecurity in her voice makes me frown.

"I've been waiting for you to do what you need to, A. You're always welcome to be with me, no matter where I am. When would you like to come?"

"It's Wednesday now, and Ivie is here helping me close up the spa. We should be done by Saturday. How does Sunday work for you?"

"What time do you want to leave?"

"Oh, I thought I'd just book a flight and you could pick me up at the airport."

"I'll come get you. I'll bring the plane myself so it's just the two of us. You can be my co-pilot."

"Is that safe?"

I laugh, excited at the thought of having her here with me in just a few days. "Okay, there may be three of us on the plane. I just have to tell you, I'm so proud of you, Annika."

"For what? Being an adult?"

"Yes, actually. And for handling everything in that classy way you always do. Seattle will be lucky to have you."

Hell, *I'll* be lucky to have her.

But I don't want to move too fast or scare her away. I just need her with me. And it's going to happen, sooner than expected.

"Well, I'll just be happy and relieved when all of this is settled and all I have to do is come back to sign closing papers in about a month. I'm getting there. So, I'll see you Sunday?"

"Absolutely. Make sure you're eating, okay? And getting rest. I know you, and you'll work yourself into exhaustion."

"Yes, sir." She chuckles again. "I'm eating. Sleeping so-so. It'll get better. I'd better go. Ivie's giving me the stink eye because she's carrying boxes, and I'm flirting with you on the phone."

"Well, I guess we can't have her giving you the stink eye. I'll be in touch. Call me if you need anything at all, okay?"

"Okay, thank you. See you soon."

She clicks off. I set the phone down and stare out the windows at the city of Seattle as it buzzes down below.

I've kept a condo in the building my family owns for several years. I've never felt the need to buy a house that I have to maintain the way Carmine does. He likes being out of town.

He's very much like our late grandmother in that respect.

Shane and I have been content with our condos in our building. But Shane is rarely here, preferring to spend his time at his ranch in the mountains of Colorado.

I've always felt that I'm in limbo. Missing something. I didn't know what I was missing exactly, until now.

Annika.

My life isn't complete without her. This condo has been fine for me because I didn't have her with me to make a home.

But that's about to change. I know I need to be patient, to take it slowly, but once I have her with me again, I'm never letting her go.

This time, it'll be forever.

"I'm going to get Annika in the morning," I say to my father as we sit in his office, finishing up some business.

"And where are you taking her?" he asks.

"I'm bringing her here, to Seattle. She sold the house and closed her business."

He raises an eyebrow. "Planning to marry her, are you?"

I hold my father's gaze. "Yes, eventually. For now, she needs a new start, and I suggested Seattle. Especially now that Nadia and Ivie will be here more often. It seemed like a good choice for her."

"Not to mention, *you've* been in love with her for years."

I blink in surprise, and my father laughs.

"I don't know why my children all think I'm blind and oblivious to what's going on. I'm not, you know. I knew why you stayed at that college all those years. So did Igor. We were not friends then."

"No." I clench my jaw and have to make myself keep my hands loose. "You weren't."

"Things change. People grow. Igor may be the only man in the world who understands my life and the pressures that go with it. We've had our ups and downs but have grown to trust and respect each other. We wouldn't allow our families to tie themselves to each other if it were any other way, and you know that."

"Yes." I nod once. "I know that."

"And you're bitter that Carmine married Nadia after you were torn from Annika all those years ago."

I stand and pace my father's office, feeling the frustration bubbling up. "I don't mean to feel that way, and it's not something I think about every day, but yes. I guess so. The game changed, and Carmine is with a great woman that he loves very much. I wanted the same."

I turn back to find my father watching me with speculative eyes.

"I *want* the same."

"Well, when the time comes, if Annika is agreeable, you won't get any pushback from me, son. She's a beautiful woman who didn't deserve what happened to her. You know your mother and I will welcome her into the family the way we've done with Nadia and Ivie."

"I know." I sit again and smile softly. "Mom's over the moon, you know?"

"All of her boys have found their match. It means more people to love, babies to come. Your mother has a big heart."

"A ruthless one," I add.

"If need be, absolutely. We can't function in this life any other way, Rocco. But at the end of the day, family is everything. To your mother, and to me. And we'll do whatever we need to do to make sure that ours is protected and happy."

"I know. By any means necessary."

"Yes." His eyes take on that gleam I've always admired when it comes to his work. Carmine shares it. It's how I know that my eldest brother will make an excellent boss someday. "By any means necessary. Now, you go get your woman and bring her back here where we can keep her safe and let her heal."

"Yeah." I swallow. "She needs that. Pop, you know I like living in the condo."

"But?"

"But I don't think it's a long-term solution. If things with Annika work out, and I'm banking on them working out, she needs a *home*."

"You're right. What are you thinking?"

I shake my head, thinking it over. "I don't know yet. I think it depends on her, you know?"

"You're a smart man, my boy." He laughs a little, his broad shoulders

597

shaking. "Get her here and get settled. She'll know what she wants. Or, you'll decide together."

I nod. "You're right. I guess I'm just impatient after waiting so long for her."

"I would be, too. Did you know that your mother turned me down over and over again before we finally got together?"

"No. I thought you guys fell in love and got married six weeks later."

"That part is true, but she made me work for it for a long while. Anything worth having is worth the work and the wait."

"Annika's definitely worth it."

"Let me know when you get home. Your mother will want to invite you both over for dinner."

I grin. "Mom's turning into an even bigger mother hen than she was when we were little."

"She always wanted a girl," Pop says with a laugh. "Now that she's getting some, she's beside herself. Humor her, will you?"

"Sure. You know I never pass up a free meal." I tap my knuckles on his desk and stand. "Thanks, Pop."

"Anytime. Be safe."

I nod, leave his office, press the button for the elevator, and ride it down to my condo. It's been cleaned from top to bottom and is ready for my girl.

I just have to fetch her.

WHY AM I SO NERVOUS? I feel like a kid on his first date.

I walk up to Carmine's door and knock. She must have been watching for me because she swings the door open and throws herself into my arms.

"You're here!"

"I said I would be." I kiss the top of her head and breathe in her citrus scent. "Are you ready?"

"Yes, everything's done. I just have to lock up the house for Nadia." She pulls back, flashes me that killer smile, and then rushes away to gather her bags and make sure everything is locked up tight. While she checks the windows, I haul her bags to the car and meet her at the door as she locks up and turns to me with a wide grin. "Let's get the hell out of here."

"You don't have to tell me twice."

I open the car door for her, then jump into the driver's seat and point us in the direction of the smaller airfield used for private use.

"It's so funny because less than two weeks ago, I planned to stay in Denver. And now that I've changed that plan, I can't wait to get out of here."

"You've worked hard the last few days."

"Yeah, I'm exhausted. But also energized. Does that make sense?"

"It does to me."

She reaches over and pats my arm. "Thanks for this. For everything."

"You don't have to thank me for anything."

"I do." She grins and bounces in the seat. "I'm ready for a new adventure."

"Well, that I can deliver."

"I'M STILL LIVING in the condo," I inform Annika several hours later as I pull my Porsche into the parking garage under our building and park in my space. "It has a good view."

"It's going to be great," she assures me. "I'll help with the bags. They're all on wheels anyway."

Between the two of us, we manage to get everything upstairs in one trip. Once we muscle everything inside, Annika takes a deep breath and soaks everything in.

"Oh, Rafe, this is *nice.*"

She walks into the kitchen where she admires the deep sink, the gas stove, and runs her hand along the big island.

"I can cook so many great things in here."

"You always did cook well."

"I'm better now." She winks and saunters over to the windows. "You're right. This is a great view of the city. I can even see the water and watch the ferries float over the Sound."

"The sunset is beautiful." I shove my hands into my pockets, feeling nervous all over again. I want to touch her, but I don't want to make her uncomfortable or move too fast.

"Let me show you the rest," I suggest and lead her through the living area to the bedrooms. "I only have the two bedrooms, but I think this is a comfortable space."

I don't mention that I had the guest room furnished last week and decorated to her tastes.

"Beautiful," she says with a nod.

"There's a bathroom right over here. That's all yours."

"Okay. Where's your room?"

"This way." I lead her down the hall to my bedroom and swallow hard. Jesus, just having her in my place is hard enough, but in my bedroom? How am I supposed to keep my hands to myself?

"This is huge," she says with a laugh and checks out my closet. "You don't have much in here. It looks empty."

"I'm a dude. I don't need much."

"All this space is just going to waste." She clucks her tongue and then pokes her head into the bathroom. "And look at that tub!"

"I can't complain about the tub," I agree and watch with a smile as she gets right into it, clothes and all, and lounges back as if she's taking it for a test drive.

"This is sweet."

"Like you."

Her grin turns soft as she gazes up at me. "Rafe?"

"Yeah?"

"What if I don't want to sleep in the guest room?"

I lean back on the vanity and cross my arms over my chest. "Well, I have a couch."

Her eyes fill with humor. "What if I want to sleep in *your* room?"

"I suppose that could work. Of course, that's where I sleep, so you'll have to share the bed with me."

She laughs and pulls herself up, then climbs out of the tub.

"That works for me." She crosses to me, takes my hands in hers, and tilts her lips up toward mine.

I never *could* resist this woman.

And now I don't have to.

I close my mouth over hers, gently sampling her. She tastes of the mint she had in the car, but more than that, she tastes of *Annika*. Like everything good in the world.

I lay my palm over her jaw, encompassing her neck and cheek, and take the kiss deeper, wanting to memorize every nuance. Each breath.

She sighs and leans into me, surrendering to me. Her breasts press against me, and I want to scoop her up and take her to bed—lose myself in her for several hours.

And I will.

Eventually.

"Rafe?"

"Yes, baby?"

"You kept asking me in those other condos if it felt right. If it was the place for me."

"I did."

"This is the one. Right here. This feels right."

I let out the breath I didn't know I'd been holding all day.

"I feel it, too."

Her smile is slow and full of pure female satisfaction. "Good."

CHAPTER
NINE
~ANNIKA~

We didn't have sex. I thought we would the first night I was in his place, but it didn't happen. We ended up ordering in Chinese food and talked for hours, the way we used to when we were kids and falling in love.

That's not to say that just because we didn't do the deed, that he didn't touch me. No, Rafe is the king of physical affection. There was plenty of hand-holding and hair-playing. He kissed me some and traced his fingers down my cheek and over my jawline.

It's safe to say that he kept me in a constant state of pleasant arousal all day and into the evening.

And when we finally went to bed, we curled up together, fully clothed, and whispered into the night.

As much as I can't wait to get naked with this man, I have to admit that our first night together was exactly what I needed.

I stretch and roll over in bed, expecting to find Rafe next to me, but the bed is empty. And when I reach out to touch where he lay, the bedsheets are cool.

He's been up for a while.

I sit up, yawn, scratch my arm, and glance around. Rafe's place is nice. It's not fancy, and he certainly hasn't done much to make it look like anything but a bachelor pad, but it's super clean and updated. I can't wait to get my hands on that kitchen.

I shuffle sleepily into the bathroom with the best tub I've ever seen and consider taking a bath, when it occurs to me that I smell...*bacon.*

Is he making us breakfast?

I hurry through the condo to the kitchen and stop short at the sight that greets me.

Rafe, shirtless with a white towel flung carelessly over his shoulder. His skin is smooth and tanned, and the muscles beneath bunch as he moves from the stove to the mixing bowl on the countertop.

He's just so...*hot.* He's big, at well over six feet, with broad shoulders. But his movements are graceful. Those clever hands crack an egg into a bowl, and he gives it a whisk.

He's so competent in the kitchen, it's as if he makes breakfast every morning of the week.

When we were together before, he hated to cook.

This new side to him is...intriguing.

"Are you going to hover, or are you going to come and get a cup of coffee?" he asks without turning around.

"I didn't make any noise. How did you know I was here?"

"I always know where you are, Annika." He turns to look at me over his shoulder, and the look he sends me makes my stomach quiver. "I hope you're hungry."

"Oh, I'm hungry." I cross to the island and sit in one of the stools, resting my chin in my hand as I watch while Rafe moves about with grace. I don't mention that I'm equally hungry for him to boost me up onto this island and have his way with me, as I am to get my fingers on that bacon. "Wait, you made bacon with no shirt on? That's awfully *brave* of you."

"No." He chuckles and then turns to pass me a cup of coffee, just the way I've always liked it. He remembers how I take my coffee? "I was wearing a shirt, but it got splattered, so I took it off."

He flips the pancakes.

"How do you want your eggs?"

"I have to say, I'm impressed, Rafe. You used to hate to cook."

"I can't eat takeout all the time like I could when I had the metabolism of a teenager," he replies. "And a man has to eat."

"I suspect your metabolism is just fine." I sip my coffee. "I'll take mine scrambled."

"Thank God. That's the only way I know to make them."

We laugh together as Rafe cracks more eggs into a clean bowl and begins whisking them with a fork.

"Did you know that if you add a little dill to the eggs, it adds a nice flavor?" I ask.

"Who's doing the cooking here?" He opens the spice cabinet and hums as he picks up little bottles and then sets them down again. "Dill is on the shopping list."

"We have a shopping list?"

"Of course. I didn't know what you might like to snack on. I remember some of the things you used to eat, but tastes change."

"Going to the store sounds good to me. I'd like to start cooking dinner in here tonight. Unless you have other plans."

"My mother invited us over for dinner." He sends me an apologetic glance. "But I can cancel if you'd like to take a couple of days to settle in first."

"I adore your mother," I reply honestly. "I can cook tomorrow. Ivie told me the other day that she and Shane are coming to Seattle for a couple of weeks. They arrive on Wednesday."

"Shane mentioned it," he replies as he sets my plate in front of me and then joins me with a loaded serving of his own. "It's been nice this fall. Not as rainy as usual. If the weather holds, we might take the boat out on the Sound."

"You have a boat?" I munch happily on a piece of bacon.

"A few, actually. My father always liked to sail. We spent a lot of time on the water growing up. It's been a busy year, so we haven't been out as often as we'd like. If the weather holds, we'll go."

"Fun."

"Do you get seasick?"

"I never have." I shrug a shoulder. "I should be fine."

"Good." He leans over and kisses my temple. "I'm looking forward to sailing with you."

"So, let me get this straight. You're a badass mobster who cooks breakfast and enjoys sailing?"

"I'm a man of depth." He chuckles. "Mobsters have lives, too, you know."

"Sure. Those lives just include killing people."

"Sometimes." His voice quiets as he wipes his mouth. "Sometimes, it does. But that doesn't happen as often as you'd think. Certainly not as often as it has over the past year."

"You really have had a busy year, haven't you?"

"Yes." He laughs, and I can't help but join in. "It's nice to know that things are calming down a bit. At least, for a little while. It gives me time to spend with you."

"I have questions."

He cocks an eyebrow. "Okay. Shoot."

"I know that Carmine is a financial planner and works for the family."

"Yes. He's a nerd."

I smirk. "And Shane does stuff for the government that we're not really allowed to know about."

"Yes, he's a meathead."

I laugh and bump him with my shoulder. "Why don't I know what you do?"

"You know." He frowns over at me. "I fly."

"For who?"

"Anyone who wants to hire me. Although I have a stable of regulars that I work for and haven't taken on anyone new in quite some time."

I sit and blink at him. "I knew you know *how* to fly, it just didn't occur to me that you did it for a living."

"I'd rather fly than do just about anything else."

"Then why don't you work for a commercial airline?"

"Because I have a demanding family, and I need to be available to them at a moment's notice. That's hard to do when you're on a rotating schedule with an airline." He shrugs and shoves almost half of a pancake into his mouth. "I'm doing what I like."

"Do you enjoy working with the family?"

He swallows and seems to think it over. "I love my family. If I choose *not* to work with them, I'd have to leave. And that's not an option for me."

"I see."

He glances my way. "But you don't like that answer."

I push my empty plate aside and offer him a shrug. "I don't know what answer I want, to be honest. I love that you're close to your family. I'm close to mine, as well. But I've never wanted to be involved with the family business. And my uncle has always made me feel that he loves me whether I want to participate or not."

"It's not like you do nothing, Annika," he reminds me as he stands and puts the dirty dishes in the dishwasher. "I know for a fact that Igor has you handy in case someone needs to be patched up."

"I don't mind that," I admit softly. "And it doesn't happen often. I guess my point is, my uncle wouldn't disown me if I didn't want to help with the family business."

"I'm a man," Rafe says simply. I start to argue, but he holds up a hand. "Call it sexist or misogynistic, but it doesn't change the fact that if I were a woman, less would be expected of me. My father wouldn't disown me, but he would shut me out of a lot. I wouldn't be privy to information, and I certainly wouldn't have the protection I have now."

"And then there's the money," I say and know immediately by the look in his blue eyes that I've overstepped. "I'm sorry, I didn't mean—"

"My father isn't the only one in this room who's wealthy," he reminds me. "The last time I checked, you've never wanted for anything. Or gone without."

"Rafe, I didn't mean to insult you."

"Well, you did. I work my ass off for this family. I kill, I run all over this godforsaken globe, and I won't have you questioning my motives. I'm here because I *love* my family. If that's not something you want to be a part of, or if it's something you find insulting, we can find another place for you to stay."

"Jesus." I hang my head in my hands and wish I could hit the rewind button to go back about ten minutes. "I'm a bitch."

"Right now? Yeah."

My head snaps up. There's not only anger in his voice. There's hurt, as well, and it makes me feel like the worst person ever. "It came out entirely harsher than I meant, Rafe. All I meant was—you know what? It doesn't matter. I'm sorry. I was out of line. Nothing you could do would insult me, and I don't want to stay anywhere else."

He blows out a breath and hangs his head.

"Forget it. Let's get ready to do some sight-seeing before we go see my parents this evening."

He moves to walk past me, and I reach out for his hand, tugging him to me.

"I'm sorry."

"I said forget it."

I wrap my arms around his middle and hold on tightly. "I have a stupid mouth, and I didn't mean it."

"Hey." He kisses my head, and it makes me feel a little bit better. "I said it's okay. Maybe I just know that you never wanted to be involved with someone who's committed to the organization the way I am. I'm not leaving it, A. And you need to know that before we go much further."

"I know it." I look up at him. "I know, Rafe. And if I thought I couldn't deal with it, I wouldn't be here. The truth is, I just want to be with you. No matter what."

He lets out a long breath and kisses my forehead.

"It's fine, Annika. Let's go have a good day."

"Okay."

"ARE YOU ENJOYING SEATTLE, DEAR?" Rafe's mother, Flavia Martinelli, asks me later that evening. "Have you been sight-seeing?"

"She just got here yesterday, Mom," Rafe says but wraps his arm around his mother's shoulders and gives her an affectionate squeeze.

"Well, we did do some sight-seeing today," I reply as Flavia fills my glass with wine. "Rafe took me to Pike Place Market, where he bought me the most amazing bouquet."

"The market really does have the best flowers," Flavia agrees.

"We wandered around downtown and just had a good day."

"And what do you think of the condo?" Carlo asks.

"It's a nice place." I smile politely and sit next to Rafe at the table, where appetizers are being served.

By staff.

I'm used to this at Uncle Igor's house, and I always forget how fancy it makes me feel until I'm in the situation again.

"I love the view," I continue. "The water is just *so* blue. And it's fun to watch the ferries float on the Sound, as well."

"It really is a nice view," Flavia agrees. "Perhaps you should buy a house near the water, Rafe."

I frown as I take a bite of my Caprese salad and turn to Rafe. "Are you looking for a house?"

"Well, you two can't live in the condo forever," Flavia continues. "It's so small. There's no room to stretch out and enjoy each other. And what about when you start having children? No, it certainly won't do for the long term. But I know of some absolutely *gorgeous* homes for sale that have amazing views. One of my good friends is a realtor. I'll give her a call next week."

"I don't think I'm in a rush to buy a house," Rafe says and eyes me warily. "I haven't even talked to Annika about it yet."

"Oh." Flavia looks between us and cringes. "Oh, dear. I'm sorry to speak out of turn. My mind just starts working, and my mouth starts to babble."

I smile, but I make a mental note to ask Rafe *many* questions when we get back to the condo. I feel like I'm missing something, something big. Like he isn't telling me everything.

And Flavia mentioned *children*. I don't know how I feel about kids. At least, kids of my own. I mean, I just got here.

We haven't even had sex yet, not to mention the fact that we certainly haven't talked about anything long term.

I thought we'd take things slow. Because while it's a fact that I want to be with Rafe for the rest of my life, I'm still healing from a lot of garbage.

"Annika?"

I glance up and realize that Flavia asked me a question. "I'm sorry, I was too busy having a party in my mouth with this salad."

The other woman laughs and then nods. "It's my favorite, as well. I was just wondering if you've thought about opening another medi-spa here in Seattle. I'd love to be your first patient."

I grin at the thought. "Mrs. Martinelli, you're lovely without my help."

"Well, then, just think about what a knockout I'll be *with* your help."

We all laugh, and I feel much more comfortable as we settle in to enjoy each other's company.

CHAPTER
TEN
~RAFE~

I could kill my mother.

I shift gears manually and merge onto the freeway while Annika sits quietly next to me.

"My mom means well."

She turns her head towards me and offers me a smile in the darkness. "I adore your mom. She's sweet and fun."

"I wish she hadn't gone on and on about me buying a new house."

Annika shifts in her seat, facing me now. "I was going to ask about that. Do you want to move out of the condo? You hadn't mentioned it before."

I sigh deeply and rub my hand over my mouth as I keep my eyes on the freeway. It's late into the evening, so traffic is light.

"I'd only started thinking about it," I admit, not sure how much to say. I don't want to scare her by talking about things that could happen in the long term. We aren't there yet. This is still new for both of us.

But damn it, I'm a planner.

"You don't like the condo?" she asks.

"I like it fine." I glance her way and find her watching me carefully. "It's convenient since it's downtown and only about twenty minutes from the airstrip."

"But?"

I shake my head with a chuckle. "I was just considering a house in a nice neighborhood. Maybe with a water view."

"When did you start thinking about this?"

I bite the inside of my cheek until I taste coppery blood on my tongue.

"About a week ago."

She's quiet for a long moment and then clears her throat. "Are you considering a house because of *me*?"

"I don't know." I blow out a breath. "Maybe. Look, I know that the condo isn't the best."

I take my exit off the freeway.

"I like the condo."

"It's small. No yard. And most of the building is used for business, so that's probably not something I'd like to have you living with for long."

"Rafe, you don't have to buy a whole house just because I'm staying with you for a little while."

I park in my space and turn to her with a scowl. "What do you mean, for a little while?"

Her mouth bobs open and closed, and then she simply sighs and closes her eyes. "I'm saying the wrong things."

"I think we're both doing a good job of that."

I jump out of the car, hurry to the passenger door, and open it for her, escorting her to the elevator. Once inside the condo, I toss my keys into the bowl by the door, and she kicks out of her shoes.

"Of course, you're not buying a house just because of me," she continues as we walk into the kitchen, and I reach for two glasses. One wine glass, and one whiskey glass.

I pour us each a drink and pass the wine to Annika.

"I mean, you have valid reasons for wanting a house *without* me."

"A?"

"Yes?"

"Stop talking." I clink my glass to hers, take a long sip of the whiskey, and then pull her in for a hug. "My mother spoke out of turn, that's all. I just have thoughts running through my head. But before I do anything that would commit either of us to something for the long haul, I'll have a conversation with you first. Okay?"

"Yeah. Okay. That sounds good."

She smiles up at me, looking relieved. I'm still stuck on her *for a little while* comment, but I decide to let it be for tonight.

We've made no promises.

But if she thinks I'll let her move away from me, she's got another think coming. But it's early days yet, and we're finally in a place of getting to know each other again—and being together.

The rest will happen in due time. For now, I'm going to enjoy the hell out of her.

At *her* pace.

"Are you sleepy?" I ask when I hear her yawn.

"I think the past week is catching up to me," she says and sips her wine as she follows me back to the bedroom. Of course, she's exhausted. She packed up her house, her business, and left her life in Denver. We wandered all over the market today, and she had dinner with my parents.

I'm surprised that she's still standing upright.

"I have an idea." I kiss her forehead, run my hands down her arms, and then lead her into the bathroom. "I think you need a hot bath."

"Oh, God, I've been *dying* to take a swim in that tub." She does a little happy dance. "You run the water, and I'll go get my things."

I take my time setting the temperature of the water, sprinkle in a generous amount of Epsom salts that smell like lavender, and light a few candles that I bought a day or two before Annika came to Seattle.

When she returns, her eyes widen.

"I might fall asleep."

"If you do, I'll wake you up. No drowning in my tub." I tip up her chin so I can kiss her softly. "Just yell if you need anything."

"Thank you. This will be heaven."

I close the door behind me so she has privacy and find my laptop. I sit in the chair by the window and open the computer. I should check my email and see if any clients need me this week.

But things are quiet on the work front. It seems everyone is happy where they are for now. And I won't complain about that because it gives me more time with Annika.

I put the computer away and use the other bathroom to take a quick shower and change. When Annika's been in the bath for more than thirty minutes, I knock on the door, just to make sure she didn't make good on her word and fall asleep.

"You alive in there?"

"Oh, yeah. I'm just in bliss. But I'm a prune, so I'll be out soon."

"No hurry, honey. Just checking."

I turn down the bed and slip between the sheets, feeling exhausted myself, just as Annika steps out of the bathroom, a whoosh of warm air trailing after her.

"That was the best thing I've done in a *long* time," she announces as she tosses her dirty clothes into a hamper and then joins me in bed. "It might become a nightly ritual."

"Nothing wrong with that." I trail my fingertip down her nose and then lean in to kiss her gently. I've been taking it slow with her. There's no need to hurry.

It's torture keeping my hands to myself. Keeping myself from stripping her bare and having my way with her.

But there's plenty of time for that.

Annika starts to unbutton her pajama shirt, but I take her hands and bring them to my mouth, then turn her away from me and press her back against my chest.

"Goodnight, sweetheart."

"'Night."

I'm just about to drop into sleep when I hear her sniffle. My eyes shoot open, and I frown as I pull Annika onto her back and cup her cheek gently.

"What's wrong?"

She shakes her head and tries to pull away, but I hold her close, panic setting up residence in my belly.

"Honey, I need you to tell me what I did wrong so I can fix it."

"I *am* too damaged," she says, her bottom lip quivering.

"What are you talking about?"

"You said that I wasn't, that everything I'd been through didn't repulse you. But, damn it, it's my second night here, and I just practically threw myself at you, and you turned me away."

She's crying in earnest now, and I feel like the biggest asshole to ever walk the face of the Earth.

"I didn't mean to turn you away." I wipe at her tears and am pretty sure I'd like to beat myself up for causing them. "I just...I'm trying to take things slow."

"Why?"

"Because you *matter*, Annika. Because you've been through hell in the past year. And what kind of a prick would I be if I just jumped you? If I pushed you against the wall and had my way with you?"

"That sounds kind of fun."

I laugh in spite of myself and kiss her forehead. "We can put that on the schedule for a later date. I hate that today had awkward moments. Especially after we spent so many years together, and it was anything but awkward back then. But things have happened since then. Things that are absolutely *not* your fault. Not mine, either. We're getting to know each other again, in a way. I know who you are, and I can tell you that I'm as attracted to you today as I was the first time I saw you on campus."

"Really?" She sniffles, but her eyes are full of hope now. "I was afraid I'd made a mistake by coming here. That I'm intruding or something."

"No." I kiss her lips now. "Absolutely, not. I don't want the first time I take you to be when you're exhausted from wrapping up your previous life just *hours* before. Call me a romantic, but I want it to be more special than that. Because you deserve that and more, Annika."

"Wow, you *are* a romantic," she whispers. "Okay, that makes me feel a little better. But the next time I move to take my shirt off, don't humiliate me by patting me on the head and telling me to go to sleep."

"That's *not* what happened."

"Felt like it."

"Then I apologize for being a moron."

She laughs a little now. "Apology accepted. I *am* tired."

"Go to sleep." I kiss her once more. "Before I say fuck it to being romantic and make you *really* tired."

"Fine." She sighs and burrows face-first into my chest. "Goodnight, Rafe."

"Goodnight, Annika."

"I REALLY LOVE THIS KITCHEN," Annika says the next day as she starts to clean up from dinner. "That oven is just amazing. When did you have this place updated?"

"It was done about a year ago, I guess. Pop had the whole building updated. He went all out."

"You're not kidding."

"I can help with dishes."

"No." She holds up a hand. "Absolutely, not. You've made breakfast two days in a row, cleaned up, *and* helped me prep dinner. I've got this."

I'm relieved that she let me off of the hook for KP duty because I have a little surprise for her. So, I nod solemnly and promise to be back shortly.

I walk to the bedroom and set my plan in motion. I have rose petals to spread over the floor, the tub, the bed. I have roses in vases. I have candles to light.

In less than thirty minutes, the bedroom is transformed into a romantic suite, complete with champagne.

I'm going to romance my girl.

When I return to the kitchen, Annika is just putting away the last of the dishes, humming to herself.

"How do you feel?" I ask.

"Pretty good, actually. Not too full, not too tired."

"Excellent. Come with me. I want to show you something."

She grins and takes my hand. "Okay. What do you have to show me?"

"You'll see."

With her hand linked to mine, I lead her down the hallway and open the bedroom door.

"Your suite awaits."

Her eyes grow wide as she steps inside, and then she turns to me.

"How in the hell did you pull all of this off? We were together most of the day."

"You took a nap," I reply easily. "I ran an errand or two."

"No kidding." She sighs and brushes her fingertips over a rose, then buries her nose in the fragrant bloom. "This is so lovely."

"Not nearly as lovely as you."

I wrap my arms around her from behind and kiss the shell of her ear.

"Do you mind if I take a bath?" she asks, and I just smile and open the bathroom door, where I have more candles lit, a full, steaming tub with more rose petals floating on the water. "Holy cow."

"I want you to relax. I want you to feel pampered and appreciated."

"Mission accomplished." She tests the water with her fingers. "I promise not to drown."

"Good idea. Because I have plans for you when you get out of this tub."

Her eyes shine with mischief and lust when they find mine. "Promise?"

"Hell, yes."

"Then let me get in the water." She shoos me out of the room, closes the door, and I take a long breath.

She likes it.

Hopefully, she likes everything else that's about to come, as well. I'm going to take my time. I'm going to relearn and examine every inch of her perfect little body.

Similar to the night before, I go down the hall to the guest bathroom. I already stocked it with my shaving supplies, so I do that first. Then I take a shower and pull on only a simple pair of black boxer shorts.

If all goes according to plan, they won't be on for long.

I've just walked back into the bedroom when the bathroom door opens, and standing as a silhouette against the light of the bathroom behind her, Annika pauses and bites her lip. She's the most beautiful woman I've ever seen in my life.

I mean, I already knew that, but with her standing there in a sexy black nighty that I didn't even see her grab earlier, my heart simply stalls in my chest. My mouth goes dry. My dick comes to attention.

"I want to fuck you in that doorway." My voice is pure gravel. The pulse in Annika's throat jumps. "But I'm not going to. Not right now."

"It's on the schedule for later with the against-the-wall sex?" she asks, her voice breathless.

"Oh, yeah. It's on the damn schedule. I want you with an ache that never really goes away, Annika." I'm slowly stalking toward her as I talk. I'm afraid to reach out for her because I know I won't stop once I touch her. "I tried for years to extinguish that desire. To tell myself that I'd never have you. That you couldn't be mine.

"But there was always something inside me, a voice or an ache, that wouldn't shut up. That wouldn't *give* up. You kept telling me no, but I knew that I'd have you with me again someday. I didn't know when or how, but I knew in the deepest part of me that you'd make your way back to me."

I swallow hard and reach out to touch just the very edge of her earlobe.

She shivers.

"Everything about you is a miracle." I step closer. "And I want you to not only *hear* that but also believe it. Because it's true. You're my miracle, Annika."

"Rafe?"

I just look her in the eyes.

"I'm going to need you to touch me now."

CHAPTER

ELEVEN

~ANNIKA~

I s someone hammering the wall next to me? Or is that just my
heart, thundering in my chest?

The way Rafe's looking at me would make any woman melt
into a puddle. His eyes, so brilliantly blue, are on *fire*. Intently watching
me as he slowly walks closer as if he's a big cat, stalking his prey.

And let me just say, I'm more than happy to be the prey. I'll gladly
sign up for that mission.

I volunteer as tribute.

"My knees are shaky," I say, surprised to hear the shake in my voice.

"Let's help you out with that."

He scoops me into his strong arms and carries me to the bed, where
he lays me on the sheets covered in rose petals.

I didn't expect Rafe to go all out like this. He didn't even do this
when I lost my virginity to him. But it's so incredibly sweet, and so
thoughtful.

So *Rafe*.

"I don't know where you bought this thing," he says as he pushes a
finger under the black strap on my shoulder and runs it up and down.
"But we're only shopping there from now on."

618

I grin and reach up to brush my fingers through his damp hair. "Like that, do you?"

"Yeah. Yeah, I like it. It's going to look fucking awesome on my floor."

I snort, all awkwardness gone between us. And when that finger glides down my chest and brushes over the tip of my breast, I sigh.

"You were hot at nineteen," he murmurs and gets to work unfastening the little black number I wear. "I couldn't keep my hands off of you. I could *wait* for you to be ready for a moment like this."

"I made you wait for a long time."

"It was worth it." He swallows hard when he uncovers my breasts, then licks his lips. "A man should have to earn this, A. And I just have to say, if you were hot then, and you *were*, you're beyond my wildest dreams now."

"Rafe—"

"It's true." His eyes fly to mine and glow in the light from the bathroom. "Jesus. Your body matured into a gorgeous work of art."

"Yeah, I'm not as skinny anymore. I have hips and boobs, and—"

"Curves," he interrupts. "They're called curves, baby. And if you say anything bad about them, I might have to take you over my knee."

"Well, that would be horrible." My dry, sarcastic comment makes him chuckle as he kisses his way down my torso. "You're just so good with your mouth."

"I'm glad you think so. Because it's going to be *all over* you."

"That sounds like a threat."

"Promise." He kisses the tender flesh just above my navel, hooks his fingers into the thin straps on the poor excuse for panties I'm wearing, and guides them down my legs before tossing them on the floor. "It's a promise. I hope you don't have plans tonight because this will take a while."

"And here I was hoping to run out and catch a late show." I grin, but then sigh when Rafe parts my legs and places a kiss on my inner thigh, about six inches below the promised land.

How often did I dream of exactly this? Long for it? Even after I moved to Denver and met the jerk that became my husband, I thought of Rafe. No matter how hard I tried to block him from my mind, it was no use.

Because being with him feels right. I belong here in his arms. In his bed.

I gasp when he blows gently on my core, and when he dips his head to brush his tongue over my hard clit, I have to grab onto the sheets to anchor myself.

"Hold onto me," he instructs. I follow his orders and plunge my fingers into his hair. When his mouth returns to me, my hands clench, hard.

My God.

My toes curl. My stomach and butt clench, making me rise off the mattress, and Rafe uses the opportunity to slip his hands under me. He cups my ass and holds me so he can feast at his leisure.

He changes rhythms, moving from quick, pulsing motions to long, leisurely licks. My body is on a roller coaster of sensation, and it just might kill me.

But what a way to go.

When he slips two fingers inside me, I come apart at the seams. I can't see or hear. I can't do *anything* except ride wave after wave of sensation.

And when my brain starts to clear, I feel Rafe move, shift his body to between my legs, and settle in over me, his elbows planted on either side of my head.

"Amazing," he whispers.

"Yeah, it was."

My eyes flutter open to find him smiling softly down at me. With those blue eyes tied to mine, he slips gently inside of me and stops to let me adjust—the way he always did before.

Rafe is blessed in the penis department. But it doesn't take long for my body to loosen. When it does, he moves in long, fluid thrusts. His pubis rubs against my clit with each stroke, and I know without a shadow of a doubt that I'm about to fall over the cliff into bliss again at any moment.

"Rafe."

"Yes, baby?" He kisses the side of my mouth, then takes one hand and pins it above my head. "I'm right here."

"Oh, God."

With three more thrusts, I succumb to the orgasm, shivering and clenching around him. With a muttered curse, Rafe follows me over.

We're panting and clinging to each other. It's been *so long,* and yet it feels like no time has passed at all.

"That was a good start."

His head comes up, and he stares down at me before letting out a loud laugh.

"A good *start?*"

"Hmm." I stretch lazily when he rolls away. I'm about to get off the bed to go clean up when Rafe walks into the bathroom. I hear the water running. When he returns, he wipes me with a warm washcloth. "Oh, that's nice."

He grins, tosses the rag into the laundry basket, and then curls up next to me.

"Rafe?"

"Yes, babe." He kisses my temple.

"I want something sweet."

He boosts up on his elbow and brushes a strand of hair off my cheek. "What kind of something sweet?"

"Cheesecake."

He cocks a brow. "We don't have any cheesecake."

"I think I saw a diner down the street. They probably have cheesecake."

"So, we're going out then?"

"Yes." I jump up from the bed, feeling newly energized. Some muscles will be sore in the morning, but deliciously so. "I'm just going to slip into some clothes."

"The more you put on, the more I have to take off later."

"You're a big, strong man. You can handle it."

"How many blue shirts does one person need?" Rafe demands as he holds out a navy-blue blouse for me to put on a hanger and add to the closet.

Since I'm officially staying in the master bedroom, Rafe offered the *gorgeous* closet to me since what he has doesn't fill even a fraction of it.

I didn't say no.

"There are many different shades of blue," I inform him and take the blouse from him. "This is navy, but that next one is cerulean."

"Cer-what?"

"Cerulean. And then you have your baby blue, cobalt, indigo, teal—"

"Okay, okay." He laughs and passes me another top. "I get it. You need a lot of blue. And every other color, it seems."

"I like clothes." I shrug and open another new container of hangers. "Just wait until we find the box full of pretty party dresses. Those are my favorite. I don't go to many parties or formal events, but a girl needs to have plenty of options on hand, just in case."

"I can't wait."

I glance at him and grin. "You know, you don't have to help me in here. I can manage all of this. I'm sure you have stuff to do."

"I don't mind." His phone rings, just as mine does at the same time. "Shane."

"Ivie."

"Put us on speaker," Ivie says as soon as I answer. Rafe already has Shane on speaker when I get Ivie set up, and then they both announce, "We're getting married!"

"Uh, we know. Shane proposed weeks ago," I reply.

"No, we're getting married *now*," Ivie says. "Well, soon anyway. We're on our way to Seattle right now."

"We haven't finished with the plans," I reply, starting to panic. "A lot goes into a wedding, Ivie."

"That's just it," Shane adds. "We don't really want a big wedding."

"So, we're going to Vegas!" Ivie squeals. "All of us. Get packed because we're leaving tonight."

"Who else is going?" I ask.

"Curt's with us, much to his dismay," Ivie says. Curt is one of

Shane's closest friends and the manager of Shane's ranch in Colorado. "Nadia and Carmine are flying into Vegas tomorrow morning."

"But they're on their honeymoon."

"They're headed back this way, on their way to some posh spot in Europe. They're going to make a stop in Vegas to celebrate with us."

"Did you invite the parents?" Rafe asks his brother.

"We talked to Mom and Pop," Shane says. "They're fine with this, as long as we let Mom throw us a big reception at some point."

Ivie's parents are dead, but my family thinks of her as ours.

"Even Uncle Igor was happy with it," Ivie adds. "It's all set. Seriously, pack. Oh my gosh, it's going to be *so fun.*"

They both hang up, and Rafe and I just stare at each other in surprise and then bust up laughing.

"So, I guess we're going to Vegas."

"Never a dull moment with this family," he says, shaking his head and tapping on his phone.

"I'll finish unpacking a few boxes, and then I'll pack. They won't be here for a while yet."

I pull the tape on a box, open the flaps, and hear Rafe mutter, "Good God."

"What?"

"Is that all *white* shirts?"

"Yeah." I look down with a frown. "I mean, you need white shirts, Rafe."

"How many? There's only one shade of white, A."

I cross my arms over my chest, knowing that it boosts my boobs and he can see plenty of cleavage. "I don't know." I tap my lips as if I'm giving it a lot of thought. "There's cream, eggshell, pearl, alabaster—"

He moves quickly, way faster than you'd expect for a man Rafe's size, and crushes me to him, pressing his lips to mine and making me forget how to breathe right.

"That shut you up," he says against my lips.

"I don't remember what we were talking about."

He laughs, pats me on the butt, and looks ridiculously proud of himself when I have to sit on the ottoman to get my bearings. But then the box at my feet reminds me.

"I really need to get this done. I can't pack if I don't know where all of my clothes are."

"Of course, not. If you have this under control, I'll go pack some things and make sure the jet will be ready."

"I've totally got it under control." I wave him off and reach for a cream blouse to hang.

"Do you want anything? A latte?"

"Oh my God, I'd give my right ovary for a latte."

"No need for that." Rafe leans in to kiss me. "I'll bring you one in a bit."

"You're handy to have around." I blow him a kiss and reach for another hanger. "I need to call Ivie back. I don't even know what she wants me to wear."

"Shit, you're right. I'd better ask Shane if he wants me to bring a suit. I'll see you in a bit."

"Okay." I reach for my phone as Rafe leaves and dial Ivie's number. I grin at the happiness in her voice when she answers.

"Hey there, bestie."

"You sound ecstatic."

"Are you kidding? I'm getting married in *Vegas*. How cool is that?"

"Very cool." Not what I would pick, but I'm thrilled that she's getting what she wants. "I need to know what the dress code is. Do I get to wear something fancy?"

"Hell, yes. I bought a gorgeous white dress that isn't technically a wedding dress, but it's going to be awesome. I know you have a closet full of nice dresses. Pick one."

"Is there a particular color you want me to wear?"

"You're beautiful in anything. Seriously, you choose."

"I'm going to bring a couple of choices, and we can decide together."

"Good idea. We're in the car headed to the airfield now. We'll be in Seattle by early afternoon. If all goes well, the five of us will be on the jet by dinnertime."

"Sounds good to me. And because I *am* your best friend, and I love you, I'm just going to double-check. This is what you want, right? You're not just doing this because you don't want to ask my uncle to pay for a big wedding?"

"No. Honest. Shane and I were talking about it, and we both think it sounds like fun. Spontaneous."

"It is that," I agree. "Okay, you sound excited, so I am, too. I'll be ready when you get here."

"Annika, I'm so happy. Like, *so happy*. I didn't think this could ever happen to me, and then Shane just burst into my life and wouldn't take no for an answer."

"The Martinelli men all have that in common." I finish hanging up the last of the *white* shirts and turn to open another box. "They're charming, and persistent."

"And don't forget sexy," Ivie reminds me. "Okay, we'll talk more when we have Nadia with us. I can't wait to hear about her honeymoon."

"Me, too. I hope they're having fun."

"Are you and Rafe doing okay?" she asks.

"Things were a little awkward at first, but they are calming down. We're growing more comfortable with each other. And now that sex is involved—"

"*Sex* is involved?" she interrupts. "Oh, man, I can't wait to hear about this. And I'll want all the details. Shane, hurry. I need to get to Annika."

"I'm going as fast as I'm allowed under the penalty of law," I hear him reply.

"Go faster," she replies. "Okay, I'll see you in a few hours."

"See you soon."

I hang up and dig in, truly wanting to be settled into this closet.

A couple of hours later, with an empty latte cup on the ottoman, all of my things are on hangers or tucked into drawers. My bags are on shelves. Shoes organized.

It's glorious.

And now, I have to pack to go see my best friend marry the love of her life.

CHAPTER
TWELVE
~ANNIKA~

"Carmine and Nadia just arrived," Rafe says as he walks into our hotel suite and sits on the bed next to me, where I'm nursing a hangover. Ivie and I had one too many celebratory shots of tequila last night.

Or seven too many.

But the drunk sex when Rafe and I got back to the room was *so* worth it.

"I brought you coffee," Rafe adds.

"Oh, thank God." I take the mug from him and take a long, grateful sip. "My God, I drank too much last night. And the worst part is, we'll probably do it all again tonight."

"You don't *have* to drink," he reminds me and pushes my hair over my shoulder. "You can pass."

"Yeah, I might do that. We'll see how things shake out. Now, I have to get myself together so I can hurry up to Ivie's suite and help her get ready."

"I'm meeting with the guys here in a little while. We're going to get ready in Carmine's room and when we're all good to go, we'll meet up with you ladies in the lobby."

"That sounds good." I take a deep breath, another sip of coffee, and lean over to rest my head on Rafe's shoulder. "I'm glad we came. It's a fun distraction."

"Did you need to be distracted?"

"No, but it's a good one all the same." I sigh. "Okay, I need to hop in the shower and get over there."

"I'd join you, but I'm worried that Shane will eat all the bacon." He kisses me on the nose, then pulls me off the bed. "Have fun. Call me if you need me."

"Same goes." I wave as Rafe heads for the door, grabbing his bag on the way out. When the door closes behind him, I take another deep breath.

I'm in Vegas, with all of the people I love the most, and I'm *with* Rafe. For the first time ever, I don't have to pretend that I don't love him. Everyone knows that we're together.

The shower helps to rejuvenate me, and by the time I wrap myself in a robe, pile my wet hair in a knot on top of my head, and gather all of my supplies to head over to Ivie's room, I almost feel like myself again. Which is good because Ivie's getting married, and I want to feel my best.

I make sure I have my room key in my bag and then head down the hall to Ivie's room. We're all staying at the Wynn, and we've taken over a floor of suites.

Because, of course, we have.

We're two wealthy families, which means that while Ivie may be eloping, it'll still be done in style.

I don't have to knock on the door because Shane's coming out of the room as I arrive.

"Hey," he says with a grin. "The other two are waiting for you."

"Thanks. How are you holding up?"

"I'm fantastic. The day can't go fast enough for me."

He holds the door for me, then waves at Ivie, who's just seen me, and claps her hands in excitement.

"See you soon, babe," he says and lets the door close behind me.

"He's about to be my *husband*," Ivie says before throwing her arms around me in a big hug. "How do you feel?"

"Hungover. Why aren't you in pain?"

"I was for a few minutes but then I took a shower. Now, I'm fine. Nadia just ordered all the food in the world, and we have hair and makeup people coming in about an hour."

"Whoa." I stop cold and stare at my cousin after rounding the corner to the dining room. She's tanned and looks damn happy with herself. "You're gorgeous. Obviously, the honeymoon agrees with you."

"I'd like to be on a honeymoon all the time," Nadia replies as she stands and wraps her arms around me. "It's going well. And this was a fun surprise to throw into the mix."

"Food's here!" Ivie announces at the sound of the doorbell.

"She's so *happy*," Nadia whispers to me. "She's giddy. I've never seen her like this. Ever."

"I know, and I like it. She's excited to marry him. He makes her happy."

"Clearly." Nadia turns her shrewd eyes to me. "When's it your turn?"

"He hasn't asked me. Besides, it's too soon."

"He'll ask," she says simply as a man rolls a big table full of food into the room. "You can leave that there. We'll take over."

After he collects his tip and leaves, we each pile plates full of food and sit at the table.

"So, you're getting hitched." Nadia shoves some melon into her mouth. "I want to see the dress."

"After I eat. I don't want to mess it up," Ivie replies. "Tell us about your honeymoon. Where have you been again?"

"Bora Bora," she says. "Let's just say it's been nothing but sex, lying in the sun, eating all the food, and more sex."

"God, that sounds horrible." I shake my head, feeling only a little jealous. "Your skin is glowing. Is that from all the sun, or all the sex?"

"Both." Nadia eats a strawberry and turns to Ivie. "Are you and Shane taking a honeymoon?"

"Not right away. I don't know where I want to go. He said we can go literally *anywhere*, and that overwhelmed me, so I'm thinking about it."

"There's a resort in Bora Bora I can recommend," Nadia says with a wink. "Do we have time to go shopping? Or should we wait until after the wedding?"

"Depends on what we're shopping for," I reply. "Actually, strike that.

No, we don't have time. When Nadia shops, it's an Olympic event. We'd better save that for tomorrow."

"I never got Carmine a wedding gift," she says. "And it's been bothering me. He not only got me this ridiculous rock but he also bought me a *new car*. Like, a whole car. A Porsche. I mean, who does that?"

"The Martinellis," Ivie and I say in unison, making us laugh.

"What are you going to get him?" I ask her.

"There's a special Rolex that I want to get him. And it's rare. But I made some calls on the down-low, and a boutique here has one in stock. They're holding it for me."

"Carmine likes watches, doesn't he?" I ask.

"Yeah. It's like me and handbags," Nadia replies with a shrug. "He'll die when he opens it. So, we'll go fetch it tomorrow morning. What did you get Shane, Ivie?"

Ivie blushes and then shrugs. "Nothing yet."

"But you have a plan." I lean forward. "Spill it."

"We're going to try to get pregnant," she says. "I want babies, you guys. And he does, too. So, we're working on it."

I blink at her. "Your wedding gift to Shane is the possibility of children?"

Ivie frowns. "Well, yeah. I guess. Damn it, is that lame?"

"Kinda lame," Nadia says. "We can do better than that."

"I don't think he needs a watch," Ivie says, thinking it over. "And he has all the electronic gadgets anyone needs. He doesn't wear jewelry. He's not fancy. Dear God, what do I get him?"

"Okay, don't panic," I say and reach over to put my hand on hers. "Obviously, there's no huge rush here. Just think it over and get him something *sometime*."

"Yeah, okay." Ivie takes a breath. "I'm going to show you guys my dress before the hair and makeup girls get here. Come on."

We file into the suite's second bedroom and watch as Ivie unzips a long garment bag, then peels it back.

"Holy shit." Nadia walks closer. "It sparkles."

"This is gorgeous, Ivie."

The dress is white and covered in gorgeous crystals that sparkle in the light. It's form-fitting and looks like the hem will hit just below the knee.

The bodice has a sweetheart neckline, and it's strapless.

"You'll be a bombshell in this," I inform my friend. "Shane will pass right out, and the boys will have to pick him up."

"I hope so," Ivie replies just as the doorbell rings again. "Okay, let's get this show on the road."

IVIE IS *gorgeous* in her dress, with her hair loose and curly, and her makeup done absolutely perfectly.

Nadia chose a red cocktail dress with a lace neckline, and I'm in a purple number that I've been *dying* to wear somewhere.

All of the guys are in suits.

Shane sprung for the best elopement package, complete with a photographer, flowers, and music.

And I have to admit, it's really beautiful.

"You married me." Ivie cuddles up to Shane in the limo, her bouquet still clutched in her hand.

"And I'd do it again," Shane says, kissing her on the forehead.

"Rafe and I put our heads together," Carmine says, catching all of our attention. "And rather than go out to eat with a bunch of strangers in a restaurant, we brought the party to us. We'll be in a private dining room at the hotel."

"That's so nice," Ivie says just as the limo stops at the hotel entrance where someone is waiting to usher us into a private elevator and up to the private suite for our makeshift reception.

The room is beautiful, with candlelight, a cake, and a table set with gorgeous flatware and more flowers.

"This was a good idea," I whisper to Rafe. "More intimate and special."

"That was the goal." He presses his hand to the small of my back. "Have I mentioned that you're stunning in this dress?"

"About a dozen times."

"Here's lucky number thirteen. You're a vision, Annika."

"Well, thank you very much. And you look dapper in this suit." I run a finger down his lapel.

"I hate wearing suits."

"I thought all mafiosos wore suits every day."

He smirks and shakes his head. "Hell, no. Only in the movies. Or if you're my dad."

"I'd like to propose a toast," Carmine says, raising his glass and catching our attention. "And maybe give a little speech. Bear with me. I'm happy for the both of you, Shane and Ivie. That you endured everything that happened a couple of months ago together and came out on the other side stronger. You clearly love each other very much and are happy together. So, here's to a lifetime of love and laughter. No matter what might come up, if you hang onto each other, you'll be okay. To Ivie and Shane."

"To Ivie and Shane," we agree and drink our champagne.

Dinner is a delicious steak with salad and potatoes and fresh asparagus. There's more food than most of us can eat.

And when it comes time to cut the cake, Ivie only gets a little frosting up Shane's nose.

But Shane gently holds the fork for her, not getting a speck on her.

"Well, that's no fun," Rafe mutters, making me laugh.

"It's respectful," I say, nudging him with my hip.

"How long do we have to stay?" Rafe asks, and I frown up at him.

"What do you mean? This is *your brother's* wedding, Rafe. We stay until it's over."

He sighs as if he's suffering.

"Why do you want to go?"

"I haven't had my hands on you in almost twenty-four hours."

His blue eyes shine as he stares down at me.

"I'm going to the bathroom. Meet me there."

Without waiting for him to reply, I walk away, through a small bedroom, and into the adjoining bath.

He doesn't knock.

He just walks right through the door, locks it behind him, and comes for me, his mouth set in firm lines. He's all business as he turns me away from him so I'm facing the mirror. He watches me in the reflection.

"This isn't going to be soft and gentle," he warns me.

"Fine by me." I shimmy my skirt up around my hips as he fumbles with his pants. The next thing I know, he bends me over and slides right inside.

"Jesus, you're so fucking wet."

"Always when you're around." I grab onto the edge of the vanity. "Oh, God, yes. Oh. This is a good angle."

"Fucking hell." His voice is a primal growl. He grips my hips, his fingers almost biting into my flesh as he fucks me hard from behind. I can't help the small cry that rips from my throat when I come, and then the whimper when he follows me over.

This might be the fastest quickie we've ever had.

But it was damn good.

And when he slips out of me and wipes off before tucking himself away, he looks mighty proud of himself.

"See?" I say as I wiggle my skirt back down into place. "Now we don't have to leave the party. But I do have to clean up, thanks to gravity. You go out first. I'll follow you."

He frames my face in his hands and kisses me long and slow. Finally, with a smile, he leaves the bathroom, and I take a moment to catch my breath and clean up.

That was unexpected.

When I walk back into the party, I'm met with sober faces and silence.

"What's wrong?" I ask immediately and hurry to Rafe. "What's happened?"

"We just got a call from Pop," he replies grimly. "Another boss and his family are dead. The Giovannis in Kansas City."

"This is a pattern," Nadia says. "Three families, all assassinated. These aren't unrelated. Someone is picking off syndicate families, one by one."

"Agreed," Carmine says and turns to Shane. "And I'm sorry that this call came in today."

"It pisses me off that it's happening at all," Shane replies. I wish I had my equipment, but I do have a computer in my room."

"I do, too," Ivie says. "We can do some digging tonight. Are the parents safe?"

"Igor said they're fine for now," Carmine says. "And I'll call Pop. I think we should have Igor and Katya come to Seattle where we can have them in one spot with Mom and Pop. Keep them all safe while we figure this out."

"My father has an army," Nadia reminds her husband. "He is capable of keeping himself and Mom safe."

"He can bring his army with him," Carmine says. "They're safer together, and we all know it."

"Let's take the cake back to our suite," Ivie suggests. "We can work and nibble on this there."

"You shouldn't have to work on your wedding night," I say, but Ivie just shakes her head.

"It's fine. Really. I had the best day ever, and now I get to do some hacking while eating delicious cake. Life's good. Let's go find the bastards behind this and make them pay."

"You've become a total mafioso wife," I accuse her with a laugh.

"Yeah, thanks." She wipes an imaginary tear from the corner of her eye. "It makes me all sentimental."

CHAPTER

THIRTEEN

~RAFE~

"Now that everyone's under one roof, security is in place, and we feel generally safe right now, let's go down and work out," Carmine suggests. We returned to Seattle from Vegas two days ago. We got our parents and the Tarenkovs settled into our grandmother's estate yesterday.

An army of men patrols the grounds at all times.

No one will get through.

And I could use some time in the gym with a punching bag.

"I'm down," Shane says. "Let's all meet down there in twenty? I could take a round with Rocco in the ring."

"If you plan on dying today," I say with a grin. "Yeah, we'll meet you down there."

I hurry up the stairs to the room that Annika used during Carmine and Nadia's wedding. This time, I'm not next to her. I'm staying *with* her. Just as it should be.

"Hey," Annika says when I walk through the door. "I was wondering where you ran off to."

"I was chatting with the brothers. Are you in the mood to work out?"

She arches a brow. "Sure. Where?"

"Just get dressed, and I'll show you."

"Okay, mysterious man." She jumps up and changes into leggings and a sports bra, then turns to me. "I'm ready."

"Not like that, you aren't."

She scowls and looks down at herself. "What's wrong with this?"

"It's a *bra*. You need a shirt over it."

"It's a sports bra. This can be the shirt."

"No."

She sets her hands on her hips and glares at me. "A bathing suit covers more. You're being a caveman. Let's go work out."

I cross my arms over my chest and stand firm. "If you think I'll let my brothers see you in that getup—"

"You're ridiculous." She flings her hands into the air and stomps to the dresser where she pulls out a tank and slips it over her head. "There, master. I'm all covered up. Happy?"

I grin. "Yes, actually."

"You know, you don't get to dictate everything I wear."

Before I can open the door of our room, I turn and pin her against the wall, my face inches from hers as I nibble her bottom lip. "Your outfit is sexy as fuck. I know my brothers love their girls, but they'd *see* that, and I don't want to have to kill them today. It's a simple tank top, A."

"Does this mean I can't wear a bikini when I go to the pool?"

"No." But the thought doesn't sit well with me. "I suppose not."

She laughs and pushes at my shoulder. "You're cute when you pout."

"I'm not pouting."

"Right. Not at all. Come on, let's work out. I didn't know there was a gym in this place."

"It's in the basement." I lead her to the elevator and refrain from pinning her against the wall, right here and now.

When we get to the basement entrance, the other four are already there, along with Curt, who's also riding this thing out here at Gram's house. Carmine is keying in the code to the heavy, iron door.

"What the hell is this place?" Nadia demands as the door swings open. "And why didn't you tell us about it before?"

635

"We were busy," Shane says with a shrug. "Okay, we have the gym over there. Through that door is the artillery vault and firing range."

"Holy shit," Ivie whispers. "It's a mini version of the ranch."

Shane turns and kisses her on the mouth. "Now you're just flattering me."

"This is crazy," Nadia breathes. "I want to see the weapons before we work out."

"Okay." Carmine presses his palm to the plate next to the door. When it opens, we all file in, and the lights automatically come on. The glass cases are also well lit, displaying all different kinds of weapons from daggers to automatic weapons.

Annika pulls her hand from mine and lifts a 9mm pistol out of the case.

"Whoa." I reach out and take the gun from her. "I don't think you should be handling this."

"Is it loaded?"

"They're all loaded, sweetheart. These are all dangerous weapons. A novice shouldn't be playing with them."

She nods, stares at the gun in my hand, and then takes it back. "Where's the firing range?"

Nadia snorts, but I don't look her way. "Over there."

"Let's go." She leads the way to one of the firing lanes, sets up a target, and sends it down the line. Then, without missing a beat, she pops the magazine out of the gun, examines it, pops it back in, loads one in the chamber, and lifts both hands. She fires a single round, pulls the magazine out of the weapon before setting it down, and pushes the button to fetch the target.

We're all quiet, watching intently.

And when the target arrives, there's a single hole in the forehead of the outline of a man.

I blink at her and then the target again.

"Nadia taught me," is all Annika says.

"Did you think I'd let the niece of a boss go through life unable to protect herself?" Nadia demands, still grinning. "Annika is a hell of a shot. And she knows her way around any weapon you have in there. She's no pussy."

I'm so turned on right now, I can hardly breathe.

"Do you have any more *mansplaining* you'd like to do?" Annika asks.

My brothers crack up.

Ivie and Nadia both high-five her.

Without saying a word, I pick her up and toss her over my shoulder.

"Hey!" Annika says and smacks me on the ass.

"I think Annika's about to get lucky," I hear Ivie say.

"Dude, you're a caveman," Shane calls out, and I throw up my hand, flipping them all the bird as they laugh and jeer behind us.

I don't break my stride as I choose the stairs rather than the elevator. I'm barely breathing hard when I reach our room.

Once inside, I put her on her feet and stare into mutinous blue eyes.

"That was *embarrassing.*"

"Why?" I trap her against the wall the way I did not long ago before we went downstairs. "Because I hauled you out of there?"

"Over your *shoulder.*"

"Damn right. It was that or drag you, and carrying you was easier."

Her eyes narrow. "What's wrong with you?"

"I'm so turned on, I can't see straight."

That stops her. Her mouth opens and closes until she settles on, "What?"

"You heard me." I nip the side of her mouth. "I had no idea you could shoot like that. It was a lightning bolt straight through me. Jesus, seeing you hold a gun like that was the sexiest thing I've ever seen. I needed you. I *need* you. And you said you wanted to have sex pushed up against the wall."

"So that's moved up on the schedule, then?"

I grin and tear her leggings at the crotch. "Hell, yes."

There are no more words as we rip our clothes from our bodies. When I sink inside her, it's like coming home. I'm an animal. I can't go slow; I can't take my time.

All I can think about is the overwhelming drive to *mate* with her.

And when she moans with that gritty, dirty edge to her voice and clamps around my cock, it's my undoing. I empty myself inside her and have to lean on the wall to catch my breath.

"Well." Annika swallows hard. "That was fun. Let's put it back on the schedule for another time."

I laugh and set her on her feet. "I always have time for this."

"I WANT to go over everything we know," Pop says later in the evening when we're all together with our drinks of choice. Pop sits next to Igor, while Mom and Katya are seated by the window, drinking wine.

Curt, Shane, Carmine, and I are seated at a table with a glass of whiskey, and the girls are on couches, lounging with their wine and eating chocolate ice cream from the tub.

It's as casual as it gets around here, and my grandmother would have loved it.

"We have three bosses and their families, all murdered, in the last few weeks," Igor says, rubbing his chin. "Not by the same methods. No notes left behind, and no family taking credit for it."

"There was a car accident," Carmine adds, picking up the facts. "Killed the boss, his wife, and their daughter in Chicago. Then, we have the family in Boston, who were all sent into the water with cement shoes."

"This last one in Kansas City is even more disturbing," Pop says, shaking his head. "The boss and his wife had their throats slashed. The children, both under the age of twelve, were drugged and left for dead. One child, the youngest son, survived and is in the hospital under constant supervision."

"Has anyone called Elena?" Mom asks, catching our attention.

"Shit, I'll do that as soon as we're done here," Carmine says. "She and Archer are in Oregon, tucked away."

"Why do you need to call your cousin?" Nadia asks, frowning. "She's been on the down-low for years."

"We'll send some extra men to keep an eye on her," Carmine replies. "Besides, after what happened to her parents, we've always been more careful where she's concerned."

"What happened to her parents again? I know someone killed them, but I don't know the story."

"My sister, Claudia, was married to Vinnie Watkins, who was the boss at the time. Vinnie was a piece of shit, but he was still the boss," Pop says, telling the story. "When Elena was about twenty, I guess, Vinnie went to prison. He got too cocky with some money laundering and got caught. It was disgraceful. He was too prideful. While in prison, someone killed him."

"Claudia was killed in a car accident," Mom says, picking up the story, "on the same day."

"It wasn't an accident," Pop insists, slamming his fist on the table. "She was murdered."

"Well, we weren't able to prove that, were we?" Mom asks. "Carlo's mother, the woman who owned this house, spent many years trying to find those responsible for her daughter's death. Also, within hours of Claudia and Vinnie being killed, she hid Elena away. From all of us. For over a decade, we all thought Elena was also dead, her body not likely to be found."

"They didn't tell you that they were hiding Elena away?" Annika asks, shocked.

"No," Pop says. "However, *I* knew. I was the only one who did. Because the men my mother hired to help Elena disappear worked for *me*. Not her. I didn't tell anyone else because they didn't need to know. The fewer who knew, the safer Elena was."

"Still not happy that you didn't tell us," Carmine says, but Pop just shrugs.

"I run my house the way I see fit, and you know that. I don't apologize for it. Elena was safer because she was gone."

"I'm calling her now," Carmine says, tapping his phone. After three rings, Elena answers.

"Hey, favorite cousin," she says.

"I heard that," I call out.

"You're all my favorite, Rocco," she reminds me and makes me smile. "What's up with you guys?"

"Are you and Archer still in Oregon?" Carmine asks.

"Yeah, we're at the beach house. It's been a nice break, but I think we're heading back to the city in a couple of days."

"I want you to stay where you are," Pop says sternly. "Some things are happening here that I don't want you around for. Stay there with your husband. I'll have some men come to keep an eye on things, as well."

"Something big is going down," Elena says, her voice sober. "Don't worry, we'll cooperate. I'm happy to spend more time at the beach."

"Good girl," Pop says. "We'll be in touch."

"I'll call you soon," Carmine adds and clicks off.

"So, the people who killed Elena's parents are killing the other bosses?" Annika says.

We all look her way and frown.

"Not necessarily," Pop says. "What happened to Claudia and Vinnie was more than a decade ago. This isn't related."

"I don't think you're seeing the big picture," Annika disagrees. "And I don't mean that to sound disrespectful. Let's outline this. Bosses and their entire immediate families are coming up dead—all murdered in different ways. Your sister and brother-in-law were murdered. And your mother feared for Elena's life so much that she sent her away. She thought it was even a secret, so she could keep her safe. Why would she think that Elena would be killed? Most of the time, when a boss is murdered, the rest of their family isn't executed, as well."

"But why would they wait so long to continue?" Shane asks.

"Everyone is always saying that the mafia has a long memory," Nadia points out. "And they're not wrong. This started all those years ago with Elena's parents. And now, someone is systematically making their way through all of the prominent families in the country."

"We're going to find them," I promise. "And we're going to end them."

"Oh, we certainly are," Nadia agrees. "But we need to know where to start."

"Gram has boxes and boxes full of research," Shane says, thinking it over. "When we discovered that Elena was alive and were trying to find her, we found the boxes. She must have hired dozens of investigators to find the killer or killers and filed everything away methodically. There has to be something in there that she missed."

"Well, we have a whole room full of fresh eyes," Ivie says. "And I don't mean to sound heartless, but some of us aren't personally connected. Maybe we'll see something that your grandmother didn't."

"You're forgetting something," Igor says, speaking for the first time as he turns to Pop. "We're in *your* home, my friend. Anything here, including the investigative reports, are proprietary to your family. If you don't want my family digging into that business, I understand."

All eyes turn to Pop, who's rubbing his chin again.

"If I didn't trust you and the rest of your family, Igor, you wouldn't be in my family's home. You know that. This doesn't just impact my family now. It affects yours, as well as all of the other organizations in the country. Perhaps the world. If something here can help solve this mystery, it's open to all of you. Your firefly is right. Fresh eyes are helpful. Our young people are intelligent. And we're stronger together."

Igor nods, happy with Pop's answer. "I couldn't agree more. Let's get to the bottom of this and terminate those responsible. No mercy on this, do you understand?"

We nod. Oh, we understand perfectly well.

The assholes responsible for killing so many people are about to be punished for their crimes.

FOURTEEN

~ANNIKA~

"That's the last of them," Shane says as he sets a box on the floor of the family room where we're all sitting, reading through old reports. There are seven moving-sized boxes stacked against the wall.

We're only one box in.

This is going to take a while.

"Some of these are just your grandmother's notes. Her thoughts," Ivie says as she stares down at a pile of papers in her lap. "She was so filled with grief."

"Yeah, and my aunt Claudia wasn't a prize," Carmine says with a wince. "I know, speaking ill of the dead and all, but she really wasn't. Pop said that Vinnie was a piece of shit, and he totally was. But Claudia wasn't much better. Maybe she was softer when she was young. I only knew her to be cold and brash."

"Elena definitely wasn't close to her," Rafe adds. "She hit the shit jackpot when it came to her parents."

"It's why she spent so much time with us." Shane sits on the floor next to Ivie and digs out some papers from the box. "She was always at our house. And in the summers, she came here to spend time with Gram. She's really more like a sister to us."

"Guys." I wave a pile of papers around. "I just found crime scene photos from the car wreck."

"Nice," Rafe says next to me. The others crowd around me as I lay the photos on a table, spreading them out so we can all look. "Man, that car was charred."

"Was it a Mercedes?" Ivie asks, squinting. "I think I see the logo in this picture."

"Yeah. Mercedes sedan." Rafe leans in to get a closer look, his hand on my shoulder. "So, she hit a tree?"

"Looks like it," Carmine says.

"And from what Gram said, the cops ruled it an accident."

I'm staring at one photo in particular. "You guys, this just doesn't look right. That tree is a good twenty yards from the road. How does she just veer off and hit it? Not to mention, there are no tire tracks on the road."

"You're right," Curt murmurs. "No tire tracks at all."

"Also, can we just talk about the fact that her front end isn't mangled?" Ivie asks. "If she hit the tree, and it set the car on fire, why isn't the front end totaled? It looks like someone just pushed it over to the tree and set it on fire."

"You think?" Carmine says bitterly. "Of course, they did. Like Pop said, she was murdered. This was no accident, and these photos prove it. Not that they prove much else."

"I'm going to keep looking at them," Ivie says thoughtfully. "Something else might pop out at me."

"Good idea." I return to my pile of papers and sit on the floor. "I could use some pizza while I do this."

"Same." Nadia reaches for her phone. "I'll order some in. Everyone tell me what they want."

"SHE SAVED *EVERYTHING*," Rafe says later after we've consumed four pizzas and made our way through two boxes. "For a woman who was so tight-lipped and didn't keep anything helpful in her office, she sure saved a lot of shit."

"I went through most of this before," Carmine adds. "But I just skimmed, looking for Elena's name since that was the focus. I should have been more thorough."

"You're one person," I remind him. "Now there's seven of us. We'll get through it."

"Your parents are here," Rafe says, checking his phone. "Security just texted me."

"Oh, I'll go say hi. I'll be right back."

I stand, jump over a box, and hurry from the room.

"Mama!" I rush over and pull my mom in for a hug. "You guys were supposed to be here yesterday."

"Your father had some things to wrap up," she says. "But we were very safe, don't worry. And we're here now."

"Where is Dad?" I ask, looking around.

"He's already off to find Igor and Carlo," Mom says, shaking her head. "He's eager to talk business."

"Typical." I loop my arm through hers. "You have a beautiful room upstairs."

"This is such a beautiful home," she replies. "I enjoyed being here for Nadia's wedding. I guess, if we have to be locked up somewhere, there are far worse places to be."

"No kidding. And you aren't exactly locked up. You just can't go anywhere without an escort."

She glances at me with eyes so much like mine and then giggles. "Yes, I see the difference. I'd like to get settled into our room and maybe take a little nap. You know what a nervous wreck I am on airplanes. I didn't get any rest at all."

"I know. You hate to fly. Well, you're here now." I show her up to her room, and once we've fussed over the beautiful décor and hug twice more, I leave her to nap.

But I'm not in a hurry to find the others. Not because we're working through all of the boxes of documents but because I could use a few minutes by myself.

I glance to my left and grin.

I'll just take a short walk through the yard.

The estate is beautiful and vast. Carlo's mother was a classy woman, and from what I gather, a little *extra*.

She loved fancy things, and that shines through in her home. Outside of museums, I've never seen so much artwork in my life. I'm afraid to touch anything. Rooms like the family room are comfortable to relax in, but other spaces are quite formal.

I'm sure it was a formidable place to host gatherings in. If she wanted to intimidate other families, all she had to do was invite them here.

I take a deep breath, sucking in the fresh air. It smells like it's going to rain, and if the dark clouds overhead are any indication, we'll have plenty of it by this evening.

But for now, the sun is still peeking through. I set off down a path that winds away from the house toward a row of trees.

I love being here. Even though we've only been in Seattle for a short time, it feels good. Like home. The air is fresh, and I just love how *green* everything is.

Not to mention, being with Rafe is a dream come true.

It was surreal last night, sitting in that room with Rafe's parents and Uncle Igor as if we did it all the time as a couple. Rafe even held my hand at one point. I almost jerked back, afraid that Uncle Igor would notice.

And then I remembered.

We can be together.

So much warmth and joy filled me at the thought, I was surprised it didn't radiate from me.

When I get to the edge of the trees, I'm surprised to find a tree house. And from the looks of it, it's pretty sturdy.

I glance around to see if anyone is watching.

I'm a grown woman. I have no business climbing up into a tree house.

I bite my lip.

"But it looks like fun," I mutter, and then decide...what the hell? Rafe and his brothers must have spent a lot of time up here when they were kids. And from what they said last night, it sounds like Elena played out here with them.

I wonder what they were like as kids? I grin as I reach the top of the ladder and step onto the platform.

I can just imagine Rafe running around here with a toy sword, playing pirate or space invaders with his siblings. I'm glad that he had the experience of growing up with a loving grandparent, and a safe haven to spend his summers.

I cross to the window and look outside at the grounds, surprised to see how far I wandered from the house.

It didn't feel that far when I walked over here.

The green grass is bright, and the house stands grandly a couple of hundred yards away.

I'm glad my parents arrived. I've been worried about them. All of them, actually. Someone out there has a vendetta against the mafia, and they're doing a good job of killing off entire families.

But why?

That's the question. Of course, every organization has done their fair share of bad things. You're friendly with some families and others you don't trust and can't stand.

But it's never *all of them.*

Is this someone who's been cast out of a family? Is this how they're taking their revenge?

I don't like it. And out here, by myself, I can admit that it scares the hell out of me. Because Rafe is a soldier in his organization. He'll go in with his brothers and do his best to kill the bad guys.

But, in the process, he could get killed himself. I suppose that's true every time he goes out on a mission for the family.

It's one of the reasons I always said I wouldn't marry someone connected to organized crime. I've seen too many women become widows far too young.

We've been lucky in my family. And the Martinellis have been fortunate, as well.

But when will that luck change?

"I don't want to find out." I take another deep breath. "And I can't help who I love. I tried to deny it for years. I told myself that Rafe was lost to me and that it was for the best. But it was *never* for the best.

Because all I did was long for him. I married Richard, hoping that I could fall in love with someone else and be happy.

"And we all know where that got me."

I swallow hard and watch as the first fat drops start to fall from the sky.

"I'm done denying what my heart and head both tell me is right. Rafe is it for me. And I'm finally with him. The fact that he's very much a part of his mafia family is just something I'll have to learn to live with. And, for the immediate future, we have to figure out who's trying to kill us and stay alive."

I refuse to be a widow before he's even asked me to marry him.

I yawn and then frown when I hear someone yelling my name. I glance around and narrow my eyes when I see Rafe running over the grass, calling for me.

"Hey!" I wave out the window and smile when he sees me. But he doesn't look happy in the least.

He runs over to the tree house, faster than I've ever seen anyone move in my life. He lifts his phone to his mouth, but I can't hear what he says.

And when he reaches me, he quickly climbs up, rushes over, and yanks me into his arms.

He's panting, gasping for air.

"Hey, what happened? Rafe, what's wrong?"

"We couldn't find you." He pulls back and frames my face in his hands. "Jesus Christ, A, don't do that to me ever again. You scared the shit out of me."

"I didn't go far."

"What if someone had nabbed you?"

"I'm *right here*."

He just rocks us back and forth, clinging to me.

"I just got you back in my life. I can't lose you again. Now or ever."

"Funny." I turn my face and kiss his chest. "I was just thinking the same. I want to wrap this all up so we can get on with our lives. And I need us both to live through it."

"We will."

"Promise."

"I promise. I have no intention of being apart from you again. And the next time you want to go for a walk, just let me know, and I'll go with you."

"I wanted a few minutes alone," I reply and then snort when he scowls as if I've hurt his feelings. "We're allowed to have a few moments alone now and again. It's healthy."

"Then just warn me so I'm not off on a frantic wild goose chase."

"Deal. I didn't mean to scare you, Rafe."

"I know. Hey, are you ever going to call me Rocco?"

I laugh and lead him to the ladder. "Hell, no."

"Why?" He's not mad now. He's just grinning. He knows the answer to this.

"Because *Rocco* is a meathead's name. And you're no meathead."

"I kinda am, honey."

"No." I bounce down to the ground and wait for him to join me so I can plant a kiss on his cheek. "You aren't. Everyone else in the world can call you Rocco for all I care, but your name is *Rafe*. So that's what I'll call you."

"Fine."

"Do you really hate it that much?"

"No, but I have a reputation to uphold here. Rocco sounds tougher. I need people to think I'm a badass."

"We all know you're a badass." He takes my hand and leads me back to the path so we can walk back to the house. "But you're not badass with me. You're sweet and gentle. Sexy. Everything."

"I like that last word the best."

I glance up and grin. "Yeah? Well, it's true. Besides, it would sound weird if I called you Rocco."

"Try it."

"Hey, Rocco, will you pass me the chips?"

He thinks about it and then starts laughing. "Okay, yeah. It sounds dumb when you say it."

"See? Told you."

"I'm hungry."

"We literally just had pizza."

"Yeah, but then I thought you were missing and used up about two thousand calories in adrenaline. I think there's some pepperoni left."

"Let's go find it, then."

FIFTEEN

"Ithought it would be easier today with fresh eyes," I mumble as I sit on the couch, Annika next to me, and another pile of papers in my lap. "It's not. Still boring as fuck."

"Drink more coffee," Ivie suggests.

"I never thought *fuck* was boring," Nadia says, her eyes narrowed thoughtfully as she sips her coffee. "I mean, if you're doing it right."

I shake my head. "Carmine, control your woman."

Nadia's face splits into a slow grin. "Yeah, Carmine. Control your woman."

"She'll kill you, man," Carmine says to me with a sigh. "Don't provoke her."

"Did anyone ever go talk to this Danvers guy?" Curt asks out of the blue. He looks up from the page he's been reading and frowns. "It says here that John Danvers killed Vinnie, but so far, I haven't heard any of you mention any research into that dude. No personal investigator interviews or anything."

"I don't know," Shane says, shaking his head.

"I'll go talk to him. Where is he?"

"Hold on," Ivie says as she taps on the keys of her laptop, which is always nearby. "He's at a maximum-security prison in Walla Walla. On death row."

"Who do we know that can get in there to have a little chat with Danvers?"

"Wait." Annika rests her hand on my arm. "I don't think it's a good idea for you to go into a prison to see a killer."

I blink down at her. "Why not?"

"Because he's a *killer*, Rafe."

"He's in *prison*," I reply. "It's not like I'm going to pose as an inmate and try to talk to him on the inside, for God's sake."

"I don't like it," she whispers with a mutinous scowl on her gorgeous face.

"Hey." I take her chin in my hand and lean in to kiss her. "I'll be fine."

"Who do we know who can get Rocco into the prison?" Shane asks.

"Archer's cousin, Matt Montgomery, might be someone to talk to," Carmine says. "He's a top cop in Seattle and probably has connections."

"Let's call Archer."

I pull my phone out of my pocket and put the call through to Elena's husband. He answers after the second ring.

"Hey, Rocco, what's up?"

"I have a question for you. Do you think your cousin Matt would speak with me?"

He's quiet for a second. "I guess that depends on what you want to talk about."

"We're doing some digging into Elena's parents' deaths," I say, quickly filling him in. "I'd like to go speak to Danvers in person. But you can't just show up to a maximum-security prison and ask to speak to someone on death row, you know?"

"Makes sense. I'm sure Matt would talk to you, especially about this. Let me give him a call and give him your number."

"Excellent. Thanks, man. Let him know he can call anytime."

"Will do."

He hangs up, and I rub my hands together. "This doesn't suck. This is a *plan*. I can't just sit here and read old notes. It's making me crazy. Is anyone else hungry?"

"Mom's making breakfast burritos," Annika says. "She'll call out for us when they're ready."

"Your mom can *cook*," Ivie says with a grin. "I'm so glad she's here."

"Me, too."

My phone rings in my hand, surprising me. "That was fast. Hi, Matt, this is Rocco."

"Archer filled me in on what's going on. I have a buddy who used to work with us here at the force who moved to Walla Walla a few years ago. His wife's family is there. Anyway, he's the warden at that facility. I'm sure I can get you in."

"Can we make it happen today?"

"I'll give him a call and ask. Are you driving over? It's a long way."

"I'll take the helicopter."

"Would you mind if I rode with you? I'd like to observe your interview. I work homicide now, and I'd be interested to hear what he has to say."

"Doesn't bother me at all, especially if your friend can help me out."

"I'll call you back as soon as I know anything. I can be ready to leave in about an hour."

"Great."

I click off just as Annika's mom walks into the room carrying a big tray heaping with steaming breakfast burritos.

"We could have come fetched these," Curt says, jumping up to take the heavy tray from her.

"You're busy," she says with a smile. "I'll be right back with some plates and stuff."

She bustles out and quickly returns with all kinds of condiments.

"This is like a delicious buffet," I mutter, my stomach growling. Before I can take even one bite, my phone rings again.

"Rocco."

"It's Matt. We're good to go. Just tell me where to meet you."

THE SMALL AIRSTRIP outside of Walla Walla is only a couple of miles from the prison. There's a car there, and a tall, dark-haired man waiting for us.

"Montgomery," he says with a smile as he walks toward us. He puts his hand out to shake Matt's. "It's damn good to see you."

"You, too," Matt says with a smile. "You look great, Middleton."

"Yeah, well, it's the armpit of the state here, but the wife's happy." He shrugs and turns to me. "You must be Martinelli."

"That's right." I shake his hand. "Thank you for letting us come today."

"Matt's an old friend. It's not a problem. I'll drive you over."

We all pile into the car, Middleton in the driver's seat and Matt next to him. I'm in the back, which I don't mind because I can get the lay of the land around us.

It's flat. Not much to see. And certainly nowhere for someone to hide, should they escape.

"Couple of things to remember when you get inside," Middleton says. "First, we'll take your weapons off your hands and return them to you when you're ready to leave. Next, this guy's an asshole. He's not physically violent, but he has a mouth on him. He'll be secured to the chair, unable to move about the room. Matt and I will be on the other side of the observation glass, and we have three armed guards on standby should he decide to *get* physically violent."

"Has anyone else come to see him since he's been in?" I ask.

"Not a one," Middleton replies. "In the nine years he's been a guest at our beautiful resort, he's had no visitors, no calls. No mail. He doesn't send anything out."

"I have Ivie doing a background search on him," I murmur. "My sister-in-law is good at research. So, to clarify, he's had no contact with the outside world at all in nine years?"

"That's right."

"Interesting."

"It's not unusual," Middleton continues. "These guys are the shit-bags of society, Rocco. They've not only murdered. Many of them are rapists, have killed family members, and did all sorts of despicable crap that embarrassed their families. Hurt them. They don't have loved ones. They gave that up long ago."

"But I've heard about women who get off on establishing relationships with dudes on death row," I say. "Do you get much of that here?"

"Yeah, some of the guys get letters now and then. I don't get it. But we don't have anyone married to someone they met while on the inside here."

"No conjugal visits?"

"Hell, no. Not on death row. Besides, these aren't the kind of guys most women want to fuck, you know what I mean?"

My stomach hardens.

Middleton pulls into his parking slot, and we walk through three sets of secure, heavy doors. Matt and I are relieved of our weapons, and we walk through metal detectors. I have to sign a book and a waiver.

Before long, we're walking down an institutional-looking hallway lined with doors. The walls are grey. The floor is grey. It smells of disinfectant.

I guess death row isn't supposed to be pleasant.

"You're in here," Middleton says and then points to the door just three feet to the left. "And we're in here. The armed guards are in with you. If, at any time, you don't feel comfortable, just say so and you can leave."

"Jesus, is he going to try to eat my face or something?"

"We never know with these assholes." Middleton sighs. "You can go in."

I'm not one to stereotype. I didn't have any preconceived notions when I walked in here today regarding what this Danvers would look like.

But when I walk through the door, the man sitting at the table is pretty much what I would expect when I think *murderer*.

He's probably fifty but looks much older than that with wrinkled skin covered in tattoos from his hairline to the tips of his fingers. His brown eyes are hard and cold. His hair's a long, tangled mess.

And when I sit across from him, he simply stares at me.

"Did they tell you who I am?" I ask.

"No."

"I'm Rocco Martinelli. I'm here to talk to you because you were convicted of killing Vinnie Watkins nine years ago."

He doesn't say anything, just stares at me.

"Vinnie was my uncle by marriage. I'd like to talk to you about the circumstances surrounding the case."

"Read the fucking case files," he says.

"I don't want to. I want to talk to *you*." I don't lean forward. I don't even blink. "I want to know who hired you to kill Vinnie."

His impassive face doesn't even twitch. "I don't have to tell you shit."

"Nope. You don't have to. But you're already here, man. It's over. More people are dying. Three bosses killed last week. And their families."

Now, his eyes narrow in interest.

"When we started looking at the big picture, it seemed like these recent murders are similar to when Vinnie and his wife died."

"Been a long time," Danvers says.

"Yeah. A long time. And in this business, people have long memories. So, I'd like to ask you, man to man, who hired you?"

"I ain't in your business, man. Maybe my memory ain't so good."

"I think your memory is just fine."

He watches me and seems to think it over. And just when I think he's not going to say any more, he sighs and starts to talk.

"Didn't nobody hire me. I didn't kill him."

I scoff, but Danvers shakes his head with impatience. "I'm telling you, I didn't kill 'im. I ain't got nothing to lose here, man. I was his cellmate. Vinnie was a stupid piece of shit. Ran his mouth, thought his shit didn't stink. Let me tell you, it did. He thought he was too good to be in here, but he got caught doing some shady shit, you know? Anyway, I didn't like the fucker, but I was only in for a couple of years, got caught sellin' some dope. Not a huge amount, just enough to get me a couple years, you know?"

Now that he's started talking, he won't shut up. And he says *you know* after every other sentence. But it's fucking fascinating.

"So, one morning, I wake up, and Vinnie's dead in his bunk. Bled through the mattress, too. Fucker. And I banged on the bars to get the guard's attention. Next thing I know, I'm being hauled off to isolation, and then I'm standing trial for killin' the son of a bitch. I dealt. I admit that. I was into some bad shit. But I ain't never killed nobody, you know?"

"Did you tell the public defender all of this?"

"Sure, but nobody wanted to listen to me. They wouldn't even let me testify on the stand on my behalf. Said it would look bad to the jury. Instead, the motherfucker lawyer they gave me just sat back on his hands and let the DA tell the jury what a jerk I was, presented evidence that wasn't true, and then I'm sentenced to die. Here I am."

I narrow my eyes at him. "John, are you telling me *no one* ever contacted you about Vinnie, about who he was, and asked you to kill him or offered to pay you to kill him?"

"Fuck no. I have a daughter. Ain't seen her in a dozen years now. Won't ever again. I was supposed to get out. Get clean. Be a dad. I wouldn't have killed nobody."

I sit back, stunned at this turn of events. Could he be lying? Possibly. But my gut tells me no.

"Thank you for telling me all of this. For being straight with me."

"You're the asshole's family. I guess you should know the real story. Not that it does any good now."

"You'd be surprised. And, John, if I can prove this and get everything resolved, we're going to work on getting you out of here and back with your daughter."

His eyes light up for a nanosecond but then dull again. "Won't work. Thanks for sayin' that, but it won't work."

"We'll see." I stand and nod at him. "We'll see about that."

I leave the room and meet up with Matt and Middleton in the hallway.

"What do you think?" I ask Matt as I rub my hand over the back of my neck.

"I don't think he's lying," Matt says slowly. "I've interviewed a shit-ton of suspects in my time, and the liars don't tend to give up that much information. He looked you in the eye. And when you said you'd help him, he looked...hopeful."

"Agreed," Middleton says. "I've never seen him like that. And if he's here because someone dirty put him here, that'll piss me the fuck off."

"I'm going to keep digging," I reply. "They may have already found something else back home while I've been gone."

"If you find any other reasons to believe that Danvers is innocent, you get the information to me," Matt says. "And I'll help get it to the people who can help him."

"Will do."

THE FLIGHT back is uneventful and quiet, with Matt and I both lost in our thoughts. Once back at Gram's place, I hurry in to check in with the others.

Carmine smashes a soda can in his hand after I recount the interview.

"Someone fucking set him up," Carmine growls.

"I mean, that's not shocking," Nadia points out. "It happens."

"Not like this," Shane disagrees. "We don't send innocent people to death row. We don't involve civilians in organization business."

"Sometimes, there are casualties," Igor says, thinking it over. "But, no, it's not something we like to do."

"I want to know who the fuck set up that man for killing Vinnie," Pop says, his eyes hard as steel. "Because I'm going to kill them with my own hands."

"I might know something," Ivie says, surprising us all. "Right before Rafe got home, I was doing some digging on the Danvers' trial. The judge was one Honorable Lawrence Santiago. He'd been a judge in Washington for only three years at the time. Relocated here from Florida."

"Okay," Pop says, frowning. "And?"

"Well, at first, it ended there. It's pretty weird to only have three years' history on a forty-something-year-old man. So, I peeled back some layers. Turns out, Lawrence P. Santiago is actually Santiago-Reyes. The brother of Phillipe Reyes. Of Miami."

Pop's eyes narrow. "Of the Reyes organization."

"That's right," Ivie says. "He has ties to the mafia family in Miami."

"Looks like we're headed to Miami in the morning," I say. "Get packed."

CHAPTER
SIXTEEN
~ANNIKA~

"I called ahead," Shane says after we land in Miami. "And I just heard back from Maceo, Phillipe's son. He said he's at the hospital, and we can meet him there."

Rafe and Carmine share a look.

"Why are they at the hospital?" I ask.

"Looks like we're about to go find out," Nadia says. "And I don't have a good feeling about this."

Because of traffic, it takes more than an hour to reach the hospital. When we all file out of the car, we find a dark-haired, dark-skinned man approaching with a grim look on his face. When he sees me, he does a double-take but then shakes his head and addresses Carmine.

"I have a waiting room set up for us inside," he says by way of greeting. "I don't want any trouble today."

"You won't get any trouble," Carmine says to the other underboss. "We just have questions."

Maceo nods and leads the six of us inside to a waiting room on the second floor, where three other men wait. When he closes the door, he turns to us.

"What is this about?"

"First, why are you at the hospital?" Carmine asks, and Maceo narrows his eyes.

"You don't know?"

"No, we've been on a plane most of the morning. Miami's pretty far away from Seattle," Rafe says.

"My father was killed this morning," Maceo replies. "My mother is in intensive care with multiple stab wounds. My young sister is on the run with her Godfather because we don't know who did this or what the motive is."

I shake my head and turn to Ivie, who slips her hand into mine.

"Fucking hell," Carmine growls. "Jesus, I'm sorry, Maceo. We hadn't heard."

"Ours is the fourth family targeted," Maceo says.

"Fifth," Shane says. "We have reason to believe this began more than a decade ago with Vinnie and Claudia Watkins."

Shane briefly fills the other man in and then says, "Where is Lawrence Reyes? The man who goes by Santiago? And why was he working in our city?"

Maceo scowls. "My father's brother?"

"That's the one," Carmine says.

"My family hasn't had anything to do with that asshole in twenty years. He's a traitor. He was feeding information back and forth to the Carlito family in Dallas. Working both sides."

"But the Carlitos haven't been active for many years," Carmine says.

"If you think that family has been sleeping all these years, you're an idiot," Maceo says, cutting to the chase. "They've been quiet, but they're not asleep. I don't know what they had on my uncle or why he decided to start working for them. It was the biggest disgrace of my father's life. Everyone told my father to kill Lawrence, but he couldn't do it. He gave his brother an ultimatum. If he wouldn't stop working for the Carlitos, he was no longer welcome here.

"He left the next day, and no one has heard from him since. I don't know why he was working in Seattle."

"He was the *judge* on the case of the man accused of killing Vinnie," Rafe tells him.

"I've honestly told you everything I know." Maceo stops and glances over at me, looking like he wants to say something, but then turns back to Rafe. "The Carlitos are dirty as hell, man. If they're behind all of these assassinations, they need to be taken out."

"I have a feeling we'll be headed to Dallas in the morning," Carmine says.

"I'd like to go with you," Maceo says.

"You have your hands full here," Shane points out. "With your father dead and your mother in the ICU. Not to mention, you're now the boss of your organization, Maceo. Let us go take care of this. We will keep you informed every step of the way."

"I don't like sending someone else in to clean up my mess," Maceo says.

"It's our mess, too. Has been for a damn long time," Carmine replies. "It's going to be handled."

Maceo nods and gestures to me as we turn to leave. "I'd like to talk to you."

"Me?" I point at myself and then glance behind me.

"Yes, you." He pins the others with dark brown eyes. "Alone."

"Fuck that," Rafe says, pushing me behind him. "If you have business with her, you have business with *me*."

"Hey." I pat Rafe's shoulder and smile when he looks down at me. "Just wait right outside the door. You're right here. Nothing's going to happen."

"No."

"I only want to have a private word. I mean her no harm. I give you my word," Maceo says.

Finally, Rafe nods once and steps outside the door but watches through the little window.

"He's in love with you," Maceo says.

"Yeah. What's up?" I ask.

"I want you to know that I've received emails from an unknown source. They contained photos. Of you."

I narrow my eyes as the blood leaves my face, and my heart hammers.

"I didn't know you at all until you got out of that car. I only recognized you from the photos. Someone is trying to ruin your reputation, and the reputation of the Tarenkov family. What you do with this information is up to you."

"What did you do with the photos?"

"I deleted them." His eyes harden. "We don't hurt women, Annika. I have no beef with you or your family. Therefore, I have no reason to keep them. But I can't tell you where they were sent from."

"Do you know if they were sent to other families?"

"No, I don't know."

I nod and offer him a small smile. "Thanks for letting me know."

"Good luck to you."

"Same to you. And I really am sorry for your loss."

I slip out the door and join the others in the hallway.

"What the fuck did he want?" Rafe demands, but I just shake my head.

"Not here."

"Let's check into the hotel and decide what we want to do from there," Carmine suggests.

"So, all this time, it's been the Carlito family," Nadia says as she kicks off her shoes and drops into a sofa in her suite.

"They're involved," Carmine agrees. "How deeply, we don't know quite yet. But we're going to find out."

"Obviously, we can't tell them we're headed to Dallas," Shane says. "We're going to sneak in and infiltrate their headquarters. Or their compound."

"I've been looking at satellite images," Ivy says. "It looks like a compound similar to your grandmother's place in Seattle."

"It'd better not be that nice, or we'll never get inside." Rafe pushes his hand through his hair in agitation. "We need to call Pop."

"Yeah." Carmine sighs warily and picks up his phone. "I'll FaceTime him."

Carmine dials, and when Carlo picks up the phone, Carmine fills him in on the details.

"Igor and I will meet you in Dallas tomorrow morning," Carlo says.

"Why?" Shane asks. "We have plenty of manpower here. We can get in and out and be done."

"Because this vendetta has been a long time coming," Carlo says. "And I'm going to look those people in the eye when they're questioned —and when they're killed."

"We can't talk you out of this." Carmine's statement isn't a question.

"No. We'll meet you there. I'll message you to coordinate the time."

"Yes, sir," Carmine says. "I'll talk to you soon."

He ends the call and shakes his head.

"This will put a wrench in things," Ivie says. "If Igor and Carlo are there, not only do we have to do the job, but we also have to look out for them."

"Look at you," Nadia says to Ivie, a proud smile on her face. "Sounding all mobster-like and stuff."

"I know, right?" Ivie asks.

"Yeah, it's going to switch it up," Rafe agrees. "We won't infiltrate anything. We'll be knocking on the fucking front door."

"Sometimes, that's not a bad strategy," Carmine says, thinking it over. "They still don't know that we're coming. Maybe we make it seem like it's a friendly call."

"I'm not feeling particularly friendly toward the Carlitos," Rafe says.

"But they don't know that, do they? We'll make it seem like we're just after some information. Because we need that, too. And then, we'll see what happens."

"I don't like it," Shane says and crosses his arms over his chest. "Something still feels off. Like we're missing a piece."

"Curt's still going through paperwork in Seattle," Ivie reminds her husband. "Maybe he'll come up with something between now and tomorrow morning."

"He's flying to Dallas with the dads," Carmine says. "We'll need him."

"And then he's done working for the family," Shane adds. "This isn't what he signed on to do when he asked to work for me. He's my ranch manager. He's done after this."

"We have no issue with that," Carmine replies.

"Oh my God, I'm so *tired*." I collapse onto the massive king-sized bed in our bedroom and long for a nap. "I feel like we've been up for weeks."

"What did he say to you?"

I crack an eye and stare at Rafe, who's standing at the end of the bed. "Huh?"

"What did Maceo say to you, Annika?"

"Oh." I take a second to take stock of how I feel about this. Turns out, I'm not embarrassed. Or even sad. I'm just pissed off.

I sit up and lick my lips. "He received emails from an unknown sender that had photos attached. Of me. The photos from before."

Rafe's hands ball into fists.

"He was warning me that someone sent them and was trying to ruin my reputation. My family's reputation. Honestly, I think he handled it really well. Discreetly. And he seemed really pissed about it. He said that he doesn't believe in hurting women."

"Son of a bitch." Rafe paces away and shoves his hands into his pockets, then stares out the window to the ocean beyond.

"Why are you mad at me?" I climb off the bed and prop my hands on my hips.

"I'm not." He doesn't raise his voice.

"You're acting mad. I didn't do anything wrong, *remember*?"

"What do you want from me?" Rafe spins and holds his hands out at his sides. "What do you expect? Of course, I'm pissed. Someone is dicking with the woman I love. Someone is trying to *hurt* you, and I don't know who it is. I thought we had this handled with the Boston thing, but I guess not. And now it's just one more thing to pile onto everything else that's happening around us."

"Well, I'm sorry that I'm such an inconvenience. I didn't plan on this, you know. It's *never* good timing to find out some asshole has intimate photos of you and plans to share them with the world. But I guess I could have put out a notice on social media and asked them to hold off for a few weeks while we clean up this other mess."

I stomp into the bathroom and slam the door shut.

He just makes me so *mad* sometimes.

"Annika."

"I need a second." I lean my hands on the bathroom vanity and take a deep breath as Rafe opens the door and steps inside. "What if I'd been on the toilet?"

"I don't care." He pulls me to him and wraps his big arms around my shoulders. "I'm sorry I'm a monstrous dickhole."

"You really are."

He kisses my head. "I know. And for the record, I'm not mad at you. I really am just pissed at whoever is still jerking you around. I want it finished. All of it."

"Yeah." I finally loop my arms around him and hug him back. "I'm not even embarrassed about it anymore. It just is what it is. And we'll figure out who's behind it. It's like they're a high school bully who leaves mostly naked photos of the popular girl on all of the lockers as a joke."

"No one ever left a naked photo on my locker," he says with a pout. "I feel left out."

"Perv." I lean my head back and pucker my lips. He doesn't disappoint with the kiss he lays on me. "Thanks for being outraged on my behalf."

"I wasn't kidding before," he says. "Someone is trying to hurt you. And I love you. That means they have to die."

"You love me?"

He frowns and then scoffs. "Of course, I love you. Have I been alone the past few weeks?"

"You haven't said it." I snuggle closer and nuzzle my nose into the crook of his neck. "And for the record, I love you, too. I always have, Rafe. I pushed you away, over and over again, but all along, I knew you were the one for me. There will never be anyone else for me."

"That's a good thing."

"Really?" I raise a brow. "Or what?"

"You don't want to know." He slings me over his shoulder and carries me to the bed, my head coming inches from hitting the doorframe.

"You almost just killed me."

"Nah, I missed by a mile."

I laugh and then squeal when he drops me unceremoniously onto the mattress.

"You're totally a caveman."

"Yes. Rocco carry Annika."

I giggle and scurry away when he reaches for me.

"I need a hot shower and some food. I'm starving. Then you can have your way with me."

"I think we need a compromise in this situation," Rafe says.

"No. I said what I said."

"How are we supposed to have any kind of healthy relationship if you're not willing to grow and respect our differences of opinion?"

I shake my head at him. "Why do you sound like a shrink now? I'm getting in the shower."

"Fine. If you love shower time that much, I'll compromise with *you* and wash your back. I'll even let you stand in the hot water so you don't get too cold. I'm a giver."

"You're weird this afternoon." I laugh and bounce out of his grasp as I hurry back to the bathroom. "And I don't need you to shower with me."

"Stop begging. It's embarrassing. I already told you I'd shower with you."

"You're such a pain in the ass."

"But I'm *your* pain in the ass." He pulls me to him, the laughter fading as he lowers his lips to mine. "And I'm going to make you forget your name tonight, my love."

"Well, when you put it like that, I guess you can shower with me."

"Great. Will you *share* the hot water spray?"

"You said I could have it."

"Don't be selfish. It's all about compromise, remember?"

"I'm reserving water privileges until I see how good of a job you do at washing my back."

"Oh, honey, I'm *very* good. There's no need to worry about that."

SEVENTEEN

~ANNIKA~

"It's still dark," I whisper when Rafe kisses my neck and drags his hand down my arm. I was lost in a very pleasant dream, and I'm not ready to wake up. "Not morning yet."

"We have to get an early start," he reminds me, his voice thick with sleep. "Big day today."

"Five more minutes." I burrow my face into the pillow, but he kisses down my bare spine, and little licks of pleasure spark over my skin, making the dream slip from my mind and all of my attention shift to Rafe. The man is insatiable. It's like he just can't get enough of me.

I'm not complaining.

Making love with Rafe Martinelli is the delight of my life.

As I turn over to face him, the covers slip down, and the cool air from our room blows over my skin. The combination of cool air and Rafe's warm skin send goose bumps over me, waking me fully from sleep. My legs tangle with his, and his already-hard cock presses to my thigh impressively.

"How are you already awake and ready for this?"

"Need you," he whispers against my neck. "More than I need to breathe."

"I'm right here." I skim my nose over his shoulder and sigh in delight when his rough hand closes over my breast. His thumb brushes back and forth over my nipple, making it come to life.

It's a slow, sweet coupling, full of heavy sighs and light nibbles. Whispers.

And just as he teases my already-slick opening with the head of his cock, he looks into my eyes, the first light of dawn casting grey over his face. "You're everything I've ever wanted. All I've ever needed, A."

Slowly, so slowly I have to bite my lip, he slides inside me and frames my face with his hands. I can feel the emotion coming off him in waves, and it absolutely takes my breath away.

"Your heart matches mine," I reply softly and take one of his hands in both of mine, linking our fingers as I hold his gaze. "We're linked, *bonded*. Together. And no matter what life throws at us, that will never change, Rafe."

"God, I love you so much." His mouth closes over mine, and his hips begin moving. But nothing about our joining is rushed. Nothing is urgent. It's the purest form of lovemaking there is. As intimate as it gets.

When we were young, we made love often, lost in each other. But now that we have our second chance, it's so much...more.

More intense.

More meaningful.

"Mine," he whispers. "Open your eyes."

I comply and find him watching me with those fiery blue depths.

"You're mine, Annika. Today and every day that I walk this Earth. You're the only one for me. Do you understand?"

"Of course, I understand. Because I feel exactly the same." My hand dives into his hair, my fingers tangling in the strands as I hold on, enjoying every moment with this man that I love so much.

With his forehead pressed to mine, he picks up speed and sends us both over that delicious crest into oblivion, where I feel so connected to him, I'm not sure where I end and he begins.

We are one.

We always have been.

"Mine," he says again before kissing me so tenderly, it brings tears to my eyes. "Why are you crying?"

"Because I thought this, you, were lost to me. And this is all the sweeter because of it."

"I'm never letting you go again," he promises and kisses my hand. "Ever. If something were to happen, and our families forbade it, we'd leave them. I will *not* be without you, Annika. I can't. I lived through that torture for far longer than any man should have to. I'll do everything in my power to always have you by my side."

"I know." I kiss him sweetly. "I know it. And I'm right here with you. Nothing's ever going to tear us apart again."

He rolls to the side, unlinking us, and then pads into the bathroom.

"Sun's coming up," he calls as he starts the shower. "Pop wants to get an early start."

"Yeah." I sigh, a little sad that our wonderful moment is over. But there will be more.

A lifetime of moments, just like this one and better.

"I want to talk a bit about today before we're with the others," Rafe says as he pokes his head out of the bathroom.

"Okay. What's up?"

"I want you on the periphery of everything that happens today. If you can stay in the van, all the better. I don't want you to see any action."

I frown, but he keeps talking.

"I'm not saying that to sound sexist. Yes, you can shoot—probably better than I can. And you're damn smart. But you haven't trained for these situations. You're a doctor. A damn good one."

"Now you're just buttering me up so I say, '*Yes, sir.*'"

"No. I'm not saying anything that isn't completely true." Steam starts billowing out of the bathroom from the hot shower. "These are dangerous people, A."

"I'm well aware of that."

"Nothing can happen to you."

"Likewise." I stand from the bed, also stark-naked, and prop my hand on my hip. "We have the same goal, Rafe. To get in and out alive while making sure the target is eliminated."

"I don't want you in the middle of it."

"Too late. I *am* in the middle of it. And I'll be surrounded by people who have far more experience than I do. I won't do anything to put anyone in harm's way. I'm not careless. This may not be my specialty, but Tarenkov blood runs through my veins. I can handle myself."

"You stick close to Curt or Nadia. You keep your weapon on you at all times, and don't be afraid to use it. And, Annika, I'm only going to say this one time... If something happens to me, you absolutely *cannot* jump into the middle of things out of pure emotion. You'll instinctively want to run to me, help me, but you will only put yourself in danger. Keep that cool head of yours on straight. It'll keep you alive."

I blow out a long breath, the thought of something happening to Rafe turning my blood cold.

"I'll keep my head on straight," I promise him. "But, Rafe, if something happens to you, I'll never forgive you."

He walks to me and pulls me into his arms, rocking us back and forth. "It's just a what-if, baby. I want you to be prepared for anything, and I need you to stay safe. That's *my* primary objective today. To keep you absolutely safe."

"I love you." My words are a whisper against his chest. The thought of *anything* happening to Rafe fills me with absolute terror. I don't think I would survive losing him again.

"I love you, too." He kisses my forehead. "Let's get ready to go. Pop's impatient."

"I'm surprised that he wants to go on this mission," I admit as I follow Rafe into the bathroom. "It's not that he and Uncle Igor are out of shape. Quite the opposite, actually. But they don't *have* to do this anymore."

"It's personal for them. I don't know all of the details yet, but that's the feeling I get. I suspect that when we're all together, they'll fill us in on everything they know. I don't know about Igor, but I know Pop can take care of himself. He's a big man, but he moves surprisingly fast, and he's deadly with a weapon. From what I understand, he was formidable in his prime."

"I've heard that Uncle Igor was the same."

"That would make sense. They're two of the most powerful men in this country."

He gets in the shower as I brush out my hair and tie it up on top of my head so it doesn't get wet when I step in.

"Now that Carmine and Nadia are married, and they were each next in line to be the boss of our respective families, what will happen if something happens to either Carlo or Uncle Igor?"

Rafe goes quiet for a moment.

"I think the two families are now merged. Considered one family. Nadia and Carmine would head both organizations."

"Holy hell, that's a lot of power."

"Yes."

I open the glass door and join him.

"Want me to wash your back again?" He grins and waggles his eyebrows.

"Good God, you're insatiable. We literally *just* finished."

"That was round one. I've had time to rest."

"No. You said yourself. Your father is impatient."

He pulls me to him, wet and slippery. "A few more minutes won't matter."

"THEY'RE ALREADY HERE," Shane says, pointing to the other private jet sitting on the jetway.

"Just arrived," Rafe confirms. "We were only twenty minutes behind them."

Shane's phone rings, and he answers right away. "This is Shane. Yep. We see you. We'll be right over."

He hangs up and turns to the rest of us.

"Pop wants all of us to go over there for a briefing. That jet is bigger, and our only office in Dallas."

"Makes sense," Carmine says as we come to a stop. We leave all of our belongings on the plane—one of the perks of being on a private aircraft—and hurry over to the much larger jet where everyone else is waiting.

Carlo and Igor are seated at a table on one side. Curt's in a chair with his laptop open on a small table. The six of us file in and find seats, all business, all ready for what's about to come.

"This could be the most important day in our organization's—or *any* organization's—existence," Carlo begins. "Igor and I have been doing some research on the Carlito family for several months on the down-low. We had to be careful and methodical because this family seems to have eyes and ears *everywhere*."

"They are sneaky," Igor adds. "And more intelligent than any of us gave them credit for, for many years. To our detriment. There's still much we don't know. We will not just burst in, guns blazing."

"We want answers," Carlo picks up. "We want to ask questions and get answers."

"We'll get them."

We all turn in surprise at the sound of Mick Sergi's voice. The New York boss steps onto the plane, his son Billy right behind him.

"What are you doing here?" Carmine demands, but Carlo holds up a hand.

"Thank you for coming," Carlo says and then nods again when Maceo from Miami follows the Sergis onto the plane. "I'm sorry for your loss, Maceo."

Maceo's eyes are hard and cold.

"Thank you."

"Please explain this," Carmine says as he pulls his sidearm from its holster and lays it on a table.

"All of our personal beefs with each other, whether big or small, are set aside for today," Igor says, watching the others. "Our only vendetta, our only focus, is destroying the Carlito family. But we have to get answers before we kill them."

"So, what's the plan?" Rafe asks. "We just march up to the front door and ring the bell?"

"Precisely," Carlo says, smiling at his son. "My three sons and I will ring the bell. Say we're there to talk, to ask questions. Be non-threatening."

"In the meantime," Igor says, "the rest of us will infiltrate the perimeter and take out their security."

"It's damn good security," Curt says, still staring at his computer. "I have it up on the laptop, thanks to a late-night email from Ivie."

"Wasn't easy to find," Ivie mutters with a mutinous frown. "Bastards."

"I have a plan in place, and I'll go over it with everyone," Curt says and nods at Carlo.

"Excellent. While my boys and I are talking with Benji inside, you'll all take out Benji's men. And once inside, Igor, Mick, and Maceo will have plenty of time to get more answers before extinguishing the Carlitos and their bloodline. They will never be an issue for any organization ever again."

"How do we know that they're behind *everything*?" Nadia asks thoughtfully.

"They're the common denominator," Mick replies. "Crime families own up to what they do. If I have a beef with someone and have them killed, I'll admit it. I don't hide. No one claimed to have issues with any of the families killed over the past few weeks. *No one.*"

"And the Carlitos haven't said a word," Igor adds.

"How many Carlitos are there?" Ivie asks. "We've only heard of Benji. We know he's young, only in his early twenties, and his father didn't have an interest in the family business after his grandfather died."

"We know that Benji is trying to run things." Mick rolls his eyes. "He's a fucking *kid*. His grandfather died twenty-five years ago."

"Who's Benji's father?" Carmine asks.

"Francisco," Carlo says. "Francisco Carlito. He was never one to be in the forefront of things. Happy to sit in his father's shadow. And when his father died, we all assumed the family went to sleep."

"They never slept," Maceo says. "They're just good at working underground."

"Is Francisco dead?" Ivie asks.

"We think so," Igor says. "We believe that Francisco's death is what propelled Benji into action."

"But it's not been confirmed that Francisco is dead." Rafe crosses his arms. "There are too many unanswered questions."

"That's what today is for," Carlo reminds him. "Now, Curt, tell us your plan for getting inside and ambushing their security, and let's finish this mission."

"I DON'T LIKE THIS." I'm sitting between Ivie and Nadia in the van, ready to jump out and set Curt's plan into motion.

It's a damn good scheme.

We watch as the four men walk down a driveway and up onto a wide front porch.

"Is it just me, or does something feel off?"

"It's not just you," Ivie says.

"I feel it," Nadia says, her eyes pinned to Carmine's back. "We're missing something here. There's a hole in all of this, and I don't like it."

I check my earpiece and hear Uncle Igor in my ear when he says, "They're in. Let's go."

Curt's in the lead, with Nadia right behind him, followed by Maceo, Uncle Igor, the Sergis, Ivie, and me. Once we're near the fence line, we web out, ready to neutralize the security and get inside.

We all want answers.

EIGHTEEN

~RAFE~

"Remember," Pop mutters as we approach the front door, "we're going to make it seem like this is a friendly visit."

"Right." Shane's voice is cool and hard. "I'm sure we look friendly. Their security has already figured out we're here."

"We will be nice until it's time to *not* be nice," Pop replies and presses the doorbell.

"Well, it's about time you got here."

A young guy answers. Looks to be early twenties. Spoiled. Weak.

I could take this kid out with my pinky finger.

"Was traffic bad from the airport or something?" he asks.

"Hello, Mr. Carlito," Pop says. "I'm Carlo Martinelli."

"I know who you are. By all means, come on in. I can't wait to see this show."

Benji steps back and gestures for us to enter.

"Oh, by the way, go ahead and leave your weapons at the door," he adds.

"You're cute," Carmine replies with a toothy grin. "And I don't think so."

We file past Benji, who's lost his cocky smile, and walk into a living room where my father stops cold.

"Hello, Carlo."

"Claudia?" Pop gasps in surprise. I look at Carmine and then narrow my eyes at the woman sitting in a high-backed chair, her dark hair swept back from her face, her legs crossed, her eyes cool and calm. "My God, have they had you here all these years? Held you against your will?"

She cocks her head to the side and then starts laughing as if she just heard the funniest joke of all time.

"Oh, Carlo. Grow the fuck up. Of course, they haven't been holding me against my will." My father stiffens beside me. "Why don't you all sit down? We'll have a nice family reunion. I'll tell you everything. I've been champing at the bit for *years* to tell you all about my adventures down here in Texas."

Out of the corner of my eye, I see Curt slip silently against the wall and give Shane a signal.

All clear.

"Oh, just let your friends come inside, as well. I always did love an audience."

"Wait, there's more?" Benji asks in disgust as the others file in. My heart calms when I see that Annika is unscathed.

Her eyes are haunted, however.

She killed.

She'll never be the same.

"Oh. Well, look at you," Claudia says to Annika. "You look so different with clothes on."

Igor moves up behind Annika, Ivie, and Nadia as I glare at my aunt.

"You were behind the blackmail," I say.

"Rafe," Claudia says with a small smile. "You grew up to be a handsome man. All three of you did. Of course, I blackmailed her. She spread her legs for literally *any* man who asked. The Tarenkovs should know who they have in their family. It's disgraceful. In fact, the Tarenkovs have a lot of bad eggs. It was just so *easy* to lure Alexander away. To get him to start the drug arm of things. He was eager to defy his father. And let's be honest, he flat-out *hated* his pretty little sister. Of course, I can understand sibling rivalry."

Claudia turns to Pop and winks.

675

"You're going to die today," Igor says coldly. "For what you did to my family and for much more than that. How does it feel to know that your life can now be measured by mere minutes?"

"Oh, please. I'm not dying today. You all might think that you took out my security outside, but I have plenty more where they came from, don't you worry." She turns to Pop with a smile. "I must say, I have missed you, brother. You've aged well. How is Flavia? Still weak and whiny?"

"Cut the family reunion bullshit and get to it," Carmine says and raises a brow at Benji when the other man steps toward him. "Oh, I dare you."

"Stop with the dramatics," Claudia says impatiently. "Carlo, I'd like to introduce you to your nephew. My son, Benji."

"Your *son*?" Pop demands.

"Yes. My *son*," Claudia replies as the others in the room shuffle around, ready to pounce and kill her. But we don't have all of the information from her yet. The energy in the room is electric, full of hatred and violence. But Claudia is as calm as ever, almost feeding off the attention, smiling at Benji like a proud mother at a high school graduation. "I suppose I really should start at the beginning, shouldn't I? Vinnie was a piece of shit. We all know that. It's not like the world lost a great man the day he died. I hope he's rotting in hell, where he deserves to be. Mom and Daddy made me marry him because he had the right pedigree, but there was literally *no* attraction there. None at all. We couldn't stand each other. We were married in name only.

"A few years after I married him, I met Francisco. Now *that* was the kind of man I wanted. He was kind and gentle. Not nearly as driven as me, but I was able to overlook that all in the name of love. I spent a great deal of time here in Dallas with him."

"Even after you had Elena," Carmine says.

"Elena." Claudia sighs. "I didn't want to have her. I wasn't interested in having a child with Vinnie at all. The sex was appalling. Ugh, just the thought of it turns my stomach. But that asshole just kept pestering me, *nagging* me to produce an heir for him. Then Mom started in, too, and I got pregnant to shut them all up. I thought about getting an abortion, pretending that I'd lost the baby. But then I thought...I'll just go through with it and hire a fucking nanny. Between the nanny and my family, I hardly ever had to see her."

"Should have just aborted her," Benji spouts off, and before anyone can react, Carmine raises his arm and shoots the other man right between the eyes.

Claudia jumps and stares in horror as her son falls to the floor, dead.

But she just keeps speaking as if nothing at all just happened. Like a cold robot.

"I had Vinnie killed in prison. Staged my death and got the fuck out of that rainy, godforsaken city. Ran to Dallas with Francisco. I had Benji about five years after Elena. Carlo, do you remember those two years or so that I was gone so much, and Mom kept calling you, wanting to know where I was?"

"Yes. I remember."

"Well, it's not like I could go to Seattle to see the family while I was pregnant with another man's child. Even *I* wouldn't do anything so dramatic."

"Because you know Vinnie would have killed you on the spot," Shane says. "He beat the hell out of Elena, almost killed her, just because she wanted to marry her high school sweetheart, and he thought that was an embarrassment to the family. If you'd shown up pregnant, he would have killed you. And you know it."

"Perhaps." Claudia narrows her eyes and then glances at Benji on the floor. "My son was the *true* heir. The *only* heir. And when Francisco died, God rest his soul, I made it my mission to get rid of all of the other families so Benji could rule, and the Carlitos would be the only organized crime family left. He had Carlito *and* Martinelli blood running through him. Who else could be more ideal to run it all?"

"You killed Vinnie and put an innocent man on death row," Pop says, staring at his sister as if she were a stranger.

"Who gives a shit about that?" Claudia demands. "He was a *criminal*. It was so easy to hire the right judge, a *dirty* one, and make sure he took the fall for it. All tidied up with a pretty little bow."

"Everything you are, everything you stand for, is exactly *against* what we're taught, Claudia," Pop says in exasperation. "My God, you're crazy."

"I am *not* crazy. I'm strong. I'm driven. And I know what I want."

"And would you have killed Elena if you'd known where she was?" Carmine asks.

"I looked for that little brat for *years.* Always slipped through my fingers. Then I found out that my mother was behind hiding my daughter from me." She examines her nails. "So, I killed her."

Pop's hands ball into fists. All of us want to pounce on her.

"You killed *my mother,*" Pop says.

"I killed *my* mother," Claudia shoots back, her eyes full of anger now. "A woman who cared more about you and your three little brats than she ever did about me. She loved my *child* more than me. It was sickening how she fawned over all of you. She didn't even like me. She *ignored* me."

"You were never around," Pop points out. "You spent as much time as you could away."

"You bet your ass, I did."

"And who do you expect was supposed to love Elena? To care for her?"

"God, you're slow, Carlo. Try to keep up here, okay? In case you haven't heard a word I've said, I'll say it again. I don't fucking care about that little cunt," Claudia says, leaning forward. "It was *me* who didn't get any love from anyone in that damn house. So, I came here where I was loved. Appreciated. The Carlitos *worshipped* me."

"So, all of this is because you didn't get enough attention?" Annika asks and sets her hands on her hips. "Really? That's really stupid."

"You'll watch your tone with me if you want to keep that tongue in your pretty little mouth," Claudia replies, her voice full of venom.

"You just try to touch her," I suggest. "I beg you."

"You blamed my family for protecting Pavlov," Mick Sergi says coldly, now that the Martinelli side of things has been explained. "Built an entire web of lies that my men believed and had dozens of them killed because they believed they were carrying out *my* orders."

"You might want to hire men who aren't so gullible," Claudia says with a shrug. "It's certainly not my fault that they believed a bunch of lies. Besides, it was for the greater good, Mick. Pavlov was a *mess*. And he was from your city. Why didn't you take care of him when he lived there?"

"Because I had him under control," Mick replies. "And then, suddenly, one day he was gone. I thought he was dead and forgot him. Until my men started disappearing and ended up dead, and it all came back to *me*."

"Well, I had to blame someone for it, didn't I?" Claudia asks. "I mean, I was building an empire for my son."

"And you killed my father," Maceo says.

"I told you. Benji was the only man who could be the boss. The Carlitos are the only family who matter."

"You killed my father and other families who never had a beef with you," Maceo continues. "My mother could still die."

"You're not *listening* to me." Claudia's frustrated now. "No one else matters except Benji."

"But it was just you and Benji. There is no *Carlito* family," I point out.

"He would have married within a few years and started a family. We would have built from the ground up. But now you've ruined that. You've ruined everything. I should have known you would. The people I came from never did anything good for me, not once in my life. Benji was going to do great things. He had his whole life ahead of him. I just had to get a few roadblocks out of the way, and the sky was the limit for him."

"By killing off the other families," Igor says, shaking his head.

"Yes. You and Nadia were next, but I couldn't pin you down. I was just going to blow you all up."

"And us?" Pop asks.

"I was saving you for last." She taps her lips thoughtfully. "I planned to put the bullets into your heads personally."

"Are you finished with your story?" Pop asks.

Claudia lets out a loud, gusty sigh. "Boy, it feels good to get it all off my chest, you know? Keeping secrets is tough. Yeah, I think that's it for now."

Without another word, Pop raises his gun.

"It's *my* bullet going in *your* head." He squeezes the trigger and kills her instantly with a bullet right between the eyes.

"Is more security on the way?" I ask Curt, who stayed on the perimeter, keeping an eye out.

"No, we got them all. She may have had more men in different locations, but I disabled the communication systems before we got here."

"We make a pact, here and now," Mick says, his eyes hard and on Claudia as she bleeds from the forehead in her fancy chair. "Nothing like this happens again. We don't let it get this far just because we're too proud to speak to each other. No matter what our issues are."

"Agreed," Igor says with a tired sigh as he looks at Nadia and then the rest of us. "You young people remember this. Let it be a lesson to you. When Mick, Carlo, and I are long gone, and you're the ones in charge, don't let anything like this happen again."

"We won't," Carmine says. "It won't be repeated."

"All because she didn't get enough attention," Annika says again. "I'm no psychiatrist, but I'd say that's psychotic behavior."

"Claudia always had mental health issues," Pop says. "But it sounds like it festered as she got older. I don't know that woman. And now that my family, *all* the families, are safe from her, I'm ready to go home and forget her."

"We have to tell Elena," I remind him. "She deserves to know."

"You're right." Pop pats me on the shoulder as we file out of the Carlito house. "We'll tell her together. She'll need all of us with her."

"I have a question," Maceo says, catching all of our attention. "Does this mean we're...*friends*?"

"Think of it like this," Mick says thoughtfully. "We've been through a war together. We fought for the same side. We won't always agree and will likely lose touch after this, but in this matter, we're comrades. I'm sorry you lost your father. I liked him very much."

"He didn't die," Maceo says, surprising all of us. "He's also in the ICU. We told everyone he died, so the heat was off him, and I could take care of this."

"Smart." Carmine nods, his face full of admiration for the other underboss. "You're damn smart."

"And we are not your enemy," Maceo says. "None of you. If you ever need us, you know how to find us. Now, I need to get back to my family."

"Let's go home," Annika says, taking my hand in hers.

CHAPTER
NINETEEN
~RAFE~

We went to her.

Pop would usually ask us to come to him. To meet at his home or his office. But for this, he insisted that we go to Elena's house on the coast of Oregon where she's been staying with her husband, Archer Montgomery.

Carmine called her this morning to let her know we'd be here today, but he didn't give her any other information.

What we have to tell her needs to be done in person. We left the girls in Seattle at Gram's house.

Just as the four of us climb out of the SUV in Elena's driveway, the front door opens, and Archer and Elena come out to greet us.

Elena immediately hugs Pop and then each of us.

"It's really good to see you," she says. "It's been too long."

"You're right," Pop says. "We need to get together more often. We'll start making that happen. Now, let's get in out of this wet."

"Come on in," Archer says with a smile and leads us into a beautiful home set on the cliffs of the Pacific Ocean. "Can I get you anything?"

"Coffee would be great," Pop says. "I take it black."

"Coming right up."

Pop wanders to the windows to watch the storm rage over the

water. It's been a harrowing twenty-four hours for him. My father can be a ruthless, cold man. But he loves family more than anything.

He loved his sister.

The woman he remembered her to be all those years ago anyway.

And despite all of the hard things he's done in his life, I know that killing her will be the thing that haunts him for the rest of his days.

"Here we go," Elena says as she and Archer bring trays of coffee with cream and sweetener for anyone who wants it. Once we're all seated in the living room, Elena smiles at all of us, takes a deep breath, and grabs Archer's hand. "You must have news for me. You didn't come all this way just to tell me there's nothing new."

"We do have some things to say," Pop says and takes a sip of coffee, then sets the mug down. "First, I need to apologize to you."

We all look over at him in surprise.

"For what?" Elena asks.

"I knew where you were hiding all of these years. I didn't question your grandmother about her motives. I didn't dig into the situation. I knew you were safe, so I let you live your life. But I did you a disservice. I hurt my entire family."

He shakes his head and stands to pace the room. Pop always did think better when he was on the move.

"Uncle Carlo, you did what you thought was right."

"I did what was easy," he disagrees with an impatient swipe of his arm. "I had three sons to see to and a family to take over. My sister and her husband were dead. But none of that is an excuse."

He turns to Elena and cups her face in his hand. "You very well might hate me after I tell you what I have to tell you."

"I won't hate you," she promises and presses her hand against his. "You can tell me."

I can count on two fingers the number of times I've seen my father look so sad. One was the day my grandmother died.

The other is right now.

"Until yesterday, your mother was very much alive."

Elena gasps and listens intently as Pop relays the entire story from start to finish. He doesn't leave anything out. He doesn't try to spare her from any of the details.

683

Except for the part when Claudia called Elena a cunt. He keeps that to himself.

"She would have killed me," Elena says as Archer rubs circles over her back. "I always knew that she didn't like me. She didn't care enough about me to be *mean* to me. She just ignored me. And I was so used to it, I didn't really care. I had good nannies, and I always had all of you."

She stands to pace the room. She always did remind me of my father.

"Should I have known, somewhere deep down, that she was still alive?"

"Why would you?" Carmine asks.

"She was my *mother*," Elena says. "Then again, I never felt a connection to her, so I guess I wouldn't have known. My father was evil. She did the world a favor by having him killed, but my God, Uncle Carlo, an innocent man has been in prison for *years* for something he didn't do."

"I already have his release in motion," Pop says. "He'll be set free soon."

"How did you manage that so quickly?" Shane asks. But Pop just winks at my brother.

"I have connections, son." He turns back to Elena. "And Danvers will be taken care of for the rest of his life. That's a wrong that we can correct."

"Good. That's good." Elena looks out at the storm and then back at Pop. "She killed Gram?"

"Yes, honey."

"I thought Gram died of natural causes?" Carmine asks. "I sat at her bedside. It wasn't a quick death."

"Poison," Shane says shortly. "She made Gram suffer."

"I want to kill that bitch all over again," I say and push my hand through my hair. "She lived too long. She was *happy* for far too long."

"I won't disagree," Elena says. "I also can't believe that I had a half-brother from the time I was five. That's unbelievable."

"I think all of this is pretty unbelievable," Archer says. "It's like something from one of Luke's movies."

"I wish it was fiction," I reply. "I wish you'd known our grandmother. She would have liked you."

"Are we going to bury Claudia?" Elena asks, not referring to the woman as her mother.

"No," Pop says. "Absolutely not. We left her for the cleanup crew. The entire house was burned to the ground with her and that little piece of garbage son she loved so much inside. She doesn't deserve to be buried alongside my parents. I won't mourn for her a second time."

"You absolutely shouldn't," Elena says. "I have to say, I'm relieved that the apple fell quite far from that particular tree in this case. I'm nothing like her."

"You're one of *us*," I reply. "You'll always be ours."

"And mine," Archer says with a smile.

"So, it's good that Gram hid me away." Elena sits and hangs her head in her hands. "I always wondered if it was necessary, or if Gram was overreacting. She didn't tell me who she was hiding me *from*, you know? Just that someone had killed my parents, and she was afraid they'd come for me, too."

Elena's head shoots up, and her eyes go wide.

"Oh, God. Did Gram know that Claudia was behind it all? That Claudia was alive?"

"We don't think so," Shane says. "I thought of that on the plane. We've been through every piece of paper that pertains to the case. More than once. We can't ask her to be certain, but she never mentions in any of her notes that she knew about Claudia. She hired many investigators over the years. If she knew about Claudia, she wouldn't have needed to do that."

"Good." Elena swallows hard as tears fill her beautiful, bi-colored eyes. "Because that would have just tortured her all those years."

"This chapter is now closed," Pop says and reaches for Elena's hand. "There's no need for you to look over your shoulder anymore, Elena. You can truly put it all behind you and live your life as you wish."

"I'm glad. It's a relief. Because I have news, too." She grabs Archer's hand again with her free one. "We're going to have a baby. And it's going to be born into peace. And love."

"Ah, little one." Pop gathers Elena close and kisses the top of her head. "This might be the most loved baby to ever be conceived. I can't wait to meet him or her."

685

"Can they call you Papa?" Elena asks. "You're the only father I've ever known."

For the first time in my life, I see my father's eyes fill with tears. "It would be my honor."

"Do you hear that?" Annika asks, making me stop on the path that runs through my grandmother's estate.

I stop and listen. "No. What?"

"Quiet." She smiles and tips her face up to the sunshine. "It's so quiet. And the air is light, like a huge weight has been lifted."

"Because it has." I kiss her hand, and we begin walking again, headed toward the pond where I spent summers splashing and swimming. Making mischief.

It's here, in this special place, that I want to do what I'm about to do.

I'm not even nervous.

Okay, I'm a *little* nervous.

When we reach the bench by the water and Annika sits down, I lower myself to one knee and smile up at the most beautiful woman in the world.

Every time I look at her, my breath catches.

"Rafe."

"Annika." I grin and reach into my pocket for the ring. No box, just a ring. When I take her hand in mine, I'm surprised to find it shaking. "I'm supposed to be the nervous one."

She just laughs and swipes at a tear on her cheek.

"I feel like this is millennia in the making. It seems like I've wanted to ask you this question for all of my adult life. And I know that there were reasons before why it wasn't possible for us to be together.

"Those reasons are gone now. And I know that if I don't ask you to be mine, as soon as humanly possible, I'll regret it. I don't want to waste any more time, Annika. You're my soul mate. I need to be with you the way I need air. And I know what you're going to say."

She just laughs and swipes at more tears.

"You're going to say that we're together. And we are. It's awesome.

But I want more. I want *everything.* I want to make it legal. I want to give you my name. I want the whole package."

"You want a lot."

I sigh and lean in to kiss her cheek. "Yeah. I want a lot. But I'll give you back just as much, if not more."

"I know you will."

"Is that a yes?"

"You didn't actually ask me anything yet."

"Oh. Right." I clear my throat. "Will you marry me?"

"Of course." She flings her arms around my shoulders and buries that sweet face in my neck. "Of course, I will, Rafe. There's nothing in the world that I want more."

"Thank God." I ease back so I can slip the ring onto her finger.

"Oh, this is *stunning.* And so unique."

"Yeah." I kiss the ring on her finger and then slide up onto the bench with her. "The big diamond in the middle was my gram's. Not from her wedding ring. My mom has that. But it was from a ring that my grand-father gave her on their twenty-fifth anniversary. She loved it very much. The green stone is from my mom."

Her blue eyes fly to mine in surprise.

"Yeah, I asked her for help on this because I didn't want to screw it up. Anyway, the emerald is from a necklace my father gave her for a birthday gift. The ruby is from *your* mom."

"The ring my father gave her when she had me," Annika says softly. "I've always admired that ring."

"That's what she said. The sapphires are from your Aunt Katya. They were earrings gifted to her by Igor."

"Rafe, this is amazing."

"One more thing," I reply. "The gold is from Ivie. It was her mother's wedding band."

Annika gasps and starts to cry again. "*Rafe.*"

"The ring is all of us, Annika. Because family is important, and they're all a part of us. They support us. They love us. And it's with huge relief that I say I asked your father *and* Igor if I could ask for your hand, and they both gave me their blessing."

She laughs as she turns her face up to me. "Well, I would have been surprised if they'd said no."

"Still, I was nervous as hell."

She sighs and settles in next to me on the bench as we quietly watch the water for a long moment. Ducks splash, but the leaves have long fallen, and winter is on the way.

"I have something else to discuss with you," I say.

"You're full of news today."

I shrug and tighten the arm I have slung around her shoulders.

"Yeah, well, I've been doing a lot of thinking. And I had a long talk with my father last night after you went to bed. I know you like it here in Seattle, but what do you think about this specific place?"

"Your grandmother's house?"

"Yes. We need a house. More space. The condo just won't do forever. And last night, while talking with Pop, I brought up the idea of you and I living here. It's been sitting empty since Gram died. We've used it as a home base these past few weeks, but for the most part, it's just sat. This house needs a family in it. And Pop agrees that, if you don't hate the idea, we would be good here."

"I have so many questions," she whispers.

"You hate the idea."

"No. Not at all. But, Rafe, this is a *huge* house for just us."

"It's big," I agree. "I can't change the size of it. We have caretakers for the grounds, and housekeepers for inside. Also, Pop's fine with us changing anything we want. He just asked that if we want to rehome some of the art, that we give it to him to see to."

"I'd like to change a few things, but it's really beautiful the way it is."

I look down at her. "Is that a yes?"

"Your brothers and Elena are okay with it?"

"Yes. I've spoken with them, as well. It's not leaving the family. And they're always welcome here. The thing is, I like the idea of *our* home being the anchor, you know? A place where the family can always come to gather together. Holidays, special events, that sort of thing. Gram would love that."

"I love that, too. I've been so at home here. I think making this our place is a good idea. Because I have something to tell you, too."

I raise a brow, waiting.

"We're going to start filling those extra bedrooms upstairs sooner than we expected."

"Are you telling me—?"

"I'm pregnant." She grins, and when I let out a whoop and spin her in the air, she laughs loudly. "Put me down before you make me throw up."

"Are you okay? Do you feel all right? Do you need anything?"

"I'm great." She cradles my face in her hands. "And I have everything I need right here."

"Let's go tell everyone all the things."

I take her hand and lead her back to the house.

"You mean they don't already know?"

"They don't know everything. Let's go share this with them."

"Good idea."

EPILOGUE

~CARLO MARTINELLI~

One Month Later

"We did it." I light my cigar and smile over at my friend as we survey the room. We're in the ballroom of my mother's home, Rocco's home now, watching the party unfold around us, celebrating the wedding of my youngest son and his darling Annika. "We managed to match them all together."

Igor grins and sips his whiskey. Our table is on the edge of the room where we can keep watch over our two families. Our wives are huddled together. And the kids are dancing, laughing, and enjoying each other.

"A good-looking bunch, our young ones," Igor says with a salute of his glass. "Smart. Strong."

"And powerful."

We share a pleased look.

We achieved what my sister longed for all along. We managed to build the strongest organized crime family in the country.

I feel the familiar pang in my chest that always comes when I think of my sister. I wish things had been different.

But they aren't. And that chapter is closed.

The new one ahead looks like the beginning of a bright future for our children and our grandchildren.

"They take after us," Igor says and clinks his glass to mine. "Do you think they have any idea that we put their matches into motion?"

"Of course, not." I sip my whiskey and then puff the cigar. "They're smart, but we were cunning. Had some surprises and bumps along the way."

"But we got here all the same," Igor replies. "And that's the important thing. My firefly is happy with your Rocco."

I gaze across the room where Rocco lifts Annika into his arms and kisses her soundly. There is nothing I love more than my family.

"It's been a long time coming."

"Unfortunate, but necessary," he says. "And I believe they'll be all the stronger because of it."

"Agreed. They'll give us beautiful babies."

"Indeed, they will. Thank you for offering them this home."

"I was surprised when Rocco asked me for it, but it made sense. He's always been more rooted here than my other children. It's the right thing to do. And I know that he and Annika will always open their doors to you and your family, just as they will to me and mine."

"We are one family now," Igor says. "Twenty years ago, I would have thought it impossible."

"And now?"

"I'm grateful."

"As am I, my friend."

We puff our cigars and watch our brood, and I know, without a doubt, that our family is safe, ready for future generations of Martinellis and Tarenkovs to rule.

Our families will go on.

And that, is the ultimate goal.

. . .

691

I HOPE you enjoyed my mafia family! If you haven't read the book where it all began, You Belong With Me, you can get it now! Elena and Archer's story is here:

https://www.kristenprobyauthor.com/you-belong-with-me

AND, keep reading for a look at You Belong With Me!

ABOUT THE AUTHOR

Kristen Proby has published more than sixty titles, many of which have hit the USA Today, New York Times and Wall Street Journal Bestsellers lists.

Kristen and her husband, John, make their home in her hometown of Whitefish, Montana with their two cats and dog.

facebook.com/booksbykristenproby

instagram.com/kristenproby

bookbub.com/profile/kristen-proby

goodreads.com/kristenproby

NEWSLETTER SIGN UP

I hope you enjoyed reading this story as much as I enjoyed writing it! For upcoming book news, be sure to join my newsletter! I promise I will only send you news-filled mail, and none of the spam. You can sign up here:

https://mailchi.mp/kristenproby.com/newsletter-sign-up

ALSO BY KRISTEN PROBY:

Other Books by Kristen Proby

The With Me In Seattle Series

Come Away With Me
Under The Mistletoe With Me
Fight With Me
Play With Me
Rock With Me
Safe With Me
Tied With Me
Breathe With Me
Forever With Me
Stay With Me
Indulge With Me
Love With Me
Dance With Me
Dream With Me
You Belong With Me

ALSO BY KRISTEN PROBY:

Imagine With Me
Shine With Me
Escape With Me
Flirt With Me
Change With Me
Take a Chance With Me

Check out the full series here: https://www.kristenprobyauthor.com/
with-me-in-seattle

The Big Sky Universe

Love Under the Big Sky
Loving Cara
Seducing Lauren
Falling for Jillian
Saving Grace

The Big Sky
Charming Hannah
Kissing Jenna
Waiting for Willa
Soaring With Fallon

Big Sky Royal
Enchanting Sebastian
Enticing Liam
Taunting Callum

Heroes of Big Sky
Honor
Courage
Shelter

Check out the full Big Sky universe here: https://www.
kristenprobyauthor.com/under-the-big-sky

Bayou Magic
Shadows
Spells
Serendipity

Check out the full series here: https://www.kristenprobyauthor.com/bayou-magic

The Romancing Manhattan Series

All the Way
All it Takes
After All

Check out the full series here: https://www.kristenprobyauthor.com/romancing-manhattan

The Boudreaux Series

Easy Love
Easy Charm
Easy Melody
Easy Kisses
Easy Magic
Easy Fortune
Easy Nights

Check out the full series here: https://www.kristenprobyauthor.com/boudreaux

The Fusion Series

Listen to Me
Close to You
Blush for Me
The Beauty of Us

Check out the entire Crossover Collection here: https://www. kristenprobyauthor.com/kristen-proby-crossover-collection

9 781633 501317